To Martin Navard
with l
Carol Br

The Lorestone

CAROL BROWNE

UPFRONT PUBLISHING
PETERBOROUGH, ENGLAND.

AUTHOR'S NOTE

Limited Edition
misprint!
Ignore pages 652-658
inclusive.

Carol Browne

THE LORESTONE

ISBN 978-184426-432-2

First Published 2007 by
UPFRONT PUBLISHING LTD.
Peterborough, England.

Printed by Print-on-Demand Worldwide Ltd.

Acknowledgments

Thirty years ago I wrote a novel. I didn't know where it came from, nor where it was going, but I knew that one day I would see it in print - and, with the help of Simon Potter and everyone at Upfront Publishing, here it finally is.

Getting to this point involved a very long and difficult journey and my heartfelt thanks go to those who helped and supported me along the way: - Carolyn Brown; Trevor J Douglas and the Penman Literary Service (1987-1990); George and Emma Windsor; Jeff Smith; Ben and Charlotte Kennedy; Beryl Sheehan; Penny and Paul Snook; Trisha Roberts; Estelle Shepherd and Riaz at PC World, Peterborough. Last but not least, thanks to my dog, Harry, who makes my world a much better place simply by being in it.

I take full responsibility for any proof-reading errors. I also hope that the reader will overlook any historical inaccuracies in what is, after all, just a fantasy.

Dedicated to the memory of

FREDERICK LINCOLN TOPPING

Chapter One
Britain - 500 A.D.

As Elgiva reached the brow of the hillock, she acknowledged in her heart the reality of exile.

She stopped and surveyed the landscape of her future and her pale lips parted to release a sigh of resignation. Somewhere ahead lay the prospect of loneliness and it crouched in ambush, like a beast of prey, and though summer still ruled in the fields below her, the mist that lingered upon the grass was clammy and sluggish and carried a chill like the breath of winter. It made her shiver in her servant's rags.

Just then, her companion reached her side, but Elgiva found that she couldn't meet her eye, for a great sadness was welling up inside her. She knew that Alison had been away from home far longer than she had intended and soon the two of them would have to part. This separation was something that Elgiva feared she would be unable to bear; but, of course, she had no choice.

She sighed and toyed with a strand of her black hair. "So, Alison Fiorin," she said, "is this … where we part?"

The Elf-horse snickered softly and Elgiva gave her a sorrowful look. She would never see her friend again and the realisation brought the smart of tears to her dark eyes. She studied the animal closely, the black mane and tail such a contrast to the whiteness of her coat, and tried to memorise her appearance, to hold it in her heart as a shield against ugliness. Then she sighed again and shifted her gaze.

"It was kind of you to come so far with me, Alison," she said, "but it does make our parting harder. I dare say you miss your children and the Royal Herd. You must go home."

The Elf-horse lowered her great head. As leader of the Royal Herd, her place was with her kind, but leaving her friend was a hard thing to do.

Harder still to conceal the truth, although it yearned to be spoken … But the time was not yet right.

Elgiva hooked her long hair behind her pointed ears and stuck out her chin defiantly. "I'm on my own now, Alison. I'll have to learn to fend for myself and there's nothing more to be said, but … there's something I would like to ask." For a moment, she hesitated, fearing to sound impertinent. "Why have you always been my friend? You favour a nar-Wardain, yet refuse to carry the King on your back."

The Elf-horse gave no answer and Elgiva knew better than to ask again. "Be on your way, then," she said with a frown. "Leave me to my fate."

But neither of them moved. Knotting her fists in her patched, grey robe, Elgiva grimaced with dismay. "Where will I go?" she pleaded. "Alison … tell me where to go!"

The childlike tremor in her voice made the great horse angry, but her anger wasn't for her friend and she knew that she mustn't speak of it. "Lord Bellic wanted you safe, Elgiva, and no-one will bother you here, but we could have travelled further, faster. You could have ridden me, yet you would not …"

"But, Alison, a nar-Wardain …"

"So be it," the Elf-horse said brusquely. "My heart would travel on with you, but duty calls me homeward. I feel the need of my kin. I can do no more for you, except to give you this advice. Oaks are lords of the forest and their wisdom is well known. Find one that is rich in years and its rede will guide you well. And do not forget the amulet. Now, Elgiva, I fear I must leave. May our paths cross again in happier times, if Lord Faine wills it so." She turned and prepared to descend the hillock.

"Alison!" cried Elgiva, her thin arms held out pleadingly. "This shouldn't be ...you know it! You know I'm not a traitor, don't you? One day they'll all realise and the King will revoke my banishment ... won't he?"

"Speak not of him. He is unworthy."

With that, the great horse trotted away, fearing that her resolve might crumble if she delayed any longer. As soon as she reached level ground, she broke into a gallop and Elgiva stared after her, lost and afraid, her vision blurred by silver tears.

"Alison ... don't leave me!"

But Elgiva's voice was no more than a sob and the mare was gone and all that remained was a lonely, young Elf dressed in servant's rags, standing on a hill.

The sun had grown warmer, but still she shivered and a rush of panic quickened her pulse. It seemed to Elgiva that her life lay behind her, like a discarded chrysalis, and unwillingly she had emerged from it, tender, vulnerable and alone. But there was nothing for it. Somehow the future had to be faced and she must find the courage to do so.

She sniffed back her tears and walked down the hillock.

At least she had something to focus on. Find an oak tree, Alison had said. That seemed like a good idea. They were wise and could be trusted. Bellic would approve ... but he wouldn't approve of self-pity. She had been banished from Elvendom, yes, and whether she had deserved it or not, she had to make the best of it. Bemoaning her lot was a waste of effort.

For a while she trudged on, deep in thought, and the morning matured around her. For the first time in her eighteen years she would have to provide for herself entirely … but how, in Faine's name, would she do that? She couldn't live off the land in winter and she had no land of her own to till. She didn't even have shelter. They had sent her away with nothing, not so much as a cooking pot or flints to make a fire. Her life had been spent as a servant and all her needs had been catered for, as long as she did her chores. Now all that was lost to her.

There was a thought at the back of her mind, a feeling that she should rejoice at her freedom, but freedom was something that carried with it a host of frightening responsibilities: self-preservation being the worst. Security was a thing of the past and that was hard to accept.

She studied the trees around her with a heightened sense of urgency. They merged into a smear of green and, at length, her eyes began to ache.

And then she stopped abruptly. Ahead of her was a massive oak tree and she gasped with relief and quickened her pace, until she stood within a few feet of its mighty, knuckled trunk. She gazed up into the branches.

She knew it was hard to talk to trees. They were deep and dark within themselves and spent most of their time asleep. Hesitantly, she reached out her hand and touched the rough bark with her fingers. She felt the need for reverence, but her need for comfort was stronger.

Pressing her body against the tree, she threw her arms around it.

"Forest-Lord, I need your help!" she begged in a quavering voice. "My name is Elgiva. My people are … my people were the Eldrakin. I need your guidance … please … if you could … if you would …"

She couldn't continue and, for a time, her slender frame was racked with sobbing, while the oak leaves danced above her head, their shadows capering on the grass, carefree as summer butterflies.

"Your arms are warm, little Elf," said the tree, "but they need to be much longer, if you wish to embrace me."

Elgiva sniffed back her tears and listened, but she felt rather than heard his voice. It flowed like dark waters under the earth.

"You've seen many things in your life," she said, a tentative smile upon her lips. "Would you be willing to give advice to an Elf who's lost all hope of home?" She dabbed at her eyes with her ragged sleeve.

"I would," he replied, "for the Elves are my friends. They venerate my race. I am Derryth and I do not forget those who pay me respect. Well I recall those others … it seems but yesterday. Druids they called themselves. Now they are gone. All gone forever. All of them slain."

Elgiva tried to be patient. She knew that time had no meaning for Derryth and he would never understand the need for haste that governed the lives of shorter-lived creatures.

"Yes, all slain," he went on sadly. "Then came others from across the grey sea. Bricks and stones and wars. They were always building, but I cared nothing for their works. And now, these Saxons … tree-slayers. I feel the anguish of the forests."

"Yes, the Wilthkin. They're cruel and selfish."

"But Elves … I like. Speak, child."

"I need your guidance, Derryth. I was a servant in Elindell, but I've been sent into exile … for treason. I'm banished from Elvendom and so I must fend for myself, but I don't know how to. Where will I live? How will I survive the winter? The food I brought with me is all gone. All I have is this amulet." She held it up for him to see, then felt extremely foolish – but Derryth had senses beyond mere vision. "It was given to me by a Wardain … Lord Bellic. He was my friend … my teacher."

"I know of him."

"You do?"

"He travels far. He speaks with the trees. His heart is good. Speak further, child."

"The amulet has the power to protect and it gives off warmth, if the giver is within three leagues of it, so I think … I hope … he intends us to meet again."

"How is the amulet used?"

Elgiva's brow creased slightly, as she thought back to the day of her leaving Elindell. Briar the wild cat had brought her the gift, had carried it in his mouth, and he told her what Lord Bellic had said. "I must speak its name and it will work whatever spell I wish," she said. "But if I use it for sport or gain or any evil purpose, it will rebound on me. Apart from this gift and my servant's rags, I have nothing else in all the world."

"You have the world," said Derryth softly.

Elgiva didn't understand. She peered up into his branches and tried to conceal her disappointment. Derryth seemed to be falling asleep; she could sense him drifting away. Her impatience made her protest far more shrill than she intended and it startled birds in the neighbouring trees.

"Derryth, I've been wrongly accused! I only ever did my duty and they sent me away from home … forever! Derryth! Are you listening?"

She felt a tremor run up the trunk, as though the great tree were chuckling.

"The Eldrakin … how they sparkle!" he said. "Be calm. I feel your innocence … but, little Elf, there *IS* blood on your head."

She pressed her forehead against his trunk and fought to hold in her tears.

"But still," he went on, "I am happy to help you. I do this in honour of Faine, your First-Father, the Founder of Elvendom. It was his love for the trees and beasts that gave us this boon of speech. Let us not squander it."

"Then tell me, Derryth, what must I do?"

Derryth drifted again. Elgiva sighed with impatience and ran her fingers through her hair. Finally he spoke.

"You must change," he stated simply.

"Change?"

"The amulet. Tell it to change you."

"But, Derryth, I don't understand."

"You may not walk abroad as an Elf. The Wilthkin will not shelter you … Kill you, most surely, I think. Your own kind have renounced you. You have no skills to survive alone and winter will be hard this year." The breeze rustled harshly through Derryth's leaves, as if to add weight to his words, and she felt a shiver skitter down her spine. "If you appeared to be … what you are not … help would be given willingly. Then safety. Until Lord Bellic comes to your aid."

"You think he will?" she asked worriedly.

"He is a Wardain, child. He will not abandon his friends."

Elgiva grimaced awkwardly at this, but she didn't wish to call into question Derryth's regard for Royal Elves and so she made no comment. "So what must I change myself into?" she asked.

"You must become a Saxon."

Elgiva's mouth fell open. Derryth's suggestion was ludicrous. Perhaps she had chosen the wrong tree. He wasn't just old, he was senile.

Another tremor ran through his trunk and his leaves seemed to crackle with laughter. "These hewers of trees are hateful, yes, but they overrun the land, little Elf. Everywhere. Like ants. You have travelled east into their domain. The Saxons are masters here. Will you elude them forever? Who will help you, if they do not? Do Elves not need companionship, too? I have no love for the race of Men … Wilthkin, as you name them … and the Saxons I like least of all, but they are most hospitable and always look after their own. Shelter will not be refused you, if you are one of them."

"Perhaps you are right," she said thoughtfully.

"The Saxons … you will learn from them, for everything is a lesson, child. They will teach you how to survive. Then, after winter, travel on. Spring will be early. Warm."

"You think so, Derryth?"

"I know it. I know many things … unknown to you … Ah!" He paused and seemed to hug to himself a secret he clearly wished to reveal.

Elgiva frowned and waited, but Derryth was drifting away once more. "Derryth! Did you have more to say?"

"Ah … little Elf," he murmured, at length, "this amulet. Tell me … how long will the spell endure?"

"Until I undo it … I dare say." She shrugged.

"Let us hope so, my child. Good. So, you have had my advice. Rest here awhile, for you need time … to decide if you will take it … or not."

She sensed that the oak tree had said his piece and that he would say no more. She could feel his consciousness sliding into sleep, so she sat herself down in the hollow between two of his thick, knurled roots and leaned her back against the stout trunk. Then she considered his words.

It was true, surely had to be true, that Bellic would one day seek her out. He had always been her teacher and friend and he was a good Elf with a generous heart; he wouldn't abandon her to her fate. But if for some reason he didn't come, she would have to find some cave or wood, far away from Elves or Men … The thought of such solitude appalled her aching heart and she quickly pushed it away. Perhaps that was something she could face, when there was no other choice. Until then all she needed to do was survive the coming winter.

It was decided, then.

The amulet of lapis lazuli hung on a leather thong round her neck. She clasped it firmly in her hand. She didn't know how to use magic, but supposed that a formal tone was best when addressing amulets and such. Self-consciously, she cleared her throat.

"Siriol, hear me and work my will! In the name of the one who gifted you to me, do as I bid you and change my appearance. Let me walk unremarked upon into the world of the Wilthkin and change me into a Saxon maid with yellow hair and eyes of blue. Do as I command you, until I bid you otherwise and ... Siriol, I, er ... so be it."

Elgiva realised that she was holding her breath, but nothing unusual happened. A stillness seemed to steal over the grass and she realised then how tired she was. She felt herself relax and her body was slowly sinking, as though it were melting into the tree bole ... and had the birds stopped singing, or were they just singing a long way off?

She sagged even deeper against the tree and tried to stifle a yawn. Her eyelids felt like slabs of cold stone, but she didn't want to sleep. Not yet. She needed to know that the spell would work.

But still her hair lay, black and gleaming, over her slender shoulders. It seemed that nothing had happened.

Nothing ... nothing had happened and perhaps her whole life had been a dream.

She yawned again, even less aware of the tree against her back. She felt that Derryth was fading away, evaporating like a mist. He seemed as unreal as the magic he had told her to call upon.

Magic.

It was hard to believe in such a thing. But her weariness was real enough and she let herself sink into it and allowed it to take her where it would.

* * *

Chapter Two

The sun was past its zenith when shouts erupted from a nearby wood and sent the birds screeching and chiding into the summer sky.

Elgiva woke abruptly. The cries were the cries of Wilthkin for there was a harshness in their calls and the underwood cracked loudly beneath their heavy tread. No Elf would cause such disturbance.

She thrust herself upright, rubbed her eyes, and her fear-sharpened hearing caught the swish of arrows among the trees. So the Wilthkin were hunting. She readied herself to withdraw.

But then she listened. These men were on foot; she couldn't hear any horses. If need be, she could easily outrun them. There was no need to panic. She felt herself relax.

Unhurriedly, she brushed the dirt and leaves from her clothes and prepared to continue her journey, but almost at once she faltered. Where had she come from? Where was she going? She felt that she had forgotten something; something most important. The fog in her brain defied penetration.

Another cry made her glance at the wood; then the cries abruptly changed and turned into peals of laughter. They sounded so inviting that she felt moved to seek out their source.

She touched the oak tree, seeking advice, but Derryth slumbered still, immersed in dreams of long-lost summers. Gathering up her courage, Elgiva set off towards the wood. Her heart was thumping in her breast, but curiosity drew her on. She crossed the meadow warily and stopped at the marge of the wood.

After a moment to wait and listen, she stepped between the trees. Her sandals sank into the leaf-littered ground as she crouched among the shadows. Peering through the foliage, she wondered vaguely why she felt compelled to seek out these Wilthkin in spite of her fear, but she felt she was on some kind of a threshold and knew she had to keep moving. There was no other choice. A tall elm creaked above her, as if it shared her tension, and for a moment she steadied herself against its sturdy trunk. Then she walked on cautiously.

In the still, green silence ahead of her, an arrow whispered through the air and Elgiva stiffened and held her breath. The Wilthkin were nearer than she had thought.

"Missed again, Elric!" came a shout. "Perhaps we should ask them to stand still for you." The voice trailed off into peals of laughter.

"Hah!" cried a second voice. "Taunt me, would you, when you've hit nothing all day yourself!"

"You're forgetting something, Master Elric," interposed another voice. "Your cousin has pierced the heart of a hawthorn and caught an old robin's nest."

"By Grim! You saucy rogue!" cried the first voice. "I'll have your eyes for gaming pieces!"

"In that case, my Lord, they'd see that you lost."

Elgiva smiled at this, then heard a gasp of pretended fury, followed by the sounds of a scuffle, while the owner of the second voice – whom she presumed to be Elric – complained at the lack of discipline.

"Come on, let's find a wild boar," he said gruffly. "We can take its head back as a trophy."

His companions agreed and followed him deeper into the wood, while Elgiva grimaced and shook her head. What coarse and clumsy creatures! Were they as ugly as their voices? She knew she wanted to find out, so she followed quietly in their wake, letting their noise be her guide.

At one point her path was blocked by a fallen tree and as she clambered over the toppled giant a mantle of silence fell over the wood; the hunters were lying in wait.

A sudden, whooping noise to her left and her heart jumped into her throat. The men were nearby, far too near. She crouched in the shadows and waited.

"By Frigg! you got him. Our luck has changed!"

She recognised Elric's voice.

The owner of the third voice sounded weary and bored. "It's just a young hare, Master Elric. He strayed from the meadow little knowing he'd end up as sport for a slave."

Elgiva's pale lips curled into a smile. This man's appearance was a mystery to her, but she could almost picture the long-suffering look he would now be giving his master.

"Even so, Godwin, that was well done."

"Well," said Godwin, "I thought I'd show my betters how it's done. After all, you can't eat an old robin's nest, no matter how it's cooked."

"Does this bastard never cease?" Deor demanded huffily. "Who said you could hunt anyway? A churl bearing arms indeed! Let me remind you, Godwin, you're supposed to CARRY our gear, be our beater, and shut your noise!"

"If I did that, my Lord, I'd make a very poor beater."

"By the blood of the gods!"

In her hiding-place, Elgiva grinned. As far as quick wits were concerned, the churl had the upper hand. As a servant herself, she took pleasure in it- but, of course, it wasn't a good idea to get too involved with these silly creatures and their petty word-games. Tucking her long hair behind her ears, she crept a little closer.

"Deor, listen!" Elric hissed suddenly. "Think I heard a large animal… over there in those bushes… if your noise hasn't driven all the game away."

Silence settled once more on the wood and Elgiva edged carefully closer and closer, until she finally spotted the hunters, crouched and unmoving among the shadows.

If only they knew, she thought.

Her Elven senses had told her that the beast they sought was some yards behind them, grouting among the ferns. It began to scent the air and its rough flanks shuddered with loathing. A muscular male with gleaming tusks, its mind held a bitter memory: a memory of men and arrows and pain.

And suddenly it moved.

"Lord Elric, behind you!"

At this, the hunters sprang to their feet. Elric span round to avoid the boar that was hurtling madly towards him. Deor fumbled to nock an arrow, but before he could aim, the beast had gone, had smashed its way back through the bushes, as startled by the warning shout as those it had sought to surprise.

"By Frigg!" cried Godwin, "that was close!"

"You all right, Cousin Elric?"

Elric glared at his companions. "Who called my name?" he demanded. The other men shrugged. "Who called?" he shouted, scanning the trees ahead of him. The lack of response sparked his anger and he drew an arrow from the quiver at his back and raised his tall, curved bow. Nocking the arrow, he flexed his muscles and drew the bow-string taut. "Who are you? Where do you hide? Come out and show yourself, trespasser!"

"But, Master, it was only..."

"Quiet!"

Crouched among the woodland plants, Elgiva felt panic race through her veins. What mad impulse had caused her to shout? Why had she cheated the boar of his quarry?

She was looking down the shaft of the arrow. She saw the sharp tip, the sleek, black feathers; felt the tension of the bow and the hunter's sinews. Elric was young and determined. She felt he would stand there all day, if need be.

Elric had heard a female voice. Perhaps he had more sport in mind, of one sort or another, but he might be in for a shock. Perhaps she could sneak away quietly...

"Show yourself and be rewarded, or hide and be hunted!" said Elric grandly. "You have nothing to fear, if you mean no ill!"

Elgiva's heart thumped in her breast, but there was nothing for it; shakily, she got to her feet. Momentarily startled, Elric lowered his bow.

"Approach," he commanded.

Reluctantly, Elgiva edged forwards, stopped within a few yards of the men.

Oh, Faine, I'm an Elf! They'll kill me! she thought.

Elric looked her up and down, his eyes an icy blue. He was a Saxon and, she guessed, a little younger than she was, but he was tall and well-muscled for his age. He had the manner of a lord sure of his authority and she had the impression that he had been allowed his own way far too often. Already on his youthful brow was the faint trace of a line, where a frown would be found more often than not.

Unnerved by her silence, he turned to his cousin, the blond hair brushing his shoulders as he did so. "What are we to make of this?"

Deor considered her in a way that would have made her servant's rags abhorrent in her eyes, had they not already been so. He, too, was tall and young, but the paunch that overhung his belt suggested a softer life than that of his companions. Twin garnet brooches flashed on his breast and his scabbard gleamed with amber studs. Elgiva considered him altogether too well-dressed for hunting.

"Don't ask me," he replied with a shrug. "Godwin has put me in a bad humour. Whatever I say will bode ill for your rescuer – if it isn't mocked first." He thrust out his chin and glared at Godwin. "But she's not one of my father's serfs and, if she isn't one of yours, she's no right to be on Lord Othere's land."

Folding his arms, Elric turned to the third man. "And what do you say, Godwin?" he asked, as though granting him an undeserved honour.

Elgiva looked at Godwin. He was, she supposed, a Briton, and a plain-looking creature compared with his betters. She thought he must be at least ten years their senior, though Wilthkin, she knew, had much shorter lives and guessing their ages was difficult.

His russet-brown tunic was patched in places; his belt was a plait of rope. His long, wide sleeves were frayed at the wrists and his boots were well-worn and sad-looking. His masters were growing immature beards, but Godwin was clean-shaven and, though not as tall or as handsome as them, he was strong and lean with a dark, gentle beauty that Elgiva found strangely appealing. His short, brown hair had a reddish sheen that reminded her of old copper.

But what struck her most were his eyes. Like the Saxons, he had blue eyes, but his were a cleaner, deeper blue. They gave him an open, honest look and she fancied she saw a light in them that had been dimmed by harsh experience.

He folded his arms across his chest, smiled impishly at Elric, but Elgiva sensed tension behind the smile. Then he gazed at her for a moment with what she could only describe as regret.

"If I wasn't a man of honour," he said, "I'd say I was glad my wife isn't here." He had said what was expected of him. Elric smirked appreciatively. "But, Master Elric," he went on more gravely, "this girl, perhaps, has saved your life. True, she's a trespasser, but a most welcome one." He inclined his head towards the Saxon, which made Elgiva wince. The gesture didn't become him, though it came to him easily enough. Then, in an instant, his tone changed again. "Besides, she's young and looks half-witted, so I think we should be merciful."

His gaze appealed to her once more, but she failed to read its message.

"How dare you!" she cried, forgetting her fear. "I have all the usual number of wits and more besides, I'll have you know!" She tossed back her head defiantly. "Don't taunt me… or I'll call back that boar and watch him make a meal of you all!"

Godwin and Elric stared at each other. "Well," said Godwin with a wry grimace, "apart from the language of my betters, I speak a few words of the Celtic tongue. I know some Roman phrases, too, I learnt from Aethelwulf the Sage. But now I find myself surpassed. I wouldn't claim to be fluent in Boar."

"And why not, for you are one?" Deor put in with a satisfied pout. "So, what do you say to that, then? I've learnt to beat you at your own game!"

Elric scowled with impatience, while Godwin regarded Deor as though he were an imbecile.

"And why not, my Lord? I beat you at yours."

Deor spluttered indignantly, but before he could respond, Elgiva intervened.

"Enough!" she cried, her small fists bunched at her sides, while three sets of eyes swivelled in her direction. "I'm tired of all your chatter. Are you men or squirrels? I saved your life, Lord Elric, and you've no right to toy with me."

Godwin lowered his gaze, while Elric's eyes glittered dangerously. Elgiva's anger quickly turned to fear and the impulse to flee made her turn on her heel.

"Stay…friend!" commanded Elric. "We did not mean offence!"

He placed a hand, half-amiably, half-threateningly, on her arm and she gave him a look that rightly belonged on the face of a startled fawn, but she swallowed the panic that clogged her throat and tried to appear affronted.

"You know what I am, Lord Elric, so why don't you put an end to me now… spare me this cruel sport?"

The three men looked at each other blankly.

"What are you, then?" asked Godwin, who by some unvoiced agreement had been delegated to speak. "Apart from another damned Saxon, a trespasser on Lord Othere's land and a saver of great men?"

Elgiva's mouth fell open. A what?

In the silence that followed, her mind laboured madly to make some sense of it all. Siriol! she thought. The spell must have worked. How did I forget?

"What's up with this girl?" asked Deor. "Surely she is Elf-shot."

Elgiva cast him a look of such hatred that he stepped back in alarm.

"Master Elric," said Godwin quickly, "this creature has a fine spirit. I think we've offended it. Your father would..."

"Speak to me not of him!" snapped Elric. "I know how to behave!" For a moment he frowned with petulance, then he bowed in Elgiva's direction and opened his mouth to speak, but the trespasser was ignoring him.

Instead Elgiva was drawn to the churl. She saw his concern and kindness clearly, but also the pain and complexity hidden behind a veil of humour. She felt the need to acknowledge his support, but "Thank you" was all she could think of.

Elric frowned, as though insulted, while Godwin looked mildly surprised. Deor merely sighed with boredom.

With his fists on his hips, Elric turned to the churl. He had lost control of the conversation and with it his air of authority. Now he didn't know how to proceed and he seemed even younger than he already was. But Godwin was preoccupied. He looked Elgiva up and down in her shabby servant's clothes and he felt that they had much in common. For her part, Elgiva wondered how he coped with the arrogance of his masters.

The first fine threads of a bond began to form between them.

She stepped towards him carefully, her voice little more than a whisper. "I see sorrow and loss in your eyes. It makes me sad," she said, and as soon as she did so, she cursed herself and lowered her eyes with embarrassment.

There was an awkward silence, in which the songs of the woodland birds sounded unnaturally loud and Elric and Deor shuffled their feet.

"You're wise beyond your years," said Godwin, his gaze both wary and quizzical. "Do you have the second-sight?"

"Er… no," said Elgiva, totally lost. "I recognise sorrow, that's all. It's my companion, too."

By now Elric had, had enough. "What's your name, girl? Where is your home?"

"My name is Elgiva," she answered, "and home is wherever I find myself. My people have banished me."

Elric gaped at the other men and they were equally shocked. Banishment from home was worse than anything they could imagine; worse than death in battle, which, at least, was an honourable end; it was worse than sickness or famine, which were eased by the help of one's kin. To be shunned by the gods was bad, but to Elric, Godwin and Deor, who seldom thought of the afterlife, banishment from home was the worst thing in the world.

"Now I feel sad for *YOU*," said Godwin, his brow creased with sympathy. "So young and so alone, with no lord to protect you. What on Earth did you do to deserve it? Was your crime so great?"

She looked at each of them in turn. She hadn't intended any of this. All she needed was food and shelter. No further involvement was required. Not with these barbarians. Why had she trusted them with the truth, when lies were all they deserved? She had committed herself too hastily. And Derryth was a fool.

"I'm innocent," she sighed. "And I will tell you my tale." Innocent, she thought, yet guilty of murder. Oh, Faine.

"Tale-telling comes later," said Godwin with a smile. "First you must sample our hospitality." He turned to address Elric. "This creature looks half-starved. Your father would be angry if we didn't offer food and shelter to an ill-used Saxon maid."

Elric's forehead furrowed, as he thought of his father's anger, but Elgiva recoiled from the prospect of help as though she had been offered a quick death.

"No… I can't!" she protested.

They were going to take her back with them, which, of course, was what she wanted, but her Elven instincts were appalled. She had forgotten who she was. These people were her people's enemies.

But … she had no people anymore.

Siriol …this was all a mistake!

Scowling at her intractability, Elric groaned with impatience and rested his arm across Godwin's shoulder. This gesture conveyed an unexpected depth of friendship and affection, throwing her further off balance.

"I'm sorry …I must go," she said shakily.

"Come, girl, let us help you," said Elric. "We shall be honoured to share our food and hear your sorry tale." Then his tone took on a sharper edge. "How can an exile refuse?"

How indeed? Elgiva was bereft of words. All she could think of was her home; the only world she knew and understood. It was lost to her forever. And now, thanks to Siriol, she had even lost herself. It was all too much to bear.

"Other tribes wouldn't be so hasty in their trust," said Elric haughtily. "Now, we must get going. We're two leagues from the settlement and I, for one, don't intend to go home empty-handed."

Elric had spoken and must be obeyed. He turned abruptly and marched away, his bow slung over his shoulder. Deor, with a grin of relief, gathered up his bow and arrows and trotted after his cousin. Godwin stooped to pick up the remainder of their gear, then he held out his hand towards Elgiva.

For a moment she chewed her lower lip, still weighing the need for shelter against the desire for escape. He sensed her apprehension and smiled at her reassuringly.

It galled her to admit it, but already she liked this man.

Reaching out, she took his hand, allowed him to lead her away. And neither of them could have known that with this simple joining of hands they had joined their separate destinies.

As they walked through the wood, Elgiva toyed with a strand of her hair. Lost in thought, it was some time before she noticed that her hair was now a golden yellow. Of course, she knew that Siriol must have brought about some change, but she had hoped for an illusion, not a physical fact and the knowledge of her transformation made her gasp with shock. Every muscle in her body tensed.

Godwin turned to look at her, concerned by the tightening of her grip. Forcing a smile for his benefit, she told him she had stumbled on a tree root. But she was frightened to be so changed: more frightened still to know the cause. Magic was something the Wardain used. It was fearsome and capricious and underlings like her could only wonder at it and seek to avoid its wrath.

However, as she left the wood and felt the clean sunshine on her skin, she chided herself for her cowardice. Though Siriol's magic frightened her, she knew it was good magic. It was as natural as the air she breathed. It was Lord Bellic's magic.

And if they couldn't be together, then at least this was something they could share.

★ ★ ★

Chapter Three

The afternoon was growing old when the four companions halted beneath the boughs of an ancient oak tree. Dark clouds were gathering in the sky and a stiff breeze ruffled their hair, carrying with it the scent of rain. Deor claimed to have seen a deer and he and Elric set off in pursuit, like excited boys at play, leaving Godwin in charge of their gear and their guest.

Elgiva looked at Godwin and he shrugged resignedly, then sat down beneath the tree.

"Will they catch anything?" she wondered, speaking more to fill the silence than for any other reason.

"I hope so," he replied. "I'd like to see my home again."

She seated herself beside him and watched him from the tail of her eye. She felt a great deal more at ease since the younger men had gone and she allowed herself to relax a little. "They're not very experienced at hunting, are they?"

Godwin looked at her and smiled. "They like to imitate their elders. Well, that's how we learn, isn't it? The real hunters will be home long since with enough meat to last us a week. As for the lads, well, we indulge them. It keeps them out of mischief... Elric especially."

"He's ...he's a bit sure of himself, isn't he?"

Godwin shrugged. "No doubt he has a right to be. His father is our lord and master. But it's not for me to say. I just do what I'm told. If that includes baby-sitting, well, so be it."

"Of course," said Elgiva. Do you despise them, too? she wondered.

"Elric's headstrong, yes, but he's a good lad at heart. He'll make a fine warrior one of these days." Godwin folded his arms and leaned back against the tree. "Mind you, I can't pretend I'm sorry to see them go. It wears me out trying to keep them amused."

She studied him for a while. There was something in his artless eyes that spoke of a deep and raging frustration, so deep that he wasn't even aware of it.

"Do you have children?" she asked.

He nodded. "Two young daughters, who take after me in colouring, but fortunately for them, not in looks." He grinned. "They are the pride of my heart."

"I thought Wil... er men looked down on daughters and longed for great broods of strapping sons?"

Godwin shook his head. "Is that what it's like where you come from? Well, I can only speak for myself, but what use are sons to me? I have no fields to till, no livestock to tend, no line to maintain. Nothing." A hint of sadness in his voice was instantly abandoned. "And why should daughters be overlooked? As Aethelwulf would often say, women can be warriors, too, and lead men into battle, when the need is great."

Elgiva felt that Godwin wore his maleness like an ill-fitting hat and beneath it was a sensitivity that he was careful to keep well-hidden, like his grievances against the Saxons. And grievances there must be, she knew, for their lot in life was similar. Their status alone gave them cause to be bitter and she felt that they would understand each other, because they both lived in servitude. This must explain why she liked him.

But there was something else.

She remembered Bellic telling her, during one of his endless lessons, that the Wilthkin were a mixture of races, not pure like the Eldrakin. He told her about the Britons, who long ago her people had named Elfryth. He said that they had magic, too, but not the kind used by the Wardain. No, this magic was more subtle. A kind of extra sense. An affinity with the Earth and the beings who lived in Spirit. Was that what Godwin had called 'second-sight'?

Bellic had grown very sad, when telling her of the Britons. They had lost much of their Earthlore and the Druids had taken their secrets and their wisdom to their graves.

When she thought of Bellic, she wondered if Aethelwulf had filled the same need in Godwin's life, taking a lowly churl under his wing and teaching him as an act of kindness, when nobody else would care. She wanted to find out more, but she knew she had to be careful: she didn't want to involve herself too deeply with the Wilthkin.

"You speak with this Aethelwulf a lot?"

"Well, not anymore. He's dead." He saw her startled reaction and laughed. "Last Winter was very hard, you see, and many elders perished."

"Oh… I'm sorry," she said.

"Don't be. He had a good, long life."

They lapsed into thoughtful silence.

"Your wife," she ventured at length, "is she of your race?" He shook his head. "Is she a slave like you?"

Godwin scowled at her. "My wife, Rowena, was born a serf and, yes, I was made one, but we're not slaves. Never that. Lord Othere treats us very well. He's like a father to us all." He shifted his gaze and looked at the sky, where the clouds were now bruised and swollen with rain. "I was almost like a son to him, when I was a child."

Elgiva sensed the tension creeping back into his voice, but she held herself still and listened.

"When Elric was born I was still a boy, but it seemed quite natural for me to become his unofficial guardian. I suppose like an older brother. And I guess I felt sorry for the lad. He had no mother to care for him. She died when he was born. Lord Othere has always trusted me to keep an eye on his only son. I'm quite a high-ranking slave, you see." He turned to her and grinned.

She marvelled at his good humour and wished she had the same capacity for accepting life's vicissitudes.

"Othere's a fair and generous master. You know what it's like to …oh, forgive me!"

Elgiva shrugged. "I don't know what it's like to have a fair and generous master, but it doesn't matter now." Even so, she felt the smart of tears and had to turn away.

Godwin didn't know how to proceed. "My wife is very beautiful," he said inconsequentially. "I'm a lucky man. I can't imagine why she chose me, but I'm glad she did." For a moment, his eyes sparkled wistfully and he seemed lost in thought.

She felt, on the one hand, like laughing at him, but, on the other, she heard Lord Bellic telling her that love could make any hardship bearable. Love was power, he had said. The only power that mattered. And she had yawned at him.

"It speaks of rain," he said suddenly. "We might even have a storm."

Elgiva was startled out of her thoughts. Reaching up to tuck her hair behind her ears, she froze. Her ears felt different somehow; small and rounded and very unelvish. Her hands fell limply into her lap and she saw that her skin had reddened, lost its pale, translucent quality. There was a coarseness about it that brought a constriction to her throat.

She had no idea what she looked like. She didn't know who she was.

Oh, Faine, she thought, this is awful… awful! I know it was the only way. I know that Siriol did what I asked. But how am I to bear it?

It didn't seem believable that in the space of a few short weeks her life could change so drastically. For eighteen years, she had led an uneventful life as a servant. A hard and lonely life it had been, but it had been secure and safe. Now she was in a different world, and she was a different person. How could she cope with this deception?

Yet she knew that if it hadn't happened, she was as good as dead.

She sniffed back the tears that were threatening to flow. Bellic wouldn't approve. She had to get on with the business of living.

And she wondered if what had died was really worth grieving for.

She realised that Godwin was looking at her.

"Is something wrong, Elgiva?"

"No… no, nothing." She forced a smile.

"The gods are planning a battle up there for us poor mortals to wonder at." He pointed at the sky. "I wonder where the lads have got to?"

Elgiva didn't care. She watched the clouds that were rolling towards them, grey as despair and edged with darkness. "A wind is blowing from over the hills that lie between my land and yours. It carries the scent of pines. I can almost smell the wood-smoke and ...I can hear the laughter. Friends are sitting around the fire. Can I still call them friends? They are laughing, but I am forgotten."

Godwin watched her guardedly. "You speak strangely," he said. Yet it seemed that he, too, could almost smell and hear the things that she described. He cast his gaze to the far horizon, not knowing what he sought.

"I can hear the harp," breathed Elgiva. "Caspell is singing in the great Hall and the hounds are sprawled beside the hearth. The ladies wear heartsease in their hair."

He reached out to touch her, but thought better of it. "Don't be sad, Elgiva. Whatever happened, you're all right now."

"It's changed for me. I am changed."

Then the first raindrops began to fall and it grew very quiet. The birds were silent in the trees, the air suddenly chill. Then both of them were startled as a flash of lightning cracked in the sky and, moments later, thunder rumbled in the slate-grey clouds above them.

"Not the safest place to shelter," said Godwin, glancing up at the tree. "Strange how the weather can change so suddenly." Elgiva looked at him blankly. "Where in Frigg's name have they got to? I suppose they've got themselves lost. Let's hope they return before we're struck by lightning."

Elgiva found herself laughing, in spite of her melancholy. How ironic it would be! How pointless her years of servitude, her exile, her transformation, if in the space of one second she ended up as a pile of ashes!

Godwin feigned disapproval. "I'm glad the idea is so entertaining."

Her giggling slowly subsided and they sat and listened to the rain.

Godwin hugged his knees and let his gaze unfocus, while Elgiva secretly watched him. The weight of things unsaid still hung in the air between them and there was something about this man that made her want to know more.

Well, it'll pass the time, she thought.

"Godwin, if we're here for a while, why don't you tell me how it is you come to be living with Saxons?"

The look he gave her was so intense that she felt she had touched an open wound, rather than asked a question.

"Godwin, I'm sorry, is that ... is *THAT* the sorrow I saw in your eyes?"

He was visibly taken aback by this. Was his pain really so obvious? "Feel like a story, do you?"

She touched his arm lightly. "Bellic says ...oh, he's a friend of mine back home ... he says it's good to talk of past anguish, or it lies within us festering. The cankerworm of care, he called it."

"Did he indeed?" said Godwin, and he felt that his tone was perhaps too sardonic. Yes, he needed to tell her, though he wasn't the sort to unburden his heart to a stranger. To anyone.

Elgiva turned away and sat twisting a coil of hair round her finger. She seemed to be waiting and he had a strange feeling that what happened next was inevitable. But he didn't know where to begin, nor if it were wise to begin at all. To tell his kind of story needed courage, but courage wasn't a virtue he saw very often in himself.

"Very well." He took a deep breath. "It was a day very much like this one," he began, "when I, son of someone I can't remember, bearing a name that time has erased, lived in a long –lost village." He paused and his generous lips curled into a smile. "The minstrels could make a fine song out of that."

Elgiva glanced towards him with a look of disapproval, made him regret his levity.

"Well," he went on," I was playing outside this village, among the trees, with my sister. My only sister, as far as I know. I may have been five years old … or six. I'm not exactly sure. But she was a little younger I think. Well, it doesn't matter now. My age, like my name, is a mystery. But I do remember blackberries. We had a basketful. Someone had sent us out to pick them. I imagine we ate more than we collected. And we had some toys. Wooden toys."

"Well, it was muggy and very still. The sky went dark and it started to rain." He paused and tried to recollect those things that only seemed clear in his nightmares. "There was lightning… then thunder. We heard cries, too, coming from our home. I must have been very afraid, but my sister, she was never afraid. She wasn't afraid of anything." He stopped and smiled fondly at the thought. "I don't remember her name either and now I can't even see her face … but I do remember her beautiful hair. It was … I can't describe it. Dark with a reddish sheen to it and she wore it in plaits tied up with green braid."

He glanced at his companion. Her features didn't betray her thoughts, but at least she wasn't laughing at him. "What happened next, it's hard to say. So many years have passed. But I do remember the noise from the village…the rain… the clouds of smoke…and suddenly everything had changed and we knew that something was badly wrong. People were running towards us. A tall man … he looked like a giant to me … came running towards us and grabbed hold of me. He hoisted me into the air and I heard my sister scream. I think she tried to protect me, but … the warrior had a broadsword … and I looked down … I looked down and saw…" He stopped and swallowed hard. "She lay among the blackberries and toys. And she was dead. That's one thing I'll never forget." He paused again and sighed. "Well, I don't remember the journey to Othere's, but that's where I ended up. As for my parents…" He shrugged and fell silent, turning his face away.

While Godwin tried to compose himself, Elgiva waited, stunned, not daring to break his line of thought, for she felt that he had more to say. She wanted to reach out and comfort him, but she didn't know how to do it.

"Well," continued Godwin, with a small smile in her direction, " I do have more than memories to remind me of the past. I have a sword, Elgiva. You know we're not allowed to bear arms, so I'm not permitted to use it… wouldn't know how to anyway. I had it with me when I was taken. I think it had a leather scabbard, but that got lost somewhere."

Fatigue and hunger were beginning to make Elgiva feel light-headed, but she tried not to show it in her voice. "You were young to have such a weapon," she said.

"Yes, it's odd, but that sword was always with me, I think. A dangerous toy for so small a child, but I can't explain it. Perhaps I was born to better things." He smiled again, but his smile only served to underscore his bitterness rather than to hide it. "But I know why the

Saxons let me keep it. They told me, when I was older. I tried to defend myself with the sword … to the great amusement of all the raiders. They thought it a handsome weapon and determined to take it from me, but when one of them tried to do so, he was badly cut. Othere told me they all roared with laughter. The warrior lost three fingers and almost bled to death."

Elgiva's eyes widened in horror and Godwin burst out laughing. "Othere said it was great sport indeed … one of their best warriors defeated by a tiny child. So he decreed I should keep the sword, as a keepsake of my past. He does have these whims from time to time. It's still the subject of a joke among the older men in the Meadhall … when they're all drunk and feeling nostalgic."

"And what of the man you wounded?"

"Oh, he was fine," Godwin assured her. "In fact we've always been friends."

Elgiva was about to remark upon the brutality of Saxons, until she remembered that she was a Saxon now.

Lightning whipped suddenly across the sky, made them both flinch and peer up at the tree. Then they looked at each other and grinned and Godwin resumed his tale.

"So I ended up at the settlement where Othere's word is law and I've been there ever since … over a score of years … bearing the name they gave me…"

"They killed your sister and made you a slave!" she exclaimed, appalled.

Godwin glared at her. "These things happen. You must know that. Have your people never gone to war? Against the Britons …against each other?"

She shook her head in disbelief. "But still, they killed your sister. Did you never think of running away?"

"Running away? To what? Isn't one place as good as another? You were a slave, too, weren't you? What made you so sorry to leave?"

She was taken aback by the anger in his eyes. "They ... they were my people. I had a roof over my head and I had food and I had ... well ...I knew no other life."

"And I have a wife, a family and a generous lord. The Saxons have treated me well. Other captives weren't so lucky. And when it happened, I was a child. I had to accept it all. Then I grew up and it no longer mattered – do you understand? The Saxons are my people now."

"Godwin ...I'm so sorry," she said. Crestfallen, she drew up her knees and hugged them to her chest.

He felt a pang of guilt at being the reason for her dejection. She may have sparked his anger, but she wasn't the root cause of it. His life was full of unanswered questions that he never dared to confront and now a total stranger had brought them all to his attention. He had the strangest feeling that his conscience had taken human form.

He touched her arm reassuringly. "Don't be... please," he said, but she still looked sad and uncomfortable. "Life's hard," he stated uselessly. But perhaps it was harder for the brave he thought. It was easier to be a coward, especially if one had no other choice.

"I was born a servant," she ventured. "If I'd been made one instead, I dare say I'd be angry, too." She glanced at him, uncertain of his mood. "But you seem to cope with it. I'm not sure that I would. Oh, I've had to accept what I am ... and I do, but ... not knowing who my parents were... who I am ... I find very hard to accept. I had a sort of guardian once." Her pert nose wrinkled with contempt. "Eldreda … she was hateful. I didn't dare ask her anything. Her answers were always the same – a couple of swipes of the cane she always carried. And Bellic wouldn't tell me, so I knew it was bad and I must have been the product of some … some indiscretion."

She shrugged, as if such things no longer had the power to hurt her, and turned to face her companion. "Doesn't it bother you, Godwin, not knowing who you are, who you might have been? Don't you hate the Saxons for taking all that away from you?"

Her eyes held a look of pleading, as though in asking him such questions she might find the answers to some of her own. His artless, blue eyes held her gaze for a while and then he turned away and drew a steadying breath. She was being honest with him and deserved the same honesty in return.

"What good would that do, Elgiva?" he asked. "It wouldn't change anything, would it? It would only make life harder. I have a good enough life. The one I might have had could have been worse. I will never know. Be reasonable. We have to accept things as they are and just get on with life."

"But I can't!" she blurted out. "I won't! What happened to me … it's wrong! It's not fair! It's just not fair!" She hid her face in her hands and, unexpectedly, burst into tears.

Godwin's experience as a father had made him an expert at dealing with tears. He put his arm around Elgiva and pulled her gently towards him. "But you'll be all right now," he told her. "Lord Othere will look after you."

"How can you be so sure?" she sniffed.

"Well, if you were wrongfully banished…"

"Of course I was!"

"I know. I'm sorry."

"What makes you think I want your master looking after *ME*? I want ... I need my *OWN* people!"

"The Saxons *ARE* your people, Elgiva."

She sobbed afresh and wished she had the courage to tell him the truth. "Oh, Godwin ... what's to become of me?"

Godwin felt a pain in his heart at the sight of her distress. He'd only known her for a short while, yet he felt a bond with her. He didn't understand it, but he knew that no-one else had ever made him look inside himself and question what he saw there.

He looked around and realised that the rain had stopped. Every leaf and blade of grass sparkled with moisture in the sunshine. The air smelled clean and new.

"Life's not been kind to either of us, so perhaps we deserve each other," he said. "If you're afraid of the future, then knowing you have at least one friend might help."

She looked up at him, her eyes wet with tears.

"Upon my oath, I'll be your friend. I'll ward you from any foe," he said, "if it's within my power. I vow to be your protector." He placed his hand upon his breast. "I pledge this with all my heart. There. Do you feel better now?" His smile was warm and comforting. "You won't need my protection, you know, but you have it all the same."

A cry hailed him from the distance and both he and Elgiva visibly jumped.

By Grim! What had he been saying?

"It's Elric and Deor," said Elgiva.

They got to their feet as the two young men came running up excitedly, their clothes soaked with rain and their blond locks dripping. Deor stumbled on a root and Godwin grabbed his collar to keep him from falling.

"You should see what we've caught!" cried Deor. "Godwin, we killed a red stag, by Thunor!"

Elric threw his bow on the grass and stood, grinning broadly, his fists on his hips. "We were successful, by Frigg! Wait till they see the brute back home! We must return at once!"

"Yes, Master Elric, we will," agreed Godwin. "Our guest is very weary."

Elric gave her a cursory glance. "Yes, well, come on, then, man. Help Deor carry the beast. We left it over there." He swung his arm out casually.

Inwardly Elgiva groaned. Now she would need excuses, when food was offered in the Hall. Though the Eldrakin used the hides and horns and bones of beasts that died in the forest, since the time of Faine's bond with the animals, they had never eaten meat. Well, that was another problem she would deal with when she met it.

As the men set off to recover their prize, she trudged behind with a heavy heart. Lord Bellic had told her how Faine First-Father had won the friendship of animals. How their mutual love and respect created a magical bond that allowed communication between them. How this bond that could never be broken had first been made with a stag. A red stag.

Gritting her teeth, she walked on.

⋆ ⋆ ⋆

Chapter Four

The home of Lord Othere's people was a well-established and prosperous place and Elgiva had never seen anything like it. Her people lived unobtrusively in their tidy forest dwellings, while these Wilthkin seemed to need plenty of space in which to live out their brief and brutal lives.

As she was taken though the gates, the stronghold opened out before her; almost thirty acres' worth of bustling activity and within it were three dozen or more rectangular dwellings of varying sizes, all with pitched, thatched roofs. There were also work-sheds and stables and pens. Smoke dawdled in the late-summer air and the stench of burning rubbish made her wrinkle her nose with disgust.

But the noise surprised her more than anything else: the chatter of people doing their chores; the barking of dogs and the bleating of goats; the raucous laughter of warriors, lounging near the stronghold's gates; the screams of children playing tag; and, somewhere, the laboured clanking of a loom.

She tried to take in all the details, as Godwin led her towards the great Hall. This building, made of seasoned oak, was large and solid-looking, and inside there were splendours Elgiva hadn't expected. The massive high-table bore gleaming goblets and golden platters, all reflecting the light. Benches stood ranked among the thick stanchions that supported the roof with its rafters of ash. On the walls hung silver-tipped drinking horns, colourful hangings and polished war-gear and by the great hearth a brace of huge deerhounds, watched the newcomer warily.

Elgiva hoped that she might get the chance to talk to these hounds while no-one was looking and learn all she could of their masters, but for now it was clear that what she believed about the Wilthkin wasn't quite true. She thought that their homes would be dirty and dismal, but the great Hall was spacious and orderly; the wooden floor had been recently swept, the torches lit and a fire blazed in the hearth. Polished and arranged with care, helmets, swords and seaxes gleamed bravely on the walls.

Of course, she thought, they're still barbarians, surrounded by the spoils of battle.

She saw few people in the Hall, apart from a handful of menials, preparing for the evening meal, and none so much as glanced at her. Godwin hefted a glass jug, poured some pale wine into a beaker, and handed it to her with a smile. Elric frowned and tapped his foot. Godwin looked at him and sighed, like an old tutor with a slow-witted pupil.

"I've served the guest first, Master Elric, as is the custom," he said.

"Yes, I know that, Godwin, but don't be so bloody slow about it, man! I'm nearly dying of thirst."

Deor ignored the formalities. Snatching the jug from Godwin's hand, he poured himself a beakerful and threw it down his throat. Then he wiped his mouth on his sleeve. "This will sharpen my appetite, by Thunor!" he declared. "Just wish we didn't have to wait so long to eat."

"I've a mind to try some sword practice first," said Elric. "What do you say, cousin?"

Deor groaned with reluctance. "Oh, well, if we must. It'll pass the time. But let's stop at the kitchens on the way. I can smell fresh-baked bread!"

Elric slapped him hard on the shoulder. "Come on, then, you sluggard!"

To Elgiva's relief, they marched away.

"Here's Redwald," announced Godwin, "Lord Othere's minstrel."

Elgiva turned to see a tall, thin man striding into the Meadhall. He had long blond hair and carried a lyre and his face was as bland as his homespun tunic. He perched himself on the edge of the dais on which the Lord's high-table stood, then he drew up his knees, like a long-legged bird in a nest that was far too small for him, and began to pluck at the lyre.

"Practising, " said Godwin, adding in a lower tone, "Well, he needs to, believe me." Elgiva grinned at this. "Some new tune, if we're lucky, but no doubt the same old tales."

"What sort of tales do your people like?"

He cocked an eyebrow at her. "*MY* people? Don't you mean *YOUR* people? You're the Saxon, not me."

Elgiva bit her lip. "Well … I meant… different tribes, different customs … I dare say." Her face felt suddenly hot.

"They like the usual stuff," he said, watching her askance. "Like Saxons everywhere, I expect. Tales of honour in battle… dragon-slaying and feuds… gods and the like… and bonds between the warrior and the gold-giver. Shall I go on?"

"No … no, I see. The usual stuff, of course," she said, twisting a strand of hair round her finger.

"As for what *MY* people like, I'm not the one to ask." He gave her an arch look.

"No, of course." What on earth was a gold-giver? She had to find out more. "So ... on the subject of gold-givers ... er..."

"We needn't speak of that," he said. "In your case it can only cause pain."

Elgiva regarded him blankly.

"Well, yours was more of a grief-giver, wasn't he?" He raised his eyebrows in a manner that suggested she would agree with him.

Elgiva's mind worked frantically. "Oh... oh, yes! And yours?"

"Othere is a very generous master to those who are loyal to him."

Bribery, she thought dismissively. Would these people serve him out of love, if he had no gold in his pockets?

But she had served Thallinore out of love and look where it had brought her.

"We take an oath to serve him and in return we have his protection, but you'd know all this, of course," said Godwin.

"Well, I don't know much about honour and oaths and all that sort of thing," she said. "All I know is drudgery. You couldn't make a heroic tale out of sweeping floors and scrubbing tables."

"Well, we won't have you sweeping and scrubbing just yet. We generally feed our guests before we stick a broom in their hand." He flashed her a look full of gentle humour and she couldn't help but smile back at him. "And you won't be a churl tonight. Your place will be at the high-table – next to Othere himself."

Her smile disappeared. "It will?"

"A stranger with a tale to tell? You're worth your weight in gold, Elgiva. My betters can't cope with a lack of war. Boredom is a merciless enemy and Othere's in need of some entertainment. We won't get many travellers now with winter on the way and the last one we had was a while ago. A wandering story-teller he was. Paid for his meat and ale with stories – the sort that would give you nightmares. Enchanters and woodland sprites and animals that could talk. Complete nonsense and fantasy, but it kept him well fed for a month. One tale I remember especially. It was all about Elves and their wicked ways."

Elgiva swallowed hard. "I can't compete with tales like that. My own is very dull."

"But true, though. That makes all the difference. But no need to worry about that now. We've some time yet before we eat, so I'd better find you a place to stay. We're a little cramped here at the moment, but we're building some new dwellings in the Spring. Of course, you must have servant's quarters." He grimaced in apology. "For the time being you're welcome to share *MY* home."

She inclined her head towards him. "You're very kind," she said.

He led her towards a side-door and together they left the great Hall and strolled across the settlement towards the servant's quarters. Godwin walked up to one of the dwellings, pushed open the rickety, wooden door, and invited Elgiva to step inside with a sweep of his arm and a grin on his face.

"There's a spare place over there," he said, pointing through the gloom.

Elgiva peered across the hut and saw a low, wooden frame. On either side were partitions of osiers.

"I'm afraid that's the best we can do for now. I'll get you a pallet from somewhere."

"I'm accustomed to nothing better," she said, hoping he wouldn't take offence.

"Neither am I." He grinned.

"Where's your family, Godwin?"

"My wife will be preparing food. I expect the girls are playing somewhere. They are usually with their friends. And I must be getting back to the Hall, but I'll light you a fire before I go."

While Godwin was busy with this task, Elgiva inspected his home more closely. There were four partitioned areas, shelves displaying pots and utensils and, against one wall, four three-legged stools stood in a row. The fireplace was a pad of clay in the centre of the room. As the fire caught hold and she had more light, her eyes were drawn to a glinting object hanging high up on a wall. It was the sword he had told her of. It seemed out of place in this meagre dwelling.

"So that's your sword," she remarked. "It looks like a handsome weapon."

Godwin walked towards the sword and grasped it by the hilt. "I polish it from time to time, but I keep it unhoned, of course."

Elgiva felt herself drawn to the blade; there was something odd about it. She felt a pulling sensation in her solar plexus, a curious feeling she couldn't explain.

"My only link with what has been ... or even might have been," he said wistfully. He ran his fingers over the hilt. "The Saxons make the finest of swords." He smiled. "But nothing like this."

Elgiva moved to his side. She saw engravings on the hilt; they were the impressions of tiny stars and, within each star, a mysterious rune.

"Unhoned, you say?" He nodded. "But it looks incredibly sharp."

He laughed. "I assure you, it's quite dull and blunt, though I keep it up here out of harm's way, just to be on the safe side. My children are young, you see. It must be the way it reflects the light. Part of the skill of its maker, perhaps." He ran his thumb hard along the blade's edge. "I couldn't cut butter with this." He laughed and replaced the sword on the wall. "Well, I'd better speak to Lord Othere. Tell him all about you. No doubt he'll be intrigued." He strode towards the door, then turned. "Stay here and rest. I'll call for you later."

Elgiva chose one of the three-legged stools and placed it beside the fire. She sat down with a heavy sigh and tried to accept what had happened. Clutching the amulet at her breast, she begged it to maintain the spell, but also she pleaded with herself not to forget who she really was.

* * *

The feasting was drawing to a close and the air in the great Hall was thick with smoke and sweat and the tang of roasted flesh. The chatter and laughter of many voices resounded within its walls. Elgiva longed for the cool, open air. She swallowed some wine to calm herself and watched the great dogs that were grouped by the hearth. They were fighting over a thigh-bone that once had belonged to some hapless beast and the manner in which they addressed each other made Elgiva sigh. Well, dogs imitate their masters, she thought.

Someone was trying to attract her attention. It was Othere, seated on her right. Godwin had brought her to him at the beginning of the meal. Elgiva's mouth had gone instantly dry and she feared that the man could see her trembling. Tall and broad and draped with fur, Othere looked like an angry bear, with strong hands and a battle-scarred face and a voice accustomed to being heard.

He had thanked Elgiva for her part in saving his son from the boar's attack, but when told of her exile, his face had darkened. He had shaken his head and his grey beard whispered against the silver chain that hung about his neck. His eyes had the sharpness of steel and she knew that deceiving him wouldn't be easy.

But Othere had said that no guest in his Hall was called to account on an empty stomach and with that he had left her alone to gnaw on the bones of her apprehension.

Now, however, it seemed that he was ready and eager to hear her tale.

"You have feasted well, child? Perhaps you will honour me with the tale of your unhappy exile? I cannot believe you an evil-doer, unless your innocent looks are deceptive."

Elgiva drew in a deep breath and expelled it quickly to steady herself. "I may have done evil, my Lord, but it wasn't my intention," she said. "You see, it was like this. I tried to protect my master. I knew he was in danger. He had placed his trust in men who were really his enemies. I chanced by their hiding-place one day and overheard their talk. They were plotting against him, my Lord."

Lord Othere drew closer, intrigued to hear more.

"I was angry," Elgiva continued. "For all his faults, he was still our master and we had sworn oaths to serve him." Othere nodded in grim approval. "I had to keep it to myself and you might wonder at that, but, to be honest, I was afraid. I'd always been a dutiful servant, only to be despised for it, and I never found out why." She paused as though it saddened her to recollect the past, but it was the effort of choosing her words that made her hesitate. One slip and she would be lost. "Who would believe someone like me, if I accused my betters?"

Bellic would, she thought. But he had been absent as usual, when he was most needed.

"I decided, if I was to save my master, that I must take action myself." She paused again and gulped some wine. "Well, my Lord, my people are skilled at archery. Even churls love to practise the art. So as I knew where my master's enemies planned to meet him ... kill him ...I left the servants' quarters and went there with a bow and some arrows. I climbed up a tree. And I waited."

Elgiva was growing in confidence now and this time she paused for dramatic effect. She took another sip of wine, while Othere sat stiffly attentive.

"My Lord arrived for the secret meeting his enemies had requested and soon his arch-enemy, who was his Chief Counsellor, turned up with his fellow conspirator."

Tarkinell. She shuddered as she remembered his gaunt, mean face and greedy eyes. He was an Elf she had never liked.

"This man diverted my Lord's attention and engaged him in conversation. Then the Chief Counsellor stepped behind him and drew a dagger from his robe. The cold metal flashed as he raised it, but I was ready. My bow was drawn and I released the string. Did I intend to kill the Chief Counsellor? I don't know my Lord, but haste does nothing for one's aim. I pierced him to the heart."

Elgiva glanced at Othere. His mouth was set in a thin, hard line, but otherwise he showed no reaction.

"My master looked up and saw me," she went on, "and, while he called for the guards, the other man picked up the dagger and hid it in his tunic. Then there was general confusion, as guards and servants appeared from all sides. I was shaken from the tree and the plotter feigned outrage and told everyone that my master had been my intended target. Nobody listened to me. The Chief Counsellor a traitor? What a ridiculous notion! And there was I, a low-born slave, with a bow and arrows, guilty of murder. I was beaten unmercifully ... the plotter egged them on to prevent me speaking up for myself. I think they would have killed me, had a high-ranking friend not intervened."

Captain Merrill, she thought with a smile. She hoped he hadn't been made to pay for standing up for her.

She sighed deeply and took more wine and by now her head was beginning to swim and the heat in the Hall made it hard to breathe freely. She leaned against the tall chair-back and tried to relax, but it wasn't easy. She could see in her mind those awful moments following her arrest; the blows and accusations and the anger of King Thallinore. She thought that he would strike her dead with his Royal Elf-magic, but, oddly, he had withheld his power, in spite of his fury. Outrage had no doubt robbed him of the capacity to act.

She swallowed to ease her tightening throat. It was easy now to look sincere. Too well she recalled the curses and blows and the feeling of helpless despair.

"At length I was dragged away," she continued. "I was put in a cruel confinement, underground in a dark, dank cell. If some sort of trial was conducted, then I was never told of it. Eventually, they hauled me out and banished me forever. Well, I thought they were going to execute me, but perhaps they thought that exile was worse. I dare say they're right, my Lord." She shrugged and took a sip of wine. "So, I can't return to my people's land. Never. On pain of death. My home is lost to me."

And Bellic had said nothing. He sent Briar with the amulet. He asked Alison to be her escort. But he had said nothing: not even good-bye.

Othere had listened carefully, respectfully, to her tale. Now he clenched his large fists on the table before him. "If what you say is true …" he began.

"I swear it, my Lord," said Elgiva.

"Then your lord is unjust and foolish, my child. He lacks the knowledge of men required for a lord to rule wisely and well. A lord must be a father to everyone, high or low, and must know their needs and value their worth. I have seen the lowliest churl shame his masters in battle with his loyalty and courage, though untutored in the art of war. A lord must give justice to everyone, regardless of the crime. Your master did not permit you to speak in your own defence. Your youth and sex at least should have earned you merciful treatment. A lord such as yours can never have the respect his title merits."

Elgiva imagined that Othere truly believed what he was saying, but, removed from them by his rank and wealth, did he really know the worth of his people down to the lowliest servant?

"It is foolish to trust without question the men who crowd around one, eager to give advice," he went on.

"Such men are often dissemblers whose hearts nourish secret ambitions. They are often not a tithe as true as the lowly vassal who tends the hearth."

He was going to chase this to its death. These creatures love to talk, thought Elgiva. No, that was uncharitable. Considering Othere's hospitality, she could at least have the grace to listen to him.

"Such men," he continued, "have much to gain by fawning, but a servant born to his lot in life is not permitted a higher rank and, having little to gain, is apt to speak the truth."

His use of the word 'permitted' made Elgiva squirm and she didn't think it was wise for servants to go around speaking their minds. Despite his claimed love of justice, he clearly didn't believe in equality, but what else had she expected? He was, after all, a lord, like Thallinore, and the reason for his existence was to keep everyone else in their place.

"Like Godwin?" she asked ingenuously. She had glanced up and seen him across the Hall, clearing away the remains of the meal, while his betters continued to laugh and swill beer.

"Ah, my favourite churl! I would trust him with my very soul. An honest wight, indeed. More so than these noble sirs you see about me, mouthing wise words. Position and wealth do not nurture humility."

She wanted to cock an eyebrow at this, but managed to look sincere. "I think he respects you very much, my Lord," she said. Which makes him a fool, she thought. After all, you cost him his family.

Othere shrugged modestly and smiled.

"Yet even so," she added, "he belongs to the race of our enemies."

He raised his hoary eyebrows. "That is so. There were many battles with different tribes at the time when Godwin was taken." He paused for a moment and the gleam in his eyes looked more like relish than recollection. "Our children were also abducted in raids. But now we live in a time of peace. Our enemies have retreated west and those that were taken, on both sides, are no doubt content to be where they are. Godwin is one of our race now."

"I dare say you are right, my Lord. Are there more of Godwin's race in the stronghold?"

"There were," he replied, "but I sent them south many years ago. To Deor's father. As a gift. Good workers are worth their weight in gold, but I kept the best for myself." He grinned.

Elgiva was appalled. She lifted her beaker to her lips, but found that it was empty. Othere reached for a jug of wine.

"Permit me to offer you more," he said affably.

He filled her beaker to the brim and Elgiva smiled to herself. Seldom was a servant waited on by a lord.

"You treat your guests very well," she said. "I am, after all, a mere churl." His eyes narrowed fractionally; perhaps her remark had been ill-considered. Hastily, she added, "And a churl without a master. As an exile, I can expect nothing from anyone, but I dare to ask something of you, my Lord Othere."

"Ask."

"I need food and a place to live. You are convinced of my innocence … I hope. Would you let me stay here and serve you… if you deem me worthy, of course?" If it weren't for the loosening effects of the wine, these words might have choked her.

Othere carefully weighed her request, while Elgiva's guts churned with impatience. Eventually, he said, "I consider you most worthy."

"Thank you, noble lord."

He chuckled. "An interesting creature you are, to be sure. You are a churl, yet your manner speaks of higher things."

"I was well-taught, my Lord."

"So it would appear. I was told you may have tales for us. In sooth, I confess that my hospitality was not entirely unselfish." He studied the rings that adorned his fingers, while Elgiva gulped down more wine. "Hearing that you were a traveller, I had hoped that you would repay me by giving us news of foreign parts, as well as a few new stories. Perhaps you know some verses?"

"I shall be honoured," she lied.

"We have few visitors these days, now that things have quietened down. Some diversion is always welcome. As you see," – he gestured towards the minstrel -,"our present entertainment has grown a little stale." He chuckled, as though this were a great jest. "So, child, from whence do you come?"

"From beyond the hills to the west," she replied.

"The stronghold of the Britons?"

"Oh, er... yes, my Lord." She swallowed, then affected a haughty smirk. "But our settlement is very large and we have many warriors. As for the Britons," – she shrugged –, "a disorganised rabble, bemoaning their lot and fighting amongst themselves. They know what's best for them and leave us well alone."

"Well, yes," agreed Othere doubtfully. "It must be as you say. I confess we do not know as much about other tribes as we should. We have grown complacent and lazy.

A very dangerous state of mind. But, enough of such matters for now."

Elgiva sagged with relief. Then a cry rose in the Hall and was echoed by many voices.

"A tale! A tale!"

"Let's have tales of dragons!" cried someone.

"No, riddles. Riddles are best!" cried another.

"Very well. The meal is ended." Othere turned to the minstrel. "Redwald, if you please, it is time we heard our favourite tale, the saga of Hengist and Horsa and how they took this land away from the High-King, Vortigern!"

A thunderous cheering greeted these words and the minstrel stood up and cleared his throat. But Elgiva wasn't listening. She wondered what Godwin thought of it all, yet she failed to catch his eye. He was staring vacantly into the fire and his arms were tightly folded.

It seemed an unjustifiably long time before Redwald reached the end of his song, but the Saxons banged their fists on the tables and called for more entertainment. Othere, grinning broadly, turned towards his guest as she was trying to stifle a yawn.

"Perhaps you have some tales for us?"

Elgiva would gladly have throttled him; instead she gave him a weary look. "Forgive me. I don't wish to offend, but I am very tired. My mind is confused by the day's events. If you have no objection, my Lord, I should like to retire."

Othere looked disappointed, but his concern to uphold his image as the affable host quickly reasserted itself. "Of course, my child. I can see your fatigue. I will not keep you from your rest."

She bid him good night, left the table and slipped out through a side-door into the evening's chill embrace. Its freshness hit her like a wall of stone, made the wine surge in her veins and she staggered for a moment or two before the giddiness passed. Her gown felt damp and cold on her skin.

The full moon had risen and the afternoon storm had rolled away to a distant sky. Leaves and blades of grass were silvered under the spell of the moon, robbed of their reality, but Elgiva's senses felt their being and she knew that she was still a part of all the things that really mattered.

It was then that she felt a pang of compassion for these Wilthkin with their narrow views. They would never see life with her Elven perception; never know the feeling of Oneness with even the smallest living thing.

A burst of fresh carousing from the Hall and her communion was profaned. She sighed and walked towards Godwin's hut. Now she wasn't just a servant, she was a servant of the Wilthkin. It was truly unthinkable. She hoped it would be a short Winter.

And what had happened to Bellic? Was he sitting in King Thallinore's Hall, listening to Caspell's harp, or reading some dull, old manuscript in his cosy, firelit room? Did he wonder what had become of her, or had the giving of Siriol absolved him from all responsibility for his former pupil, from the guilt of letting them drive her out?

But he wasn't responsible for her at all. He had only been her friend. Friends weren't responsible for each other ...were they?

Even so, he was still a Wardain, a Royal Elf, and he had power. He could go wherever he pleased, do whatever he liked. Surely one day he would seek her out?

Yet could it be that even he believed she was a traitor?... No, he knew her better than that ... Well, she hoped he did.

That night Elgiva went to her bed feeling lost and alone, but the days that lay ahead of her weren't as bad as she had feared.

Many months passed and a hard winter came. The rivers were choked with ice, the mean huts scoured by blizzards, but in the great Hall there was food and warmth, and company, of sorts, and she did her duties without complaint and became a special figure in the ranks of Othere's menials, delighting him with verses and tales.

Her skill in handling livestock was generally admired, and no-one ever suspected that being able to talk to the animals was the reason for her success. She saw this as her chance to gain a little privacy and asked if she could have a pallet in the stable. Her devotion to her master's beasts thus earned her further praise. Who would have thought that she preferred the company of animals to the company of men?

Guilt, however, gave her no peace; guilt at living a lie. She wasn't used to the feeling; it was something she hadn't expected. After all, they were only barbarians. What had she to feel guilty about? Didn't she work hard for her keep?

And with the guilt came anger at the situation she found herself in. Her life should never have been like this. It wasn't right. It wasn't fair.

Soon the winter was growing old and still there was no word from Bellic. Still the amulet's spell endured, and Elgiva longed for the first signs of Spring, for the time when she could leave this place, undo the spell and be herself again, running free in the leafy woods.

But the time for her departure was nearer than she thought.

* * *

Chapter Five

It was a grey dawn near the end of winter, when tragedy fell upon the settlement. An army of warriors appeared in the east, came marching over the frosty fields, their minds fixed on the same grim purpose. Cold sunlight flashed on their shields and swords.

Panic scattered Lord Othere's sentries, for peace had made them complacent and they were late in sounding the alarm. The people were jolted out of their sleep, not knowing quite what the danger was, and they were unprepared for the threat of bloodshed.

Elgiva, however, was aware long before the sentries knew what was happening. In the deep straw of the stable, she was dragged from her sleep by a premonition. She sat up and listened intently. Her companions were restless and a small, nervous pony nudged her with its muzzle.

She laced her feet into her sandals and buckled her belt round the waist of her robe. Then she set off for Godwin's hut.

Once there, she found all the occupants sleeping. She shook Godwin by the shoulder and tried to convince him that they were in danger, insisting they hurry to find Lord Othere. Confused and frowning, he pulled on his boots and yawned his apologies to his wife, Rowena, then he stumbled after Elgiva as she ran towards the Hall.

By the time they reached it, the alarm had been given and warriors were starting to take up arms. A half-dressed servant came tearing towards them, still wrestling with the buckle of his leather belt. He thrust them aside and barged into the Hall.

"Have you heard? We're attacked!" He threw them a look of terror over his shoulder.

Godwin's jaw dropped, then he pulled his wits together. "Kern, wait!"

But the man was already on his way to rouse Othere, his bare feet slapping on the wooden floor.

Elgiva stood before the high-table, chewing her lip with impatience. Godwin hurried to her side. At that moment, Othere appeared at the curtained entrance of his chamber, a mighty scowl upon his craggy face. Kern came scuttling in his wake and Othere rounded on him angrily.

"By all the gods, what's toward, you rogue? Why am I tumbled from my bed at this hour? Is the settlement ablaze?" With one mighty hand he combed back his hair in an effort to look more dignified.

"It … it's Beortnoth!" Kern almost shrieked, "With a great army … a very great army, my Lord … and almost upon us!"

"By Grim!" roared Othere. "That murdering bastard is after my lands again!" He gave the servant a mighty shove with his hand. "Don't stand there gibbering, Kern! Get my sword and helm and see that everyone is awake!"

Kern darted off in terror and Othere strode towards the dais, a dangerous frown upon his face. "A dawn attack!" he thundered. "There is no honour in that!"

"My Lord," ventured Godwin, "they'll be here before we're ready. Can we hold the gates against them? Perhaps we should talk …"

"Talk?" Othere glowered at Godwin as though he had crawled from the woodwork. "How much talk has there been with that bastard and his mercenary scum ? How many truces has he broken? Did he not agree to keep to his side of the river? He covets my land, Godwin. It is good land and he means to have it. He won't give up until he has everything I own. But I will see him dead first!"

Godwin lowered his gaze. "Yes, Lord."

"He has been biding his time, gathering strength. Now he means to finish it. It is a blood feud and must end in blood. We must commit ourselves to battle and pray that the gods are with us. We must hold the gates, Godwin, and, if we cannot, then we will fight to the very last man." His keen eyes narrowed with resolution. "Whoever is sound in limb must take up arms – even you, Godwin."

A spasm of anxiety passed over Godwin's face, but he merely nodded.

"Hurry, man!"

Godwin straightened himself, gave Elgiva a brief, tight smile, and hastened from the Hall. She stared after him blankly, wanting to express her concern, but finding no words for the purpose.

At that moment, another side-door flew open and in its throat stood a trembling Kern, behind him a background of chaos.

"My war-gear!" cried Othere, as though he were greeting a long-lost friend.

Elgiva watched him from the corner of her eye. You're actually enjoying all this, she thought.

As if for the first time, the Saxon lord seemed to notice Elgiva. "Find yourself a place of safety, child, " he commanded gently. And with that he hefted his broadsword in both hands and strode towards the Hall's main doors, Kern trotting in his wake.

Elgiva sighed and leaned heavily against the high-table. Now what? she wondered. This seemed like a good time to leave. This world was one of violence and mayhem and she had seen the awakened savagery in Othere's ice-blue eyes. He thrived on warfare: they all did. Without it what were they but farmers and storytellers, growing fat and bored?

Well, she didn't intend to shed *HER* blood in the name of some petty, territorial dispute. If she sneaked through the rear of the Hall and out across the compound ...

Her plan got no further, as Bellic's stern face rose suddenly into her mind and in his wise, old eyes she could see more than a hint of reproach. He would no doubt have reminded her that she owed a great deal to Godwin and his family, and even to Lord Othere. To run away now would be an act of betrayal.

For a while she wrestled with her feelings, but she knew that there was only one honourable course to take, and at length she made for the main doors and stood on the threshold, looking out.

People were running everywhere and it was impossible for her to make sense of the chaos that lay beyond the doors. The clash of swords rang in the distance. That could mean only one thing: the raiders had already forced their way in and were fighting with Lord Othere's men. But what could she do to help?

She drew the air deep into her lungs in an effort to steady herself. She needed to consider her part in defending the people who had given her shelter, but she knew that any help she gave would have to be limited to those she considered her friends.

She wondered what had become of Godwin, who had gone unskilled to join the defenders of the settlement. Perhaps, already slain, his corpse lay, spilling blood, before the gates of the stronghold. She wasn't prepared for the indignation that such a thought provoked, but she knew that, Wilthkin or not, he didn't deserve to die like that. More irksome still was the fact that she was powerless to help him. But perhaps she could render him some service indirectly; at least she could ensure that his family were safe.

Knowing now what she must do, Elgiva stepped over the threshold and hurried to Godwin's hut.

But in her haste to get there her own safety was forgotten.

Suddenly she found herself hoisted into the air. Twisting round, she came face to face with a tall, blond warrior. His fierce eyes glittered with triumph.

"You'll make a fine gift for my father-in-law, Othere's dog!" he snarled.

Elgiva kicked out angrily and caught him on the shin. He howled with rage and loosened his grip, but recovered before she could struggle free.

"Siriol, curse him with the Pox, the Blister and the Scab!" she screamed.

The raider laughed and slung her over his brawny shoulder. She beat her fists against him but his muscle-hard torso barely noticed. Restraining her legs with one hand and clutching his short sword with the other, he strolled away with his prize.

"How dare you!" she cried. "How dare you!"

In the distance she saw the servants' dwellings, and she was being carried in the opposite direction. Tears of frustration welled in her eyes. Godwin had been her friend and she had to help his family!

When she thought of Rowena and the two, little girls, desperation stirred up all manner of wild imaginings: scenes of destruction, slaughter and rape.

"Siriol! Siriol! Why don't you help me?"

But the amulet didn't respond. It seemed unaware of her plight.

Try harder, she thought. Try harder.

Perhaps the amulet wouldn't help, if in doing so it caused harm to another? But her heart was so full of hate … HATE! She must get free. She must help Rowena. Inwardly she raged at herself. Concentrate. Try harder. Do you want to end up as a spoil of battle?

Siriol, she pleaded, why don't you do something? You're supposed to obey me!

Could she penetrate the amulet's passivity with her mind, forge some kind of link between her need and Siriol's power?

She needed words to awaken its might, but her mind was completely blank. She needed the words she had never been taught …

What were the words? What were the words?

"Stop struggling now, Othere's dog, or my sword will spill your guts," snarled the raider.

His threat provided the spark. Her anger suddenly flared with a heat that she felt would consume her, if it found no release. She poured it into Siriol in a moment of exquisite focus.

"In the name of Faine, protect me, Siriol!"

A glow of power responded to her need. At first, she thought it centred on the amulet, but then it grew more vague, more diffuse. A strange warmth spread throughout her body. It set her nerve-ends tingling and her skin shivered with gooseflesh. She hadn't expected this. For one awful moment, she feared that Siriol couldn't separate its mistress from her enemy. The use of the amulet had never been explained to her. And now it was too late.

The power grew. There was an excruciating moment of calm and Elgiva felt that she was poised on the lip of some bottomless chasm. Did Siriol feel her hesitate?

She surrendered herself to the power.

"Siriol, strike him now!" she cried.

Something contracted inside her. Then she felt an explosion, which seemed to be in her mind. An intense stab of heat-pain passed from her body into that of her captor and she was instantly flung aside. She heard his yell of agony as he fell to his knees, hugging his chest.

For a moment, everything went black in her mind, and she didn't know why she was sprawled in the dirt. Then she forced herself to her feet. Her legs felt weak and boneless. Her head reeled and nausea griped her guts. Holding the amulet in a trembling hand, she glared upon it angrily.

"Whose side are you *ON*?"

Her gaze flew to the stricken raider, who was rolling on the ground in pain. She stared at him for some time, forgetting everything else. A strange desire to gloat on his agony rooted her to the spot. She felt as though she were witnessing some personal achievement, yet she also felt sickened by what she had done and longed to be as far away from the horror of it as possible. She knew that he had deserved his pain ... but, surely, Siriol, this was too much?

Finally, she had control of herself and tore her gaze away. She left the man moaning on the icy ground and ran to the servants' quarters.

★ ★ ★

Othere's men stood before the attackers; a human wall of strength between the gates of the stronghold and the dwellings within. Their eyes flashed no less keenly than their broadswords. Men of lesser rank stood their ground among the warriors and held whatever weapons they had managed to find. All fought with the same determination, the same need to save their world from harm.

Godwin was flanked by Elric and Deor. Luckily he had found a broadsword in the armoury, but he prayed that better men than he would have dealt with the enemy long before his own fighting skill was put to the test.

Many of the raiders had been beaten back already and their corpses blocked the gateway. A fresh wave clambered over the bodies and the archers on the stronghold's walls fired into it repeatedly. Those who broke through into the compound met a sturdy barrier of resistance: the steadfast ranks of Othere's men, whose war-cries froze their blood.

"We've stemmed the tide!" cried Elric above the din of battle.

Godwin's relief soon turned to dismay, as a warrior charged towards them, plunging through the smoke and noise, his features taut with panic.

"They're breaking through on all sides!" He clutched at his chest and fought for breath. "Beortnoth ... he has mercenaries! We fight like gods, Master Elric, but we're outnumbered three to one. They mock us with fire and iron!"

"Grim's Blood!" cursed Elric. His face was flushed and his breathing ragged. He wiped the sweat from his brow. "Tell me, where is my father?"

"I do not know, my Lord."

"The gods protect him, " gritted Deor.

My family, too, thought Godwin. He was torn agonisingly between his duty to his master and his duty to his kin, yet he felt that at a time like this it was all one and the same.

* * *

Rowena and her two small daughters were huddled together inside their hut, like mice that have heard the tread of a cat. Rowena felt as brittle as the embers in the hearth, but she knew she must be brave for the sake of her children.

What was happening? Where was Godwin? If Beortnoth won, would she and the girls be taken as slaves or put to the sword? Their world, for so long safe and secure, seemed to crumble to dust around them. She drew her daughters closer and soothed their fears with words that seemed to tear her throat like shards of glass.

Suddenly, they gasped in fear, as the door of their hut flew open. A figure stood in the doorway; a vague, dark shape against the grey, winter light. It made some kind of plea, but the words were lost in the noise of battle.

Then the figure darted forwards and all three of them shrieked in terror.

"It's me! It's only me, Rowena!"

Rowena's heart leapt. "Elgiva …my friend!"

The children clutched at Elgiva's robe, bleating like frightened lambs. She hugged them reassuringly. "Don't be afraid. We'll be all right." She glanced towards their mother. "Rowena, they might ransack the huts. You must find somewhere safe to hide. Where they won't find anything worth the bother of searching. The defences are breached. We must move quickly!"

Clasping the Saxon's hand, she dragged her out of the hut, the children's fingers still clamped to her robe. Fires blazed everywhere, as they burst into the stark, cold light. A premonition of danger made Elgiva unduly brusque, as she urged her charges behind an overturned cart.

Within seconds, three raiders came tearing past, one brandishing a torch. They were searching all the huts for treasure, though the servants' dwellings had little to offer. But Godwin's proved more lucrative. To the cheers of his companions, a raider emerged with Godwin's sword and flourished it triumphantly.

Elgiva frowned and clenched her fists at the sight of his greedy smirk. Godwin's only link with his past was now in the hands of scavengers. And she could do nothing about it.

The man with the torch set flame to the thatch. As the fire took hold, his lips drew back in a fierce grin of pleasure. Then he joined his companions and they dashed off again on the trail of plunder.

Elgiva watched through narrowed eyes as the figures were lost in the billowing smoke. Rowena gaped at the loss of her home and the children whimpered and clung to her robe. For a time they watched the little hut burn, as though they were paying their last respects.

"Huts can be rebuilt," said Elgiva. "And you're all safe … and not in there."

Rowena's lip trembled as she tried to smile. "Elgiva... yes. We must thank the gods. For that ... for you. You saved us!"

Elgiva lowered her gaze. Rowena's gratitude stung her conscience. After all, she was merely discharging a debt. That and nothing more. "Come on," she said. "Follow me."

They trotted behind her obediently, as she led them towards the stables. The fences were smashed, the animals taken and, for the moment, all was quiet. She ushered them all inside.

"I can't think of anywhere better," she told them. "If you hide in the straw perhaps you'll be safe. They can see the place is empty. Nothing here for them to steal. But, Rowena, keep a look out for men with torches." Then she turned to the children. "You must be very, very quiet. Still as two hares in a meadow." She placed a finger on her lips and they nodded, eager to please.

She hugged them again and turned away. She had been of some use to her friends and now she could leave with a clean conscience, but Rowena grabbed her by the sleeve.

"You are leaving us, Elgiva?"

"Well, I..."

"Stay, please! I'm afraid!"

Haven't I done enough for you already? Elgiva thought, but said instead, "Don't be. You're safe here. Be strong for *THEM*." She nodded towards the girls.

"But, Elgiva, my friend, what of *YOU*? You must stay with us and hide."

Elgiva hadn't expected this. She had tried to keep her distance from these people, but she realised now that she had failed. Why did Rowena's concern surprise her? After all, why had she saved Rowena, if she were being honest?

In discharging a debt to these people, she had only become more involved with them. She wished that Bellic had given her a lesson or two in friendship.

There was nothing for it but to sit down and wait.

Rowena peered out of the shelter. "I wish I knew if Godwin … if …" She swallowed thickly and turned away.

"He can take care of himself." Another lie, thought Elgiva, but what else can I say?

Rowena turned to face her. "He's no warrior," she said, and her face was streaked with tears.

Elgiva sighed loudly and got to her feet. "I'll find him and bring you news."

The Saxon tried to grab her arm, but Elgiva was far too nimble. Ignoring Rowena's pleas, she left the stable at a run and was soon swallowed up by the greasy, grey smoke.

She hadn't intended any of this and she certainly didn't want it, but she had to escape from her ties with these people. They had reached her in ways she hadn't expected. Yet still she needed to prove her integrity; to herself, if to no-one else.

And then she would be free.

As she pelted towards the Meadhall, she made herself a promise. If she escaped from this place with her life, she would march straight back to Derryth and give him a very large piece of her mind.

* * *

Chapter Six

Deor, fatally wounded, lay stretched at the feet of his comrades. They couldn't move him to a place of safety, for the battle was raging all around them, but they tried to shield him as best they could. Their battle-cries still rang bravely in the air and their swords were slick with the enemy's gore.

Beyond the wall of the stronghold, just out of the archers' range, Beortnoth sat on a great, black horse that raked the earth with its hooves and he watched the embroilment like a god of war and laughed at the missiles that fell short of their target. Where he had found such a fearsome steed, no-one could imagine, but the sight struck terror into Othere's men.

Godwin glanced down at Deor. "My Lord, how do you fare?"

"I'm dying, you stupid bastard. Forget me, man … the foe!" He choked on the blood that rose in his throat, his face as white as the frost.

A fresh wave of raiders surged to attack. Godwin parried blow after blow until his head was swimming. That he still lived amazed him, but years of hard work had given him the muscle to wield the mighty broadsword. And he had Elric beside him. Many times he had thanked the gods for the younger man's quick reactions. Now they were part of a sturdy line of battle-seasoned warriors and, while these veterans stood at his side, Godwin could count on their protection.

He swung at his assailants, trying to disable them before they came too close, but he was growing more fatigued. Only the need to survive kept him going, gave him the strength to keep hacking and slashing with the ponderous blade for all he was worth. He clung to the image of his family: he was doing it all for them.

And he was glad to have left his own sword behind. Too short, too blunt for this bloody work.

Weariness warped the world around him, but he battled on, compelled to keep the flashing blade in motion. It seemed that he had always been here, whirling this blade, and always would be. The foe kept coming, the foe would keep on coming, and at his feet Deor's lifeless body mocked him with its sightless gaze.

The shock of knowing that the man was dead caused a break in his concentration.

"Godwin, look out!" cried Elric.

Godwin looked up and saw a long, long blade poised in the air above him. Numb to the core and unable to move he watched his death descend.

Suddenly, he was knocked aside and thrown like futility among the corpses on the ground. A battle-hardened warrior now stood in his place and with practised ease despatched the marauder, as if such things were the linchpin of his life.

Having saved Godwin, the grey-bearded veteran flashed him a grin of fellowship. It was Cerdic, Elric's tutor in swordplay, a good-natured man who had always treated Godwin like an equal.

For there was a bond between them.

He tucked his broadsword under his arm and, with his right hand, helped Godwin to his feet. His left hand was unfit for the task, as three of its fingers were missing. Briefly, they grinned at each other, then Godwin retrieved his broadsword and staggered back to the line of warriors.

He gritted his teeth to keep his fear in check and held in his mind's eye the images he fought for; his wife, his children, his lord. His home. He clung to these symbols of permanence and applied the sword to its work. It was the only reasonable thing to do.

Oh, Grim, he thought, don't let me die like this.

He fought on. He mustn't stop. He couldn't stop. Too many people relied on him and needed him to be brave. Only death could halt the broadsword that threatened to tear his arms from their roots.

Yet perhaps he was already dead. If he could bear to focus on the warriors around him, he might see nothing more than a gathering of ghosts, too fixed upon their purpose to realise that they were in another world entirely; a world beyond the grave.

He wondered how Rowena would break the news to his daughters. At least they would be proud of him. He had died with a sword in his hand. Like a warrior.

* * *

Lord Othere was despondent. Beortnoth's men were within the defences. How many women and children were taken, how many warriors killed, dwellings gutted? He feared to even guess the answer. Screams reached his ears from every side and he heard the brave cries of his men. He yearned to be among them, but he had suffered a painful blow to the shoulder. There was a time when such a wound would merely have goaded him on, made him reckless and bold and eager for combat. But now he was just an old man, weakened by loss of blood and, as he sat in the Meadhall's shadow, leaning heavily against the wall, he knew he had never in his many years felt such a sense of defeat.

His tribe were doomed and all he could do was watch and bemoan the loss of his people... his lands...his gold... his youth.

With an effort that wrenched his heart, he tried to portray a semblance of courage. He mustn't allow the churls around him to see how helpless he really felt. If he must die, it wouldn't be as a coward. Even so, shameful though the idea might be, perhaps it would be better if he fell on his sword, rather than face the prospect of being a prisoner of Beortnoth.

Suddenly, he saw Elgiva running towards him over the smoke-blurred compound, and concern for her safety briefly banished his despair. His raised a hand in greeting.

"My Lord!" she exclaimed. She thrust the twittering menials aside and knelt before their master. "I'm glad to see you still alive ... but hurt! Here, let me help you."

As she tore a strip of cloth from the hem of her servant's robe, she studied his battle-stained face. Then she smiled at him grimly "I fear you have surrendered in your heart, my Lord, but the day is not yet lost."

Othere winced at this observation, then his grey eyebrows knitted together. "My wound pains me sorely. It is hard to think clearly ... to know what to do for the best."

"Indeed." She staunched the flow of blood with the piece of cloth torn from her robe. "The wound is deep," she said. She knew that her tone was unsympathetic, but she was worried about Godwin, not him.

No. Othere had been kind to her. At least she could show some respect.

"But you'll live, my Lord," she went on more gently. "You're too weak to fight, but don't give up. Your warriors battle on and they draw their strength from you. Don't let them down. You are their guide." She squeezed his hand reassuringly. "Believe that good will triumph, my Lord."

He looked at her intently. There was a certain authority in her tone, a certain compulsion in her large, blue eyes, and the pressure of her handclasp renewed his hope. No, he wouldn't give up. He couldn't forsake his duty. He was a foolish, old man, and she was right.

He drew a cleansing breath, then bringing her hand to his lips, he kissed it.

Once again Elgiva found herself embarrassed by the affection of a Wilthkin, but she mastered her desire to pull back her hand.

"Your presence is magical," he said, and a grim smile lit up his rugged features. "A blessed day indeed, when I permitted you to join my household. I have spent my life in warfare and in warfare I will die. You have lifted the veils from my eyes." He hauled himself to his feet and turned to face the churls. "Go, arm yourselves. I need you no longer." The servants dithered anxiously. "Are you all cowards?" he asked them.

Elgiva's heart stiffened in her breast and she touched his arm reproachfully. "Don't scold them for that, my Lord. It's Nature's way to feel fear … is it not?"

They regarded each other and he was suddenly ashamed.

Was it the code by which they lived that made these people so callous, she wondered, or were they simply stupid? "The mouse hides from the hawk, my Lord, knowing he's met his match," she said. "It would be cruel to send these men out to meet theirs, would it not?"

Othere thought then of Godwin, whom once he had loved like a son.

And he knew in his heart he still did.

"But if they were really cowards, my Lord, would they still be here with you?"

He frowned at this. What did she mean? Was she insulting him now, or was this some jest to lift his mood?

Elgiva grinned at him. "I know nothing of warfare," she went on," but I have heard it said that one way to beat an enemy is to make him leaderless. If that's the case, Lord Othere, you are Beortnoth's prime target."

The servants gaped in panic, but their master's face relaxed. "It's true what you say, little churl," he agreed.

"So you must preserve yourself," she told him. "Inspire your men with your presence and give them cause for hope."

He straightened himself and squared his broad shoulders. Pain winced briefly across his face and Elgiva reached out to take his arm, but he declined her support.

"Keep out of the battle," she said. "And these servants would be better used giving aid to the women and children and tending the wounded, too." *And pray that they never tell a soul that a servant reminded you of your duty.*

"And what of you?" he asked. "We must find you a place of safety. You have more than proved your worth, Elgiva. I will not lose you, child."

"I have to find Godwin, my Lord. Rowena is desperate for news of him. She and the children are hiding in the stables." She touched his arm respectfully. "They would benefit from your protection."

He nodded, "Of course, my child. I will send men at once to bring them to the Meadhall. But as for Godwin, he stood before the gates. The battle is thickest there. You cannot go to him. I do not permit it." Confident that she must obey, he moved to instruct the servants.

As soon as he had turned his back, Elgiva span round and took to her heels.

Othere extended his arm, as if to draw her back. "You cannot go there, Elgiva! I do not permit it. Come back!"

She stopped and grinned at his scowling face. "Stay angry, my Lord," she shouted. "It will put armour on your courage!" With that, she darted away and her slender form was soon lost to him behind a wall of smoke.

* * *

Elgiva soon found the hub of the conflict: a seething mass of warriors battling for control of the area before the stronghold's gates. The latter hung from their hinges, like the broken wings of some great, trampled bird.

Drawing closer, she spotted Elric. His face was grey with effort and his broadsword smoked with blood. For a moment, she felt a pang of compassion. Though he looked like a man, he was younger than she, and it crossed her mind that he shouldn't be forced to risk his life in so desperate a manner. His courage made her stand back and look at her own.

She searched the turmoil feverishly, trying to make some sense of it all, but the chaos defeated her gaze. The air blew about her in acrid gusts, sharp with smoke and the reek of gore and her eyes stung and watered so much that all she could see was a meaningless blur.

Scrubbing away the tears, she edged carefully forwards. The ground was churned and trampled by combat, strewn with weapons and injured men. And then she saw Deor, twisted and still, stretched on the earth in the company of Death. A trail of blood ran from his mouth and matted his neatly-trimmed beard: the immature beard that would never know manhood. His eyes were wide and staring, but he saw no more of this world, and never would again. In his white, clenched fist he gripped his shattered sword. Not even death could part them.

Elgiva gasped at the sight of him, at the promise of youth that came to nothing, and she lifted her hands to stifle a cry. But then she averted her eyes. No. These Wilthkin didn't concern her. Frantically, she resumed her search for the only man who mattered, determined to pay all her debts to him in one single act of friendship.

It was then that she saw him; lying beside the wall of the stronghold – alive or dead she couldn't tell. The intensity of her reaction came as a surprise to her, but inwardly she knew that of all the Wilthkin she had met, Godwin was the one she most wanted to survive.

Avoiding the blades that sliced about her head, she ran to his side and knelt beside him. His hand still gripped the haft of his sword and it filled Elgiva with dread, as a picture of Deor flashed into her mind.

"Godwin!" She shook his arm and the weapon slid from his grasp. "By Faine, you're alive! Listen! Godwin, listen! I've hidden your family. They're safe, do you hear me? Godwin!" She found herself shouting, angry at him, at herself, at everything else. "Wake up, Godwin. Wake up … damn you!"

His eyelids flickered open and he gave her a vacant look.

"You can't stay here. You'll be hacked to pieces." She shook his arm again.

"Am I not … already …then?" His voice was hoarse and weak.

Sighing with impatience, she struggled to heave him upright. Slowly, they crawled and stumbled away from the thick of battle and then she let him rest.

"Your head is bleeding, Godwin," she said, her smooth brow creased by concern. "Is that your only wound?" He gaped at her as though she had accused him of a crime. "You're covered in blood. Not all yours, I hope." She felt her nose wrinkling at the stink of gore.

"Something hit me," was all he could say.

She tore another strip from the hem of her robe and began to bandage his head. At this rate, I'll soon be naked, she thought.

"You said they were safe," he ventured.

"Your family? Yes. I hid them in the stables and Othere will send men to rescue them. They'll be all right. Don't worry."

She smiled at him and he relaxed. His artless eyes beamed gratitude at her and she wished that she'd been less abrupt with him.

"Othere's hurt, but he'll be fine, too," she told him.

"I'm glad, Elgiva. While he's alive, there's hope for the rest of us."

She arched her eyebrows. "Hope, Godwin? He's an old man. Old and stupid. Your warriors … well, they're dead, they're wounded … they're outnumbered. Can't you see, it's only a matter of time?"

He gazed at her, as though bewildered. "We'll be taken, then, Elgiva. We'll be slaves of Beortnoth." A look of horror widened his eyes. "Elgiva ... they'll take my daughters!"

She saw his fear and, suddenly, she also saw herself, making pies in the kitchens with Godwin's wife, while his two little children played with the dough, and she remembered laughing with them, and for a while she had known what it felt like to have a family.

Her pulse was pounding in her throat, as she fought to control conflicting emotions. She ran her fingers through her hair, trying to compose herself, but his pain, her anger, demanded her attention. And not merely her attention.

Abruptly, she jumped to her feet. "This has gone on long enough!"

Something she had said to Othere now spurred her into motion. It was the only solution and though she might not be the only one to see it, perhaps she was the one best placed to take the proper action.

"You stay here," she commanded.

"Elgiva!...Where are you going?"

Elgiva didn't respond. She crept towards the stronghold's gates, her back pressed to the wall, and all the while she searched the ground for the weapon that she needed.

With a major effort, Godwin stood and tottered in her wake. His vision swam at the exertion, but, when it cleared, he saw his friend lift the tall, curved bow from the body of a fallen archer. Then she selected a single arrow and ran towards the gates.

The warriors at the entrance were too engrossed in battle to notice the girl who darted among them. One swung his axe half-heartedly, but she ducked beneath his arm; no-one was going to stand in her way. Godwin pursued her as best he could, too numb to care for his own well-being. He only knew he must follow his friend: he couldn't remember why.

Elgiva ran through the shattered gates and came to a halt about thirty yards from the line of thegns that were ranked around Beortnoth. They bristled with contempt at the sight of the girl, her slight form dwarfed by the bow. Their master's eyes narrowed above his hooked nose and for a moment he considered the threat, then he let out a roar of mirth.

"My lords, we are undone!" he cried, in a booming voice that was edged with malice. "A fierce war-maiden is upon us!"

Hoarse chuckles of laughter greeted his words, though secretly the men admired the little archer's courage.

With a grimace of effort, Elgiva struggled to nock the single arrow.

"By the time you have that weapon under control ... if you can, little churl … my warriors here will have cut you down," Beortnoth promised sternly. "Othere must be desperate indeed, to send his half-grown serving women to fight his battles for him!"

His men raised their bows and nocked their arrows, while others unsheathed their swords, unhurried in their complacency.

"Siriol, hear me," whispered Elgiva. "Raise a wall of power before me, so that their arrows will not strike me."

Planting her feet firmly on the earth, she drew a steadying breath and her Elven instincts focused upon the mastery of the bow.

The speed with which the Saxon girl armed and fired her weapon was such that Beortnoth's warriors were hardly aware that it had happened; could hardly believe that their haughty master was pierced to the heart.

Godwin staggered from the stronghold just in time to see Beortnoth drop slowly from his horse's back. The animal reared and galloped away, while the warriors stood open-mouthed and gawped at their fallen leader. But several had the presence of mind to let their arrows fly.

Godwin stumbled forward, as the missiles swished about his friend. Each step he took jarred the throbbing in his head. Vaguely, he realised that he had left his sword behind. He was weaponless, defenceless, but it didn't matter now. Concern for his friend was his only thought. And he was too late to save her. He hadn't kept faith with his vow.

Horns blared the news of Beortnoth's death and the ranks of the enemy scattered in confusion. Godwin watched them, as they made their retreat; the thegns on their horses, the rest left to flee as best as they could. He shifted his line of vision and gasped when he saw his friend. She lay stretched on the ground, like a sacrifice, and a bristling of arrows pierced the earth around her, like carelessly planted saplings. In his haste to reach her, he tripped and fell and stumbled to his knees.

When he had regained his feet, he found himself facing the stronghold, and the sight that met his eyes made the breath catch in his throat. Like a broken dam, the gates spewed forth a flood of retreating men. Some were injured, some carried plunder, and many were fighting still, as they tried to get away. A few had taken captives; children who squirmed in their captors' arms and screamed to be released.

The retreat emboldened Othere's men and cries of triumph rang in the air.

Godwin stood transfixed by it all. It seemed that a tidal wave of men was bearing down upon him, and he knew that he had to reach Elgiva, but before he could summon the strength to move, the surge of marauders had swamped him. He was carried along with them all.

Someone grabbed hold of him, encircled him with rope. He struggled but was overwhelmed by the crowd of fleeing men. As if from a long way off, he heard the horns of the settlement bellowing victoriously. He fought for a last look at his home, but all he could see was a pall of grey smoke that rose from the stronghold, like a gasp of exhaustion.

Bewildered and bereft of hope, he allowed himself to be dragged along by the yelling mass of raiders. A blur of armour and bristling swords blocked everything else from view. They hauled him down a grassy slope and over a narrow brook. A raider, his thick arms cradling booty, crashed heavily into him and they fell into the water. Goblets and plates clattered and splashed. His captors jerked him upright and urged him on with curses.

Ahead of them were ponies and wagons, waiting beneath the trees. The animals neighed in terror at the sight of the angry horde and their eyes glittered white, as the men milled around them.

Godwin was bound securely, then hurled into one of the wagons, where he lay among the sacks of booty; just another spoil of battle. Blood from his head-wound leached through the bandage and trickled down his face.

He felt the sticky wetness itch his cheek, like tears of despair. All around him the air was thick with the clatter and cries and curses of an angry, defeated army.

Then, with a sudden and sickening lurch, the wagon began to move.

★ ★ ★

Chapter Seven

Night had already fallen by the time that Godwin floated up from a darkness of his own. He lifted his head and gasped at the pain that seemed to pierce his skull, but gradually his vision cleared and he was able to focus on his surroundings.

He found himself at the edge of a clearing. He was slumped on the cold earth, leaning against a tree and bound to it with rope. His chilled body was stiff and bruised and a crust of dried blood tightened the skin of his face. He ached to stretch the cramps from his limbs.

As bewilderment sloughed off him, the night's icy breath crept into his bones. He shivered and scanned the trees around him, but he had no idea where he was, nor how he came to be there. He remembered being in a wagon and reason told him that he ought to be at the settlement of Beortnoth's people by now, but clearly he was in the middle of nowhere.

About four yards from where he sat, a small fire blazed invitingly and above it was a cooking pot raised on a makeshift spit. A delicious aroma wafted towards him from the pot, made his stomach clench. He had eaten nothing all day – assuming it was the same day – and a void inside him yearned to be filled.

Beside the fire squatted a man he assumed to be his captor, or one of them, at least. The man was rubbing his hands to warm them, his scowling face weirdly lit by the flames. He glanced impatiently over his shoulder and searched the surrounding trees, then with a curse he turned to the pot and stirred its contents with a stick.

Godwin tested his bonds, but they were far too secure. Wearily, he resigned himself to whatever his captors had planned for him. Suddenly, a noise in the undergrowth snatched away his attention. Then a man in a cloak emerged from the shadows and strode towards the fire. His companion looked up with a grunt of annoyance.

"Have they fixed that wheel yet?" he asked morosely. "At this rate we'll never get home."

The newcomer warmed his hands by the fire. "Stop moaning," he said. "That's all you ever do. I told you, it's a tricky job. Harold thinks it's past repair."

"Well … shit. That's all we need. This jaunt's been a nightmare from start to finish. We've had more bad luck in one day …"

"Shut your noise," said the newcomer, "and give me one of those oatcakes. I'm starving."

The first man ignored him. "We should have left the ruddy wagon. Gone back with the rest of them."

"And leave all that stuff?" said the second man. He seated himself by the fire. "I'm not going home empty-handed. Anyway, there wasn't room in the other carts for us and all the spoils. How many times must I tell you?"

"No room, aye, and why is that? All those kids they took, that's why. What use are they? Take adult prisoners, that's what I've always said. The higher ranking the better. You get more ransom, then." He glared at his companion, daring him to disagree, but the other man merely shrugged beneath his cloak. "In Woden's name, where are they?"

"Have patience, damn you. Harold has to see to the horses."

"Horses? That's another thing. Those nags we took are no use either. Like the rest of the stuff. We should have dumped the bloody lot. We could be home by now."

The second man sighed loudly. "For Frigg's sake, let it rest. We're here for the night, so get used to it. Besides, would you fancy being home right now, with the news they've just had?"

His companion grimaced. "Aye," he said, "I never thought of that. There'll be sparks flying in the Hall tonight!"

"And we'll not get the stick for it. So, let's have some of that stew."

From the distance a sudden howling noise shattered the calm of the glade. The marauders stiffened, drew close to the fire.

Godwin dragged his tormented gaze away from the cooking pot. His mind was clearer now and some of his strength was returning. He decided to try his bonds again, but still it was no use.

The howling sounded once more in the darkness. A solitary wolf.

Now that his eyes were used to the dark, Godwin could make out more of the clearing. He noticed something to his left and thought that he detected movement. Was it a small figure he could see, tied to a tree like himself?

What happened next would have made him leap up, had not the ropes prevented it. His fellow captive let out a howl so similar to that of the wolf that the men by the fire sprang up in alarm and fumbled for their swords.

"By the gods!"

"A wolf!"

"Too bloody close for my liking!"

The men peered round in all directions and another howl reached their ears, this one from the distance. They sagged with relief and reseated themselves, convinced that one wolf had made both the sounds.

"Night air playing tricks on us!"

"Aye. A wolf won't come this close to a fire."

But from Godwin's perspective the last howl had seemed much nearer than the first. Whatever had made it was drawing closer and Godwin had the strangest feeling that it came in answer to the other captive's call. An insane idea, he told himself, but one that he couldn't shake off.

The first man prodded the stew with a stick. "It's ready now," he said, but then he jumped to his feet in horror and stared across the clearing.

His companion followed the line of his gaze and his mouth fell open in shock.

Emerging from the shadows was a wolf with silver-grey fur. A moment later, Harold appeared from the opposite side of the clearing, another raider at his side. Their thoughts of supper were soon abandoned and they threw down their torches and fled. The two marauders by the fire were quick to follow their example.

"They always travel in packs!" screamed one. "Let them eat the captives!"

They crashed through the bushes in a frenzy of fear, desperate to make their escape. Beyond the trees was a scuffling and cracking, the nickering of horses and the bellowing of oaths, and Godwin listened as they galloped away, leaving both their prisoners to the mercy of wolves. He held his breath and prepared for the worst.

For a long, long moment nothing happened, and the night and the silence seemed to thicken around him.

Then the great wolf turned slowly towards him and a visceral panic lurched through his body. He felt as though all his organs were rushing to his feet.

But the wolf wasn't joined by others of its kind, nor did it seem in a hurry to eat him. It paused, sniffed the air with its long, grey muzzle. The full moon, rolling free from clouds, turned its fur to an eerie silver and its amber eyes gleamed thoughtfully. Paralysed and helpless, Godwin watched it consider him.

Then suddenly the great wolf turned, its large paws soundless on the frosty grass, but Godwin found no relief from his fear, for the animal was striding across the glade towards the other captive. Once there, it stopped and lowered its head and its jaws opened and fastened on something.

Godwin felt that his heart would stop: the other captive was being devoured!

He struggled wildly in his ropes. Then, breathing hard, he stopped and listened. There were no screams, no sounds of tearing fangs. All he could hear were his own ragged breaths – and the wolf was wagging his tail!

Suddenly, a voice exclaimed, "Thank you, Greyflanks," and, shaking off the chewed ropes, the captive got to her feet. She stretched herself exquisitely, then stroked the animal's head.

By Frigg! … Elgiva! Godwin gaped at her, stupefied, as she strolled across the glade.

Kneeling beside him, she untied his ropes.

"Elgiva?"

"Yes, that's right." Her lips curled into a mischievous smile. "You look as though you've seen a ghost."

"But … I was sure you were dead!" Liberated from his bonds, he rubbed his wrists and flexed his arms. His mind was so crowded with questions that he couldn't give voice to them all.

"I pretended to be," said Elgiva, "and, if I'd done so for a few minutes longer, I wouldn't have been taken. Curiosity overcame me."

He shook his head and stared at her. "I … don't understand. What's going on?"

She tucked her hair behind her ears and smiled to ease his confusion. "Are you all right?" she asked. "Can you stand?"

"Yes," he said vaguely. "I'm fine." With her assistance, he climbed to his feet.

"Godwin, this is Greyflanks," she said, pointing towards the wolf. "And we were very fortunate that he was in the area. I recognised his voice at once and … er … sent him a cry for help." Her eyebrows drew together and a tentative smile touched her lips. "I spoke Wolf, of course, so I didn't alert the raiders."

"Of course." Godwin frowned in bewilderment.

The animal leaned against Elgiva and she fondled his large, soft ears. "You see we … we're old friends."

"Old friends." Godwin feared that his grip on reality was not as firm as he had believed.

"Godwin, I …" but then she stopped, her features fraught with misgiving. "You should sit down. You don't look well." Her small hand cupped his elbow. "Our captors left their supper. A shame to waste it, don't you think? And I'm sure you must be hungry." She led him unresisting to the camp-fire and they seated themselves in silence.

Gradually the warmth restored the feeling to his limbs and Godwin felt his stupor recede. Automatically, he ladled some stew into a wooden bowl and, as he did so, he tried to grasp the strangeness of his plight. He offered the food to Elgiva, but she pointed towards the wolf.

"Serve the guest first, as is the custom," she told him with a grin. "Then yourself. I'll eat these oatcakes." To the question in his eyes she said, "Haven't you ever noticed? I don't eat meat."

"Why not?"

"Well ..." She stopped herself. Perhaps this wasn't the time to explain. "It's not the custom of my people." She hoped this would suffice.

"Oh."

He stared at her vacantly for a moment, then gingerly placed the bowl of stew before the wolf. Then he reached for a second bowl and filled it for himself. The wolf regarded him briefly, as though in silent thanks, then set about devouring the stew with obvious enjoyment.

Elgiva sat chewing an oatcake and staring into the fire, her large eyes reflecting the flickering flames. Godwin watched her while he ate and his mind worked frantically.

A young girl having a wolf as a friend? A wolf as docile as Othere's hounds? He had once suspected that she was different, that there was something a little strange about her, but up until now he had always found her behaviour fairly normal. And why was she being so quiet? They had been involved in a battle, abducted from the settlement and miraculously saved by a wolf, but it didn't seem worthy of comment, as though such things were commonplace. He felt there was an awkwardness between them that had never been there before and he couldn't cope with this silence. What was she hiding? Had he offended her?

"Did you rear him from a whelp?"

She was startled out of her thoughts. "What?"

"Your friend. You tamed him, did you? Does he do tricks as well?" Perhaps it was all quite plausible really. What were Othere's dogs after all, but domesticated wolves? As for her claim to have spoken Wolf, that was clearly a joke.

"Tricks?" Her tone conveyed annoyance.

"Well, Redwald had a dancing bear once."

The flash of anger in her eyes brought an end to his questions. He sighed and stared at the fire.

Elgiva knew that he deserved an explanation, but he was still a Wilthkin. The things she needed to tell him he would surely disbelieve, for they lay outside his experience. He could never understand. At best, he would simply make fun of her.

When finally she spoke, her tone was harsher than she had intended. "He's completely wild – as he should be. I met him a few years ago. He was half-grown then and his leg was caught in one of your people's traps. They had no business laying their vile snares so close to my people's lands." Her voice was rising in scale with her anger. She checked herself and drew a deep breath. "Well, anyway, I freed him and Bellic tended the wound. It was lucky I found him when I did, or he might have lost half his leg." She glared at Godwin, who suddenly felt the need to apologise, as though he had set the trap himself. " We haven't seen each other since, but he hasn't forgotten me, and I haven't forgotten the sound of his voice."

Now Godwin was even more baffled. How had she found the courage to approach an injured, wild animal? And how could she tell one wolf's howl from another?

Elgiva lifted her gaze. For a moment she looked at Godwin with something approaching hatred in her eyes, but his open stare confounded her. She had expected some quip, some callous or dismissive remark. Regret softened her features. "I'm sorry," she said, with a sigh.

He managed to smile at her. "What for?"

"I thought you were like the rest of them, but, of course, you're not, are you?"

His eyebrows drew together. He had no idea what she meant.

"I'm going to tell you something ... something you ought to know. You've been a good friend to me, Godwin, and perhaps you will still be my friend, when I've told you the truth." Her assumption sounded more like an appeal. Then she shrugged her slender shoulders. "Or perhaps you'll hate me. I don't know. I just know I must tell you my secret. This lie ... this disguise ... I hate it." A threat of tears thickened her voice. "And, when I've told you, I'll leave you in peace. I'll go to the forests, to where I belong, or to wherever ..."She swallowed hard and turned her face away. "I'll never bother you again."

"Elgiva?" He reached out to touch her, but she recoiled from him, so he sat back and waited, concerned by her sadness and desperate to know its cause.

She shifted her position. Drawing up her knees, she hugged them to her chest. It was then that Godwin noticed the tear in her sleeve just above the elbow, the smear of dried blood caked around it. One of the arrows fired by the raiders must have snicked her flesh. Frowning, he got to his knees.

"You're injured. Let me tend the wound."

"Please," she said steadily, "sit down and listen."

Godwin acquiesced with a shrug. "Very well, you can have your say, but that wound should be tended to. After you've told me ..."

"After I've told you, you won't care, believe me! You'll have run for your life … or you might want to kill me!"

"What in Frigg's name are you talking about?"

"Just sit down and listen!"

She glared at him and refused to go on until he complied with her wishes. The wolf was watching him, too, and Godwin felt that any offence he gave Elgiva wouldn't escape the notice of her canine companion.

"I didn't want to deceive you," she said, with a pleading look in her eyes. "Believe me, I meant no harm. It was something I had to do … to survive. I needed food and shelter and there was nowhere else to go. What you see … my present form … it's one I took upon myself by the agency of … magic." She paused and ran her fingers through her hair and Godwin felt his heartbeat quicken. "I'm not what I appear to be. I'm … one of those beings feared by your kind. I'm …" She hesitated once again and her eyes begged for his understanding. "Godwin, I'm an Elf."

That knock on the head had clearly done him more harm than he realised. None of this made any sense. If Elgiva hadn't looked so sincere, he might have laughed out loud. He didn't know how to answer her, but he knew that he had to say something.

He looked at her intently. "Elgiva, is this a jest?" Her scowl told him plainly that it wasn't. "Forgive me … I don't know … I've no idea what you expect me to say. I'm not even sure this is really happening."

Godwin wanted to lighten the mood, to make her the friend he knew, but everything seemed to have changed between them. He didn't know how he should react and she appeared unwilling to help him. He hadn't yet recovered from the trauma of abduction and his mind was still at the settlement, where Elves lived only in tall tales and sagas.

"I thought you were different once," he ventured. "Well, a bit mystical … something like that. But this…" He looked bewildered. "If you really are an Elf, I guess you could put a hex on me, but it wouldn't be a bad one, would it? You'd never do that to a friend."

He raised his eyebrows expectantly, but perhaps he was being presumptuous. Elgiva was frowning at him.

In reality she was taken aback by his matter-of-fact response.

"I can't anyway," she said lornly. "Only the Wardain – the Elves of Royal blood – have the gift of magical power. I'm just an underling. Ordinary. In Elvish we say 'nar-Wardain'."

"But you talk to wolves!" he protested.

"That isn't magic."

"It isn't?"

"Yes, well, it is … and it isn't. Basically, Elves and animals are able to speak to each other. It all goes back to our Founder, Lord Faine. His love for animals, and theirs for him, created a magical bond. It happened a very long time ago. It comes from the spirit … a feeling of Oneness…" She realised that he was totally lost. "Well, let's just say that there are many different kinds of magic and some of them are commonplace."

"What else can you do?" he asked. He might as well be discussing the weather, and where his emotions should have been there was nothing but a great, black void. He knew that fatigue was partly to blame – and perhaps he had actually fallen asleep and this was all a dream.

"My senses are very acute. I can talk to trees, if they're willing, but sometimes I think it's better not to." She paused for a moment and smiled to herself. "Some Elves can see into the future. I can't. I don't think I'd want to either. I dare say mine isn't worth the looking. Well, apart from all that, I can't do much, but I'm good at household chores." She gave him a sideways look.

"You forgot to mention one thing," he said. "Your skill at archery. You saved the settlement, you know."

Yes, Elgiva thought ruefully, I make a good assassin.

Godwin found his attention shifting, as images of the day's ordeal went dancing through his mind. Had he actually fought in a battle? He saw a man falling from a horse, warriors running, huts belching smoke and pools of gore on the grass. Had he been a part of all that?

"You're taking this very lightly," she said. "Have you listened to me at all? I've just confessed to being an Elf. An Elf, Godwin! Don't you believe me?"

"What?" Despite her insistence, it still seemed quite unreal. "I've known you many months," he said, "and now you confront me with this! What in Frigg's name do you want me to say? I'm sure I've no idea!" He looked to her for guidance, but she turned her face away, "Well, then, why don't you tell me how you managed to change your appearance? You said it was with magic, yet you say you don't have any."

Leaning towards him, she showed him the amulet and explained its purpose and origin. "Bellic is a Wardain. The great-uncle of my Lord … I mean King. King Thallinore, who is ruler of Elindell, where we live. Well, where I used to live. Bellic gave up his rights to kingship in Astorill – that was his home – so he can follow his chosen pursuits. He is a seeker after knowledge, so is often absent from Elindell. He likes to wander and talk to sorcerers and animals and even Wilthkin – that's our name for men –and he often wears a disguise so he can go where Elves aren't welcome. I guess I've followed in his footsteps." She gave him a hesitant smile. "Bellic is wise and compassionate and he taught and befriended me, when I was a child. He didn't have to do it. A nar-Wardain doesn't need much education, you know. Perhaps he took pity on me for some reason. Perhaps I even amused him."

"And perhaps, like you, he needed a friend."

She reflected on this in silence. At length, she said, "Well, he gave me this amulet. Its name is Siriol. I used it to change my appearance, but something went wrong at the settlement. I believed it was protecting me, when I went to kill Beortnoth, but, as you can see, it wasn't."

She looked down at the gash on her arm and probed it with her fingers. A grimace of pain winced across her face. It was deeper than she had thought. However, what hurt her most of all was her loss of faith in the amulet and, by association, in the giver.

"Perhaps it doesn't know you now, if you've changed your appearance," said Godwin.

She smiled at him warmly; he was trying to help. "While it's in my possession, it must work my will. That's the way with amulets, Godwin. They can't be fooled by outward appearance."

"I wish I could say the same."

He hoped that his humour would lighten her mood, but her pained look told him otherwise. A period of thoughtful silence loomed. He decided to forestall it.

"We've talked enough for now," he said. "I just want you to know I'm still your friend, but I need more time to take in what you've told me."

She accepted this with a weary nod, sighed and climbed to her feet. " Stay here and rest. You look exhausted. And I … need some time alone." Turning away, she headed towards the encircling trees.

Godwin didn't want her to leave, but he couldn't find the words to call her back; he was weary beyond endurance. Confusion fogged his thoughts and his head throbbed with pain. Reaching up, he touched the bandage and then he remembered his friend's ministrations. He smiled at her concern.

Greyflanks lay stetched on the ground beside him, warming his silver-grey belly by the fire. It seemed the most natural thing in the world to join the wolf and fall asleep, and, without a moment to think about it, Godwin did just that.

⋆ ⋆ ⋆

Chapter Eight

Godwin awoke and stretched himself. The morning sun had melted the frost and bird-song filled the trees. He sat up slowly and gazed around him and it took a few moments for him to remember exactly where he was. How different everything looked in daylight!

In front of him a heap of grey ash was all that remained of the fire. It seemed incapable of heat. Had two marauders really sat there, warming their hands at this very spot? Had a wolf really answered a summons for help; dashed to the rescue at his friend's request? His friend … who was an Elf!

He inspected his wrists; ropes had chafed them raw. The cooking pot still hung from the spit. Two wooden bowls lay beside him on the grass.

Well, some of it was real.

The sound of laughter drifted towards him, like music beyond the trees, and he turned in time to see Elgiva step from the bushes and walk towards him. The wolf pranced beside her like a fawning puppy.

"I wish you could speak to wolves, Godwin. They know so many pleasing tales." Her smile was more carefree than any smile he had seen on her face before. "How do you feel today?" She sat at his side, her golden hair like sunshine about her face. He noticed that she had torn the sleeve from her robe and used it to bandage her arm. "I'm sorry, I let the fire go out, but never mind. It's such a lovely morning. And you've missed the best part of it already."

He pulled his wits together and smiled. "The best part of morning is breaking one's fast. Have I missed that, then?"

"There wasn't any breakfast to miss. Sorry I can't conjure up a roasted swan for you – or whatever it is you Wilthkin prefer."

"Oh, don't apologise, Elgiva. Roast swan never agrees with me at this time of the day."

They looked at each other and grinned.

"Greyflanks and I found roots," she announced, opening her hands to reveal a collection of small, grey objects. "I brought some back for you."

"Can I eat them?" He grimaced. "They look like bits of wood."

She laughed. "Yes, you can eat them, and you'll be surprised how sweet they taste."

The lightness of her manner showed no trace of the previous day's ordeal. It was almost as though she wanted to forget the secret that she had shared with him and he had no wish to darken her mood.

"Later we'll look in the wagon," she said. "There may be food in it."

"Do you know where we are, Elgiva?"

"I've no idea. And neither has he." She nodded towards the wolf. "He and the pack got separated several days ago. They were out hunting and, being the fastest runner, he lost them all. Got carried away in the thrill of the chase, I dare say." She lowered her voice to a whisper. "And he'd had a brief illness. Lost his sense of smell."

Godwin cocked an eyebrow at this. "I see. That wouldn't help."

"What worries him the most is that his mother will fret."

"Yes. Well. She would."

"She's leader of the pack now. His father was murdered last summer. By Wilthkin."

"Ah."

"He was after their lambs, I dare say, and, of course, that's not allowed. Everything belongs to the Wilthkin, doesn't it?"

He refused to be baited and said nothing.

"Greyflanks has a reputation for getting himself into trouble. After all, that's how we met."

Godwin had ceased to listen. Something of desperate importance had leapt into his mind. How could he be so thoughtless?

"By Frigg! Elgiva, my family! What about my family? Roweña and the children! What's become of them?" He grasped her arm in his panic.

"Oh, yes. The settlement." She sounded bored.

"Don't you care?" he demanded. "I must find out … how … if …"

"I'll see what I can do." She got to her feet and squinted at the sky.

He watched her with a puzzled frown. What on earth was she doing? Was she mocking him?

"Look!" she cried. "I think we're in luck!" She pointed at the clouds.

"What?" He followed the direction of her arm, but saw nothing of any interest. And yet … what was that dot he could just make out, circling lazily above them?

"Hey!" Elgiva waved her arms and the black dot spiralled down.

Soon Godwin saw that the dot was a hawk. It hovered awhile then swooped towards them and landed in a tree. Elgiva walked towards it, while Godwin stood with folded arms, not knowing what else to do. He could see Elgiva talking to the bird, but he couldn't imagine why.

At length, Elgiva returned to his side. "She flew over a settlement yesterday. Many hours before dusk, she says. She stopped to rest in a tree and watched. There were fires being put out and people dead or injured. She remembers seeing a large building and a Saxon woman in an amber-coloured robe. The woman had two little girls at her side, and they were dressed in blue. And a tall man with them, bleeding at the shoulder. The granary had been pulled down and there were loads of mice …"

"Forgive me, but I have no interest in the fate of Othere's mice!"

"As you wish." Elgiva looked away haughtily.

He sighed. "Sorry. Thank you for this news."

"Don't thank me," she sniffed. "I've only told you what the hawk said. There are other details, if you care to hear them."

"No. It sounds like home. Where else?"

"The bird saw truly. She has keen eyes. The reputation of hawks is well-known. Surely, even to Wilthkin."

Godwin scowled at her supercilious tone, but kept his anger in check. "Yes, even to us, Elgiva. So … my family are alive, at least. And Othere, too. How far away is the settlement?"

"About two leagues due west."

"When do we leave?"

"We?"

"We can't stay here. Be reasonable, girl! Beortnoth's men are bound to return. They've left a wagonload of booty. Where else can we go but home?"

"Home?" Her tone was edged with acid. "Your home, perhaps, not mine." No, not even that, she thought. She cocked her small fists on her hips and made her position clear. "I told you, Godwin, I'm an Elf. My home is in the woods. That's where I belong – and should have stayed, but for some very bad advice. I can't return to Othere's. I must help Greyflanks find his family. Then I'll fend for myself."

"But you saved the settlement! They'll hail you as a heroine!"

"Is that a fact?" she snapped.

He was taken aback by the force of her reaction.

"You'd have me pile deceit upon deceit. Not only would you have me lie about my appearance,you'd have me pretend to be brave, too. I told you, Godwin, I believed the amulet would protect me. Do you think I'd have been such a fool otherwise?"

"Perhaps I do. You're fool enough."

His remark stunned her, but his steadfast gaze showed no hint of apology. Abashed, she looked away and ran her fingers through her hair. Then in a calmer voice, she said. "There's nothing for me among your kind. I don't need their adulation. I don't belong there. I never did. It was all a great mistake."

"By Frigg! We fed and sheltered you! How can you be so arrogant?"

She almost spat with anger. "How dare you judge me, Wilthkin? By Faine! why can't you just go home and let me live my life?"

He shrugged and sighed. "Very well," he said grimly. "You must do as you please. You saved my family, so I've no right to stand in your way. I'm in your debt." He seated himself beside the dead fire and stared at the cold, grey ashes.

Elgiva hesitated for a moment and then she joined him and, for a while, no-one spoke.

"You're not in my debt," she ventured, at length. "And … and I'm glad your family are safe."

He smiled at her and nodded. "Where will you go?" he asked.

"That's not your concern. Go back to Rowena. It's your duty, Godwin. But you'll have to go alone. I won't go back to Othere's. I can't." She got to her feet. "Have a safe journey home." She turned her back on him.

Godwin quickly got to his feet and, as he did so, he grabbed her arm, made her look at him. "Is that any way to say farewell to a friend?"

Despite the frown that marked his brow, his tone was gentle. He was desperately trying to understand, but her only desire was to escape.

"Friends should be curt in their good-byes and spare each other pain," she replied.

"You do have feelings for me, then?"

She flashed him an angry, embarrassed look. "That's neither here nor there! By Faine! What do you want from me? Your family needs you. I need no-one. All I want is my freedom! Let go of me!" She snatched her arm from his grasp. "If you need me to admit that I've felt friendship for a Wilthkin, then I admit it. Satisfied?" He nodded slowly. "Now, let us part!"

No, thought Godwin, not like this. "We shall, "he said, "but before we do, grant me one favour … in the name of friendship."

Elgiva narrowed her eyes. "What might that be?"

"I want to see you as you really are. You owe me that. I've never seen an Elf. I need convincing that such things exist."

"Still you don't believe me!" Her face was flushed with rage.

"Indeed I do," he protested.

"What good would it do?"

"If I don't know the truth, it'll haunt me forever. I don't deserve that, do I?"

Her smooth brow wrinkled with doubt and frustration. What was she to do? Bellic had told her that there were Elves with the power to enchant Wilthkin simply by their appearance. And if that happened, would she ever be free of this man? But how could she refuse him? He was her friend … and they would never meet again.

"If I do," she said uncertainly, "will you accept that we must part … forever?"

"I never knew your heart could be so cold."

"My heart is not your concern!" The wolf began to fidget uneasily, eager to be away. He fixed Elgiva with his amber eyes and she couldn't ignore his plea. "We need to be going," she said. "This delay distresses Greyflanks."

"Then change now. Please."

Elgiva thought for a moment, torn between anger and fear. "But what if I can't? What if Siriol won't obey me? What if … you don't like what you see?"

He held her gaze as steadily as he could. "There's only one way you can answer those questions."

She shrugged resignedly and drew a deep breath. Very well. There was nothing else for it. She would do as he had asked. It was the only way to be free of him; of the guilt he made her feel.

She turned and put several yards between herself and her friend. Filling her lungs with air to stop herself from shaking, she folded her hands around the amulet. Her throat felt as dry as the ashes of their fire.

"Siriol!" she cried in a quavering voice, "hear me and work my will. I beg you, reverse your enchantment. Restore me to my true appearance." She cleared her throat, then tightly closed her eyes, more from fear than from a need for concentration.

Despite his wish to see her as an Elf, Godwin felt his entrails knotting with trepidation, but he clenched his jaw and ignored the inner voice that urged him to run for his life.

"Siriol," continued Elgiva, more strongly, "tear away this deception. Take the dawn's blush from my skin, the summer sky from my eyes, the autumn gold from my hair. I no longer need the protection of this disguise. I wish the spell undone. So be it."

She waited, her breathing quick and shallow. Would the amulet's magic affect her as violently as it had when she used it at Othere's settlement to free herself from the marauder? So far there was no giddiness, no nausea or weakness. The merest sensation of passing wafted through her soul, but it had no more power to alarm her than the draught from a butterfly's wing.

Beside the dead camp-fire the wolf whimpered softly.

"Well? Has anything happened?" she asked, but Godwin wasn't listening. Her eyelids snapped open. Her friend looked like a man bereft of all his wits. "I take it something has," she said and her dark eyes watched him warily.

Godwin stood motionless and seemed struck dumb, but there was a look of wonder on his face. Elgiva had to admit that she was relieved that it wasn't revulsion, then the depth of her own vanity made her angry.

"By Faine! Don't stare at me like that!" And to her surprise, she stamped her foot.

"You're beautiful," he said.

Her pale lips parted, but astonishment left her mute. For a while they stared at each other, neither knowing what to say. Then Godwin gathered himself together.

"If it wasn't for those strange ears, I'd mistake you for a Briton."

"Strange ears?" Her hands came up to cover the offending articles and, as far as it was possible for an Elf to blush, she did. Her forehead creased with indignation. "Are you satisfied now?" she cried. She strode towards him and searched his face. "You can understand what I'm saying, I suppose?"

"Of course I can," he replied a little distantly.

"I may be able to understand other languages, but Wilthkin can't seem to do that, so I'm speaking Saxon, just for your benefit. I've spoken it for long enough – it came quite naturally along with the disguise ..."

"You speak it very well," he said.

"Of course I do!" she retorted. "I'm an Elf. Such abilities are not beyond me!" She tilted back her head in a gesture of dismissal and her black hair fell about her shoulders, gleaming in the morning sunlight. "Now, in the name of Faine, be gone!"

She held herself still and waited, but Godwin didn't move. Unable to endure the intensity of his gaze, she turned her back on him and folded her arms.

"Elgiva ..." He hesitated. He knew what he ought to do, but what he wanted to do carried far more weight. "Let me come with you. Just a little way."

With an angry glance behind her, she shook her head at him.

"Please, Elgiva, I could be of help in finding Greyflanks's family."

She threw up her hands in despair and span to confront his plea. "I thought the matter was settled? What about *YOUR* family?"

"I know they're safe and they'll believe that I'm held captive at Beortnoth's. They won't expect to see me until Othere bargains for the return of prisoners."

"And will he?"

"Of course he will! He's our master! He wouldn't abandon any one of us."

"And what help could you be to me, or Greyflanks?"

Godwin regarded her blankly. His fascination for the creature that had magically appeared before him drove all other considerations out of his mind. Elgiva shook her head with exasperation. She had feared that this would happen.

"You're enchanted, aren't you?" she sighed.

He ignored this remark. "I have to see you settled somewhere. How can I leave you now? I'd never know where you were or if you were all right."

"Would it matter?" she asked him wearily.

"You protected my family! You saved the settlement! You probably saved my life! Don't I have a right to care in return?"

"Of course you do, when the caring is real. But this is just an enchantment, Godwin!"

"I don't know what you mean."

She knotted her fingers in the dark splendour of her hair and fought with her growing impatience. "If it's adventure you're after, you'll get no adventures travelling with me."

"To me, freedom itself is an adventure, and anyway, I made ..."He flinched from her dark gaze, suddenly bashful. "I made a vow to protect you. I can't go back on it now. Not until you are safe somewhere."

"Excuses," she fumed. "So, my friend, you made a vow, but now you're enchanted and you don't know what you're saying. And how could you possibly protect me?"

Secretly, Elgiva was overwhelmed by the honour he had done her, though it made her annoyance all the keener. The more she loathed his race, the more they provided her with proofs of friendship. Guilt had become the foundation of her life.

"You can't really stop me anyway," he said.

He smiled ingenuously and Elgiva shook her head. "You're a fool, Godwin, but I see I have no choice. I can't stand here forever arguing about it. I've tried to dissuade you, but it's your life and you must do with it as you please. I dare say I should be flattered by your concern. Well, so be it. It might be quite pleasant to have some company – at least for a while. I'm sure you'll change your mind sooner or later." She looked him up and down, then shrugged resignedly. "Right then. There's a stream beyond those trees where you can bathe and wash the blood from your clothes. But don't be too long, Godwin. We must be on our way."

She turned on her heel and left him.

Godwin hurried to join her and an unnamed gladness filled his heart. But suddenly he faltered, looked back at the clearing. At the dead embers of the camp-fire and the empty cooking pot. From her perch in the tree, the hawk eyed him warily.

He had an odd feeling that he had left something behind, something very dear to him, but he couldn't unravel his thoughts. Nor did he wish to try. Adventure, she had said. Yes, and so it was. Even if nothing happened, it had to be different from the day-to-day existence that he had drifted through for as long as he could remember.

And he was free.

But he had left something ... No, wantonly abandoned it. He pictured Rowena through a haze of wood-smoke on a summer evening, her smiling face and the laughter of his children. But these images were losing their power to hold him. He ought to make an effort. They mustn't slip away like dreams that are vanquished by the morning.

Then another face rose into his mind: the face of a Saxon girl whose hair carried a crown of golden sunshine. He knew that he had lost her, too. His friend had gone forever. Worse still, she had never even existed. This alluring stranger had taken her place. What seemed like fantasy now was in fact reality robbed of its disguise.

Well, what did it matter? What was past, what was lost, none of it mattered now. Something unfamiliar beckoned him to follow and it was irresistible.

"Godwin, have you changed your mind?"

Elgiva stood at the edge of the glade, her head cocked questioningly, and her voice was alarmingly real. The hawk left the tree with a flutter of wings and Godwin visibly jumped.

"No ... I was just..."

"Never mind. Come on!"

Chapter Nine

Godwin had bathed his wound in the chill water and scrubbed the gore from his grey, woollen tunic and he knew himself to be far from clean, but this was the best he could do. He joined Elgiva, as she searched through the spoils that the raiders had left in the wagon. They found two water-skins, some dried fruit and bread and a large, round cheese that was wrapped in a cloth. Godwin put them all in a sack, which he volunteered to carry, and, all the while, the wolf padded round them, trying to contain his impatience.

With a grimace of satisfaction, Godwin uncovered a small knife and he thrust it into his belt. Then, for a moment, he felt himself drift. When he returned to his senses, he found that he was staring at Elgiva, as though she were something precious and beautiful. Her long-suffering expression told him better than words that he looked as foolish as he felt.

"Are we ready to leave?" he asked.

"*WE'VE* been ready for ages," she told him, "but *YOU* were somewhere else."

"I'm sorry." He slung the sack over his shoulder and turned to walk away.

"A moment, if you please."

He turned and saw that she hadn't moved. She was leaning against the wagon with an arch look on her face. "Something wrong?" he asked.

"Well, two things. Firstly, where are you going?" Godwin frowned at her. "We haven't decided which way to go yet and I think our friend is the one to choose. His instinct is better then ours."

Godwin nodded. "Of course."

"Secondly, are you blind?"

Godwin looked at her questioningly. Her answer was to reach into the wagon and snatch aside a piece of cloth. When she lifted her arm again, it was with a gesture of triumph.

"My sword! Elgiva, they took my sword!" He dropped the sack, ran to her side and grabbed the weapon gratefully. He gazed at it in disbelief, as though it were an old friend he hadn't seen in years. "This is good fortune indeed!" he cried. The weight of the blade reassured him and somehow he felt whole again.

Elgiva smiled at the joy in his artless eyes. "Now we really are ready for the road that lies ahead," she declared. "Greyflanks, lead the way."

* * *

Dusk was falling, as the three companions stopped for the night in a sheltered clearing. Following Greyflanks's instincts, they had walked many leagues in a north-easterly direction, though they had no way of knowing where they were nor exactly how far they had travelled.

The land they were in was thickly wooded and the absence of tracks made the going hard, but at least there was plenty of wood for their fire and Godwin found a stream of clear water with which he replenished their water-skins.

Elgiva and Greyflanks flopped down on the grass, while Godwin set about making a fire, striking sparks from a stone with his knife and using moss for tinder; it was a laborious business and soon his forehead was slick with the effort.

Elgiva watched until the fire was lit, then she tried to comfort the wolf. "When morning comes, I'll stop a bird and we'll ask it if it has seen any wolves. Do you feel we're going in the right direction?" Greyflanks snuffled dejectedly. Elgiva sat up and hugged her knees. "Well, tomorrow will be better. We'll be rested then." She caressed his large head gently and the wolf leaned against her and licked her face. "We'll soon get used to travelling and then we'll pick up more speed. Then we won't be holding you back. But … perhaps you'd rather go on alone?"

Wolves don't care to travel alone, said the large, sad eyes that were lifted to hers. It's not in their nature. Alone is bad.

Elgiva knew the truth of this, but didn't care to confront it. Then she had the feeling that she was being observed. She looked towards Godwin, who sat rubbing his hands by the fire, and he was looking straight back at her, his eyes glazed with adoration. Elgiva drew a long breath and leaned towards the wolf.

"There," she said, "is one who, as yet, knows nothing of his aloneness, for he's seen an Elf and dwells with enchantment. This is all a dream to him. I feared it would happen and I did try to warn him, didn't I? He should have remembered me as I was, but Wilthkin won't be told." A ridge of concern furrowed her brow. "And when the enchantment finally fades, reality will come as a shock. I wish I knew what to do for him, Greyflanks. I wish Lord Bellic was here." She slumped back down on the grass with a sigh and in the sky above her, the shadow of night pursued the sun towards the western horizon.

"Elgiva, I'm starving," Godwin complained.

"You'll have to get used to it," she said. "We have to be sparing with food. We're not in the Meadhall now."

"Perhaps we could hunt?" he suggested.

"Hunt with what? Your sword?"

He shrugged and lowered his eyes.

"Have a piece of that bread, if you must," she said. "Greyflanks might hunt tomorrow. Perhaps he'll share the kill with you. At least the enchantment hasn't robbed you of hunger, unlike your common sense."

"What enchantment? What do you mean?"

"Some Elves have the power to enchant, merely by their appearance, and I seem to be such an Elf. Don't ask me to explain. I can't. I believe it wears off, given time." Godwin smiled at her indulgently, as though she were talking nonsense, and this provoked her anger. "No-one explained such things to me! I don't know how to end the enchantment, but I do know that you've left your family because of it … because of *ME*! You've abandoned your home and your kin, and you just sit there, Godwin, as if it didn't matter at all!"

But Godwin continued to smile at her and she felt her hands clench into fists. A sudden focus of passion glimmered in her eyes. "By Faine! I wish I could end this enchantment. I wish you'd see sense and go home! I won't be responsible for you, Wilthkin. I just won't stand for it!" His eyebrows lifted slightly, as if in mild surprise at her ranting. "Oh, in Faine's name, Godwin, just wake up!"

Her tone made him jump and he frowned at her, but then he felt like laughing, for she seemed to be talking nonsense again. Then he saw the vehemence in her gaze and the dusk seemed to thicken around him, draw into focus with sickening speed, and he couldn't make a sound.

Elgiva felt suddenly weary; her flare of temper seemed to have drained her reserves of strength. But she stopped in mid-yawn. Godwin was staring about him and he appeared to be wondering where he was. She leaned towards him eagerly.

"I don't believe it," she said with a tentative smile. "Is the enchantment fading?"

His blue eyes swivelled towards her, wide with bewilderment and a hint of fear. He didn't seem to know who she was.

Elgiva turned to the wolf. "I didn't expect it to fade this quickly, but I dare say the length of enchantment depends on the gullibility of the one enchanted, so, in Godwin's case, it probably lasted longer then usual." She giggled, but it was more from relief than from genuine amusement.

"By Grim! Where am I?" cried Godwin. "Elgiva ...what's going on?"

She saw his distress and her smile faltered and she was more than a little ashamed. Crawling to his side, she grabbed his sleeve, anxious to dispel his confusion. "Godwin ..." she began, but the sentence went unfinished.

Something large was heading towards them, slashing through the bushes. The wolf sprang up, his hackles raised and a snarl about his lips, and Elgiva and Godwin jumped to their feet to confront the unknown threat.

Then a huge figure burst from the trees and blundered into their midst. He wielded an axe that would have tested the strength of three average men. His massive shoulders were draped with furs, which added to his bulk, and from his chin hung a great, blond beard. He was a Saxon and he was a giant: seven feet tall, at least.

He planted himself before them and the firelight glowed on his cheeks. “Intruders!” he roared, lifting the axe, and his brows drew together into a scowl.

Then he took a few steps forwards… and they took a few steps back.

While he looked them up and down, Elgiva and Godwin stood holding hands, like two small children caught robbing an orchard, each comforting the other.

Greyflanks moved slowly, as though he intended to circle the threat to his friends, but the giant flourished the mighty axe and made a bold sweep before him. Clamping his tail between his legs, the wolf slunk off behind his companions.

For a long, tense moment, they all stood in silence.

There must be some place in this world that doesn’t belong to someone, thought Elgiva bitterly. Once again, she was trespassing, but this time she didn’t have a disguise. Well, somebody had to do something and it might as well be her. She peeled her hand from Godwin’s grip and stepped towards the giant. Then she halted and swallowed hard.

He planted the axe before him, its edge a flash of gold in the firelight. From underneath his craggy brows, he watched Elgiva guardedly. She made a small bow and looked up with a grimace that tried to be a smile, but failed. His stern expression didn’t waver.

“My Lord,” she ventured, her heart thumping in her breast, “I’m Elgiva. I’m an Elf, as you can see. These are my friends. Godwin, a Briton, and Greyflanks, son of wolf-queen Whitefoot. We're sorry to trespass and we meant no harm. We can move on, if you wish."

The giant studied each of them in turn, but made no move to answer.

"Perhaps we can make amends for our intrusion," said Elgiva, "and invite you to join us in a humble meal?"

Elgiva moved back to Godwin's side and they glanced at each other worriedly. She saw in his eyes the fear that the giant would eat all the food they had and, despite their situation, her lips curled into a smile. She cursed her Elven sense of humour, but the giant responded to her grin.

"Joskin, I'm called," said the giant. "You one of Tandrin's Elves?"

"Er … who is Tandrin, my Lord?"

"Ha!" said the giant. "I'm no lord!" The companions flinched, but the giant beamed as though Elgiva had done him an honour. "Tandrin," he went on. "King of the Elves. Round here, that is. Nice bunch they are. Not very chatty, though." Despite his deep and resonant voice, he spoke in an awkward, jerky manner, as though he had little practice with speech.

"I'm from Elindell," Elgiva said.

"What you doing here, then?"

"Well … I … lost my way."

The giant nodded knowingly. "Happens to the best of us. What you got to eat, then?"

He tucked the axe under one arm and sat down cross-legged by the fire. Elgiva and Godwin looked at each other and then they followed his example.

"Is … is there a settlement near?" Godwin asked him carefully.

"East. Ten leagues," said the giant.

"So … you live alone?" It wasn't that Godwin cared if the giant were lonely or not, but he was concerned that more of his kin might be lurking in the bushes.

"Have to," responded the giant. "Understandable, really. No fun being different. Even as a lad. Always so tall. Don't know why. Parents, a bit on the small side, see? Always seemed to frighten people. And there's another thing. About being big. People think you're special. They want to have a go at you, too. You get no peace. Lord had me marked down for his champion. Might have had to kill someone. So, I ran away."

Godwin grimaced nervously and held out their sack of provisions. The giant helped himself to some bread with a courteous nod of thanks.

"Not a bad bit of bread," he opined, laying down his axe. He saw Godwin's look of relief and laughed. "Don't worry, man. Use the axe to chop down trees. Or scare people off. Never to hurt. Can't stand the sight of blood, you see. But who's to know that, eh?" He laughed again, an honest laugh that held no trace of malice. "Gave you lot a fright, at least! But if you'd all ganged up on me, don't know what I'd have done."

The three companions looked at him sheepishly. Yes, they all thought, you were lucky to have stumbled upon three cowards. The wolf put his head between his paws to hide his long, sharp teeth and Elgiva hid Siriol deep in her robe. Godwin turned sideways to hide his sword.

"How come you're travelling with a wolf?"

"He lost his family," Elgiva explained. "We're trying to help him find them."

"Very obliging, I'm sure," said Joskin. "Poor thing must be fretting. Tell you what, come back to my cave. Better shelter than here. A good night's sleep, set you up for travelling. I've got Elf-wine, too." He winked at Elgiva. "How'd that suit you?"

Elgiva looked at Godwin and he nodded his agreement. "You're too kind, Joskin," she said.

"Bless me!" exclaimed the giant. "You can never be that!"

"We'd be honoured to stay at your home."

"Good. Don't get many visitors. Well, none really. Food, back home. Meat and stuff. Elves leave me some things now and then. Very grateful I am, to be sure. Only wish they'd stop for a chat. But Elves are wary. Never mind. I've got friends, why, yes! Bless me! There's Shredwing and one or two others who pop in now and then. Many a creature old Joskin has raised that fell from the nest or lost its kin. Animals never forget, you know. Don't care what you look like either."

Raising a piece of bread to his lips, he nibbled at it daintily. Godwin fought the urge to stare, but he couldn't help himself. He had fully expected the food to vanish in one almighty gulp, instead he found himself put in mind of a great, bearded hare chewing grass.

"Perhaps I'm a lord, as you said," chuckled Joskin. "Lord of the Beasts! Yes, I like that!" He laughed his hearty laugh. "Course," he went on, "you can't talk to them. Unless you're an Elf, that is. 'Cause they don't follow, you see."

He brushed the crumbs from his golden beard and drew a small handkerchief from his tunic. Then he wiped his mouth with it, as though he had eaten a feast.

"Think we'll be off now, if that's agreeable. Don't like to leave the old place too long. Especially at night. Understandable really. Never know who's abroad, do you?" He rose to his feet and towered above them. "Nice evening for the time of year. Still a bit chilly, though. Take a brand from the fire, if you would, little Elf. To light us on our way."

Elgiva did as she was instructed. Godwin kicked dirt onto the fire and picked up their sack of provisions and Greyflanks padded softly behind them, as they followed the giant's lead.

⋆ ⋆ ⋆

The cave where the giant lived had been carved from a stony ridge of land and was hidden from view by the ancient trees and undergrowth around it. Before the entrance stood six tall rowans that he had planted in an orderly line; they were trees that had power against hexes he said. The cave was also Joskin's doing. He had hewn it with his powerful hands out of the shallow escarpment.

"Ruined all the tools I had. Just the axe left now," he said proudly, smiling at his own accomplishment.

He guided his visitors inside and set about making a fire a few feet from the entrance. While he worked, he told them how the Elves had spied on him, admired his perseverance and left him gifts outside the cave when he was fast asleep. Sometimes they left food or wine, sometimes knives or pots or beakers. On several occasions he found injured birds, which he cared for until they had recovered.

Each time he released one back to the wild, the Elves would leave him a special gift. Usually something good to eat – fruit cake was a particular favourite!

The cave was a cheery, comfortable home, despite the cold, unyielding rock. Two stone ledges, waist-high, ran parallel to each other down both sides of the cave and at intervals they were draped with furs. Rough niches in the walls accommodated flagons and bowls and there were brackets for holding torches.

Elgiva noticed a number of tapestries pegged to the walls of the cave and enthused about their detail and colour, unprepared for the giant's response.

"One of them was an Elvish gift, but did the others myself," he explained. "Elves left me some stuff, you see, so thought I'd have a go. Suppose they're okay. Makes it look cosy. Only one problem, the spiders. Spiders get behind 'em. Can't stand spiders, can you?" His massive frame shuddered, but then he laughed. "They probably can't stand *US*! And spiders need a home, too, eh? Anyway, cobwebs, good dressings for wounds." He raised his eyebrows knowingly.

Elgïva was charmed by his eccentricity. "You have a lovely home," she said. "In fact, I've never seen better."

A glow of pleasure and modest pride mantled the giant's cheeks. "Well, though I say so as shouldn't, it's true. Make all my own clothes, too. Don't like to kill for the skins, of course. Elves don't like it either, so I take things already dead, if I can. But now and then," he shook his head sadly, "have to set some traps. Understandable really. Got to eat, you know."

By now the fire had taken hold. Joskin lit four torches and positioned them on the walls. A cheery glow spread into the cave and, near the back, the travellers saw more of Joskin's handiwork: a smooth perch fastened to a stave of wood. And on this perch, blinking in the light, was a bird – or something resembling a bird. Its wings hung down like tattered rags.

"Aye, that's Shredwing," the giant said, following their gaze. "He was a fledgeling. Wild-cat got him. Saved his life, but couldn't fix him. Did what I could, but ... as you see. Wings beyond repair."

"He's some kind of falcon," said Godwin. "My lord had one just like it."

"He may have been a falcon. Now he's just my friend."

Shredwing inspected the visitors and his black eyes gleamed like polished pebbles, but having spotted Elgiva, the vigilance left his gaze.

A sweet scent suddenly filled the cave, mingling with the wood-smoke. Joskin grinned, when he saw his guests thoughtfully sniffing the air.

"Burn herbs with the wood. Nice, eh? Please sit down. I'll do you a meal. Just have to warm up that comfrey soup. I've a stew of winter vegetables. Bread, too, and some honey somewhere. And, by the looks of you two, I need to find fresh bandages. You've been in the wars, I'd say. Well, a noggin or two of Tandrin's wine ... Soon put you to rights!"

* * *

Chapter Ten

The night was waning when Elgiva woke suddenly, wondering where she was. The dark ceiling of Joskin's cave appeared to be hanging above her, as though preparing to fall, and everything had a reddish glow, cast by the embers of the fire. Sliding from under the fur coverlet, her skin tightening at the loss of its warmth, she searched for her leather sandals. Something had awoken her, something that waited outside the cave like a vague threat poised for utterance. A runnel of dread ran down her spine.

She had no idea why she felt so strong a sense of impending danger, but it was too insistent to ignore. For a moment she thought of alerting her companions, but was stopped by some unnamed instinct. She felt, inexplicably, that she must dare this menace alone.

She stepped from the ledge and moved out of the cave as quietly as she could. Her heart was pounding in her throat, as she peered between the rowan trees and searched the night for whatever was out there. And, whatever it was, it beckoned. She held her breath and listened, but her ears detected nothing, save for a silence as dark and empty as an abandoned crypt.

It would soon be daybreak, but the sun had yet to rise, and the dark beyond the cosy cave swarmed with potential horrors. Elgiva needed all the acuteness of her senses to make out her surroundings, as she stepped out from among the rowans. The night was gripped by an unnatural calm and, as her sandals whispered against the cold grass beneath them, they sounded abnormally loud.

She feared that they would betray her presence and wondered why she felt such a need for stealth.

After a while she came to a stop and searched the benighted trees without knowing what it was she sought. Thin strands of mist curled along the ground, cold and clammy, like an exhalation of sickness.

She hugged her shoulders, knotted her fingers in the cascade of her hair, and her body shivered in its ragged robe. All around her the silence seemed to be drawing into focus.

"Who is it?" Her throat was too dry for her purpose. She swallowed and licked her lips. "Who's there? I know you're there. I can … I can feel you!" Feel you, she thought, and shivered, as though a host of insects were crawling on her skin.

A flash of silver sliced through the dark and made her gasp in fear. Her arms came up to shield her face, as the beam struck a rock several yards ahead. It exploded with a whooshing sound and sent up thousands of splinters of light, which fell to the ground and sizzled in the mist.

A shape now stood upon the rock, its form concealed in a black, hooded cloak.

Elgiva locked her knees to keep herself upright and, as she clutched the amulet to her breast, her hands were white with terror. "In the name of Faine, who are you?" she cried. " What sort of trick is this?"

A soft, sly voice spoke back to her. "Why should you fear magic?"

"Magic?"

"Magic."

"What do you want?" she pleaded, her voice a croak of fear.

"To see for myself."

"To see what?"

The dark shape sniggered but made no answer, instead it swept its cloak aside and a cloud of sparks flew out from it and covered the ground with beads of light. She stepped back unsteadily, resolved to flee.

"Stay!"

The creature raised a skeletal hand and the forefinger swung towards Elgiva and pinned her against the darkness, held her like a rivet of bone. No Elf, no Wilthkin, ever owned such a hand. Her legs were beginning to buckle beneath her. This had to be a nightmare; she was still asleep in the cave. But she knew that it was all too real.

"Who are you? What do you want?" she cried. "I have … I have an amulet!"

The creature laughed derisively. "I am Death and I have come for *YOU*."

It began to radiate a sickly light, enveloping itself in a caul of brilliance that glowed like verdigris. The light pulsated with force and grew in size until the trees behind it were bathed in its angry glare. Stealthily, it reached for Elgiva, like a foul stench creeping along a breeze, and she felt herself helpless in the grip of some coercion. The creature's power throbbed in the darkness.

Within the taut coils of her fear, her instincts screamed at her to run, but her limbs had turned to stone.

Siriol, Siriol, help me … help…

The creature sensed her silent cries, greeted them with a shriek of glee and increased the throb of its power. She felt a sudden, quivering shock as the force poured into her mind. Then she became divorced from herself and watched from a great distance, waiting for the horror to unfold.

Then something broke inside her. A dam burst open and a flood of defiance surged to her assistance. "You're not Death! No-one dies like this!" She pulled herself back into focus. "In the name of Lord Faine, whoever you are, you have no right! I'm defenceless. Stop this!"

The hooded opponent merely intensified the probing of its power, renewing its attack on the barriers of her mind and behind its virulence she felt a thrill of laughter.

How dare you!

She didn't know how she mastered her fear, how she found the strength to resist, but she felt she must fight for her very life. Her enemy's power was narcotic, lulling her into a trance, but part of her mind was feverishly active, gathering might of its own. An inner resource she couldn't name was pleading for recognition.

She forced herself to concentrate. She must expel this being from her mind.

It seemed that they were revolving round each other, like autumn leaves caught up in a gale, though she knew that they both stood motionless, rooted to the earth, like impossibly ancient trees. Within her breast was an unfamiliar feeling, a growing heat like a guttering candle bravely defying a tempest. The flame expanded in desperation and then flared with a boundless joy, as if it were nearing some long wished-for focus. It filled her with strength ... but how it seared! Like scratching an open wound.

Stop it, please ...stop it.

The creature's power only probed the greater, but, as it breached the privacy of her mind, it revealed something of its own.

Elgiva recoiled momentarily, alarmed at the discovery that this being was a Wardain. But who?

Frantically, she strengthened her will and kept the creature at bay, but his power still battered at the threshold of her mind. Self-defence required so much effort that she felt that the blood was boiling in her veins and her mental anguish scaled upwards, became physical pain.

Why are you doing this to me?

She couldn't stand this any longer. She prepared herself to die.

Suddenly, there were shouts in the distance, a hundred leagues away. Someone was calling her name. Someone she knew: the voice of a friend. She made a mighty effort and strove to gain her freedom and a great light flashed in her brain.

Then she was herself again, on her hands and knees with the shock of the cold grass on her skin and the world canting madly around her. She was free … free … but engulfed by fire and soaked with sweat. Her robe clung to her skin, like a membrane, and her scorched lungs heaved for air.

She managed to lift her head. Through a throbbing, red mist she saw her attacker, standing calmly on the rock, his concentration either broken, or willingly curtailed. His cloak was wrapped around him and a sheen of spent magic shivered along his form.

"Excellent," he said softly. His voice had changed completely, its edge of malice gone. "I'm sorry about the theatricals, but that was an entertaining battle. I think we shall meet again."

As she watched through the tears that were stinging her eyes, his flesh seemed to grow transparent. Gradually he faded and melted like mist and then, in a moment, was gone.

Her limbs folded beneath her and she fell face down in the dew. Between her ragged gasps she vaguely heard someone running in her direction. Then she was gently rolled onto her back and relief flooded her mind, for in the first light of dawn she recognised Godwin.

"Elgiva, by Frigg! Who was *THAT*? What happened?"

Elgiva couldn't respond.

"Are you all right? … Elgiva?"

"I'm sick," she croaked. "I feel … so sick." She felt herself being cradled in his arms; it was a good feeling.

"Who was that?" persisted Godwin. "What did he do to you?"

"Hold me … hold…"

She floated on a sea of nausea and clung to Godwin as her only anchor, until the heat within her gradually dwindled and the world decelerated around her. As the dizziness passed, it left her with a feeling of violation. Moreover, she knew that some change had occurred at the very core of her being. Some inexpressible wrath or madness hungered for release. She didn't understand it; but whatever it was, it scared her. She pressed herself closer to Godwin, desperate for warmth and strength.

"Greyflanks woke me," he explained. "He seemed upset. Tried to drag me from my bed. Being dragged out of bed by a wolf wakes you up a lot quicker than a cock-crow, I think." He smiled at her but she looked at him blankly. "Well, he stood there, snarling at the cave-mouth, but he wouldn't go out himself. Then I noticed that you had gone. Elgiva, are you hurt?"

"Oh … no, not hurt," she said shakily. "It wasn't that kind of fight. It was … it was all in the mind." She took a deep breath to compose herself. "He was looking for something. Something in me."

"Did he find it?" asked Godwin carefully.

She looked at him, confused by his tone, and decided to skirt around the question. "He was thinking 'easy prey', but I wasn't." She paused, slowly shook her head. "I defended myself … but I don't understand. Perhaps it was Siriol. I just… don't know."

"Who was he, Elgiva?"

"He was a Wardain, Godwin. Very powerful, too. I thought … I thought he would turn me to ashes. But he didn't. I felt him … I felt him holding back." Her forehead creased with effort, as she tried to explain what she had endured. "It was almost as though he was testing me."

"Testing you? Why?" Battles in the mind? These were things that Godwin couldn't even begin to understand.

"I've no idea," she said forlornly.

"How did you defend yourself?"

"I don't know that either. Somehow I just … did. All of my strength fought half of his, but somehow I defied him. It must have been the amulet." She pulled away from him, sat up and combed the hair from her face with a hand that trembled badly. She felt that she must try to regain some composure. "He was holding back. Was he waiting for me to weaken or just prolonging the sport? I was done for, I know that, but then you shouted and broke his concentration." She looked at him, her dark eyes wide with horror. "Godwin, if you hadn't …!"

Overcome by exhaustion and fear, she needed his support again. His strong arms held her in a tight embrace and they sat in silence for a time. All around them the darkness was lifting and birdsong announced the dawn.

Godwin was happy to hold Elgiva until her terror had passed. It gave him time to consider something that puzzled him. When he had found her lying on the ground, he had seen a strange light in the depths of her eyes, like the luminous gaze of some fierce, wild creature. Had he merely imagined it? Was it a trick of the light?

"Come back to the cave," he advised her. She nodded weakly and allowed him to help her to her feet. "We must continue our search for the wolves and you'll need some rest before we go."

She gazed into his honest, blue eyes, her features raw with protest. "Godwin, no, you must go home! That Wardain said we'd meet again. If he returns…"

"Go home, Elgiva?" He glared at her, as though she had questioned his mettle. "Be reasonable, girl! Do you think I would leave you, when your life is in danger? I vowed to protect you and I intend to be true to that vow, if to nothing else."

"What could you do against power like that?" she demanded, and tears welled into her eyes.

But Godwin would hear no more of the matter. Life had made him an expert at the art of hiding his feelings and now he gratefully acknowledged the skill. Feigning courage, he took her small hand and guided her back to the cave.

⋆ ⋆ ⋆

Joskin had slept soundly and knew nothing of the night's events. His sole concern was that his guests should be better equipped for the journey that lay ahead of them. With that in mind, he presented Godwin with a thick, brown cloak as protection against the chilly nights.

"Elves made it for me," the giant explained. "A fine thing it was, till I washed it. It's wool, you see. It shrank!" He laughed his generous laugh. "Now it's your size. That's lucky, eh? Keep the wind out, won't it? Here's a linen shirt. Put it over your gown, little Elf."

Elgiva did as she was told, but her hands were lost in the sleeves. Godwin rolled them up for her, a broad grin on his face.

"Do up your belt," said Joskin. "There. That looks a treat, you know."

The giant patted Greyflanks's head and wished him success in his quest. He was trying his best to be cheerful, but the prospect of being alone again made his great heart ache with sorrow.

Before they left, Elgiva bade good-bye to Joskin's pet, Shredwing, whose squawks of excitement filled the cave.

"There's something he wants to tell you, Joskin, while he's got the chance," she said.

The giant's eyebrows lifted expectantly.

"If only you understood his language! He's picked up most of yours."

"Bless me!"

"You see, my friend, they *DO* follow much more than you imagine. He also says he's sad when you're lonely. He tries his best to comfort you, but you think he's just making a noise. And he says he'd rather have pigeons than hares."

Joskin chuckled. "Anything for Shredwing." He stroked the bird's head fondly.

"What's more," Elgiva went on, "he wishes you knew how grateful he is. He'd have died but for you. But he's sorry to be such a burden. He can't hunt and he can't sing and he's often very sad, you know. He can't spread his wings and soar among the clouds." She paused for a moment and lowered her eyes. "He dreams about clouds. About blue skies and riding the warm air currents, just like his parents did."

"Poor wings," murmured Joskin.

"But he's proud to be your companion. He feels you were destined to be together. A couple of outcasts, he said." Well, the word he used was 'misfits', she thought, but no need to hurt you with that.

However, looking round, she felt that Joskin and his pet were in good company.

"Dear bird," said Joskin tenderly.

Godwin caught Elgiva's eye and gave her an urgent look. She nodded slightly and turned to the giant. "We should be on our way," she said.

Joskin sighed resignedly, while Godwin collected their sack of provisions.

"I'm sure this is heavier than it was," he said, looking somewhat puzzled.

The giant's hearty laughter echoed round the cave. "Forgive old Joskin. Took the liberty. Added some things. A bit of dried meat and some honeycakes. Bread and some good, strong ale. A small bowl to drink from. And flints and some tinder. Need them to make fire, you see."

"Joskin, you're worth your weight in gold," declared Elgiva brightly.

"Bless me," he said, "then I'm worth a fair bit!"

"I'm sorry we have to go."

"Understandable really," said Joskin. "Poor wolf. Must find his family. Bad to have no family, eh? At least I've got Shredwing."

Yes, it's bad, thought Elgiva, sadly. She glanced at Godwin, but he turned away. "I hope Tandrin's Elves come to visit more often. Perhaps one day they'll stay for a chat. You never know with Elves," she said.

Laughing at this, Joskin placed a huge hand on her shoulder. "A safe journey, then, my friends. Perhaps one day we'll meet again. Who knows?"

"Who indeed," said Elgiva.

The three companions left the cosy cave, turning once to wave to the amiable giant. He stood and watched in thoughtful silence until the forest had closed behind them. And continued to watch long after they had disappeared from view.

⋆ ⋆ ⋆

Chapter Eleven

They had travelled two leagues before noon, but saw no sign of wolves, and the birds Elgiva questioned offered little in the way of help.

"Your family must have moved," surmised Godwin, while Elgiva translated his words. "They could be looking for better hunting. Perhaps they're looking for *YOU*." He felt like an idiot, talking to a wolf, but knew better than to say so.

They travelled on, stopping once to eat. The sun had a cold and liquid look and lay among the grizzled clouds like a monstrous, broken egg. An east wind stung their eyes and chilled their skin, leaving them weary and dispirited.

Late afternoon saw them dragging their feet along a narrow valley, where a thin stream bubbled over stones and rocks, when suddenly they were brought to a halt by a faint cry in the distance. The cry was that of a wolf. Greyflanks stiffened and lifted a front paw tentatively, as though preparing to follow the sound.

"It's Blacktail!" he cried.

Exhilarated by the distant call, he threw back his head and howled his response. They waited for an answer, but were to be disappointed.

"He's a long way off," said Greyflanks. "The wind is against me. He hasn't heard." He pawed at the sparse grass dejectedly, then suddenly he brightened and his wet nose scented the air. With a wag of his tail he span to face his companions. "So long since I hunted!"

He streaked off down the valley, while Godwin sighed at his retreating form. "Might as well make camp," he said.

"Why not," said Elgiva. "We've walked enough for today."

Together they clambered out of the valley and searched for a sheltered spot. They were in an area where scything winds had levelled the shrubs and twisted the trees. A group of large boulders stood in a heap, like a family gathering of stones in the wilderness, and they set up camp beside them.

It was nearly dark by the time they had gathered enough wood to make a fire. Greyflanks returned soon after. He had caught and eaten an elderly goat, but he spared Elgiva the details, and, while his friends ate their own, meagre supper, he told them all about Blacktail.

Blacktail was an elder of the pack, an uncle of Greyflanks and a veteran of many battles. He had only one eye and his snout was badly scarred. His restless spirit made him often absent, wandering and exploring. Greyflanks guessed that the old wolf had been off on one of his expeditions, when they had heard his call, and he might be as lost as they were. To Blacktail, of course, this wasn't something that called for lamentation.

Night darkened the sky by degrees, as the travellers sat huddled before their fire, each thinking of the homes they had left or lost.

Greyflanks elation had faded. Not even a stomach full of goat was compensation for the absence of his pack.

For Elgiva, however, the longed-for meeting with the wolf's family wouldn't be so welcome. What was she to do with her life, once their quest was over? Could she live with the wolves? Living life as a nomad was unthinkable. It might be fine for Bellic and Blacktail, but it held no appeal for her. Yet what else lay in store for a nar-Wardain like herself, banished forever from her people's lands?

Had Thallinore discovered the plot against him? Did he now regret the expulsion of the only person who had managed to thwart it? No, that was unlikely. And, even if he had, recalling her from exile would make him look a fool in the eyes of his subjects. Thallinore was too proud to admit that he had made a mistake. And, after all, why should he bother? She was no-one of any importance, when all was said and done. He had always despised her anyway and was probably glad to have her off his hands.

She thought then of Eldreda, the old crone who had been Elgiva's guardian. She was overseer of the King's Household and had taught Elgiva her domestic duties. Drunk more often than not, she answered every question and rewarded every mistake with a swipe of the cane she always carried. She had repeatedly told Elgiva to be grateful, for the King had given her a status far in excess of her merits.

No doubt the cruel hag had fallen down a well one night after a bout with the Elf-wine. No-one had ventured an explanation for her disappearance and Elgiva wouldn't have dared to ask for one, even if she had cared.

As for herself, Elgiva had accepted that her origins were somehow shameful. Even Bellic had evaded her questions on the subject. Either he didn't know, or he couldn't bear the truth. Perhaps her parents were criminals and she was the last in a long line of traitors. The irony was that *HER* treason was warranted.

Now, added to all her unresolved questions about the past and her fears for the future, was a new and undeserved terror: a powerful Wardain had chosen her for his sport. But why?

Feeling that tears were very close, she lay on her side and curled herself into a tight ball of anguish.

Godwin glanced down at her. Firelight gleamed fitfully on the silken hair that fell across her cheek, obscuring her delicate features. Her slender form looked frail and childlike in the tattered gown and over-sized shirt. She looked like a beggar's daughter, or some lorn and hapless infant abandoned to the mercy of the world. He wished that he had a blanket to protect her from the malice of the night.

Her vulnerability hurt his eyes, so he tore them away and studied the camp-fire. Despite his fatigue, he was wide awake. He felt restless and edgy, poised between his past and his future, like a man who has abandoned one and can't find the other. He hugged his knees and shivered, but it wasn't the chill of darkness that filled his veins with ice, rather it was the burden of the guilt he carried.

Why hadn't he returned to his wife? The question stung him like a dart of self-loathing. She must surely believe him dead or enslaved. And his dear, little daughters, what were they thinking? Why had he found it so easy to run away from his responsibilities?

He scratched the stubble on his chin; it rasped against his fingers and he found it vaguely offensive. Somehow, he felt sure, only warriors should have beards.

He wondered if he would ever find his way back home.

Home …

A picture of Elric flashed before his mind. What had become of the lad? He knew that Othere had survived, but the fate of his master's son was a mystery. And what of Redwald, Kern and Cerdic? What of the countless others; childhood friends and fellow churls? How he longed for news of them all, for some assurance that the security of home was the same as it had always been.

He gritted his teeth to stifle his frustration. His sword lay beside him, glinting in the grass, and he touched it with his finger tips, as though it were his only anchor in an ocean of anxiety.

Home ...

Where he was merely a churl, a man of little consequence, the lowest of the low. Where he wasn't even allowed to wield the sword that was his birthright. Hadn't he earned one brief taste of freedom after all those years of service?

He looked down again at Elgiva, now safe in the arms of sleep. Why was he following her? Did he honestly believe in the inviolable nature of vows, or was that just an excuse? What made him trail in her wake, despite his dread of the unknown, while all the time he longed for his former state of slavery? No, not slavery. That was too harsh a word.

He shrugged at the chaos in his head and sighed. Small wonder he felt ill at ease. There was no daily routine anymore. No moil and toil of chores and duties. No landmarks to help him get through each day. No need to act a part. For the first time since he could remember he had no master but himself. He'd been a churl for so long that the possibility that he might enjoy another kind of life had never even occurred to him. Never before had he had the chance to find out if he could be anything other than what he was. It was a thrilling, frightening thought. Physically he had never been in fetters, but in his mind…

In his mind a flower was growing, spreading its petals like the fingers of a welcoming hand. He faced hunger, fatigue and danger, but to compensate for that he at last had freedom of choice. Freedom to choose between home and the unknown. And home would always be waiting for him once he had exhausted his desire for adventure.

Freedom of choice. There was something dignified about it. He must enjoy it while it lasted.

⋆ ⋆ ⋆

For three more days the companions travelled on, but they never heard Blacktail again. Despite the advent of spring, winter refused to leave without a fight and scattered frost and rain in equal measure.

Godwin became resigned to the fact that hunger and cold were his constant companions, but he had chosen them of his own volition, so he forced his sore feet onwards and kept his complaints to himself.

On the third night they made camp under an ancient elm. Lord of a desolate kingdom, it stood alone on a wind-scoured plain of thin and scrubby grass. In the distance lay a nebulous shape; a large, dark blur of forest.

They had eaten the last of their rations, but drew comfort from their blazing fire. They had gathered wood throughout the day, determined not to suffer a cold and cheerless night.

Even so, Godwin's mind was elsewhere. It had wandered over the mirthless miles to the Meadhall of Lord Othere. There men would be drinking and laughing and joints of meat would be dripping juice onto the silver platters, ignored by a rabble already too full to move. His mouth watered at the image.

For a while Elgiva and Godwin talked, till weariness and the warmth of the fire compelled them both to sleep.

Much later, in the dead of night, a gathering wind blew across their camp, carrying the scents of the forest.

Greyflanks awoke in an instant and lifted his head from between his paws. He sniffed the air, then sprang to his feet. There was a pleasant, familiar smell, faint but unmistakeable: the scent of wolves. It tasted like home and he knew he had to investigate, but he decided not to disturb his friends.

He padded towards them. They were still asleep, but the fire was burning low. For a moment he felt it was wrong to leave them; they were vulnerable all alone. But the call of his kin was in his blood. With a silent promise that he wouldn't be long, he quickly trotted away.

Greyflanks wasn't the only creature following a scent that night.

Crawling shadow-like over the grass, a great beast moved carefully through the darkness. Over its canines flashed a thick, black tongue, as it slavered with anticipation.

Travelling alone for many months, it had finally detected its favourite scent and the scent was that of an Elf. Its nose was as keen as any wolf's and its appetite for Elf-meat knew no limits. Some half-forgotten instinct had told it not to leave the hills, for it was vulnerable in the open, but food was scarce up there in winter. At least in the valleys and woods there were mice and hares to eat, if it could catch them, though such things were no substitute for the food it craved the most.

And tonight it was fortunate: an Elf, unprotected by others of her kind.

With a low rasp of pleasure, it approached the travellers' camp.

Dragged awake by the intervention of instinct, Elgiva opened her eyes. She listened for a moment, then struggled to her knees. Her movement disturbed her companion.

"What's up?" he wondered drowsily.

He levered himself up onto his elbows, surprised to see Elgiva on her hands and knees, listening to the night, like a terrified animal.

"Quiet!" she hissed.

She picked up some of their surplus wood and threw it onto the fire.

For a moment the crunch of grass that sounded in the dark could have been nothing more than the sighing of the wind, but it soon became apparent that something slow and ponderous was drawing towards their camp – was about to breach the firelight that strained against the night.

"What's that noise?" grated Godwin. "And where's … By Frigg!" He sprang to his feet in alarm.

Elgiva joined him, as the shape of the intruder shambled into their midst. It lumbered out of the shadows, a materialised horror, bear-like and monstrous. Halting, it scented the air, then raised its bulk on stout, hind legs. Cords of drool hung, sparkling, from its jaws.

"What on earth ..?" cried Godwin.

Elgiva swallowed hard. "A Fellkin … Faine, no!" The words tore her throat and her blood had turned to ice.

Since childhood, she had been warned of these eldritch beings. The obscene experiments of a long-dead

Wardain had given them life, Bellic had told her, but she had always suspected that such tales were inventions, designed to make naughty Elf-children behave. Now the truth stood before her, clothed in flesh and all too real to dismiss.

The large, brown eyes of the Fellkin swivelled towards Elgiva and fastened upon her with carnivorous glee.

Godwin was on his hands and knees, scrabbling for his sword.

Despite her fear and revulsion, Elgiva stood firm, refusing to flee. One thing at least she remembered from Bellic's interminable lessons: the Elven Incantation against Onfliers and Evil Magic, which he had made her learn by rote. There was power in the words, he had said. Now, silently, she thanked him.

Her own blood seemed to be roaring in her ears, but she clenched her fist around Siriol and forced out the words as steadily as she could.

"Though you be dead or living, foul or fair,
"Though you bring poison to the loam or air,
"Keep you no dwelling place but your own lair.
"Pine thou even as,
"And wilt thou even as,
"And cringe thou even as
"A bloom beside a tare.
"Though you be flesh or vapour, strong or weak,
"Though you have claws or feathers, flews or beak,
"No matter what you be or what you seek,
"Shrivel thou even as,
"And fade thou even as,
"And dwindle thou even as,
"Tarn-mist, fog and reek.
"Though you be tall or tiny, one or ten,

"Though you be in the mountain or the glen,
"Depart from here and never come again.
"Shrink thou even as,
" And sink thou even as,
"And spoil thou even as
"The moonlight on the fen."

As she spoke, the words provided a basis on which to plant her courage and her voice became stronger, as it drew authority from the verse. Godwin was now at her side, his sword dangling in his grasp, but she paid him no heed. Her awareness was centred on the creature before her, on the incantation and the tightening of her will. The camp-fire became an insubstantial flicker, the encircling night a swart blur of irrelevance.

The Fellkin appeared to be visibly affected and it listened raptly, while its claws raked the air. Frustration shuddered in its shaggy hide. The skin on its snout wrinkled and its lips curled back from its yellow teeth in a snarl of impotent rage.

Godwin fought for self-control and turned to Elgiva in supplication. The sight of her hit him like a bludgeon. His friend was no longer a small, frail figure, but appeared to have blossomed in stature and presence. She glowed invisibly with a smouldering power and her eyes were shining with vehemence. He couldn't name the force around her, but he felt it all the same. The very air was taut with it; it throbbed all around him like a tortured nerve. The night pressed down upon him like a weight he couldn't carry, but he fought to stay on his feet.

The incantation spoken, Elgiva drew a brand from the fire and flourished it at the beast. The tips of the flames flared momentarily blue and echoed the glint in her eyes.

"Be gone!" she commanded.

The creature reared for a moment in a last gesture of defiance, then it was on all fours again, watching her with its large, brown eyes; eyes surprisingly soft and sad. Their innocence seemed incongruous in such a feral face. They held a look of pleading that made Elgiva falter. Her confidence guttered and the breath caught in her throat.

But then the Fellkin turned away and sloped off into the darkness.

Godwin felt terror drain away his strength and his legs folded beneath him. He was suffocating with awe. He had seen something impossible, unreal, and, while its horror still hummed in his ears, he failed to notice the wolf calls in the distance.

Suddenly, the violated night was filled with the sounds of howling and yapping. Dark shapes whirled past the camp-fire and pelted after the Fellkin. Hugging his chest, Godwin listened to the snarls of the wolves and the screams of the Fellkin, as the pack leapt upon it and tore it apart. The noise of rending made the gorge rise in his throat. Was this really happening, or had he gone insane? He shot his companion a terrified look, desperate for reassurance.

"The gods protect us!" he cried. "Elgiva?"

She placed her small hand on his shoulder, but didn't meet his gaze. "It's all right," she said in a trembling voice. Her fingers pressed his flesh. "It's all over now, Godwin."

Then weakness overcame her. She covered her face with her hands and began to sway where she stood. Before she lost her balance completely, he roused himself and got to his feet and grabbed her by the shoulders.

Shortly, she raised her head and her hands fell to her sides and she took a shuddering breath.

She looked at Godwin and his artless gaze washed over her like solace. She tried to smile, to thank him for his friendship, but could only gape at him dumbly. Her eyes were mirrors of exhaustion.

Gently, Godwin clasped her hand: it was hot and damp and trembling. Neither of them felt able to speak, but presently their stupor was broken, as Greyflanks came trotting towards them and announced his news with joyful barks.

"He's found his family," stated Elgiva. Her voice sounded flat and abraded. "You were right when you thought they had moved. To the forest over there in fact. He brought them back to meet us – fortunately for us!"

Godwin sighed deeply with relief. He never thought he would be so glad to see a pack of wolves. "They've killed that thing, then? They'll dine well tonight."

Elgiva snatched her hand from his grasp and let out a cry of protest.

"No natural creature eats Fellkin-meat!"

Godwin's brow knotted with incomprehension. "Why not?" he demanded. "What is it? I've never seen its like!"

"Never mind that now," she said sharply. "I haven't … I can't explain." She rubbed her forehead and screwed up her eyes, as though her head were splitting. "We're being escorted to the wolf-camp now. There's food and shelter there."

Turning stiffly, she stumbled after Greyflanks. She had the air of someone fleeing unbearable truths and Godwin stood and watched her go, while he tried to summon the strength to follow. His head was spinning with hunger and fear and his recent experience had appalled him. He ached for knowledge or guidance, for anything that would help him come to terms with what had happened.

But no-one was there to help him. A monster that couldn't exist had attacked them, had been chased off by a magical spell. A pack of wolves had swarmed to their rescue. Not even Redwald could invent a tale like this.

Forcing himself into motion, he kicked out the campfire and followed Elgiva into the brooding darkness.

⋆ ⋆ ⋆

Chapter Twelve

Godwin held fast to Elgiva's hand and trusted her to lead him to the wolf-camp. Her superior night-vision was equal to the task, though they stumbled over tree roots and their progress was slow. At last they reached a clearing where a den beneath a mound of earth lay half-concealed by ferns.

"We're here," she said.

He set to work and gathered wood for a fire. Hunger, cold and darkness made Godwin's movements clumsy and the noisy greetings of the wolves only worsened his unease. Explaining to their hosts her companion's need for heat and light, Elgiva went to help him, and they had soon collected sufficient wood to build a substantial fire.

Once the fire had taken hold, Godwin could see the wolves more clearly. To his surprise Queen Whitefoot personally thanked him for playing his part in the return of her son. Elgiva conveyed the wolf's gratitude to him and he bowed politely – and self-consciously - in the animal's direction.

By now his need to talk with Elgiva was the only thought in his head, but she seemed too busy with the wolves and he didn't want to intrude. He knew that he was totally out of place and all he could do was content himself with warming his bones by the fire. At length, despite his anxiety, he resumed his sleep where he'd left it.

He awoke with a start sometime later and found himself completely alone, the fire a hot glow of ashes and the stain of dawn in the sky. He gaped at the forest around him and his heart lurched with panic at the absence of his friends. Surely they hadn't abandoned him?

He clambered to his feet, yawned and stretched. As the sun rose higher behind the old trees, the promise of a mild, clear morning filled him with renewed vigour and he set off into the forest to look for a brook or stream.

He didn't have to go very far before one crossed his path; a fresh, clean runlet of water that meandered between the trees. He drank the water in grateful gulps and splashed it onto his face. It was then that he heard wolves howling behind him. Instinctively he stiffened and his hand flew to his sword. But then he remembered. They were friends.

He shook his head at the strangeness of it all and made his way back to the camp.

Elgiva and the wolves were waiting for him; at their feet the body of a deer.

"Good morning," said Elgiva, in a strangely toneless voice. "Our friends have been hunting and they'd like to share their food with you."

With a grin, he hurled more wood on the fire, his mouth watering at the prospect of meat. He looked round at Elgiva and parted his lips to speak, but she had turned her back on him and was strolling into the forest, as though she had no use for his company.

He folded his arms and scowled at her back. It seemed that his questions would still go unanswered. With a long-suffering sigh, he directed his attention towards building up the fire.

When that was accomplished, he took out his knife and sharpened it on a stone. Then, kneeling beside the body of the deer, he started to slice it open. The preparation of meat was something that he knew from long acquaintance but, while he was carving the hapless creature into manageable chunks, he was pulled up short by a sudden realisation.

An Elf wouldn't care to witness this.

His eyes scanned the surrounding trees. He wanted to call Elgiva back, wanted to tell her that he understood, callous Wilthkin that he was. Of course, there was no sign of her and so he returned to his task, selecting a chunk of meat for himself and placing it on the edge of the fire. He sat cross-legged before it and tried to contain his impatience, his stomach grumbling painfully at the smell of the sizzling flesh.

He drew his sword and used it to turn the roasting joint, the weapon quite content, he hoped, to double as a cooking aid. The wolves milled around him, sharing the rest of the kill. One of them snatched up a severed hind leg and dragged it away to the underground den where the hungry cubs were waiting.

As Godwin sat prodding his breakfast, his mind fathoms deep in thought, he hardly noticed the number of wolves that had joined him in the glade. They sprawled or sat, chewing on bones, as if he wasn't there. It seemed that travelling with an Elf made him someone they could trust. He looked up suddenly and smiled to himself. If only Othere could see him now, dining with a pack of wolves!

⋆ ⋆ ⋆

As the day wore on, Godwin became more reconciled to being on his own. Elgiva's absence galled him, propelled him towards infuriation, but he balked at the idea of searching for her. He didn't want her to realise how forlorn he was without her, nor did he relish the prospect of getting lost in the forest.

So he sat, he dozed, he replenished the camp-fire. He strolled around the glade and watched his furry hosts. Despite a gnawing impatience, he told himself that the Elf would return, that he wasn't abandoned in the middle of nowhere.

An afternoon hunt was a welcome distraction. He watched the young wolves race off together and marvelled at their stamina. Later he laughed at the antics of the cubs as they were led from their den to romp in the sunshine. Some of them came to stare at the stranger, their heads on one side and their wet noses quivering. Then a bird swooping low overhead sent them tumbling off in mad pursuit.

Yes, he decided, they were fine, noble creatures; dutiful at home, merciless with prey. Not much different from Saxons. Or was it the other way round?

Well, they were still only wolves and he couldn't talk to them. As beings in their own right they had little to hold his interest and the fact that Elgiva could converse with them made her even more alien in his eyes. He wondered if he would ever come to terms with the strangeness of his friend or with any of the things that had happened to him.

Never mind. It was good to relax and watch the clouds drift; inhale the scent of pines and the perfume of the grass; good to hear the songs of the birds over the tranquil forest. Nothing to do. And no-one to tell him to stop doing it.

The day seemed like an endless calm, but, at length, the sky was raddled by the sun as it fell towards the west.

It seemed to Godwin that never before had he seen such a beautiful sunset.

Or perhaps it was just that he had never looked.

⋆ ⋆ ⋆

As evening fell upon the wolves' encampment, it carried with it a cloying dampness. Mist coiled among the trees and the black trunks rose from its fleshless grip like the bare bones of a mirage.

Godwin congratulated himself on his attention to the fire; it was all that preserved him from the chill, black night. Even the wolves had deserted him. Some had gone to their underground dens, while many patrolled the forest. Occasionally an eerie howl fractured the evening calm.

Though Godwin missed the company of the wolves, part of him had been relieved, when at last they had stalked away. Pretending to be perfectly at ease in the presence of so many sets of sharp teeth had been something of a strain.

When Elgiva suddenly appeared from the trees, tendrils of mist fleeing from her tread, Godwin was startled and visibly jumped, convinced that she must be a ghost. He seemed to have been without her for so long that part of him had forgotten she existed.

Recovering quickly from the suddenness of her arrival, he struggled to his feet, determined to have his questions answered, or die in the attempt. But when he saw her hag-ridden features, there was only one he could ask.

"Elgiva, are you all right?"

With a weary nod she sat down beside him and held out her hands to the fire. He seated himself next to her and waited for her to speak.

"I'm sorry I was away so long. I lost all track of time," she said. "Did you mind? The wolves don't bother you, do they?"

He shook his head. "Don't fret about me. Where have you been, Elgiva?"

"Oh," she shrugged. "Just out there. Thinking."

"A lot to think about, I expect." He rested his forearms across his knees. "Do I have your attention now?"

She turned her head, one eyebrow arched questioningly. "Yes, of course," she said.

He shifted his position so that he could look at her more comfortably. "Would you care to tell me what a Fellkin is? I've never seen anything so hideous!"

"Of course you haven't," she said with a frown, as though the idea were foolish. "They keep their distance from your kind. You hold no interest for the Fellkin. They only have one aim in life – if life it can be called." She paused and he saw her shudder. "To slaughter Elves and eat them." His eyes widened in horror and he looked so aghast that she wanted to smile, but instead she cursed her perverse sense of humour.

"Well? Go on!"

"Are you sure you want to know?"

"By Frigg, that's why I asked!"

"Very well." She drew herself closer and folded her hands in her lap. "Fellkin aren't animals. And yet, they are."

"Riddles are all very well in the Meadhall…"

"If you think I'd waste my time on riddles, you're very much mistaken!" she snapped.

He sighed. "I'm sorry. Please carry on."

"Thank you. As I was saying, they're not true animals. Bellic calls them,"- she paused thoughtfully for a moment –"corrupted hybrids. Yes, well, an evil Wardain called Smirill created them, many generations ago. Royal Elves do sometimes go bad ways and he went further than most. He dabbled in things Faine warned us against … have I told you about Faine First-Father?" Godwin looked confused. "Oh, well, I dare say I'll get round to it. Now, Smirill lived in Misterell. It's a strange place shunned by other Elves, a place that breeds legends … but, that aside, it was a very, very long time ago that Smirill spawned these creatures by interbreeding natural beasts in the presence of dark magic. The animals he chose were freaks and all essentially flawed and in due course his vile experiments left us with the Fellkin. Smirill was mad but believed himself a creator, a genius. He thought he had the right as a Wardain to pervert the natural order of things, but he became so corrupted by the forces he thought to control that, one day, according to legend, he exploded."

Godwin couldn't help himself and burst out laughing. Elgiva threw him a hurt and angry look.

"I'm finding this impossible to believe," he said. "Well, the bits I understand, that is."

"Don't blame me!" retorted Elgiva, thrusting her pert nose in the air. "It was you who wanted to hear it!" She turned her back on him indignantly. "As I was saying, Smirill exploded because the pressure of the evil within him was too great for his flesh to contain. The forces he thought to master merely rebounded upon him. So, he was no more, but the evil lived on in the things that he created. They are few in number, I'm glad to say. They're sterile, too, and slow and elusive, but they don't die like natural beasts. A strange power sustains them. Some part of the dark might that Smirill invoked is still at work, defying mortality."

Godwin shivered. "At least, they can be killed, like other animals."

"By a pack of wolves certainly," she agreed, "but many an Elf, caught alone by a Fellkin, hasn't had the good fortune to have a pack of wolves to hand. We, indeed, were lucky." She paused and shook her head. "You know, for a moment I doubted my eyes, Godwin. I was as shocked as you were. I've never seen a Fellkin before, though I've heard all the tales. I suppose I didn't really believe them. It's hard to believe in something you've never seen and the Fellkin rarely come close to our forests. They prefer to pick off lone travellers and an ordinary Elf, lacking magic, is helpless."

"But," he said carefully, "you weren't helpless."

"Bellic taught me the incantation. He made me learn it by rote from something he called The Book of Weirds, and he made certain I had it by heart. He said there was power in the rhyme, enough to hold a Fellkin at bay, so an Elf can escape. Fellkin are slow, clumsy things, easy to outrun."

Godwin wasn't convinced. "So, why didn't you run?"

She lowered her eyes evasively. "Well … I wanted to."

"You didn't stay on my account?"

"No, Godwin, you were always safe. You're not a Fellkin's idea of good eating."

"Is that a compliment or not?" he asked, trying to lighten her mood.

"It's a very good thing for you and your kind!"

She fell silent, reluctant to continue, but Godwin's curiosity had yet to be satisfied.

"Tell me, then, Elgiva, if these things were created by some mad, old Elf, why do they want to eat Elves?"

She thought for a moment and toyed with her hair. "Revenge perhaps? Who knows? You know, I feel sad, when I think of them, Godwin. After all, it's not their fault. They are abominations of Nature, the work of madness. Surely they have no peace?"

She looked away and stared at the fire. The panic caused by the Fellkin's attack had now faded away and all she could see was its hideous face with those disturbingly beautiful eyes. There was a wrongness about it that appalled her to the marrow of her bones and she wished that there was something she could do to answer the plea in the Fellkin's gaze.

"No, perhaps not," agreed Godwin thoughtfully.

"This is what happens when we get above ourselves and think we can defy the laws of Nature, Godwin. Bellic told me that the Wardain are well-schooled in such matters and know that there's a natural limit they mustn't go beyond." She hesitated and a frown creased her brow. "Schooled or not, I wouldn't want the responsibility of such power. I mean, it must be a temptation to see how far you can go … I dare say."

She changed her position again, sat hugging her knees with her back turned towards him, as though she were closing the door on his questions, but Godwin hadn't finished.

"You still haven't answered my question," he said. She looked at him sternly, unsure of his meaning. "Why didn't you run?"

"There was no need," she replied with a shrug. "The incantation sufficed."

"From whence came your courage?"

She frowned at him, puzzled. "The words gave me courage and I … I had Siriol."

"Words! Amulets!" His tone made her start, but then he softened it. "Elgiva, they had nothing to do with it."

"What do you mean?" she countered. "It's the only explanation. You didn't run either. So what? Let's be honest, shall we? We were both too scared to move."

His frank, blue eyes watched her steadily. "Yes, let's be honest, Elgiva. It was *YOU*, wasn't it?"

She glared at him as though he had hit her. His suspicion would have seemed totally mad, had it not been an echo of her own and she couldn't find words to refute it. Something was happening that made no sense. Life in Elindell had left her ill-equipped to deal with her experiences since being banished, but these same experiences all seemed to lead to the same crazy conclusion. There were things she needed to understand, but they defied comprehension. Why had she felt so weak and dizzy after using the incantation, as though some part of her own self had been actively involved? From whence came that searing inner heat, and the strength that had protected her when she was trying to free herself from Beortnoth's marauder back at the settlement? And again, when attacked outside Joskin's cave? Was it Siriol? If so, why had she felt nothing when the amulet altered her appearance – and changed it back again?

At that time, of course, she hadn't been in a state of terror. Were the nausea and giddiness merely the after-effects of her own cowardice? Was she really so craven?

Or was the magic of amulets and incantations too much for the frail flesh of a nar-Wardain?

She scowled darkly at the fire. One thing she did know for certain: Siriol couldn't be trusted.

Her rigid posture told Godwin not to question her further, but in truth he didn't know how to. He knew nothing of Elves or incantations and even less about Fellkin. But one thing he did know; when Elgiva had spoken the potent rhyme, the force he had felt came from her, not the words. How he knew this was yet another mystery. He had hoped his friend would explain it, but now was not the time. Her confusion seemed worse than his.

"I wish Bellic had told me about magic … about this wretched amulet," she said. The anguish in her voice made him look at her. "It frightens me!" She took the amulet from around her neck and clenched it in her fist and Godwin saw that there were tears in her eyes. Then a frown of determination seamed her brow. "I can't use this again! I won't!"

She drew back her arm, but before she could hurl Siriol at the fire, Godwin seized her wrist.

"No!" he exclaimed forcefully. "By Frigg! There may be purpose in it yet. Wasn't it the gift of a friend?"

"I used to think so … yes," she sobbed.

"So is there any wrong in it?"

For several long moments, her dark eyes opposed him, then suddenly she relaxed and he loosened his grip on her arm.

At length she said tentatively, "I just don't know … what's happening. Godwin … I feel … different."

With that, she stumbled to her feet and dashed towards the forest. He didn't know how to call her back, nor even if he should. He was left, once more, with only his thoughts for company and the doubts and fears he harboured began drifting to the surface of his mind.

Now that Greyflanks was back with his family, this was the end of the adventure and perhaps it was time for Godwin to go back to his. He had seen the unknown and he wasn't disappointed, and being at the wolf camp was an interesting experience, but it wasn't the place for a human. Moreover, this Fellkin businesss frightened him. It was all outside his ken, weird and unfamiliar. And now his friend had grown distant and strange and he didn't like it at all.

But hadn't he sworn to protect her? And what of the threat from that unknown Wardain?

Wardain. Even in his own thoughts the word sounded strange.

What should he do? In this world that was so different from everything he knew, he felt lost and alone. There was magic in it certainly, and though he hadn't believed in it before, it was real enough now to both fascinate and worry him. It intrigued him, of course, but he was defenceless in the face of it and whatever threat it posed. If it couldn't be explained, and if it couldn't be destroyed by the sword, it challenged the subtle balance of his mind, distorting his conceptions of reality. He didn't think he was equal to such a challenge.

He drew out his sword and studied it. There was something reassuring about a sword, even if one lacked the skill to use it. It was real, hard, irrefutable. With a sword in his hand – this sword – he felt inexplicably safe. The touch of cold metal stilled the jangling of his nerves and soothed his apprehension.

But what use was it here?

No, he thought, this isn't my world. None of this has anything to do with me.

But there was still his vow to be honoured and ahead of him on the open road lay the freedom denied him for so many years.

Bitterly he acknowledged his inability to make decisions. Other people had always made them for him. How he wished he could be in two places at once!

He was still agonising over the future and his role in it, when Elgiva returned in the early hours of the following day with roots and herbs for them to eat. He was more than glad to see her, having finally resolved to confront her with the fact that he wanted to go back home. He knew he was taking the coward's way out and he tried to think of the best way of announcing his decision without sounding selfish.

But once again, when he looked at her face, he found himself lost for words. She had a peculiar glint in her eyes, a glint he had seen there before. It was disconcerting and elvish – and also strangely appealing- so he dumbly accepted the food she offered and waited for her to speak first.

But the chance for discussion never arose, for there was a sudden commotion beyond the trees. Howling and yapping rang through the forest as the pack swarmed into the glade. Their tails were thrashing with excitement and they chased each other about.

Elgiva smiled at the celebration. "Blacktail has returned," she said.

At that moment an elderly wolf trotted proudly into their midst, followed by a rabble of delighted youngsters. He pranced towards Elgiva, nuzzling his kin aside, and seated himself before her. His snout was raked by old scars and his left eyelid sank into an empty socket.

Seeing the animal's battle-scars, Godwin found himself reminded of Cerdic.

Elgiva inclined her head towards Blacktail and he greeted her with throaty growling.

"What's he saying?" Godwin asked.

"If I am Elgiva of Elindell, then he has a message for me!" she exclaimed, her eyebrows lifted in surprise.

"I have travelled far," began Blacktail, "and, as is my wont, I spent a day with a lady who befriends all woodland folk. She was glad I had called, for a stag had come to see her some weeks before with a message from an Elf."

"An Elf?" said Elgiva. "Who?"

"This she did not say, but she said he was a great Elf and that he was in peril, foiled by evil magic. His plans had been ruined and he spoke of you and said you would need help. The lady was to find you and give you food and clothing and whatever else you needed and tell you many things he wanted you to know. He had planned to search for you himself, but now that is not possible – though, of course, for short forays he can venture out in spirit."

"In spirit?" repeated Elgiva.

"This she said, but how shall I, a mere Wolf, explain the doings of great Elves? Well, I am strictly adjured to guide you to this lady and to suffer no delay."

"She talks to animals? Is she an Elf?"

"She is," replied Blacktail. "And she is not."

Elgiva frowned at this. "Can I trust her?"

"Only as much as you can trust the sun to rise each day. She would not entertain evil or the company of evil-doers. Her house is under Elf-ward."

"Elf-ward?"

"We must talk no more," said Blacktail impatiently. "Prepare to leave, Elgiva. Gather your baggage and say your farewells. I go to tell the Queen where I am bound. Life is one long journey, my friends." So saying, Blacktail hurried away, while Elgiva told Godwin what he had said.

"If this woman can be trusted, as Blacktail maintains, then perhaps I've found shelter at last," she said cheerfully. "I dare say the great Elf he spoke of is Bellic. There's no-one else who would bother to help me." She smiled. "I hoped I wasn't forgotten."

"But Blacktail said that your friend was in trouble. How can he help you?" protested Godwin. "Perhaps he needs you to help him!"

Elgiva's smile vanished and she narrowed her eyes, anxiety etched on her face. To Godwin she looked like a child chased by ghouls with nowhere left to run. His protective instincts rose to the fore and his cowardice cringed in their shadow. She was his vulnerable friend again and needed his support and all thoughts of parting would have to be shelved.

"Perhaps Bellic intends this woman to shelter you, but there's definitely something wrong," he said. "If he's as powerful as you say, then why is he in trouble? Instead of finding a place of safety, you could be walking into danger. Might the Elf you met outside Joskin's cave …"

"No!" she cried. "Don't speak of it. I've no idea what's going on, but if it *IS* Bellic who summons me, then I have no choice. And, if I can help him, I will. At least I must find out what's wrong."

"We must both find out."

She stared at him with fear-widened eyes and he thought that she was going to object, but she said nothing, and he suspected that facing danger all alone was something she couldn't bear, that secretly she desired his company but was far too proud to admit it. Her fear reassured him. It made him feel wanted and useful. When she was distant and strange, he was lost, but at this moment she was in need and this need made him strong. It was something that he understood and could fight. Weakness and fear were well within the scope of his mundane powers.

He took her hand and squeezed it. "We'll find out what's going on," he told her. "If Bellic's in trouble, then perhaps his purpose in sending this message is to make sure that you, at least, are safe. Maybe he can get himself out of the mess he's in and, when he does, he'll know where to find you. No point in looking on the black side just yet."

Elgiva nodded despondently. Godwin began to collect their belongings.

"Blacktail is back," he said, looking up. "He seems eager to get going." He shouldered the sack and held out his hand and Elgiva took it glumly. "Come on," he said, "let's make our farewells."

⋆ ⋆ ⋆

For the rest of that day and the next, they followed the old wolf through woods and fields with no idea where they were going, except that they knew they were heading north. The awakening earth waxed green about them and buds swelled on the trees, yet still the hem of Winter's gown trailed across the land and, unaccountably, on the second day it snowed. It seemed like an act of malice against the tender shoots and ripening buds. The dark sky glowered above them and the freshly fallen snow sparkled in the rays of feeble sunlight, coldly mimicking heat with its crystalline gleams.

That night, cold and hungry, they sat huddled around their fire. They spoke little, slept badly, and were awake at dawn eager to continue, if for no other reason than to keep themselves warm.

It snowed again during the morning, leaving the air fresh and clean, but so sharp that it burned their lungs and drew water from their eyes. As they plodded on wearily through a snow-draped wood, a cheery voice greeted them, jolted them out of their gloomy thoughts.

On a branch a few yards above them sat a young male blackbird, his dark eyes twinkling.

"Hail, travellers, and well met!" he cried. "Hail from the leader of the dawn chorus! I am Deryn yclept. If you are Elgiva of Elindell, I am come to bid you welcome in the name of my mistress!"

"Hail, Deryn!" called Elgiva brightly. "I am who you say and honoured to be so greeted by the fairest songster of the woods."

The clear, pure notes of the blackbird's voice trilled like laughter from his throat and he swooped low over their heads, alighting on a tree stump beside them. "Across these fields before you and over that rise yonder, you will come to a plain that slopes down to a wood," he said. "There dwells my mistress in her little house. Before dusk you will reach it. Tarry not. Supper awaits. I must go and tell her you are come."

With that the blackbird twitched his tail and soared into the air.

"Deryn, wait!" Elgiva cried.

"I go!" whooped the bird. "I fly! Follow me!"

And he was gone, winging his way erratically over the fields before them, his dark body swooping and climbing with ease.

Blacktail studied his companions from out of his one good eye and saw them hesitate. Nuzzling Elgiva's hand with his dry, scarred nose, he sought to reassure her.

"The bird speaks truly," he said. "Follow his directions and you will not go astray. As for me, I must go home. You have no further need of my guidance." He turned and picked his way through the snow. "Farewell my friends," he called over his shoulder. "I hope we shall meet again."

* * *

Chapter Thirteen

Alone in a wilderness of white, the small house squatted darkly, its back to the frozen woods. The weather-warped walls bulged slightly at their base, then tapered up towards the coarse, brown thatch with its covering of snow. A fillet of grey smoke plumed upwards from the roof.

Despite its dismal aspect, the dwelling was cosy within, and its occupant sat by a cheerful fire, mending her tattered, grey shawl. A pot of gruel simmered on the fire and the smaze from the cooking curled up towards the ceiling where dried herbs hung in bunches from the rafters.

The old woman raised her head and listened. Upon the roof was her sentinel, Deryn, and she heard him call her name. Her visitor was arriving at last! Smiling, she looked at the leather-bound book that lay on the floor beside her. Now finally Elgiva would know the truth and the task of the telling was hers. The stars were in a favourable aspect and the scattered runes were agreeable. Everything was happening as it should.

She put the shawl aside, got stiffly to her feet. Patting her long, grey hair into neatness, she shuffled towards the door. She lifted the latch and the doorway grinned at the flat, white plain ahead. She squinted across the brilliant landscape. The sky had a brownish tint; dusk would soon be falling.

Then she saw them; two figures in the distance, wading through the snow. One was taller than the other and – judging by its clumsy gait – this person was a

Wilthkin. Well, who was she to criticise? She chuckled to herself. Elgiva had chosen an unusual companion. Then they drew nearer and the old woman saw that the man was a Briton, and she smiled with understanding.

She called to them and saw them stop and peer towards the sound. She called again and waved her arm. Had they overlooked her little den, tiny in its nest of ancient trees, like an old addled egg abandoned by a long-forgotten spring?

The figures pushed on through the drifts of snow and she hobbled out to meet them. As Elgiva approached, she bustled forwards and threw her arms about her.

"My dear, how good it is to see you after all these years!" she exclaimed, and she spoke in the Celtic tongue. "And how you've grown … and so pretty, too!"

Startled, Elgiva pulled away brusquely. "We'd rather you spoke Saxon," she said warily, "if you can."

The old woman raised her eyebrows at this, but then she shrugged and nodded. She asked for no explanation, but, regretting her earlier curtness of manner, Elgiva offered one. "My friend was brought up by Saxons."

"My dear, I will speak any language you wish, for you are as dear to me as if you were my very own child."

"I've never met you before in my life!" retorted Elgiva indignantly.

The old woman laughed. "Well, how could you remember, indeed?" She looked them up and down. Their clothes were torn and filthy, their faces pinched with hunger. In the wounds of their eyes she saw their shared sense of misery and bewilderment.

"By the stars!" she exclaimed with maternal concern, "a fine pair of scarecrows you look, poor chits! Yet, never fear, there's room inside my little house for all of us and a nice, warm fire and a good, spiced caudle to warm the blood. There's water to wash and clean clothes, too. Come inside, my dears, please, and let us thaw you out!"

Her arm gestured towards the door, but the travellers waited hesitantly and looked at each other for guidance. "Come," she beckoned, with a good-natured smile, while tugging at their sleeves.

They both regarded her blankly.

"Who *ARE* you?" asked Elgiva, determined to resist the enthusiasm of the welcome.

"Why, I'm Kendra," said the woman simply. "Has Bellic never mentioned me?" Elgiva shook her head. "By the stars, he's not ashamed of me, I hope!" Kendra laughed and hugged herself, but the jest meant nothing to them.

Elgiva gave her a puzzled look. "You clearly know who I am," she said. "This is my friend, Godwin."

"A fine-looking lad. A Briton, in sooth! They have such wonderful eyes. No-one but a Briton could have a look like that." Kendra chuckled at Godwin's embarrassment. "Forgive me, my dears. No doubt you're wondering what kind of creature I am?" She glanced at each of them quickly, measuring their response. Her large, dark eyes had an honest gleam, but there was mischief in their depths. "My parentage perhaps makes me somewhat strange in manner. My mother was a Briton, but my father, on the other hand…" She chuckled to herself again. "My father was an Elf." She laughed at their astonishment and took them both by the arm. "Ah, did you think such unions impossible? Did you not know that they of the Elven and Celtic races are drawn together by the similarity of their natures? Well, no matter. Let's get inside. The air's as chill as death."

Reluctantly, they obeyed her, wanting to trust this unusual creature who wore her good-humour like a well-loved cloak, yet uncertain of her intentions. At the threshold she turned and held up her hand.

"Young man, I think you to be an honest wight, but be aware if you have evil in your heart, for my home is under Elf-ward and none who seeks to do me harm may cross this threshold scatheless."

Godwin gaped at this and looked to Elgiva for guidance, but she was unable to give any and all she could do was shrug.

He drew a deep breath, closed his eyes and stepped inside the house.

Nothing happened, except for a strange sensation, as though he had walked through a membrane of gossamer, but almost immediately he became aware of the warmth of the fire and the smell of the gruel. His stomach also noticed and began to growl appreciatively.

Kendra bustled after him and beckoned to Elgiva. When her guests were both inside the house, she closed the door and moved towards the hearth. She lowered herself upon a stool and indicated that they should take the other two beside her. Elgiva and Godwin glanced at each other before they took their seats, then Elgiva sat down beside Kendra, while Godwin took the stool nearest to the door, as though he were readying himself for escape.

"Did you feel nothing?" asked Kendra, at length, reaching over to stir the gruel. Unsure of her meaning, Godwin shook his head. "Ah, that is odd. You can't feel the Earth-magic? You sensed it, Elgiva, when you stepped through the door? A shivering sensation, at least? I'm surprised that your friend is so … unattuned. The

Britons well know the feeling of magic. They have an affinity with the Earth, you see."

"As I said," Elgiva reminded her tetchily, "Godwin was brought up by Saxons."

"I confess I know nothing of Saxons," said Kendra, "but perhaps they think more of war and the getting of gold than they do of mystical matters."

"That's not true," put in Godwin, and then he faltered, not knowing how to continue or why he felt so defensive.

Kendra smiled. "No matter," she said. She reached across and patted his arm and the wrinkles at the corners of her eyes tightened with good humour. Then she got to her feet and hobbled towards a set of slanting shelves. "You both sound hoarse, my dears. This weather's bad for throats. But I've some horehound will cure that. We can't have you getting coughs, when there's a remedy to hand. Ah, here it is." She picked up an earthenware jar. "Now, my dears, I'll make a potion anon, but first some fuel for your bellies."

Setting the jar upon a table, she gathered up two wooden bowls and carried them back to the fire. "I like to think of my den as a sanctuary. I never turn away any creature that needs a bit of help. That's why we're here, to help each other, and by the looks of you two poor waifs you arrived here just in time. You've met young Deryn, of course. He was blown in by a storm. A sorry sight he was. A small, brown thing, not even had his first moult. Well, I sheltered him and fed him up and he seemed to like this place so much he hasn't left it since! I keep telling him he should find a mate, but no doubt he'll get round to it."

While she ladled gruel into the bowls, her amiable chatter put her guests at ease. Then she made her way back to the table, where she cut up a round loaf of coarse, brown bread. She offered thick slices to each of her guests, then sat by the fire with a grimace.

"By the stars, my back is a bane and a burden! Too well I know the penalties of having Wilthkin blood. In weather like this 'tis best I bide indoors to fend off the rheumatics, and it's cold for the time of year, is it not? Well, no matter. No use complaining. I'll live a bit longer yet, Faine willing, and for a woman who's had too hard a life, I don't look bad for 74." She chuckled at their astonished faces. "Eat, eat, my dears! You look half-starved! My caudle will melt the ice in your bellies and give you the strength of ten!"

Godwin sniffed warily at the contents of the bowl, hoping she wouldn't notice, but her eyes missed nothing and her peals of laughter filled the cosy room. It was so infectious that Elgiva joined in.

"Trust me, lad," chuckled Kendra, "I'll not poison thee, for you're Elgiva's friend and there's too little good in this world. I'd poison bad folk, I suppose, and think no more about it, but they poison themselves as it is, I think, and don't need my assistance."

Godwin flushed with embarrassment and started to eat the gruel.

For a while Kendra sat nibbling on some bread and staring into the fire, but, at length, the silence galled her. The chance to converse with her fellow creatures didn't often arise. It would be a shame to waste it.

"That's a fine sword you have there, Godwin," she said. "Do you think I could take a look?"

Godwin was using a chunk of bread to mop up the last of his gruel. "What?" he asked, looking up. "Oh, yes. I suppose you can."

He drew the weapon from his belt and handed it to her without a second thought. Any ideas of mistrust he had felt had been overcome by the cosy fire and the satisfying meal. She studied the blade with interest and followed the patterns on the hilt with her fingers.

"From whence does it come?" she asked. "Who made it?"

Busy with chewing, he merely shrugged.

"'Tis a fine thing indeed," she said, nodding sagely. "But, indeed, by the stars, this is odd! Know you the meaning of these patterns here?"

Godwin swallowed. "Er … no," he said.

She nodded to herself. "Most odd."

By now Elgiva had also stopped eating and she and Godwin stared at Kendra, perplexed by the reverential way in which she handled the sword.

"A rare gift," she murmured. "Has it always been yours?"

"Why … yes. I've had it since I was a child."

"I see."

"Is there … is there something wrong?" he asked worriedly.

Kendra's eyes darted towards him, as though he had startled her. "Wrong? Ah, no! No wrong in this." She looked at her guests and read the anxious questions in their eyes and smiled dismissively to ward them off. "No matter, my dears, I should say no more." She returned the sword to its owner and slowly got to her feet. "Help yourselves to more bread and gruel. I must feed the goats. It seems I'm a little late today, but I think they'll understand."

Kendra shuffled towards the door where a mantle hung from a peg in the wall. She draped it round her shoulders, smiled and made to leave. But then she hesitated and turned to face them. "One thing, my dears, I must ask you. Are you travelling on together?"

For a moment they were taken aback by this unexpected question and the strangeness of the old woman's tone. Then Elgiva ventured an answer.

"Godwin was planning to see me settled somewhere before returning to his home. From the message you sent with Blacktail, I had hoped that you …"

"Though you are welcome to stay here, that's something you cannot do," said Kendra. "And if you were to part from your friend, I think that would be unwise. I feel that, somehow, your destinies are linked."

Elgiva and Godwin gaped at her, but before they could question her cryptic remarks, the door had closed behind her.

* * *

It wasn't long before Kendra returned, her arms laden with firewood. The night now crept close round the little house and a sly wind whispered under the eaves. Inside, however, the cheery fire threw soft, blurred shadows upon the walls and filled the room with a smoky warmth.

Kendra put some wood on the fire and sat on the stool by Elgiva. On the hearth lay a long, iron poker, its tip blackened by years of use. Kendra leaned forwards and picked it up and began to poke at the fire. Her eyes had a distant, dreamy look and she seemed quite content with the silence, but Elgiva had questions she needed to ask.

"Kendra," she ventured, "are you going to tell me why I'm here? Blacktail said you had things to tell me."

Kendra replaced the fire-iron, then reached across to her left. Lifting the leather-bound book from the floor, she placed it on her lap. As she turned to face Elgiva, a gleam of anticipation lit up her kind, old eyes.

"Yes, my dear, you have been very patient, but now it is time, I think. Do you know what this is?"

Mystified, Elgiva shrugged her shoulders. "Well, a book, I suppose."

Kendra laughed. "A book, indeed! But a most important book. Elgiva, 'Tis the Ninth Book of the Chronicles of the Eldrakin."

Elgiva frowned dismissively. "There are only eight," she said. Kendra gave her an arch look and her certainty fell apart. "Aren't there?"

"So it was believed for many generations, my dear. Ah, me, I have so many matters to relate. Where to begin? Forgive me, if my talk grows wearisome and confusing. 'Tis a complicated story."

Kendra looked at them both in turn, then she cleared her throat importantly and opened the book on her knee.

"You know, Elgiva, that the chronicler, Silvanuil, left eight manuscripts in which he had written the history and lore of Faine and the Eldrakin. Bellic taught you all this, I think, when you were just a child. But some time ago another manuscript came to light and this is it, the Ninth Book, and this is the Book of Prediction. And can you guess who found it?"

Elgiva looked at her askance. "Lord Bellic, I suppose?"

"The very same! His wanderings have resulted in this gift – though he was not the very first to find it. Well, before I tell you my story, let me show you this." She turned several pages and indicated that Elgiva should look at the words.

Raised by a race unfamiliar with writing, the book held no interest for Godwin. All he could do was watch Elgiva and let her reactions guide him.

"This is a copy," said Kendra, "one of only two that exist. The original is in Misterell."

"Lord Bellic went to Misterell?" Elgiva was astonished.

"Yes, and he has the other copy. The original has decayed and parts are missing, but see you this?" She pointed at a passage in the book. "Read."

Elgiva leaned forwards and began to recite;

"The Stone's Discoverer,

"Orphan and slave,

"Shall unlock the door..."

She stopped and frowned at Kendra. "What does it mean? What stone?"

"One thing at a time, my dear. As I said, the original was decayed and the rest of the verse has been lost, but it says in the passage before this that the Stone will be found in the thirty-ninth generation of Elindell – you see, it mentions Elindell specifically – and you, my dear, are the beginning of that generation. You look baffled, but it will all become clear. The contents of this book of prediction were given to Silvanuil by Zallic, prophet of Faine First-Father. He spoke what he foresaw and this Stone is the Lorestone, left by Lord Faine to redeem his people at a time of future peril. It was his parting gift to Elvendom. And perhaps the time of peril is upon us – but more of that anon."

"Many years ago, Bellic chanced to find the legendary land of Misterell and he met and befriended the king,

Eldruin. They shared a common interest in histories and lore and, some years later, on a subsequent visit, Eldruin told Bellic of a remarkable discovery.

"You know that Misterell was the home of Lord Faine, the very first kingdom of the Eldrakin and the seat of the Founder's power. A Royal Hall has stood on the same site there for as long as anyone remembers, but the present building was threatened by subsidence. The foundations needed attention. It was during repairs that an iron-bound box was unearthed and within it were the remnants of the Book of Prediction. Eldruin had a copy made, which he gave to Bellic in the name of friendship. Though like all Misterellians he preferred isolation from the rest of the Eldrakin – they bethink themselves rather special, I ween – he was a good Elf, I am told, and not averse to sharing knowledge for the sake of the common weal. I do not think it meant a great deal to him, but Bellic read the manuscript and in it he saw many things of importance."

"As I said, it is a book of predictions made in the time of Faine, and afterwards. It seems that many good and evil things lie in store for the Eldrakin, but such is life, a constant battle between these two forces. Well, there are gaps in the text and we must interpret what is left as well as we are able. In the deciphering of this book, I trust Bellic, as I trust him in all things, and this Lorestone is, he believes, to be found by you, Elgiva. This legacy is to be used now, by you, to save Elvendom from the evil that threatens it."

Elgiva made to protest, but Kendra reached out and patted her arm. "It will all become clear, Elgiva." She shifted her position on the stool, placed the book on the floor beside her and folded her hands in her lap.

"The Lorestone is a thing of awesome and unknown power," she went on, "and Bellic is convinced that it is hidden in Misterell. But as to where exactly and how it may be found is unclear. In the Ninth Book there is mention of the forest's heart and something about passing through water to a door that is not a door." She pondered for a moment. "Yes, something along those lines. It is in the passage before the one you read, Elgiva, and there are many omissions. Bellic, no doubt, is still working on it." She studied the faces of her guests. They appeared to be totally baffled. "Ah, my dears, this tale surpasses you somewhat. Let us drink a little ale together and I shall tell you of Elgiva's past. It may prove of greater interest." She rose to her feet and shuffled into a corner of the room, where she seemed to merge with the shadows.

"My past!" exclaimed Elgiva. "Do you know who my parents were?"

"I do, in sooth," said Kendra, returning to the fire. In one hand she held a tall clay jug that she set upon her stool; in the other, a long, thin spill that she used to take flame from the fire. Returning to the table, she lit a tallow candle. "I must have more light," she muttered, as though addressing herself. "My eyes are not what they were."

Presently, she was back with her guests, and in her arms were three silver goblets. Elgiva toyed with a strand of her hair, trying to control her impatience, as Kendra gave them a goblet apiece and filled them both with ale from the jug. She smiled at their reaction to the richness of the drinking vessels.

"A gift," she said. "From … a friend of mine." Her lips curled with some secret amusement. She sat herself down upon the stool and took a long draught of the dark ale, then she smacked her lips with pleasure. "Ah, this bog myrtle was gathered at just the right time." She looked at them both and chuckled. "You look so glum, my dears. Drink up! This is the finest Gale Beer you ever will have tasted. It will do you good."

Elgiva held the old woman's eyes and in her own was a look of frustration. Kendra leaned forwards and patted her hand.

"Yes, my dear, and now for my tale. I fear I have postponed the telling. Perhaps I know it will shock you, and it will sadden you, too. You want to hear it … and you don't."

Elgiva turned her face away, determined to hide her feelings.

"Your forebears, Elgiva, are the Wardain of Elindell and, I suspect, you will prove to be the finest fruit produced by that particular family tree."

Despite her decision to remain aloof, Elgiva jumped to her feet in disbelief. The goblet fell from her fingers and clattered across the floor. "Kendra … what are you saying?"

"Ah, such a waste," said Kendra, shaking her head at the pool of ale that was slowly seeping into the floor. "My fault, I think. I knew this would alarm you. Sit down, Elgiva. Please."

Elgiva hesitated and looked at Godwin. He was staring at her in speechless amazement. Then she ran her fingers through her hair and her voice was raw with emotion. "Forgive me," she said, reseating herself.

"No need, my dear," soothed Kendra. "Forgive *ME*, if you can. I am making this harder than it should be. I have no gift for tact. Mine is a meandering mind and when I try to be direct, I do not do it well."

"Kendra, please!"

The old woman held up her hand in a gesture that asked for patience. "I tell you that you are a Wardain, child, and the king who sits on Elindell's throne is a fool, a knave, a usurper … and he is also your cousin."

"Thallinore, my cousin? He can't be! I don't believe any of this!"

"I … I do," broke in Godwin.

They looked at him, as if they had forgotten that he had the power of speech.

"Well, I do." He lowered his eyes. "I know Elgiva's a Wardain. I know she has power. I've … felt it."

Kendra nodded vigorously and smiled with satisfaction. "Then you are not totally blind to the Earth's magic, Godwin? I am glad. So, Elgiva, you have used your birthright already?"

"No!" Elgiva protested. "I haven't! It was Siriol." She drew out the amulet and showed it to Kendra, whose eyebrows lifted a little. "Bellic gave me this … to protect me."

Kendra touched the amulet thoughtfully, and then she shook her head. "I think not, my dear. You are mistaken. There is no power in this."

Elgiva scowled at her, refusing to believe it, but Kendra's eyes were adamant. Glaring at Siriol, as though it had betrayed her, Elgiva thrust it back inside her robe.

"I feel that the amulet has a link with Bellic, if that is some consolation," said Kendra.

Elgiva didn't respond to this. She turned away and frowned at the fire and for a time the three of them sat in a gloomy silence. Godwin drained the last of his ale, desperate for intoxication. Somehow he felt that, if he were drunk, this whole situation might seem more acceptable.

Kendra sighed deeply. It saddened her to be the cause of Elgiva's loss of trust, but she had a duty to perform. "This is my tale," she said, at length. "Try not to interrupt. I have digressed more then enough already. Pour some more ale and listen well." She set her own goblet on the floor and glanced at them both in turn, making sure that she had their attention.

"Now," she began, "I left Astorill with your great-uncle Bellic twenty years ago – yes, your great- uncle, Elgiva. Strange to hear him called that, I am sure. We journeyed to Elindell, he as escort for his niece, Erlina. Elindell's king, Modron, had a younger brother, Ner, who was next in line to the throne and was to marry Erlina. I went along with Bellic, being always uneasy without his protection – and I wanted to see the wedding.

"Now, Modron had a bastard son – that's Thallinore, of course. Yes, Elgiva, a bastard, begat of a wench called Eldreda, herself a mere nar-Wardain. Modron had never married and had no legitimate heir, but the lack did not concern him. You see, it falls to some, like Zallic, to see what lies ahead, and such a one was Modron. After the wedding, he took your great –uncle aside and told him what he had seen in his many prophetic dreams. Ner and Erlina would have but one child, a daughter, and she would have power to surpass all other Elves and this power would come to her in the form of a gift, but what kind of gift, he knew not. He felt that this future child was ordained to be a great ruler of Elvendom – its redeemer, in fact. How unfortunate that he should say all this within earshot of his jealous son, but Thallinore's true nature had not then been revealed,"

"Though there are many who discount prophesies, Bellic respected Modron and always kept in mind what he had said. After the wedding, Bellic decided to stay in Elindell a while until his niece was settled in her new role and I do not need to tell you that he grew to like the place so much, he has been there ever since. As a scholar and a wanderer, one place suits him as well as another, I expect.

"Well, he grew very close to Modron and Ner and, having no hope of ruling in Astorill, where his brother and sister had many children, he decided to abstain from kingship there – not that the title of king would ever have appealed to an Elf like him. So, he set up home in Elindell and devoted his life to study and learning.

"In the fullness of time, Erlina conceived. We were all delighted, of course, but happiness is never meant to be permanent." Kendra shook her head sadly. "No. Poor Modron caught an ague and died and Ner was suddenly king. Thallinore had by this time fallen in with Tarkinell – a rogue, an arch-manipulator. I hated him from the first. I think he has aspirations to greatness and the fact that he is not a Wardain has no doubt driven him mad. So Thallinore was in good company. Tarkinell knew he was weak and greedy and they became close friends. What passed between them, who can say, nor who did the deed that followed? I suspect that Tarkinell convinced his friend of his right to rule as Modron's only child."

"So we may never know who poisoned Ner, but poisoned he was, and he left this world before his time. We were numb with grief and none more so than Erlina.

The shock induced delivery." Kendra paused for a moment and looked at Elgiva with eyes that were moist with remembered sorrow. "I was with her when she birthed you, child, and I was the first to hold you in my arms. Yes, poor chit, Ner and Erlina were your parents. Sadly, your mother died soon after you were born. I think her heart was broken."

At this point Kendra was obliged to break off from her narrative to wipe the corners of her eyes with her sleeve. She drew a deep breath and tried to suppress the surge of painful memories that time had left undimmed. Glancing at Elgiva to offer some comfort, her heart was wrenched still further by the young Elf's tortured gaze.

"At least in you those two fair creatures live again," she said fondly. "You have your mother's beauty, Elgiva. The same delicacy of feature. And in your eyes I see the same fire and will I saw in your father's. How cruel it is that they should not have lived to see the jewel their love created."

Elgiva lowered her head and a curtain of dark hair concealed the tight frown that marred the smoothness of her brow. Kendra reached out and patted her arm consolingly.

"Before Erlina died, she asked to see your great-uncle. She begged him to protect you. She told him she suspected that her husband had been murdered and she feared for the safety of her babe. You may not know this, Elgiva, but the Wardain do not attain magic till puberty – and a good thing, too, I'm sure! Imagine power in the hands of naughty Elflings! Erlina wanted Bellic to ward you until you could fend for yourself, so he put you in my care and for many months I tended to your needs."

"After your mother was…" Kendra paused and swallowed down a knot of grief. "Afterwards, Bellic spoke to Thallinore, concerning the fate of the kingdom. At that time he had no reason to suspect your cousin of any duplicity or malice and, when Thallinore offered to be the regent until you were of age, your great-uncle gladly accepted. According to Elven law, of course, Thallinore could not be king, for he is half-Wardain. Well, there was no-one else with a claim to the throne and Bellic was an outsider, related to the Royal house by marriage, so his right to interfere was limited."

"It was then that Bellic heard from Eldruin and was invited to Misterell on a matter of some importance. And so, my dear, he left you in my charge and was away some time. Alas, in his absence, Thallinore proclaimed himself king. No doubt Tarkinell egged him on. No-one in Elindell was able to oppose him – he does have powers, you see, be they somewhat weakened by his mother's blood. So we had to accept it. Of course, we had no reason then to believe that he did it for any other end than the good of the kingdom."

"As for myself, it became increasingly clear to me that I was despised for my Wilthkin blood. I was an outsider. With your parents dead and Bellic away, I realised that I had no friends in Elindell and would not be used with kindness. Sadly, I have not found favour with any race. My strangeness has always set me apart. You see, it is hard to conceal one's ancestry, my dears."

She raised her hands and hooked her long, grey locks behind her ears: they were pointed, like Elgiva's. Grinning, she continued, " Of course, you know why Bellic went to Misterell. The Ninth Book. When he returned, he found your cousin secure in kingship and so he confronted him about Elindell's future."

"He learned that Thallinore objected to my presence and so he agreed to send me away. Indeed he was glad to do so, knowing that I would be safer elsewhere, especially as he himself would often be away. This is the home he found for me." She spread out her arms and grinned contentedly. "I like it very well. Anyway, Thallinore told Bellic that he had plans to found a dynasty of his own and you would be excluded from the succession. In his heart, Thallinore feared what you might become, for he remembered his father's prediction, no doubt. So, too, did your great-uncle, but he alone had read the Ninth Book.

"Your cousin told Bellic that he was welcome to stay in Elindell, as long as he took the oath of fealty to the king - as all Elves must do, or be forced to leave the kingdom. Your great-uncle agreed, but only if Thallinore promised that no harm would ever befall you. He expected your cousin to be honourable, no doubt. Well, having taken the oath, which is always made in the name of Faine, Bellic may not act against the king. To break such an oath is unthinkable. You yourself, surely, took the same oath, when you were old enough to do so, Elgiva.

"Thallinore had you put in the care of Eldreda, until it could be decided what should be done with you. Fear for your safety no doubt prompted the idea that sprang into Bellic's mind." Kendra paused for a moment and looked at Elgiva, as if she feared that her next disclosure would be the worst so far. "He suggested that an announcement be made to the effect that Erlina's babe had died of a childhood illness, and meanwhile you should be brought up in the Royal Household as one of the servants, that, indeed, you should be a lowly churl, knowing nothing of your origins. So it was done. What is one more parentless babe in the servants' quarters? … No, Elgiva, do not speak. I know your heart and it misjudges Bellic. Do you not see, my dear, not only did this keep you safe and allow your great-uncle to stay in Elindell and keep an eye on you, it also fulfilled the prophesy – 'Orphan and Slave'. And, as you grew up, Bellic taught you as much as the time allowed and whenever he could without arousing suspicion. He taught you things unknown to other menials. And to him it all seemed to fit. He was preparing you for your destiny and he, in turn, was able to travel when he wished, having no need to fear for your welfare. My dear, do not scowl. Think you not he had another aim in mind?"

Elgiva flashed a look at Kendra, at once both puzzled and angry.

"Do you not think, child, that a wielder of great power must be a creature of humility, a being mindful of the needs of others and aware of the importance of justice and mercy? Would not a slave know more of such things than someone accustomed to wealth and flattery and selfish indulgence?"

Elgiva's expression softened and, turning her head, she gazed into the fire. In the dancing flames she seemed to see Lord Othere's face and almost heard him echo Kendra's words.

"But … I have no power," she said quietly.

"You are unpractised merely."

They fell silent. Kendra sighed deeply, while Elgiva continued to stare at the fire. Watching them both was Godwin. He was overwhelmed by what he had heard and wished that he could offer some comfort to his friend, but these were matters beyond him and he didn't know what to say.

"Perhaps Bellic presumed too much," admitted Kendra, " but there was no-one else to protect you. He could have gone away and taken you with him, but Thallinore would have tracked you down; you were a threat to his sovereignty. And it was better you should stay where you were and come to know the workings of Elvendom and of the kingdom you would one day rule. Bellic is a Wardain and wise, my dear, but, by the stars, he is not infallible. Do not hate him, for he loves you dearly. In you his dead niece lives again."

Elgiva didn't move, but a sigh escaped from her lips and there was a dampness on her lashes, a dew of sadness.

"Well, my dear, your childhood passed and no-one knew your true identity, except for Bellic, your cousin and Eldreda… and Tarkinell, of course…"

"And Alison," Elgiva broke in. "I think that Alison always knew." Kendra and Godwin both looked at her quizzically and a fond smile touched her lips. "The leader of the Royal Herd."

Kendra smiled and nodded. "Well, you showed no signs of magic, Elgiva, but no more should you have, for you believed yourself a nar-Wardain. If peculiar feelings stirred within you, no doubt you dismissed them as symptoms of growing up. Without a tutor in magic, your powers did not develop. But you were being watched. Tarkinell was always alert to the stirrings of your power, ready to advise his master that the time had come to dispose of you – as Eldreda was no doubt disposed of, when her love of Elf-wine and mischief-making threatened to loosen her tongue. Bellic made more frequent journeys, searching for somewhere to hide you away, where he could teach you the application of magic. He felt that the first part of your training was over and he also suspected that Tarkinell was planning a little accident, something that would rid the king of your presence without giving rise to suspicion.

A small smile touched the corners of Kendra's mouth. "But, no sooner had Bellic found the ideal place, when you did something quite unexpected. You know to what I refer. You got yourself banished. Well, in many ways it was well timed. There was no need for Bellic to spirit you away, inviting suspicion and trouble. Tarkinell, of course, had a hand in the plot that, but for you, would have succeeded. He was second only to the Chief Counsellor and probably thought it was time to move upwards, where he would be nearer the throne. It would have availed him nothing, of course. As a nar-Wardain he would have been deposed sooner or later, but Tarkinell is mad, I think. And I suspect he has interests elsewhere, but I must keep to the matter at hand.

"As you know, Bellic did not follow you. He wished to appear indifferent, perhaps even ashamed. It suited his purpose. He had no wish to leave Elindell at that time, for he was fearful for its future and he believed it would be easy for him to find you when he wished. And he gave you the amulet, of course, but I must leave the explanation of that to him, when you both meet, as I hope, by all the stars, you will."

"Shouldn't we?" asked Elgiva.

Kendra shrugged and her expression was grim. "Who can say what meetings the future holds? Things in Elindell are not what they were."

"And Bellic is in trouble."

Kendra nodded. "From what I hear they are all in trouble. Let me tell you what I know, when I have found a good place to start." She stooped awkwardly to pick up her goblet and, after a long drink and a moment to arrange her thoughts, she continued. "You realise that, when you slew the Chief Counsellor, the position went to Tarkinell?"

"I helped him!" cried Elgiva crossly.

"Yes, you did, but be that as it may, he has told his master that documents exist dating back to Faine knows when, according to which the kingdom's nearest neighbour, Urith-Endil, was once a province of Elindell. He has persuaded Thallinore that it is time to claim it back. 'Tis absolute nonsense, of course, but for now, a state of war prevails between the two kingdoms."

Elgiva gasped in disbelief. "War? That's madness, Kendra!"

"Madness, indeed," said Kendra. "And meanwhile your cousin grows more grasping and more cruel and severe penalties are meted out to anyone who opposes him. He means to destroy those he cannot bend to his will. But there is something else I must disclose and it is the main reason why your uncle cannot leave."

"Several days after you left, my dear, a traveller came to Elindell with a retinue of Elves. He claimed to be Vieldrin, Misterell's new king. Since Eldruin's death he had been putting his realm in order, he said, and had now decided to visit other kingdoms and lay to rest the reputation of his own. He maintained that his mission was one of friendship and peace. Your great-uncle no doubt knew him from his visits to Misterell in the past and may already have had some inkling of his true nature

– I did hear that Eldruin's death was suspicious. Well, Vieldrin fell in with Tarkinell and Thallinore and I'm sure he soon knew everything that they did, but being Eldruin's son he alone had access to the Ninth Book. I believe that Bellic spoke out against Vieldrin, or his cronies, and certainly the war, but whatever transpired, he made himself an enemy. His last message gave me little cause for hope, Elgiva. He asked that I help you and tell you all I know, for he himself is unable to act."

"But why?" demanded Elgiva.

"I know not. I know only that he cannot leave Elindell."

"Kendra, Bellic is a Wardain. He has great power!"

"To you, little Elf, mayhap. But your great-uncle is ninety-five – three times Vieldrin's age, I'm sure. He is weary and has spent his life in study, not in the practice of magic. While you have seen him as some kind of god, his powers as a Wardain are no more extraordinary than those of any other."

"Why are you telling me this?" cried Elgiva with a passion that made Kendra flinch. "I can't bear it!"

"Be calm, my dear. You have work to do in this world. Things to learn and a destiny to fulfil. Perhaps the future of Elvendom is in your hands alone." She reached out to touch Elgiva's arm.

"No!" snapped Elgiva, pulling away. "I have no power! Modron was wrong … and Bellic, too! And the wretched Ninth Book!"

"I did not expect you to react so selfishly," chided Kendra sternly. "Bellic is relying on you."

"How else can I react?" Elgiva stood up and paced back and forth, her eyes flashing angrily. "One minute I'm a servant, a nothing, and the next I'm a Wardain with magical powers ordained to rescue Elvendom. How can I save Elvendom? It's ludicrous. What am I supposed to save it FROM? And if this Vieldrin surpasses Bellic, then he'll surpass me, too. Kendra, I have no magic!"

She came to a halt behind Godwin and, after a moment of hesitation, placed both her hands on his shoulders, as though he were her contact with reality. A soft smile lifted the corners of his mouth, for he was pleased to be entrusted with her need

Kendra watched her with a mixture of feelings, torn between love and vexation, and then she exclaimed, "No courage either."

Elgiva sprang forwards, uncertain of what she meant to do, her face dark with rage. Godwin quickly caught her arm and held her back and she twisted round to confront him, her eyes pleading, lost. His eyes narrowed fractionally, urging forbearance.

She sagged against him, her arm around his shoulders.

Kendra acknowledged his intervention with a small nod of her head, but, when he looked at her, his gaze held the same gentle reproach he had used to calm his friend.

For a while they were grimly silent, then Elgiva spoke. Her voice sounded small and defeated. "What must I do?" she asked lornly.

Smiling with relief, Kendra held out her hand. Slowly, Elgiva reached out and clasped it, then she knelt at the old woman's side. Kendra looked down at her and compassion moistened her gaze. With her free hand she stroked away the angry tears that stained Elgiva's pale cheeks.

"My dear, " she said softly, "it seems that there is but one thing you must do. Find the Lorestone and use it."

"Yes, Kendra, but how?"

"Let us hope that Faine will show you the way." Kendra smiled, but then her expression hardened. "You ask what the danger is. I do not know, but it is certain. It is great. The Ninth Book would have it so. And it is Bellic who told me of this. I may not doubt him."

"The King of Misterell, is he the danger?" wondered Elgiva.

"He may be. Or part of it," said Kendra.

Elgiva tightened her grip on Kendra's hand and her eyes brimmed with fear and revulsion. "I think we have already met."

Kendra nodded. "He is bound to know all about you."

"He's evil, Kendra!" protested Elgiva. "Am I to oppose *HIM*? I can't!"

"What happened, when you met?" Elgiva shook her head and pulled back her hand. "No matter," soothed Kendra. "Do not tell me, if it pains you."

"Tell her," urged Godwin, leaning forwards. "Tell her how you protected yourself."

She darted a look of annoyance at him. Then her anger melted into fear and self-doubt and she took a shuddering breath. "How can I?" she begged him. "I just don't know."

Godwin's forehead creased with concern and he looked across at Kendra. He decided to take it upon himself to tell her what had happened. Kendra listened attentively and nodded her wise, old head, as though it all made sense.

"She told me he could have destroyed her, but he refrained," said Godwin. "But why? Is she more powerful than he expected?"

"Sadly no. Elgiva is only a Wardain, Godwin, and unschooled in the use of magic," said Kendra. "However, when the need is great, magic can rise up to protect its possessor, and how strong it will be the opponent cannot know. You were deeply afraid at the time, Elgiva? Indeed. Your powers responded to that. Bellic will tell you that magic resembles the body. Without use or exercise it does not develop. Your powers are weak, unpractised, diffused, and, what is worse, you do not believe in them. But when you are overcome by violent emotions, then instinct rules your actions and your magic is shocked into being. Small wonder if it hurts you and leaves you exhausted. Your body is unused to it. You have not been tutored. Magic must be properly channelled, or it flies off in all directions. It may even hit an unintended target, which could be most unfortunate." She gave Godwin a wry smile and saw him swallow hard. "These are things that Bellic would have taught you."

"Can't *YOU* teach me?" asked Elgiva.

Kendra lowered her eyes and smiled as though trying to hide some private amusement. "Think you that I have magic, child?" She glanced at them both, but her gaze was drawn finally to Godwin. His blue eyes regarded her archly and Kendra's smile broadened. "It is not for me to teach the uses of power. I have the gift of healing. I read the stars and the runes. I am a maker of medicines and potions and a keeper of arcane knowledge. I talk to trees and animals. There are many kinds of magic, my dears. That a tiny acorn can become a great oak, what is that but magic? But I know nothing of real power, the sort that Royal Elves use. One thing, however, I do know," – her eyes widened warningly -,"is that you must not play with it. Magic is a gift; not a sport, not a toy. It must be used wisely and for all the right reasons. There is always the danger, without proper schooling, of magic being misused."

"You say you know nothing of power," remarked Elgiva wryly, "but be honest, Kendra, you know a great deal about everything."

Kendra chuckled. "By the stars! Much knowledge may be gained by study, they say. By study and thought and observation. There is no mystery in that. But 'tis wrong to credit my poor pate withal. My sources are not extraordinary. Perhaps my knowledge, too, was ordained and we have all been chosen for a purpose."

"Who chose us?" asked Elgiva. "Faine?"

"Who can say, my dear?" replied Kendra. "Perhaps the Founder's spirit wanders still among the forests of this land, watching and guiding his people. His magic was greater than any and perhaps he even cheated death and still walks the Earth in flesh. His leaving was mysterious, an end that was not an end, as you will have read in the Chronicles, Elgiva. Forsooth, we could talk of this all night and still be none the wiser – and Godwin would be even more baffled than he already is." She smiled at him warmly. "Well, suffice it to say, if we are chosen, we must accept our destiny and strive to fulfil it."

Elgiva drew a long breath. "Misterell."

"Yes, my dear, the Lorestone."

"But where *IS* Misterell?"

"To the north-west. Many leagues ... I think," said Kendra hesitantly. Something in her tone made them look at her.

Elgiva frowned. "Don't you know exactly?"

Kendra shook her head, half in ignorance, half in exasperation. "Why can things never be simple?" she complained. She looked at Elgiva and shrugged, as though asking pardon for her lack of knowledge. "Life is a maze and amazing," she chuckled. "Give me some more of that ale, my dear. I am hoarse from all this talking. A moment or two to gather my wits, and then we shall speak of Misterell."

⋆ ⋆ ⋆

Chapter Fourteen

Kendra held out her goblet and Elgiva filled it with ale. She watched the old woman quaff the Gale Beer, watched the firelight glinting on the silver goblet, and struggled with her impatience. At length, the ale had been consumed and, with a sigh of contentment, Kendra wiped her mouth on her sleeve and placed the empty goblet on the floor.

"Misterell," she said suddenly. "Only Bellic knows the way. He uses magic to find it."

Elgiva sucked in her breath and released it with a sigh of frustration.

"You see," continued Kendra, "'tis the most magical of all the Elven kingdoms. Everything about it is strange and it is a place that breeds legends and myths. Faine First-Father loved it…"

"This I know!"

"Yes. Be patient, child." Kendra reached out a placating hand and stroked Elgiva's hair. "Other kingdoms have always feared it. Thus did its rulers seek to protect it and ward off the outside world. The land that lies about it is enchanted and 'tis a hard place to find, for it has turned in upon itself and withdrawn. Perhaps it is not for you to find Misterell. Perhaps Misterell will find *YOU*. Bellic is the only Elf I know ever to have been there, but he would not tell me what it was like. Whatever lies within Misterell, you must find out for yourselves."

"Is it really an evil place?" asked Elgiva anxiously.

"I do not know," answered Kendra. "Some legends would have it so, for it turned against the Founder, despite his love for it. All I do know is that the spell that surrounds it makes travellers stray from their path. Bellic tried to find it many times before he succeeded. He told me that something always made him turn back or change direction. Bushes and trees sometimes changed position, or so he thought, and before he knew it, he was on the wrong road and totally lost. The forest wove a spell of confusion to protect the dark trees from outsiders. Eventually, Bellic ignored what he saw and felt. He focused his mind on the enchantment itself and followed it to its source."

"But if he entered Misterell and left unharmed, it can't be an evil place," said Elgiva. "And wasn't Eldruin a good king – his friend?"

"So I was told," replied Kendra, "but we can all appear to be what we are not." Silently, her guests agreed. "And Misterell can do likewise. If Bellic returned scatheless, perhaps it was only because Misterell wished him to."

"Or because Eldruin wanted to trick him," suggested Godwin self-consciously, "and the Ninth Book … is … a lie."

Elgiva and Kendra gaped at him and he shifted in his seat. Uncertainty hung in the air above them and doubt coiled in the shadows, as dark as despair. At length, Kendra straightened herself and shook her head in denial.

"No," she said confidently. "Bellic would not be so easily duped."

"But you said he wasn't infallible," Elgiva reminded her.

"Why, by the stars … so I did!" admitted Kendra, somewhat disconcerted.

For a time they all sat pensive and quiet, listening to the crackling fire and the moaning of the wind that scythed across the darkness. Kendra stabbed half-heartedly at the fire with the iron poker, her brow furrowed with thought.

"Of course, my dears," she said after a while, "there's only one way to find out the truth about Misterell. You'll have to go there and see for yourselves."

"If Bellic wouldn't tell you what the truth was, it must be something bad. I don't think I want to go there," said Elgiva. She gave Kendra a sullen, sideways look, then glared at the fire, her shoulders hunched forwards. "I don't think I want any part of this." She felt the tension inside herself increasing, becoming too much to bear, and, rising to her feet, she glowered down her nose at the old woman with all the petulance she could muster. Her fists were concretions of anger at her sides. "Why can't someone else find the Stone? Someone with real power? Why me? Why pick on me?"

"Is this self-pity now?" asked Kendra.

"Insult me all you like," returned Elgiva, tossing back her head.

Kendra smiled indulgently. "Elgiva, don't be childish. Someone has to find the Lorestone. Why shouldn't it be you? Think you that other Wardain can leave their lands without protection to go gadding about after legends? Has Bellic had the time or the opportunity to tell them all he knows? Would it be wise for him to do so? And would they find the Lorestone, if they tried?"

"Why shouldn't they?" snapped Elgiva.

"Because it's not their destiny, child."

"Destiny! I'm sick of that word. I don't believe in destiny!"

"Nevertheless, it is a fact. I am older than you, Elgiva, and have seen and heard and felt many things. I have discovered that too often we disbelieve, when there is no solid proof, and all we achieve is to close our minds to the unknown wonders of this world. We narrow our vision and are left with nothing but the bare bones of existence. I have learned that it is better to keep the mind open."

She reached down and picked up the leather-bound book. While Elgiva mulled over her words, Kendra searched for the passage she wanted.

"The Stone knows,
"The Stone shows,
"And who shall lose,
"The Stone shall choose."

Kendra looked up with a gentle smile, but Elgiva's face was a mask of indifference. At length, in a flat, doleful tone she said, "I have no choice, do I?"

"We all have that," said Kendra. "We all have the freedom to act in whatever way we think is best."

"As I said, I have no choice. But I tell you, Kendra, the very name of Misterell fills me with dread, and I won't pretend that I can see any sense in going on this fool's errand. It seems that to find Misterell, I must follow my nose, but I don't think I can smell evil."

Kendra saw fit to ignore this remark. "Apart from the trouble in Elindell, other Elven kingdoms may soon fall prey to Thallinore's greed and the schemes of Vieldrin and Tarkinell." Kendra glanced worriedly at Godwin. "Wilthkin lands as well, perchance. For those who desire to take and possess, boundaries have no meaning. The Lorestone may be the only hope for us all. Be it a legend, or a lie, it must not go unexplored."

"Yes, yes! Don't go on!" retorted Elgiva fiercely. "The position I'm in I can only escape at the cost of my integrity. No more persuasive words, just tell me how to get there and I'll leave first thing in the morning."

Kendra tutted and shook her head. "You neither trust nor believe me."

"I do not know you!" cried Elgiva.

"Your great-uncle Bellic..."

"I don't know him either, though once I thought I did."

"Well, he is not as young as he was and I'm sure we'll both become doddering old fools, chatting about the past, as though it were yesterday, and forgetting what happened yesterday, as though it were centuries ago, but all we can do is our best..."

"By Faine, Kendra! Get to the point!"

"You have no respect for my age or my wisdom and you are too quick to anger. If Bellic were here..."

"Well he isn't! And I'm quickly losing my patience. And I'm also wondering what the connection is between the pair of you. Why are you such intimate cronies? What are you, Kendra? Lovers?"

Kendra let loose a shriek of laughter and slapped her palms on her thighs. Her reaction made her visitors jump, though Godwin felt his lips curl with amusement and he had to hold back a desire to laugh.

It took Kendra some time to recover her composure. "Forgive me, my dears," she said, still chuckling. "He told me to make you angry, if I could, to see if it roused your powers. Then I could tell how they are progressing."

"If I'm a Wardain," said Elgiva, "wouldn't that be risky?" In the firelight her smile appeared somewhat cruel.

Kendra gave her an arch look. "It seems not, my dear. Your powers are in a far worse condition than we had even expected."

Elgiva scowled angrily, made to speak, but instead decided to sulk. She kicked her stool across the room and turned her back on Kendra.

The old woman let out a long-suffering sigh. "At first I said that you had power and then you were annoyed, now I say you have no power, and still you are annoyed. You cannot have it both ways, child." She reached across to touch Elgiva, who instantly recoiled. "Fear not. The magic will come in time. Retrieve your stool, if you please. I can see that you are a complicated and sensitive creature, my dear, and I meant you no offence."

After a moment to think about it, Elgiva righted her stool and sat down. Kendra nodded appreciatively. "Now, Misterell," she said. "You must go north-west till you reach a great forest. Not only is this forest large, but long and narrow, too. It sprawls like a serpent across the land and you will have to decide if you are going to walk through it or go round it. The latter course will cost you a day of travel at least, but to cross the forest will take a few hours. That seems straightforward, no doubt, but it may be unwise to brave that place without the protection of magic. Bellic calls it the Forest of Shades. It lies under some kind of spell – perhaps the influence of Misterell. Well, you will have to decide for yourselves. Only you will know if you have the strength for it. But if you cross it, be aware, and do not stop until you are safely on the other side. I think that even the trees are dangerous."

"How can trees be dangerous?" Elgiva's eyebrows arched in surprise.

"I dare not imagine, for I have never been there. Well, when you are through the forest, keep going north-west and hope that you find what you seek. I cannot give directions. Landmarks may be inconstant. Be ever on your guard against danger and deceit." She glanced at her guests, then nodded, as though her task was done. Then she got to her feet. "All this talk has made me hungry. I made a fruit cake yesterday. I think it's time we ate it." She turned to walk away, then stopped. "You asked me a question, Elgiva, which I have yet to answer. Forgive me for forgetting. You wanted to know the connection between your great-uncle and myself."

"Kendra, I'm sorry, I didn't mean…"

"Bellic is my father."

Kendra turned to hide a sly grin of amusement and shuffled towards her shelves, while they stared at her back in silence. This was just one more unexpected and amazing disclosure to add to all the others and their store of astonishment was already so depleted that they were unable to react to her statement with anything other than dumb acceptance.

"Aye," chuckled Kendra quietly from the corner of the room, her voice as soft as the shadows, "there's more magic in me than meets the eye."

⋆ ⋆ ⋆

As the night matured, Elgiva and Kendra continued their discussion of Elven affairs. Lulled by the warmth of the cosy room and the potency of the ale, Godwin's attention was drifting away, and he became increasingly superfluous to their talk. Sensing this, his companions lapsed into Elvish. A gulf had opened between them that seemed too great to be bridged and Godwin felt confused and excluded, and a little selfish, too. Elgiva surely missed her home and was anxious for any news, but Godwin missed his home as well and no-one seemed to care about that.

Yes, of course he was envious. Here was Elgiva finally aware of the truth about her past and that was something he could never even dream of.

He turned away from his companions and gave his grievances free rein.

The past was one thing, but what about the future? Great danger loomed ahead, apparently, and, once again he was forced to consider his part in it. If he went with Elgiva and lost his life, he could never return to his family. He had already been absent from home for … how long? He couldn't even remember. It was more than a week. Was it nine days, ten? They had drifted past him unrecorded, as though he had been living a dream.

His family. He had deserted them. He had wilfully divorced himself from the people he loved. They must surely believe him dead by now. Perhaps at this very moment they were mourning their loss and inconsolable. Was Redwald even now singing in the great Hall in praise of those who had died in the battle, and was the name of Godwin on the list of fallen heroes? Did Othere bewail the loss of his churl? Did Elric miss his amenable guardian?

You selfish, irresponsible bastard! You and your thirst for freedom.

Slyly, he glanced at Elgiva. Sitting there in her tattered robe and the over-sized shirt, she seemed so small and frail, despite the powers she supposedly possessed. He noticed how her fingers toyed nervously with the strands of black hair that fell about her shoulders. She looked like a vulnerable child. How could he be envious of such a tormented, self-doubting creature? And he had made an oath. And Kendra had advised them to stay together. Elgiva still needed his protection. To abandon her now...

To abandon her now would be churlish indeed, he thought with a smile of bitterness.

But how could he protect her in a world of magic and unknown, evil forces? He was just one man. A powerless Wilthkin. A coward with a bold-looking sword, who lacked the skill to use it.

The problem was, Elgiva didn't believe in destiny, but, for his part, he did. Deep inside in a secret place where dreams and hopes were hoarded against a time of emotional famine, he felt it to be true.

He realised that he was frowning. What a serious fellow he had become! What had happened to the Godwin he knew, always ready with a humorous quip? He didn't know himself anymore.

Yet now, perhaps, he was himself, had grown up years too late. Had he ever been a compliant servant, or had that been a mask, a defence? With Elgiva, he never needed a disguise. She accepted him as he was. She relied on him to be sensible and strong and she heeded his advice.

Yes, he had always ignored it, but his bitterness seemed finally to have broken through the surface. As if for the first time, he realised how deep his anger ran, how much he hated Othere and all he represented; his jealousy of Elric, who had landed like a cuckoo and ousted Godwin from his master's paternal affection. The shock of it staggered him.

But Othere had been a fair and generous master … and yet, by Frigg, what right had he to make slaves of others? What right had anyone?

They killed your sister and made you a slave. Didn't you ever think of running away?

He had been born a free man and the Saxons had warped him, made him a serf and taken by force whatever inheritance had been his birthright. They had murdered his sister. It wasn't even their land, it was the land of *HIS* people, and these invaders had stolen and pillaged it!

And this Elf beside him, she knew. She knew what it felt like to be a slave, parentless, robbed of liberty: to be seen as inferior for so many years that one came to believe it oneself. To give up one's self-respect because of the will of others. No-one had the right to do that to another. Death was preferable to self-effacement. Couldn't Othere see that? Couldn't Bellic see that?

No, he could never return home as a slave. He would go with Elgiva and risk all the Fellkin and demons and beasts and anything else that stood in their way.

And what if they succeeded? What if she did win the throne of Elindell? What if the Lorestone were real and her powers were real and they both survived the quest? His friend would be a powerful queen. She would reward him for his help and he would go home in splendour with gold, a fine horse and a retinue of retainers. He could picture it all quite clearly. He would take the settlement by storm. Pranked out with gems … polished leather … a silver shield …a snorting steed … and he himself clad like a warrior, riding into the stronghold. He would sneer as he trampled their crops; he would sneer at Othere's hoary beard and laugh at his stolen trinkets. He would be the master and make them all dance to his tune, for marching behind him would be a host of armed men, and servants by the score, scuttling to obey his every whim. Yes, he'd show Othere what slavery was. He'd make the Saxons pay for their arrogance!

No, by Frigg, this was madness! What was he thinking? Did his hatred run so deep? The gods should strike him down. Servants? Revenge? He didn't want that. That was their way, not his.

He stared at his empty goblet. He was clenching it so hard, his knuckles were white. This was all fantasy. It must be the ale. He couldn't be such a hypocrite; he couldn't be like *THEM*. Why was there so much venom in his heart? And did he plan to help Elgiva merely for some reward? A reward that would enable him to exact revenge on the Saxon lord who had treated him so well? Did he think so little of his wife that he wanted to make her people pay for merely being what they were?

After all these years of hiding his hurt was he finally losing control? It seemed that he had acted his part so well, he had even convinced himself. Only in dreams had he been aware of the darkness of his thoughts. Yet, even then, he fancied that he understood himself. Now he wasn't sure.

As he sat there, immersed in the turmoil of his thoughts, a small voice called to him from the distance. Then a hand touched him gently on the arm and jolted him back to reality. He looked up quickly and his eyes were burning with dry and impotent tears.

"Godwin, are you all right?" asked Elgiva. "You're trembling. Are you ill?"

"Ill?" he said dourly. "Perhaps I am."

"What's wrong, my friend?"

He shrugged. "I'm all right," he lied. He couldn't tell her about his thoughts. She mustn't know that he was basically corrupt.

She wouldn't accept his answer and she didn't spare him the penetration of her gaze, but her touch on his arm was warm and forgiving. He wasn't corrupt. Merely human.

"I was thinking," he said quietly. "And … I didn't like what I thought. I'm weak."

She smiled at him. "So are we all. But is it weakness to question oneself, or is it moral strength?"

"You read my mind!" he flared at her.

"Oh, if only I could!" she responded with a grin. "No," she went on more seriously, "I didn't need to read your mind. I recognised the look in your eyes."

"Oh, I see. I'm sorry."

Elgiva sighed and stared at the floor. "I recognised myself."

She looked up and their eyes met, and in that moment they were suddenly both aware of a new depth in their relationship: aware of how fragile the barrier is that exists between friendship and love.

Shyly, Godwin looked away and found himself being observed. Kendra smiled at him knowingly and he felt that she saw right through him with her wise, old, Celtic eyes.

"We have been cruel, Elgiva," said Kendra, "excluding this poor, young man from our talk. No doubt he is bored and, when folk get bored, their minds start to wander and who knows what they might dwell on. He has things that trouble him, just as we do. Forgive us, Godwin." She turned to Elgiva. "I think, my dear, we have talked enough. 'Tis late and you two look fit to drop. I've some soft, straw pallets in there." She pointed towards a curtained chamber. "A good night's rest is what you need."

"What were you talking about?" asked Godwin, ignoring Kendra's advice and the ache of his fatigue. He felt that he needed to be involved, to assert his usefulness and offer his support to Elgiva.

"We were talking about the Wardain I met outside Joskin's cave," Elgiva replied in muted tones. "If it was Vieldrin, why did he let me live, and does he know I will try to find the Lorestone?"

"It all depends on whether or not he believes the Ninth Book and the prophecy Modron made," said Kendra.

"So everything hinges on prophecies," said Elgiva, "and we're all chasing moonbeams in the dark."

Elgiva gave Kendra an arch look and the old woman shook her head, as though she were exasperated, but a slight smile touched her lips. "Well, my dears, it's time for slumber."

Suppressing a yawn, Elgiva stood up and bid good night to her friends, then she made her way towards the curtained chamber. Godwin pushed himself to his feet and prepared to follow her lead, but Kendra had more to say.

"Before you retire, Godwin, there is something else that arose in our discussion and it is only proper that you should know as much as we do." Kendra opened the Ninth Book and squinted at the pages in the fire's dwindling light. "Though there is no mention of how this Lorestone may be used, one thing is very clear. As it says in this passage, 'Use it once, then it is done'. So, whoever uses this precious gift, they must know what they are about. Now off to bed with you. I'll sit here a while and take a potion. My head is aching. This has been a night to tax my poor, old pate beyond the limits of its humble power."

Godwin cocked an eyebrow at this, but she gave him an innocent smile. He inclined his head respectfully in her direction, then silently took his leave.

★ ★ ★

The morning was well advanced, but the sky was dark with the threat of snow, when Elgiva and Godwin ventured out from Kendra's snug, little home.

During their preparations for leaving, Kendra gave Godwin a stout, sacking bag for carrying their provisions. It had leather straps and fitted well between his shoulder blades. Then Kendra insisted on filling it with whatever she could spare and he hoped his spine would be fit for the burden.

But this was a minor annoyance. He felt refreshed after a good night's sleep. He had bathed and shaved and eaten a large breakfast and had sharpened his sword with a whetstone. He felt as fresh as the crisp, new day.

Kendra had also kitted them out with clothes she had found in a seemingly bottomless trunk in the depths of the curtained chamber. Godwin now wore a thick, woollen tunic over a shirt of white linen. His woollen leggings were blue, like the tunic, and the new boots that reached above the ankle were thick-soled and roomy. These were simple yet serviceable garments and, with Joskin's cloak to complete his outfit, Godwin judged himself ready for travel.

Elgiva's robe and shirt were replaced by a long-sleeved, grey, woollen kirtle; at her waist a thick, brown cord. Her feet were laced into dainty, brown boots and the brown mantle that fell to her calves was held at her throat by a silver clasp. The hood of the mantle was hidden beneath a shining cascade of newly washed hair.

Before she bade them farewell, Kendra delved once more into the cavernous trunk and produced a black, leather scabbard, which she proudly offered to Godwin. "A fine sheath for a fine blade. 'Twas made in Astorill."

He accepted her gift with a nod of thanks and fitted it to his belt. Inwardly, he smiled to himself. The old Godwin had been discarded along with his servant's rags and now he fancied he had the aspect of an errant warrior intent on bold deeds. But not just any old warrior: a warrior with a giant's cloak and a scabbard made by Elves.

Everything had changed since their meeting with Kendra, taken on a different perspective. They were starting out on a new adventure, but one with a worthy and serious purpose.

⋆ ⋆ ⋆

Chapter Fifteen

Godwin's elation was starting to waver. The weight of the pack he carried was impinging upon his sense of adventure and he knew that he was still playing the servant's role, for he had volunteered to carry all their gear, while Elgiva bore nothing but a small, cloth bag that held enough food for a couple of days. Well, it was too late to start complaining now, and there was no point in feeling resentful. It was entirely his own fault for wanting to appear so strong and dependable.

Elgiva was walking some way ahead of him, deeply cocooned in thought, and she seemed to have forgotten he existed. He noticed a tension in the way she carried herself, a stiffness in her shoulders that was so unlike her usual graceful posture. Clearly, she was worried and preoccupied and perhaps he should leave her in peace, but he couldn't cope with this protracted silence. Partly to lift her spirits, but mostly to vanquish his boredom, he caught her up and tried to set a conversation going.

"This snow's a nuisance, isn't it?" he said.

She merely nodded, her eyes upon the ground.

"By Frigg! it's damn cold! I thought we might be in for warmer weather by now."

She smiled in spite of herself. "We are. Be patient. You Wilthkin are obsessed with the weather. Believe me, this is the last snow we'll see before next winter."

"Are you sure?" he asked.

"Kendra said so. She knows much about weather-lore."

"I see."

This conversation was leading nowhere and Godwin decided to abandon it, but the ensuing silence galled him. He needed to be more direct; his friend was troubled and there was no sense in skirting around the problem.

"Do you think Kendra spoke truth?"

Elgiva glanced at him, puzzled. "About the weather?"

"No! You know!"

Elgiva drew a deep breath, frowned and gazed towards the horizon, as if she were reluctant to confront the facts but knew that she must. "I'm confused," she admitted. "I can't believe it, yet I have to. I'm wondering if I dreamed it all, or if it was the Gale Beer. If it's all true, then it's too much for me to take in. How can I say if she spoke the truth? I don't know her."

"Well, she knows a great deal about you. And, besides, she has the Ninth Book."

"What she knows she could have found out by some means or other and, as far as I'm aware, there is no Ninth Book. It could be just an invention. The trouble is I suspect it *IS* all true and I must face a challenge that will undo me." She turned towards him with a look of helpless anger. "How could they do this to me, Godwin? They keep things a secret for all these years, then suddenly they tell me who I am and what I'm expected to do, like it or not. I've got these powers, so I'm supposed to act accordingly. No time to adjust to it. Here we are searching for a place that may be impossible to find, a Stone whose location is totally unknown, and we're doing it because two long-dead Elves had visions. Doesn't it all seem a bit vague and pointless? I mean…"

She stopped suddenly in her tracks and spread out her arms in a gesture of despair, as though her thoughts defied expression. "We've got nothing definite to guide us. It's not fair, Godwin, and they could … they could at least have given me time to get used to the idea of being a Wardain. They expect me to act differently, but I'm still just me. Imagine, Godwin, if someone came up to you and said, 'Oh, by the way, you can fly, but we didn't want you to know until now, because now we need you to fly to the moon for us."

Godwin nodded his understanding and smiled sympathetically.

"Godwin, if we abandoned this quest and sneaked away somewhere, would anyone notice? Would anything dreadful happen? I wish I knew."

"Of course it would," he replied. "Kendra said that your people were in danger."

"But why must they leave it all up to me?" she demanded. "I know nothing of power."

"Maybe that's all part of the plan," he suggested.

"Plan? Destiny, you mean? If it's all ordained, then what we do has no meaning. If it's all going to happen according to a plan, then it really is pointless. We might as well be pieces on a gaming board."

He shrugged. "Well, I don't know. But we do have minds. We can make choices to alter things."

"Hollow and senseless choices made from some desperate need for self-justification. And all the while we're fooling ourselves, because we can't see that it doesn't really matter. When we're all dead and buried, what will our choices mean then?"

He frowned at her reproachfully. "You're talking nonsense and you know it. Be reasonable, Elgiva. What's the matter with you? I thought you were stronger than this? Just look what you've been through already. This is no time to wallow in self-pity."

She glared at him, her hands on her hips. "How dare you talk to me like that!"

"And what are you going to do about it? Strike me down with magic perhaps?" He folded his arms and regarded her steadily, but inwardly he knew he was still a little unsure of her. "I know it's been a shock for you, but there's no reason why you should take it out on me."

To his relief, he saw the anger fade from her eyes. Abashed, she looked away.

"I'm sorry." She bowed her head and carried on walking. "It's just that sometimes I wonder, if the world just vanished in a blinding flash, would it really matter?"

"Well I, for one, wouldn't exactly be pleased about it. Come on, Elgiva, this isn't like you at all."

"Isn't it?" She shrugged. She walked on in silence for a while, then she turned to face him. "I shouldn't have shouted at you, but … it annoys me when you play father to my child." She looked at him shyly from under her dark lashes.

"You need it."

They smiled at each other, then walked on again. The snow was still drifting about them, like pieces of shredded clouds, and they trod on a crisp, white carpet, marked by their footprints alone.

"Perhaps I'm too hard on you," said Godwin, at length.

She looked at him questioningly, her eyebrows arched and her black hair dusted with crystals of snow.

"If I'd found out about my past the way you have," he said, "I guess I'd be a bit angry, too. I wouldn't know how to react. But the thing is, when you say everything's pointless, well…" His eyes scanned the landscape, as he searched for words, then he continued hesitantly. "You see … I have enough doubts about my actions as it is. You only make it more difficult for me." He looked at her intently and hoped for some gleam of understanding.

"So, you've made the wrong choices," she answered smugly. "A bit too late to worry about it now though. What made you choose to come with me to Misterell anyway? Because Kendra told you to, or do you have something to prove?"

He scowled at her. "You don't trust me."

She refused to answer his question.

"Look," he said sharply, "perhaps I do have something to prove. Perhaps I need to find out what's important … to find out what I really want … what I really am!"

"And you expect to find the answers?"

The condescension in her tone was like a dagger in his heart. Sometimes, he decided, she could be insufferable.

"For Frigg's sake, girl, Can't you see that you and I are driven by the same need?" He looked at her askance and her silence seemed to invite him to continue. "We need to fill some emptiness inside us. An emptiness where self-knowledge ought to be or …I don't know … just self-respect."

She thought about this for a while and then she nodded. "Well," she said, "we'll be lucky to fill that emptiness, whatever it is. I can see us drifting aimlessly, without a reason to be and never finding a home. Not one we're happy in."

"But you *DO* have a reason to be!" he insisted. "You'll be … you *ARE* the Queen of Elindell! You'll put your lands to rights. Is there no reason in that?"

"What if I do? Another wicked Elf will come along, another danger, and it might all be generations ahead, but all the good will turn to evil. Then someone else will have to end that evil and so on, like some never-ending circle. If we all gave up and broke the circle that might not be such a bad idea."

"Death is the only way to break the circle," he said. "Does life really frighten you that much?"

She avoided his gaze, as though this remark were too close to the truth.

"Perhaps life has to be a struggle," he went on. "Without evil, good has no meaning. And the gods have instilled a purpose…"

"Your gods would find other toys to play with."

"Now you're insulting my beliefs!" he flared, battling to control his anger.

"They aren't your beliefs," she told him, "but those of your masters. Can you really believe in a bunch of warlike gods, riding chariots through the clouds and throwing thunderbolts about?" Her alien eyes challenged him, made him sigh with infuriation.

"Why are we quarrelling, Elgiva?"

"We're not. You Wilthkin take umbrage at the slightest thing."

"You really hate us, don't you?"

She refused to answer, but in her eyes was a look of doubt, or regret.

"Well, then," he said wearily, "as you seem to think I'm not the sort of man who can believe in a bunch of warlike gods, what sort of man do you think I am?"

She studied him for a moment. "I don't know. You're different. The Saxons were narrow and boorish and stupid. You could easily be like them, but somehow you're more … sensitive. Something inside you reaches out to something better. You didn't fit in with the Saxons any more than I did." And sometimes, she thought, when

I look at you, I have the strangest feeling that I am looking at myself.

Godwin smiled wryly. "You insult me one minute and compliment me the next. I'll never make you out. Are all Elves so unpredictable?"

"I'm not sure," she said glumly. "I'm not sure of anything."

"No? Well, talking of the beliefs of our masters, you have yet to tell me about yours. Who is this Faine First-Father?"

"Faine?" Elgiva looked taken aback, and, knowing that she was quick to anger, Godwin wished that he had phrased the question more tactfully, but she didn't appear to be annoyed. "Ah, Faine," she said softly, and her black eyes had a misty look, as though it pleased her just to say the name, "the Founder of Elvendom. He wasn't a god, but a living being. We didn't invent him out of a need to have something to believe in."

"But that's something we all need," said Godwin carefully.

She ignored this remark and quickened her pace. Adjusting his pack, Godwin strove to keep up with her, the snow-crust cracking beneath his feet.

"Faine," she continued, "founded our race – the Eldrakin – as we know it now. I don't know where we came from, but we lived in this land long before any of the Wilthkin. Faine united us into one kingdom and he was our first king. In those days, we knew nothing of magic, but it fell to him to discover it."

"How?"

"Bellic said that Faine understood that all things are One. He was One with the Earth and its power. They communed with each other."

"I still don't understand."

She smiled at him in apology. "Sometimes Bellic's lessons were a bit beyond me, too," she confessed. "It's difficult, but … let's just say that by being what he was Faine earned the respect of the Earth Spirit, and so was granted a share of the Earth's magic. And he became a great leader and king, but, even so, he himself was only a servant of a much higher power."

"Which is?"

She shrugged. "Call it Good, or Love, or what you will, it is the life force of the Universe."

Godwin frowned thoughtfully and tried to stretch his mind around the concept of anything larger than a settlement. "Kendra implied that his spirit may still be working for the benefit of your race," he said, knowing himself to be surpassed by the topic, but eager to show his interest.

"It may be so," said Elgiva. "My people believe that life in some form continues after death."

"So do mine," he said.

She looked at him archly. "The Saxons or the Britons?"

"They both do, I think," he replied with a grin, "though Aethelwulf told me that the Britons now worship a single god and their former beliefs have been abandoned. I guess they couldn't believe in a bunch of warlike gods either!" Godwin chuckled at this. "Well, that's according to Aethelwulf the Sage, though I suppose I should say 'Aethelwulf the Dead'. Well, he'll know the truth of it all now, I expect!"

He hoped she would share his humour, but she seemed unamused.

"Wilthkin are strange," said Elgiva. "How can they believe in a load of old gods that no-one has ever seen? And how can they then change their minds and start to worship something else?"

"And how can you make such sweeping statements, when you know so little about us?" he asked, his indignation rising.

"How else can I learn? Bellic told me to see all sides of every subject, but he didn't show me how to. You're my opportunity for finding out about Wilthkin. You're the only one I've ever been able to talk to like an equal, but sometimes, Godwin, you disappoint me with the narrowness of your vision and it's not helpful when you take offence at everything I say."

"By Frigg! Your arrogance is beyond me," he said with a frown of vexation, "however, I can make allowances. Being a father, I am used to ignoring childish behaviour."

She halted in her tracks, glared at him and readied a cutting reply, but the indulgent gleam in his honest eyes softened the edge of her anger. However, she had no intention of letting the matter rest.

"Why must you take everything so seriously?" she asked. His eyes narrowed and he looked away, determined not to be baited. "Why is it so hard for you to stand up for yourself?"

He scowled at her, both hurt and annoyed. "Why is it so hard for you to use magic?"

For an instant, she faltered and tugged thoughtfully at a lock of dark hair, as though considering some deep and complex truth. Then, unexpectedly, she smiled. "Well said."

"No, I'm sorry," he said. "That was cruel. I had no right…"

"You had every right. We're friends, aren't we?"

"I hope so," he replied.

"Then I value your opinions, even when we disagree. Bellic says that true friends can disagree and still be friends."

"You know, Elgiva, I'm sick of hearing what Bellic says," declared Godwin, careless of the consequences. "Don't you have any opinions of your own?"

For a moment, she looked hurt and abashed. She searched his face thoughtfully. "I know one thing," she ventured, "we've spent all our lives being told what to do, what to think, what's right and wrong. We accepted it all. We just listened, but we didn't question any of it. Now we have the freedom to think and say what we please and look what a mess we're making of it."

He relaxed and acknowledged her statement with a nod.

"However," she went on, grinning mischievously, "Bellic says that they who listen learn far more than they who talk. You must have learned a great deal, listening to Othere and his noble counsellors – assuming it was worth the trouble."

He laughed at this. "Some of it was. I was fortunate in being so trusted that he allowed me by his side, when other servants were excluded."

"Like one of his faithful hounds," she said, giving him an arch look.

"Ah, but I had one advantage over them, whenever Othere needed someone to agree with him – which was most of the time. The hounds couldn't talk."

"Or so you believed."

He cocked an eyebrow at her. "I think that all my beliefs are being overturned."

"I know what you mean."

Godwin smiled, then looked up at the sky. "It's past midday. Shall we stop here and eat? I could do with a rest."

"As you wish, but we mustn't stay long. We can cover a lot more ground before dusk."

"I think," said Godwin wryly, "that we've covered more than enough for one day!"

⋆ ⋆ ⋆

They travelled for three more days, while the snow melted around them and the grey clouds fled before the strengthening sun. The leagues drifted by unrecorded in their minds and though the spring unfolded around them, it couldn't distract them from their gloomy thoughts, from the dread that dogged their footsteps.

On the third day, emerging from an ancient wood, they saw the ruins of an abandoned fortress on a flat-topped hill to their left. It had an air of hopelessness about it and did nothing to lighten their spirits. The grimness of their situation wasn't alleviated on the fourth day, when they spied a dark mass on the horizon. Instinctively, they knew that it was the Forest of Shades. It sprawled across the land, like a monstrous animal; sleeping, or lying in wait.

As they approached the outer marge of the forest, it seemed almost to rear up at them, as though frozen in the act of pouncing, and, in the late afternoon silence, they fancied that they could hear the old trees chuckling softly to themselves. They knew that it was only the breeze rustling in the dry, old branches, but still they were uneasy. They hadn't expected to find the forest so soon, nor to find it so grim and forbidding. Now it stood before them, not like an ordinary forest, teeming with natural life, but like a huge, quiet beast with a simmering mind, brooding in the shadows. They were overwhelmed by its size, by the density of the trees, the thickness of the canopy of leaves. Young saplings marched out from among their elders in straggling two's and three's. They looked like sentries, alert for any intruders, and an atmosphere of coiled hostility hung above them like a pall of smoke.

"Not the most welcoming of places," said Godwin.

"I think we've heard too much about it, or perhaps too little," said Elgiva. "We're afraid of the unknown, that's all." She tried to ignore the icy shiver that skittered up her spine.

"I'm not so sure," said Godwin. "I may be a thick-skinned Wilthkin, but it doesn't feel right to me, yet what I can see looks normal enough." He turned to Elgiva and smiled. "Of course," he added, "I've been fooled by appearances before."

Elgiva ignored this remark. "It's a natural fear of dark forests and wild beasts and nothing more."

"Maybe so," he agreed, "but the beasts in this particular dark forest are a bit too quiet for comfort."

They stood and listened, both holding their breath. The forest was still and deathly calm, as though it, too, were listening. Elgiva chewed her lower lip. She wasn't familiar with forests like this, with such a sinister silence.

"What shall we do, then?" she wondered. "It blocks our path to Misterell. You can see how big it is. Can we spare the time to walk around it?"

"Why should we?" asked Godwin. He folded his arms and glared at the trees. "I think we'd be mad to be scared of a forest. The trees can't hurt us, can they?"

Elgiva shrugged. “I don’t see how. But I don’t like it, Godwin. It doesn’t feel right to me either. Night’s drawing on. Perhaps we should make camp here tonight and cross it in the morning.”

“No, let’s carry on,” he said. “If we let this get the better of us, when worse things lie ahead, how shall we cope with those? Come on, Elgiva. I thought Elves lived in forests?”

“Not ones like this!” she declared.

Godwin extended his hand, palm upward. “It’s starting to rain. That settles it. I’m not getting soaked out here. We’ll have more shelter among the trees. Kendra said it would only take a couple of hours to cross the forest, so we can walk through it now and make camp on the far side. We’ll sleep much better, knowing it’s behind us.”

Elgiva’s large eyes were full of misgiving. “Remember what Kendra told us? We mustn’t stop for any reason. Do you think we can make it? It’s getting dark.”

“We can try,” he replied. “There’s a few hours of daylight left yet.”

“Are you being sensible, or just very brave?”

“I’m trying to be both,” he replied with a grin.

Elgiva considered the dark forest and then turned to look at her friend. “Very well,” she said, “lead on.”

* * *

Inside the forest it was much darker than they had expected. Branches coiled like snakes above them, blotting out the light. A strange gloom filled the air, a chill as dank as a dungeon, and the soil gave off a rancid odour beneath their wary feet.

They felt obliged to carry on, despite the darkness and unnatural calm, but the underwood grew thicker and they gradually lost their sense of direction, and soon they began to appreciate the folly of their decision.

They knew they shouldn't stop, but it was useless to continue. When they reached a glade that offered relief from the tangle of thorny shrubs, Godwin suggested that they stop and make camp. Reluctantly, Elgiva agreed and together they gathered wood for a fire.

Slipping his arms out of the straps, Godwin dropped his pack to the ground with a sigh of relief, then he spread out his cloak beneath a towering elm. "The soil's damp," he said, frowning. "I hope it doesn't seep through my cloak."

Elgiva sank down upon it. "I'll soon complain, if it does," she said. She watched him as he built a fire a few yards further off. His movements were quick and competent; such menial tasks held no mystery for him. Soon the wood was crackling with flames that nudged the darkness back against the trees. "What have we left to eat?"

Godwin stood up and strode towards her, inspected their pack of provisions.

"Some cheese … oatcakes … dried fruit … bread." As he spoke, he shared out the food between them. "And there's something I've been saving for a time of extremity!" With a grin and a flourish he drew out a jug with a stopper in the neck. "Gale Beer!" Removing the stopper, he sniffed expectantly at the contents. "By Frigg, it might have gone off! Actually … smells like horse linament."

Elgiva swallowed the bread she had been chewing and let loose a peal of laughter. It echoed through the brooding forest, then faded into silence. Godwin drew his breath in sharply as a chill ran up his spine.

"The fire won't last long," he said. "We're going to need more wood." He shuddered at the thought of being plunged into darkness in this cold and gloomy place. "Perhaps the ale will warm us, before it rots our guts." He tasted it warily and screwed up his face. "It's not so bad," he said.

They sat in silence, pretending to be brave, and shared the food and ale, and, before they knew it, the latter was all gone. Godwin emptied the last of it into his mouth and cursed at the bitterness of the dregs. In a sudden flare of temper, he swung back his arm and hurled the jug across the glade with all the strength he could muster. It struck against one of the nearest trees and broke into jagged pieces.

Elgiva sighed at his outburst, but it didn't claim all her attention. She was focused instead on the sound of the rain, as it sifted through the leaves above them. It resembled the angry hissing of serpents.

Both of them were quietly aware of the forest's oppressive aura and Godwin felt suddenly queasy. He blamed his nausea on the ale, but suspected that fear was the real culprit. If only he could hear the hoot of an owl, the scream of a fox; natural things, things he understood. But this creeping darkness wasn't right. This dread of something intangible had no remedy known to him.

He wrapped his arms about his chest, trying to maintain control. Silently, he cursed Kendra for putting ideas into his head.

"I don't feel very well."

Elgiva's announcement startled him, but he pulled himself together. Sliding his arm around her back, he drew her to his side. As though she were an ailing child, to distract her from discomfort, he began to tell her a tale her had once heard in the Meadhall: a hundred years ago, it seemed. But he found he couldn't look at her. The effort of focusing made him feel giddy.

He chattered on, being dimly aware that his friend was listening raptly, and, as he continued to tell her the tale, a saga of valour in battle, a change occurred in his mood.

He ceased abruptly and looked around like a man who had lost his way. Then he scowled at the encircling trees. Elgiva tugged at his sleeve.

"What happened next?" she asked him.

"What?"

"The story, Godwin. You were telling me a story."

"Frigg take the stupid story! What about this forest?"

"I don't know what you mean."

"If there are any monsters here, I bet they're too scared to come out."

He struggled clumsily to his feet, while she watched him through half-closed eyes. "What monsters are these?" she asked wearily.

He cocked his fists on his hips. "That old crone Kendra has frightened us stupid. Come on, now, admit it."

"I don't know…" She sighed. Her head felt suddenly heavy and needed support from her hands.

"What if she made it all up?" he persisted. "There's nothing wrong with this forest at all. It's lies, by Frigg! Just lies."

"If she lied about the forest, then she lied about…"

"Dangerous trees? Shit. We've been here ages and they're not attacking us, are they?"

Elgiva arched her delicate brows, baffled by Godwin's manner, but then she gasped as he drew his sword and waved it at the shadows.

"If you're so bloody dangerous, come on then, do your damnedest! You know who this is?" He flung out his arm, swaying drunkenly, and pointed at Elgiva. "This, my friends, is an Elf-queen … no … *THE* Elf-queen, the Ordained One!"

"Godwin, please…"

"This is a Wardain, you stupid bastards, and, if you give us any trouble, she'll sort you all out, don't you worry."

"You're drunk," she said. At the back of her mind, Kendra was saying 'danger and deceit', but she felt strangely bold and a strong desire to burst out laughing took her by surprise.

Godwin span round to face her, hoping to see her eyes alight with the stirring of magic and the very idea made a thrill of dark pleasure course along his veins. He couldn't resist the urge to goad her. "You're the greatest of Elves. Why don't you prove it? Kendra would want you to practice."

"But you said she made everything up."

"What are you waiting for? Are you afraid?"

"Kendra said not to…"

"What right has she to tell you what to do?"

"What right have you?"

He looked at her for a moment, then he shrugged with indifference and sheathed his sword. "I'm disappointed," he said sulkily. "I thought to find some courage in that icy heart of yours."

She pushed herself upright. Beside the elm, discarded branches lay among the shadows and she stooped and grasped one. Then she turned to her friend.

"Courage enough to knock your brains out!"

She circled him threateningly, waving the branch, but he merely laughed at her. "I don't expect you to blow up the world or anything half so drastic," he said. "Something small will suffice. Can't you do something about the fire? It'll soon be out and we'll be cold. Seems like a sensible idea to me. That's using magic wisely, I'd say."

Elgiva looked deeply into his eyes, afraid and puzzled and indecisive. She knew that she was swaying where she stood. The influence of the ale, no doubt, or was it something else? Something she couldn't identify was slithering into her mind.

"Of course, if you can't ... If it's too much for you..." He looked away with apparent disinterest, but inside he was churning with fear and excitement. "Perhaps you're not up to much after all."

A sudden lust for violence took possession of Elgiva. It was odd. It appalled her. But it couldn't be resisted. She gripped the branch with both hands and exerted enough force upon it to snap it in two.

Godwin appeared briefly perturbed by what Elgiva had done, but recovered his wits sufficiently to quip, "We can all snap rotten twigs, you know. Is that the extent of your powers?"

A wicked grin spread over his face and Elgiva matched it with one of her own. The air reeked of conspiracy and they knew that it was aimed at them, but also that they were a part of it. There was both such hatred and love in their hearts that this chaotic mix of feelings went beyond all the bounds of reason. There was no going back for either of them. The game must be played out for good or ill.

* * *

Chapter Sixteen

Elgiva hurled the riven branch angrily into the shadows, swept back the gleaming darkness of her hair. "You want fire, Godwin?" she asked with a chilling softness. "Then you shall have it!"

She threw her mantle aside, as though preparing for combat, and her eyes smouldered with a fierce, determined light. As she looked at Godwin, her gaze was feverish with the possibilities of power and it made excitement seethe in his breast. His legs felt boneless, incapable of support, and anticipation left him breathless. As if entranced, he watched her turn towards a tree behind him. Then she raised her arms, as though in greeting.

Imprisoned in a dark chamber, deep within his mind, a tiny voice pleaded no, no, no, but he pushed it down even deeper and crushed it into silence.

The tree was a veteran of many winters; the trunk gnarled and brittle-barked. Its denuded branches strained upwards to the canopy above, where they burst into leaf, as though the air below the forest's roof were poisonous to life.

"I know no suitable incantations, so this will have to do," said Elgiva. "I command you, denizen of the dark forest, I compel, I order you to take fire and perish. I, Elgiva, Queen of Elindell would have it so. It is my will"

Her voice began strongly, confidently, but soon trailed away to embarrassed giggling. After a while it became apparent that nothing was going to happen and a silence fraught with apprehension swooped into the glade. Elgiva glanced furtively at Godwin, who frowned with frustration, his expectations thwarted.

"You've not done it right!" he protested.

"I've not been taught!" she snapped. "I don't know what to do. I feel … I feel silly."

"And so you are, by Frigg!"

"Damn you, then I'll try again!"

Inhaling deeply, she flexed her fingers, trying to grapple with her inexperience. Closing her eyes, she strained to focus her will upon the tree. A furrow of effort appeared on her brow and her hands became clenched into fists.

By Faine! she gritted, I will find the power. This spell will not surpass me!

Then she felt a tightening within her, a shiver of passion that ran down her limbs. It was a strange, alarming sensation, but it pleased her, even so. It thrilled along her nerves, yearning for release.

Suddenly, her eyes sprang open, shining with confidence, and, tossing back her long hair, she once more confronted the tree.

"You hideous, evil tree!" she cried, "I command the Earth-magic and you will obey me. I order you to take fire and perish. As I say, so mote it be!"

Still nothing happened, but time passed and the sky grew heavy with darkness.

Elgiva's impatience flared upwards, boiled like magma. She stamped her foot in frustration and, almost at once, she felt the heat leave her in a dizzy rush of madness that sucked the strength from her limbs.

"This is ridiculous!" Godwin fumed, spinning round to face her. "How can a tree just burst into flames?"

Hardly had he spoken these words, when a roar of hot air sent him staggering. In amazement he turned and gaped at the tree, which was now engulfed in fire. Grinning with delight, he rushed up to Elgiva and grasped her by the shoulders. "You did it, by Grim! You did it!"

Elgiva pushed him away and stepped back and her face wore a look of horror. "Faine, oh, Faine! Just look what I've done! Godwin … this is murder!"

"What do you mean?" he demanded, unable to comprehend her remorse. "Elgiva, look! It's wonderful!"

She gaped at him, as though he were loathsome. "But the tree is alive …alive!"

"So? It's only a bloody tree. Trees don't feel, you stupid girl."

She stepped forward quickly, knotted her small fists in the fabric of his tunic, and tried to shake him, though she hadn't the strength. "Of course they do!" she cried. "I know, damn you! Because your senses don't stretch that far, you dismiss the suffering of other creatures. How do you know what a tree feels? You're not a tree. You're a pompous, selfish Wilthkin!"

He grabbed her by the wrists and easily unhooked her hands from his tunic. "And not so long ago, I was different. I was sensitive. Now that I don't agree with you, I'm suddenly pompous and selfish."

"And so you are! And this is all your fault. You provoked me!"

"You were easily provoked," he countered.

"You wanted me to do that," she said, gesturing wildly towards the tree, "to satisfy your need for excitement. You're just like all the rest of them. A bloody barbarian.

You're cruel. I hate you!" Her dark eyes flashed with loathing.

"Don't think the feeling isn't mutual. You think you have all the answers, don't you? You and your Faine and your bloody magic. You're an arrogant, little sprite from the woods and you've no right to preach to me!"

She flew at him in a desperate rage, kicking and scratching and flailing her fists, while he tried to fend her off. The shadows billowed up around them, gyrating about the burning tree, and flakes of its blistering flesh wafted skywards, while the rain steamed in its branches.

Caught between darkness and light, Elgiva and Godwin struggled; struggled with each other and with a will that was not their own. And all the while the burning tree screamed out its rage and anguish, but they were deaf to everything, save the thunder of darkness in their minds, and paid it no heed.

But its brothers and sisters heard it. The earth and the sky heard it.

The shadows heard it.

As the rain grew in strength and momentum, it began to sift through the lattice-work of branches and its whisperings cooled the frenzy in the glade.

Suddenly, Elgiva felt a mist leave her mind and she reeled with the pain of awareness. Panting, she pulled away from Godwin, her muscles slack with exertion.

"Stop! Godwin, let me stop it. Let me save the tree!"

He was deaf to her plea and didn't reply. Without warning, he struck her hard across the face and sprawled her in the grass. Stunned by the blow, she was helpless to resist as he pinned her to the ground. Her vision occluded by whirls of darkness, she watched him unsheath his sword. Firelight danced along its edge like glee.

No, she protested weakly. You can't! But she couldn't say the words.

The forest shivered in its cloak of darkness and a pulse of desire left its murky heart and rumbled along the forest floor.

Elgiva fought the blackness in her mind and struggled in Godwin's grip. "The forest is angry," she managed to wail. "Listen! Can't you hear it? I've done murder. It will kill us both!"

"I'll save it the trouble of killing you!" he said, with laughter that was not his own.

Leaning forwards, he pressed the edge of the blade against her neck, with the pressure of a kiss and the spite of an old adversary. As he did so, his arms were trembling, as though they feared to obey him, but his mouth was set in a grim line of cruelty.

He dragged the blade across her throat.

Elgiva winced as her soft flesh felt the bite of the cutting edge and a sticky wetness trickled down her neck. The smart brought tears to her eyes. "Fool," she croaked. "We'll die …we trespass!" She grabbed his wrists to hold him away.

"It's all your fault," he snarled at her. "Everything is your doing. You seduced me from my family."

"You seduced yourself."

"An answer for everything, haven't you! You're evil clothed in flesh. As all Elves are. Cajolers of men. You're demons. You're filth. Every last one of you!" His blue eyes burned with a fearsome intensity that was nothing short of madness and it left Elgiva so empty of will that she could hardly recall who she was. "It's my duty to free the world from the tyranny of evil Elves. It's my duty... it is ... my duty..."

He slowly raised his sword arm. For a moment, he held it high, trembling and poised to strike. For a moment, a blood-lust boiled in his breast, his mind devoted to her destruction.

But, no ... no ...Not his mind...

Not *HIS* mind.

His eyes widened suddenly in horror. "Oh, Grim, Elgiva! The gods know ... the gods know ... I can't! I could never..." He hesitated, shivering, in the grip of conflicting desires, as if torn by some inner struggle. Then lowering the sword, he looked at it with a grimace of disgust, seeming to see it for the first time. "What...?"

Finally, he hurled the blade aside. It span through the air with a flash of silver and landed in the bushes. Aghast at his hunger for violence, he looked down at his friend and her stupefied stare made him cringe with self-loathing. Filled with remorse, he snatched her to his breast.

"Elgiva, forgive me! Am I mad? What in Frigg's name was I thinking of?"

"It wasn't you ...The forest ... the forest..." she insisted hoarsely. "It's using you. You must fight it, Godwin."

He pulled away from her, studied her face, and a frown appeared on his brow. Still he fought to subdue the turmoil in his mind, and still the strange voices invaded his brain with their sly, seductive whispering.

"Don't let them," pleaded Elgiva. "The trees are making sport with you. You mustn't let them use you."

But even as she implored him to be strong, Elgiva felt the forest's coercion seizing hold of her again. Its madness was flooding into her mind. She was aware of it now; knew what it was. She felt the collective intelligence of the trees. It was their only defence against intruders, but, also, it was their sport. Together, their warped and savage wills became an awesome weapon.

And she knew herself inferior in the face of such dark power. She had no defence against the malice of the trees. They toyed with her and her friend, wrapped them up like flies in a web, and their might was irresistible. Appalled though she was, she didn't have time to wonder at the unknown ill that lay behind this corruption, that had spawned such unnatural spite. All her mental resources were needed to try and block out the forest's will. She had to close her mind to it somehow, so it wouldn't discover her weaknesses and turn them all against her.

But it was a battle she couldn't win.

As she looked at Godwin, she became aware of his lean strength and the way his hair gleamed red and gold in the light from the burning tree. She thought she saw passion shine in his eyes, his honest eyes so intensely blue, and she realised that he had beauty she had never noticed before. And she… why she had power. Power to compel, to take, to possess…

"Use me?" cried Godwin suddenly. "No-one uses ME! I'm free to do as I please. Free to be the master of any I choose!" He gripped her slight body in a firm embrace and a look that was neither hate nor love took possession of his eyes. "Elves are beautiful really," he murmured. He pressed her to the ground and lowered his weight upon her. "In fact, I think I'll kiss you."

"Don't!" she begged him. I want this, she thought. I don't want this. "They'll force me to use my powers against you."

He laughed softly, scorning her words, and she knew that it was the will of the forest that drove him to act in this way.

Or was it, she wondered, like the truth found in wine?

No, no, she must ignore the voices that chattered in her brain. This wasn't Godwin; he was her friend. And part of him was fighting, trying. To use her power against him would be cruel, disloyal and cowardly. It was what the forest desired. The forest would drive them insane and watch as they killed each other. The trees were feeding upon their emotions, drugging themselves with vicarious pleasure. She must deny them, but...

But, oh, how she wanted to hurt him.

He pressed his mouth upon hers and she struggled and beat at him with her fists, but he held her arms without effort. His strength filled her with longing and, abruptly, she relaxed, her mouth yielding to his.

The trees around them thrashed their limbs and the air was filled with their creakings and rattlings. The forest was one dark mind, with one emotion, one desire, and it stood round its prey like a circle of malice. In its depths strange wailings echoed, like the cries of souls that were long ago lost. But for all their power and lust, the trees were still mere rooted things, fixed till death in the earth, and their venomous sap seethed with frustration. The coalition of their wills was their only weapon, their only sport, their only hope of joy.

Godwin released Elgiva suddenly. Drawing away, he grew still and alert. A wordless voice had warned him of danger, but from whence did it come? He frowned in confusion. Somewhere in the undergrowth there lay a feeling of abhorrence, but he couldn't identify the source of the protest. Perhaps he had imagined it, but the cries in the distance were real enough.

"Wild beasts," he whispered.

Reaching out, Elgiva knotted her hands in the fabric of his tunic, as though their separation filled her with chagrin.

For a long moment of anguish, Godwin forgot who and where he was; forgot what lustful act he had planned to commit. He looked down at Elgiva, his heart thudding with panic, and she regarded him strangely, a smile on her lips and mischief in her alien eyes. Reaching up, she ran her fingers softly down his cheek.

"No," she breathed, "not beasts. The trees are mocking us."

He snatched her hand from his face. "That's impossible!" he cried. "Why should they?"

Her eyes held his unflinchingly, though their focus seemed elsewhere. "Because they can." She giggled softly.

Scowling, he stumbled to his feet and the forest whirled dizzily around him. "Those bushes … they've moved! They're closer!"

"Illusion," laughed Elgiva.

Brusquely, he dragged her upright and shook her by the shoulders. "By Frigg! What's going on?" he demanded.

Elgiva fought for self-control. "We must leave this place … at once. Or never leave at all." Her voice was lacking in intonation, though her eyes reflected the pain of self-mastery. "Can you get our stuff together?"

He stared at her for a moment, perplexed by the tone of her voice. She seemed indifferent to their plight. She gave him a crooked smile, devoid of warmth or humour, and he quickly let her go. He didn't want to look at her and a shudder convulsed his muscles.

As he went to collect their belongings, a calm as cold as the grave seemed to settle into his bones. He felt as though he had woken from a dream, as if some part of his mind had been absent. While he hoisted their gear onto his back, Elgiva approached the discarded sword, which lay in the shadows, strangled by briars. She reached down slowly and grasped the hilt.

A shudder of revulsion shivered from the blade into her arm and stung her. Surprise and bafflement narrowed her eyes and fanned the flames of her anger. How was it possible that this miserable hunk of metal could protest at being handled? She felt its denial like a physical force.

She grinned to herself. More tricks.

She turned to watch the burning tree. Whips of fire lashed its neighbours. Holding the sword up before her face, she whispered to the blade. "You will work my will."

Briefly a doubt crept into her mind and the grin died on her lips. The sword seemed to deny her, to accuse her with its metallic integrity.

But the forest tightened its grip.

She glared at the tangled underwood. So, you *HAVE* moved closer, she thought. Or *IS* it all illusion? I'm not a fool and I'll make you pay for trying to deceive an Elven queen. I could reverse the spell and save your friend, but I won't. Your tricks will avail you nothing."

"Are you ready?" called Godwin anxiously.

He was waiting some yards from where she stood, impatient to be away. Slowly, she turned to face him.

"So, you would kill me, would you?" She touched the cut on her throat and he gave her a puzzled look. "Defile me, would you, Wilthkin scum?" She stepped towards him and lifted the sword. "I have no need of this. I could deal with you as I dealt with that tree, but I'd rather do it your way."

"Elgiva ...what...?"

Running forwards, she drew back the sword, then swung at Godwin with all her might. The weapon sliced through the thick, smoky air. Godwin, taken by complete surprise, made a desperate attempt to avoid the blade as it slashed towards his head, but his body felt suddenly numb and leaden and it caught him on the shoulder. It fell from his attacker's hand and landed on the grass.

He staggered under the impact and stumbled to his knees, but he felt no pain, just disbelief. He knew that his shoulder must be cut to the bone, but it didn't seem to concern him. He saw Elgiva flit away, like a shadow among the trees, and he knew only that he must follow her. And he must catch her; she had to be stopped.

As he ran from the clearing, his sword lay behind him, forgotten, on the grass.

* * *

Deep in the forest, creatures were stirring; unseen things that crawled and slithered. Drawn to the forest's evil aura, they had driven out its natural inhabitants. Now intruders were in their midst and must be rooted out,

As Elgiva ran, laughing, through the trees, she knew that hideous, hapless creatures followed in her wake, but she was far too bold with power to pay them any heed. Magic pulsed in every vein and her mind was awash with reckless endeavours. She felt herself proof against any threat; capable of any madness. She could blow up the world, if she wanted to. She could turn it upside down.

But where was the fun in that?

She slid to a halt in a broad glade densely flanked by ancient trees and the moon's mottled face looked down at her from a ragged patch of sky. She turned around slowly and laughed at the trees. "I'll turn you upside down instead!"

They faced her in their silent ranks, encompassing her slight figure like a wall of gnarled and twisted stanchions, leprous in the moonlight.

"How would you feel with your roots in the air? Don't think I can't do it. I've got magic now," she jeered. She laughed at their silence, their impotent rage. "I'll teach you all a lesson!" Spreading her arms, she turned in a circle and summoned up her powers. "I command you all to be uprooted and upended in the name of Faine, in the name of the Queen of Elindell! I command you all to turn upside down!"

The old trees simmered with helpless rage, yet secretly they laughed. They saw their adversary's lack of skill, her petulance and fatigue, and they knew that her magic was weak and unfocused. And they had seen far greater power. They were well acquainted with mature magic, with the evil powers of the Elven lord who held them all in thrall. It was he who had taught them to hate and destroy and the pleasure that it brought. Let this feeble creature do her worst with her puny, childish magic. When the Elf-lord learned of this violation, she would suffer pains unending.

Elgiva stamped her foot in frustration and screamed at the towering trees. "I know what you're thinking, you evil trees! You want to turn my power against me, but you can't … you can't! It's mine!" She sank to her knees and beat the earth with her fists. "I commanded you and you will obey! You will be overturned!"

It was then that Godwin dashed out of the shadows. As he stood awhile to catch his breath, he heard Elgiva's wild demand, saw the fever of effort that slicked her brow and he wondered what he should do. Fearing to intervene, he dreaded more the outcome of allowing her to continue.

And there was an added danger. A quickening breeze had started up and was fanning the flames of the burning tree. Godwin now sensed the fire at his back, heard its distant roar, as the flames leapt from tree to tree. They had to flee the forest.

"Defy me, will you?" cried Elgiva. "Damn you. Curse you. Wither and die, you ugly, unnatural spawn of rotten fruit!" Picking up twigs and clods of soil, she threw them at the trees, and tears of vexation spilled from her eyes, like the tears of a thwarted child. "You think I'm weak, but I'll show YOU! I've not been taught, that's all. All I need is practice, then you'll tremble at my name. Then you'll know what fear is!" She lowered her eyes and sniffed back her tears. "Stop laughing at me … you monsters."

Seeing the childish behaviour of his friend, Godwin's anxiety melted away and he found himself actually smiling, like a father who, intending to scold, was moved by love to forbearance. Concern for Elgiva chased away the last of the forest's enchantment and he felt whole and sane once more.

"I have your measure," he said out loud, "and you won't fool me again. Silly, old forest, you've had your fun and I've had enough of your tricks. By Grim! What a dismal collection of tired, old ruins you are!"

Elgiva glared at him in protest. "They dare to defy me, but I'll find a way."

"Be silent, girl," he commanded sternly. He strode towards her purposefully and dragged her to her feet and she stared at him in anger and surprise. "Be reasonable, can't you! We've more important things to do than waste our time on these sad, old sticks of firewood. Where is your will-power? For Frigg's sake, come to your senses!"

She clenched her fists at him. "How dare you!"

"I dare, Elgiva. Don't be so bloody pompous. You have no more idea of how to use magic than I do, but I promise you, when you have mastered your powers, if you ever use them this way again, I personally will kill you. So help me."

Elgiva gaped at him, completely abashed and unable to speak.

"This is a place of madness," he said, "but now it must end. The forest is alight." He grasped her shoulders and shook her firmly, but his words were gentle and soft. "Can you understand what I'm saying?"

She blinked at him, clearing the tears from her eyes, then nodded, and he released her.

"Forgive me for what I did to you … for what I would have done," he said, ashamed. "I'd never, never hurt you. It was the will of the forest. At least … I have to believe that."

She shied away from his gaze and clawed the strands of hair from her face. "Godwin … listen …I…" She looked about her, as though bewildered to see the shards of her reason scattered at her feet. "Who can say what lies hidden in the shadows of the mind?"

She drew a deep breath and looked at him and, for a while, they stood with their eyes locked together, sharing their shame, and their understanding. Then they hugged each other for their mutual comfort, welding their different natures into an alloy of strength.

Reluctantly, Elgiva broke the embrace. "I fear the trees haven't finished with us yet. I think we'd better leave."

As if in answer, a distant growling rumbled through the forest. Something large was smashing its way through the trees and strange cries echoed in the darkness. Smoke rode the back of the freshening wind and an orange glow flared between the tree trunks, as flames gnawed their way through the forest, leaping from bough to bough.

"There may be Fellkin here!" cried Elgiva, knotting her fists in Godwin's tunic, her large eyes round with terror.

He grabbed her arm and they turned to run, but, to their horror, a mass of brambles reared up in their path. The underwood had crawled towards them, stealthy and silent and rife with barbs. On what had been an open stretch of ground there stood a tangle of thorny shrubs.

"By Frigg! It's impossible!" Godwin cried. "We're trapped … the forest has trapped us!"

Elgiva span round. Wherever she looked, their path was blocked by shrubs and briars and weeds. "It knows it's going to die and it's making sure that we die with it!"

"We have no choice, Elgiva. We must get through these brambles. Look … it's thinnest here!"

He grabbed her hand and pulled her along and they struggled through the briars. Behind them they heard the fangs of the fire devouring the old, dry wood, but Elgiva also heard the trees, screaming as they burned. She was moved to pity and stopped in her tracks.

"What is it?" demanded Godwin.

"The trees," she moaned, "the trees! They're helpless ... they're screaming! Perhaps I can..."

"What? What can you do?"

Bewildered and anguished, she shook her head and fresh tears spilled from her eyes.

"You can do nothing!" he told her sharply. "This is an evil place, Elgiva. Better to let it burn!"

"Evil ... What is evil? You said that without it, good has no meaning."

"We haven't time for this!" he shouted, tugging at her arm.

"But don't you see ... to this forest, evil is good and good is evil. It knows no other way!"

"I don't give a damn!" he cried.

"It's all my fault," she sobbed, hiding her face in her hands, and her legs began to fold beneath her.

"By Frigg!" He seized her roughly and dragged her along. "Debates about good and evil can wait, and you can't reverse the spell. Not now. In the name of Frigg, be reasonable. Would the forest have cared about *US*?"

Reluctantly, she stumbled on through the tangled vegetation.

Brambles tried to snare their legs and branches thrashed at their faces and they scrambled on in desperation, unsure of the way ahead. The further they went, the thicker the brambles, and their strength was beginning to flag.

Elgiva stumbled and couldn't get up; the sharp thorns held her down. As Godwin tried to wrench her free, the cruel barbs ripped their hands and faces.

"I can't do this!" she wailed. "I can't! Just leave me here to die!"

Godwin tried to calm her, but his throat was clogged with panic. He could plainly hear the fire behind them. "Don't struggle!" he pleaded, and his voice cracked with stress. "You'll only get more entangled!" He seized her hand firmly and felt the sticky warmth of her blood mingle with his own. "Wrap your cloak about you ... tightly... Protect yourself from the thorns."

Somehow he succeeded in hauling her upright. Putting his arm around her, he pressed her body close to his and guided her through the briars, groping ahead with his free hand. Their progress was slow, but now they had plenty of light, as the fire drew ever closer. Smoke stung their eyes and rain hissed like malice in the canopy above. The smart of their cuts and bruises was agony.

They knew it was hopeless. The forest had won.

Then a brave hope flickered in Godwin's brain, one that he hardly dared voice. "If I only had my sword, perhaps I could hack a way out of this mess."

He looked at Elgiva and she clutched at his tunic. "Perhaps I could ... Why not?" Her large eyes gleamed in the ochre-tinted darkness.

"Could you?" he wondered, gasping with fatigue.

"I have to try. I know I couldn't clear these brambles, but retrieving your sword ... well ... there is need!" She felt her pulse thudding in her throat and she gulped down air to steady herself. "I need some words to help me focus."

For several moments she stood in silence, trying to find the place within where she knew that her magic slumbered. She clamped her hands over her ears to blot out the roar of the fire and her body shook with the extremity of her plight.

Siriol, Faine, somebody … help me.

"Sword of steel, hear what I say,

"Hie to your master without delay.

"Leave the place where now you sit.

"I have spoken; so be it."

She felt a faint, warm tingling in her limbs; a brief flare of giddy excitement, but it passed so swiftly she feared that she had failed.

Suddenly, Godwin heard a thud, as something heavy fell at his feet. His gasp drew Elgiva's gaze towards him. Stooping awkwardly, obstructed by briars, he touched the object and instantly recoiled.

"Ow! It's hot!" he declared. For a moment, they both laughed with relief. "Thank the gods I sharpened it! When it's cool, I'll make short work of these bushes."

Elgiva looked down at the glinting weapon. Retrieving the sword had been easy. Too easy. She felt that it had wanted the summons. She wiped the sweat from her eyes with her sleeve.

"It's cool now," she said. "You can pick it up." He looked at her and hesitated. "Trust me," she said, with a smile.

* * *

Chapter Seventeen

A golden sun peeped over the horizon and daylight illumined the dim, grey land. Godwin and Elgiva found themselves lying on open ground, where exhaustion had left them the previous night. Godwin sat up slowly, feeling stiff and sore and bewildered. He had no idea where he was. His face and hands were covered in scratches and his clothes were torn by brambles, but his sword was in its scabbard and his knife was in his belt. Their pack lay beside him on the sodden earth. It seemed that all he had lost were his wits.

Elgiva sat up, stretched and yawned, as Godwin got to his feet.

"I'm soaked," he complained.

"Where are we?" she asked.

She rubbed her eyes with her knuckles and scanned the landscape hopefully, as though seeking a friend in a roomful of strangers. As she pulled herself to her feet, Godwin glanced at her sheepishly.

"I suppose I should apologise. What happened in the forest was all my fault. We shouldn't have crossed it so late in the day," he said.

"Do you think it would have been safer at any other time?" Elgiva shook her head. "I think we should forget it." She tried to smile to assuage his feelings of guilt. "We survived, didn't we? Let's put it behind us."

They both looked back at the forest and to their surprise it was now transformed into naked, black and smouldering spars, where once whole trees had stood.

Some of them had survived on the margin, but the heart of the forest was gone.

"A blaze like that would have been visible for miles. We couldn't have done a better job of announcing our arrival. I mean, we're close to Misterell, aren't we?" Godwin scanned the landscape ahead and his eyes narrowed thoughtfully. "North-west, Kendra said. We'd better get moving. We'll have to skirt around that hill, past those clumps of willow. But we should have some breakfast before we go."

Elgiva followed the line of his gaze, while he knelt on the ground and rummaged through their pack. "What clumps of willow?"

He straightened up and squinted at the hill. "I could have sworn…"

"Perhaps my great-uncle's not an old fool after all, unless you're both prone to seeing things."

He handed her a chunk of bread. "Elgiva? I know you said to forget it, but…"

She turned to face him. "What?"

"What happened in the forest … did it really happen?"

"Haven't we the wounds to prove it?" She lifted her chin and bared her throat. Across the smooth, pale skin was a shallow, red cut, covered by a crust of dried blood: the work of Godwin's sword.

"Elgiva, I could have killed you!"

A sudden realisation widened her eyes. "And … and I YOU!" Her hand flew to her mouth in sick horror.

Godwin touched the wound on his shoulder, which, until this moment, they had both forgotten. Nauseated at what he might find, he explored the site of the injury and the colour drained from his face. Elgiva snatched his hand away, determined to see the extent of her crime, but then she gaped in bewilderment. Although the fabric of his tunic was slashed, the skin beneath it was unmarked.

"I don't understand!" she cried.

"Elgiva ... how...?"

"I don't know, Godwin. I just don't know! But I know it happened. All of it did. I hit you with all the strength I could find, though it shames me to admit it. I should have taken off your arm! And look, we're covered in scratches. It must have happened, but why I'm injured and you're not, I just can't explain."

Did it really happen, she wondered, that night of panic and madness? If not, were the powers she had used a mere illusion, a trick of the forest?

"Dwelling on it isn't going to do us any good," she said. "And if we're close to Misterell, weirder things might happen yet. We need to doubt everything we see."

"Including the evidence we leave behind us?" He nodded towards the forest.

"Can we believe what our eyes tell us in such a place as this?"

"It's hard not to," he replied. "How else will we know what is and what is not?"

"Our hearts must guide us, as Bellic's guided him when he sought the kingdom of Misterell." Abruptly she ceased and turned away. "I sometimes wonder if it isn't *ALL* an illusion. Life itself, I mean. Do you ever feel that way?"

He smiled and took her hand. "I may have lost my bearings, but I can't doubt reality or the fact of my existence. I have substance and so do you. Last night..." His expression grew more serious, as he tried to recall their ordeal, "if all else was illusion, I touched your blood. My blood and yours, they mingled, and … something we shared was real. I know that as surely as I know my own name…" He checked himself abruptly and frowned. "But I don't really know that, do I?" He dropped her hand and sighed. "It's not easy for me, Elgiva. This world is so unlike the one I know."

"And mine. Magic has always frightened me, but now that I know I'm a Wardain, there's something that frightens me more."

"What's that?"

"I've no solid proof that I *HAVE* any magic … and no hope of learning to use it, if I do."

"Well, there's only one way to find out." He hoisted their pack onto his shoulders. "Truth won't come to us. We must go and find it."

He extended his hand towards her and she took it gladly and smiled, and together they set off on their quest for Misterell.

* * *

For the rest of that day and the next, they travelled on with grey clouds and grey thoughts for company. On the third day, the sun warmed and burned off the clouds and the landscape around them glowed with new vigour. Woodland plants stretched out their soft, new leaves and danced in the sun-haze beneath the trees and the air was vibrant with the sounds of spring and heavy with its perfume.

As they emerged from a wooded area and crossed a sun-filled meadow, they saw two figures some way ahead. One was a dun-coloured pony; the other an old man in a dirty, grey robe, who sat on the ground beside the animal, looking woebegone. As Elgiva and Godwin approached him, he rubbed his ankle with arthritic fingers and muttered to himself. He seemed to be frail and harmless and Godwin ventured to speak to him.

"Hello, old man. What's amiss?"

Startled, the man's eyes widened in fear. His thin, white hair, standing stiff on his skull, gave him an air of distraction. Godwin approached him carefully.

"Can we help you?" he asked.

The old man grinned at him, revealing stained and broken teeth. "Oh, what a blessing to see you, lad! Yes, indeed, what a place to be lost in," he said, his voice hoarse with age and distress.

"Are you hurt?" asked Elgiva gently.

"Ye gods! What kind of creature's this?" exclaimed the old man and he clutched at an amulet of amber that dangled around his neck.

"Don't be afraid," said Godwin soothingly. "You're safe with us, I promise."

"By all the stars! A Briton and an Elf! Strange company for an old Saxon to fall in with. An' I'm safe, say you?"

"I promise you," said Godwin. "Now, what's wrong with your foot?"

"Fell an' twisted it on some rocks. By the ancients! But what I'm doin' out here, the gods wot not. An' this ole pony be no use nor ornament. Stubborn, that's what she is."

"Where are you bound?" Elgiva asked.

"Like I told you, I'm lost," he replied. "Sure as skies are blue. Travellin' for days an' here I be, lost, with a twisted ankle an' this ole bag o' bones. Was e'er a man so tried? I was off to sell this vermin at market, but the eyes,

I suppose, they've led me agley an' I can't see the right road for lookin'."

"Where are you from?" Elgiva persisted.

"Many days to the north. I've got this little homestead, see. Some acres of land. Do a bit o' farmin'. I was on my way to the neighbourin' village. Should have been there two days since. Must have took a wrong turn back at the crossroads, but I'm a born fool, I reckon. If I don't sell some stock, I'll starve. Times are bad, see. The wife she joined her ancestors. A cold snap took her, just like that, and my only son, he died last harvest. Got the bloody flux, he did. I had two lads helpin' out an' they ran off one day. Well, I ask you, how's a man to live? So here I be, lost and alone, wi' a twisted ankle an' a stubborn nag what's no use but for hound meat. I think the gods have punished me for gettin' in the haystack wi' the weaver's wife, when I were but a lad."

Godwin smiled, but Elgiva looked thoughtful and her eyes were fixed on the dun-coloured pony.

"What manner o' place is this?" asked the Saxon, frowning and scratching his head. "Movin' bushes an' all sorts. Have you seen 'em? Weird it is. I can't fathom it at all, but 'tis no wonder I've lost my way. I thought the eyes was playin' tricks and then methought, if 'tweren't no trick o' the eyes, then the ground was boggy or some such an' things kept slitherin' about. But the ground's as hard as the muck back home, where I have to scratch a livin'."

"Let me see your ankle," said Elgiva unconcernedly.

"Well, I don't know…"

"I'll not put a spell on you, if that's what you're thinking," she snapped.

Godwin quickly looked at her, surprised at her asperity, but the man gave her a peculiar grin and held out his injured leg. Godwin tried to lighten the mood. "If we had any food left, you'd be welcome to share it, but all we have is water."

"The moment I set eyes on you, I knew you was kind-hearted," said the Saxon. "There's few as would stop for a codger like me, except to rob me, of course. But don't you worry. I've plenty of food an' I'll be honoured if you'll partake. I've bread an' meat aplenty in that pack on the pony's back an' you'll dine well this night – an' you, Grimalkin!" he shouted hoarsely, half-turning towards the animal, "you can get off up that hill an' fill your belly wi' grass." The animal eyed him contemptuously with her large, bloodshot eyes. "I call her Grimalkin, for she's as spiteful an' wayward as an ole she-cat." He looked at Godwin and chuckled, then he shook his fist at the pony. "Get on, wilful beast, or you'll feel the end o' my boot."

"There's nothing wrong … that I can see," announced Elgiva suddenly, her tone strangely sardonic.

"Eh?" The old man narrowed his eyes at her.

"Your ankle. There's nothing broken. Perhaps you should give it a rest."

He looked at her blankly, then slowly nodded his thanks. For a long moment, she studied him, then she got to her feet with a sigh and, giving Godwin a look that he couldn't decipher, she walked towards the pony.

"There's some nice grass up on that slope," she said softly. The pony allowed her to lead it away.

The Saxon indicated Elgiva with a sideways nod of his head. "That creature has a way wi' animals, but she don't care for men."

"Well," shrugged Godwin, "she's an Elf."

"Suspicious, eh?"

"What? ... Well ... yes. Of us perhaps and probably with good reason. She'll come round sooner or later."

"Hope so. Can't stand bad feelin'. Puts me on edge, it does. At least you seem a friendly sort. What do they call you, son?"

Godwin smiled ironically. "A great many things, no doubt, but mainly they call me Godwin. My friend is called Elgiva."

"An' I go by the name of Oswald. Oswald Elricson."

"Elricson," mused Godwin. "I knew an Elric once. I ... used to work for his father." Inwardly, he smiled at this.

They chatted until Elgiva returned, the pony at her side. She had a troubled look on her face. Oswald smiled in welcome, but she quickly looked away.

"Well, Oswald," said Godwin, "what are your plans?"

The Saxon shook his head indecisively. "Can't say for sure. To one that's lost any path will suit. I could travel with you aways ... if you don't mind, o' course. Might find my way back home."

Godwin was about to reply, but he didn't get the chance.

"We travel alone," said Elgiva brusquely.

Godwin winced at the tone of her voice. "It's better we do," he said hurriedly, making amends for his friend's curt manner. "We follow a dangerous road."

"Well, by the gods!" Oswald declared, "I've been on many a dangerous road an' most had more holes than these rags I'm wearin'."

"How odd that someone so widely travelled should get lost going to market," remarked Elgiva wryly.

"Look here, I never said I was widely travelled," Oswald protested, looking offended. "I've been about a bit, you know, but not all over the place. An' goin' to market, well, that's different. It's on a road I don't much use. Never fell on hard times till now an' had no reason to go to market to sell off my only chattels." He shook his head slowly and sighed. "You was right, lad, when you said Elves was suspicious."

"But! …" Godwin's attempt at an explanation was silenced by the hurt and angry look he saw in Elgiva's eyes. He blanched under their venom. "Well, er, best be on our way. I suppose you can travel with us a short while, until your ankle's better." He glanced at Elgiva sheepishly, but she turned her back on him. "Can I help you onto your pony, Oswald?"

"Nay, lad, I can shift for myself, as long as she stands still. Perhaps you'd hold her head, son?"

Godwin took hold of the leather bridle, while Oswald struggled to perch himself upon the animal's back.

"Are we ready, then?" asked Godwin.

Elgiva glared at him icily and began to walk ahead and Grimalkin trotted after her, as though she had heard a spoken command. Feeling somewhat dejected, Godwin brought up the rear, the image of Elgiva's reproving gaze refusing to fade from his mind. He felt like a betrayer.

For a while they travelled in silence, but Godwin found that he couldn't bear the burden of his guilt and Elgiva's manner worried him. He quickened his pace and caught up with her.

"I'm sorry about that," he whispered, so that Oswald wouldn't hear. "Elgiva, it's not what you think…"

She shrugged. "It doesn't matter."

"Well, then, what's wrong?"

She looked at him, but he was aware that he had only half her attention. "That pony. She won't talk to me."

"What?"

But Elgiva seemed too preoccupied to pay him further heed. He sensed her unease, but misunderstood, and thought that his friend was annoyed because the animal had snubbed her. He dropped back, shrugging his shoulders, content to let her sulk alone.

They had covered almost two leagues, when Elgiva stopped abruptly. Ignoring Oswald, she said to Godwin, "We'll stay here for the night."

"But, lass," protested Oswald, "there's several hours of daylight left."

She gazed at him contemptuously. "I think your pony is tired."

"And I'm hungry," Godwin declared, adding under his breath, "not that anyone cares." He quickly surveyed their surroundings. They were standing in a shallow dell, sheltered by a few small trees. "A good enough place to set up camp." He held out his hand to help Oswald dismount.

The old man shrugged and clambered down awkwardly. "By the gods! I'm stiff!" he complained, massaging his bony rump. "Like sittin' on top of a sack full o' stones!"

Godwin turned to speak to his friend, but stopped when he saw her expression. She was watching Oswald closely and seemed to be quite perplexed. Then her gaze slid towards Godwin and became immediately blank. She strode off towards the lip of the dell and sat down with her back towards them.

With a sudden lurch, the pony moved and lumbered after her.

Godwin shook his head at her sullen demeanour, then forced a smile for Oswald's benefit. "Would you like some water?" he asked, lowering his pack to the ground.

"That I would," said Oswald cheerily.

He handed the old man a water-skin, then carried the other across the dell to where Elgiva sat; the pony beside her, munching grass. "Some water for you," he stated tightly.

"Thank you, my friend," she said, investing the title with a strange solemnity. For a moment, she searched his face, before taking the water-skin and satisfying her thirst. Then she poured water into her hand while offering it to the pony.

"Can't that clapped-out beast find its own?" he demanded.

"Why don't you shut up!" she said. She thrust the water-skin back at him and flashed him a look of ire. "Go away. I have to think."

He snatched the water-skin from her hand and stormed back to Oswald, muttering curses.

"I'll get some wood for a fire," he grated, trying to hide his annoyance, and failing.

Oswald chuckled throatily. "Prefers her own company, does she?" he said. "Look, son, while you're getting wood, have a rummage in that pack on Grimalkin. You'll find enough food for the three of us."

Godwin nodded and set to work collecting wood for a fire. He glanced at his friend, but the rigour of her back defied communication. He felt as if a leaden weight had taken the place of his heart. Since their ordeal in the Forest of Shades, he had come to feel that they were equals, had almost forgotten that she was an Elf, but now her aloofness called to mind her perplexing, elvish nature. She was a being from a magical world, who talked to animals and hated men and perhaps he was only with her on sufferance.

But then he chided himself. His friend had a great deal to worry about and he was being feeble. A proper meal and a good night's sleep would soon put things to rights.

* * *

By the time that dusk had fallen, a chill breeze tugged at the trees around the dell. Godwin and the old man sat before a roaring fire, grateful for its warmth, while Elgiva continued to sit apart, like a sentinel watching the gathering night.

Hating their separation, Godwin was beginning to resent the Saxon's presence. The sight of Elgiva sitting alone in the cold was more than he could bear and he decided to try and persuade her to join them. Leaving Oswald to finish his meal, he casually strolled across the dell and sat beside his friend.

"Elgiva?"

"What now?"

He frowned. "Come to the fire and eat."

"Leave me alone," she said coldly. "I don't want his food."

"Why not?" he demanded. "Why do you sit here? Have I offended you?"

She looked at him and her features softened. "No … no," she said, lowering her eyes. "I don't like *HIM*. I don't know why. I just don't trust him, Godwin." She sighed and ran her fingers through her hair. "He has an unpleasant aura."

"Well, a bath wouldn't go amiss," he jested.

She cut him dead with a glare. “It’s not funny!”

He sighed with exasperation. “I’m sorry. Look, I don’t want him here anymore than you do, but we’re stuck with him for the night. Tomorrow we’ll send him on his way.”

After an awkward pause she said, “Perhaps Elves *ARE* suspicious.”

“I had to explain…”

“Only I can explain my own actions!”

“Can you?” he asked sarcastically. “I’m not so sure of that. Be reasonable, Elgiva. You were far too rude.”

“And you were far too friendly.”

“By Frigg! I had to be! Poor, harmless, old man. One of us had to show him some pity. Besides, Elgiva, he’s one of my kind.”

“He’s a Saxon!” she snapped.

“He’s a human being!”

She looked at him and, for a moment, her eyes reflected something torn between hurt and envy. Then she smirked sardonically, “Is he?”

“Yes, and I felt sorry for him. I suppose … really … it’s good to talk … to a normal person again.” Godwin regretted this statement, as soon as he had uttered it.

“I see.”

He gave her a hesitant smile. “I do believe you’re jealous.”

She scowled at him indignantly. “How you mistake me, Wilthkin! But I warn you; be on your guard. Something is wrong here. I feel it. What will it take to teach you caution?” She turned her back on him dismissively.

“I … By Frigg! You’re impossible!”

He snapped to his feet and stamped back to the fire, where Oswald sat, unconcerned, chewing on an oatcake.

⋆ ⋆ ⋆

Chapter Eighteen

Despite the coming of spring, a cold, sharp night lay in store for the travellers sheltering in the dell, but thankfully there was no rain or snow to add to their discomfort. The sky was clear of clouds and the bright stars glittered like shards of glass.

Beside the cheery camp-fire, Godwin lay wrapped in his cloak, his body aching for sleep, but Oswald was a lively character, who seemed to need no rest. As soon as darkness had fallen and they had settled down for the night, the old Saxon had begun a seemingly endless monologue. The history of his thrilling life was a tale long in the telling and Godwin felt a wave of relief, when finally it crawled to a close. But Oswald hadn't finished.

"You know, what puzzles me, young man, is what you two are doin' out here. You're in the middle of nowhere. You could be attacked by wolves an' there's robbers on the road. You're miles away from the nearest village." He paused and threw more wood on the fire, then looked at Godwin askance. "You runnin' away from somethin'?"

Godwin floundered at the change of subject.

"You're not lost, surely?" Oswald went on. "Such capable folk as you? Folk like me get lost all the time." His manner was affable, matter-of-fact, yet Godwin felt suddenly ill at ease. "By the way, if you want some real strong ale, there's some in Grimalkin's pack." He glanced about him, then drew a little nearer. "Or, if you're a man as likes somethin' a bit different, well, I've got these mushrooms … you know." He grinned grotesquely in the firelight. Godwin raised his eyebrows, then shook his head ingenuously. "Well, as you please," said Oswald with a shrug. "They're not easy come by, so I don't mind keepin' 'em all to myself. There's few pleasures left at my age. Not like you young folk, eh? What was I sayin'? Ah, yes. Seems to me you're ill-prepared for travellin'. No food an' no pack animals."

Godwin swallowed hard and his mind laboured frantically. "Er … we had some trouble in that quarter."

"Robbed on the road, no doubt?" Oswald surmised, with a knowing nod. "That happened to my brother, when he was about your age. These rascals stopped him in the wood, took all his clothes an' money, they did, an' threw him in a bog. The bastards beat him black an' blue before they threw him in. You never saw the like of it. I was only a lad then and it just seemed funny to me, but Mother she fell down in a heap, screamin' bloody murder."

Godwin raised his hand to stifle a yawn.

"There's some bastards about an' no mistake. Robbin' ain't good enow for some, they need their sport as well. Lone travellers are good sport, you know. Aye, you never can tell who you'll meet far from home, on a lone track … in the dark."

Godwin rolled over and pretended to sleep – a pretence easily maintained – but Oswald's elbow jabbed at his ribs and forced him to turn around.

"So, you was robbed. Now where are you headin'?"

"We're lookin' for … a village," said Godwin evasively.

"A village? What, Saxon? What village is that?"

"Where … where they breed the best pack-ponies in the land. My father wants six for his farmstead." Godwin was rather impressed with this invention, but the look of doubt in Oswald's rheumy eyes gave him second thoughts.

"Goin' to buy nags? What with? Got some gold stashed away, have you? I thought that you was robbed?"

"Yes, but … well … you see…"

"So your dad has a farm then? How come you took up with that Elric's father and didn't work for your own?"

Excuses fell from Godwin's lips in a desperate rush of panic. "We fell on hard times. We had a bad harvest. We needed the money. You know."

Oswald nodded in sympathy. "It happens to us all, lad. But won't you have your hands full, bringing six big ponies back on your own? What if they're twelve hands or more, like ole Grimalkin there? They can be fierce, unruly beasts."

"I thought they were quite gentle?"

"Gentle?" Oswald laughed uproariously. "Some appear so, lad, but it's all a trick. Once your back's turned, they bite it! Know much about horses, do you?"

"Yes, of course," lied Godwin with feigned indignation.

"Well, keep your wits about you an' don't be fooled into buyin' no clapped-out nags. Don't you be duped. You don't want nothin' that's cow-hocked or ewe-necked like ole Grimalkin, do you?"

Godwin cleared his throat, totally baffled. "Er … no."

Oswald shook his head. "Aye, if I ever get to market, I'd best find a blind man, if I want to sell *HER*." He chuckled to himself. "An' mark me well, you don't want nothin' wi' too much spirit. That's one of her failin's, too. Her ancestors pulled chariots, you know. Well, you'd know that, bein' a Briton. Great stamina an' strong as a bull, these Celtic ponies, you know, but mean as a pack o' wolves. Like to think they're boss. No use takin' a stick to 'em. Just makes 'em more defiant. Mean buggers, an' no mistake. But you know about horses, so you'll not be tricked."

"No … no, I won't." For a moment, in his drowsiness, Godwin believed his own invention.

"An' there's another thing. I don't know why you're with an Elf, but if I was you I'd drop her. You can't go into no village wi' an Elf. Folk would run a mile. There'd be a bloody riot, son. Ain't you afeard of Elves?"

"I was," said Godwin, "but now I know better."

Oswald drew in his breath sharply, like a man whose knowledge weighed heavily upon him. "Wish I could say the same, I'm sure. I've heard some tales o' the fairy folk, but, well, best not to say."

"What sort of tales?" asked Godwin, his interest reviving.

"Nay. Happen it's all tittle-tattle."

Godwin sat up attentively. "No, go on," he urged, "but," he lowered his voice to a whisper, "more quietly, if you can."

Oswald drew closer and glanced right and left, as though afraid that the shadows had ears. "Have you ever heard of, or seen, a man what's Elf-shot? I mean, really?"

"I've heard many claim it," said Godwin, "but they were fooling themselves, I think. Some people always need someone to blame for their problems, rather than blame themselves."

"Well, son, believe me, I've seen it an' I don't want to see it again." Oswald shivered and his white hair seemed to stand up on end. "Young Eadric it was. A good-lookin' lad from t'other valley. Neat-herd for his uncle Wilfred, who was a good neighbour to me. Well, one fair mornin',

Eadric went out to the wood behind the farm, collectin' berries an' such. We all knew there was Elves there, but Eadric he didn't give a crone's cuss. Well, that night he came staggerin' home, like a man who's been chased by demons. Wild-eyed he was, an' his handsome face as pale as a linen clout. Said the Elves bewitched him for trespassing on their land. He wouldn't say what they did to him, but he took to his bed that very night an' he never got up again. We all knew he had been cursed with the Blister an' sure enow, he was covered in blisters an' tossed an' turned all night. Burnin' up wi' fever he was. Terrible to see.

"Well, as soon as I got wind of it all, I rushed straight over to help, but I saw him breathe his last. Off to the ancestors in his prime. An' if you'd seen the body, son; a bloated mass was all, covered in great purple blisters. It fair turned my stomach an' I'm not the squeamish type. To think he was once a fine young lad – not unlike yourself – the pride of his kin and loved by his friends."

"Perhaps it was the plague," said Godwin, anxious to end the tale.

"Plague? Forsooth! He was Elf-shot! An' his mother, a poor widow lady, weren't right up there ever again." Oswald tapped himself on the skull in a gesture of explanation. "An' his uncle went to pieces."

"Was he Elf-shot, too?"

Oswald frowned at Godwin's sarcasm. "Nay, lad, you mock me." He looked away for a moment. Was it a trick of the firelight, or was there really a sly grin on his face? "I'm tryin' to warn you of perils your young mind is ignorant of."

"Well, I'm much obliged," said Godwin. "It's a strange tale, indeed, by Grim." He lay down and made himself comfortable, hoping that Oswald had finished for the night.

"An' all the stranger for bein' true. An' there's another thing. I knew a man once whose kine was hexed by Elves. A whole herd dropped down dead as stones, 'cause this man had tilled land that belonged to them."

"There are certainly a great many Elves where you live, and all of them very unpleasant," remarked Godwin. "A wonder you've lived so long."

"Well, I'm careful, see," said Oswald. "I keep myself out of trouble. I know right well that Elves are hidin' in every bush an' cave an' tree, just waitin' to play their tricks."

"Well, I don't know about that, but Elves wouldn't kill a herd of cows," Godwin informed him crossly. "They wouldn't make beasts suffer."

"Kine what fall down dead in a flash don't do much sufferin', son. An' you can't gainsay the fact that not all Elves is good. How can they be, when we ain't?" Godwin couldn't argue with that. "You don't know much about Elves, lad, an' I'm afeard for you, 'cause all you do know comes from your friend. Elves is devious creatures an' can make a man believe aught that suits 'em."

"But, listen here…"

"An' there's somethin' else, though it isn't easy to talk of, but I see you'd best know about it – just to be on the safe side."

Oswald frowned and hesitated, as though debating whether or not it was wise for him to continue. Godwin sat up and stared at him, his curiosity roused.

"What is it?" he asked worriedly.

"Well, you see, son, these Elves, so I do believe, they have a way about them. They're enchanters, see, an' can poison your mind. They take on disguises to fool us." He nodded authoritatively and folded his stick-like arms. "Seems to mean something to you, lad?"

"No, no. Please go on."

"Well, they're damned clever, see, an', well, sensual. To them seducin' a mortal man is the height of entertainment. They have strong passions, you understand, an' a likin' for trickin' innocent lads into their beds…"

"Now just a minute! …"

Godwin tried to protest, tried to find the words, but his logic had forsaken him. He eyed the old man thoughtfully. He had no reason to lie and like all old men he loved a good tale. And there was often truth in tales, and he himself was well aware that Elves were jealous, gloating beings who hated to be crossed. He travelled with one, didn't he! Elgiva had magic, too, and cursing a man with blisters might not be beyond her reach. He remembered also with a sudden pang her Saxon disguise and the way she had enchanted him, when he saw her true appearance.

But when it came to seduction, the guilt lay at his door. He remembered his lust in the Forest of Shades and his cheeks burned with scarlet shame.

For a moment he peered across the dell. His friend still sat beneath the moon, like just another shadow. The thought of her cold and lonely vigil filled him with remorse and he knew that, in many ways, he had betrayed her.

"Mind you," said Oswald, "you can take care of yourself, I'm sure. Took you for a warrior at first. Can't understand what a farmer's lad would be doin' wi' a sword like that. A goodly, bold weapon indeed. I've been admirin' it, so I have. Would you mind if I had a look?"

Oswald's eyes grew large and round and Godwin saw a gleam in them that smacked of greed. He clasped the sword tightly and shook his head. "No!" He drew a deep breath and forced a smile. "No, it's dangerous. Very sharp."

Oswald shrugged, as if it didn't matter. "Well, son, we'd best get a bit o' sleep. Nice talkin' to you, but," he held up his hand in gentle reproach, "an ole man needs his rest, you know. You young folk don't think o' that." Opening his mouth wide, he yawned extravagantly. "Good night, then. Sleep well." He pulled the thin blanket over his chest and settled down to sleep. Then he chuckled softly. "Happen I'll sleep wi' one eye open, lest your friend gets a funny mood on her in the middle o' the night."

Muttering oaths under his breath, Godwin lay down once more. He covered himself with Joskin's cloak and cursed his own stupidity. Fatigue had made him gullible and he had lapped up Oswald's chatter like the credulous dolt he was. Yet, though he refused to believe it all, some doubts still lurked in his mind, doubts that sprang from his fear of things he didn't understand: Elves and magic and the unknown horrors that crouched at the marge of reality.

⋆ ⋆ ⋆

Finally, after an age of restlessness, Godwin fell asleep.

At his side, the old man sat up slowly. Sure that his movement had gone undetected, he shrugged off his blanket and got to his feet. Then he strolled across the moonlit sward to the lip of the dell, where Elgiva sat, her chin cupped in her hands. She heard him approach and raised her head.

"Your ankle has made a remarkable recovery," she observed, without turning round.

Momentarily taken aback, Oswald chuckled softly. It seemed that she had been expecting him. "Thought you'd fallen asleep," he said. "I was restless, see. Needed to stretch the ole legs. My ankle was only twisted. The rest must have done it good. Mind if I join you, lass?"

"As you please," she said.

"Stars are bright tonight," he remarked. He seated himself upon the grass. "You're keepin' a lonely vigil out here. What you watchin' for? You got enemies?"

Something in his tone made her look at him. She paused, then said, "We all have enemies."

"Yet you're travellin' wi' one. Elves an' men don't mix, you know. Sad, I reckon, 'cause Elves ain't bad folk. No worse than us, at least. You ain't the first I've seen, you know. The woods are teemin' wi' Elves back home, but they keep to themselves an' don't cause no trouble." He chuckled and shook his head. "Aye, less trouble than them damned Britons. They're a funny lot. Can't be trusted at all. But Elves, they mind their own business."

He looked at her for some response, but all he got was a sigh of boredom. "You know, I once was told that only Royal Elves have magic an' I've always wondered if that's true. Would you be Royal, by any chance?" Elgiva merely shrugged. "Don't give nothin' away, do you? But you needn't fear ole Oswald. I'm just expressin' an interest."

He paused and shuffled nearer. "You know I think it fittin' I give you some advice. Be careful o' the company you keep, lass. That friend o' yours has a runaway tongue. It doesn't matter in front o' me, 'cause I'm an honest wight an' take it all wi' a pinch o' salt. But there's some folks might wonder a bit. Might think his wits had gone wool-gatherin'."

"Really?" she asked indifferently. "Tell me, what did he say?"

"Funny things they were to be sure. Said you was lookin' for some stone or other, though I've plenty back on my homestead as would save you all this trouble. An' he said you had great magic. Well, that intrigued me, I can tell you. An' what I thought was, could I have a demonstration, if you're up to it?"

Elgiva turned and regarded him steadily, her dark eyes slightly narrowed. She knew that he was playing a game and enjoying it all immensely. She also knew that his appearance was false, but though she saw something in his eyes, it was gone before she could name it. The spell he had woven was far too strong. She knew that sooner or later he would drop his disguise and she also knew that she had to be careful.

"Your friend seems wary of you," he told her. "Said Elves did awful things to a man. Made him act against his wishes. I didn't like to tell him it was all in his mind. He said he'd have to split wi' you soon or he might lose his reason. Britons are superstitious folk." He paused a while and watched her. She seemed to be ignoring him. "Look, I'm on your side an' all I ask is to see a bit o' magic. Go on, make an ole man happy."

"You underestimate me," Elgiva said at length. "Especially my sense of hearing. I know what's passed between you. I might have found it entertaining, had your sport not been at my friend's expense." She turned and gave him an icy glare. "What game are you playing?"

Oswald feigned innocence, then he laughed.

"I'm not a fool," Elgiva assured him. "What's the meaning of this act of yours and, furthermore, who are you?"

"I'm a poor, ole man," moaned Oswald, "an' if my mind sometimes wanders, then 'tis no fault o' mine."

"You can do better than that," she said.

There was a brief, tense silence.

"I should need to do a great deal better to fool you, little Elf. I have nothing but praise for your perspicacity."

Elgiva's jaw dropped and she stared at Oswald, amazed at the change in his voice. He smiled at her; a cruel and cunning smile that had nothing in common with humour. Then he sighed and stretched himself, as though set free from a tiny cell.

"This is a most uncomfortable shape. The worst I've ever tried," he said. "It needs a major effort of will, but, of course, does not surpass me. The greatest difficulty is the voice. I am always seeking knowledge, but confess that I know little of Wilthkin dialects. I thought that your friend would see through me there, but he's an ingenuous fool. I'm amazed at you, consorting with him. The Wilthkin is just a barbarian. Mind you, for someone so gullible, he is very hard to corrupt. Nevertheless, he gave me good sport."

"Who are you?" demanded Elgiva, but she half-feared that she knew the answer.

He raised a sinewy hand and stroked her cheek. Though filled with revulsion, she couldn't pull away.

"I am not as I appear, of course, " he said. "You knew that something was amiss, but this is such an excellent disguise that you could not pierce the illusion, could you? Well, I'm not a Saxon. Neither am I old. What am I then, think you?"

"I … I…"

"Come now, little Elf, you do not need to fear me. I am your friend. Your only true friend in all the world, though as yet you cannot see it. I know your heart."

His vivid, blue eyes gleamed and grew larger, and seemed to emit an inner glow that animated his features. Suddenly, his hand snaked out and fastened on her arm. Drawing her towards him, he rested her head upon his lap and stroked her forehead with a silken touch. Mesmerised, her limbs relaxed. A warm, narcotic glow spread throughout her being and she lay as defenceless as a fly caught in a web.

She gazed up at her captor, her eyes struggling to focus, and, within the nimbus of power he had thrown about himself, she saw a male Elf, neither young nor old, but strong and lean and supple. His features were so perfect that they could have been sculptured out of marble by a master at the art. His high, intelligent forehead was crowned by glossy, black hair, which fell to his shoulders in gleaming waves, while above his large, black eyes, his eyebrows arched wickedly, full of dark humour.

Yet, despite his beauty, his face had a contradictory appearance, for it seemed at the same time both cruel and kind. When he spoke, his voice was as sweet as honey; but as sour as vinegar, too.

"Forgive my little disguises," he purred, "but sometimes I grow bored and, when I do, I must make mischief. But this is preferable, is it not? A handsome fellow, would you not say? I assure you that this is my true appearance, yet gladly will I assume another, if it does not please you. Great magic knows no limits."

He continued to stroke her brow, his touch as soft as a butterfly's wing, as soothing and warm as a mere in summer, yet as numbing and cold as a winter frost. Elgiva's eyes refused to stay open.

As she lay helplessly sprawled in his lap, she felt herself floating over fields of flowers, the Earth a pageant of colour below, the mountains glimmering in the sun…

No, this was an illusion…

She opened her eyes and blinked at the night.

"Do not oppose me," he murmured. "I do not mean you harm. You see how magic can be used to subdue, how easy it is to beguile? I regret your inexperience, but I, Vieldrin, can teach you." He felt her resist, felt her muscles contract and saw a feverish gleam in her eyes, a spark of awakening power. "The King of Misterell is your friend and you are safe with me. Quite safe."

He lowered his head and kissed her mouth and the pleasure of his embrace melted her resistance. She felt a tingling in her lips, the coercion of magic that made her his thrall. He released her slowly and studied her face.

"We are two of a kind," he breathed. "We are Eldrakin. And you are safe with me. And you are safe with me."

"Yes."

"And you are content. I am your friend."

"Yes."

"You trust me."

"Yes."

"Thallinore is a fool. He talks too freely and I know all. It did not require a great stretch of my intellect to work out what you are up to. And I know you for what you are. A precious jewel of Elvendom. Mine, dear heart. My jewel. What would I want with a dolt such as he, with magic dulled by unworthy blood? He believes I am his protector, but he is useful to me. That and nothing more. But you I would not use. You would not be taken in, I think. Clever, little Elf. But here I must apologise, for one of my disguises frightened you – though even then you knew it was a trick. However, it was cruel of me, but I had to test your mettle, to see what you were made of. You have potential, I admit. And you intend to find the Lorestone, do you? Unhappily, so do I."

Elgiva struggled to speak and fought the spell that cocooned her. "You were afraid of me," she gasped.

"Afraid, dear heart?" He laughed scornfully. "Wary, nothing more. Wary and respectful of your little powers, my sweeting. If I feared anything, it was that I might harm you. I wanted to assess your strength. Thallinore thought you had no powers, for, when you were banished, you did not use them. You let those scum abuse you. But even then he feared you, for he is a cringing coward. I also wanted to determine your heart's true inclinations. How distressed I was to find it set so resolutely against me! It pained me, little Elf, for I wished only to be your friend."

"My heart will always … be set … against … evil…"

He laughed. "Your heart has been warped by weak Elves and Wilthkin. But I will win your heart, as I will win the Lorestone. You do not know your true self, but I do. Power will excite you. Power is a drug you will come to crave."

"Never."

"Be that as it may, dear heart," he sighed condescendingly, "you will come to realise that what I am to tell you is the only way. It is inevitable. Mark me well. You and I together, with the Stone, would be invincible. As allies, we could rule the Earth. What could we not achieve together? As King and Queen of Misterell, we would build a powerful dynasty and our children would inherit our conquests. The stain of Wilthkin would be removed from this land and all Elves would kneel before us. Even Faine would seem weak in comparison to our power."

Elgiva was aghast. "You can't deceive me … you can't. You know I'll find the Stone … the Ninth Book says…"

"The Ninth Book comes from Misterell. How do you know that it is genuine? But harken to me, Elgiva, I will give my kingdom to you as a gift to seal the alliance between us. It was a disorganised kingdom, when it fell into my lap. My father was weak and foolish." Vieldrin's lip curled disdainfully. "But now I have it all in order. My subjects resented the rule of law and stuck to their idle ways. They thought to oppose me, as you do, but were soon to discover the extent of my wrath. They are a mere handful now, but they always do my bidding." His lips twisted into a smirk of cruelty. "They have learned the wisdom of obedience. A king must be strong and brook no insolence from a rabble of inferiors."

"You murdered your own people?"

"I did what was necessary," he replied affectedly. "Do not trouble yourself with such thoughts. The loss of a few silly Elves is beneath consideration. I have set my sights on higher things."

"You won't succeed! … I'll find it … I'll find the Stone and I'll defeat you!" declared Elgiva, but her voice sounded too feeble for her purpose.

"Poor, misguided creature. Would you risk your life for those who do not love you as I do? I am King of Misterell and have never found the Lorestone. Small hope have you, and even less of using it with your adolescent powers. But, so be it. It shall be a game between us. A contest. I shall enjoy that. Yet, if you do not finally see the sense in what I have said, and if you persist in opposing me, then regrettably, I will destroy you, as I would do now, had I not a kind heart."

"A kind heart … without a conscience?"

He laughed merrily and his teeth glimmered like pearls in the moonlight. "Having a conscience is like having a twisted ankle. It impedes one's progress. Power, they say – those who have none – is a corrupting force, but I know it will divert you to a truer path. A path that leads to my friendship. How sweet would be the union between us! We are so alike, dear heart. And there is none to equal you in Elvendom, none as worthy to be my queen. You will realise that I am your only hope, in fact, I am your destiny." He tutted, then frowned in mock apology. "In the name of Smirill, how remiss of me! Here I am, chattering on, and quite forgetting an important disclosure I had come here to make. It is most inexcusable. Will you forgive me? I have good news for you, my dear – though it will make your obstinacy even more unthinkable." He stroked her hair for a moment and gazed up at the night sky, sighing affectedly.

"You see," he went on in silken tones, "I was charged to tell you that your banishment is revoked."

Elgiva tensed beneath his touch, but was powerless to move.

"Furthermore, the King of Elindell has given you to me. You are your master's gift to me to seal the alliance between us. As the property of your betters, you must do as they decree. So you will be my bride. The oath of fealty you made to the King in the name of that old fool

Faine still applies, so you are bound to honour your master's pledge."

Elgiva struggled to rail at him, but her voice was a croak of helpless ire. "You lie!"

He shook his handsome head. "Whether you like it or not, dear heart, you belong to me. Would you dishonour your vow to Faine?" His eyebrows arched with glee. "Well, I will leave that to your conscience. It is time for me to go."

He bent and kissed her on the lips and she felt his power draw back, the spell of coercion lifting. Shaking the mist from her mind, she pushed herself away from him, her features raw with revulsion.

"I don't believe you! You're using me to get to the Stone and once I've outlived my usefulness…"

"Do not even think such thoughts. I am your friend, Elgiva."

She tossed back her hair, made anger the shield for her fear and abhorrence. "Your spell has faded. Is that the best you can do?"

He smiled and got easily to his feet and his stately frame towered over her. "A weak spell sufficed to subdue you, my dear. Now I must go. I eagerly await our next meeting." He paused and looked at her thoughtfully. "But before I leave, should I draw your attention to something that you may already have noticed?"

She merely frowned at him.

"Your friend, Elgiva…"

"What of him?"

"That sword of his…"

"I know."

"Of course." He turned to leave, but then he stopped. "By the way, please keep that pony. She is a true beast, not a fiend in disguise, but you probably know that, also. I placed a spell of silence on her, but it is lifted now." He paused to snap his fingers. "I took her from this awful, old man who was on his way to market – as I took his name and appearance. I had to dispose of him, naturally, for he was loathe to part with his old bag of bones. He had only himself to blame, daring to trespass so near to my lands." Vieldrin laughed with relish. "The poor, stupid worm never expected a murderous attack from a harmless, old crone! But such scum deserve to die. What use are they? Yes, keep the flea-ridden beast. I despise it no less than the beast I took it from. And the food also. I do not wish to see you starve before the start of our contest. Where is the fun in that? Do not worry, dear heart, none of it is poisoned. I fully intend us to meet in Misterell."

He strolled away gracefully, tall, lean and imposing, along the lip of the dell.

"You may as well kill me now!" cried Elgiva. "I will never be your ally! Never!" She tried to conceal her distress, but her voice was broken by sobs.

"We shall see," he said with a cunning softness.

His laughter hung in the darkness, but he had vanished, like an illusion.

⋆ ⋆ ⋆

Chapter Nineteen

Godwin's eyes focused on another day and he noticed at once the absence of Oswald. Elgiva was also missing. At least the pony was keeping him company. She stood a few yards away from him, large-eyed and raw-boned, regarding him with perfect indifference. In fact, as her jaws munched a mouthful of grass, she seemed to be looking straight through him.

He sat up, stretched and yawned. The camp-fire was a mound of grey expenditure, as empty and forlorn as the blanket beside him. He rubbed his eyes with his knuckles, while the pony continued to watch him aloofly.

"Can't you stare at something else?" he asked. The animal tossed her head and snorted. "Where has everyone gone?" Grimalkin snickered half-heartedly. To Godwin it sounded like a man chuckling at the antics of an insect. "Stop that silly noise!" he snapped.

Godwin got stiffly to his feet, feeling as though the contours of the ground were now impressed forever into his flesh. "By Frigg, you're an ugly brute!" The animal flashed the whites of her eyes at him disdainfully. "If I was an Elf," he went on, "we could have a chat to pass the time. There's no-one else to talk to round here and, when there is, they either bite your head off or bore you to death with their endless prattle." He looked about him and frowned. "Perhaps I've been abandoned." He shrugged. "Well, no reason why I should starve."

He walked towards the pony, intending to take some food from her pack, but she whinnied at him and backed away. Sighing with impatience, he carefully stepped towards her. This time she showed him her large, yellow teeth, her brown eyes round with the promise of violence.

Godwin cocked his fists on his hips. "Well, perhaps I will starve after all."

Whinnying triumphantly, the pony turned and kicked out her legs, just missing him with her hooves. Then she galloped out of the dell, leaving Godwin alone with his hunger.

Muttering oaths, he picked up his cloak. He threw it around his shoulders and wandered out of the dell through the trees behind him. A short walk took him to a bubbling stream, where he splashed cold water onto his face. The sun was newly risen and its rays slanted like threads of steam across the land before him. It was a fresh, mild morning and the emerald vistas called for his appreciation, but his hunger was gnawing painfully. He decided to wander back to the dell with the hope of somehow procuring breakfast.

When he arrived, he saw Elgiva already preparing food. The pony lounged beside her, her jaws still munching grass.

"Hello," greeted Elgiva, "I wondered where you were."

"Me?" returned Godwin. "Where were *YOU*?"

"Just a short walk. To clear the cobwebs. It's a beautiful day."

"You haven't slept, have you?"

"By Faine, does it show that much?" Elgiva laughed light-heartedly.

"Well, it seems to have done you good," he said. "You seem a bit more ... cheerful. You should go without sleep more often."

Her eyebrows drew together and she muttered a brief apology.

Godwin shrugged. "I understand. Don't worry. I forgive you."

"I don't need forgiveness from a Wilthkin!" she retorted tetchily. "And your understanding is given without knowledge."

Godwin bowed with mock servility, then he turned to face the pony. "You see, Grimalkin, when it comes to saying the wrong thing, you can always rely on me."

The animal snickered at this and Elgiva threw her a look of annoyance. Godwin yearned to ask her what the pony had said, but he thought it inadvisable.

Sighing, Elgiva looked at Godwin, then she handed him a bowl of oatcakes, liberally spread with honey. "Sit down and eat your breakfast."

Godwin gladly obeyed her command. "Where's Oswald got to, then?"

Elgiva looked away and grinned. "I believe he was on his way to market, when an old woman stole his pony."

"Well, pardon me if I don't follow any of that," he said with a frown of exasperation.

"I'd better explain." She seated herself beside him, a mischievous glint in her eyes. She hooked her hair behind her ears, folded her hands in her lap, then she told him what had happened while he slept. He completely forgot about the longed for breakfast.

"Frigg! I had no idea!"

"Neither did I, for certain," she said.

But he felt that she sounded rather smug. "So, now you can laugh at my expense. I was completely taken in. I should have been more guarded. Now I guess you'll have to gloat."

She seemed slightly taken aback. "You're a Wilthkin, Godwin. How could you possibly see the truth behind a glamour of magic? How can I berate you for lacking a skill your kind don't possess?"

"This is one of the few occasions when I have been thankful for my native stupidity," remarked Godwin wryly. "It has spared me your condemnation. But, Elgiva, couldn't that nag have told us what was going on?"

"Vieldrin silenced her with magic."

He nodded and chewed on an oatcake. "So, Vieldrin sees this as a game," he said.

"A game he intends to win." She hugged her knees and stared at the ground, the splendour of her hair like a shawl about her shoulders. "He was trying to turn us against each other, but probably just for his own amusement. He tried to tempt me with power and marriage and he threatened me with a broken vow. It would have been easy for him to kill me, but I know why he refrained. I think he really does believe the prophecies, so I dare say he'll wait until I've found the Lorestone. Whatever his motives, there's a lot more sport to be had in waiting. Watching us struggle towards our goal, knowing he's going to kill us at the end." She sighed and lay back on the grass. "The worst part for me in all of this is that he's right. In Elven law I do belong to him."

He looked at her askance. "No, surely you don't believe that. He's using your integrity against you."

"Perhaps, but I think … you know something about the nature of vows, Godwin." She looked at him carefully.

"Perhaps I do," he agreed.

"If I'm no longer exiled, I am bond-servant to the King. Upon my oath I am his to command. If he decrees

I belong to Vieldrin, then I am required to obey. I vowed such obedience in the name of Faine. No honest Elf would break such a vow. Vieldrin is using my love for Faine to force me to be his bride."

"He's cunning and cruel, Elgiva. But Faine wouldn't hold you to such a vow."

"No, I know. But, nevertheless…" She lifted her torn, sad gaze to the sky and for a while she didn't speak. Then she pursued another line of thought. "Godwin, those tales he told you, when you thought him just a lost, old man, did you believe them all?"

Godwin looked furtive. He felt that the truth might be hurtful, but he didn't want to lie to his friend. "It's a rule of mine to take the words of Saxons with a pinch of salt," he said.

"Perhaps you should have believed them. You should know what Elves are capable of."

"I may have had second thoughts," he confessed, "but I knew you weren't like that."

"Indeed?"

"You wouldn't hurt a living thing without a very good reason. Of course, I know nothing of other Elves." He glanced at her guardedly. "You might be the only good one among them."

Elgiva thought, with a sudden rush of shame, of the Chief Counsellor, of Beortnoth. She saw, too, the Saxon raider, felled by her Elf-bolt and writhing in pain. And she was solely responsible. She had burned a forest alive and the screams of the trees still rang in her ears. Their anguished cries filled the background of her mind, while in the foreground the eyes of a Fellkin begged her for something she couldn't give, the sounds of its slaughter just one more part of the screaming in her brain.

Killing was just too easy. With power it could only be easier. Perhaps Vieldrin was right about her.

She sat up suddenly, hugged her knees. "I'm a good Elf, am I?" Her tone was more savage than she had intended. She swallowed hard and tried to smile. "Then, if I'm the only one, you're lucky I'm the one you're travelling with. But make no mistake, I'm still an Elf. I have my faults, as you have yours, but mine are potentially far more dangerous, because I'm also a Wardain and because I'm unschooled in the use of magic. With my powers I could easily become the kind of Elf that Oswald described." She paused, then added quietly. "It would make life so much simpler."

"But you won't," he said.

"You're sure?"

"I won't let you." Then he smiled at her warmly.

Elgiva looked away. His loyalty and support filled her with remorse. "I must confess something, Godwin," she said in a small, shy voice. "When I was cold towards you … well, I knew that Oswald wasn't as he appeared. I felt that he would try to turn you against me, manipulate you in some way, but I had no idea why he should. Now that I know who he really was, I realise that he could have used an enchantment. It would have been much easier, though I dare say not half so amusing for him. It was wrong of me, but … well, I thought it would be a test of your friendship." She paused, but couldn't look at him, fearing his reaction. "After what happened in the Forest of Shades … Look, I'm set on a perilous course and I have to know who I can trust." She buried her face in her hands. "A test! Faine help me, as if you needed one! All the time you've stayed with me, when you should have been with your family, and I've been cruel and made you suffer even more. Who knows if I may not do so again? Yes, I'm suspicious, Godwin. Perhaps I'm jealous, too. I'm insecure and vain and selfish and lots of other things, but how can I measure friendship, when I've known so little of it?"

She turned and looked at him then and tears of shame clung to her long lashes. "I've failed you, Godwin," she sobbed. "Betrayed you. When I suspected Oswald, I should have been straight with you."

Mention of his family had wrung Godwin's heart, but he swallowed down his hurt. Leaning towards Elgiva, he put his arm around her. "Perhaps you did right," he said soothingly. "Perhaps I needed a test. I'm the first to admit that I'm weak."

"No!" she protested. "You're stronger than *ME*!"

"Well, whether I am or not, you gave me a warning, remember? But I was too proud to accept it. Besides, had we thwarted Vieldrin's game, who knows what he might have done for his sport?"

"Nevertheless," she sighed, "I fear you must find me very wearisome. Perhaps time will cure me of many things – if you have the patience to wait." She touched the hand that cupped her shoulder and he gave her fingers a gentle squeeze. "You're the truest of friends and I value that … more than I can say…" She faltered, avoided his gaze. "So … I would also value your forgiveness … if I may hope to have it."

"Always," he said softly.

⋆ ⋆ ⋆

The companions travelled for the rest of the morning. Elgiva talked to Grimalkin about her life on Oswald's farm, while Godwin watched them enviously from the corner of his eye. He could have felt superfluous, but the sight of them made him smile and for a time he forgot the gravity of their quest.

It was later in the afternoon, when Godwin became aware of an odd sensation in his mind, as though someone were talking to him just beyond the range of his hearing. He froze, listened intently. The voice was telling him to turn aside and follow a southerly trail. Straightening himself, he glanced at Elgiva, who was walking some way ahead. He wondered if she were experiencing the same thing, but decided not to mention it for fear of appearing foolish. To keep his attention focused, he thought of verses he had heard in the Meadhall, reciting them silently to himself to block out all distractions.

He became so set on closing his mind to all external forces that, when Elgiva called his name, she had to repeat it several times before it claimed his attention. He looked around. The dusk was falling and on the horizon a sprawling mass lay dark against the sky.

Elgiva and Godwin looked at each other, sharing a common thought. It could have been any forest, but, inwardly, they knew that it was Misterell: the object of their quest.

Their dread meant little to the pony. The air was heavy with the scent of water and she cantered off in search of it. When Elgiva and Godwin caught up with her, they found her lapping at a small, shallow pool, its edges broken by rushes. The sun was falling into the west and they both decided to stop and make camp.

Godwin struggled out of his pack, but he couldn't find the energy required to make a fire. Instead he strolled to a nearby alder, whose limbs reached out across the pool, and sat himself down at the water's edge. Elgiva, too, was abnormally tired. She slumped against the trunk of the alder and let out a weary sigh.

Soon, the act of sitting up seemed far too much of an effort. Godwin stretched out on the ground, supported by one elbow, and dipped his fingers into the water. He watched as the ripples fanned outwards in lazy, gentle curves. In the distance a trilling blackbird announced the advent of evening.

At length, Godwin fought his languor and returned to a sitting position, but the will was being sucked from his mind and his muscles felt almost useless. "I think there's something wrong," he finally managed to say.

"Yes," sighed Elgiva. She stretched herself exquisitely, as if to crack the torpor that seemed to bind her limbs. "Yes, I feel it, too." His eyes drifted towards her, but he was too fatigued to voice his question. "The enchantment of Misterell saps our will. It wants us to leave. Do you remember?"

"Bellic."

She combed her hair with her fingers and gazed at the darkening sky. "I'm convinced we should turn back … but it will pass. We must ignore the enchantment."

"It's growing dark," he observed tonelessly.

"It's been growing dark for a long time."

He drew a deep breath and got to his knees. Her last remark had bewildered him. He wanted to speak of his fears, his dread of what lay in store for them, but instead he decided on something safer.

"I think I should build a fire."

Grimalkin suddenly raised her head and stamped one hoof on the ground. Elgiva leant forward and gripped Godwin's arm.

"Be on your guard!" she whispered. "We have company!"

"Where?" hissed Godwin, spinning round. He scanned the foliage worriedly.

"That bush over there." She nodded to the right. "Someone's hiding in it."

"I see nothing."

"Neither do I, but Grimalkin and I can sense it."

Godwin fumbled for the hilt of his sword, his fingers clumsy with haste. "Shall we see who it is?" His brow was furrowed with apprehension.

She shook her head. "No, let it be. I feel that it's harmless," she said quietly. "Let's wait and see if it declares itself."

"Whatever you say." Godwin relaxed, his hand spurning the sword.

"No, draw your sword, Godwin," she advised. "Keep it at the ready. We'll have some supper then we'll pretend to be asleep."

He raised his eyebrows, but voiced no objection, and Elgiva went to fetch their provisions. Together they made a small fire, then they ate without haste and talked awhile, as casually as possible. Soon it was time to bed themselves down and they wrapped themselves up in Oswald's blanket and resigned themselves to waiting.

Silence settled over them and soon their pretence of sleeping began to approach the reality, but, at length, whatever had hidden itself made a move towards them.

Godwin tightened his grip on his sword, every muscle tensed. Elgiva hardly dared to breathe and Grimalkin cocked her ears, the whites of her eyes flashing in the firelight.

Suddenly, a small, dark shape crawled out into the open. It crept up to their pack of food and began to rummage inside it. Instantly, Godwin leapt to his feet, seized the intruder and pinned it down, raising his sword above him. The captive emitted a pitiful squeal and struggled with all its might.

"He's an Elf!" cried Elgiva.

The intruder began to beg for mercy.

"Stop struggling!" shouted Godwin. "We won't hurt you!"

The Elf relaxed a little and his thin chest heaved as he fought for air. Shortly he said in the Saxon tongue, "All I wanted was food!"

"We'll give you food," said Elgiva calmly. "Don't be afraid. We mean no harm." She turned towards Godwin. "You'd better put some more wood on the fire, so we can see what we've caught."

Godwin stood up and sheathed his sword.

Later in the fire's glow, they were able to study their captive more closely, as he bolted the food that they gave him. He seemed very young, an adolescent, grimy and barefooted, and his skinny frame was clothed in rags, his hair tangled with burrs. On his left cheek was an ugly scar that ran from his eye to his chin. His features were gaunt and pinched with malnutrition, which made his black eyes seem unusually large; they looked like wells of sorrow in which his hopes had drowned.

"Now," said Elgiva, at length, "if you've finished eating, perhaps you could tell us your name."

The Elf swallowed and wiped his mouth on his sleeve. "T-Trystin. My name is Trystin."

"Well, Trystin, this is Godwin, and I am called Elgiva."

The Elfling's eyes grew larger. "The one the wise man spoke of?"

Elgiva was taken by surprise. "What did the wise man say?"

"That someone would come to … free us." He glanced about him warily. "He said it was you. But I mustn't tell. And I've kept my secret, Lady."

Elgiva regarded him steadily. "How old are you?" she asked.

"Fourteen … fifteen … I'm not sure, Lady."

"Why are you out here? Where are your parents?"

He lowered his melancholy gaze and his bottom lip trembled. "Dead. A long time. Killed."

"The King?" she asked him gently.

He nodded and turned away. Elgiva reached out and took his hand. "I know your king. He's an evil Elf. Are you a slave of his?"

"We all are," he said solemnly. "We're cursed and starved and beaten. There's nothing but slavery in Misterell." His red-rimmed eyes were wet with tears and they gazed at her in supplication. "Have you come to help us, Lady?"

She shouldered his question aside. "This wise man, Trystin, where does he live?"

Trystin's disappointment was naked in his gaze. "In the hills beyond the river," he sighed. "He came to Misterell a few months ago. He wore a cloak and a hood, so I don't know what he looks like. I was out collecting mushrooms, Lady, near the edge of the forest. He wouldn't tell me his name, but he talked to me and I liked him. He told me of you and said I should meet you. He said I should help you … but … I couldn't stay." At this, the tears fell freely down his cheeks, leaving trails in the grime on his skin. He smudged them away with the back of his hand. "He was kind to me and he trusted me. He promised to visit whenever he could and I saw him twice, at night. It was good to talk to him. I could tell him things. There was no-one else." Fresh tears spilled from his eyes. "There was no-one else I could talk to. But I haven't seen him for weeks, Lady."

"Is he an Elf?"

He shrugged his thin shoulders. "I don't know, Lady, but he spoke in the Elven tongue. He asked me what was happening in Misterell and he said no-one must know we had spoken. The King has lots of spies, he said. I was told to keep watch for you and, when you arrived, I was to help you, but I couldn't stay in Misterell. So … I've failed him, haven't I?"

"You've run away," she said matter-of-factly.

"I was afraid!" he exclaimed, his dark eyes round with terror. "They caught me stealing bread in the kitchens. They beat me with a stick. So, yesterday I ran away, because … because…"

"You've had enough of beatings."

He sobbed into his grimy hands. Elgiva and Godwin looked at each other, sharing a surge of compassion. Then Elgiva touched the young Elf's cheek.

"Who did this to you?"

He clapped his hand to the damaged flesh and pulled away from her, as though ashamed. "The Captain of the Guard," he sniffed. "Two summers ago. For … insolence."

Elgiva frowned at this. "Don't back away from me. Come here." She seized his thin arm and drew him towards her. "Whatever happens, trust me," she said. "I will not hurt you." She pressed her palm against the scar.

Elgiva focused inwardly, ignoring all distractions. For what she wanted to do, she needed to find belief in her powers, to cast aside all previous doubts. No thought of failure could be allowed to spoil her concentration. It was time to consciously summon the magic and bend it to her will.

She had no strong emotion, no threat of danger to trigger her might, so she focused on the ugly scar; the disfigurement of healthy flesh and the cruelty that had caused it. Soon she felt her anger stir in response to this unjust act. She brought her will, her ability to heal and her hatred of cruelty to a point of convergence.

As she focused upon the scar, Trystin trembled in fear.

Elgiva smiled to herself, as the magic blossomed in her limbs, quickened and gathered strength. Power hummed along her nerves. It wasn't magic apt for destruction, but warm and controlled and sanative, and, when she felt that the time was right, she willed it to flow into Trystin's face.

He felt it flooding into his skin, saw the flare of power in Elgiva's eyes and involuntarily he recoiled, terrified of magic. Godwin, kneeling beside Elgiva, leaned forwards and seized the Elfling's wrist and, to his amazement, he felt the magic faintly in his hand; a brief and subtle shivering of power, attenuated by distance. For a moment he felt aglow with health, then the magic was gone.

Elgiva sat back, breathing hard. "Now, little Elf," she said with a smile. "Tell me what you feel."

Gingerly, Trystin lifted his hand and lightly touched his cheek. What his fingers found he dared not believe; that what had been an ugly seam of skin was now as smooth as the rest of his face. He gazed at Elgiva in wonder.

"It's gone! It's gone!" he shouted with joy. "Oh, Lady Elgiva, thank you!"

He threw his arms about her and hugged her for all he was worth. Elgiva pushed him away.

"Don't take on so! It was nothing, Trystin. Godwin, give him some more to eat. He's so thin it makes me shudder."

"You've healed me, Lady, with magic … good magic!" His eyes were large with worship and astonishment.

She looked away, slightly embarrassed, and her eyes met Godwin's. He smiled at her approvingly, then handed more food to the Elfling. Trystin gladly accepted and grinned at them both in turn. As he ate, he stopped repeatedly to thank Elgiva and praise her, and he hummed a little tune to himself while his mouth was crammed with food.

Godwin warmed his hands before the fire. "You'll choke, lad," he remarked. "Eat more slowly, Trystin, for your stomach's sake."

"I'm sorry, my Lord," said Trystin shyly.

Godwin laughed at this. "My name is Godwin, and I'm no-one's lord, merely a runaway servant. Just like you in fact. And Elgiva. We've all escaped from slavery. Why even our pony, Grimalkin." He chuckled to himself. "Quite a collection of churls we have here."

Elgiva caught his eye and grinned.

"You're not from the village, then, Master Godwin?"

Godwin looked puzzled. "What village is that?"

"A day's walk on the other side of Misterell," Trystin explained. "South-west. In the river valley. The people who live there look like you. We trade with them. But it's not fair. This trade is the King's idea. They give him kine and half their crops and in return he leaves them alone and doesn't use magic against them. But even so, they're under a spell. Grandfather calls it Elf-bane. It won't let them leave the valley. I think if they try it will kill them. We were their friends once, Grandfather says. And now their chief is old and ill. Poor Wilthkin, their lives are hard."

"Have you any news of Elindell? Did the wise man ever speak of it?" Elgiva asked him hopefully.

Trystin screwed his face up thoughtfully and tried to remember information that made no sense to him. "King Thallinore has a mind fever. He wanders the forest all day and makes toy warriors out of twigs. Slow poison, the wise man says. Who is this king?"

"It doesn't matter, Trystin. He's just a watered down version of Vieldrin. Well, I'd like to meet this wise man, but the main thing now is Misterell."

Trystin gasped and stumbled to his feet, as though preparing to flee. Elgiva stood up, placed her hands on his shoulders and looked him in the eye.

"We're looking for the Lorestone. Did the wise man speak of it?"

Trystin looked sheepish, then nodded.

"Does he know where it is?" she asked.

"He … thought he knew where it might be," said Trystin, chewing his lower lip. "A place deep in the heart of the forest … where Faine would go for solitude. That's what the legends say. I told the wise man of this place. He said it sounded right."

"So you could take us to it?"

This was the question that Trystin had dreaded the most. He chewed his badly-bitten fingernails and avoided

Elgiva's eyes. "He made me promise to show you, Lady. It's well-hidden, but…" He looked up at her pleadingly. "I can't go back. I can't!"

"Be reasonable, lad," said Godwin. "It's vital you show us where it is and both of us will protect you."

"No, please, Master Godwin, I'm afraid. Please. You don't understand."

"I understand that you've broken your promise."

"No," said Elgiva, "let him do what he likes." She turned to her friend with an arch look, hoping that he'd guess her meaning. "So, Trystin, where will you go now?"

"I was going to the wise man to beg for shelter, but now … but now I can't. Well, I don't care, as long as I'm away from Misterell. I'll find a cave or wood to hide in and stay there forever, if I have to."

A memory from the past flitted like a shadow across Elgiva's mind. "A sad end for one so young," she sighed. She looked at Godwin, who seemed to know what was required of him.

"You'd be better off with us, fighting for freedom, than hiding in a cave for the rest of your days, afraid to stick your head out, like a snail that fears being trodden on. But I guess you know what you want." He shrugged.

"The wise man was cruel," said Elgiva, "making you promise to risk yourself."

The Elfling looked at them both in turn with a lost and anguished expression. "No!" he protested. "He's not cruel! The wise man was my friend."

"So it is with sages," Elgiva went on, frowning. "What do they know of the real world? They spend all their time with books. They get children to do their dirty work instead of going out in the world and putting their knowledge to good use."

"No, Lady, no! He's not like that! The wise man is clever and good!"

"If he were good, he'd have rescued you. Instead he entrusted you with a mission. You're much too young for such a burden."

Trystin frantically chewed his nails.

Elgiva turned to Godwin. "What do you think, my friend?"

"I think we're wasting our time," he replied, "and we should get some sleep."

Elgiva nodded. "A good idea. Well, Trystin, you can stay here tonight and breakfast with us before you leave tomorrow."

Trystin made to answer her, but his mind was in turmoil and he couldn't speak.

His companions then lay down and readied themselves for sleep and Trystin felt himself dismissed. He lay down and curled up before the fire and closed his weary eyes.

But some time later he was still awake, his mind refusing to rest. He was torn in two directions: on one hand, his fear of going home and, on the other, the promise he had made. And there was no-one in the world who could help him reach a decision. He knew what he ought to do, but he didn't want to do it. Tears welled up in his eyes again, as he touched the cheek that was healed and whole.

The effort of stifling his sobs hurt his throat and he could bear it no longer. Abandoning the warmth of the fire, he went to the shadows to weep unheard. But he didn't get very far. A large shape barred his way. For a moment, he was greatly alarmed, but he quickly realised that it was only Grimalkin. He reached out his hand to stroke her neck. She swung her head round, stared at him, and snorted with disdain.

"Want to hear a riddle, child?"

He nodded, tried to smile.

"What must you keep after giving it to someone else?" she asked.

He shook his head.

"Your word, stupid!"

Snickering triumphantly, the pony sidled away.

* * *

Chapter Twenty

When the travellers awoke the next morning, the sun had just risen and the sky was flushed with pink and gold.

While Godwin rebuilt the camp-fire, he listened to the birds. The trees were full of their music and he felt a surge of vernal hope that pushed aside his dread. After breakfast was eaten, he emptied his pack onto the ground and he and Elgiva took stock of their provisions.

They had two water-skins and Joskin's bowl and flints and these they transferred to the pony's pack, along with the remaining bread and cheese and a small amount of dried fruit left over from Oswald's provisions. At the bottom of the pack, nestling in a leather pouch, they also discovered an odd collection of shrivelled fungi.

Elgiva grinned at her friend. "I think you'd better dispose of them."

Godwin nodded and smiled. "Yes. There's plenty of strange things going on as it is, without resorting to these." He scattered the mushrooms into the bushes. "We've enough food left for one more meal, two perhaps, if we're careful. No need for this anymore, I think." He picked up his back-pack and threw it away.

Elgiva leaned on Grimalkin's shoulder and followed the wispy clouds with her gaze. The morning sunshine was warm on her skin and she allowed herself to revel in it. Godwin sensed that she wasn't yet ready to set off on their quest. Something told him to sit by the fire and keep himself occupied by sharpening his knife.

Trystin was sitting a few feet away, looking downcast and chewing his nails. He had just returned from bathing in the pool and his face looked even younger without its layer of dirt.

"A wonderful time of year, spring," mused Elgiva suddenly. "Don't you agree, Trystin?"

Trystin looked up and parted his lips, but he merely smiled in an awkward manner and continued to chew his nails.

"Buds on the trees and birds building nests. Wherever you look, there's life and power, and the strange thing is," Elgiva went on, "it arises out of decay."

"I wonder what tells the birds to make nests," said Godwin. "What makes the green things start to grow again?"

"The need to survive," she said. "But in the natural world there's a balance. The needs of all creatures must be considered. In Elves and Wilthkin, it corrupts. It makes the strong cruel and the weak faint-hearted." She cast a quick glance at Trystin and was pleased to find him listening intently, though pretending to be indifferent. "Some in order to survive run away from whatever threatens them and they are doomed to run forever, never finding peace of mind. Good creatures must act or the bad ones will flourish, but they don't realise that. It's much wiser to face our fears than to drag out the torment day after day and live in some self-imposed prison." Elgiva paused for a moment and thought of her old friend Bellic and she fancied that he would be proud of her eloquence. "Better to try and fail than never to try at all and wonder always what might have been. Wouldn't you say so, Godwin?"

"Why, er, yes, Elgiva. Better to die once than die a little every day, I suppose, but what? ..."

"Well," said Elgiva briskly, "if we're ready, we'd best be on our way. Perhaps, Trystin, you could give us some directions before you leave?"

Trystin stared at his legs and seemed unaware that she had addressed him. Then, slowly, he lifted his head and looked at them both with an expression of grim resignation.

"Lady, you're right," he admitted. "I could never escape the King. I could run a thousand miles away and he'd always be in my mind. I'm terrified of Misterell, but I love it, too, and my friends, and I've left them behind. That was wrong of me."

Elgiva walked towards him and drew him to his feet. "I've tried to get you to come with us, Trystin, because the search for the Lorestone is so important, but I know I've been very selfish. I haven't considered your fears at all. And that was wrong of ME. I have no right to force you to act against your will."

"Oh, no, you haven't, Lady," he assured her, "it was what you said about spring. It just made me think of ... home." His eyes misted a little and then he smiled; a sorrowful smile but one that was full of warmth. "But you shall see for yourself."

Elgiva rested her arm on his shoulder. "Very well, my friend," she said. "Let's be strong together."

* * *

They departed for Misterell as soon as Grimalkin had completed an extensive breakfast, which involved sampling most of the local plant-life. She wasn't a creature to be hurried. Godwin wondered at the tolerance of his companions; personally, he would have given the beast a wallop on the rump to get her moving.

The sun grew warmer as it climbed towards noon and, when it was at its zenith, the travellers stopped to rest. They sat in a meadow of tall grass, Grimalkin standing over them, like some wary matriarch. Elgiva talked of Elindell and Trystin listened raptly, but Godwin soon found his attention drifting.

His eyes drank in the landscape, the vegetation sprouting green shoots. The patches of woodland that bordered the meadow blossomed with new leaves and soon the land around them would be a riot of colour. He lay down on his stomach, his chin cupped in his hands, and his mind began to wander.

For a while he was lost in thoughts of summer, how his children would skip through the fields that surrounded the settlement, dancing among the poppies with daisy chains on their heads. Then a sudden rustling noise some yards upwind dragged him back to the present. Two young rabbits darted out of the grass and crossed his line of vision. He watched their antics for a while and grinned.

"Look at those two," he whispered. "They don't even know we're here."

Elgiva looked up and smiled. "They're babies," she said.

"Sometimes," mused Godwin, "I envy you Elves, being able to talk to animals. I wish I could talk to them, too. I wonder what rabbits have to say to each other?"

Elgiva's eyebrows arched mischievously and, leaning closer to Trystin, she whispered in his ear. "Shall we give the Wilthkin his wish?"

The Elfling grinned with glee. "Oh, yes, Lady! Can you?"

Elgiva considered the matter. Her earlier success in healing Trystin had given her more confidence in the usage of her powers. "I'll try," she said. "Let's hope it works." She chewed her lower lip thoughtfully. "Well then, here goes."

Elgiva doubted the outcome, but she felt her power respond at once and knew that something would happen.

"Mother won't half give it you, if you run off again!" declared the smaller rabbit.

Godwin's eyebrows shot sharply upwards.

"Mother said you must stay in the burrow. You're real bad, that's what she said."

Godwin raised himself from his elbows and his mouth hung open in disbelief.

"You're too young to go gadding off," continued the smaller rabbit. "Get yourself eaten up by an old fox and you'll be sorry, you will!"

"No fox is going to get me!" retorted the larger rabbit. "I'm faster than any old fox or anything." And so saying, he hopped away, while his brother dashed off in the opposite direction and disappeared in the long grass.

Godwin was now on his knees, his eyes wide with amazement, unaware of the giggling of Elves. "You won't believe this…" he began, spinning round to face them. "What are you laughing at?"

His companions couldn't answer, for they were helpless with mirth.

"Oh, Godwin!" cried Elgiva, giggling like a child, "you ought to see your face!"

"No, spare him that," snickered Grimalkin. "It's not a sight bears close inspection."

"I see!" said Godwin crossly. "An Elf's trick, by Frigg! Well, thanks for including me in the joke, though I seem to be the object of it." His hurt and angry frown erased the grin on Elgiva's face.

"Don't be such a bore, Godwin. You're not really angry, are you? I gave you your wish. The gift of a friend." For a moment she seemed uncertain, then she flashed him a charming smile.

Godwin pretended to be aloof, but he saw in her eyes a sense of wonder that even surpassed his own. Knowing that she was pleased with herself, he concealed his indignation. "How long will this spell of yours last?"

Elgiva shrugged her slender shoulders. "I can't be sure. As long as you live, I hope. From now on you will understand animals, Elves and men, and they will understand you." She tossed her head back haughtily. "That's quite a gift, you know. Aren't you going to thank me, at least?"

Her stance rekindled Godwin's anger. "Thank you? For making a fool of me?"

"Cabbage hearts!" snorted Grimalkin. "Don't credit her with Nature's work!"

This unexpected sarcasm from a supposedly dumb beast made Godwin scowl with fury.

"You should be thankful!" snapped Elgiva. "I could have turned you into a rabbit instead of letting you speak its language. Perhaps the thought did cross my mind!"

Her black eyes flashed with anger and for a moment they stared at each other, the tension growing between them. Godwin, however, could see the wisdom in lightening the mood, so he cocked his fists on his hips and pretended to be indignant.

"Turn me into a rabbit, would you? Well, we'll see about that!"

He darted after Elgiva, his arms outstretched to grab her, but she skipped away from him, laughing. Trystin danced like a carefree child, giggling with delight, as Godwin chased her through the grass and up and down a shallow knoll. And for a time they were children again, their burdens cast aside.

Godwin knew that he would never catch his friend, although it didn't spoil the game of tag he had initiated, but, as he prepared to spring at her again, she suddenly drew up short. Seizing the opportunity, he grabbed her by the arm.

"Got you!" he cried triumphantly. "Now let's see you turn me into a rabbit, shall we!"

Elgiva ignored him; she was listening, and Trystin was on his feet, alert and afraid.

"What's wrong?" asked Godwin, suddenly alarmed.

But then he heard it, too: a strange, unearthly noise was floating over the fields and it came from the forest of Misterell. Godwin had never heard anything like it and it turned his blood to ice. It was like the wailing of many harps, shrill and sad and distorted by distance and punctuated by the blare of horns. It seemed as weird and frightening as the eldritch forest itself.

"The harps of Misterell!" Trystin exclaimed, covering his face with his hands. "Vieldrin has returned!"

"What do you mean?" asked Godwin anxiously.

Trystin looked up with fear in his eyes. "He travels often, Master Godwin, and, when he returns, the harps and horns must sound in welcome. By his order."

"You mean, he's actually home," said Godwin scanning the landscape. "That is … he won't come this way, will he?"

"Who can say which way he comes?" said Trystin, wringing his hands. "On foot? In a chariot? With an army or on his own? Sometimes he's invisible, to catch us unawares. He changes all the time."

"Yes," said Godwin, "we've met him. We know his love of disguises. He pretended to be an old man and travelled with us awhile."

Trystin almost choked at this. "W-with you, Master Godwin?"

"Yes," said Elgiva grimly. "He tried to persuade me to be his ally."

"And we met him once before that," added Godwin.

"He's had two chances to kill you, Lady, but you still live!" Trystin was astonished. "All who oppose him are killed. That's Vieldrin's way."

"But I haven't opposed him!" protested Elgiva. "I can't! I don't know how and Vieldrin is fully aware of that. He knows my power is limited. Had he used all his force against me, I wouldn't be standing here now."

"Perhaps you aren't a threat to him now, but you will be," stated Godwin.

Elgiva lowered her gaze. "He … he means to corrupt me first."

"You have no faith in yourself at all," observed Godwin gently.

Trystin approached Elgiva slowly and slid his arm through hers, his large eyes moist with worship. "You should have faith," he ventured. "I've never seen magic put to good use and it seems to be all the stronger. Evil can only destroy. Where's the strength in that, Lady?

Good magic turns pain to joy." He touched his cheek for emphasis and a smile lit up his face. "I'm glad I've lived at least this long to finally see good magic. For the first time in my life I know that there's such a thing as hope."

Elgiva shunned his gratitude. "You just don't understand. These powers I have are new to me. They're weak and I can't control them."

"I don't care, Lady. I have to trust them. I can't live with evil magic. Come what may, I pledge myself to you as friend and servant. And I'll have faith in you forever."

Elgiva looked to Godwin for guidance, not knowing how to respond.

"Can Elves enchant other Elves?" he asked, giving her an arch look.

Elgiva sighed with resignation. "All right," she said. "Now we are three."

"Four," snickered Grimalkin.

"Four!" exclaimed Elgiva. "And if we are to prevail against evil, we'd better make a start. Let's place out trust in the powers of Good. Misterell awaits." She tossed back her head in a gesture of defiance and the sunshine gleamed on her dark hair. Taking Trystin by the hand, she briskly led the way. Grimalkin lumbered after them and Godwin brought up the rear.

Godwin knew that their quest had now reached the point of no return and, while his friends' determination seemed to have strengthened, the spectre of an unknown future grinned at him with carnivorous glee at the limit of his vision.

He clenched his hand firmly on the hilt of his sword.

★ ★ ★

As the afternoon wore on, a mild south-westerly breeze blew up and clouds rolled sluggishly overhead, but the companions paid little heed to the possibility of rain, for Misterell lay ahead of them and dominated their thoughts. The harps and horns had long since ceased and a cold, grey silence floated out from under the forest's skirts, spreading like sea-fog over the grass.

But despite her gloomy thoughts, Elgiva noticed, as they drew nearer, a strange and puzzling fact. The ancient trees were impossibly verdant, as if they had heard the call of spring some weeks before the surrounding land.

All too soon, they found themselves standing before the edge of the forest, confronted by a wall of trees that stood together like sentinels. Their branches overlapped and meshed and their roots were buried deep beneath a tangle of shrubs. The travellers listened for hostile sounds, subdued by the aspect of the towering trees, and in the shadow of the mighty forest, they felt their insignificance.

For her part, Elgiva wondered still at the forest's vernal splendour. The branches above were rife with leaves and, despite the eerie calm surrounding it, inside the forest a host of birds filled the boughs with song. It was almost as if the birds had flocked to the enchantment of Misterell.

She gazed up at the trees; they were dour and forbidding. There was a feeling of power about them. But when she probed them with her Elven senses, she found no wrong in them.

Yet beneath their quiet murmur of life she felt their stern command: turn back.

She looked at her companions, her forehead lined with doubt. Trystin chewed his fingernails, while Grimalkin fought the urge to shy. Godwin stood and hugged his chest and gazed at the forest before him, as though it were a forty -foot wall and he had been asked to climb it.

"Well, here we are," he stated uselessly. "How far must we go into the forest?"

"To the middle," snickered Grimalkin. "After that, we'd be going out."

"The trees aren't so crowded inside," said Trystin. "There are many paths and glades. I know the way, Master Godwin." He looked at his friends and gave them a nervous grin, caught between fear of going home and excitement at being their guide through the forest.

Elgiva peered up at the lofty trees, like an ant inspecting a bulrush. "Very well, Trystin. Lead the way."

★ ★ ★

Chapter Twenty-One

In single file they threaded their way between the knuckled trunks of the ancient trees and, once this initial barrier was breached, an astounding sight met their eyes and they stopped and gazed around, astonished. Trystin grinned with pleasure, delighted by his companions' response.

Inside the forest, the air seemed warmer and bird-song filled the treetops. Wherever they looked the shrubs and plants were prematurely in bloom and a rich, moist, peppery perfume rode the silken breeze. There were tangles of elder and hawthorn and clumps of hazel, heavy with catkins. Rowans stood proudly between the old oaks and the emerald sward was ablaze with coltsfoot, daffodils and daisies. Fungi clustered in the shade beneath the grey-barked beech trees and the sun that pierced the branches above seemed to lie on the shrubs like powdered gold.

Godwin stared about him in wonder, as hundreds of white petals, the discarded blossom of many trees, drifted down around him like snow. On every side he saw throngs of harebells and clouds of feathery ferns and they seemed to dance beneath the trees in an almost dreamlike shimmer. And the trees themselves seemed to grow together in defiance of their natures. He was used to woods were one type of tree dominated over the rest, usually oak or beech, but this was like an ideal forest, a vision of health and beauty. It seemed to him that Misterell was a haven for green, growing things; a sanctuary for natural life.

Elgiva's heart was filled with joy at the sight that greeted her gaze. Now she knew why the birds had forsaken the neighbouring land and flocked to this forest. Now she fully understood the power and pride that hummed in the oaks, the air of prohibition that Misterell put forth. This wasn't a natural forest, but a supernatural one.

She turned to her companions, her eyes almost sated with beauty. "No wonder this place is enchanted," she said reverently. "It guards itself against intruders. This is a special place."

"It's wonderful," agreed Godwin. He inhaled deeply, savouring the scent of the rich, dark earth, the radiant flowers and the woody perfume of the trees. It was as life-affirming as the first breath after birth.

Grimalkin's nostrils flared with delight. "It smells delicious," she said.

"Spring always comes early to Misterell," explained Trystin proudly. "One of the Founder's gifts to us. This place is good and beautiful. There is no forest like it in all the land."

"I never expected this," said Elgiva. "My people fear Misterell as a place of evil."

"Perhaps it is evil now," sighed Trystin, "but it wasn't always so. Misterell is enchanted and other kingdoms have feared it, because it's a powerful place, but they don't know the truth. The wise man feared to come here, too, but when he did he realised that Misterell is sacred, not evil. He said the enchantment comes from Faine and we should feel honoured to live here. Faine brought all the people together at a place we call the Hill-Shrine and he did great magic there long ago. We used to go there to worship his memory and share our love for the Earth, but that's forbidden now. The penalty for worshipping Faine is death. Grandfather says that Vieldrin is jealous of the Founder."

Elgiva frowned indignantly. "Misterell has been fickle before. Bellic told me some of the legends, how Misterell turned against the Founder and so he left them and never returned. And when they realised their loss, they knew it was too late. All they had left were guilt and remorse."

"So it's said, Lady," said Trystin sadly, "but before he left he blessed the forest and Faine wouldn't take back such a gift. Not even in anger, Grandfather said. I don't believe we lost his love either. The elders still argue about it, but I'm sure that Faine forgave us." He paused and tried to smile at them. "Grandfather told me our forbears repented and so the Hill-Shrine was consecrated and dedicated to Faine." He sighed deeply and looked away. "But then," he went on, "the guilt of the people began to infect the forest. It withered and shrank back into itself. So, when the spring returns each year, it makes us both happy and sad. As Grandfather says, we remember Faine's love and also how that love was spurned. Now the enchantment that Faine gave to Misterell has become a thing of fear. The forest is warped by guilt."

Elgiva grasped the Elfling's arm and made him look at her. "This is a sorry tale indeed, but I do think that you are forgiven. The Founder wasn't easily spurned and it seems to me that he trusted you above all his other kingdoms, because he left the Lorestone in your keeping."

Trystin stared at her hopefully. "If the Lorestone's really here..."

"That's what we have to find out. But, first, I'd like to see this Shrine."

Trystin's gaunt features brightened and he took her by the hand. "It's this way, Lady Elgiva." His steps were brisk and purposeful, as he led her into the forest.

Grimalkin trotted after them, wafted along by the heady scent of edible greenery, but Godwin followed with some reluctance. Delay was the last thing they needed and it made him apprehensive. He tried to respect Elgiva's wishes, but they had no meaning for him. A Shrine to Faine was all very well, but where could he honour his own beliefs? Where could he find some spiritual guidance in a world of Elves and enchanted forests?

Yet how could the gods of his masters aid him? Would Woden, god of magic and valour, have any time for a cowardly churl? Woden had more in common with Elves. If anyone earned a seat in Valhalla, it would be Elgiva, not him.

The companions walked through a coppiced area, then crossed the ford of a shallow stream. A well-trodden path took them on through the trees, through clumps of sowthistle and betony, then skirted a group of abandoned huts that had fallen into decay. Trystin moved at a quicker pace and averted his eyes from the crumbling huts, as though some horror were crouching there. A cloud of memories darkened his gaze and he touched his healed cheek, as though it helped to steady him on his course.

At length, the path snaked out into a clearing and at its centre was a shallow knoll. Rowans grew around its base and buttercups swarmed on the grass below it. Trystin stopped and grinned at his friends.

"The Hill-Shrine," he announced.

Elgiva prepared to climb the knoll, but Trystin tugged at her sleeve. "No, Lady Elgiva, it's forbidden! The penalty is death!"

"I will climb this knoll, no matter what!" she said vehemently, and she tossed back her long hair, her eyes bright with purpose.

Godwin smiled grimly at this. He watched her turn and stride up the slope to the summit of the knoll, and he admired her spirit, but not her lack of wisdom. Shaking his head, he sat down heavily, resigned himself to waiting, but he kept a wary eye on the forest and his hand on the haft of his sword.

Trystin chewed his finger thoughtfully, his tormented gaze flinching back and forth between Godwin and Elgiva. Then finally he made his choice and scampered off up the knoll.

The flat crest of the Hill-Shrine bore a crown of flowering plants, a ring of purple self-heal nearly a foot in height. Trystin stepped into the circle and stood at Elgiva's side.

"They always grow here like this, Lady." He pointed at the flowers. "Grandfather says Faine ordained it. They represent the counsellors who stood with Faine at his first court here."

Elgiva merely nodded at this simple explanation, but to herself she mused upon the meaning of the Shrine. Self-heal. Was that the Founder's message, his legacy to Misterell? To Elvendom itself? And what about the rowans, the trees with power over death?

She knelt upon the thick grass and her veins were filled with a sudden surge of energy and courage. The earth beneath her seemed charged with power and, when she placed her palms on the ground, it seemed to share itself with her.

Yes, she thought, there's power here, and something else; some memory. A residue of something. A feeling of love, of oneness.

Tears sprang into her dark eyes, though her heart was brimming with joy.

"Faine First-Father," she said softly, "I am committed to your service, yet I need courage to face the future. My heart is weak. Don't let me fail." She clenched her hands in the grass beneath her and closed her eyes in prayer. "Grant us your guidance and protection and let us find the Lorestone and free your people from the evil that threatens them. Let Misterell be once more proud to praise your name. And, as for myself, whatever happens, I pledge to serve you always."

Trystin was moved to kneel by his friend in deference to the Founder, yet it was hard for him to refrain from glancing at the encircling forest, hard to suppress the dread of being discovered.

Godwin waited patiently. Out of respect he stifled the yawn that threatened to crack his jaw, but he longed to stretch himself full-length upon the deep, rich grass. The forest's balmy, fragrant air was making him feel drowsy.

At length, their prayers completed, Elgiva and Trystin walked down the slope of the knoll, holding each other's hand, and their faces shone like children who were on their best behaviour.

Godwin clambered to his feet and tried to look alert.

"Should you make a sacrifice or something?"

He felt pleased at being able to make a contribution to the proceedings, but Elgiva's pert nose wrinkled slightly, as though he had uttered an oath.

"What sacrifice do you have in mind? We don't shed blood in the name of Lord Faine. He taught us to love our fellow creatures, not take away their lives."

Suddenly, her face darkened, and her brow was creased with remorse, but Godwin couldn't find the strength to ask her what was wrong. He merely shrugged and said, "But you asked much of him."

Elgiva turned to face him and she flinched under his artless gaze. "Yes, I need his help, Godwin, and I want to be worthy of it ... but I'm not worthy. I've shed blood." She wrapped her arms about her chest and struggled with her feelings of self-loathing. "I'm a murderer, Godwin."

"You had reasons to do what you did. I don't call it murder."

"No? But I did destroy the Forest of Shades and where was the reason in that? I did it deliberately and how quickly I've forgotten that!"

"Be reasonable. You did Faine's work, Elgiva," Godwin protested, growing annoyed. "You put an end to an evil place ... and that self-same evil made you do it."

She dismissed this with a quick shake of her head. "That's neither here nor there," she said. "The forest couldn't help itself, but I had a choice. I could have shown mercy. I could have tried to help the trees. I misused my powers for my own entertainment. I was showing off." She lowered her gaze as though ashamed. "It was an act of pure vanity."

She stood for a moment toying with her hair, while Godwin wondered how to console her, then her sudden demand startled him.

"Give me your knife, please, Godwin!"

He grimaced apprehensively. "What are you going to do?"

"Don't worry," she reassured him. "But you were right … as usual." The smile that lit up her delicate features was unashamedly deferential. "I can't shed blood to honour Faine, but a sacrifice of some kind is required."

Perplexed and concerned, he took out his knife and gave it to his friend. Elgiva tested its edge with her thumb then turned and ascended the knoll. Once on the summit, she took the blade in one hand and her long, black hair in the other and, without a moment's hesitation, she severed the gleaming tresses. Then she scattered them carelessly on the grass, as though they were contemptible.

Godwin winced at this desperate act and Trystin gasped in horror.

"Oh, Master Godwin! Elven ladies never cut their hair!"

But Godwin wasn't listening. His attention was totally drawn to his friend as she stood on top of the knoll.

"I have been guilty of vanity and I've misused the power you gave me, Lord Faine. So I sacrifice this symbol of vanity to make amends with you. Forgive me, if you can, and guide me to a truer path." Elgiva drew a deep breath and straightened herself, as though shrugging off a burden.

Godwin felt that he understood the necessity for her action, though it galled him to see her hair despoiled. He placed a hand on Trystin's shoulder and opened his mouth to speak, but then his attention was snatched away by a rustling in the shrubs nearby and he span to confront the unknown threat.

Trystin's thin hands flew to his face and Grimalkin let loose a snort of alarm, as three Elves sprang into the glade, each one carrying a spear. They halted several yards from the knoll and assessed the situation. Spangles of sunlight flashed on their spears.

"So!" cried one. "Intruders! You defy the laws of the King"

"The penalty is death!" yelled another.

Two of the Elves levelled their spears and strode towards Godwin and Trystin. Their faces wore grins of anticipation.

"Be gone!" commanded Elgiva. "Leave us alone or I will attack you!"

"Yah!" jeered the first Elf, and he and his companion marched steadily on.

Godwin thrust the Elfling behind him and hastily drew his sword. He knew that his hand was shaking badly, but the effort of trying to steady it only made it worse, and, while he tried to look menacing, the third Elf stalked towards the knoll.

"In Faine's name, stop!" Elgiva cried. " I do not want to harm you!"

But her warning was ignored. The two Elves got ready to throw their spears. Hampered by Trystin's clinging presence, Godwin couldn't move.

Elgiva, palsied by anger and dread, didn't know what to do, then she looked at the knife still in her hand and was seized by a sudden intuition. She pointed the blade at the two attackers.

Faine, help me! I can't let them kill my friends!

This thought had barely left her mind, when a beam of force streaked from the blade and seared across the clearing. Godwin and Trystin fell to the ground as the ray of destruction spiralled past. When they could bear to open their eyes, they saw two bodies on the grass.

The remaining Elf was taken aback but he soon threw off his shock. With vengeance gleaming in his eyes, he started to climb the knoll and, before he reached the summit, he drew back his arm to strike.

Godwin scrambled to his feet and ran to save Elgiva, but the spear had already been released and was sailing towards its target.

The weapon, however, did no harm. It appeared to hit an invisible wall and Godwin watched in disbelief, as it tumbled to the grass.

The attacker gaped slack-mouthed at this and watched the spear roll down the knoll, as though it had betrayed him. For several moments his eyes flipped back and forth between Elgiva and Godwin and it was then that they noticed the ridge of scar that twisted the length of his right cheek. Recovering his wits, the Elf then scuttled back down the knoll and fled into the forest.

Hastily, Godwin sheathed his sword and bounded up the slope. When he reached Elgiva, he seized her by the shoulders and turned her round to face him. Spent magic glimmered in her eyes and her face looked strangely puzzled. The knife slipped from her grasp.

"Are you hurt?" demanded Godwin.

She shook her head slowly. "No, I'm fine."

He took a deep breath and smiled with relief. "By Frigg! Don't look so thunderstruck. Does your power amaze you that much?"

She seemed unable to focus her gaze and confusion wrinkled her brow. "But … I didn't do anything!"

"Didn't you kill those two?" He pointed at the two dead Elves lying on the grass.

Elgiva recoiled in horror. "Yes," she affirmed, "oh, Godwin, yes! I keep on killing, don't I? But I had to …you know I had to…! You and Trystin…"

He shook her gently. "Stop. It's okay."

Desperately, she searched his face, and then she steadied herself. Godwin stooped to retrieve his knife.

"I used the blade to channel the power," she said in a small, tired voice. "Iron must be a good medium. Perhaps too good. I kill too easily."

Godwin pushed the knife into his belt. "You saved our lives," he reminded her.

"Yes, well, I'm glad of that, but I could do no more."

"I assure you that was quite enough," said Godwin with a grin.

"No, no, I mean … I used up my strength with that first bolt of power." She looked at him intently. "All my strength. I was desperate."

Godwin's composure was shaken. "What?"

"When the Elf attacked me with that spear, I didn't defend myself … I couldn't." She glanced around her, searching for words. "Something … something helped me. Something stood between us and knocked the spear away." She shivered and placed her hand on his arm, as if his solid presence were an antidote to her fear.

Neither of them knew what to say, but they knew that they must face an impossible truth and, as they stood in silence on the knoll, they felt that they were not alone.

Some moments passed before they felt able to move and descend to level ground, where Trystin sat staring at the dead Elves, frantically chewing his nails. He ran to greet them and threw his arms around Elgiva, babbling thanks for his deliverance, but she was appalled by the sight of the dead Elves and couldn't return his embrace.

Godwin pulled the Elfling aside and enlisted his help in dragging the bodies into the underwood. Together they hid all trace of the Elves.

Elgiva suddenly gasped in panic. "Godwin! Where's Grimalkin?"

Trystin was startled. "Oh, Lady Elgiva, she was scared. She must have run away!"

"She can't have gone far," said Godwin. "No doubt she's found something to eat."

"We'd better find her," Elgiva decided. "Trystin and I will search for her. We know the ways of forests. Stay here and rest awhile, Godwin – you look like you could do with it. I'm sure we'll be back before that scarred Elf returns with reinforcements." She touched his arm reassuringly.

Godwin wasn't entirely convinced, but Trystin agreed with Elgiva.

"The Elf will have gone to the Royal Hall, and that's a long way off, Master Godwin. And they won't come back here looking for us. We'd be mad to stay after what we've done."

Mad indeed, thought Godwin. Reluctantly, he acquiesced and watched his friends depart.

When they had gone, he sat down by the knoll and he tried to relax, but it wasn't easy. He drew out his sword and stroked the blade and mused to himself that, as usual, his dubious skills as a warrior had been completely superfluous. Magic had saved the day.

Beneath the warmth of the afternoon sun, the forest was very still, but Godwin had disquieting thoughts, despite the pervasive calm. Perhaps his friends would never return. Perhaps they had never existed. Perhaps he was really in the throes of an illness and would wake up back at the settlement, his lumpy, straw pallet beneath him and his travels but a dream.

He got to his feet and stretched until his bones cracked. The dream, however, persisted. Turning, he looked up at the Hill-Shrine and decided to climb to the top. What prompted this move he didn't know, but he told himself that the top of the knoll was a much better vantage point, where he wouldn't be taken unawares. But inwardly he knew that this was only a part of the reason. He felt too sleepy to be on guard.

He lay down in the circle of Self-heal, like a sacrifice to the spring, the gleaming lengths of Elgiva's severed hair strewn around him in the sunshine. Laying his sword upon the grass beside him, he let the warmth soak into his bones.

Birds trilled in the treetops and insects droned in the tepid air. Warmth, drowsiness and enchantment flooded like a sleeping draught into Godwin's limbs and his eyelids closed contentedly, cradling him in darkness.

Drifting for a time, as though freed from all his fears and doubts, he suddenly became aware that a figure was strolling through the blackness towards him. It drew into focus and he could see that it was Rowena. She was talking to an unseen companion and behind her the Meadhall sprang into being, its walls shivering like a mirage. As the vision sharpened, he found himself listening to his wife's words.

"Yes, our Lord says he will bargain for the captives' return. In my heart I know that Godwin will come back home to me."

She was smiling. That well remembered smile. The long, flaxen hair. The blue eyes like sapphires. If only he could reach out and touch her … touch…

He sat up with a start and the vision burst like a bubble, leaving him bewildered and lost. He gasped at the pain of separation.

Rowena!

Now he really was dreaming. He rubbed his eyes and looked around. There was no sign of his friends. No sign of enemies either. The glade was deserted and quiet; an island of unimpeachable stillness in the tangled, lush-leaved forest.

Before he could wonder at the strangeness of his dream, something compelled him to lie down again. Whatever it was, he couldn't resist it. His eyelids felt like slabs of marble and he was forced to close them. For a time he floated in a lazy warmth, like a ship becalmed on a tropical sea, a silken breeze caressing his skin and filling his lungs with the scents of the forest. Lulled by a bone-deep feeling of security, he was suddenly surprised to hear a voice, a voice that seemed to be in his mind, a mild and soothing voice that spoke to him without words: somehow he felt the meaning. It seemed to hum around him and within him, like the very air he breathed; a voice of authority, but gentleness, too. An anodyne that flowed into his veins like peace. He fancied that, if the Earth could speak, she would speak in such a voice.

"They who persecute evil shall prosper
"And come to their inheritance.
"The sword now sleeps,
"But, awakened, the sword shall guard the good.
"The iron shall be invincible,
"The brand shall be bold,
"The glaive shall be glorious,
"The metal made mighty,
"The steel strengthened.

"The Light-Of-Battle will protect its lord."

Godwin rolled over onto his stomach. He knew that he was dreaming still, but the smell of the earth was so vivid beneath him. Surely, he must be awake? Why couldn't he open his eyes? The ground he lay on seemed to yield and his body sank gladly into it, as though it sought oneness with the Earth. The sun on his back was soothing, narcotic, negating all thoughts of resistance. He opened his mind once more to the voice.

"'Tis time thy natal gift to claim.

"A warrior's fame and place to take;

"And, when in peril, say its name,

"Then Taranuil shall awake."

⋆ ⋆ ⋆

Chapter Twenty-Two

"Are you asleep, Master Godwin?"

Godwin struggled to wake himself up. Shafts of sunlight sliced through the clouds, dappling his vision with the shadows of leaves. He sat up slowly, fighting his confusion. He couldn't remember where he was, but he felt as though he had slept for many hours.

"It didn't take long to find her," announced the Elfling brightly.

"Oh, it's you, is it, Trystin?" mumbled Godwin. "By Frigg, I must have been dreaming!"

"What's that?" called Elgiva from the foot of the knoll, "sleeping when you should have been alert? You could have been slain where you lay."

"It skills not," he said distantly. "The light-of-battle will protect its lord." He grasped the hilt of his sword and suddenly felt, or thought he felt, a tingling in his arm. He pulled his hand away quickly.

"What?" called Elgiva with a puzzled frown.

"By Grim! I've got pins and needles."

"I think Master Godwin is still dreaming," laughed Trystin, helping him to his feet. He handed the sword to its master. Godwin took it cautiously and followed him down the slope.

"We found Grimalkin," Elgiva informed him. "She cast off most of our baggage in her hurry to get away and we were forced to retrieve it. Luckily she left us a good trail to follow and, as you predicted, the local plants were much too tasty for her to stray very far."

"How long were you gone?" he asked.

"Not long at all," she said.

"We found some mushrooms, too," declared Trystin.

Elgiva held out Joskin's bowl, which contained a variety of evil-looking fungi. Trystin snatched it from her hand and thrust it under Godwin's nose.

Godwin averted his eyes in disgust. "Those are toadstools!" he exclaimed. "Do you want to poison me?"

Trystin looked crestfallen. "I'm sorry, Master Godwin. I didn't know that Wilthkin can't eat them." His lower lip began to tremble, as though he were owning up to having committed a horrible deed.

Godwin put his arm around him. "Never mind, lad. No harm done."

The Elfling smiled at him gratefully.

"We'd better make a move," said Elgiva. "We've tarried here too long."

Godwin nodded his assent, though he felt that he needed more time to gather his wits together. His recent dreams had clouded his brain, but he had to acknowledge the need for haste. He followed his friends, as they left the glade, but his mind was wandering still in visions.

Hardly had they left the clearing, when a skirl of shrill cries snatched their attention back to the top of the knoll. A host of birds had descended on the Shrine and each one picked up a hank of dark hair before taking flight again. Their cries rang with triumph, as they bore their spoils aloft. Elgiva seemed briefly taken aback, but then she laughed with delight.

"At least I have some use in this world, even if only for lining nests!"

Her companions shared her amusement and, with Trystin leading once again, they set off through the forest.

As they threaded their way through the undergrowth, it grew increasingly thicker, thwarting their need for both speed and stealth.

"We're making no headway at all," complained Godwin, stabbing at the shrubs with his sword. He suspected that Trystin was leading them astray, but he didn't want to offend the Elfling's overly sensitive nature with ill-considered criticism.

"They'll be looking for us, Master Godwin," said Trystin, as though he had read his mind. "We must avoid the paths."

"Perhaps," said Elgiva, "we should startle Grimalkin. I dare say she'd make a fine path for us in her frenzy to escape."

This remark was greeted with horsy disdain.

"With our luck she'd go in the wrong direction," Godwin said with a sigh. To ease his frustration, he took a swipe at a low-hanging branch with his sword. The weapon cut cleanly through the bough, as though it had been a twig. Satisfying though this was, Godwin berated himself for his foolishness. The blade could have been damaged.

"This fellow was sired by a seax!" he said. "Whoever forged this weapon gave it the temper of stone."

"Must you mutilate the trees to prove it?" asked Elgiva behind him.

He didn't deign to answer this, as his answer would have been hurtful. Perhaps it was an answer that she deserved for having deflated his pride. No. What happened in the Forest of Shades was something best forgotten.

"Shameful for a warrior to have so sharp a sword," he mused. "It should be blunted by frequent battle."

He plied the blade once more to the vegetation that blocked their way, clearing the path of obstructions. Trystin gave up the position of leader and followed meekly in his wake.

"A good thing he's shameful," whinnied Grimalkin, "or we'd be stuck in this lot till autumn."

Godwin ignored the animal's sarcasm.

At length, they came to a small clearing. Daylight was leaving the forest, but there was enough to threaten their safety away from the underwood's concealment. For a moment they looked at each other, but then, by some unspoken agreement, they decided to cross the clearing.

Suddenly, as if from nowhere, a tiny figure appeared from the trees, a sackful of firewood strapped to its back. At once, the four companions melted back into the arms of the forest.

A flock of rooks cawed stridently across the darkening sky and the tiny figure jumped in alarm. She watched them speeding home to roost and then, as silence drifted down once more upon the glade, she went on with her chore. The sack she carried seemed cruelly large, but she continued to fill it with twigs, as if inured to the task.

"That's Kinchine!" declared Trystin. "She's my friend!"

Without further consideration, he broke from cover and ran to meet her. His companions shared a thoughtful look, then cautiously followed his example. When Kinchine saw Trystin running towards her, she dropped the twigs she was carrying and covered her mouth with her hands.

"Kinchine, what's wrong? It's me. It's Trystin!"

"Go away!" she wailed, stepping back. "You ran off. They'll catch you! They'll kill you … and Kinchie, too! I mustn't talk to you. Haldrin said so."

Trystin turned to his friends for support, his large eyes full of hurt.

"Don't be afraid, little Elf," said Elgiva, smiling warmly at the child.

"Kinchie not afraid of YOU!" Kinchine cried indignantly. "Kinchie afraid of warriors! Kinchie wants to go home now!" Her eyes darted about in panic, seeking a way of escape.

Godwin put his sword away and approached the Elf-child slowly. "There's really no reason to be afraid." He gave her a generous smile. "Nobody saw us come to this place, so Kinchie is quite safe."

She pouted at him charmingly with a child's expression of doubt and he saw that the edge had left her wariness. Moving forwards, he scooped her up and held her in his arms. A tiny squeal escaped her lips and she tried to pull away.

"Don't make a fuss," said Godwin calmly. "We won't let them get you and we won't hurt you either, but you'd best be quiet, or someone might hear." He squatted on the grass and sat her on his knee and, at length, the tiny Elf relaxed. "There we are," he said. "That's better."

She looked at him from under her lashes. "Wilthkin," she said, in a small, awed voice.

"That's right," said Godwin cheerily. "What a clever girl you are. I'll bet it's the first time you've seen one, isn't it?" A tentative smile touched the child's soft mouth. "Do you think we could be friends?"

Kinchine nodded uncertainly, while her small fingers plucked at the hem of her robe.

Godwin looked at Elgiva. "The poor mite's afraid to trust anyone."

"She trusted me … once," sighed Trystin.

Kinchine regarded him coyly. "Kinchie never forget you, but you look funny now."

Trystin's hand flew to his cheek and he wore an expression of pleasant surprise, as if he had actually forgotten that his ugly scar had gone.

"Where did you go?" asked Kinchine. "No-one to share the badness with now. Kinchine was sad when you left." She sniffed and lowered her eyes, twisting her little hands together, as she struggled with her sorrow. "Haldrin sad, too," she added. Then she began to sob.

Trystin sidled up to her and held her hand in his own. "Trystin ran because he's a coward. He's ashamed that he made you sad," he confessed. "And the nasty scar was taken away by Lady Elgiva here. She's a Wardain and she's my friend and, Kinchie, she can kill our master."

The Elf-child's eyes widened at this and Elgiva grasped Trystin's arm.

"Say no more!"she commanded. "Don't burden this child with dire intelligence, Trystin. Leave her young mind in peace."

Trystin looked abject. "Yes, Lady. I'm sorry. I'll get Grimalkin and we can leave."

Elgiva grinned at the Elf-child. "Time you went home. It's getting dark."

"Good-bye, Kinchie," Godwin said, setting her on the grass.

"No!" she protested. "Let Kinchie come, too, and ride on that great, big horse!"

Grimalkin snorted loudly and wrinkled her nose with amusement.

"Take Kinchie home, please, Lady? It's not far."

Elgiva considered the Elf-child's appeal and ran her fingers through her dark, shorn locks. "Perhaps it might be a good idea to meet the other Elves," she said. "What do you say, Trystin? Will this child's kin embrace our cause?"

"Oh, yes!" he affirmed. "They all hate the King, though they're too scared to say so."

"Very well, " decided Elgiva. "Godwin, put Kinchine on Grimalkin's back and we'll see her safely home." She cocked an eyebrow at the pony. "I'm sure you won't object, Grimalkin?"

Grimalkin submitted grudgingly and, as the gloaming deepened around them, she shambled after her two-legged friends.

* * *

Kinchine's home was a sprawl of huts, dwarfed by a ring of elms and oaks, and to the four companions in need of some comfort, it wasn't a welcoming sight. The circular huts, two dozen or so, were warped and weather-worn, their thatched roofs thinning with age. Above them the trees seemed to sag with despair, as though their roots were buried in gloom, and the air was thick with the smell of decay.

"What keeps this collection of daub and wattle dog-holes from falling apart?" wondered Godwin.

A paltry fire burned fitfully in the centre of the settlement and before it sat an elderly Elf, his shoulders slumped forwards dejectedly. He seemed to have been fashioned out of what was left over from the building of the huts. Upon hearing the arrival of strangers, he raised his hoary head slowly, but seemed too apathetic to show his surprise.

"Look at Kinchie! Haldrin, look!" squealed the Elf-child happily. "Kinchie's riding a great, big horse!"

"Where've you been to, spindle-shanks?" demanded the old Elf, not unkindly, his wizened face a sullen mask in the firelight. "'Tis late. Who's that with you?"

"Kinchie met nice friends in the forest. Trystin's come home, too. Trystin's naughty, isn't he?"

"Trystin's a fool, " said the old Elf gruffly. "Come here by the fire all of you. Don't skulk in the shadows like thieves. What's your business here?"

Trystin yanked at Elgiva's sleeve and urged her towards the fire. Lifting the Elf-child and her burden of firewood from Grimalkin's back, Godwin strode towards the elder.

"My name is Godwin," he announced, setting Kinchine gently down. He held out his hand, but it was ignored and he looked at his friends for support. "This is Elgiva from Elindell and our pony is Grimalkin."

"From Elindell, you say?" An expression of mild curiosity flitted across the elder's face.

"Er … yes," replied Godwin. He folded his arms across his chest, wondering how such a shrivelled creature could make him feel so ill at ease.

"Come here, girl," said the elder crossly. "Stand where I can see you. I can't abide skulkers. Now you're back, Trystin, make yourself useful. Go and find some food for these folk and put that gnat to bed before she falls asleep where she stands." He turned to face Elgiva and Godwin and looked them up and down. "Sit down beside me, the pair of you."

Trystin scuttled to obey his commands. He seized Kinchine's tiny hand and led her away. Elgiva and Godwin sat down by the fire and subjected themselves to the old Elf's careful scrutiny. Without regard to their feelings, he studied them intently, as though they were items on a market stall and he a wary buyer.

At length, he deigned to speak. "Now, you're from Elindell and he's a Wilthkin. What else have you to say for yourselves?"

"We'd rather not say too much," said Elgiva. "This is a dangerous place to be and I fear that your King has many spies."

"What?" croaked the elder, his temper rising. "If all you can give me is insults, you can go on your way at once! If he has any spies or supporters, I am not among their ranks. I may be a menial now, but I have my conscience and my principles, no matter what you think. I was a free Elf once, you know, until I defied our so-called King. May Faine tie his entrails in a thousand knots!"

Elgiva and Godwin looked at each other, taken aback, but also reassured, by the elder's outpouring of wrath.

"You said 'Faine'," Elgiva ventured.

"Oh, I see!" he cried contemptuously. "The light has suddenly dawned! You're spies of that jumped-up jackanapes yourselves and you've come to trick me, have you? Well, he might think he's a deity and better than the Founder, but the filthiest heap of dung on the earth would avoid his foot for fear of being tainted. There! Take that back to your master. I've lived too long as it is!"

Godwin had to smile at this. The scrawny-limbed ancient had climbed to his feet and was flailing his arms about angrily and the sight of such infuriation, dancing about in a tattered robe, struck Godwin as being both sad and amusing. The elder's behaviour was excessive and his courage pathetic, for it seemed to be no more than the death wish of a foolish old man who could well afford a reckless concern for what life he had left.

"He's a flint-hearted, swaggering scoundrel," the elder ranted on. "He should have killed me long ago, but it's better to have slaves. It's better sport to gloat on us, for he knows he's broken our spirit." He shook a sinewy fist at them both. "Broken it, I say!"

Elgiva quickly climbed to her feet and reached out her hand to the elder, but he recoiled from her touch. "Calm yourself, please," she begged him. "We think the same as you do. Vieldrin is our enemy. In fact … I mean to challenge him."

The old Elf cocked his fists on his hips. "Hah! I never trust the words of strangers. I know Vieldrin and his tricks. You may have fooled Trystin and Kinchine, but it's not so easy to fool me." He jabbed a finger in her direction. "How can you prove what you say?"

"Elgiva's the Queen of Elindell," broke in Godwin, somewhat vexed. He got to his feet and stood at her side, as if to show his allegiance. He would have said more, but the elder forestalled him.

"What proof is that, then?" he demanded. "I'm not too keen on Royalty!"

"I had hoped for your support, but if you don't trust us, so be it," Elgiva said. "I dare say we can live with it. All we ask for is your silence."

It was at that moment that Trystin returned. He carried a loaf and a jug of ale, which he placed before his friends, painfully aware of the hostile atmosphere into which he intruded. He stepped back, trying to smile.

Elgiva frowned at the offered food. "If this is all you can provide, how can we take what little you have?"

"If our food isn't good enough, that's your look out," snapped the elder. "Vieldrin keeps us short of food to make us weak and pliable. Eat it or not, I don't much care."

"There's really no reason to be so rude," Godwin told him crossly. "We came here in peace and are used like enemies."

"If you don't like it, you are free to leave and find better company elsewhere. I still don't know exactly what you're doing here, so why should I welcome you with open arms?" Haldrin glared at Godwin with blatant contempt, then he hitched up his robe and sat down.

After a short and uncomfortable silence, Elgiva and Godwin followed his example, while Trystin stood nervously chewing his nails.

Elgiva considered the unease of her friends; the hopelessness of their situation. For good or ill, they now found themselves here. Perhaps it was meant to be. Though the search for the Lorestone was their special quest, if they could glean some hope or help from the Elves of this strange kingdom, it mustn't be discounted. Yet the old Elf's unfriendly manner disturbed her. She had to convince him of her integrity.

She turned towards Godwin. His friendship was the only thing she felt she could rely on and in his gaze she saw an echo of her own thoughts: it was time to take some kind of action, to make some kind of statement.

She got to her feet, her sudden movement startling those around her. "Haldrin," she said solemnly, "we can't accept your hospitality and it seems to me that we should leave you in peace, but, before we go, let me make amends for any offence we have given you."

"How?"

She shrugged. "My magic is unpractised, but it is at your service."

"Now just you harken to me, girl!" Haldrin pushed himself upright, his face creased with annoyance. "I am leader of the Eldership of Misterell. In youth I was chief mentor to the late, good king, Eldruin. I was Ministrant of the Rites of Faine First-Father!" His head snapped back importantly, as though he expected his audience to gasp at the sound of these appellations. "And I tell you this, I will not be mocked by magic trickery!" He drew a deep breath and puffed out his chest.

Elgiva admitted defeat. "As you wish."

"No, Grandfather!" bleated Trystin. "Lady Elgiva would never mock you! She is good and has great magic. Good magic, Grandfather, look! " He tugged at the old Elf's sleeve. "She healed my scar! She healed me!"

"I know what the Wardain can do!" snapped Haldrin. "They conjure up things to make us afraid. They use us for their sport. She healed you, did she? So? A small demonstration of magic and you become her willing thrall! You are too gullible, boy. Did Vieldrin not promise us many things, when he set the dead king's crown on his head? We trusted him and were betrayed."

"Elgiva's not like that!" Tears of frustration welled in his eyes, as Trystin went on brokenly, "You alone of the elders … you knew Eldruin well. You said he was a good king. And Faine … Grandfather, Faine … wasn't *HE* a Wardain?"

"Be silent, boy!" commanded Haldrin, his eyes livid with outrage. "Don't dare to argue with me! You ran away and now you presume to tell us what to think. Good Eldruin might have been, but he sired an evil monster, so there was something rotten in him, for all his good intentions. Let go my sleeve, you silly knave, or I will cuff your ears!" He pushed him away indignantly. "Magic can kill as well as heal. Have you forgotten so quickly the murder of your parents?"

Trystin covered his face with his hands. Frowning at Haldrin's callous outburst, Godwin quickly sprang to his feet and drew the sobbing Elfling into a warm embrace. Angered by her friend's distress, Elgiva knotted her fists in her robe and felt the coils of her power unfold, like a serpent preparing to strike.

Then she reached a decision. Something had to be done, if only to mollify Trystin's pain; if only to purge herself of anger.

Turning on her heel, she walked several yards, then span to face the fire. She threw back her mantle and spread her arms out before her. A frown of concentration deepened on her brow, as she focused her will on the wielding of magic, her anger the spark that kindled the flame.

Her companions watched expectantly, while Haldrin cocked his fists on his hips, a dark scowl on his face. He wanted to walk away from the scene, but he felt compelled to watch.

There was nothing of power in Elgiva's stained, grey kirtle. The tears in her cloak and the tangle of her hair made her look like a beggar pleading for alms, and her slight form spoke of weakness rather than strength. But Godwin could see the gleam in her eyes, the light of a fierce determination, and he felt a thrill in the pit of his stomach.

Elgiva's magic was now fully awakened and it ached to obey her commands, but hesitation held her back. Poised on the brink of eruption, some self-doubt or fear seized her heart. What was she doing and why was she doing it?

Why was it so hard to let go?

From the shadows that flickered beneath the trees a snort of amusement reached her ears.

"Show the old bastard what's what."

A mischievous grin lit up her face at Grimalkin's wicked suggestion. Confidence flooded into her brain and dissolved the dregs of her doubt. Drawing a deep breath to steady herself, she gathered words for a spell.

"I think this fire does not suffice on such a night to melt the ice,

"So I will try to be precise and make it brighter in a trice."

Bringing both hands together, palms down, she levelled them at the fire and sent magic coursing down her arms. "Stand back!" she warned. Her friends obeyed at once and even Haldrin made no protest.

Suddenly, the fire hissed, then flared with an angry roar. It began to grow in size and soon the flames were over ten feet tall. The night drew back, as though startled, and the shabby huts were illuminated by a billowing, orange glow. Their shadows capered in the underwood, like the dancing souls of dwellings.

Then Elgiva began her incantation, pausing between each line.

"Fire dance and flames arise.

"Mirror the colours of the skies.

"Red, orange, yellow and blue,

"Imitate the rainbow's hue.

"Change to violet, then to green.

"Now all together they are seen."

As she spoke these words, the turgid flames obeyed her commands. Their colour began to change and, as it did, it softened. Her companions were no longer dazzled by the brilliance of the fire, but could watch the display without shielding their eyes. The darkness around them thickened once more and took on a rosy hue, as the fire billowed scarlet.

The flames rippled like tongues of blood and their crackling pulsed with vigour. Then the flames were streamers of a rich orange light, filling the glade with amber warmth. A moment later the fire became a dazzling cowslip yellow, a citrine coruscation as clean as summer sunshine.

Godwin gasped at the sight of it. Visually it staggered him, but the heat of the blaze seemed more penetrating than that of a normal fire. It flooded into his night-chilled bones and made him think of poppy-filled fields and drowsy afternoons. He shot a glance at the old Elf. Haldrin was unimpressed.

The aureate splendour of the flames deepened, translated itself into azure. Like a cloudless sky, it spoke of freedom, and the onlookers felt tiny before the fire, as though they beheld the vast tracts of the heavens. Trystin clung to Godwin's tunic and his thin face glowed with wonder, but Haldrin, still unmoved, stood like a pillar of granite.

The azure melted to lavender, then modified to purple. The wall of flame swarmed with magical power and hinted at earthly opulence: it was at the same time the cloak of a sage and the banner of a king.

It was then that Godwin heard movement behind him, but he couldn't bear to drag his gaze away from the beauty of the magical fire. Its enchantment seemed to stultify all fear of being discovered.

With a sudden flare, the fire changed again, and now it was green; a bright, luxuriant emerald so redolent of the pulse of spring that the onlookers could actually smell its leafy, growing life. The essence of green health itself was captured in the blaze, as if in celebration of the power of the Earth. The trees around the clearing stiffened and Godwin felt them strain towards the fire, as if they meant to feast upon the vigour of the flames.

Godwin waited patiently for the final change to come, confident that, when it did, he would see an earthbound rainbow. Elgiva was still standing, arms levelled at the blaze, and her dark eyes flashed with power. But the last line of the incantation had been ineffective. In a sterner voice, she spoke it again, but the green sheet of flame remained unaltered.

The air seemed to hum with the striving of magic that strained to the limit without success. Godwin could see Elgiva trembling, her small fists clenched with effort, as she stood in the eerie, emerald glow. He glanced at Haldrin, who stood blank-faced, and was taken aback by the number of Elves who now stood in the clearing. Aware that some magic was at work, they had crept from their beds to investigate. They now stood cowed and silent and in their eyes Godwin could see both fear and wonder in equal measure, as they gaped at the grass-green blaze.

Then Elgiva's voice ruptured the silence.

"Fire obey and flames be true!

"Reflect entire the rainbow's hue!"

She scanned the fire hopefully, chewing her lower lip. Mirrored in her feverish gaze, the green flames were unchanged. She lowered her arms despondently. "I'm sorry," she said. "Have patience. I'll try a little harder." She closed her eyes and lifted her arms, her forehead glazed with sweat.

"Mighty fire of Mother Earth,
"Be kind to one who knows your worth.
"Forget your roots are in the land.
"A rainbow be, as I command."

A grimace of pain appeared on her face and the fire writhed with violence, but its colour didn't change. "A rainbow be, as I command!" Elgiva's voice broke with the effort and trembling racked her limbs. Her body, unaccustomed to magic, began to protest at the strain. And still the fire refused to respond.

"Stop it," hissed Godwin urgently. "You'll hurt yourself. Enough!"

The green glow flickered and faded and then, with a tremendous whooshing sound, the fire shrank back to normal. Darkness swooped triumphantly back into the glade.

Elgiva staggered, lost her balance and fell to her knees with a groan. Godwin felt his muscles tense, as he fought his desire to run to her aid. He didn't want the Elves to see how badly she needed support, how inept she was at magic. Inwardly he felt that this display had cost them the trust of the Elves, but acknowledging Elgiva's weakness would only make things worse.

Elgiva slowly opened her eyes and looked around the glade. When her vision swam into focus, she was startled to see so many Elves, and all of them apparently dumb. They watched her with their mouths agape and she looked vacantly back at them, panting with fatigue. Her lungs felt scorched and her stomach churned, but she struggled to her feet. The forest canted crazily round her for several sickening moments.

Sweeping the tangle of hair from her face, she turned towards the fire, as though considering one more attempt. But then she shrugged. "You win," she said.

Ah, well, she mused, so much for trying to impress people. All she had succeeded in doing was to demonstrate unreliable power and her lack of control in its use. The Misterellians would never see her as a serious threat to their King.

She mopped her brow with the sleeve of her robe and stared at the crowd of Elves. An embarrassed silence stifled the air. Why didn't somebody speak?

Into the feverish calm she said, " I have to ask your pardon. I've over-taxed myself."

Helplessly, she looked at Godwin and he folded his arms and grimaced with a smile of wry amusement. He wanted to hug her with relief, because she was unharmed, but he felt it would be wiser to appear to be unperturbed. Elgiva tried to smile at him, but the muscles of her face weren't working and she feared that her grin was a little lopsided.

"A fine thing, by Frigg!" said Godwin, sighing with disappointment. "All these folk assembled here, hoping for entertainment." He shook his head slowly. "And you call that magic?"

Godwin would never know how grateful Elgiva was for those words, for his supportive humour. The tension was lifted and she sagged with relief. The faces of the gathered Elves made her think of bewildered sheep, staring wide-eyed at the antics of a brace of large, mad dogs, and despite her empathy for them and her guilt at causing their consternation, her need to giggle was irresistible.

Careless of the consequences, she sat on the ground and laughed.

The Misterellians muttered in the shadows, but Haldrin snapped at them to be quiet. Then he strode forwards stiffly and stood before Elgiva.

"Forgive me," he said, with the hint of a bow.

Elgiva peered up at him quizzically. He glowered down his nose at her, jealous of his dignity, despite his humble manner.

"Perhaps I misjudged," he admitted. "If you can find such amusement in failure, then I'm inclined to trust your intentions." He felt he should say that he had been wrong. Strange how such a little word could be so hard to utter. "Perhaps not all the Wardain are evil. Vieldrin would have torn us all limb from limb, had we been witness to a failure of his power. You ask pardon for your weakness. You greet your companion's disdain with laughter. We have seen all this and yet we still live. And above all that…" He paused and in his mind he saw once more the thrilling sight of the clean, green fire of health and he decided that failure was hardly the word to describe what he had been privileged to see. "And above all that, you honour Faine."

Haldrin smiled and his wizened face seemed almost embarrassed at having to use a blatant expression of pleasure. He turned and let his eyes wander over the Elves in the glade, and then he nodded to himself, as though he had reached a decision.

"Well, fellow thralls, it seems to me that we're not in the mood for sleep," he said. "So why don't we have some food and wine in honour of our guests? It seems there may be work afoot and we should be apprised of it. The time has come to take counsel together. You know me well. I lead the elders, but I am also a slave who has had enough of slavery. All things must change, my friends. That is as it should be and I believe that they will change for the better in Misterell. I don't speak lightly. We have seen good magic here this night and in it there is hope for us all. What say you? Shall we cast off the yoke of serfdom? Shall we drink to the death of Vieldrin? He is an abomination in the eyes of the Founder!"

His audience muttered and glanced at each other, aghast to hear their respected leader give voice to the hatred they secretly shared.

"Come, ditherers!" he exhorted them. "We have been slaves too long. We have forgotten our oath to Faine. Vieldrin had no right to take our liberty away, to forbid us to worship the Blessed Founder. It's a wrong we have endured too readily. We are Misterellians! Cowardice does not become us! Wencel, you know where the wine is hidden. Eltheyn, fetch that pot of stew. Everil, where's that bread you baked? And those cheeses you hoarded were meant to be eaten. Let's all gather together as we did in the olden days, when Eldruin was still on the throne. It is time to renew our bond with Faine!"

Still the Elves wavered and looked at Haldrin as though he had gone mad. But he squared his shoulders proudly and gave them all a defiant grin.

"So, you fear discovery? But what do we have to lose? If we are slain tomorrow, then we will die free Elves, not slaves. In our hearts, if nowhere else. Our souls will fly to the First-Father and he will greet us as his people, not as his betrayers. If it must be our one last act, let it be a brave one!"

Though they valued Haldrin's wisdom, the Elves were shocked and uncertain, but finally it was the prospect of food and conversation with strangers that stirred them into action.

★ ★ ★

Chapter Twenty-Three

The fire had been refuelled, the tables and benches dragged out onto the grass, and, under a star-filled sky, the slaves of Misterell were gathered for a feast: a feast that would leave them short for tomorrow, but, living in Misterell had taught them that tomorrow might never come.

The chance to speak to them all together was one that Elgiva welcomed, but she felt that it would be unwise for her to give her trust too freely. Their sudden change of heart was odd and perhaps it didn't ring true, however, she felt responsible for it and she couldn't just walk away.

"My fellow Eldrakin," she said, "your hospitality gives us strength for the challenge that lies ahead of us, and for that we are very grateful. Misterell must be purged of evil and her people must be free once more. Your King is a tyrant who breaks the laws of the Founder. If we are to be free of him, we all must do our part. Mine is to oppose him. I hope I have the strength for it, but your support will help me."

The silence that followed was filled with the noises of eating and slurping wine, but a few apathetic murmurs greeted her remarks. Only Trystin's worshipful gaze and Godwin's generous smile offered her any encouragement, but they weren't enough. She seated herself dejectedly.

Then an Elf with steel-grey hair caught Elgiva's eye.

"May I, Lorac, be so bold as to comment on your words?" He linked his hands together, his elbows on the table. "What you say is all very well, but Faine, you know, is spirit now and we are flesh and bone. My dear, what spirit may endure the flesh and bone cannot. You say we all must do our part. You speak of strength, but you are a Wardain. To you such things come easily. We, however, have no power, merely the strength of our sinews and limbs, and most of us are too old to boast of any prowess there. Too old or too young, my dear. The fittest among us were chased away or murdered by the King. He brooks no threat, however slight. What kind of support do you expect? We are old Elves and infants. What use are we in the fight against evil?"

"And we're forbidden to worship … you know," another Elf broke in. His eyes peered warily from under a mop of thick, white hair. "If we are seen to be praising him … to be seen praising F-F-Faine, we have earned ourselves a speedy death."

"Can't you worship him in your hearts?" asked Elgiva angrily.

"The spies of the King are everywhere," Lorac said with a smirk. "I should not be at all surprised if that included our hearts."

"Lorac, I think she has a point," said Haldrin with a frown. "I believe that we should listen to her."

Lorac shrugged his shoulders and started to pick his teeth.

"Old fool, " snorted another Elf from an adjoining table. She seemed much younger than the other Elves. "When have you ever believed, or trusted, even in the early times, when we were still free Elves? What's made you change your hide so quickly? Has one display of magic robbed you of your wits, or are you going senile?"

Haldrin prepared a curt response, but Trystin intervened.

"I wish you wouldn't argue!" The depth of his feeling drew everyone's gaze and he was suddenly overcome by shyness and had to press himself close to Godwin in the hope that he could draw some courage from the nearness of his friend. "I love Elgiva. She healed my scar and I trust her with my life. She wants to help us. Why won't you listen?"

"Help us, hah!" spat the white-haired Elf. "Help us stir up Vieldrin's wrath and put us in our graves! I want it known that I, Aldric, want no part of this."

"It's better ... better to die once, than die a little every day," Trystin ventured, chewing his lip nervously. "You ... you're elders ... you're wise, aren't you? Can't you see the wisdom in that? Lady Elgiva is good. I know. She hates the King and so do we. So ... we should stand together."

Hearing his own words repeated by Trystin, Godwin smiled warmly, but the elders seemed to have taken offence.

"Look, lad," said Lorac, "you fail to see the danger we are in. Yes, we know she possesses magic. We may even accept that it is good magic. But, good or bad, is it strong enough? I think we already know the answer. One Wardain against another and one of doubtful skill, and I think we know which one would win."

Trystin pouted sulkily. "You're blind," he muttered. "A chance of freedom tries to take your hand and you smite it in the face."

"Chance, aye," said Lorac gloomily, "and chance isn't good enough. What we need is certainty."

"Excuse me," interposed Godwin, "but as to the strength of Elgiva's magic, your King doesn't doubt it as you do. He has tried to make her his ally." Their cold eyes looked him up and down, as though he had spoken without permission, and his confidence deserted him, but he felt that he must continue. "I know I'm only a Wilthkin, so all this is beyond me, but I know what I know. I know what I've seen. We've met your King, not once, but twice. And we're alive to speak of it. That's not Vieldrin's way."

"What would a Wilthkin know of his 'way'?" Lorac demanded with a sneer. "He is a creature of caprice, yet there is method in it."

Godwin pretended to ignore this. He took a large swig of Elf-wine and, much emboldened, he pressed on. "Perhaps great magic isn't required. Perhaps there's other help to be had." He paused to clear his throat. "Haven't you heard of the Lorestone?"

Elgiva grabbed his sleeve in protest, but he shrugged her hand away. The elders merely stared at him, totally perplexed.

"The Lorestone," Godwin persisted. "It's a stone of great power to be used against evil and legend has it that Faine left it hidden…here."

"Legends?" protested the female Elf. "What use have we for legends?"

"Well we …we're looking for it."

As soon as he had said this, Godwin knew that he had made himself look ridiculous. Elgiva and Trystin, too. The striving after the Lorestone had totally consumed them and it came as a shock to realise that, in the eyes of others, they looked like lunatics chasing moonbeams. Sit down and shut up, said an inner voice, but, even so, he didn't listen.

"Legend or not," he continued, "if Vieldrin gets the Lorestone first, then he'll be invincible."

"He already is," sniggered Lorac.

A murmur of bitter laughter greeted Lorac's words.

"He believes it exists," said Godwin, undaunted. "He's searching for it now."

"Not now, I think," yawned Lorac. "If he's any sense he'll be in bed, which is where we all should be."

"He mustn't get his hands on the Stone," Godwin went on bravely. "You have to help us … you must help us, if you want your freedom, and … what's more…"

His voice cracked under the strain of pleading with an audience who reviled him. Why was he pleading with them anyway? When had it been decided that they needed the help of these downtrodden Elves? He raised the beaker of wine to his lips and, though he knew he had drunk quite enough, he drank a good deal more. Then he straightened himself and continued his speech, ignoring Elgiva's angry glare and the tugging on his sleeve.

"The time for action has come. We all know what it's like to be slaves. It's insupportable. And you, Lorac, you speak of danger and yet you haven't the faintest idea what real danger is."

"What is it, then?" asked Lorac, his head cocked condescendingly. "Enlighten us, Wilthkin, do."

"Well, I, er…"

Before he dug a pit for himself, Godwin resumed his seat, and somewhat heavily in Elgiva's opinion. He folded his arms across his chest and glowered at the table, refusing to meet her gaze for fear of seeing her look of sufferance. The elders muttered softly and their eyes were wells of disdain.

It was then that a tiny Elf-child tottered towards them across the sward. In her long, white shift of linen she looked like a wraith that wanders the night, searching in vain for peace. She rubbed her eyes with her knuckles and her soft voice stunned the darkness.

"I wish Mamma would come home. Aunt Everil, where is Mamma?" She looked at the Elf-woman pleadingly and the phantasm of a nightmare glimmered in her dark eyes.

Elgiva stood up and stepped towards her and, taking the child's tiny hand in her own, she turned to face the eldership. "This is innocence," she said. "A sight to gladden the Founder's heart. Can you stand by and see it corrupted, trampled on, despised? Will you sacrifice her right to be free for the sake of your hoary fears? The old should prepare the way for the young."

She stared at them accusingly, while the elders shook their heads and muttered. Suddenly, Trystin sprang to his feet.

"Let's celebrate!" he shouted. "Let's celebrate good magic and look to the future and freedom!"

He raced across the grass to the huts. Curious but wary, the elders watched in silence. When he returned he held a reed pipe, which he then began to play.

"Quiet, lad!" hissed Aldric. "We've made enough din for one night! Someone is bound to hear us."

"A curse on the spies!" cried Everil. The elders visibly jumped. "Why should we be quiet? What's wrong with merry-making? Let the forest ring with laughter and song and these sad, old trees will be proud again!"

Haldrin nodded gravely. "Indeed we must honour the Founder," he said. "We have not been true – I least of all. I was always the first to praise his name, now I am the most disloyal. My friends, we have sinned against our lore, our duty, our very natures. Our shame is great indeed."

Haldrin straightened himself in his seat. He seemed as though restored to his former authority, when he led the Elves in their devotions, and now, instead of bitterness, he wore a look of zeal.

Aldric frowned, then nodded doubtfully. "Praiseworthy Faine," he muttered, glancing at the encircling trees.

The elders looked at each other in silence, as though they were sharing their thoughts. Then, as one, they rose to their feet, animated by a common spirit: a decision had been made.

A surge of long-suppressed energy now brought them all to life. They hastened to their dwellings, woke their grandchildren, nephews and nieces, and searched for their pipes and lyres. They built up the fire to a roaring blaze and fetched more flagons of wine.

Godwin looked at Elgiva, a warning in his eyes, but he was dismayed by her lack of response. She seemed unaware of the recklessness that was slowly unfolding around them. Across the glade, the drowsy children stumbled from the huts, puzzlement on their faces. Then Trystin ran to join them and very soon they had formed a ring and were dancing round the fire.

Godwin felt a stab of fear, as Trystin left his side. He wanted to shout, 'Come back' at him, but he couldn't quite think why. Yet there was a feeling of imminent madness hanging in the air. The elders were smiling and tuning their lyres. Some hugged each other, while others danced or laughed at the children's antics. The change in their behaviour made Godwin feel uneasy.

Haldrin turned to Elgiva, took her hand and kissed it. "We will defy Vieldrin," he promised her. "You are right. Elves can't deny their nature and live as servile cowards. Misterellians least of all! We were born for music and dancing and the freedom of the forests. So many years of laughter suppressed! We can't make up for it all in one night, but some of us will try! And Faine will see how we repent. We must pay tribute to all that is good and free in this wicked world!" Then he wandered off with a smile on his lips.

It's the wine, thought Godwin. Can't you see? I feel half-crazy, too.

Again he turned to Elgiva, but she didn't seem to share his fears. The laughter of children bubbled about him, but he felt that it was wrong. In such a place, where the trees dripped night onto the firelit sward, where unseen enemies might be lurking, joy was out of place.

"Elf-wine's too strong for Wilthkin," Elgiva remarked with a grin. "But you look more worried than drunk."

He grimaced awkwardly in reply. It seemed that she took a perverse delight in reminding him of his race, whenever he began to accept that they were friends and equals. Would he ever understand her? His palms were suddenly clammy with fear and he felt very alone.

"You don't understand them, do you, my friend?" Her unexpected softness unsettled him even more. "The passions of Elves run very deep. Haldrin's people have only half-lived. They've given way to apathy. Years of it, Godwin, eating at their hearts. Elves can't live that way."

Nobody can, he thought, but we can't all let go just like that. "Be reasonable, Elgiva, what if they're heard by the King's patrol's? What if the guards investigate and find them worshipping Faine?"

His words were drowned by a burst of song, as the elders sang in praise of the Founder, as if to add weight to his apprehension. The children tried to sing along, but knowledge of Faine had long been forbidden and they didn't know the words.

"They renounced the Founder," Elgiva said crossly, raising her voice to be heard above the noise. "They broke their oath to him. Now they must renew their faith. In the days of Faine this kingdom was the heart of Elvendom. The body can't be healthy if the heart is weak and this heart must be strong again."

"Is this you talking, Elgiva, or are you reciting a lesson?"

She rounded on him angrily. "Do you condone the breaking of a vow? I seem to recall you saying once that such things must be honoured, or were you reciting a lesson? What is death compared to broken faith?"

For a while they held each other's eyes. He thought that he saw hatred in hers, but he hoped he had imagined it.

"How can a Wilthkin understand?" said Elgiva, at length. There was an unpleasant edge to her voice that Godwin found disturbing. He wanted to speak in his own defence, but then her expression softened. She shook her head in self-reproach. "And yet, my friend, why should you?"

Abruptly, she turned and made her way to the fire and the dancing children, leaving Godwin all alone to battle with his dread.

Yet he thought that perhaps he did understand, even more than he cared to acknowledge. The intoxication of freedom.

The pipes and lyres sang out, like birds released from their cages. Festivity was King and the Elves were his willing subjects. A group of dogs stood barking in a ring of dancing elders, but only Godwin heeded them.

"What's going on?"

"Have you all gone mad?"

The Elf-wine was like lead in his veins. He turned and walked unsteadily towards the edge of the glade. There beneath the cool, dark trees, Grimalkin stood, munching grass.

The chill beneath the trees was balm to Godwin's sweating limbs. His body was on fire. He placed his hand on the pony's back, inebriation making him bold, and leaned his weight against her. Grimalkin swung her head round slowly, fixed him with a glare.

"You're drunk, I see. No self–control."

He blearily tried to return her stare, but she seemed to have four eyes.

"And you're not the only one, Briton. Celery stalks! Just look at 'em! Someone should get a pail of water. Give 'em all a dousing." Casually she lowered her head to snatch at a tuft of grass, but Godwin sensed her unease. A tremor of nervousness ran down her neck.

He tried to clear the brume from his brain, divorce himself from the Elves' carousing, but, as he stood there, watching them dance, the music called to his soul. He longed to join the revelry, but he feared to let down his guard. Someone had to stay alert; darkness was everywhere.

The Elves were dancing like butterflies and even the oldest were agile enough to make him feel clumsy and hateful. But he felt guilty, too. The shadows reeked of hysteria and the blame for it all was partly his. Were they doing it all for Faine, or was it merely pent up anger finally breaking through; the death-wish of a dying race?

Elgiva, he noticed, stood apart and her face was solemn and blank. You can't let go either, can you? he thought.

Grimalkin snorted and fidgeted and a muscular ripple ran down her spine. Were they the only ones aware of the danger that lurked in the shadows? He feared for the Elves, as helpless as Wilthkin and prey to the whims of their betters. Once he had lived like that. But he also knew that he feared for himself, that this was his main concern. The depth of his selfishness sickened him. There was no honour in it. He had to admit that he was basically a coward, but cowardice was the right of slaves and now he was free and armed like a warrior.

Yes, a warrior's sword, but not his heart.

But he had been a warrior; he had fought beside Elric and Deor – of course, he reminded himself bitterly, that was out of duty and he had performed it with terror, not joy. If he wanted to be a warrior, he had to accept the risks it involved and the honour of dying in battle. But how could he accept such a creed in this glade full of laughter and green, growing things? It was easier to be a slave and have one's cowardice taken for granted. Being a slave meant that a man wasn't forced to stand on his own two feet. A slave was freed from such responsibility. He could go about the business of life and know that his conscience was clean.

A slave, of course, didn't have a conscience. Whatever he had, it belonged to his master.

The music and dancing continued. How long would it be before the King's guards came bursting into the glade? Had he been a warrior, Godwin would have relished the thought, the chance to engage in his favourite sport. But combat wasn't his favourite anything.

Oh, Grim! So now he wasn't a slave, but he wasn't a free man either. He wasn't a noble or a vagabond. But he had to be something. He must have some use, some place in this unjust world. His past and his future were mysteries and his role in the present unclear and he was one small island in a large and lonely sea.

How he envied the Elves their catharsis, their daring!

He must find something to divert his mind or his thoughts would drive him mad. He decided to sharpen his knife. He hunted round for a flat stone and, having found one, he sat down cross-legged on the grass. Grimalkin edged nearer and peered at him, as he used the stone to whet the blade. He worked at this for quite some time, while blasts from the pony's nostrils scorched the back of his neck. The concentration of mind and body released him from disquieting thoughts and loosened the grip of the wine.

At length, he finished and held up the knife, examining it with care. The effort of focusing made him dizzy.

"You going to kill someone with that?" Grimalkin enquired indifferently.

Godwin winced at the very idea. "I need a sharp knife," he retorted. "I might … I might want a shave or something." He scratched at the stubble on his chin.

She snorted at this. "Why bother? Hair's meant to grow there, isn't it? You trying to look young and virginal? It just wouldn't suit you. Not at your age."

He scowled at this. What right had this ungainly beast to make him feel ridiculous? "I know what I'm doing!"

he snapped. "Mind your own business, you stupid, old nag."

He ran his thumb along the knife to test its edge for sharpness, but instantly he pulled back his hand, as the blade bit through his skin. Angrily he looked at his thumb and saw a bubble of blood.

With a snort of derisive humour, Grimalkin resumed her supper.

Godwin sighed. He drew out his sword and lovingly stroked the blade, as though it were the only friend he had in all the world. It eased his distress and made him feel stronger. But even the sword was useless, he thought, in the hands of a man like him. If someone had trained him in swordsmanship, then things might have been different, but a churl cleaned the weapons, he didn't use them. When his masters had practised their fighting skills, he had merely stood and watched, amazed by their strength and agility and their disregard for wounds.

He pictured Elric and Deor playing at war together and it depressed him all the more. They had taken such pleasure in it and it marked them out as real men, made them look special in the eyes of women.

But Deor was dead. There was always someone better, quicker, more cunning. And perhaps their courage had been nothing more than arrogance in disguise. Arrogance or stupidity.

Then there was Lord Othere.

As a child Godwin had revered his master, who seemed to embody all the heroic, manly virtues, and even old age hadn't dimmed the light that gleamed in the Saxon lord's eyes. How cruel that the man he had loved like a father should send him unskilled to the horrors of battle.

A sense of ill-usage burned through his brain.

You took me from my father, so I loved you in his stead. I loved you, Othere, yet to you what was I but a churl? Another spoil of battle to show that you were a man. Who gave you the right…?

He swallowed down his anger, his surge of bitter hatred. Such feelings served no purpose. They only hurt the one who felt them. Instead he focused on his sword.

This is my past. It's who I am.

He ran his finger carefully along the edge of the sword. He needed to know that it was ready to protect him. But his heart sank. It couldn't be! He pressed the sword edge harder, but the blade felt thick and dull, as though it had never been sharpened. He shouldn't have used it earlier to hack a path through the trees, but a weapon that was so easily dulled was a useless thing indeed.

He felt the tears well into his eyes and he cursed himself for his weakness.

⋆ ⋆ ⋆

Chapter Twenty-Four

The night was old by the time that Elgiva decided to seek out her Wilthkin friend. Godwin didn't notice her standing at his side, so lost was he in his gloomy thoughts, and the sound of her voice made him start.

"You look unhappy, my friend," she said. An understatement, she knew. His eyes were like wounds of sorrow.

He searched her features, gauging her mood. Her face was etched by fatigue. Her reserves of energy had all been squandered, performing tricks to amuse the children.

"They're certainly in high-feather," said Godwin, inclining his head towards the Elves, "but Vieldrin is still their master and they are still his slaves. Nothing has changed, Elgiva."

"And that has made you unhappy?"

He skirted round the question. "I fear for them in their madness, don't you?"

"Haldrin says they can't be heard. The Hall is too far away. Of course, there are patrols, but they are usually small and we could overcome them. There are so many of us."

Godwin wasn't so sure. "But they're looking for us!" he protested. "Be reasonable, Elgiva, Misterell is a bloody, big place, but they're bound to search here sooner or later."

"And they'd expect to find us here, with Elves too scared to shelter us?"

He shook his head in despair, knowing that it was useless to argue. A wan smile touched Elgiva's pale lips and she sat down beside him with a weary sigh, clutching his shoulder for support.

"Some of the elders welcome discovery."

He looked at her archly. "Really?"

She ignored his cynical tone. "They believe that even Vieldrin's guards secretly hate their master and with a little encouragement they'd willingly change sides."

Godwin found this hard to accept. "I think we should be more cautious."

"Perhaps," she said, "but it's too late now. The elders are determined. I talked with them and they told me things … things that I'd rather not know…" Godwin's pulse raced with a sudden panic and he steeled himself for some dire disclosure. "There will soon be more against us than Vieldrin's evil powers. Much more and much worse, too. Remember I told you of Smirill? Vieldrin venerates his name and wants to follow in his footsteps and destroy the balance between good and evil. There are powers hidden in the Earth, good and bad, and the bad are better undisturbed. But Vieldrin will disturb them, you can be sure of that. And he will bend them to his will."

Godwin felt that he had heard enough, but Elgiva hadn't finished.

"Many ages of knowledge and wisdom lie between us and Faine, but in his day there was goodness and love. Now there is hatred and greed. Knowledge has corrupted our race and our path has reached its conclusion in Vieldrin. He's as lorewise as my great-uncle, and his personal power surpasses any Wardain in the land, but, worst of all, he has no conscience. Vieldrin doesn't care.

He'll do whatever he wants to do and he'll do it because he can. If he frees the dark things in the Earth…" She left the sentence open.

"But the Lorestone, Elgiva…"

"If the Stone holds the key to Faine's power and Vieldrin finds it, then we're lost indeed," she said grimly. "What is my power against the might of the Lorestone combined with Vieldrin and the powers of darkness?"

"But he doesn't have the Lorestone. He hasn't beaten us yet!" Godwin tried to subdue the note of hysteria in his voice. "We can't give up now, no matter what the odds, and what the elders say … well, is it just conjecture? They've frightened you with gossip. They don't know what Vieldrin's up to any more than we do. And he's flesh and blood, by Frigg! He can be destroyed, can't he?"

The arrival of Haldrin curtailed this discussion. He approached them with confidence, Trystin at his heels, and his voice was calm and steady.

"Now is the time we should make plans. We've renewed our bond with Faine, and though we risk what little we have, we will help you all we can. Trystin says that tomorrow he'll guide you to a place he knows where the Stone may be hidden."

"If it exists," said Godwin glumly.

"Better if it doesn't," said Elgiva. "At least then Vieldrin wouldn't find it."

"I trust the wise man," Trystin said. "I'm sure he was right. You shall have the Lorestone, Lady!"

"And while you search," continued Haldrin, "the rest of us will stage a rebellion to occupy the guards. Word will be sent to the other slaves who live in Misterell. Let's hope they will join us. The guards won't know which way to turn." He smiled with satisfaction.

"But how many warriors does he have? You might all be killed!" said Godwin.

Haldrin seemed unperturbed. "He has perhaps ten score at home. A great many more were sent to Elindell."

"How many are *YOU*?"

"Few, but enough to distract the guards. Vieldrin has personal servants, too, but most of them are honest Elves who serve unwillingly out of fear that Vieldrin will harm their kin. Kinchine's father is among them." Haldrin saw Godwin's look of doubt and smiled like a man who welcomes his fate. "No-one is immortal. We will do what we have to do. Why should our fate concern you, Wilthkin? Isn't your own fear a great enough burden?"

Godwin scowled at him. Had Haldrin been younger and stronger, and Godwin less awed by his presence, he might have struck him for his impertinence.

Of course, the truth always hurt.

"Vieldrin can't kill us all," said Haldrin, as though this fact somehow reduced the gravity of the situation. "Who would be left to serve him? And he's too preoccupied with other plans in other places. He wouldn't waste his personal power in crushing a rebellion. With luck we shall have just nar-Wardain against us."

At that moment the music ceased and the revellers clapped and called for more, though their mad carousing had passed its crisis. The night had grown cooler and Haldrin suggested that they all return to the fire, but as they were strolling across the clearing, Godwin's worst fears came to pass.

An ominous rustling among the trees made all the Elves turn to face its source. A silence fell massively over the glade and no-one dared to move. Suddenly a band of Elves came striding out of the night, two of their fellows bearing torches. Their swords were drawn and the firelight gleamed upon their leather armour.

The elders stood and watched, slack-mouthed, as the warriors marched into the glade and looked about them sneeringly. Godwin caught sight of the leader's face and he felt his heart miss a beat. Too well he remembered that twisted scar.

"Here they are!" exclaimed the leader. "Never thought they'd be hiding here, skulking with this rabble. These are the ones I told you of, Captain. Worshipping Faine, they were. And they killed Rancill and Vendriel, too. Look out for that one. She's got magic!"

The guards edged nearer with scowls on their faces and firelight on their swords, and, as they did so, the elders retreated.

"What's going on?" demanded an Elf, who appeared to be in charge. He took a step forward, his fists on his hips and a deep frown on his brow. He had the look of someone kept reluctantly from his bed. Crossing him would be unwise. Clearly he outranked the others, for they cringed when he spoke. "A rebels' get-together, eh? Making an infernal noise. Enough to wake the sun up. And Wilthkin! This is serious, lads!"

"Captain!" hissed the Elf with the scar, "I'll wager they're worshipping Faine!"

"Shut up, Snarkin, I know what's afoot. If you hadn't done such a rotten job, we wouldn't be scouring the forest in the middle of the night. Spare me your bloody opinions."

Grinning sheepishly, Snarkin drew back.

"Now then, I want the ring-leaders. They'll pay for all this and they'll pay in blood. Sound the horn for assistance!" The Captain strode forward menacingly. He searched every face for a sign of guilt, then he turned back to glare at Snarkin. "Damn you, Snarkin, are you asleep? Sound the horn, I said!"

Snarkin made haste to obey the command. The clarion blare made everyone jump, but Elgiva stepped calmly forwards.

"Listen," she said, "we want to help you…"

The Captain snorted with laughter. "Gah! Shut your noise, lest I use your guts to lubricate my sword. I'll do the talking here."

Elgiva was undaunted. Uplifted by the support of the elders, she looked at his face unflinchingly, defiance sparkling in her eyes. "Threaten and bluster all you like. We will worship Faine no matter what."

"You have signed your own death warrant, my girl," the Captain snarled, with relish.

"And furthermore," Elgiva went on, "I will rid this kingdom of Vieldrin."

The Captain laughed derisively, span round to face his warriors and their faces clenched with terror. "You hear that, do you, dogsbodies? Treasonous talk that is! She wants to rid us of Vieldrin, but he's a generous master. We don't want rid of him, do we?"

One of the warriors ventured to make an ill-considered reply; his companion nudged him in the ribs.

"Do we?" bawled the Captain.

"No, Captain," said the warriors feebly.

The Captain's gaze whipped back to the elders and his mouth was a smirk of cruelty. He threw words back over his shoulder to his men. "Well, my lads, do you fancy some sport? We'll take that one there for a start." He pointed at Elgiva. "She seems to be their leader. Then the old codgers should give us some fun, before reinforcements arrive. Snarkin!"

"Captain?"

"Take her, Snarkin. Alive if you can. By the King's decree, he is to question any intruders, before we lop off their heads."

"But Captain, she killed Rancill and Vendriel! She struck them both dead with a glance!"

The Captain span swiftly and slapped his face. "Don't question an order, milksop! Why can't you do as you're told?" He grabbed Snarkin's collar and thrust him forward. "Now get her, worm. We're wasting time. And mark me, cretin, I said alive. We must learn all the names of her fellow conspirators. But if she gives you any trouble, you have my permission to show no mercy."

Snarkin moved forward slowly and began to stalk Elgiva. "Now you … you make no trouble for Snarkin."

Elgiva confronted him, clenching her fists, but then her soft lips parted and she cast her gaze back at her friends, searching for one in particular. In her eyes Godwin saw a horrified look; a look that said, I have no strength.

Oh, Frigg! he thought. We're done for!

He knew that he was shaking from head to foot, but he fought to gain control of his limbs and ran across the clearing. He halted between Elgiva and Snarkin and, looking into the Elf's scarred face, he raised his sword with a hand that shook and said in a quavering voice, "Another step and you die!"

"Yah, Wilthkin!" Snarkin spat upon the ground like a snake discharging venom. "Hey, Cadrinell, get over here and sort him out for me!"

Another Elf crept forward and stood at Snarkin's side. Then the three antagonists faced each other, reluctant and uncertain. Even the tips of their swords were trembling.

"What are you dithering for?" barked the Captain. He folded his thick arms across his breast and grimaced with impatience.

Thoughts raced madly through Godwin's mind. He saw himself fighting to defend the settlement; he saw his masters practising swordplay, but none of it seemed to help him now. He didn't know what to do. If only he had a broadsword to swing at his attackers! Then he could have cut them down before they got too close. But all he had was this dull, blunt blade, a body made of lead and no sense of timing whatsoever. And if they both attacked at once … and would it be slashing or stabbing? … What would Elric have done? … Where was Cerdic, when you needed him?… Frigg! He couldn't move a muscle. Rooted to the spot like an idiot. Rooted to the spot and only half sober. The elders were old and weaponless. Elgiva had used up her strength. So much for their fanciful notions! Craven, old fools! How in the name of all the gods had he ended up like this?

Sensing his fear and hesitation, Cadrinell made his move and thrust his sword at Godwin's chest. Instinctively, Godwin parried the blow, swung his sword from left to right, amazed at his own reaction. Its flat edge clashed with Cadrinell's blade. Though his arm was twisted uncomfortably, he managed to knock the weapon aside and deflect it from its target.

Angrily, Cadrinell struck again, and Godwin parried blindly. Inexpertly handled, his sword glanced off the Elf's. Then together they swung and stabbed and sliced, while Snarkin stood grinning, his own sword poised an inch from Elgiva's throat.

Godwin's heart was pounding and Cadrinell was feeling bolder, buoyed up by Godwin's lack of skill. His Elven agility gave him the edge and to Godwin it seemed that he had winged feet.

"Cadrinell, he's tiring!"

"You'll soon finish him off!"

Godwin heard the jeers of the guards and he knew that they were right. His strength was slowly failing, he couldn't clear his head, and he felt himself retreating, inch by inch, towards the fire. He heard the shuffling of feet behind him, as the Elves moved out of his way. Trystin's terrified pleas were ignored and a child sobbed in the shadows. He heard these sounds from a distance and they didn't seem important; his only concern was to save himself and to keep Elgiva from harm, though an inner voice begged him to flee for his life and end his involvement with Elven affairs.

At the edge of his hearing were shouts in the forest. Other warriors summoned, he knew, by the blare of Snarkin's horn. The gods! He was going to die like this! Pierced by the blade of this leering wretch far away from home. Why didn't somebody help him? Why was he on his own?

As he continued to back away, panic flooded his brain and an image, unbidden, sprang into his mind: a hill with a crown of purple flowers and words that made no sense. Yet one word floated uppermost on a sea of desperation.

Without knowing why, he couldn't resist the need of this word to be spoken.

Under his breath he gasped, "Taranuil."

Like a startled animal torn from sleep, his sword tensed in his hand. Its edge took on an eldritch gleam, as though fresh from the forge. Still edging backwards, he drew the blade across the pad of his thumb. It felt as dull as ever and his forehead creased with bewilderment. He could see its lethal trenchancy, yet the blade felt thick and blunt.

His enemy moved in for the kill and, as he sprang forward, Godwin prepared to meet a painful death. He raised his sword in what he believed would be his last act on the Earth. His legs were too leaden for flight. He had no choice but to die, and die well.

Then to his utter disbelief, he felt himself pulled forwards. His sword denied his cowardice, urged him into battle, and his veins were flooded with confidence. With impossible ease, he parried the blow that would have struck his head. Cadrinell didn't have time to strike back. Godwin quickly slashed at him, from left to right, and upwards.

Cries of horror escaped from the Elves, as Cadrinell's head was struck from his neck. It rolled several yards and came to a halt, wearing a look of surprise.

But the person most surprised by this didn't have time to wonder at it. Godwin turned to face Snarkin.

While Godwin had fought with Cadrinell, Snarkin had been so engrossed with it all, it had put him off his guard. He now raised his sword to threaten Elgiva, but she had edged away from him. Godwin sprang at him, raising his sword, and Snarkin clumsily parried the blow. Deep down, Godwin was glad of this. He didn't want

Snarkin to die without the chance of defending himself. Secretly, he knew that he was invincible.

Snarkin swung at Godwin again. This time the edge of Godwin's sword clashed with Snarkin's blade. The latter broke in two and Snarkin stepped back in ashen-faced horror. The warriors gasped in unison, while their captain swore with rage.

Now Godwin felt that he could show no mercy … for they who persecute evil shall prosper. He lunged at Snarkin with all his strength and impaled him on his sword. Snarkin sagged against him, his face a grimace of pain. Godwin pulled the sword from his guts and watched him sink to the ground, excited and sickened by what he had done. He didn't want to watch the Elf die, but he was the victor; it was his right.

The warriors gaped at each other in confusion and the Captain fought to rally them, but none was prepared to take Snarkin's place. The elders clamoured excitedly, inspired by Godwin's triumph, but then they heard the blare of a horn and loud voices in the forest.

The Captain flashed them a cruel grin, as the underwood burst open and a party of Elves sprang into the glade, carrying spears and swords. Emboldened by the reinforcements, the warriors brandished their weapons.

Panic seized the eldership and they snatched up the children and scattered. Tables and benches were overturned in the hope of foiling pursuit. The torches were extinguished and dirt kicked onto the fire. In his frenzy to get away, Haldrin collided with Godwin.

"Too many to fight now!" he shouted. "Flee!"

Godwin span round madly. Darkness occluded his vision. Objects were flying through the air, hurled by the fleeing Elves, and dim shapes ran past him, left and right. Eager to help the elders, the dogs were milling about, snarling at the warriors and snapping at their heels. Godwin couldn't make any sense of it all.

Grimalkin came charging into the glade and galloped round in a rage, her hind legs kicking at everyone, regardless of who they were. She whinnied stridently, "Bastards! Bastards!"

Godwin knew that they couldn't escape, but they must at least find a safe place to hide. He looked around for Elgiva, his pulse pounding in his throat, and was relieved to find her beside the fire. She was standing like a statue, staring at the embers. He ran to her side, grabbed her hand, and dragged her across the clearing. She neither complied nor resisted.

They passed Grimalkin as they fled and he whacked her on the rump, urging her to gallop away out of reach of danger. The thought that he could have told her to run didn't register in his mind.

They ran for a while, then Godwin stopped to clean his sword on the grass. His stomach clenched with thoughts of gore that made him want to retch. In the clearing they had left behind, the warriors had scattered, the dogs still nagging at their heels.

There was madness in the forest. Elgiva and Godwin heard it, as they pressed on through the trees; cries of panic and promised violence echoing in the night. Soon the sun would rise again and hiding places would be few and the rebels couldn't run forever.

Then, without warning, both of them had stumbled into a dell. Its sloping sides were covered with ferns, its edge disguised by willows. Sliding and slithering down the bank, they came to a halt at the bottom. Their nostrils were assailed by the stench of rot, but, despite the murkiness and filth, they knew they were well hidden. Motionless and hand in hand, they crouched in the stagnant water, trying not to breathe too loudly, though their need for air was great.

After a while the sounds of pursuit seemed to pass them by and very slowly they relaxed. Then Elgiva stiffened, withdrew her hand.

"Well, that's that," she said. Godwin could sense her anger mounting. "Our allies have scattered in panic. The whole of Misterell knows we're here and we've lost our companions." She inclined her head towards him and he tensed with apprehension. "Why did you drag me away like that? I ran away like a frightened mouse. They'll think my magic's all show and no substance!"

Godwin couldn't believe what he was hearing. "Well, isn't it?" he countered. He felt that he had more than earned the right to give a hurtful response. "How can you say such a thing, Elgiva? After I saved your life! You used up your strength on magic tricks. Showing off again, by Frigg!"

"How dare you!" she cried hotly. "I could have put the fear of Faine into all of them!"

"Perhaps one of us did just that!" he snapped.

Only a whisper of moonlight penetrated the dell, so neither could see the face of the other. They sat a few moments in silence, like two silhouettes of anger, then Elgiva drew a deep breath and ran her fingers through her hair. She leaned against Godwin's shoulder.

"I'm sorry, Godwin. You did well. You were very brave. I didn't know you were such a warrior."

"I'm not," he said, "but what else could I do? The elders were scared and you couldn't help me."

"You didn't need my help."

Something strange about her tone made Godwin look at her. "No, Elgiva, but…" He searched the dark blur of her face. A feeling of secret amusement seemed to cross the space between them and his senses reeled with a sudden horror. "You mean you could have...?" He gripped her by the shoulders and angrily pushed her away. "By Frigg! you just stood there and watched …!"

"Forgive me," she said softly. She pulled herself towards him, knotted her hands in his tunic so that he couldn't thrust her away. "There was a reason. At first, it's true, I had exhausted my powers, but while you fought with Cadrinell, I felt my strength return. I decided not to intervene, because … because, my friend, you doubt yourself and it's destroying you. I know how it feels to doubt your own power. Now you know how much courage you have. Do you think I 'd have just stood by and watched, had you been in any real danger? Can you really believe that of me?" She paused and withdrew her hands. "And now I know that, when magic fails me, I need have no fear with you at my side. You made a vow to protect me and you have honoured that vow. Better than I have honoured your friendship."

Silence stretched between them. Godwin felt torn by conflicting emotions and promised himself that he would understand Elves or die in the attempt.

"I suppose … I suppose I should thank you, then, for giving me faith in myself."

She shrugged. "I'm only returning a favour."

Was that all it meant to her? "But, Elgiva, there's one thing … You don't understand. You see, it wasn't me. I couldn't have done what I did without … without the help of…"

"The help of what?"

He faltered, expecting only derision for what he had to disclose. "Of…" No, he couldn't say it. He didn't understand, or believe, what had happened in the glade. He looked away and lowered his voice. "Without the help of my sword."

Elgiva laughed merrily at this, but it was laughter devoid of malice. Even so, it made him sigh. To his surprise, she put her arms around his neck and hugged him tenderly.

"Poor Godwin, I am cruel, aren't I? Wilthkin say such funny things, but silly Elves should learn respect. Please, don't be offended. It wasn't you I was laughing at."

She yawned and snuggled up to him, succumbing to her fatigue.

"What were you laughing at?" he asked.

"I sensed it," she said drowsily. "In fact, I've always known. Why are you so shy about it?"

"What … what do you mean?"

"It's nothing to be ashamed of. You own a magic sword."

He started, utterly taken aback. He needed to question her further but, before he had recovered his wits, the chance had passed him by. Elgiva was fast asleep.

⋆ ⋆ ⋆

Chapter Twenty-Five

Godwin awoke and blinked at the light, trying to recall where he was. He had fallen asleep sitting up, leaning against the slope of the dell. Elgiva lay across his lap, her face concealed by a tangle of hair, and he couldn't think how they had slept so long, considering their discomfort. The bottom of the dell was like a trough of rank and slimy water.

He lifted Elgiva gently and propped her against the bank. Strands of sunlight, piercing the trees, spangled her hair and face. Though her skin and clothes were daubed with dried mud, her beauty shone through the dirt and her sleeping face resembled a child's; vulnerable and soft. Godwin considered the power that she had at her disposal and he feared that her body was too frail to contain such might and use it. It wrenched his heart to think that her power might be her undoing; might break her like a toy.

She showed no signs of waking, so he climbed up through the willows and ferns to assess their situation. Perhaps there were friends in hiding nearby.

The morning was young and the air was fresh with the smell of flowers and broken earth. Rain had fallen while they slept and the drops that lingered on the leaves gleamed in the sun like jewels. There was birdsong in the trees above and the sky was a clean and cloudless blue, stretched overhead like a great expanse of newly washed linen hung out to dry.

But his clothes were wet and filthy. About him hung the smell of decay and the cling of his garments made him itch. He draped his cloak on a bush to dry, then he scanned the encircling forest. It was quiet and still and he saw no Elves, friendly or otherwise.

He cast a quick glance back at the dell, then walked a short way across the grass. He spied a path ahead of him that snaked between the trees and for some reason it intrigued him. It was little more than a ribbon of earth, with clumps of grass growing down the middle, but he felt a strange compulsion to set his foot upon it and follow it to its end.

He walked for a while on the beaten track, till a nagging doubt made him falter. Perhaps he ought to return to the dell. What if Elgiva awoke in his absence? She wouldn't know where he was.

He turned to retrace his steps, then a noise from beyond the trees to his right made him stop and listen. It was the sound of water; a fresh, tinkling murmur that called to his thirst invitingly. It couldn't be ignored. He left the path and hurried towards it, wading through the bushes and a profusion of flowering hogweed taller than himself, and, as he approached it, the sound deepened, hinted at refreshment.

Suddenly, the shrubs drew back and he found himself in a tree-ringed glade. A swarm of daisies carpeted the grass. Across the glade was a waterfall, cascading down a shallow escarpment, which sloped off into the distance, carrying a crowd of trees on its back. The waterfall, a torrent of silver, plunged into a pool, and the overspill formed a bubbling stream, which seemed to dance across the glade and vanish into the forest. Reeds cooled their feet in the shimmering pool and, on either side of the waterfall, the rock-face was covered with flowers and shrubs.

As Godwin walked across the glade, he felt as though he had entered a temple. The air about him was languid and rich and filled with the perfume of flowers. He drew it deeply into his lungs and a feeling of peace washed over him. It was the sort of inner calm he had searched for all his life.

Hastening forward, he knelt by the pool and drank the clear water in grateful gulps. It was cold, sharp and invigorating. Then he lay on the grass and listened to the birds and the soothing gush of the water. The beauty and calm of his surroundings gave him a feeling of optimism: it seemed to conceal some unknown hope. He tried to pinpoint the source of this feeling, but it slipped away from him.

Then he remembered his filthiness. How could he stay in this beautiful place, bemired as he was with mud and sweat? An urgent need for purity hauled him to his feet and he stripped off his clothes and tossed them aside without a second thought. Then he lowered himself into the water, like a soul in need of baptism. Its iciness made him gasp, but soon he grew accustomed to the chill and revelled in his weightlessness, while the dirt was sloughed away.

He forgot about Elgiva, Saxons, armed patrols, battles, Misterell, Elves and everything.

Then he noticed the bundle of mud-caked clothes beside the pool. Finding their filthiness offensive, he dragged them into the water and scrubbed at the shirt and tunic with zeal, while dark clouds billowed around him in the pool, like liquid smoke.

For a time, the business of cleaning his clothes was the only thought in his mind, but then some instinct made him stop. An uncomfortable prickling on the back of his neck told him that he wasn't alone and a lapping noise behind him made his heart pound and his muscles tense. He tried to spin to confront the intruder, but his feet slid on the slippery stones and he fell backwards with a splash.

Shaking water from her eyes, Grimalkin stood by the pool.

"Oh, by Frigg! … It's you!" spluttered Godwin. "Must you sneak up on people like that?"

She tossed her head disdainfully, water dribbling from her lips. Godwin scowled at her and pushed the fringe of wet hair from his eyes. "Where've you been, you old nag?"

She stared in a bored, superior fashion and Godwin felt an irrational need to fold his arms to cover his nakedness.

"I don't like being thumped on the arse." She shook her head for emphasis. "You going to piss about in there much longer? You could have had the decency to wait till I'd had a drink. Cabbage hearts! The water's like pitch!"

With a sigh of exasperation, Godwin clambered from the pool and began to wring out his sodden clothes. He looked around for somewhere to dry them and cursed the obsession with cleanliness that had over-ridden his common sense.

"By the way, Brit, I found Trystin," Grimalkin informed him matter-of-factly. "Here comes the little whingebag now."

Godwin looked up and saw the Elfling walking across the glade. His face lit up, when he saw his friends, and he skipped towards them, grinning. He halted at the edge of the pool.

"Master Godwin, you found it, then?"

"Found what?" demanded Godwin, struggling into his clothes.

"The place the wise man spoke of. Faine's Lynn – the heart of Misterell."

"What?" Godwin tried to dress himself, hopping about in frustration. Everything seemed to be inside out and his wet clothes clung to his skin. What prompted such a stupid idea, washing his clothes with nowhere to dry them? Savagely, he thrust his arm into the sleeve of his shirt and there was a rending noise. "Shit!"

"Hurry up, Master Godwin! Let's climb up here and start our search!"

Trystin scampered towards the escarpment, while Godwin was still adjusting his clothes. He buckled his belt, forced on his boots and made to follow the Elfling. Gazing up at the rock-face, he saw that Trystin had reached the top.

Damn your agility, he thought with a frown, but he shrugged off his irritation and moved towards the cliff. He looked up at it worriedly. "Trystin, it's too steep!" he called. "I don't think I can climb it."

"Plenty of footholds, Master Godwin!"

Godwin shook his head. Reluctantly, he began his ascent. The cliff was as sheer as the side of a barn and the rocks were slick with spray, but, nevertheless, by sheer physical strength, he managed to scramble half way up. It was then that his strength deserted him and he knew that he would never make it.

"Trystin!" he cried between ragged breaths, "What is the point of climbing up here?"

"Point or not, I should make less noise," Grimalkin whinnied gloomily. "The whole of ruddy Misterell will know what you're about."

Forgetting how precarious his hold was on the rocks, Godwin twisted round to hurl an insult at the pony. Suddenly, his foot slipped and he began to slide. He scrambled to find a purchase, his muscles taut with strain, but before he knew what was happening, he was slithering downwards through the plants into the path of the waterfall.

Then he lost his footing completely and braced himself for the inevitable.

The impact stunned him for a moment. Trying to regain his feet, he found himself pummelled by gallons of water and the breath was pounded from his lungs. He lost all knowledge of who he was or what he was trying to do. Blinded by water, he crawled on all fours, knowing only that he needed air.

All at once, the pressure ceased, left him gasping in a cool, moist shade with red specks flashing before his eyes. Beneath him, his fingers clutched soaking wet soil.

Gradually, his dizziness faded. He looked up, astonished to find himself kneeling behind the waterfall in a tiny chamber of solid rock several yards in diameter. Though straight, the walls of the chamber looked as if they had been gouged from the rock by some incredible heat. In places the surface of the stone ran like solidified wax.

Shakily, he got to his feet. Between him and the outside world the waterfall fell like a silvery curtain. In his confusion it seemed impenetrable and he fancied that he was lost forever.

But he wasn't alone for long. Trystin, wearing a look of concern, squeezed his way past the waterfall and hurried to his side.

"Are you all right, Master Godwin?" Runnels of water ran down his face and his features looked as though they were melting.

Godwin gathered himself together. "Yes ... yes. No harm done." He drew a deep breath to compose himself. "We'd better continue our search."

Trystin stepped forwards. "No, wait!" he cried. He studied the walls of the chamber, as though he were searching for veins of gold. Then he turned to face Godwin, a look of delight on his face. "Don't you think this would be a very good hiding place, Master Godwin? Somewhere safe and secret?"

Godwin cocked an eyebrow at this. "Be reasonable, lad. These walls are solid. You couldn't hide anything here."

Trysin gazed round with an expression of wonder. "But these walls, Master Godwin, they don't look right."

Godwin walked to the end of the chamber, explored the cold stone with his fingers. "Well, no, they're odd, but they're still solid rock. If anything lies behind these walls, there's no way we'd ever find it."

Trystin grabbed his arm imploringly. "But it must be here!" he protested. "It wouldn't be out in the open for anybody to find!"

"How do you know?" asked Godwin impatiently. He pulled himself free from the Elfling's grasp. "Look, Trystin, lad, we can't walk through stone and I can't see a door. Can you? We'll have to search elsewhere."

Trystin, however, was adamant. "No, Master Godwin. Where's Lady Elgiva? She'll know what to do. Perhaps we need magic to get through this stone."

"Trystin, lad, we're wasting time."

But the young Elf refused to leave the chamber. "Faine loved this place," he said.

"No doubt."

Godwin turned to walk away, but Trystin barred his path. "I can feel his love," he insisted. "I can feel it … here."

The strange and wistful gleam in his eyes made Godwin hesitate. Then, with a groan of exasperation, he unsheathed his sword. An idea had suddenly entered his mind. He suspected that, once awakened, his sword could penetrate anything.

"All right I give in. If it's magic we need, then there's magic in this."

"Yes, yes! I saw!" beamed Trystin.

"If this won't do it," said Godwin, "will you be satisfied?"

Trystin nodded and grinned.

Godwin brought the blade to his lips and whispered 'Taranuil', then he walked towards the back wall of the chamber and in his heart was a firm conviction: the blade would be unharmed. Without hesitation, he stabbed at the rock with all his strength.

As steel and stone made contact, an explosion of light and a blast of air knocked Godwin and Trystin off their feet. It felt as though an enormous door had been blown in by a gale. Taranuil sang like a bell, sent shivers up Godwin's arm and he was forced to drop it. Cries of terror thronged in his throat, but the force of the blast had left him mute. Both he and Trystin shielded their eyes, as the brilliance raged about them, and the rush of air sucked the breath from their lungs.

Suddenly, it was over and a cold, damp peace filled the granite chamber. Godwin and Trystin got to their feet and stood for a while, catching their breath. The waterfall sounded unnaturally loud, but louder still was the pounding of their hearts.

When they could bear to look about them, their eyes grew wide with amazement, for in the wall of stone ahead a tall, arched doorway had appeared. Beyond this lay another chamber, bathed in a ghostly light. They stared at each other, open-mouthed, both speechless with astonishment.

Godwin summoned what courage he could and approached the doorway's threshold. Trystin followed close behind, his fingers fastened on Godwin's tunic.

They peered inside the inner chamber.

It was perfectly round with a sunken floor and the walls were of polished stone. After a brief inspection, Godwin managed to extricate himself from Trystin's grasp. He retrieved his sword, half expecting it to sting him again with power, but the blade was cold and inert; mere metal. For a moment, he and the Elfling shared a look of caution, then, brandishing Taranuil, Godwin returned to the doorway.

As he crossed the threshold, Trystin tiptoed behind him, as though he feared to awaken whatever nameless horror might be lurking in the cavern. Three stone steps beyond the doorway led them down to the sunken floor. There they stood and looked about, waiting for their eyes to grow accustomed to the dimness. The smell of cold stone and damp earth made them shiver in their sodden clothes.

Though the chamber walls were sheer and round, the ceiling was made of dark, wet earth, enmeshed with a writhing of tree roots, and, here and there, were a few fine cracks that let in strings of sunlight. The only feature in the cavern was a pedestal made of polished stone. Godwin and Trystin stepped softly towards it.

An oaken casket stood on the pedestal, bound with bands of iron. They looked at the casket and then at each other and then at the casket again. Finally Godwin straightened himself, transferred his sword to his other hand and slowly lifted the casket's lid. They sucked in their breath simultaneously, when they saw what lay within.

A smooth, round opal, as large as an apple, lay nestling on a bed of white silk and beneath its milky surface were suggestions of blue, green, yellow and red. A ray of sunlight pierced the globe, lit up the casket and bounced off again, spangling the walls with muted reflections. The light flashed and winked on Godwin's sword, as though they shared some arcane communion. And Godwin knew that their bond was magic.

Stunned by the opal's beauty, neither knew what to say. Godwin felt like a trespasser, a defiler of ancient relics, while Trystin nervously chewed his fingers and stared at the opal's perfection, as though it were an elixir that could heal his anguished past.

Eventually, Godwin found his voice. "By Grim!" he whispered. "The Lorestone."

Trystin clutched at Godwin's arm, his face alight with joy. "I knew it, Master Godwin! I knew it wasn't a myth!"

Godwin glanced at Trystin and his own sense of accomplishment glowed in the Elfling's eyes. A thrill of excitement ran up his spine and he fumbled as he sheathed his sword. Steadying himself with a deep breath, he reached out to touch the globe. Its cold, smooth surface glimmered under his admiring gaze.

"By Frigg! it's beautiful!" he gasped.

"How shall we carry it, Master Godwin?"

"Carry it?" Godwin scowled at him, as though invited to commit a crime. He regarded the Lorestone dourly. Move it from its quiet abode? Seize it with rough, mortal hands? The idea was appalling, but, of course, it was why they had come. "Carry it, yes. Well, I don't know. We must keep it somewhere safe."

He lifted the opal carefully. It looked as fragile as a dream, but it was surprisingly heavy. Then he noticed a piece of parchment lying underneath it. Replacing the Stone on its bed of silk, he took out the parchment and studied it, but the words it contained meant nothing to him, for he was unable to read. He handed it to Trystin.

"Can you make any sense of this?"

Trystin began to read.

"The Stone's Discoverer,
"Orphan and slave,
"Shall unlock the door
"With a magic glaive.
"Let him be honest,
"Sure and leal,
"And take it for
"The Elven Weal.
"Whoever should wish
"To light its flame,
"Must seek and find
"The Lorestone's name.
"The sacred grove,
"The sarsen ring,
"Where Nine Wise Men
"Are heard to sing.
"There stands the tallest,

"Like a tower;
"Beneath his feet
"A word of power.
"This word invoke
"To weave the spell.
"But have a care
"And use it well."

They looked at each other for a long moment, baffled by the verse, then Godwin picked up the opal and made to leave the cavern, feeling a sudden need for haste. Trystin padded behind him, the parchment in his hand. As they left the second chamber, the doorway vanished behind them, became once more a wall of solid stone.

Grimalkin was still devouring the plants, as they edged round the tumble of the waterfall, her ragged tail lashing at the flies that swarmed about her rump. She lifted her ungainly head and flashed her companions a look of annoyance.

"Celery stalks!" she snickered morosely. "I hate the coming of warmer weather. These wretched bugs are eating me alive!"

Trystin capered up to her and hugged her scrawny neck. "Grimalkin, we've found the Lorestone!" he cried, and he danced about with joy.

"Well, that may be," she snickered. Her eyes looked first at Trystin, then slid to the ground at his feet. "But that's no reason to tread on my dinner."

⋆ ⋆ ⋆

Chapter Twenty-Six

Sleep was a fathomless pit of oblivion in which all care was cast aside and Elgiva was sorry to leave it. Her senses were sluggish, her mind was fogged, and discomfort registered slowly. She stretched herself and scanned her surroundings.

Her nose was assailed by the stench of the water that was seeping into her clothes. Her hair and skin were stiff with dried mud, her kirtle torn and soiled and her cloak was wrapped about her body like a filthy cerement. Broken fern stems pricked her limbs and she seemed to itch all over.

Pushing against the bank of the dell, she heaved herself to her feet, wincing at the effort. She flicked the dirty hair from her eyes and searched around for Godwin. His absence alarmed and puzzled her and she realised how much she needed her level-headed friend. Her aloneness felt like panic.

She peered up through the branches. The sun was high in the sky and she knew that she had slept too long.

A rustle of leaves on the edge of the dell made a vague hope quicken her pulse. She squinted through the foliage. A dark shape sat on the top of the bank.

"Godwin?" she whispered. "Is that you?"

There was no response. Scrambling up through the trees and ferns with the sun drawing water from her eyes, she wondered at the sudden dread that writhed in the pit of her stomach.

Then she reached the top of the dell.

"I could have assumed his appearance, dear heart," Vieldrin said with a smirk. "An amusing subterfuge, I think, but rather underhand." The arch of his eyebrows sharpened, as he savoured the fear in her eyes. "In any case, such shape-shifting tends to be demeaning. Those Wilthkin are so ugly."

Elgiva reeled at the sight of her foe. The forest seemed to spin like madness and terror churned her stomach. Vieldrin sat in a long, black robe, disturbingly handsome and wearing a grin of cold and malicious triumph.

"And how could I be so cruel?" he said. "I know how much he means to you. I see it in your heart. Why, I could almost be jealous."

"What … how did you find me? What are you doing here?"

"Faine-worship has reared its ugly head. The guards who reported back to me had news of an insurrection. Who else would be behind it but you?" He smiled and exposed his perfect, white teeth. "And, as for seeking you out, dear heart, I merely followed my nose." The disgust in his gaze was palpable and, despite herself, Elgiva felt loathsome. "But I would have found you, filthy or not. Magic has an odour all of its own, but I would not expect you to know that."

Elgiva raised her head defiantly. "This disguise of yours, I've seen it before. Are you running out of ideas?"

The Elf-king chuckled merrily. "You amuse me greatly, dear heart. This is no disguise." He spread his hands affectedly. "Will you not believe it? Is it too good to be true? I was blessed at birth with a handsome appearance, the features and form of a king. I was destined to rule by looks alone, if by nothing else."

"Spare me this. What do you want? I believe our contest is not yet over." She tried to maintain an icy calm.

He smiled at her slyly and smoothed back his hair with a strong but elegant hand. "How quickly you reach such serious matters. I had hoped for some lighter conversation on so fine a day."

His smugness made Elgiva frown. She looked away and secretly she searched for the easiest route of escape, but then Vieldrin's arm snaked out and his fingers closed around her wrist. She was forced to look at him.

"I shall speak of our contest soon enough. There are other vexations I wish to discuss, the most recent being that little rebellion. Well, your attempt to incite my subjects was, fortunately, a failure, and soon they will all be rounded up. I have assured them of my leniency, providing that they abandon their foolishness and return to their duties. However, it would appear that four of my warriors managed to get themselves killed. Four of my best, you understand, and I do not feel inclined to show mercy to murderers."

Releasing her wrist, he leaned back on his elbow and glared at her down his nose. His contempt and the bitter sting of failure stirred Elgiva's anger. With a primitive hatred, she clenched her fist and raised it to attack him, but he grasped her arm and twisted it, then pulled her towards him effortlessly.

"I mislike your hostility, dear heart," he said in a calm, soft tone. "That is no way to treat a friend."

For a moment his eyes were aflame with power, then fire lanced up Elgiva's arm, pierced her heart like a dagger. The pain, though brief, left her gasping with shock and far too stunned to retaliate.

"If you … if you harm my friends … I promise you, I'll kill you!"

He laughed and released her. "Well, dear heart, what are four puny warriors? I can be generous, Elgiva. I can forget such trifles. I will think about it. They were all cowards anyway." He looked at her with unsettling softness from the depths of his large, dark eyes. "If only they had your mettle, my dear. I have five hundred warriors in Misterell and none has courage like yours."

"Five hundred?"

"Someone has told you differently?" He feigned a look of astonishment. "Well, no-one can be trusted."

"You least of all."

He grinned at this. "Your presence is so refreshing. You never agree with me, while everyone else…"

"Everyone else has neither the will nor the power. You're nothing but a tyrant with a kingdom of terrified slaves."

"I know," he said matter-of-factly. "It has been a labour of love, my dear, to get the old place how I want it."

"And Elindell?"

"Is coming along. My plan to take Queen Gilda's lands is also well in hand. Tandrin's, too, eventually. Astorill will be next, I think, then Eiriol in the north. The king of Eiriol is a barbarian and really doesn't deserve to keep all that gold he has managed to hoard. But enough of all that. It is tiresome. Let us return to the list of your crimes, and let us start with the Forest of Ethephon – the Forest of Shades as some have called it. I wish you had spared it, Elgiva. That was my favourite haunt. For ages untold the Wardain of Misterell ruled the Vale of Ethephon. Its destruction hurt me deeply, you know.

Very deeply, in fact." His gaze sharpened like a whetted blade.

"The forest was evil!" she exclaimed, and then she understood. "It wasn't the forest … it was you!"

"In my younger days I practised there. Ah, the spells I wove, the enchantments I learned! How easily I could invoke the bitter wrath of the trees!" He leaned a little closer, as though to divulge a wonderful secret. "A whim came upon me to torture them. Rooted and helpless as they were, they were just right for my purposes. But how to torture insensate creatures? I pondered on it. My powers grew. I learned new tricks. Soon I gave those dull-witted trees awareness of the outside world. I prodded them out of their sleepy ways and gave them a higher consciousness. I taught them pain and anger and hate and the power of coercion. Who would ever have believed that trees could go insane? But indeed they can. I taught them to hate themselves, because they could not walk abroad and appease the desires I instilled in them. They hated themselves for what they were and, naturally, they went mad."

Elgiva's whole body went cold with revulsion. A gyring emptiness sucked at her mind and she was forced to swallow the gorge that rose into her throat. When she was finally able to speak, her words were like gouts of abomination.

"You had no right! … You had no right…!"

"No right?" he snarled. "I had every right! The world belongs to those with power, to those with the strength to take what they want. The forest was mine by inheritance and mine by conquest, too. How can you talk of rights, Elgiva, when you destroyed the forest? You set flame to the living trees. What are you but a murderer?"

"The trees ... the trees were in torment..."

"Some misguided notion of mercy-killing? Silly Elf, they were but things of wood."

"Then why did you bother to torture them?" Tears stung her eyes and ran down her cheeks and she cursed herself for showing such weakness.

"Don't split hairs. It bores me."

"You have no respect ... no respect for Nature..." Her voice trailed away in sobs.

"Nonsense. I respect its power and I intend to use it!"

"Like Smirill used it?"

"Smirill was a fool." His eyebrows arched disdainfully. "Smirill made too many mistakes. I intend to make none."

Elgiva strove for self-control, to find the focus she needed. "You have Royal Elf-power. Nothing more. What can you do with that?"

His answer was unexpected. "How beautiful you are, dear heart." His voice was like a lake of acid overlaid with honey. "Cover yourself with mud more often. It is most becoming." His strangely cruel yet benevolent face gave her a perfect smile, but the hunger in his dark eyes made Elgiva wince.

"Stop it! Stop it ... kill me now! I can't stand this. I've heard enough." She turned away from him, hiding her tears.

"Kill you, dear heart?" He looked surprised. "I cannot pretend that such an idea has never entered my mind, however..." He paused, willed her to turn and face him. "However, since our very first meeting, I have always known it. Fate has chosen you for my bride. I want you. I shall have you."

She glared at him in sick horror. "Filthy wretch, I'll never…"

"You dare not refuse me, dear heart. You are mine, in the name of Faine."

She couldn't find words to refute him and merely shook her head in despair.

"You pretend to hate me," Vieldrin went on, his tone now soft and indulgent, "because you think you should. Even the Elven Vow to Faine cannot change your mind. I fail to understand, my dear, no matter how I try." A look of mild exasperation flickered in his eyes. "But what I cannot comprehend is why you refuse to acknowledge the fact that you find me so appealing. I do not mistake the look in your eyes. I am well acquainted with desire, little Elf." He held up his hand to silence her protests. "But that aside, Elgiva, if desire and vows have no effect upon your stubborn heart, there is one thing that will." He grinned at her for a moment, then lay back on the grass, his hands behind his head. "I have risen above mere Royal Elf-power. Forgive me for ending the fun so quickly, but our contest is concluded." He sighed with feigned regret. "Elgiva, I have found the Lorestone."

"I … don't believe you…I…" She could barely find the strength to keep breathing.

His sensuous lips stretched into a smile. Then suddenly he sprang erect, seized Elgiva's upper arms and dragged her to her feet. For someone so slender and elegant, he was also frighteningly strong. He studied her face with the manner of a father vexed by a stubborn child.

"Yes, it exists," he smugly announced, "and I have always known it. I have spent much time in the search for the Stone and now I am rewarded. I win, Elgiva, and you must surrender."

"You can only use it once," she gasped, as she dangled in his grip.

"Once will more than suffice!" he returned, his tone hinting at future horrors. "Then Faine's power will be unleashed and it will enter me, increase my might a hundred-fold!"

He tightened his grasp and Elgiva's arms throbbed with the pressure of constricted blood. The realisation of weakness and failure squeezed fresh tears from her eyes and runnels of sweat ran down her spine, but the need to escape from his evil grip burned in her brain like panic. She drew her being into focus.

"But meanwhile," she said, "you have mere Royal Elf-magic."

A flare of angry, scarlet fire blossomed from her arms, made Vieldrin gasp with pain and he was forced to release her. Scowling dangerously, he stepped back and prepared a bolt of his own. Power blazed from his finger tips with concentrated violence and it sent Elgiva reeling backwards, rolled her like a wind-tossed leaf upon the forest floor. For several long moments it clung to her skin and burned her with white-hot agony before the power was spent.

Vieldrin laughed, his fists on his hips. "Before you presume to do battle," he jeered, "consider with whom you do it. I am your senior. In my prime. And I have had years of practice." He stepped forwards lithely, seized her arm and hauled her to her feet. "Yours is the magic of infancy."

Her vision was smeared with tears of pain and she tried to focus on his face, but all she saw was a blur of evil. "You think you're clever with your tricks and threats, and you might have the Lorestone," she cried, "but you won't be allowed to use it!"

He pushed her away from him, laughing with scorn. "And who is going to stop me? Queen Gilda? Tandrin? How would they do it? They must confront me face to face, but they could never enter my realm without alerting me. I would have the advantage and be the first to attack. And, anyway, Elgiva, who will protect their people and lands, if they come after me?"

"This war … it's a diversion…!"

"Allow me to finish, dear heart!" he snapped. "It seems that no-one has taught you manners, but I will rectify that. Where was I? Yes. The list of my opponents. Your uncle – I hesitate to call him great - that old fool Bellic. He will prevent me, will he? I have him in chains in Elindell, chains that cannot be broken save by magic stronger than his. He is defeated, little Elf. He is a husk, dried up and futile. Then there's that Wilthkin friend of yours with his puny, little sword. I would not waste my power! Then there's you, my sweeting. Who would win in a duel of magic? I think we know the answer, do we not? I have your measure now." Folding his arms across his breast, he gazed at the forest, as though he were bored.

She combed her fingers through her hair and her mind ran in panic through a host of escapes, alternatives and choices, but time and again the spectre of death blocked her every move.

"Why don't you use the Stone?" she asked. His eyes swooped towards her, but he said nothing. "If you are to be the master of all, why do you delay? Why don't you stop the war, Vieldrin? There's no need for any bloodshed."

"What care I for bloodshed?" He glanced away indifferently, but she thought she saw a flicker of something; doubt or vexation, she couldn't tell, but she drew courage from it.

"The truth is, you can't use the Stone! You don't know how to use it. Nobody does, do they!"

"Be silent!" he snapped with an angry frown. "These are matters beyond you. I do not have to explain myself to you or to anyone else. All that need concern you is that I now have the Lorestone and I have the power to kill your uncle and your friends. Know also that they will be spared, if you become my queen."

Elgiva needed time to think, but her mind was completely numb. She swallowed hard. It seemed that there was only one way forward; it was purely a matter of survival. Pride, anger, revulsion, such things must be pushed aside. If she and her friends could stay alive, at least some hope would flicker on somewhere in all this darkness. Owning the Lorestone was one thing; using it was another. Until its mysteries were unlocked, she must play along with Vieldrin.

But it wasn't going to be easy!

"Well?" he rasped impatiently. "Do you agree to become my queen, or will your uncle be flayed alive?"

Faine, Siriol, somebody, help me, Elgiva thought desperately, struggling for composure.

"I am waiting, little Elf."

Elgiva drew a deep breath. Cunning and compliance were now her surest weapons. "I have no choice," she sighed. "I can't argue with what you've said. I'm no match for you and I admit it. I'd be a fool to oppose you now." She averted her face and sniffed back her tears. "Do with me as you will."

"That was always my intention," he said, with a casual wave of his hand that implied inevitability. "You are bound to me by your oath to Faine and I could have forced you to keep that oath, yet, little churl, I much prefer that you accept of your own volition and common sense. It is far more gratifying."

She gave him a lost, defeated look. Inwardly, she was baffled by the logic of his reasoning, the sudden change of moods.

"I have no wish to inflict more pain upon you than I must," he said, as though his own cruelty were abhorrent to him. "I am not a monster, my little enchantress." The savage triumph in his eyes conflicted with his words. "But all must eventually submit to me. My will is irresistible." Suddenly, his features changed, twisted into a scowl. "For I shall be the master of all. This land is mine and no-one shall stop me. No-one who defies me will live!" He knotted his fingers in her hair, wrenched her towards him viciously. "And defiance, my dear, I will not brook. I will not stand for defiance. It will be crushed, is that understood?"

His eyes pierced her like daggers and she nodded, trembling with terror. Her bones had turned to effectless jelly, while his dark eyes promised her pain and torment.

Then, in an instant, his features softened, adopted a pleasant smile. Slowly he unclenched his fist and, as he withdrew his hand from her hair, he trailed his finger tips down her cheek.

"But I won't hurt you anymore. There is no need, is there? You will not disobey me now. It would not be prudent, would it?" His voice was reassuring, as though he were soothing a child.

Elgiva frowned with confusion. The unpredictability of his moods was too extreme, even for an Elf. There was more than a taint of madness in it.

With disconcerting gentleness, he took her hand in his own. Elgiva was careful not to recoil. "Now we must be going," he said. "The Royal Hall awaits. I will have the servants clean you up, if they can bear the stink. Once you are dressed as befits your rank, I am sure you will look every inch a queen, though no amount of finery could make you anymore beautiful than you already are, my love." He gave her a condescending nod.

Give me one chance, just one, thought Elgiva.

"Don't scowl, dear heart, you are betrothed to Elvendom's future ruler. I will be the Elwardain and basking in my shadow will give you cause to rejoice." He laughed, as though this were a jest. "Look not so glum, my sweeting. You will not rue alliance with me."

She gave him a shy, uncertain smile.

You're quite insane, she thought.

* * *

Chapter Twenty-Seven

"I can't understand where she's gone," moaned Godwin.

He was sitting near the dell, Trystin beside him, solemn-faced. A small fire spat and crackled before them, its ration of branches nearly consumed. They had waited several hours, perplexed and worried by Elgiva's absence, but neither knew what to do about it. He turned to the Elfling with a frown of concern.

"Are you sure there are no messages? No marks? No Elven signs?"

Trystin sighed. He was used to answering this question by now and there seemed little point in answering it again. He stood up slowly and stretched his legs. "We both know, Master Godwin. Something has happened to Lady Elgiva."

"How much longer must we hang about here?" demanded Grimalkin irritably. She tore up a bunch of centaury and lumbered towards her companions. "Cabbage hearts! I'll get cracked heels, standing in all this mud. Why don't you do something? Why don't you search?"

"Because it's far too dangerous," said Godwin angrily. "Vieldrin's patrols are everywhere, and where would we search? It's a bloody big forest. Or hadn't you noticed, you stupid beast?"

"Call me stupid, would you?" she snickered. "Me that can jump higher than a tree."

"Don't be ridiculous!" he said.

"You ever seen a tree jump?"

The sound of someone running towards them brought their banter to an end. Godwin leapt up, sword in hand, ready to confront the intruder. An Elf was hurrying along the path that ran parallel to the dell and Godwin immediately recognised him: Aldric of the eldership.

"Aldric, stop!" called Godwin.

The old Elf started visibly and span to face the sound, but when he saw who had hailed him, his furtive look changed to one of anger. With his white hair flying about his head, he stumped towards the companions and wagged a reproachful finger at them. "It's all your doing!" he hissed. "Betrayers!"

"What in Frigg's name are you on about?"

"Have you not heard?" sneered Aldric. "You led us all a merry dance and now your plan has borne fruit. I thought we were wrong to trust you."

Folding his arms over Taranuil, Godwin sighed with frustration. "Explain yourself!" he snapped.

Aldric seemed anxious to be away. His brow was creased with vexation and his feet could barely keep themselves still. "Look, Wilthkin, your friend has betrayed us. She's going to be Vieldrin's queen. It's just been announced. What treachery!"

This information was so absurd that Godwin felt like laughing. "What?"

"Yes, it's true. What, didn't you know? Deceived you, too, then, has she? The two of them are going to be wed and all of Misterell – what's left of it – must go and pay them homage or be slain for disrespect. Tomorrow at noon, if you want to know. They're announcing their betrothal. Pah! No more chatter or I'll be late. When Vieldrin commands attendance, only a fool would disobey. If I'm not there before dusk falls, then my head's off, for sure!"

"Why you?"

"Why me indeed? Hah! Vieldrin wants something special for his wedding." He jabbed his finger at Godwin. "I wasn't always a slave, you know. I'm a weaver by trade and a good one, too, and he's made me an offer I can't refuse. Either I weave the finest cloth that Misterell's ever seen, or I get a knife in my guts." He turned to go.

"Wait!" cried Godwin, raising his sword.

The elder began to move away, but Grimalkin butted him in the back and thrust him forward with her nose, until he stood within an inch of the tip of Godwin's sword.

"Are you mad or lying, or what?" Godwin asked him angrily.

"I tell you it's true," bleated Aldric, flinching from the sword, "and my advice, for what use it is, is that you go and pay homage, too, or be found by the guards and slaughtered."

"I don't believe it," Godwin said, slowly shaking his head.

"Please yourself," snapped Aldric impatiently, "but there's something else you ought to know, though you won't believe that either. That Lorestone you spoke of… he's found it."

"Found it?" Godwin looked at Trystin, not knowing how to react, and Trystin stared back in bewilderment.

"A murrain upon him!" cursed Aldric. "I suppose that's why your friend gave in so soon. I always suspected she was a coward, but it strikes me she changed sides a bit too quickly. Not altogether unwilling, I think. I've heard about these Elindellians. Power-mad … and that's not all…"

"I think you've said enough!" declared Godwin.

"Vieldrin's a looker and a charmer, too," Aldric persisted with a knowing smirk. "They can't resist that, Elindellians…"

"By Frigg! Will you shut up!" Godwin thought how easy it would be to take off Aldric's head where he stood. "For a man who's anxious to take to his heels, you've a ruddy good lot to say for yourself. Now, tell me this. Where are we to pay homage?"

"The Royal Hall, of course. Where else?" Aldric retorted huffily.

"All right," said Godwin. "Be off with you, then, or be well acquainted with the edge of my sword."

Aldric glared at him with contempt, then he turned and fled into the forest. Sighing, Godwin sheathed his sword, musing on the nature of the Misterellians. He decided that they were cowards. But it was easy to think such thoughts with anger in his heart and a magic sword; easier to chide and bluster than to try to understand. He sighed at his own hypocrisy and turned to his young companion. The gods be thanked, Trystin, at least, was always on the side of right. Or was he just besotted with Elgiva? He was, perhaps, too easily swayed.

Trystin smiled at him cautiously. He knew that Godwin was deep in thought and was anxious not to distub him. Godwin put his arm around the Elfling's shoulders. Trystin with his starved body and melancholy eyes seemed to embody everything that he and Elgiva were trying to save. Such innocence must be protected. The right course of action had to be taken, and taken soon, he knew, but he wasn't quite sure what that action was.

"Well, lad, what do you make of all this?"

"Stuff and nonsense!" proposed Grimalkin.

"I wasn't asking you."

"Why not? Never heard of horse-sense?"

"Master Godwin," ventured Trystin, "I agree with Grimalkin. Lady Elgiva must have been tricked. She wouldn't do this willingly. She's playing along with the King."

"Yes, it must be so," agreed Godwin. "In which case, Trystin, we must make sure that she knows we have the Lorestone. And somehow we have to do this ourselves. No-one else can be trusted."

"Hate to get on my high-horse," snickered Grimalkin sardonically, "but, exactly how, may I ask?"

"Well," decided Godwin, "we'll have to go and pay homage and perhaps we can speak to her privately."

"Some hope of that!" she snorted. "More likely they'll grab us, Brit!"

"Shut your noise, you ugly brute! You're always so pessimistic."

"You wanted to talk to animals, so now you're stuck with it."

Godwin knew himself justly chastised and pretended to ignore her. "Trystin, it's going to be a long, cold night. Do you know where we can get some food?"

The Elfling stiffened like a frightened hare. "Everil will help us. But it means going back..." He paused and drew a deep breath, then his eyes lit up with purpose. "But I'll go, Master Godwin."

"Good lad, but wait till dusk," said Godwin. "As brave as you are, Trystin, bravery won't conceal you from the King's patrols quite as well as darkness."

Trystin's features tried to convey surprise, delight and embarrassment all at the same time. He couldn't have been more taken aback had he found the crown of Misterell discarded in a ditch. Inwardly, he hoped that he wouldn't disappoint his friend's good opinion.

⋆ ⋆ ⋆

Elgiva stepped out from the Royal Hall into the lambent morning. She stood ankle-deep in the rich, green sward and gazed down at her clothes. Her blue, silk gown rustled in the breeze and its train was a swathe of sky upon the grass. It seemed too light and ethereal to be a part of the Earth and she had never worn anything so exquisite.

Vieldrin's female servants had washed and brushed and curled her hair and done their best to tidy it up. They wondered why she wore it short, but were far too timid to ask. It wasn't the custom for Elven ladies to crop their gorgeous tresses, so they covered her head with a square of white silk, held in place by a circlet of gold that was shaped like a snake with two heads. It sparkled fiercely in the light and the white silk flowed and fluttered beneath it. A brooch set with garnets gleamed at her breast and, when she moved, frail chains of gold adorned with tiny trinkets tinkled like bells on her ankles and wrists.

She resumed her walk across the grass and only one thing marred her delight, cast a grim shadow over the day: Vieldrin. He sauntered behind her in equally regal attire, his jet- black outfit studded with pearls.

She shuddered as she felt him approach. His dark power reached out to hold her back and the fleshless fingers of his coercion gripped her with their unseen talons, held her still while he strolled to her side.

She turned to face him, smiling demurely, and took the arm he offered.

Two oaken thrones stood on the grass and they made their way towards them. Vieldrin had decided that the Elves would pay homage out-of-doors, for the weather was pleasantly fresh and mild and he fancied that his propective bride would look even lovelier in the sun.

Floating somewhere in the mire of his heart was a vestige of pride untouched by evil. Gazing at his future queen, he was dazzled by her radiance, though even so it troubled him to find such pleasure in beauty. As her large, dark eyes looked up at him, he wondered if the affection that he pretended to feel had some small shred of truth in it.

He laughed to himself. No. Idle thoughts. Remember who you are, Vieldrin, what you have to do. This pleasure comes solely from gloating. When those slaves see their avowed ally, the good and lovely Elgiva, sitting beside her enemy, helpless and submissive ... and soon to share his bed ... how they will despise her!

Mentally, he rubbed his hands together, congratulating himself on the way things had turned out. Now Elgiva had abandoned her quest to find the Stone and that left him more time to search for it himself. Of course, there were those prophecies, but if destiny really did intend Elgiva to be the Stone's discoverer, then, what did it matter? He would be there to take it from her.

As they neared the thrones, Elgiva stopped and gave him a quizzical look. "When are you going to show me the Lorestone?"

Unnerved, he quickly recovered himself and flashed her an evasive smile. Taking her small hand in his own, he raised it to his lips, but it was deliciously perfumed and only increased his unease. He dropped her hand with a frown of displeasure and she stepped back in alarm.

"Later, my dear," he promised, forcing himself to sound gentle and calm. "After the oath of fealty. Be not so impatient." He grasped her hand again.

She offered him a mysterious smile. Was this artful creature playing games with him? Did she really believe that he had won? Well, it would be a small thing to kill her, if she gave him any trouble.

"Will you be going to Elindell?" asked Elgiva lightly.

Vieldrin turned to face her and gave her a questioning look.

"You'll take me with you, won't you?"

He shook his head with feigned regret. "You will stay here and rule in my stead, should I decide to leave. These scoundrels need to be constantly watched." And so do you, my dear. And I would not allow you anywhere near Bellic or Gilda. Who knows what tricks you would perpetrate in such meddlesome company?

"They appear to me to be totally cowed," she remarked matter-of-factly.

"A mask. An illusion merely," he said. "They are prey to any rebel-rouser keen to talk of freedom. They revel in rhetoric, dear heart." She lowered her eyes, as though embarrassed. "They are stupid and impressionable. Gossamer in the wind."

"How fares my cousin Thallinore?" she asked inconsequentially.

"Ah, none too well, I fear."

"What poison do your agents glut him on? Hemlock?" she asked, her tone still light and casual.

"Poison? What need of poison? Mix Royal blood with that of a churl and you have an unstable compound. Poor Thallinore is mad and weak and not long for this Earth."

Elgiva seemed to consider this and then she nodded slowly. Stepping lightly away from him, she strolled towards the nearest tree, the train of her luxurious gown dancing in her wake. Placing her hand on the rind of the trunk, she stood for a moment, lost in thought. Vieldrin watched her guardedly.

"How is … my great-uncle Bellic?" Her fingers traced the patterns on the bark, but her eyes were focused elsewhere.

"Old," Vieldrin said with a smirk, "but otherwise quite well. He is not ill-treated, but he is helpless. His powers are blocked by the chains he wears … a clever spell of mine. I have allowed him to live, dear heart, but if you decide to turn against me…" His voice deepened, hinting at horrors.

She shrugged, leaned back against the tree. For a while she wriggled her toes in her sandals, watching their movements with interest, then, without looking up, she spoke. "What's the use?" The chain on her slender wrist tinkled, as she lifted her hand to toy with her hair. "I knew this was all a waste of time. Anyway … Why should I care?" She turned her dark eyes full upon him and he saw that they were livid with anger. He summoned up his powers, preparing to defend himself. "Why should I be the only one to take responsibility? This burden was dumped at my door by those who once despised me. I can't be held responsible … because … you see … I can't. I haven't the power!" She seemed distracted. "You can see it, why can't Bellic? All those years I spent as a slave! They had no right to do that. But I have the right to enjoy my life, just like anyone else."

"My dear…?"

She strode towards him purposefully and he tensed, uncertain of her mood.

"Bellic let me find things out the hard way and, while I suffered, a fool sat on my throne. Was that just? Wasn't I entitled to any respect? Should a queen be treated like a slave? And, fool that I was, I tried to save the life of my so-called master, and what did they do, they banished me! Sent me out to fend for myself. Did anyone help me? Did Bellic? Oh, no. But then I'm told I have a mission and I'm sent on a dangerous journey to help a bunch of stupid, old men, who run away at the drop of a hat. I go from one form of slavery to another and nobody ever asks my opinion. How dare they do this to me!"

With a shaking hand, she massaged her brow, as if to erase the deepening frown there, then she sighed and lowered her gaze. "Bellic doesn't realise how hard it is using magic when you've never been taught. He doesn't realise how much it hurts … how terrifying it is."

Vieldrin watched her aslant, but said nothing.

"Strange," she murmured distantly, "but I was never treated like a queen when I lived in my own kingdom." She paused and stroked the fabric of her gown and her fingers trembled, as though aroused by the decadent touch of the silk. "I never wore fine clothes like this and I never had homage paid to me, until … until I agreed to…" She looked up at Vieldrin, her eyes dilated with anguish. "I tried to be good, but being good gets you nothing but abuse. All the things I ever wanted, they denied me and … and I loved them for it."

"And it pleases you, of course, that I can so easily provide you with all the trappings of power," he said. "Whatever you want shall be yours."

She averted her face, but he caught her chin and forced her to look at him. Silvery tears ran down her cheeks and, when Vieldrin saw them, he experienced something unfamiliar. He stumbled mentally for a moment, but then he was able to name the unsettling sensation: compassion. It threw him completely off balance and confusion wrinkled his smooth, high brow. For a second he thought of striking her, but her doleful gaze seemed to plead for restraint. He wanted to hold her in his arms…

Confound the bitch! He would show no weakness! He would not jeopardise his plans for the sake of a fleeting and misplaced sensation, nor would he stoop to her level. He would be a figure of purpose and power and she would always fear him.

And she could never be trusted, no matter how genuine her change of heart.

Of course, if it were genuine, it was further proof of the axiom by which he lived his life; everyone could be corrupted by flattery, power or wealth.

Vieldrin grinned inwardly. Of course the little fool's tears were sincere. Either they were tears of frustration or tears of self-disgust. Whatever the cause, he was glad of it. It boded well for his plans. Perhaps it was odd how quickly she had changed to his way of thinking, but she was young and impressionable and years as a servant had left her with a weak will and a damaged heart. A good thing for him, but sad, too. He had bargained on a worthier foe, a more experienced bride. At any event, it seemed to him that she would be willing to help him, would even enjoy using her power against the ones who had spurned and abused her.

But, be on your guard, Vieldrin, he thought. She may get ideas of her own advancement, when she has had her fill of revenge. Of course, by then she will have served her purpose.

He saw the path ahead of him, all obstacles swept aside. With Elgiva's power to aid his own, he would rule Elvendom. He would be the Elwardain. Then all he needed was an heir and he could dispose of his queen.

Dispose of her; it would have to be. He had to be free of these strange emotions that clouded his mind and dulled his purpose.

"You no longer wish to be Queen of Elindell?" he asked her carefully.

"When you are Elwardain, I shall be queen," she said, with her usual power to unnerve him. "And Queen of Misterell, too. And Queen of wherever I choose. Why cling to the hope of one throne, when you can give me so many others and make them a reality?" She looked at him intently. "You said I'd see sense and you were right, but you are older than me. I should have heeded your wisdom. I've been a fool to uphold my ideals, because they weren't mine at all. They belonged to other fools who wanted to keep me in my place. They made me a churl then expected me to be noble and unselfish. Such attributes belong to a monarch." She smiled at him ingenuously.

Damn the little bitch, he thought. Was she being sarcastic?

"Would it be so very wrong to take the easy way out?" she wondered. "I see no point in struggling, when all the odds are against me. And anyway, Vieldrin, we might make excellent rulers. Elvendom could be strong again." Then she looked at him strangely and edged a little nearer. "I hope…" Her voice had an edge of panic, which took them both by surprise. "I hope," she continued more calmly, "that you haven't put a spell on me to make me think like this, to make me talk like this … No, no, I hope you have, because, if not, then how can I cope with the truth … Oh, Faine, I wish…"

"No spell," he put in quickly, unnerved by her change of mood. "We all must accept what we are."

"I don't know what I am!" she exclaimed. "I've never known! It's so confusing and I'm so tired of it all. I can't go on like this. If I just had time to sort out my thoughts…" She turned away and her body trembled.

He regarded her for a moment with a hungry look in his eyes. She was beautiful and vulnerable and he knew it would be easy for him to crush her with his bare hands, to snap her bones like twigs.

On an impulse he grabbed her shoulders, pulled her towards him roughly. Then he lowered his head and kissed her. She tensed in his embrace. Was this revulsion or merely shyness? He would not tolerate either. She had agreed to be his queen and must fulfil her duties.

Summoning up his powers, he span a web of coercion about them, an aura of sensual fire, and felt her revel in the heat of his passion. She seemed to melt in his embrace, but he saw in her mind a hint of reluctance.

Wordlessly, he told her, you cannot comprehend the pleasure I could give you.

For a moment she seemed about to yield, but then she stiffened in his grasp and reasserted her autonomy.

No!

Her power flared in self-protection and his web of coercion melted.

"No … please," she gasped and pulled away. Her eyes were dark with abomination.

"Coy, dear heart?" he murmured slyly.

She gave him a tight and nervous smile, though her eyes reviled him and her body quivered. For a time they looked at each other and then Vieldrin shrugged, decided to dismiss her resistance. Perhaps some beakers of Elf-wine would make her less intractable.

"Come, my dear," he said affably, "let us take our seats. The horns are sounding in the forest. The slaves will soon be here."

He sauntered towards the oaken thrones, expecting her to follow, but she had ignored his request. He turned to see her twirling round, like an excited child, delighting in the billow of her gown. When she came to a halt, she was smiling, a faint flush of pink on her cheeks and her tear-polished eyes sparkling like gems. Vieldrin scowled in irritation. Confound her beauty! he thought.

* * *

Vieldrin and his future queen watched from their thrones as their subjects arrived, drifting reluctantly into the glade before the Royal Hall. A satisfied smirk curled the Elf-king's lips, as the slaves were marched in in scattered groups, impelled along by the warriors. Their shoulders were hunched in their ragged clothes and their dejection pleased him, as though it were further proof of his right to be their lord and master.

Godwin was one of the last to arrive, Grimalkin nagging in his ear and Trystin trudging behind him. Godwin's scabbard was empty, which seemed to betoken peaceful intent, but in fact he had hidden Taranuil in a nearby grove of oaks to prevent it being confiscated by Vieldrin's guards.

Elgiva saw them and looked away quickly. Her face didn't betray her thoughts and Godwin feared he might never get a chance to speak to her.

They mingled with the crowd of Elves.

Warriors stood around the throng, facing inwards, their swords at the ready. Their Captain stood on Vieldrin's right and folded his arms across his chest. He looked out over the gathering of Elves with a scowl that promised torment should anyone dare to step out of line. Then an Elf at the front of the crowd turned to face them and bellowed an order and the slaves obediently humbled themselves and knelt upon the grass.

Vieldrin thrust himself to his feet, his dark eyes flashing with menace, and he made a brief oration, praising his future consort for the excellent choice she had made. His only reservation was the fact that she would have to rule a collection of miserable dogsbodies. Having completed his monologue, he commanded his subjects to pledge their fealty and renew their oath to serve him.

When their half-hearted mutterings trailed to an end, Vieldrin nodded with satisfaction, a perfect smile on his perfect lips, and reseated himself on his throne. He scanned the assembly for several minutes, relishing their wretchedness, then he reminded them of the Lorestone and the absolute power he now possessed.

While the elders muttered in consternation, Godwin smiled to himself, knowing that the Lorestone was wrapped in a piece of sacking and stowed in Grimalkin's pack. Perhaps he'd been foolish, bringing it here, but he doubted that anyone would suspect, and, as far as Vieldrin knew, the Lorestone had yet to be found. Its secret presence excited him. If only Vieldrin knew just how close he was to the Stone!

Vieldrin enjoyed the crowd's dismay, then he turned towards his captive and placed his hand upon her arm in a gesture of ownership. "Your companions are here," he said softly.

"I have seen," said Elgiva tonelessly.

Vieldrin frowned. "I am annoyed. What are they doing here?"

"They worship me," she calmly explained. She turned her face towards him, a hint of a smile upon her lips. "I dare say they're waiting for me to trick you."

His eyebrows lifted warily. "But you cannot, my dear," he hissed.

She looked at him with outraged innocence. "Will not, my Lord," she said. She flashed him a charming smile. "They will have to accept that things have changed."

He nodded. "Will you address the slaves, dear heart?"

"If it pleases you," she said.

She got to her feet and surveyed the assembly. The gelid indifference of her gaze froze them all where they knelt. Then her voice rang out like mockery. "So, you surrendered like cowards and now you are cringing before me. Is there an ounce of courage among the lot of you?"

Several sneering faces glared back at her from the crowd, but no-one dared to speak. Briefly she glanced at

Godwin; he was frowning and seemed perplexed and his honest, blue eyes were pleading with her. She snatched back her gaze and found herself looking straight at Haldrin. The glint of triumph in his eyes made her hesitate, but she didn't have time to wonder at it.

"Why I wanted to help you, I really can't imagine." She tilted her head back haughtily. "Now, everything has changed. Thanks to my future husband, I will have what is rightfully mine. I was born a queen, but I lived like the bastard child of a beggar. They made me feel unworthy, fitted only to serve. Such a life has a great effect on the mind…"

Her voice trailed into silence and her gaze became unfocused, as though some revelation had made her look within: There were mutterings in the crowd of Elves and Vieldrin, vexed and impatient, drummed his fingers on the arm of his throne. Then she surfaced from her confusion.

"Well, no matter," she went on. "Elindell will be rewarded for what I have endured. I despise it. I despise you…"

"Do you despise Lord Faine?"

There were gasps of horror among the crowd and Elgiva's brow clenched with dismay. Too well she knew the owner of the voice.

"Who dared to interrupt me?" she demanded angrily.

"I did," said Godwin. "You know it was me." His voice was much steadier than he had expected.

Vieldrin sat bolt upright, a cruel smirk on his face.

"Come forward, Wilthkin!" ordered Elgiva.

Godwin's legs felt suddenly weak, but he obeyed the command. He knew the risk he was taking, but he had to speak to Elgiva and tell her about the Stone and, despite her angry demeanour, and the speech that she had given, he felt he could trust her, whatever happened.

He wove his way through the crowd of Elves and walked towards his friend. A space of three yards lay between them, when she held up her hand to stop him. He wanted to be nearer, to look into her eyes and see the covert messages that she was bound to send.

"I've heard your little speech," he said. "I don't believe a word. You wouldn't change sides like this."

"Why not?" Her voice had an edge of ice. "This is the way – the only way – for me to get what I want."

"Are we no longer friends?"

Despite his anxious expression, his voice and manner were calm. Elgiva bit her lower lip and considered her reply. "We can be," she informed him, "if you swear you are loyal to me, whatever path I choose."

"I don't think I can follow this particular path," he said.

"That is most unfortunate."

Her mouth was set in a hard, cruel line, but he fancied that her eyes were laughing at him, sharing some secret joke. He hoped that he didn't mistake their meaning. He laid his mind wide open to her, begging her, somehow, to reach him.

"Do you think this is a game?" she asked. "Do you doubt my intentions?"

Godwin wasn't certain how he should react, but she spared him no time for deliberation.

"Well?" she snapped. "Do you doubt me?"

"It seems I can't, but I don't believe it. You can't be so false-hearted." He confronted her with a look of outrage, believing that that was what was required. "Is this what

I've been striving towards? So you could be with him?" He nodded towards Vieldrin.

"Striving, Wilthkin?" she said mockingly. "What is your striving compared with destiny? Destiny can't be over-ruled. I have always believed that."

His lips drew apart, but he couldn't speak. Only his eyebrows questioned her. She laughed and gave him an arch look, and then her expression changed to anger.

"You should never have interfered with the lives of the Eldrakin. Your meddling has been your downfall. Were the trivial affairs of your own kind not enough for you?"

For a moment, Godwin faltered. The ground at his feet seemed suddenly unsafe and his heartbeat quickened with panic. Had he done the right thing in coming here?

"There's no need for this," he said coldly. "You have no further use for me. I had better return to my trivial affairs."

"You can't do that," she told him. "Oh, no. I won't allow it. I may not have a use for you, but I can, at least, have my revenge."

He gaped at her, "Revenge? For what?" You told me not to doubt you, but you're not making it easy! he thought.

"An Elf's memory is long, my friend. I haven't forgotten the Forest of Shades. Remember when you attacked me? First you wanted to cut my throat, but later you had lust on your mind."

Vieldrin leaned forward in his seat a look of glee on his face.

Godwin's artless features were raw with hurt and embarrassment. "Evil magic made me do it!"

"You would have me think so."

The ground seemed to sag beneath him once more and this time he felt that nothing could save him. "How can you be so petty, so unreasonable?"

"How dare you!" she cried.

Her fiery glare made Godwin wince, but the mischievous twinkle in her eyes seemed to contradict it. Godwin knew himself totally lost.

"I ought to kill you where you stand!"

Hardly had she said these words, when Trystin fought his way through the crowd and stood at Godwin's side.

"No, Lady Elgiva, please don't!"

With a frown of genuine annoyance, Elgiva raised her hand. Godwin saw power leap through the air, saw Trystin grow suddenly wide-eyed and rigid. Then with a groan the Elfling sagged and slowly fell to the ground, where he lay as still as a stone.

Godwin was speechless with horror. He fell to his knees at Trystin's side. How could this happen? This was impossible. Elgiva wouldn't do this! But his friend's limp body said it was so.

He stared up at Elgiva, unable to comprehend what she had done. "Elgiva, you … you've killed him!"

He couldn't decipher the look on her face. She seemed about to speak, but Godwin didn't want her words. He jumped to his feet and staggered towards her, uncertain of his intentions. Vieldrin leapt up to forestall an attack and raised his hand to lash out with magic, but before he could do so, Elgiva's power stopped Godwin in his tracks. He crumpled and slowly fell to the ground and lay motionless on the grass.

Vieldrin studied his future queen. Her face was flushed, her eyes were bright, and her lips were stretched by a strange, grim smile. The sating of vicious desires, he thought. The addiction of magic will teach you the truth about yourself, my dear.

And how well she used this power! How swift and dramatic it was! He felt it growing, unfolding, and its after-glow made him shiver.

Of course, he must not let her know how adept she was becoming.

Elgiva sat down heavily, gripping the arms of the throne, while Vieldrin gazed across the crowd, pleased to see them mute with horror.

"Well done, dear heart," he whispered. He seated himself on his throne. "The fools are frightened out of their wits."

"As they should be," she panted. A distracted expression slackened her features and a gleam of wetness shone on her cheeks.

"Tears, my love?"

She smiled at him. "Ah, no. It's nothing. Power hurts." She scrubbed away the evidence, as though her tears had betrayed her.

He raised his eyebrows fractionally. "I think that you have tired yourself."

"Oh, no, my Lord. The use of power has left me a little dizzy. It's a new experience … one that I like." Catching sight of her fallen friends, she quickly looked away.

"I will have the bodies removed, my dear."

Elgiva span to face him. "They're not dead!" she blurted out, and then she managed to compose herself. "I couldn't let them off so lightly." She looked at him as though his assumption had been an act of folly. "I intend to have more sport with them. I will have my revenge and I will savour it. They'll suffer before they die." Her face lit up with anticipation. "We can do anything now, my Lord. With power, we can do anything! I never knew it could be so easy to make others do one's bidding!"

Indeed, little fool, how right you are. He patted her hand indulgently. "The easiest thing in the world, dear heart."

⋆ ⋆ ⋆

Chapter Twenty-Eight

Godwin was floating back to the world from a distant time and place, where colours were brighter, scents were sweeter; where pain and sorrow had no meaning. He had wandered through sun-swept meadows, floated through fields of cowslips, where the air was alive with enraptured bees, and, rising before him, a stately hall had opened its massive doors and he drifted through them, like a ghost, into an atmosphere vibrant with laughter.

And there … was it Woden, the High-God, Grim, the Masked One … rewarding the warriors for their valour? And was he welcome in their midst?

But he had no need of that. The fields beckoned and their corn-coloured hair was beribboned with scarlet butterflies and it moved like a sinuous river of gold beneath a smalt-blue sky.

And in that sky the stainless clouds became snow-laden landscapes, and over the snow marched a long-dead legion, its banners upraised by the wind. And the banners changed into eagles. They spread their wings and wafted skywards, their eyes of jade and their beaks of gold, and Godwin floated with them, laughing as he soared. Below him were fields and farmsteads, villages and forts, twisting streams of polished steel and hills ablaze with heather. And he was One with all of it; all things were One with him. And in the air around him shimmered a soft, familiar voice.

Be at peace, Godwin. All is well.

Suddenly, clouds of petals fluttered down upon him. Each petal reflected the sun like a chip of coloured glass and he found himself on the boundary between what is and what should be.

Then he opened his eyes. A narcotic languor clung to his mind and he stretched himself and murmured, "How soft are the clouds … how soft…"

"Master Godwin!" hissed an urgent voice.

He turned his head lethargically to find the source of this irritating noise and discovered that it was Trystin, but he was fuzzy round the edges and clearly not important. "Go away," he sighed. "You're dead." He tried to return to the land of his dreams, but the vision was lost forever. His mind abruptly cleared and he sat up, startled, and looked around. "Dead? But you're … What's going on?"

"Don't be afraid, Master Godwin. I'm alive and so are you, thanks to Lady Elgiva."

Godwin struggled to focus. He had no idea where he was. He appeared to be in a small, wooden building, but he couldn't gauge its height or width. The stump of a candle stuck to the floor was the only illumination. But one thing he knew for certain, the creature kneeling at his side was definitely Trystin.

"Trystin, what's going on?" he gasped. "I saw her strike you down!"

The Elfling shook his head emphatically. "No, she only pretended to! I heard her voice in my mind. 'Fall down. Feign death. All is well,' she said. A good trick, Master Godwin. But you knew that all along."

"I did?"

"Yes, you made to attack her. That was a good idea. It made it look more believable. Vieldrin would have killed you, but she was too quick for him. She made you fall asleep. Now Vieldrin thinks he can trust her, because she turned against us. But we knew we were safe, didn't we?"

Godwin smiled to hide his shame. "Where are we, lad?" he asked.

"In a hut near the Hall. It's dark outside. There are guards everywhere, too. Would you like a drink of water?" He handed Godwin a beaker. "Lady Elgiva said we'd make good slaves. That's why we haven't been killed. They even let us have some light." He pointed at the solitary glim as though it were a beacon and his face wore a grin of triumph.

As Godwin gulped the water, he thought of something and almost choked. "Trystin, by Frigg! … Grimalkin!"

"She's tethered outside, Master Godwin. Don't worry, she still has the Stone. No-one suspects we've got it. No reason why they should."

Reassured by Trystin's confidence, Godwin tried to relax, but then a noise outside the hut made him tense with alarm. As he and Trystin watched with dread, the heavy drape that covered the doorway fluttered and moved aside and bearing an oil-lamp before it, a cloaked and hooded figure stepped in, chased by a giant shadow,

For a moment the captives and their visitor confronted each other in silence, then Elgiva set the lamp on the floor. "Hello, you two," she greeted them. "Are you both … all right?"

"Yes, Lady," responded Trystin.

Godwin sighed with relief. "Elgiva!"

She knelt down beside them and pushed back her hood. She no longer wore her fine silk gown, but was dressed in a pale-green, linen robe, pulled in at the waist by a thick, black belt.

"Vieldrin's a little the worse for wine," she told them with a knowing smile, and she paused to savour some secret victory. "He's sleeping so soundly nothing will wake him, but he won't be left in peace for long. There's been some trouble near the Hall. Some fighting, I think, but I don't know the reason. I told the guards to investigate and said I would keep an eye on you. They weren't exactly willing to go, till I threatened to complain to their lord and master. But I must be brief. I daren't stay away from the Hall too long."

"I suppose I should thank you for saving my life," put in Godwin sheepishly. "I wasn't thinking sensibly, when I came forward like that, was I?"

Elgiva looked downcast for a moment, as though she shared his guilt. He noticed a tension in her movements, as if she no longer trusted her limbs, and it seemed to him that the strain of their quest was beginning to show in his friend. The light from the lamp underscored her features, made them look heavy and tired, and her eyes had developed a fitful gleam, as though too much energy had been tapped.

"You both put me to a great deal of trouble." She ended the sentence with a smile to show them that she wasn't angry. "In a way it was a good thing. It put you both in my power, so to speak. Now at least I know where you are and hopefully I can protect you. But you didn't make it easy for me. I was lucky, Godwin, to make a move before Vieldrin did. You realise that, don't you?"

He preferred not to think about it. "I must confess, Elgiva, you had me worried for a moment."

"Only for a moment?" She grinned at him mischievously.

Godwin ignored her frivolity. "When I saw Trystin fall…"

"I told you not to doubt me, Godwin."

He shifted his position and looked at her obliquely. "Another test?" he asked.

"A test of my skills at deception." She lowered her eyes evasively. "Even Vieldrin was convinced. There were times when I almost convinced myself."

"You don't have to worry about him now!" gushed Trystin, his face aglow. "Lady Elgiva, you won't believe it, but … we've found the Lorestone!"

"Hush, Trystin, not so loud!" warned Godwin.

Elgiva drew nearer and grasped Trystin's arm. "What? You've found it? It *DOES* exist! But … are you sure?"

"It must be! It's so beautiful! And we found this with it, Lady."

Trystin slipped his hand inside his tunic and drew out the piece of parchment. With a grin of triumph on his face, he offered it to Elgiva. They all lapsed into silence, while she scrutinised the contents.

The whisper of a freshening wind carried through the darkness. It forced its way under the drape at the door, overwhelming all other noises.

"We have to find this place," said Elgiva, handing the parchment back. "But where it might be, I've no idea. If I could contact my uncle Bellic, perhaps he'd know where these Nine Men are."

"And then you could use the Stone!" said Trystin. "And free the people of Misterell."

"And kill Vieldrin," added Godwin.

It was then that they froze: there was someone outside. Godwin heard a protracted scraping, the sound of a sword being drawn from its sheath. His nerves winced at the sound.

"Come out, conspirators!" shouted a voice.

Then Grimalkin's frantic neighing filled the air.

"Be still, you beast!" cried a second voice. "Let go of my sleeve or I'll slice you!"

The neighing, however, persisted. At first it was muffled by the sleeve, but then it rose in volume and became a string of invectives against all two-legged creatures.

Godwin bristled with anger at the sound of a bludgeon thudding down upon the pony's back. There followed an outraged squeal of pain. Careless of the consequencies, Godwin dashed out of the hut.

Seizing the Elf who had hit Grimalkin, he swung him around with a snarl of contempt and struck him on the jaw. Then, to his utter dismay, he saw that he was greatly outnumbered. Two more guards stood by the hut, their torches searing the night, and two more sprang from the shadows, each one holding a spear. One of them pelted towards him, let loose a chilling scream. Horrified and helpless, Godwin staggered backwards, but a kick from Grimalkin's hind legs lifted the warrior into the air and sprawled him on the grass.

This wasn't enough for Grimalkin. Her blood was up and the pain in her back had blotted out all else. She trampled on the fallen Elf and her hooves slammed down like vengeance, crushing out his life. Godwin tugged at her straggly mane.

"Stop it, Grimalkin! Listen!" The sounds of purposeful movement echoed through the forest. "Run!" hissed Godwin into her ear. "You must save the Lorestone!"

"The Hill-Shrine!" she snorted. "I'll wait!" With one final stamp on her victim, she turned and sped away.

Godwin glanced down at the mangled Elf and almost retched at the sight, then he turned towards the hut. Should he tell his friends to flee? Should he attack the other guards? Perhaps he should run away? But none of these choices was feasible. They were unarmed and outnumbered. Then the decision of what to do was taken out of his hands, when a band of warriors broke from the trees and quickly took him prisoner.

Elgiva came running out of the hut and felled three guards with a blast of power, but others soon took their place. She prepared another Elf-bolt, but one of the warriors swung at her with his heavy, wooden staff.

Godwin heard himself cry out, as his friend collapsed on the grass, and he knew that any resistance was pointless. He watched in despair as Trystin was dragged from the hut and beaten and kicked to the ground, where he lay in a sobbing heap.

"Stop it!" moaned Godwin. "He's only a child!" But he prayed that they wouldn't beat him, too.

As they bound his hands behind his back, he cursed the day of his birth. He felt that he should have put up a fight, rather then let them drag him away, unresisting, to meet his doom.

Now they were done for. This was the end. And Grimalkin would have a very long wait.

* * *

All too soon the guards and their captives had reached the Royal Hall. Its grim shape loomed up out of the darkness, the massive doors flung wide. A crowd of Elves came out to meet them, many bearing torches, and watched as the prisoners were dragged inside. More Elves filled the space in the Hall and spoke in nervous whispers, while the air grew thick with the smoke from the torches and the great dogs stood in the corners, trembling.

At the end of the Hall was a dais and on it an empty throne. The guards hauled Godwin and Trystin towards it and threw them to their knees. Elgiva's limp body was dumped beside them, her head wound seeping blood. Godwin, unable to help her, could only watch as the thin, red rill dripped onto the wooden floor.

Only the worst could happen now.

Drugged by despair, Godwin failed to notice the sudden stillness, the bowing of heads. He dragged his gaze away from his friend and, through a mist of hopelessness, he vaguely perceived that the King had arrived.

Vieldrin looked magnificent in a robe of midnight-blue, but his face was a mask of fury, as he glared down at the captives. But all that Godwin could think of was the precious blood that was draining away, of the hopes that were smashed like footling trinkets; that he would never see his family or his home again.

Lightning flashed in the Elf-king's eyes. "So, you plot to kill me, do you? It seems I should have known better than to trust the words of that false-hearted bitch." He clicked his fingers. "Rouse her, someone!"

A female servant bowed obsequiously and ran for a jug of water. Scampering back, she lifted the vessel and poured it over Elgiva. Elgiva gasped and opened her eyes and squinted at the light and, once she had gained a sitting position, she looked around the Hall. Godwin tried to meet her gaze, but she shied away from him, as though she expected an accusation. Raising her head, she peered at the King and a deep frown creased her brow. It seemed that she was trying to remember who and where she was.

"So, little rat, you thought to fool me, did you?" raged Vieldrin, anger reddening his cheeks. "A pity that no-one told you that I choose my guards for their excellent hearing. They have good noses, too, when it comes to sniffing out rats. Those guards you sent back to the Hall did not trust you, as I did, and they, at least, are loyal. Wilthkin!"

Godwin's heart raced fitfully, as the cold eyes swivelled towards him.

"Tell me about the Lorestone!"

For a moment, Vieldrin waited, then he hefted a silver goblet from the table beside him. He snapped his fingers and a servant ran forward, bearing a jug of wine. While the goblet was filled, emptied and replenished, Vieldrin watched his prisoners closely, searching for signs of weakness and stretching out the seconds to increase the fear in his audience.

He kicked the servant aside with his foot. Godwin's relief at not being made to answer the Elf-king's question was suddenly overshadowed by a feeling that some appalling event was about to be revealed.

"It may interest you to know, dogsbodies, that this is not the first time I have been dragged from my rest tonight. You three were not the only ones hatching a plot against me, so do not think yourselves privileged, though it may have been your example that set other fools on a suicide course." He gulped down the wine and motioned for more. "Apparently they had some notion of killing me while I slept, but, their conspiracy being discovered, they were captured outside the Hall. A small band of elders, easily dealt with. The ring-leaders were brought to me, so I could question them. Of course, they were palpably guilty of treason. You remember Haldrin, I suppose? I had my guards tear out his tongue before I dealt him a lethal bolt. And the other rebel … dear me, I forgot to ask her name … she made such a fearful caterwauling, but fortunately one of my lads had the presence of mind to run her through with his sword. Well, we can't have such a deplorable din in the middle of the night."

Trystin sobbed distractedly. "Grandfather … Everil … No!"

Godwin heard Trystin's anguish, but it seemed to reach him from a distance. He glanced at Elgiva obliquely. Her legs were folded beneath her and her head was bowed, as if in prayer. Her hands lay open on her lap, as though despair had taken their strength, and a drop of blood splashed onto her robe, but she seemed beyond the touch of grief.

For Frigg's sake, Elgiva! Do something!

Trystin's sobs rose in volume, tears streaming through the blood and dirt on his hunger-sharpened face. There was nothing that Godwin could do for either of his friends and his anger was like a furnace within him.

If only he had Taranuil! One quick thrust and that grinning fiend would be lying dead before them.

"We trust you feel contrition for the trouble you have caused," Vieldrin went on smugly. "And this is not the end of it. I see that an extensive purge of Misterell is required. I will remove all opposition." He seized the jug from the quivering servant, poured himself another drink, and the dark-red liquor splashed onto the floor.

Like blood, thought Godwin. Spilt in vain.

"However, we seem to have overlooked a most important matter … Look at me, scum, and pay heed!" cried Vieldrin.

Elgiva slowly lifted her head and saw the King through a throbbing, red mist.

"The Lorestone, Elgiva. Where is it?"

Silence settled like a heavy fug, while everyone looked at Elgiva, but it was clear that she had no intention of answering the question.

"Do not play games with me!" warned Vieldrin. "I know you have the Stone!" He reached inside his robe and drew out a piece of parchment, which he waved at his prisoners accusingly. "This was found on Trystin, that traitor, slave and coward who follows you like a dog. If you have this parchment, you also have the Lorestone. So tell me, where is it hidden?"

Godwin ventured to reply, but his throat felt like dust and his voice croaked out like a cry for help from the bottom of a well. "We thought you had it," he said.

"Damn you, worm, my lads heard you. What have you done with it? It is hidden somewhere, curse you!"

"Then you'd better look for it, hadn't you?" Elgiva suggested softly.

"Death and destruction!" roared the King. He hurled his goblet across the Hall and everybody ducked. The vessel struck the wall with a clang and scattered the terrified servants. "You WILL tell me where it is. Willingly or under torture. I will get the truth out of you. Guards! A pox on you, dogsbodies, come here and do my bidding! Take that Wilthkin and the brat and tear them limb from limb if you have to. Just get me the Lorestone!"

Four guards stumbled forwards, clumsy in their haste to obey, and seized the hapless prisoners. Vieldrin strode towards Elgiva, grasped her by the elbows and hauled her to her feet.

"As for you, little rat," he snarled, "we cannot allow you to stay alive, or our plans will be imperilled. But let it not be said that Vieldrin did not give his foe a sporting chance." Releasing her, he stepped back, his fists cocked on his hips and his mouth a curve of anticipation. "Come on, then, noble adversary. Work a spell against me!"

The gathered Elves sucked in their breath and the guards who were holding Godwin and Trystin, unwilling to miss a contest of magic, were frozen in their tracks.

Swaying with fatigue and despair, Elgiva looked too weak to work a spell, and Vieldrin was well aware of this, but while he smirked triumphantly, conflicting emotions churned in his breast. He would have to kill her, wanted to kill her, but what about his plans? What about the progeny that would carry on his work? With dissention at home and the war going badly whenever he was absent, he knew that he was stretched too thin: he was alone against the world. He must have the Lorestone to guarantee his right to rule Elvendom.

Confound you, Elgiva, I almost believed that we could work together … but there are others with whom I can work. Oh, yes. I have only to set them free. These friends of mine… they would turn the blood to ice in your veins. He grinned to himself. I will have allies aplenty, he thought, once I have the Lorestone, and then all the world can fall to rot and ruin.

"Come now, dear heart," he said softly. "Just one little spell, that's all I ask." Sad that she would have to die, but she would not see reason. What made her persist in opposing him, when she knew that she was beaten? Such foolishness surpassed him.

And he wished that he could explain his desire to reach out and touch her injured forehead, reach out and heal it with magic…

"Vermin!" he raged. "You shall know the wrath of Vieldrin!" He circled his victim like a bird of prey. "Do you remember what you once said about not letting people off lightly? You will regret you ever said it."

Then he noticed with a twinge of alarm that Elgiva's eyes were fully open and anger brooded in their depths. As she shook off her stupor, her finely-arched brows took on a fiercer aspect. Casting his cloak aside with a flourish, Vieldrin planted himself before her and adopted the air of a noble monarch facing an ignoble foe.

"Do not hope for a quick death."

The warning had barely left his lips, when Elgiva found the strength to attack. Vieldrin staggered backwards, as though a fire had blazed in his face. Scowling at the humiliation, he raised his arm and a shower of sparks shot from his finger- tips. Their light was so dazzling that everyone was forced to shield their eyes. Then, like a swarm of maddened wasps, the sparks enveloped Elgiva and forced her to her knees. Her hands flew up to protect her face, as the sparks spat out their magical poison and the air thrummed and crackled as they gyred around her.

Then suddenly the vortex of sparks was stretched by a barrier of force. It thrust them outwards as it expanded. The sparks glowed white-hot, as they tried to burn a path through the shell of power, but Elgiva's might enveloped them and they burst like harmless bubbles.

She rested on her hands and knees and appeared to be exhausted, but Elgiva had power in reserve and, before Vieldrin could make a move, she threw out a volley of force. It whirled about the scowling King, like a boiling thunderhead, and lashed at him with bolts of lightning.

Fending off the shafts of power, Vieldrin, confused and maddened, fell back against the table and his face was taut with pain. Then a power-surge of terrible strength exploded from his hand. It slashed Elgiva's storm-cloud, sent chunks of it wheeling about the Hall. Tables and benches were caught in the blast and hurled in all directions. Jugs were smashed upon the floor and the Elves drew back with howls of fear and dodged the flying plates and beakers. The tapestries flapped against the walls, the torches scattered sparks and the great dogs scrabbled at the doors, desperate to escape.

The tumult grew as magic countered magic, but then, when it seemed that the turmoil had reached an unbearable height, the hurricane exploded with an ear-splitting bang. In an instant, the magic exhausted itself and everything caught up in it fell to the floor with a crash.

Elgiva collapsed and lay gasping for air, her strength completely gone. The Elves recovered themselves from the chaos and turned to watch Vieldrin with eyes that flinched in fear from his gaze. He swayed a little and his handsome face was slack and grey with effort, but otherwise he appeared unaffected. He drew a deep breath and straightened himself.

"So that is the best you can do," he said calmly. "The magic of a child. A great display, admittedly, but there was little substance to it. Now I shall complete my work."

He turned and sat on the great oak throne and glared down at his prey. Elgiva raised herself on her elbows, watched Vieldrin helplessly and prepared herself for the worst. She gritted her teeth against the pressure of blood that pounded in her ears.

Child's magic, yes, she thought grimly. But stronger. I'm getting stronger.

"Rats should be poisoned," droned Vieldrin, "but they should suffer, too. Slow poison is my weapon of choice. An incurable sickness that finds no relief. A fatal fever that lingers on, making each minute an age of misery, wasting the body and tormenting the mind. To go mad with thirst, yet fear to drink. To be tortured by slow incineration and then to die in pain and despair. That is the way we deal with rats who invade our homes with their insolent cunning."

He made a series of gestures before him and his hands sliced through the air like knives. A thread of darkness curled throught the air and hovered round Elgiva. Then it settled upon her.

"The spell is done and cannot be undone, except by magic greater than mine, which means that you will die, little rat, for no-one in Elvendom can surpass me. Two days I give you to wait for death."

Elgiva's lips parted, but she couldn't speak. Her face was blank, as though she had known that this would be her fate, and as she sank to the floor, the sigh she made sounded like relief.

Trystin staggered on the verge of fainting and Godwin felt that his legs had lost the will to hold him upright. There seemed no reason for his heart to keep beating and a darkness moved across his vision, but he grappled mentally with himself, refused to let his senses forsake him.

"Hurl this trash out of the door. It has no further use," cried Vieldrin. "And get this accursed mess cleared up!"

He turned on his heel, his blue robe swirling, and went back to his bed. Some of the Elves followed his example, but others were galvanised into action by the King's departure. As they set about clearing away the debris, relief shone on their faces. They would live to see another day.

The great oak doors were opened wide to admit a cool night breeze and two of the servants lifted Elgiva and took her from the Hall. Godwin and Trystin were marched outside and, as the Hall doors were closed behind them, the cold, unfriendly darkness made Godwin think of a grave. Ahead of him, the servants carried his friend, like a broken doll, intending to abandon her somewhere in the forest. A third Elf lit their way with a torch. Godwin struggled to twist himself round so that he could plead with his captors.

"Please," he begged, "let me say good-bye. A final farewell. I beseech you!"

The four guards looked at him in silence.

"I can hardly help her escape, can I? What would be the point?" He almost choked on the words.

"All right," said one, "but just for a moment. No tricks, you understand? Hey, you two!" The Elves ahead of them stopped and looked round. "Put her down for a minute. Let this one say his farewells." He jabbed his finger at Godwin.

The guard loosed his hold on Godwin's arm and impelled him roughly forwards. The servants lowered

Elgiva, stepped back and folded their arms. As Godwin knelt beside her, he saw that she already had the symptoms of a fever.

Was this the end of all their strivings?

"Elgiva," he gasped, "my dear…" He fought to hold back his tears. She whispered something in a thin, hoarse voice and he drew a little nearer. "What is it? I can't hear you."

She stared at him but her eyes were unfocused. "No sentimental nonsense. Not dead yet. Keep talking. They mustn't hear. Listen…"

Godwin fought to master himself, although it wrenched his heart. "Elgiva, you can't … you mustn't die!"

She licked her lips and struggled to speak. "Something … I can do for you. My fault … all this. Make amends. Keep talking."

He swallowed down a knot of anguish. "We must say farewell," he breathed. "But my hands are tied. I can't even hold you." Whatever you're trying to do, don't do it. Don't torture yourself for my sake! he thought.

The guards began to shuffle their feet and one of them cleared his throat in a manner that hinted at impatience. Godwin's heart was thudding with panic and somewhere behind him he heard Trystin sob.

"I've found … your sword," Elgiva whispered. "I summon it. Keep talking!"

Acid tears blurred Godwin's vision and he knew he should keep talking, he knew she needed more time, but all he wanted to do was weep.

"Get on with it!" growled one of the guards.

"The sword comes to your aid!" she sighed. "Now … kiss me, Godwin. Take the magic … while I have some left…"

Godwin didn't understand, but refused to ignore her plea. He lowered his head and kissed her mouth; her lips were hot and dry. Almost at once he felt a wave of force surge into his body. It flared in his limbs like vitriol and was almost too much to bear. Tears of pain sprang from his eyes as magic, raw and powerful, shuddered through his flesh.

He felt the ropes fall from his wrists.

Elgiva turned her head away, released him from the kiss. "Use it. Can't last," she said faintly.

Godwin saw a flash of silver in the air above him and suddenly something heavy fell into his hand. His fingers closed around cold, hard metal.

Taranuil!

He felt like laughing. And he had the feeling that he was ten feet tall.

"What's going on?" shouted one of the guards.

Godwin span round to face the Elves. He felt that nothing could stand in his way and he had never been so wide awake, never seen so clearly. There was nothing he couldn't do.

The warriors gaped at the sight of the sword, then they drew their own weapons with practised speed.

"Taranuil," whispered Godwin.

The metal rang with power and the might it contained merged with the magic in its master's veins; an ecstasy of avenging force.

The servants, unused to fighting, backed away in horror, but the guards strode forwards, their swords upraised.

Godwin's strength was that of ten, as he fought with his attackers. Two lay dying at his feet and a third keeled over, spurting blood. The fourth guard ran at Trystin, but Godwin reached him first. Taranuil struck his sword with a jarring crash that broke the blade and left its owner helpless. The guard stepped back and fumbled for the dagger in his belt, but he was far too slow. Emboldened by magic, Godwin lashed out, slicing through flesh and bone, and the guard was dead before his body tumbled to the ground.

Taranuil hummed with pleasure; its edge was a gleam of relish, ready to slay its master's enemies.

The servants had slowly edged their way towards the margin of the clearing and, when Godwin looked in their direction, they turned and ran for their lives. Godwin caught one by the arm and quickly slit his throat, but the other two made good their escape and he knew it was folly to chase them. He and his friends must get away and they didn't have much time.

He sprinted over to Trystin, who was kneeling on the grass. His face was a mask of bewilderment, but, when he saw his friend approach, his large eyes glowed with wonder. Godwin dragged him to his feet. With one swipe of his sword, he severed the ropes that bound Trystin's hands. Trystin continued to stare at him.

"Now, let's get out of here!" Godwin wiped his sword on the grass and slid it into his scabbard. Rest now.

"Master Godwin … you…!"

"Don't be afraid. It's only magic." Godwin smiled at the admiration in his young friend's eyes. Then he regretted his smugness. "And it isn't mine."

Trystin was shaking with shock and exhaustion, but there was no time for sympathy. Surely someone in the

Hall had heard the clash of swords? They might be too scared to investigate, but they'd soon find someone who wasn't.

And Godwin knew that the magic was fading. He felt sick, as though he'd been spinning round and come to a sudden halt. His limbs felt cold and heavy and the sweat seemed to turn to ice on his brow. But he had to make one last effort and get his friends to safety. He grabbed Trystin's shoulder and thrust him forwards roughly.

"Damn you, get moving!" he rasped.

Trystin shuddered at his touch, at the ache of bruises he had forgotten. He stumbled forwards on legs that seemed to be devoid of bone.

The flaming brand the servants had dropped still guttered in the grass. Stamping out the last of its fire, Godwin stooped to lift Elgiva and his head reeled at the exertion.

"Leave me … fool. I'm dying," she croaked.

"I still can't hear you," he said.

⋆ ⋆ ⋆

Chapter Twenty-Nine

Dawn had broken on the eastern horizon, but, in the depths of the forest, the trees were wrapped in a pearly mist and they guarded the dregs of darkness. The companions had stopped for a much needed rest, concealing themselves in a hawthorn thicket, and for a while they sat in silence, listening for sounds of pursuit.

Godwin was past exhaustion. His eyelids felt like great iron gates. Elgiva lay motionless in his lap, dark shadows beneath her eyes and her face as pale as the mist. Trystin, sniffing back tears of despair, rested his head on Godwin's shoulder. Godwin felt that he hadn't the strength to support them both, but he knew he must.

"What shall we do, Master Godwin?"

Godwin looked up and sighed. Above him the sky was lightening; the tree-tops were limned with orange and pink and the brightness hurt his eyes. "We'll meet Grimalkin at the Shrine. We'll take the Lorestone to Elindell." His eyes felt suddenly full of grit and he scrubbed at them with the back of his hand. All he wanted to do was sleep. "But first, let's lie low and rest awhile."

"But … what about lady Elgiva?"

Godwin looked at the inert body stretched across his lap and struggled with a surge of panic. "If she … dies … we must make sure that the Stone is in safe hands. Her uncle…"

Trystin sat up abruptly. "I don't care about the Stone! Curse the wretched thing!"

Putting his arm around Trystin's shoulder, Godwin tried to be strong. "Calm yourself, lad. Elgiva would want us to finish the work she started, because if we don't, it's all been for nothing. Be reasonable, Trystin. No use getting angry. That won't get us anywhere."

Trystin pulled away sulkily and glowered at the ground, as though it had done him some grave offence. Godwin closed his eyes and forced himself to relax, but it wasn't an easy matter with the nausea of expiring magic pulsing in his veins, and, though his body ached for sleep, he felt that he should stay alert. He wondered how long it would be before Vieldrin's warriors found them. Misterell was vast and thickly wooded, but for those who knew it well it would be no more difficult to search than an orchard.

Then Elgiva opened her eyes and stared at the trees above her, as though shocked from sleep by a cruel dream and her pale, cracked lips began to form words. Godwin inclined his head to hear her.

"A spell once spoken cannot be broken. Cannot be broken. The web is woven."

Godwin sighed sadly. "Elgiva, can you hear me? You used up all your strength on me, foolish, little Elf."

"Take me further from the fire," she pleaded. "I'm too close. I'll burn." She struggled in his arms, but he held her fast.

"Master Godwin, can't we do something?" Trystin begged, rising to his knees. "Is this the end of … everything? I don't think I can bear it!"

"You must," said Godwin sternly. "This isn't like you, to give up hope."

"Lady Elgiva *IS* our hope and now she's dying, Master Godwin!"

"Trystin, she's not dead yet! There's still a chance. We can't give in!" Godwin's hand itched to slap his friend. He saw a gleam of hysteria in the young Elf's eyes and he hoped that he wouldn't go to pieces and add to their predicament. "Pull yourself together!" he snapped. "I'm relying on you!"

Trystin looked downcast and slumped on the grass and a lump rose in Godwin's throat. Was he being too hard on the lad? He was little more than a child, after all. Gently he touched the Elfling's shoulder.

"Trystin, we must have faith."

"Faith," moaned Elgiva weakly. "You and your faith. Faith in me and look where it's brought us. You and your faith."

"Be still," said Godwin soothingly. "Rest."

"Rest in death. I wither. Fallen leaves … kindlewood. Water, for Faine's love…"

"If only we had," lamented Godwin.

"The Lorestone!" she cried. "The Lorestone!"

"It's safe, don't worry," he said.

"Haldrin's dead. Everil's dead. It's all my fault … I'm guilty…"

"By Frigg! You're guilty of nothing! Be still. We're leaving soon. We're going to Elindell."

Her expression changed to expectation. "Through the flames?" she wondered. "The red ones … the yellow ones … the blue ones like flowers?"

"Save your strength now. Sleep."

"I commit my body to the flowers." She closed her eyes and was silent, but her breathing was painfully rasping and shallow, as though her lungs were scorched.

Godwin felt as empty and brittle as a corn husk. He heard Trystin sobbing and didn't dare meet the reproach in those tear-filled eyes. He clasped the hilt of Taranuil, seeking some kind of solace, and tried to clear the shambles that filled his aching head. His mind was all chaos and darkness, save for one tiny spark…

"They who persecute evil shall prosper

"And come to their inheritance…"

Frowning at the unnamed hope that flickered in his brain, he drew his sword and gazed at it, as though it held the answer. And he saw the Hill-Shrine in his mind. It was a place of power and perhaps its secrets had been forgotten.

But that didn't mean that they were lost.

He well remembered the blissful sleep that had overtaken him there. The peace. The circle of nodding flowers. But was he right to believe, to have faith in…?

His hand was clumsy with excitement and he struggled to sheath his sword. Optimism flooded his limbs, thrusting him to his feet. He lifted Elgiva into his arms; she felt as light as his heart. "Trystin!"

"Master Godwin?" The Elfling sat up straight with alarm.

"Get up, lad, I've got an idea! We're going to the Hill-Shrine … Now! If we want help, we must ask for it. Remember what Vieldrin said?" Trystin looked at him blankly. "Well, there *IS* magic stronger than his. The magic of Faine! It's our only hope!"

All Trystin could do was stare at him. Did the Wilthkin really believe such powers could be summoned? After so many generations …and by someone not of Elven blood?

"Don't sit there with your mouth open! We've no time to lose!" Holding Elgiva in his arms, Godwin strode away.

And Trystin scampered after him with fresh hope in his heart.

★ ★ ★

Vieldrin was in a dangerous mood.

Roused from his slumber yet again by menials who winced from his gaze, he instantly knew that someone was about to make a confession that would cost them their existence. While he paced up and down in the Hall and heard the account of the prisoners' escape, he bared his teeth in a wolfish snarl and scowled at the Elves who had brought him the news.

Chief Counsellor Crellin, looking dishevelled, clasped his hands behind his back and watched his master's anger mounting and he pitied the servant now telling his tale in the face of that smouldering gaze.

"And where have they gone?" demanded the King.

"Into the forest, Sire … I think … I don't know," spluttered the servant.

"And why was I not informed of this sooner?" Vieldrin's tone was controlled and menacing, like a volcano that waited for the right time to erupt.

"Well, Sire…"

"Yes?" Vieldrin stopped pacing.

"We went to get help … and then … we searched."

The King span round to face the servant, his long cloak sweeping the floor. Hate and frustration boiled in his gaze. "Gah! You miserable piece of shit!"

An arc of flame shot from his hand and both the guards and menials ducked. A tapestry on the wall behind them fell to the floor in burning tatters.

"The Stone is hidden out there and they have gone to retrieve it!"

"We'll find it, Sire, we promise you!" the quivering servant assured him. He glanced at his companion, hoping for support.

"Oh, will you?" said Vieldrin, a chilling edge to his voice. "You snivelling son of a cross-eyed crone! I'll tell you what you'll do! You'll go outside, the pair of you, in the company of my guards and they will impale you on their swords. That'll teach you to run from a Wilthkin. Get out, you cowardly bastards!"

The servants gawped in stupefaction as four guards marched towards them and Vieldrin's lip was a curl of contempt, as they were dragged away. The other menials in the Hall made shift to look like part of the furniture.

Vieldrin turned to the other Elves assembled in the Hall and he drew a deep breath to regain his composure. "Everything goes badly," he said, "and soon I must leave for Elindell. The war needs my attention. It isn't going to plan. The cowards don't seem to want to fight." But first I'll visit those Nine Wise Men. My enemies cannot use the Stone, if only I have knowledge of its name. He cast a quizzical look at Crellin. "Any news of Tandrin?"

"Yes, Sire!" squeaked Crellin. "The austral Elves have offered their help to Queen Gilda."

"Confound the vermin!" spat the King. "At least they are a lazy lot. Being warlike would not suit them. They will merely add to the number of rats I have to slaughter." His lips were stretched by a feral grin and he seated himself upon his throne, ignoring those around him. For a while he thought about his plans and his mood appeared to lighten. Then his gaze swooped outwards. "I will need a retinue of guards, when I set out for Elindell. A small one should suffice. See to it, Crellin, at once."

"Yes, Sire! And ... what about the Lorestone, Sire?"

Vieldrin thought for a moment. "Send out a search party, Crellin. Find the escapees. But not too many warriors mind. We need all our lads to patrol the forest in case of another revolt. Begin the search among Haldrin's lot and, if the rats are holed up there, I want their protectors killed. As for the Stone, I can but hope that Elgiva will retrieve it before she is recaptured. That would save us a great deal of trouble. She cannot use it without its name and I will find that first. Keep a close guard on all the horses." He rubbed his hands together and smiled. With only two days to live at most, Elgiva would never reach the Nine Men. "Whatever happens, I want the Lorestone brought to me in Elindell." He glanced at them all in turn. "And should anyone try to use the Stone, or take it to someone who can, they would, of course, be wasting their time, would you not agree?"

A row of terrified faces suggested that they did. Vieldrin leaned back in his throne and continued, as though he were thinking aloud. "Elgiva is no longer a threat. Her days on the Earth are numbered. And even if her friends escape, they will take the Stone to Elindell and no-one there can use it. Apart from me, of course!" He laughed. "My position is still secure."

He smirked at the prospect of triumph. "Crellin, the purge of rebels must wait until I am home again. I would not want to miss it! When I have destroyed the rulers of Elvendom, then there will be ample time to punish those who opposed me." With a frown of impatience, he waved them away. "Now, you gaping imbeciles, go about your duties. I have much to think about."

⋆ ⋆ ⋆

Dusk was falling upon the forest. Godwin knelt on the Hill-Shrine, Elgiva cradled in his arms, and many yards below stood Trystin, Grimalkin beside him munching the grass. It had taken them some time to reach the Shrine. They had frequently stopped to hide themselves to avoid approaching patrols and had kept away from the paths and glades, so the going had been slow. At intervals, Trystin found edible plants, which he shared with his Wilthkin friend, but they were barely enough to still the nagging of their hunger. Godwin had felt Elgiva growing heavier in his arms, though she was a burden he willingly carried, and he knew that his strength was almost gone.

Now he lifted tired, dry eyes to the stars that winked in the sky. It seemed that he had been here forever, waiting for something to happen. He had fully believed that some healing power would manifest unbidden. Now he feared that he would be disappointed.

Elgiva suddenly stirred and her eyelids fluttered open, but she seemed not to know who he was. Instead she stared blankly at the sky and her eyes were like bruises in her face. "Darkness … it calls," she murmured.

Godwin hugged her feverish body tightly to his breast; he wouldn't let death snatch her away. "Don't talk like that," he pleaded lornly. "I won't let you go."

"Tomorrow … a broken promise. Night calls me to the grave."

He tightened his grip on her slender form, shook her slightly in his frustration. "Faine *WILL* hear us, Elgiva." He looked up at the sombre sky, not knowing what he sought. "Faine, release her from this spell!"

"Fetters," she sighed faintly. "Death … the key. Unlock them."

"Faine, First-Father," Godwin prayed.

"Why cling?" she said. "Let go."

"Faine, I believe in you," gritted Godwin.

"Water!" gasped Elgiva, struggling in his grasp. He lifted a water-skin to her lips; she drank a little, then pushed it away. "Poison … poison!" she groaned.

"I have faith," said Godwin. "I have faith in good magic." But his heart was sobbing in his breast.

Night deepened all around them. Elgiva writhed in Godwin's arms and her body was burning with fever. She was like kindling, it seemed to him, apt for immolation, and the tears ran freely down his face; but he had made a vow and he would uphold it to the last.

"Elgiva!" he cried, and he shook her more roughly. "Elgiva, believe in Faine!"

"Faine … good … peace … death…"

By Frigg, I'm not going to lose you, girl! He shook her again and his anger tightened his grip like cruelty. "Focus, damn you! Concentrate! One last effort of will! Think of Faine. Believe in Faine!"

"I do believe … I do," she gasped, "but you … you're hurting…"

"Ask Lord Faine to help you!"

"It's hot. It's far too hot!"

"Forget the fever. It will pass. Lord Faine will release you."

"Yes … release my spirit."

"No, Elgiva, release you from Vieldrin's spell!"

Elgiva went limp and her eyelids closed and Godwin slackened his grip. His hands were shaking badly, as though he had lost control of his muscles. He brushed the sweat-slick hair from her face, allowed her some moments of peace. He hated himself for his ferocity. It would be kinder to let her drift, to let her succumb to the spell and die, but he well knew the heartache of forcing sick children to take the potions that tasted foul but made them better. He had the strength for such things, and he had an inner conviction that what he was doing was right. To be deserving of help, one must first ask for it.

"Elgiva!" he said forcefully.

When she didn't respond, he turned her head towards him and said her name again. The merest breath soughed through her lips. Gritting his teeth, he drew back his hand and slapped her on the cheek. This time her eyes flew open and she looked at him with such fear and surprise that he almost abandoned his purpose. Gently, he cupped her face in his hands.

"Elgiva, please, you must ask Faine to release you from the spell. Say it!"

"Faine … release me from this spell."

"Faine, heal me."

"Faine … heal me."

"Good magic is stronger than bad. Believe it." It has to be. It has to.

Her eyes closed again and she drifted away and this time he left her in peace. He felt that nothing more could be done. He lowered her gently to the grass; her limbs were heavy and still, her skin so pale that it seemed translucent.

Overcome by his own exhaustion, Godwin allowed his gaze to wander. At the foot of the Shrine, Trystin lay sleeping. Grimalkin, her head bowed, was standing beside him, the Lorestone safely in her pack

If only Elgiva could use it, thought Godwin.

Yet he knew that she would never use the Lorestone merely to save herself. A breeze stirred the branches of the trees and at first he inhaled the cool air gratefully, but as the darkness thickened around him, its chill breath made him shiver. The thought of summer crossed his mind, and it seemed so far away, and what would summer be without Elgiva? And what would become of this beautiful land, if Vieldrin weren't destroyed?

Two images vied for his attention. One, his daughters dancing in a meadow full of cornflowers; the other was Elgiva, cold and lifeless in the grave. He couldn't reconcile the two.

He thought then of the prophecies that had brought her to this sorry end. The prophecies ... orphan and slave. But *HE* had found the Lorestone. A slave indeed, but an orphan, too? Sadly he dwelt on the parents he couldn't remember; now dead, unattainable. Doubly lost.

So prophets were fallible after all and Bellic had been wrong. But Godwin couldn't use the Lorestone. He had no magic, save for his sword. He drew the weapon from its sheath and peered at it in the darkness.

Then he remembered finding the Stone. Taranuil had been the key that opened the door of the secret cavern where the opal lay concealed. The sword had been the trigger. The sword and the cavern were worlds apart, but they had one thing in common; magic. The magic of the Earth...of Elves...of Faine. The sword had no active power itself, but as a spark for other forces...

There were energies in the Earth, he knew, and here at this sacred spot perhaps they came together, focused. This was the heartland, the hub, of Faine's power.

It had to be worth a try.

"I believe," he whispered to the night. "Faine's spirit will answer me." He lifted the weapon in both hands and cried out "Taranuil!" The sword gleamed gladly in response and he plunged it into the earth. Godwin lay down with a prayer on his lips and stared at the star-flecked sky. A half-moon seemed to smile at him.

He was overwhelmed by drowsiness, but he fought off sleep, anxious for proof that magic was at work. But all that stirred were the leaves on the trees, as they rustled like slivers of darkness.

Oh, for a flash of lightning, an otherworldly voice, the sight of something supernatural!

But the knoll lay quiet beneath the sky and the hand that Godwin clasped in his own was clammy-cold and limp and dying.

"I have faith," he whispered.

A sensation of floating came over him and he could resist his fatigue no longer. He let the world slip calmly away.

And Taranuil, embedded in power, communed with the hallowed earth.

* * *

Chapter Thirty

Godwin had barely surfaced from sleep, when something large blocked out the light and he heard a snuffling noise. He pried his eyes open with alarm to see Grimalkin's yellow teeth grinning inches from his face.

"By Frigg!"

"You getting up, your lordship?"

"Must you always creep up on people?"

"His lordship's a little grumpy today. Anyway, thought you'd want to know, the kid and me heard noises.."

Godwin sat up and rubbed his eyes. "What are you talking about, you old jade?"

"Noises in the distance, Brit. Could be warriors. We'd better hoof it. No need to worry though, I've had breakfast." Casually, she turned away. "I expect they're armed to the teeth, so you'd better make your peace with God. Or Woden. Or whatever." She slithered down the slope.

Godwin felt that he had slept too well. For a moment he didn't recognise the concern that nudged at his mind, but then he reached for Elgiva, hardly daring to look.

To his surprise, her skin was cool. He scanned her sleeping face. The dark stains of illness circled her eyes and her skin seemed even paler, but she had an air of recuperation and, under the dried blood in her hair, her wound had almost closed. He listened gratefully to her breathing, which now was deep and regular, and for a while he smiled with relief and gazed at Taranuil.

Trystin came bounding up the slope and in his eyes there was only one question.

"The crisis has passed," said Godwin. A spasm of conflicting emotions crossed the Elfling's face. Godwin looked at him thoughtfully, his blue eyes misted by gladness, "Yes," he said. "I know." He got to his feet and straightened his tunic, then carefully drew his sword from the earth. For a moment he smiled at the slumbering blade. "We'd better leave. We've stayed too long. And yet," he added, "not long enough."

"Yes, Master Godwin," Trystin agreed. In his voice was a new, a deeper, respect.

Sliding the sword back into its scabbard, Godwin drew a cleansing breath, filling his lungs with the morning air. "How does one give thanks?" he wondered, almost to himself.

Silently, Trystin watched him. He was in awe of powerful magic and saddened by his own lack of knowledge. And at that moment Godwin also felt a chill run up his spine. They had witnessed something that neither understood; something great and terrible.

Godwin pulled himself together and smiled at his young friend. "Go and tell Grimalkin that she must carry Elgiva until she can walk unaided. Take the water-skin with you, lad."

Trystin hesitated. He needed reassurance. He wanted to throw his arms around Godwin, to cling to him as though to a father, until the nightmares that hovered around him paled into harmless illusions; but he knew that he was being childish. He picked up the water-skin, turned on his heel, and scurried down the knoll.

As Godwin lifted her into his arms, Elgiva opened her eyes. This time she knew who he was.

"You'll soon be well again," he said and his tone was light and full of relief. "But, my dear, we are being hunted and we mustn't tarry here. I must put you on Grimalkin's back. No doubt she'll complain about it!"

Elgiva smiled at him wanly and he carried her down the slope of the knoll and hoisted her onto the pony's back. For a moment he feared to let loose his hold, but she was stronger then she looked and supported herself without effort.

Shortly they set off and soon they were wading through lush grass and spring flowers. Finding a bubbling rill of water, they stopped to replenish their water-skins, and watched as the thin stream tinkled away into the forest's green embrace, followed by a retinue of slender reeds. Despite the beauties of Misterell, the travellers were ill at ease, not knowing if they were being pursued and, if so, by how many. This feeling sharpened as they neared the forest edge. Ahead of them lay a vast tract of land that would leave them prey to hostile eyes.

Far, far in the shimmering distance stood the purple-hued hills and, beyond them, the forest of Elindell.

Godwin remembered the village that Trystin had spoken of and was overtaken by curiosity. In that village lived people of the same race as himself! He remembered Othere telling him that his people had fled to the west and north, running for their very lives from the Saxon war-machine. Othere had said that the Britons were cowards and Godwin had accepted this dumbly, but he felt that in isolated places those of his kind still flourished.

Godwin asked Trystin if they would pass near the village.

"It's on our way, Master Godwin. It's in a valley, before the hills, and the village lies on the west bank of a fast-flowing river."

Godwin nodded. "I see."

"You wish to go there?" asked Elgiva in a voice still drained of energy.

"If there's time," he said with a shrug.

Elgiva smiled. "I understand. You want to meet your own kind."

"No time for social visits!" Grimalkin snorted testily.

"Time enough, I dare say," Elgiva returned. "We hold the Stone."

"We need food, too," piped up Trystin. "Perhaps they'll let us have some."

"That's settled then," whinnied Grimalkin. "Food it is. Let's go."

"I don't see that it should worry you," Godwin said with a frown. "There's enough good grass around here to feed a hundred lazy nags, be they never so greedy."

"Sometimes I am full of concern for the appetites of others," snorted Grimalkin tartly, tossing her matted mane from her eyes. "And grass lies heavy on the guts. Perhaps they'll have some spring greens. All I get these days is grass. Grass is boring stuff. And meadow grass, very coarse. I'd sooner eat windlestraw."

A sudden noise behind them drew them up abruptly and while they listened with thumping hearts, Grimalkin tasted the air.

"Fox," she announced. "Smelly bastard."

With much relief, they travelled on and Grimalkin took the opportunity to tell them about the vixen that paid nightly visits to Oswald's homestead, and how, one night, Grimalkin had kicked down the wall of the poultry shed on the understanding that the vixen would grab the resident cockerel.

"That taught the bugger," she said. "No more shit in my hay and a good lie in every morning."

Her humour lightened their burden of dread, but Elgiva saw that Godwin wasn't giving the tale his full attention. His eyes were glued to the ground, as though some message were written there, waiting to be deciphered.

"Godwin," she ventured, "I've yet to thank you for my return to health, though I don't remember that much about it."

He continued to stare at the forest floor. "I did nothing. It was Faine." Elgiva merely smiled. "I've witnessed the impossible, seen things that just can't be," he said. "Good magic cured you … somehow."

"We all have the power to heal, Godwin. We just don't always know how to use it."

But he wasn't listening. "It's difficult to know what to believe in. How many gods *ARE* there?"

"In the end all gods are one god. The power of Good exists in many forms, but we can't usually see it, and, when you can't see something, it's hard to believe in it. So, if there's no proof, all we can have is faith."

He felt the irony of her words, for he was doubting the very thing he had told her to cling to on the Hill-Shrine. "But wasn't your healing proof that Faine … well, his spirit, still acts in this world?"

In a manner typical of her kind, she shrugged and looked away. Had he said the wrong thing? He yearned to tell her of the voice that had entered his mind on the sacred knoll, that had told him the name of his sword, the voice that still inspired him; but he couldn't find the words. The episode lost its actuality outside the confines of thought and made him think he had dreamed it all. And he feared that so personal was the experience it would lose its precious flavour once it was revealed.

"You remember when we were attacked at the Hill-Shrine?" she asked him, turning round.

"Yes?"

"The Earth remembers, if we do not."

Godwin was disappointed. He didn't know what she meant and he felt that the answers he needed so badly were being denied to him.

As they pushed on, the trees thinned out and on either side were tracts of grass that swarmed with nodding bluebells. Silence drifted through the mist like the spirit of the forest. Misterell was hard to leave.

At length, the trees were behind them and they stood before the prospect of the open plain ahead. Godwin looked at Elgiva, but her thoughts were elsewhere, her gaze unfocused, and her hand was clenched around Siriol.

"Elgiva, is something wrong?" he asked anxiously.

With an effort, she lowered her eyes to his, but the struggle to focus herself upon him seemed to deprive her of speech. He felt a sudden desire for haste. Briskly he led his friends towards the uncertain future.

They had travelled less than half a league, when Grimalkin drew up with a snort and her large head swung towards the forest. Elgiva and Trystin followed her gaze and Godwin winced at the fear in their eyes.

"What is it?" he asked.

"Shut up!" hissed Grimalkin, her long ears swivelling back and forth.

Godwin listened, his muscles tensed, but his effort was unrewarded; he lacked the sensory range of his friends.

"Vieldrin!"gasped Elgiva.

"What do we do, Lady?" bleated Trystin.

"Sprout wings and fly seems a good idea," said Grimalkin resignedly.

Godwin searched about him, seeking some way of escape. Ahead of them stood a clump of oak trees, their branches lifting new leaves to the sun. "Elgiva?" he pleaded.

She nodded. She, too, had seen the trees. She urged Grimalkin into a canter. Snatching hold of Trystin's hand, Godwin stumbled after them. As they approached the nearest oak tree, Grimalkin stopped at Elgiva's command.

"It's no use!" cried Elgiva. "We can't hide here. They'll see us."

Hoof-beats sounded in the earth.

"Elgiva, by Frigg!" begged Godwin. "You must do something … quick!" He peered at the distant forest.

"I don't think I have the strength," she confessed. She seemed to look inside herself and a grey anxiety sharpened her features. "Perhaps … perhaps if you help me … Yes, you must help me. All of you!" Her sudden authority calmed their panic.

"Lady Elgiva, we'll do anything!" promised Trystin, his eyes bright with trust.

"Grimalkin?" asked Elgiva. "Are you able to concentrate on anything other than food?"

The pony snorted disdainfully.

Elgiva drew a deep breath. "Very well," she said. "Godwin, stand on my right side. Trystin, on my left. We will make a circle of power. We must be in physical contact." She held out her hands to them. "Put your free hands on Grimalkin. No matter what happens, don't let go until I give the word. Do NOT break the circle!"

Nervously, Godwin glanced at the forest and saw a score of horses dashing out from among the trees. The desire to unsheath Taranuil almost overcame him, but he forced himself to obey Elgiva. Trystin had seen the horses, too, and he trembled in his rags.

Elgiva's voice rose over their fear and it steadied them with a promise of power.

"Believe that we are invisible. Close your eyes and concentrate. Think till it hurts, but you must believe it. I tell you, we are invisible. We are nothing but air. Not even a shadow on the grass. Our enemies shall pass, but we will not be there. Believe it, my friends. Don't fail me."

Godwin wanted to feel secure, to trust in Elgiva's magic, but it was hard; so hard. It was as though closing his eyes had left him alone in the darkness, while peril thundered towards him, like a huge beast of ravin.

How on earth could he be invisible?

He thought as hard as he could, bullied himself into the notion that flesh and bone could be transmuted into something unseen, transparent. It was hard to imagine what help he could give by a mere exertion of will, and, once again, he was placing his trust, his life, in the hands of magic.

I am air, he told himself. Not even a shadow. I am air.

Then he heard the rumble of hooves, the exhalations of galloping horses, and in his mind they were slavering beasts with barbed tails and flaring nostrils. More like dragons than horses. His legs buckled, but the earth at his feet assured him of its permanence, its readiness to uphold him, and a strange throbbing in the air closed about him like a shield.

Air. Not even a shadow.

Then he felt the tightening of Elgiva's magic and its desperation churned his guts. The hooves came nearer, pounding the earth, and his heart was beating in time with them. How long must he think? His head was aching. He was air. When would it stop? He was air. Not even a shadow.

Shuddering, febrile bursts of magic buzzed about his ears, made the skin crawl over his flesh. This caul of force was stifling him, but he knew it held no malice. He wondered how Trystin fared.

Silently he pleaded, Trystin, lad, this is good magic! We must help it. We are air!

Elgiva strengthened her grip on his hand. She trembled and her palm was slick. He shared her pain as she forced her power to the limit and beyond. He feared that the cords of her soul would snap. She was untutored. How much longer could she maintain this spell? And surely Vieldrin could see them? Perhaps he could sense their presence? No. They were invisible. They weren't even a shadow on the grass.

The ground vibrated beneath his feet and he heard the crack of a whip. Godwin winced, but he heard no complaint from the horse receiving the smart. All he could hear were explosive snorts and the thunder of hooves, as the riders dashed by in a frenzy of speed. And then they were gone.

The thunder receded swiftly. What felt like an age of terror had lasted less than a minute. Godwin waited patiently, but he felt no slackening of the power and continued to convince himself of his invisible status.

They stood awhile, cloaked in silence, and then Elgiva's hand loosened its grip and the very air around them seemed to plunge to the ground with relief.

"Relax."

The small voice above him wasn't Elgiva's. To Godwin it sounded weary and hollow, drained of every response. But it was also the voice of someone who had survived an ordeal and gained from the experience. It had passed through fire to purity and there was a strange duality in it: enervated, yet charged with power. Had Godwin looked, he would have seen the after-gleam of magic that writhed in his friend's dark eyes; magic that still boiled with frustration. It glittered for several moments more, then it shrank into angry darkness.

"Will you take your hot, little hand off my back!"

Grimalkin's remonstrance startled him. He sighed and scrubbed the sweat from his eyes. "It seems to have worked," he said. Somehow their wills had strengthened the magic, impossible though that seemed. He looked across at Trystin, who was ashen-faced but managed a smile.

But Godwin had no time for him. Elgiva was all that mattered. Her face was blanker than a cloud, her eyes surrounded by circles of sickness. He offered her his hand and, after a moment's hesitation, she seemed to return to herself and allowed him to help her dismount.

They looked into each other's eyes and there was no need for words. He had shared her magic in Misterell; he understood how it felt.

Suddenly, her legs gave way and she fell into his arms. He carried her to the nearest oak tree and laid her gently down. Taking off his cloak, he covered her with it to keep off the morning chill. Then he made to rise from his knees, but she grabbed him by the sleeve.

"There's something I must tell you. When the slaves paid homage, I realised it then. Kendra was right … and Bellic, too. They tolerated my treatment, when I was a servant. Why? Because it taught me humility. What might I have been without it? I thought that then, back in Misterell." Her hand slipped from his arm and her eyelids began to droop. "So much power and wealth to be had … there for the taking." So many temptations. "Yet it held no appeal for me. Does suffering give one strength after all? Does it make you more considerate … and perhaps more cunning, too?" She smiled, but then her eyes flashed open. "But, Godwin, my powers … my powers are stunted! I can't develop them to the full. I don't even know what that is! Perhaps I'll never know!"

Elgiva fell back with a sigh of exhaustion. Godwin didn't know what to say. She needed a Wardain's guidance, something he couldn't provide.

"Don't worry," he soothed. "We'll go to your uncle. He'll know what to do."

"But Vieldrin will get there first! He might…"

"Rest now," said Godwin firmly. "We'll worry about that later. The danger's passed and we have the Lorestone."

A smile skimmed her lips, like a shadow, and she fell fast asleep

Godwin pushed himself to his feet and suddenly realised how hungry he was. When had he eaten last? "Trystin, we're going hunting!"

"What with?"

The voice that had answered him was Grimalkin's. Godwin turned to face her and it was then that he saw the Elfling strewn upon the grass. He had the look of someone who had fallen asleep from a great height and inanition clung to his bones.

Godwin swallowed thickly and walked to where he lay. Having knelt beside the Elfling, he tried to make him more comfortable. Trystin whimpered at his touch and, as if for the first time, Godwin noticed how bruised he was. It seemed to have escaped his attention, when he had been preoccupied with Elgiva, but now he observed with a pang of disgust the cruel abuse of Vieldrin's guards. The purple marks on Trystin's limbs were more then he could bear.

You selfish bastard! he thought.

He turned away angrily, met the pony's knowing gaze.

"Little whingebag wants fattening up. Always has," she said. "He's a growing lad, you know. Can't you see he's starving, Brit?"

"Yes, I can see that!" Godwin snapped.

"Needs his food at his age. Liable to grow up stunted."

"Stunted?" The word made Godwin shudder. Frowning, he scrambled to his feet. "Shut up, you hideous beast! I'll get some food. I'm going to hunt."

"Course you are, Brit," she snickered. "Behold the herds of fat deer running across the plain. Spoilt for choice, I reckon. Anyway, Brit, Elves don't eat meat."

"Well, I DO," he said. He strode towards her menacingly. "In fact, you idle creature, you'd feed me for a fortnight."

"You can't kill me," she snorted.

He stopped within a few feet of her, grasped the hilt of his sword. "Why not?"

"Because you're far too fond of me." She stretched out her neck and nuzzled his ear and he pushed her away in annoyance. "What are you hunting, then? Mice?"

"I need to think, so shut your noise."

Godwin looked around him. The flat land sloped off under his gaze and seemed devoid of life, but then a magpie flew overhead and he watched it, as it fluttered past, and his eyes were drawn to the cluster of oaks. Hearing birdsong, his features brightened. Purposefully, he made for the trees. Grimalkin trotted after him.

"What you up to now?" she asked, when they had gained the oak trees. "Going to make a bow and arrow?"

"Don't be silly!" he snapped. He folded his arms and looked up at the branches.

"Well, plenty of birds up there," she said. "Blast 'em from the skies, I say. Stupid, squawking bastards."

"I don't want the birds," he said, "just their eggs."

"Eggs? I can't eat eggs!" she whinnied. "Horrid, slippery things they are!"

"They're not for you. You're fat enough."

Grimalkin snickered to herself, then let out a loud, excited whinny that deafened her companion. "Look! A nest, right at the top! You going to climb up there?" She shook her head from side to side. "You'll break your bloody neck."

"Come and stand here by the trunk."

"Why should I?"

"Never mind. Just be helpful and do what I ask."

Grudgingly, the pony complied and he clambered onto her back. She swung her head round and snorted wetly.

"Must you stick your knees in my spine?"

"You *ARE* a beast of burden."

"Aye, that's my lot, Brit. Burdens galore. But Mother didn't tell me I might get used as a ladder."

"Was your mother like you," he wondered, "or are you a freak of nature?"

"All I remember of Mother is that she had a leg at each corner and, underneath, the sweetest milk you ever could imagine. But she taught me, soon as I could stand, to watch out for two-legged creatures."

"Shit!"

Grimalkin chuckled as a branch above her broke with a mighty crack.

* * *

Elgiva didn't sleep for long. Some nagging sense of urgency dragged her back to the world. She opened her eyes and looked around. In her mind she pictured Vieldrin, racing towards his destiny, and she knew herself to be a part of whatever that involved. She was wasting time, had to be moving.

And Siriol had been warm.

Supporting herself against the tree, she struggled to get to her feet. Her head reeled and her legs felt weak, as though their bones had melted. Her body felt scorched by magic. Her powers were certainly growing stronger, but she lacked the strength and skill required to protect herself from their intensity. She felt like a shallow river, broken-banked and choked with stones, unable to cope with a fierce, spring flood. She cursed her weakness and also the fever that had cost her so much energy, yet she smiled at the irony of it all. The more she exercised her powers, the stronger they became; the stronger they became, the more they threatened to destroy the wielder.

She was on a downward spiral that could only end in death, and, perversely, there was pleasure in it.

But it was pointless bemoaning her weakness and she had no time to convalesce. Only magic mattered and she was born to serve it … and if it destroyed her, so be it.

Perhaps she was being too hard on herself.

She turned her attention outwards once more. The threat of rain had darkened the sky, but that was the only menace, and so she allowed herself to relax. She saw her friends among the trees. Godwin clung to a swaying branch, while his legs kicked out at the air; Grimalkin was neighing derisively and a group of birds wheeled overhead, filling the air with their cries.

Then she saw movement some yards to her right and Trystin stirred and sat up.

"I heard birds," he said, rubbing his eyes. "They were calling for help."

Relinquishing the tree's support, Elgiva walked towards him. She knelt at his side and tried to smile. "I think our friends are robbing nests."

"Stealing eggs?" cried Trystin, horrified.

She drew a deep breath that hurt her lungs. "Needs must, I dare say," she replied. Because I'm weak and useless. Sudden anger flared in her breast and she fought it down; she had to. She felt the stirring of magic, yearning for release.

No. This was too much. How could she learn control?

Trystin appeared to accept her words, but really he lacked the strength to argue.

"Trystin, you look sad," she said, reaching out to stroke his cheek. A trite remark to make, she knew. In fact, her friend looked dreadful. He seemed to be even thinner and his bare, bruised limbs were like sticks. His hair was a wild and dirty tangle around his pale, gaunt face. It wrenched her heart to look at him.

"I'm tired and I think of ... former friends."

He hadn't intended any reproach, but she felt it nonetheless. If only she hadn't intervened, Haldrin and Everil and countless others wouldn't have lost their lives.

They sat in a thoughtful silence and Trystin chewed his nails.

"Well," said Elgiva, at length. "It seems to me that you need cheering up."

She smiled, hoping that he would do the same, but his sadness ran too deep. Placing her arm around his shoulders, she gave him a gentle hug. She longed to lift his spirits; he was too young to be so sad. But how to go about it?

Of course, there was only one way.

But she wondered if she would be doing it more to punish herself than to gratify him.

"I need some serious practice," she said. "What magic shall I perform, Trystin?"

His eyes grew large with reviving interest. "Oh, Lady Elgiva.... I don't know!" Then he saw the birds that were circling the trees and he turned to her with a grin. "Lady Elgiva, I've always wondered ... what's it like to fly?"

Elgiva arched her eyebrows. "Fly?"

"Yes! I've always wanted to know what it feels like to be really free."

She thought for a moment, then swayed to her feet. "Stand up. I'll see what I can do." She straightened herself and held out her arms, while Trystin grinned with excitement.

"Rise, little Trystin, take to the skies.

"Size is no object, when Trystin flies.
"Light as a winter moth in the night,
"Wingless, arise, ascend, take flight!"

They waited for something to happen and Trystin chewed his nails expectantly. All of a sudden he felt himself being lifted off the ground and he hovered above it for several moments.

"That's not good enough," said Elgiva.

Without some strong emotion to fuel it, the magic seemed sluggish and weak, but it would be no use to her, if it waxed and waned like the moon. It had to be controlled.

"Be spry and fly; be light, take flight!
"Soar in the ether, though lacking feather.
"A blur, a streak, though lacking beak.
"In air be fleeter than any worm-eater!"

Her mind sharpened with sudden clarity and she felt a rush of force in her limbs, a gleeful burgeoning of power. It was savage, alive and wonderful. Confining it within the bounds of her will, she directed it slowly outwards. The magic was a sparkling river and she the valley through which it flowed, no longer blocked by the dregs of disuse.

Now you will do my bidding.

But still she was holding something back. The magic frightened her.

Trystin began to rise from the ground and she heard him squeal with delight. The magic lifted him higher and higher and he began to dance in the air, spinning around like a wind-tossed leaf. His laughter made Elgiva laugh, too.

"Oh, Lady, this is fun!" he shrieked.

For a while she giggled at his antics, at the grimy tunic that flapped round his legs, like the feathers of a windswept crow, but then she felt the power ebbing.

"I'm sorry … you must come down now, Trystin."

Slowly the Elfling descended and once his feet were on the earth he ran to Elgiva and hugged her. "Oh, Lady Elgiva, you're so clever!"

Elgiva wanted to return the embrace, but a wave of giddiness made her gasp. Her vision swam with scarlet motes and the blood throbbed in her skull. Tears sprang unbidden to her eyes at the knowledge that power was killing her, yet she was compelled to use it. It was almost as though she enjoyed the pain.

Then she looked at Trystin's beaming face and it seemed a small price to pay.

⋆ ⋆ ⋆

Chapter Thirty-One

The sun was hidden behind the clouds that toiled towards the valley and the river seemed grey and sluggish, as though it were clogged with detritus. Between the river and the hills lay the British village, a sprawl of shabby dwellings, like the refuse of a bygone age.

The winter had been hard and food was in short supply, but what was the point of planting crops? It would only prolong the agony. Their former prosperity was in ruins. The Elf-king had taken their ponies, their silver and gold, their jewels and swords and, worst of all, their handsome kine. And who dared oppose this agent of Satan with his Elf-bolts and his web of enchantment?

And now a new pain had joined the old: Gwion, their chief, was dead.

Elgiva and her companions looked down at the village from the east bank of the river. They were weakened by hunger and exhausted by travel and the village's gloomy aspect did nothing to lift their spirits.

"More of Vieldrin's work," said Elgiva. "Yes, there is some enchantment here."

"Shall we go and say hello?" wondered Trystin, trying to be cheerful.

"You and I had better stay here … Well, at least for the moment. They might mistake us for friends of Vieldrin." Elgiva paused, wondering if they had been wise to come here, but their need for food left them little choice. "Godwin?"

"Yes, I'll go."

He made his way down the slope towards the rickety bridge that spanned the river. Unbidden, Grimalkin trotted behind him.

"Wait for me! Don't want to miss anything!"

A number of villagers looked up in alarm, when they heard the sound of neighing, but the sight of the two intruders seemed to reassure them and by the time that Godwin had crossed the wooden bridge a gathering of people had turned out to meet him.

He stood before the silent crowd and smiled at their sullen faces and he tried to recall the only words he knew of his people's language, but then he abruptly checked himself. Of course, it wasn't necessary, because of Elgiva's gift.

"My name is Godwin," he explained and his mouth went suddenly dry. Nervously, he moistened his lips. "I'm of your race, but as a child I was taken by the Saxons, so I was taught their customs." They continued to stare suspiciously and he realised that language wasn't the only difference between them. "Forgive me, if I appear ill-mannered, I ... er..."

They looked him carefully up and down, curious yet wary. Then an old woman in a grubby, brown robe stepped out from their midst. She stopped a few yards in front of him and thrust her staff in the earth, as though to indicate the point beyond which he mustn't go. Her wispy, white hair was like a cloud and it spoke of age and frailty, but her sharp, blue eyes were keen as a blade and suggested hidden fire.

"For someone unfamiliar with our ways, you speak our language well," she said, a frown of mistrust on her brow. She shared a look with the villagers and their silence invited her to continue. "Ceara is my name and I speak on behalf of the tribe. What is your business, stranger?"

The villagers stared unblinkingly and Godwin felt awkward and shuffled his feet. He didn't know where to begin.

"Courage, son," hissed Grimalkin.

"I've come to help you!" he blurted out.

"Cabbage hearts! It's food we're after!"

"Have you, in sooth?" scoffed Ceara. "My friends, it appears that we are saved!" Humourless laughter greeted her words.

"I'm not alone," said Godwin, crossing his arms defensively. "The powers of good are with me."

"You are an angel?" mocked Ceara.

"I don't know what you mean!" snapped Godwin, annoyed by the old woman's stance. "I heard you were in trouble and I've brought good magic to aid you."

"A half-wit," muttered Ceara.

"I know about the enchantment! And Vieldrin of Misterell is the source!" The villagers fell silent and glanced at each other through narrowed eyes. "But there are good Elves, too," added Godwin. "One such travels with me and she is determined to kill Vieldrin."

A young man stepped forward and sneered at him. "And who is this saviour?" he asked. "Is she too afraid to meet us?"

"She is an Elf," hissed Ceara, "and they are all agents of Satan."

"She is the Queen of Elindell!" Godwin told her angrily.

"We know of no such place!"

"Never mind," sighed Godwin. "We've stopped on our way to Elindell to offer you some assurance that your plight can't last forever."

"In sooth it cannot," she said bitterly, "for we cannot live forever!"

"Why don't you ask about food?" nagged Grimalkin.

Godwin ignored this remark. "We heard that your chief is dying…"

"He died a week ago!" snapped Ceara.

"Well," said Godwin, "I'm sorry for that. I had thought to bring him hope."

"Hope?" she exclaimed. "He is past hope! He is well out of it!" She hobbled towards him and raised her staff and Godwin stepped back warily. "From whence do you come with this hope?"

"From Misterell," replied Godwin. The villagers muttered in consternation. "We escaped from Misterell."

The young man turned to address the crowd. "They've sent him to spy on us!"

"No, Aled!"

Godwin looked up to see who had spoken and saw a young woman with dark-red plaits moving through the throng.

"You are too quick to judge, brother." She stopped at the young man's side. "What has become of our hospitality?"

Aled turned away haughtily and the young woman smiled at Godwin. "My name is Angwen, stranger, and I am niece to Morvyth, sister of our late Chief. Morvyth is our leader, but she is old and sick, so I will speak in her stead. I know she would aid a traveller before she questioned his purpose." She glanced at her people reproachfully and they shrank beneath her gaze. Clearly they respected her in spite of her obvious youth. "Godwin, I bid you welcome, both you and your elvish friend, and I hope our hospitality will make amends for the slights you have suffered." She gave him an open, honest smile, then turned back to her tribe. "My friends, he is a stranger, true, yet he is of our race. Is it his fault the Saxons took him? And have you forgotten that once we lived with the faery folk in peace?"

Godwin was touched by her gracious manner and bowed his head towards her. "Thank you, Lady. We're hungry and tired, but we aren't welcome in this place, so, to spare you any conflict, I think we'd better move on."

"Move on?" cried Aled. "You'd run away without more explanation? I don't like the look of you, despite what my sister says, and I'd like to see this Elf of yours!"

Angwen sighed deeply. "Excuse him, Godwin. Our people have lived here in isolation for many years. The Saxon marauders drove us here and we lost our link with the wider world. We dwell as if on an island, suspicious of anything new, but I hope we are not all as hostile as my dear brother, Aled."

"Perhaps I do well to be so," snapped Aled, "when newcomers are heathens!"

"Aled!"

"Rather than be a Saxon's dog, a Briton would fall on his sword, heathen," declared the young man fiercely.

Godwin's hand flew to his sword in anger. Sunlight glinted on the blade, and the metal gleamed with the promise of sharpness.

"Aled, how dare you!" Angwen exclaimed, her eyes wide with shame and outrage.

Aled glared at her peevishly, then, muttering, he turned away. Angwen looked at Godwin, a crease of concern on her brow.

"Godwin, please … forgive us."

Slowly, Godwin sheathed his sword, but his anger stayed honed and ready.

"Call your friend," said Angwen gently. "No harm will befall her."

Godwin looked at Grimalkin and her eyes seemed to echo his decision; Elgiva could take care of herself in a rabble such as this. He walked over to the bridge and beckoned with his arm.

"There are two Elves," he said to Angwen. "My friend is called Elgiva and the boy with her is Trystin. He was born in Misterell and has lived life as a slave since Vieldrin murdered his parents."

Angwen frowned sympathetically and watched as the figures crossed the bridge. "Welcome," she said, as they drew near. They nodded in her direction. "Godwin has explained your purpose. Please eat with us and rest awhile. My name is Angwen and it would please me to hear your story, if you would care to tell it." She stepped towards Trystin and took his hand. "Poor child," she said with a look of concern. "So young to be an orphan and a slave."

She moved away and the villagers drew apart before her. Unsettled by her final remark, Elgiva and Godwin shared a look, then they followed in her wake.

⋆ ⋆ ⋆

Night was falling like a cloud of dust and a mist-ring hugged the moon, but inside Angwen's cosy dwelling, the fire threw warmth against the walls and tallow candles bravely glimmered. Elgiva had told what she deemed wise to tell of their adventures and a meal of goat's cheese, bread and ale had chased away their hunger. Now they sat before the fire, at ease in Angwen's presence.

Angwen moved gracefully round the hut, lighting candles and refilling beakers, and always attentive to the words of her guests. Alone among the villagers, the gloom in the valley seemed hardly to touch her. Yet there was a trace of sadness in her lucid, blue eyes. For a while she was full of wonder for the tales that her guests had brought to her door, but, at length, her sadness reasserted itself and she was forced to speak of it. She sat beside them and watched the flames as they danced cheerily in the hearth.

"As you know, my friends, Gwion, our Chief, died seven days ago. He was much loved by us all. So long had he been our leader and guide that I think we forgot he was mortal. His death was a terrible shock to us – more so to Aled and myself, for Gwion was our father."

They made to convey their condolences, but she waved their compassion away with her hand. "Death comes to us all. It must be so. There is a saying: death is not the end of a short life, but the centre of a long one. And do not grieve for Gwion. He acquitted himself with honour while he lived in this world and he died a very old man. Now he dwells with God. It is we who suffer by losing him, for we are bereft of his wisdom and love. Perhaps you have heard of him, Godwin?" She turned her face towards him and her hair gleamed like copper in the firelight. "In his youth he was famed for his courage and skill, as a leader of men and a warrior. Even the Saxons respected him, for Gwion knew no fear."

Godwin shook his head.

"Well, you are young," she went on, as though she were older than she appeared. "Now, Morvyth is our Chief. When Morvyth dies, I shall take her place, but I cannot rejoice at that. I would rather she lived forever. Not only do I love her dearly, but I fear the burden that is my inheritance." She paused and a soft sigh escaped from her lips.

"Well, we have suffered much, but perhaps our sufferings are for a purpose. We may be a conquered race, but, please God, we will rise again."

"And your village, Lady," ventured Elgiva, "is cursed by an enchantment. I've felt it and, I'm sorry to say, my magic can't undo it."

Angwen didn't seem surprised. "It is as you say," she said.

"Yet you are undaunted."

"I pray to God for endurance."

"My great-uncle once told me that some of your people are blessed with a special gift. You know the Earth's magic and it protects you."

Angwen raised her eyebrows. "It is said that the Druids believed such things and I would not deny their wisdom, but God protects us now."

Elgiva acknowledged this with a smile. "God has many names."

Angwen regarded her thoughtfully and then she nodded her head.

"You doubt your fitness to lead this tribe – you who are the most worthy to do so! There's a power in you and strength," said Elgiva. "Surely you've always known it?"

Angwen was totally taken aback and Godwin decided to change the subject to save her from further embarrassment.

"I noticed on the way here that there were two Saxons in your village. Er ... well, they looked like Saxons."

Angwen thought for a moment, then smiled. "Old Gunderic and his brother! Yes, they were taken by Gwion in a night raid years ago. They are part of our tribe now ... but they are fortunate."

"Why?" asked Godwin.

Angwen's eyes held a gleam of humour, a mischievous, girlish humour that till now she had kept in check. "The elders tell us that, long ago, their bodies would have been left for the crows, while we would have taken their heads!"

Godwin's mouth fell open in horror and Angwen's expression changed. Once again she appeared to be far older than she was. Humour dropped from her face like a veil, to be replaced by regret. "Strength lies in the head," she explained. "To take the head of your enemy was to take his strength, or so it was believed. It was a very long time ago and, with God's help, we may forget such things."

Godwin realised that changing the subject had been a bad decision. "Well," he said, at length," each day we learn something new." He smiled at Angwen uncertainly and nervously cleared his throat. "There's a lot I don't know about my people. Perhaps I ought to meet your Chief. Pay my respects. If there's no objection."

"You may indeed, if you so wish. I'm sure she would be honoured," said Angwen. "But I doubt that you will learn much from her, for she is old and wanders in her mind, more so since Gwion died. I think her heart is broken." In her beautiful eyes there was a gleam of sorrow. Sighing, she got to her feet. "Now I will leave you to get some rest. I will sleep at Morvyth's."

With a weary smile, she walked to the door, but then she stopped and turned to Elgiva. "Tell me, my friend, are elvish folk mortal?"

Elgiva didn't seem surprised by the strangeness of this question. "Indeed we are," she answered, "but we are a long-lived race, Lady Angwen. An Elf who has seen a hundred summers will expect to see many more. Yet in the end all things must die."

"One hundred summers? That is cruel. One hundred winters, too," said Angwen. "Surely there are times when Elves must weary of life, like the rest of us. A shame that they must wait much longer for their heavenly rewards."

For a moment, she stood in the doorway, a pensive expression on her pretty face, and Godwin's heart went out to her. She was too young to be so sad. He noticed also, with a pang of shame, the grace of her movements, the sheen of her skin and the soft, round curves of her body beneath the plain homespun of her gown. For a moment, he thought of Rowena and the joy to be found in the arms of a woman and he drew a deep breath and turned away. A wave of loneliness made him sigh.

He shouldn't let her leave like this without a word of comfort. But it was too late; Angwen had gone.

Elgiva was watching him curiously and he felt himself flush with embarrassment, believing that she had read his thoughts.

For a time, they sat in silence. Trystin leaned against Elgiva, feeling warm and drowsy, and she put a protective arm round his shoulder.

"Angwen is special," Elgiva said suddenly. "Someone should try to persuade her to be the chief when Morvyth dies." Godwin stared at her questioningly. "She will be good for these people. She is One with the Earth, Godwin. Didn't you notice?"

"Notice what?"

She smiled. "I didn't enchant her."

⋆ ⋆ ⋆

The cosiness of Angwen's dwelling granted them untroubled sleep, the first for many a night, and they slumbered longer than they had intended. The morning was old by the time they awoke and ventured out of the hut.

A promise of rain weighted the clouds and they hung in the sky, like clumps of grey wool, and the air was warm and clammy. The villagers kept their distance, but a woman in a grubby gown saw fit to offer them breakfast. Her manner plainly told them that she did this on Angwen's orders, not from concern for their welfare. Before she left to return to her duties, she dumped a pile of clean clothes at their feet.

They ate the stale bread in silence and even Grimalkin had nothing to say. Was it the gloom of the overcast sky or the draining effects of enchantment that left a feeling in the air that stifled conversation; a feeling that something unpleasant might happen? The travellers didn't know, but the atmosphere seemed charged with tension. It turned the food to hard chunks in their bellies and made them fidget uneasily, and they drew together mentally against an unknown menace. Finally Grimalkin could bear it no longer.

"What's that shit you're eating?" she asked.

Briefly, the spell was broken and Godwin hurried to say his piece before the gloom reasserted itself. "The food's not up to much," he said.

"Don't I know it!" grated the pony. "Their hay is older than I am! Celery stalks! I wish you'd seen what I saw earlier on. They even eat rats, you know. Filthy mixen-dwellers! Don't know what they're cooking for later. Smells just like stewed puke."

Godwin threw his bread at her. "Sometimes you go too far!"

"I'd go a lot farther, given the choice. Far away from here."

"Grimalkin, that's enough," said Elgiva. "These people have to eat something. If all they can find to eat are rats, that's Vieldrin's fault, not theirs."

"I never thought it would be like this," said Godwin sadly, shaking his head. "I had some idea ... my people..." He couldn't finish the sentence; disillusionment filled his mind. The Saxons had sneered at his people, laughed at their weak and desultory ways, but in the privacy of his heart he had cherished a different picture; one of nobility, courage and strength. But perhaps the Saxons had been right.

He glanced towards Elgiva and she smiled with understanding, but all he could see was the grip of fatigue, the pallor of her skin. "You're ill yet, my dear," he said softly. "Too little food and too much travel. You haven't recovered your strength."

She twisted a curl of hair round her finger. "My mind fares worse than my body," she sighed. "These Nine Wise Men ... I wish I knew just who or what they are. Our quest has become an aimless trudge." Her hand slipped down to the amulet and she clasped it cautiously. "And there's something else that puzzles me."

Suddenly, Trystin got to his feet and pointed towards the hills. "The wise man is at home!"

They followed the direction of his arm and saw on the top of the highest hill a ribbon of dark-grey smoke.

"So that's where he lives?" said Elgiva.

"So he told me, Lady."

Elgiva toyed with the amulet. "I think ... I think I should meet him."

"Do you think he'd know where the Nine Men are?"

Elgiva looked at Godwin, as though he were speaking an alien tongue. "What? Oh, yes, the Nine Men."

"He's bound to know!" declared Trystin. "He knows everything, Lady Elgiva!"

Elgiva grinned at his confidence. "Well, I dare say he knows me."

Quickly Elgiva got to her feet, her pale skin flushed with excitement.

"We're going now?" asked Godwin.

"I go alone," she replied.

Godwin was unprepared for this. "Alone? But why? Be reasonable! Those hills are practically mountains!"

"Yes, Lady," put in Trystin. "They're very steep and covered with scree. You'll have a difficult climb."

"Don't worry," she told them. "I'll get there." She touched them both on the shoulder, then her gaze returned to the hills. "It looks so quiet and cool up there and the solitude will do me good."

"Elgiva," protested Godwin, baffled by her manner, "we should be heading for Elindell. Vieldrin may not have the Stone, but he can still cause trouble..."

"I'm going now and I'm going alone." Her voice was quiet yet charged with authority and her friends realised that further objections wouldn't be well received. "Stay here and rest and wait for me. I must be alone. I need to think."

Godwin took her hands in his own. "You will be careful, won't you?"

She smiled at him reassuringly. "Guard the Lorestone while I'm gone, and please don't worry about me." She squeezed his fingers affectionately. "I'll soon be back, my friend."

Reluctantly, he let her go.

She threaded her way between the huts and set out across open land. Beneath a canopy of cloud, the tall hills lay ahead of her, and to Godwin she seemed too small and vulnerable to confront such weighty eminence, but he had to respect her wishes.

Godwin looked at Trystin. He saw no reason to put into words the feelings that both of them shared. "I'm going for a walk," he said flatly.

Trystin merely nodded and withdrew inside the hut.

"And you, " Godwin said to the pony, as he inspected the pile of clothes at his feet, "stay here and don't wander off."

Grimalkin snorted loudly. "Everyone's going their separate ways. What kind of a quest is that?"

⋆ ⋆ ⋆

Chapter Thirty-Two

Godwin walked parallel with the river, a bundle of clean clothes under his arm. The air was growing warmer, more humid, and the water beckoned invitingly.

He was still within the village boundary when laughter stopped him in his tracks. It sounded oddly out of place in such a dismal setting. He looked around for the source of the noise, convinced that he had imagined it, then two tiny children came into view and raced across the open ground where Godwin stood transfixed. They were barefoot and dressed in shabby tunics, but their hair flew out behind them, as though rejoicing at freedom, and happiness sparkled in their eyes. Godwin was mesmerised by the sight. He hadn't expected children in such sad and solemn surroundings.

The children flew past him like cherubs. The girl had a small, wicker basket, from which she scattered daisies, and the boy flailed a battered, wooden sword at invisible enemies. Neither of them seemed to notice the stranger, lost as they were in their own private worlds. And then they had vanished among the huts.

For a long time after they had gone, Godwin stood and stared, gripped by a feeling of timelessness, and something began to edge its way to the forefront of his mind. He frowned in concentration, but he couldn't capture it. Then his heart sank into an abyss of sorrow, as the image of his daughters emerged like a guilty secret. A sensation like panic churned in his guts and forced him back into motion, as though he meant to outrun his thoughts.

But they scuttled behind him and caught him up.

What kind of a father would abandon his children and go off seeking adventure?

When he thought of his daughters, his throat constricted and he felt that he would choke on his shame and he stopped once more, brought to a halt by the gravity of his crime. If Godwin had learnt anything from the Saxons it was the importance of kin and the duty one had to one's family. His daughters were his responsibility. They depended upon him. And they were so far away.

What on earth was he doing here?

He knew if he persisted with these thoughts that his heart would surely break, so he trudged on through the tall, coarse grass, leaving the huts behind, and lost himself in motion.

Head down, the clothes clamped under his arm, he almost blundered into the willows that formed a clump at the river's edge. Their delicate limbs, adorned with new leaves, drooped languidly over the shimmering water. He slid in among them, cast off his cloak, and sat on the sloping bank.

Thoughts re-emerged to trouble him, so he pushed them away and inspected the clothes. He had chosen a long-sleeved tunic, trousers that narrowed at the ankle, and both were tough linen dyed russet-brown. He laid his sword, sheath and knife beside him, then rose to his feet and unclasped his belt, dropping it on the grass. He threw off his stained and ragged clothes and ran to the water's edge. Then, as though seeking oblivion, he plunged into the river.

When he returned to the world of air, he was gasping and chilled to the bone. He shook the water from his hair and eyes and, cleansed of all his emotions, he clambered up the river bank and flopped onto his cloak.

He had to await Elgiva's return. Better to wait in this sanctum of trees than to spend the day listening to Trystin's bleating or Grimalkin's continual grousing.

For a time, he lay staring into space, enjoying his aloneness, while the warm air dried his skin, then he snatched up the trousers and put them on, knotting the cord at his waist. As his wet hair flopped across his eyes, he realised how unkempt he was and he walked towards the water's edge to look at himself on its surface. The quivering image that stared back at him appeared to resemble a scarecrow, with a mass of wet, untidy hair and many days growth of beard. He couldn't work out how long it had been since he had last seen his home, but at a rough guess it was nearly four weeks; long enough to transform him into something that looked like a poor, mad hermit who lived in the woods and terrified tiny Elflings. As he swept the annoyance of hair from his eyes, an idea sprang to his mind. He searched for his sword and drew it out.

"Your sharp edge is just what I need, Taranuil!"

He felt the sword hum at the sound of its name and its edge took on a trenchant gleam. Seizing a hank of wet hair in his hand, he sliced the blade across it, careful to avoid his fingers. But, strangely, the sword made no impression. Frowning, he made another attempt, but still it wouldn't cut his hair.

He stared at the weapon in puzzlement. Surely he wasn't mistaken? The edge of the sword looked impossibly keen, thin as a sliver of sea-shell. Gingerly, he ran his finger down the length of the blade. His finger told him that it was dull, as blunt as a rusted ploughshare. Was there something wrong with his vision?

"I don't understand!" he exclaimed aloud. "Damn it! I've awakened you! Why are you so dull?"

He stood up and walked to the nearest tree, drew back his arm and brought the weapon down upon a slanting branch. Taranuil gleefully cut through the bough and those beneath it, as though wood and air were the same, lacking any substance. So easily was this act performed that Godwin had to grab the trunk to stop his own momentum, or take his second bath of the day.

The severed branches fell away and half the willow flopped with a splash into the river below. Godwin watched the amputated limbs drift downstream with the current. His mind refused to grasp the sight and he scowled at the shining blade.

"By Frigg! Don't toy with me!"

Angrily, he gripped the blade and closed his fingers round it. He squeezed, but felt no sharpness. He clenched his fingers tighter, until the pressure hurt him, but, when he uncurled his hand again, he could see it was unmarked.

He sat down heavily on his cloak and stared at the silent river. He badly needed an explanation, but there was none to be had. He looked at the sword, at its razor-sharp edge, and confusion gave way to fear. Quickly, he flung the weapon aside, as though it were something loathsome.

The sword hummed pleadingly in the grass, but he refused to listen.

Then he heard movement through the trees. He snatched up his knife and twisted round to confront the unknown threat. Angwen emerged from the willows, her long hair braided with pale-blue ribbons. She glowed like a flower in early spring, despite her shapeless, linen robe with its belt of plaited rope.

Embarrassed by his startled expression, she clasped her hands at her throat. "Forgive me," she ventured uncertainly. "One should know better than to creep up on a warrior."

Godwin dropped his knife on the grass and pulled himself together. "Good morning, Lady Angwen."

She moved to his side, smiled and sat down. "The sky is full of rain," she observed.

"Yes, indeed," he said.

Her blue eyes drifted across the river. "I spoke with Morvyth earlier. She would like to meet you today."

Godwin tried to sound casual and the effort it took surprised him. "How is she, Lady Angwen?"

Lowering her gaze, Angwen stared at her hands that were folded in her lap, and when she spoke her voice betrayed the fear she tried to keep in check. "Her time diminishes swiftly. She wanders in strange realms. Yet sometimes she speaks and sees so clearly … but it is often thus with the dying. For now, thank God, she sleeps."

Godwin wanted to sympathise, but could think of nothing to say. Whatever he did say was sure to sound trite. Angwen was clearly a person well acquainted with death and the loss of her kin. Embarrassed by his own awkwardness, he waited for her to continue.

Suddenly Angwen raised her hands and pulled the ribbons from her hair and the gleaming, dark-red tresses flowed like a river of polished bronze. She sighed, as though she had been freed from some unbearable constraint.

Godwin swallowed hard.

"My Aunt is so good, so full of wisdom," Angwen continued despondently. "How shall I cope, when she dies? We have lost too many elders and have no-one to guide us. How shall I lead these unhappy people? I have no husband to help me." She raised her beautiful, lucid eyes and turned their gaze upon him.

Unsettled by her scrutiny, he quickly looked away, drew up his knees and hugged them to his chest.

"There is no-one eligible for my hand and even if the Elf-King permitted us to leave, I do not know where I would search for others of our race. Aled is not fit to lead. It pains me to admit it, but he is too impetuous and has no common sense. And I am the tanist. As eldest child of Gwion, this burden must be mine." A worried frown disturbed her brow. "Our village cannot last much longer. We are diminishing, dying … like our chief." Then she looked up with regret, placed her hand on his arm. "But I am thoughtless, Godwin. At least I have a tribe. I know where I belong, but you…"

Godwin smiled inwardly; he knew where this conversation was heading. "My people must still live somewhere, Lady, but where they are I'll never know. And perhaps it's better I don't. I've been taught the Saxon ways and I think I'm too old to learn new ones."

"Was life hard for you with the Saxons?" she asked. "Being apart from your own people must have made you sad at times."

"Only when I thought about it," he replied, half-seriously. Pictures swam up from the mirk of his memory of the time when he and Elgiva first met and her absence was like the loss of a limb.

"I should like to hear about it."

Angwen waited for his answer, but Godwin shrugged dismissively. "Another time, perhaps."

"Of course," she said. "Forgive my curiosity, but we are isolated here. News from the outside world is all the more valued for its rarity. I did not intend to pry." She paused and lowered her eyes dejectedly. "Sometimes I find myself wondering if there really *IS* an outside world."

"There is," he said, "but that doesn't mean it's something worth talking about."

An awkward silence stretched between them.

"Do not judge our race by what you see in this mean valley," said Angwen, at length. "My father told me how it used to be. How proud we were, how fearless, with our ponies and our chariots, going into battle."

Godwin hid his sense of relief. Tearing about in a horse-drawn conveyance didn't sound very appealing and he was glad to have missed the experience.

"What will you do, my friend?" she asked.

"Do?" He looked at her quizzically.

"When you have helped your elvish friend. If you succeed … what then? Elves and Men cannot live together and surely you would not return to the Saxons?"

But he had to. Rowena … the children…

He opened his mouth, determined to tell her the reason why he must go back, but somehow the words wouldn't come. Gazing into her lucid eyes, eyes so like his own, he knew he needed his own kind, knew he needed her…

But the image of Rowena refused to be suppressed and he stood up, abruptly, shakily. All he wanted to do was escape. To escape from Angwen, from everyone, from all their demands and needs.

Quickly, Angwen got to her feet. "Dear God, I have offended you?"

"No!" He glanced about him wildly. No. He had offended himself. He had been false to himself.

There were too many vows to be kept. He had a duty to his family. He had pledged to protect Elgiva. And, for himself, he had promised freedom. Why were there so many choices, when once he had none at all?

He drew a deep breath to steady himself. No, he mustn't be false to Angwen. Perhaps he had used Rowena to mitigate his loneliness, to make himself feel secure and accepted. Perhaps he had used Elgiva to escape from the very security Rowena had provided and to satisfy his need for excitement. Yet he loved them both, or so he believed.

He wished that he had gone with Elgiva. He should have ignored her protests. He had made a vow to protect her and he should have stuck to it.

But he knew to his shame that, at this moment, he would rather be with Angwen than scrambling up a hill. His motives were horribly shallow: no wonder he hated himself.

If I was a true Briton, he thought, I'd fall on my sword. If it would let me.

No, he mustn't use Angwen. He mustn't betray his own people. And she alone had defended him against the hostility of the tribe. He decided to tell her about Rowena, but Angwen suddenly grasped his arm and looked into his eyes.

"In you I see loss and loneliness."

Please don't, he begged her silently. You sound just like Elgiva.

"I, too, am lost and lonely," she said. "Forgive me, if I seem over-bold, but it is the custom of our race to speak what is in their hearts."

He looked at her. I have no heart.

"I feel there is a bond between us," she said.

The touch of her hand on his bare skin and the glow of affection in her soft eyes were altogether too much. He grabbed her waist and pulled her towards him and kissed her on the mouth. She threw her arms about his neck and returned the kiss with hungry lips.

He held her away from him, appalled by her need, and looked into her eyes.

Oh, Grim! I could die for you! he thought. A wave of love washed over him and he reached up to stroke her hair.

"I knew," breathed Angwen, "one day, I knew, if I had faith, there would be someone ... someone special ... for me."

You deserve much better than me, he thought bitterly, and he was about to tell her so, but something stopped his voice. For a moment he saw another face superimposed upon hers, but it vanished before he could tell who it was, yet he found it profoundly disturbing.

Angwen smiled and clasped his hand and pulled him down to the grass. They sat and watched the sun-dappled water lapping against the river- bank and she leaned her body against him. "Could you find it in your heart to love someone like me?" she asked, a tremor in her voice.

Who couldn't? he thought. He looked at her sheepishly. "Angwen, you're very beautiful and, well, if things were different, I'd stay by your side forever, but..."

"You are my warrior," she broke in.

"I'm nothing of the sort!" he said.

"But I can see!" she insisted. "You are a true son of our race!"

He wanted to deny this, but her trusting gaze stifled his protest. In her eyes he could do no wrong.

You don't even know me! he wanted to shout. We wouldn't even be able to talk, if not for an Elven spell!

Angwen knew nothing of his past, his self-doubt and his cowardice. All she knew was that he was a man who travelled with Elves, a man who braved hardship and danger, apparently because he wanted to. She seemed to take his valour for granted, because he carried a sword and was born of a race of warriors. She also assumed that, because he was older, he was wiser, too. He was something exciting and new to her, a welcome change from the dull routine, a mature man she could lean upon after so many years of supporting others. She didn't see him as he was, only the ideal that he embodied; the escape he seemed to offer.

He was to Angwen what Elgiva had been to him. How could he shatter her illusions, when she had little else?

For his part, she had stirred in him long-forgotten feelings; feelings that must have lain dormant since childhood. Perhaps with her encouragement, he might become the kind of man she believed he already was, might finally realise whatever potential the Saxons had denied him.

He held her protectively in his arms. The instant attraction between them was odd, but it seemed to go deeper than that. There was something strange about her, something indefinable that filled a need in him. Something lost had now been found – how else could he explain it? It was almost as if he had always known her.

He hugged her to his breast and kissed her forehead, his heart brimful with yearning for her; she made him feel complete. Then he gazed down into her eyes and had the sudden conviction that even their souls were united in a tender embrace.

At that moment someone called him from the distance and Godwin heard his name, but it took some time for him to give the summons his full attention. It was Trystin and the urgency of his plea demanded an answer. As he pulled away from Angwen, he felt a great abyss yawn between them and it sent a shiver down his spine.

"By Frigg!" he cried. "What now?"

"Your friend sounds very distressed," she said.

He grimaced. "That's nothing new." He got to his feet and pulled on his tunic. "Trystin, over here!" He buckled his belt and then held out his hand to help Angwen to her feet. Gathering up his knife and cloak, he led her out of the trees.

Trystin stood on the river-bank, nervously chewing his nails.

"What is it?" demanded Godwin, controlling his anger as best he could.

"Come back to the village, Master Godwin! You must … Grimalkin … she's … there's trouble!" So saying, the Elfling took to his heels and, with a sigh of infuriation, Godwin made to follow him, still holding Angwen's hand.

Then he heard a voice in his mind and it made him pull up sharply.

Master, don't leave me!

Oh, Frigg! The sword! "Angwen, please go on ahead. I must go back and fetch my sword." He smiled to dispel her anxiety. "Don't worry, I won't be long." He squeezed her hand reassuringly, then he dived back into the trees.

Curse that wretched animal! Her timing was exquisite.

* * *

As Godwin neared the village, he heard Grimalkin calling him and her neighs were both urgent and angry. Soon he saw her, kicking and bucking, surrounded by a ring of people. A length of rope dangled from her neck.

"Piss off, you turds!" she screamed at them, "or my hooves will churn your guts!"

He thrust his way through the noisy crowd and stood before her, angry and breathless. "What in Frigg's name is going on?"

"Your beast ran off, so we brought her back," a middle-aged woman explained.

"It's that time of year," remarked an old man. "She must have got wind of the wild nags that live beyond the hills."

The villagers nodded knowingly.

Godwin cocked his fists on his hips and gave the pony a menacing glare. "Damn you," he muttered under his breath. "You were left in charge of the Stone!"

"We all need to sow a few wild oats," retorted Grimalkin, tossing her head. "I saw her sneak off after you."

Godwin was speechless with rage.

The old man scratched his scanty beard and shook his head at Godwin. "She's a stubborn brute. A killer. Never seen a more mettlesome beast."

The villagers muttered agreement.

"You'll have to give her the stick," said the woman, offering her staff for the purpose. "Show her who's the master."

Heads nodded knowingly in the crowd.

"The first dog as takes a stick to me gets his nose bitten off!" cried Grimalkin.

"Shut up!" hissed Godwin. "You've caused enough trouble."

"Listen, Brit," she whinnied, "you only know their side of it. The bastards wanted to eat me!"

"Don't give me that. You're full of tricks."

"My withers are unwrung!"

"Seeing as she's unmanageable, stranger, would you care to sell her?" The old man looked at him hopefully.

Godwin turned to confront him. "Sell her?"

"I've nothing much to barter with, just a couple of trinkets, but my family are starving, you see."

"She'd feed a great many of us!" cried another man in the crowd.

"Told you," snickered Grimalkin.

Godwin looked round at the hungry eyes and saw the lean faces taut with desire; some even licked their lips. A shudder ran down his spine. "No, I'm sorry, I can't. She's too useful."

Then Ceara hobbled towards him, waving her staff in the air. "You would see us starve, then, stranger? The Saxons taught you well!"

Torn between Godwin and her people, Angwen could bear it no longer. "Ceara, please, the pony is his, and this man is our guest!"

Ceara's lip curled disdainfully. "Did we send him an invitation?"

"You can't make me sell her!" Godwin exclaimed. He placed his hand on Grimalkin's neck in a gesture of ownership. "Don't panic," he whispered. "I'll protect you."

"And who'll protect YOU?" she whinnied. "Look at 'em. They're getting nasty!"

"You have no charity, stranger," Ceara said with a sneer of contempt. "You have eaten our food, which we cannot spare, and what need have you for a pack-horse? Your covetousness is a sin."

"Why don't you hunt, or grow some crops?" Godwin challenged her. "Are you so lazy you'd steal a man's transport rather than work for your food?"

"Heathen!" spat Ceara. "Elf-lover!"

He folded his arms and thrust out his chin. "Insult me all you please," he said. "You shall not have my pony."

Angwen touched Ceara on the arm. "It is not fitting that we should fight," she reminded her. "And if we abandon our courtesy, then we become barbarians." The two women looked at each other. Respectfully, Angwen inclined her head and, after a moment's consideration, Ceara smiled at her. "Whoever harms this animal will answer to me," said Angwen. "Now, back to your work all of you."

Slowly and with much muttering, the villagers dispersed and Angwen turned to Godwin, her hands spread out in apology. "Forgive them, Godwin," she said, "but they are broken and dispirited. They were not always so callous."

"I understand," he said.

"I think you had better tie up your beast. I wonder that this was not done before."

"I trusted her too well."

He glared at Grimalkin, but her large, brown eyes regarded him with indifference, as always totally unaccepting of any blame or imputation. He moved to her side and tugged at the pack, pretending to check that it was still in place, but really to reassure himself that the Lorestone was safe and undamaged.

Then the woman who had served him breakfast came walking towards them and stopped before Angwen. She made a slight curtsy and muttered something that Godwin couldn't hear.

"Thank you, Angharad," said Angwen. The woman trudged back to her duties. "Morvyth has asked to see you now," Angwen announced and she held out her hand. "Let us first secure your animal, then I will take you to my Aunt's dwelling."

Taking her hand, Godwin followed her, and, when they reached the meagre hut, they found Trystin hiding behind the door. Frightened by the angry crowd, he had run indoors to prevent himself from witnessing Grimalkin's fate. Seeing Godwin, he sighed with relief and threw his arms about him.

"Go and fetch a bale of hay to keep her out of mischief," said Godwin, as he pried himself from the Elf's tight embrace.

He tethered Grimalkin and gave her a scolding, though he knew that he was wasting his breath, then he followed Angwen across the village to the home of the dying Chief.

* * *

Chapter Thirty-Three

Inside the dwelling was a sunken room, a low fire hissing in the hearth. There were shelves laden with heirlooms and ornaments and from the rafters hung bunches of herbs, adding their sweetness to the air. The vague shapes of benches and chests squatted in the shadows.

Godwin stood beside the door while Angwen stepped softly across the room and stopped beside the raised bed on which her aunt was lying.

"Aunt Morvyth," she said gently, "the stranger, Godwin, is here to see you."

A frail hand fluttered on the coverlet, beckoning Godwin to approach. Angwen drew up a three-legged stool and stood it beside the bed.

"Greetings to you, Lady," said Godwin.

"And to you, traveller," said the old woman. "Will you sit awhile?"

Her voice, though feeble with sickness, had a warm, maternal quality and Godwin felt at ease in her presence. Smiling, he lowered himself onto the stool.

"Some light, Angwen," croaked the old woman, "then you may leave us, my dear."

"Yes, Aunt."

Angwen lit two torches in the wall beside the bed, kissed her aunt on the brow, and tiptoed out of the room. Now that Godwin could see her more clearly, he saw how ill the old woman was. Her skin was wrinkled, sallow with illness, and her lips were drooping and slack.

Upon the pillow was a cloud of soft hair, as white as virgin snow.

She studied him closely, with smiling, blue eyes; they gleamed like defiance in her dry, pale face. “I forget your name, stranger,” she murmured.

“My name is Godwin, Lady.”

“Well, Godwin, I am pleased to meet you. Angwen has told me some of your tale, but, forgive me, my memory cannot be trusted, and I go soon to meet my maker.” The candour of her statement caught Godwin off guard and she smiled at his discomfiture. “Be of good cheer, young man. I do not worry, nor should you. Now, it would please me to hear you talk. I do not lack for visitors, but they tell me nothing new.”

Godwin thought for a moment, wondering where to begin. “Angwen told you I was brought up by Saxons?” Morvyth nodded fractionally. “I was very young,” he went on, “when I was taken in a raid, and my sister … they killed my sister. I don’t know what became of my parents, nor do I know what tribe I’m from.” He paused, as the old pain came to the surface. Odd that it still had the power to hurt him, after so many years, he thought. “I dream of it still,” he continued, “though I don’t remember all of it. I’ve always hoped … well … I’ve longed to meet others of my race.” He looked away, avoiding her gaze.

“Ah, be not sad, my son. Curiosity is natural and such ordeals as yours were all too frequent once. I lost my husband, Verica, and Gwion, my brother, fared even worse. We are no strangers to loss, but life must go on for the sake of the tribe. We may be a persecuted race, but we are not defeated yet. I believe we will rise again.”

"But, Morvyth, somehow I feel … cheated. I'm ignorant of my people, their customs, their beliefs, and there's an empty place inside me…" He stopped himself. He hadn't intended to talk this way, but there was something about this woman that made him want to unburden himself, and she seemed quite happy to listen.

"I can tell you nothing of other tribes, only the history of ours."

"I'd like to hear it, Lady."

"And I should like to tell it." Morvyth chuckled softly. "My memories of the past are sharp and elders love to tell tales, do they not? But do not worry, I hope to be brief." Her thin lips curled with humour and Godwin felt himself smiling, too.

For a moment she paused and gathered her thoughts.

"We are of the Gododdin tribe – the Votadini, as the Romans called us. A race of proud warriors, of whom we here are surely the most unworthy, the lost ones who strayed too far from home." She shook her old head sadly. "Cunedda, our chief, brought us down from the northlands and in those days, many long years ago, our people were free and they prospered. My father was among their number, a tender of horses who aspired to live as a warrior among warriors, though he was merely a stripling who had barely seen ten summers. Yet he attained his heart's desire, and, in his thirtieth year, he fathered Gwion, my brother, the heir to the settlement our father had founded. Eftsoons, I followed, and 'tis strange to think that this worn out husk before you was once a carefree child." Morvyth smiled at her memories, recalling the long-dead days of her youth. Presently, she continued.

"At that time our race was widespread and we ourselves lived further east. The Romans had abandoned this land, but they left us their houses, their towns and roads and we were wealthy and strong. We were the masters then. But all too soon the invaders came. The Angles, Jutes and Saxons. Sea-wolves and marauders. They were warlike, wild and savage and hungry for our land. Many of our kind fled west and we were forced to follow, leaving our homesteads behind. But the Saxons could not be stopped. How it pained us to hear that the High-King himself had made a treaty with the invaders! We knew they were treacherous and were not surprised when they broke the pact and laid waste the land, destroying the towns and villas. There was no hope or help for us and the future promised us nothing but conflict. In one such battle my father was slain and Gwion became our chief. Ah, such a man, my brother! So tall and straight and fierce! No finer warrior ever lived!"

She turned to Godwin and a glow of pride glimmered in her eyes. "He married late in life, you know. Young, she was, and beautiful. Ethne was her name. She gave him a son and then a daughter. Ah, those two! I loved them. As dear to me as if they were my own. I can see them now. They were tiny chits, when their father became our chief. And they were always together." Her eyes grew misty with sorrow. "Alas, poor Verica never knew the joys of fatherhood, for I have always been barren."

Godwin reached out and laid his hand upon the old woman's arm, but she didn't seem to notice his attempt at consolation.

"If I recall aright," she went on, "it was in the year of 478 that a party of Saxons fell upon us. A terrible day … a most terrible day!" She closed her eyelids tightly against the images that still disturbed her. "Gwion lost not only the children he adored, but his good and brave wife, Ethne. And I … I lost my Verica. The raiders stole what they could and burned our homes and then they went, leaving us ruined and bereft. Gwion and I sought solace together and wept for those we had lost … Many long, long nights of grief. And for a time our will to live deserted us." She swallowed painfully and licked her lips.

"But still the tribe remained. We could not forsake our people and they, like us, had kin to mourn. So, we decided to retreat further north and Gwion threw off his sorrow, for he was a dutiful man and the plight of his people sustained him. He knew that without his leadership, they would be lost. And he seemed to recover his youth – indeed, he took a second wife. Her name was Caronwen – half his age and the temper of a wild cat! But she was good-hearted and he loved her. She bore him Angwen and, later, Aled, and it seemed that God had rewarded us for what we had endured and Gwion had given back to him the son and daughter he had lost."

"For some years, all went well, and our tribe moved on, as tribes must do, and we made our settlement here. Foolishly, perhaps, we had come too far from others of our race, but in those days there were fortified towns, well-tended roads, and we saw many travellers. We did not lose touch with the ways of the world and we were safe from the Saxon menace. But then there came a great famine and a pestilence that covered the land and took so many from us. Caronwen … she was one who succumbed, and Gwion was left a lonely, old man, trying to hold his tribe together- the remnants of it, at least- while his own grief seemed too much to bear." She motioned to a table beside the bed. "Some water, if you please," she croaked.

Godwin lifted an earthenware jug and poured some water into a beaker, then, raising Morvyth's head from the pillow, he helped her to drink.

"Thank you, young man." She lay back on the pillow, breathing hard, and her thoughts seemed to wander for a while, but, at length, her blue eyes flitted to his.

"Not long after we came to this place, we discovered that there were Elves nearby, but our race and theirs have ever been friends and we had no cause to fear them. They left us undisturbed. About two years ago, I think, our people rallied and there was a great battle. The barbarians were defeated. Word was brought by a kindly Elf, or we would never have known of it. This victory brought us peace, but this peace does not touch us here, for we live apart from the outside world, and the Elves, as I said, had been our friends, but, alas, a new king ascended the throne."

"Vieldrin," muttered Godwin.

"I believe that is his name. He took our cattle and horses, because we refused to acknowledge him sole master of these lands and, rather than destroy us, he placed an enchantment upon our village. Should any try to leave this place, it compels us to turn back … indeed, I fear that if we could defy this spell, the result would be certain death. So, Godwin, we are trapped here and time has stopped for us. The price of our freedom is to worship Vieldrin as our lord and master, but that we can never do, for God is our only master. But this Elf-king will not kill us. He requires submission first and he knows that our race scorn death. It has no meaning for us save to make us part of the next, great plane of existence. We would be one with Our Lord. And Vieldrin, he is insane. An agent of the Devil."

"Morvyth, did Angwen tell you that my companions are Elves?" Godwin asked her cautiously, unsure of her reaction.

Morvyth nodded slowly. "They are good Elves, she said."

"And one is very powerful. Our intention is to destroy Vieldrin. If he can be slain, we will do it."

"My son, such a hazardous task! And we cannot help you, for we are helpless ourselves! Whatever we had of value was taken from us by force, by the Saxons, the plague and the elvish king." Her eyes were mottled mirrors of sadness and she shook her head in dismay. "All I can give you are my prayers and my blessing, such as it is. God guard you in your quest."

"This god you worship," ventured Godwin, "I have no knowledge of him. Aled said I was a … heathen?"

Morvyth frowned at this. "Aled has no manners. No blame attaches to you, my son. Each man must follow his heart."

"The Saxons have many gods, Lady Morvyth, and I have believed in them, but…" Godwin thought of the Hill-Shrine and he knew that since Faine had touched his heart, Father Woden had lost all claim to his soul.

"Godwin," said Morvyth softly, "when our people abandoned the old religion, some say that we lost our will, our oneness with the Earth. I cannot say, but I know that God helps me. He gives me comfort and strength. We all seek different things in life. We must all tread different paths. Are the Saxon beliefs too shallow for you? I would not presume to advise you. Faith and belief are private things, which you must discover for yourself."

Her hand sought his upon the coverlet and squeezed it reassuringly and for a while they sat in silence, both buried in their thoughts. Godwin feared that he would tire the old woman and wondered if he should leave, but her wise, calm presence filled him with peace and he was loath to go. At length, he needed to talk.

"It's strange the things I remember," he said. "When the Saxons took me from my tribe, my sister and I were outside the village. I think we were sitting under a tree and we'd been picking blackberries … we had a basketful." He didn't notice Morvyth lift her eyebrows at these words. "I was carried away by a tall, blond man and the basket was scattered on the grass. And there were some wooden toys, I think. It all seems part of a single picture, as though everything happened at once. I see it more clearly in dreams, but also I see … my sister…" He swallowed and turned his head away, as the old pain tore his heart.

Suddenly Morvyth clutched at his sleeve and her eyes were wide and staring. "Blackberries, you say?"

He wondered at her reaction, but he felt that he should continue. "Why … yes. Apart from those cruel memories, this is all I have of my past."

He carefully drew his sword from its sheath and held it up before him and the smooth steel gleamed in the torchlight. Morvyth raised herself stiffly, propped herself on one elbow, and there was a wildness in her eyes which filled him with alarm.

"Please, Morvyth, I'm sorry! … Don't be afraid!"

"No, let me see it! Let me see!"

He lay the sword on the coverlet and she touched the hilt with fingers that quivered uncontrollably.

"Is it you?" she gasped. "After all these years? Brave blade, you have been true to your master!" She turned her gaze upon him and her eyes were awash with tears. Her frail body shook with emotion. "Oh, God be praised! Indeed … we are saved!"

Godwin jumped to his feet, baffled and shocked by her flow of words. "Morvyth, what is it? What's wrong?"

She gazed at him, as though stupefied, and her sallow skin had a hectic flush. "Nothing … nothing is wrong, my son! No … Godwin … it is wonderful!" Then Morvyth fell back on the bed, torn between weeping and laughing.

"Be calm, Lady Morvyth. I'll fetch your niece."

Morvyth grabbed him by the sleeve. "No stay, my son!" she begged, between sobs. "Sit down … please! You must not leave me … not a second time!"

Frowning, Godwin hesitated, then he complied with her plea. She held out her hands and he took them in his and her agitation slowly waned, her breathing returned to normal. She stared at him fixedly all the while and tears ran down her cheeks.

"Bear with me, Godwin. Do not be alarmed, for I have another tale to tell and, when I have told it, I am sure to die happy!"

She released his hands and took a long breath, while Godwin watched her, confused and uncertain, impatience gnawing at his guts. He tried to keep still and hugged his chest tightly, seeking to hold down the sense of panic that told him he was going to hear something astounding: something unbearable.

"Many years ago," said Morvyth, "while our father was still alive, Gwion went out one day alone, searching the land for allies. He travelled west and found a great forest lying beyond the hills. Suddenly he heard the cries of a child in distress and he urged his pony in her direction. He found a little Elf-child who had fallen into a ditch and broken her tiny foot, poor babe. She was fearful of the warlord, but he soothed her and calmed her, then he bound her injured foot. The little Elf was afraid to go home, as she feared she would be scolded for wandering off on her own, so Gwion lifted her onto his pony and offered to take her there and ask her elders to be lenient."

"He entered the dark forest and the keen-eyed Elves soon spotted him. A party came out to meet him with the Elf-king's beautiful wife at their head. Gwion asked pardon for trespassing and asked that the child be spared from punishment, for she was so tiny and had been hurt. Admiring his courage and compassion, the Elf-queen thanked him for what he had done and promised that she would send him a gift to repay him for all his trouble. For indeed, you see, the child he had rescued was the Elf-queen's very own daughter. The lady asked him to dine with her, but Ethne was very near her time and Gwion was anxious to hasten home. She asked him the whereabouts of his tribe and promised the gift would be sent to him there, then she and her retinue, all white and gold, galloped away on their beautiful horses."

"So, Gwion returned to his Ethne, and two days after his homecoming their son, Aidan, was born. The babe was brought out for us all to admire and we celebrated and danced till dusk. Much wine and ale was drunk that day!" She paused and smiled, then beckoned him closer, as though she feared that her frailty would lessen the import of her words.

"Then the next evening, a stranger arrived. A handsome Elf in gold and white came riding into our village. The Elf would not dismount and said he would only speak to Gwion. When Gwion duly appeared, the Elf held out an object wrapped in gold-coloured cloth. He offered it to my brother. 'We know of your joy, my lord,' said the Elf, 'and my Lady, the Queen, has sent you this gift to reward you for your kindness. It is for your son and it will protect him always,' he said, 'and it is his alone, for by the magic employed in its making, it can never leave him, save by his express command. Likewise it was forged in such a way that it will never injure him, regardless of who wields it.'"

"So, Gwion thanked the Elf, but the messenger's errand was not yet complete," Morvyth went on, "and he said to Gwion, 'In accordance with custom it has a name peculiar to itself by which its magic is released. Released for as long as is necessary to serve the one who wields it.'"

"Then the messenger beckoned Gwion closer and he leaned from his horse and whispered, so that no-one else should hear. Then he sat upright and said, 'My Lady the Queen also undertakes to welcome your son as her own, should he ever lack for home, help or kin. He need only ask for her protection and it shall then be his.'"

"The Elf then looked at him sadly," said Morvyth. "Was this a foreknowledge, perchance? Well, Gwion did not heed it. He asked the Elf to thank his queen and they bowed towards each other and the Elf rode off, while we stood watching in wonder."

Morvyth paused awhile, as if reliving a moment of magic, then she turned her attention to Godwin. "Gwion unwrapped the Elf-queen's gift and we gathered round to see it, and from the cloth he took a fine sword. A sword with silver cross-guards and strange runes on the hilt. An Elf-sword, Godwin … Yours!"

The very foundations of Godwin's being seemed to crumble inside him. A weird, aching numbness filled his body, as though his organs had been sucked out and all that was left was an empty shell. The room seemed to sway around him and he leaned against the bed, digging his fingers into the coverlet. His mouth fell open uselessly and formed a silent 'no'.

"Aidan, you have returned!" cried Morvyth. "Gwion knew you would!" The old woman fell to fresh weeping. "Ah, had you but reached us sooner, you would have heard these things from your sire! A cruel, cruel destiny to keep flesh and blood apart for so long, then cheat them at the last!"

Godwin was sure that his anger would choke him. Hot tears scorched the backs of his eyes.

"Gwion knew!" sobbed Morvyth. "He knew you would return to us! He prayed … and God has answered him! Oh, Aidan, dear nephew, even when he lay dying, his mind was as sharp as ever and he never forgot his first-born son! His last words were of you. He called to you on his death-bed. There were many things … many things …you father wanted to tell you. The most important of all, dear Aidan … how much your father loved you!"

Godwin tried to get to his feet, tried to escape from this torture, but she gripped his arm and held him fast with a strength that belied her frailty. Her eyes were burning like beams of anguish and they scalded his heart with their intensity.

"He intended to tell you about the sword, when you were man enough to use it. Oh, Aidan, alas that it should be me..." Her voice trailed away in distress. "Ah, Gwion! So brave, so fearless, a champion of our race. A warrior leading warriors!" Her eyes flashed wildly about the room, as though it thronged with the shades of the dead.

Please, don't shame me with *THAT*, thought Godwin.

"And you, his son, a warrior, will lead us out of darkness!"

"No ... I can't!" he protested.

"Yes, yes! This sword has power!" she cried. "Can you not feel it, Aidan? It is a power for good. For good! This is the sword you carried, when they took you away from us. I remember ... I remember only too well! They could not take it from you ... it would not let them take it! Forged never to leave you, it exerted its power over them. To take the sword away from you, they would have had to take your life..."

"No!" he protested desperately. "I was never so brave ... and they were never so cruel! And they did ... they DID take my life, don't you see?" The tears rolled freely down his face and he struggled in her grasp. "Morvyth, by Frigg! Please ... let me go!"

"You defend them," she gasped, "but perhaps you are right. Your father, despite his grief at your loss, told me that all things have a purpose, so there might be a purpose in your abduction. It was an old custom among our race to foster our children with others. In this way, we thought to enlarge their minds, teach them things we could not, to widen their skills and experience. Perhaps you have learned many things with the Saxons?"

He shook his head in despair.

"Now you will lead us, Aidan!" she cried.

"No, Lady Morvyth, I can't."

She didn't hear him; wouldn't hear him. "Here ... take this." She fumbled to unclasp a thin chain at her neck. It carried a ring of silver on which was a tiny red dragon, fashioned from chips of garnet. Unable to undo the fastening, she broke the chain, drawing blood from her flesh. She thrust it into his hand. "This is the symbol of our race. It was your father's ring. Wear it, Aidan. Put it on!"

He took the ring with a shaking hand and Morvyth lay back upon the pillow with a sigh of spent emotion. For a moment, contentment softened her gaze, but then she frowned with concern.

"But, Aidan ... the sword! Without its name it cannot be awakened ... and I do not know it! I do not know it!" Her eyes flashed panic at him. "Only Gwion knew its name ... and he took it to the grave!"

Godwin returned the sword to its scabbard. "Morvyth, listen, I know the name."

She gaped at him incredulously.

"I know it, Morvyth. Be at peace."

Tormented by infirmity, Morvyth sobbed and moaned and her body was seized by spasms. Godwin placed his hands on her shoulders, trying to calm her down.

"Gwion!" she cried out, "Brother! Your son has returned! Do you see...?"

"Morvyth, you should rest."

"These aching jewels fear to rest. They must have their fill of you, my Aidan ... Home at last!" She sobbed, as though her heart would break. "And now … at least … I can die happy. Angwen! Angwen!"

Her eyes became glazed and awareness of Godwin seemed to fade from her mind. He stepped back, shaking with the shock of what had been revealed, and then a sudden realisation hit him like a bludgeon.

Angwen!

He made for the door and flung it open. A rush of daylight dazzled him and some moments passed before he saw that someone was at his side.

"Godwin, what's wrong?"

His sister reached out and touched his arm.

"She … she needs you," he croaked.

He blundered past her and ran through the village to the hut where Grimalkin stood tethered. She lifted her ungainly head, tufts of hay jutting from her mouth. He had no intention of giving her any opportunity to vent her spleen, so he hid himself behind the hut and sank brokenly to his knees.

So, these were his people, the once proud Gododdin! And Gwion … had been his father! If only he'd reached here sooner. Just one short week in a lifetime of loss … before he found the Lorestone. His father had called to him on his death-bed. He alone had occupied his father's last thoughts on Earth. But Godwin would never hear from his lips how much his father loved him.

He hugged his chest, his aching heart. This couldn't be happening, could it? Could destiny really be so cruel? Had all his dreams been leading to this? His people … head-hunters. His sister, his uncle, and, worse, his own mother, murdered by Othere's men. Perhaps by Othere himself. Taranuil, an Elf-sword. And Angwen …

His father had been a warrior, had led men into battle. He had called to his son … and his son was a slave and a coward. His son was a man who deserted his children, a man who felt lust for his own father's daughter.

He had to take a very deep breath to quell a rush of nausea, then he clambered slowly to his feet and began to stagger away, supporting himself on the wall of the hut. He needed some dark and secret place in which to hide his anguish, but as he rounded the corner of the hut, a large shape blocked his path.

"Gall and wormwood, Brit!" it said. "What did that old hag do to you?"

He gave the pony an outraged look. "By Frigg, leave me alone!" he cried. "I don't need you … Not now!" He put his hands on her flank and pushed. "Damn you, get out of the way!"

"Not till you tell me what's wrong," she snickered.

"Grim take you!" He leant against her body and drew a shuddering breath.

"It seems these scum have offended you."

He glared at her in amazement. "You dare to insult my race!"

"How often have you insulted mine and then thought nothing of it?" she said.

"You don't understand," he protested thickly.

"Then make me," she persisted.

"Grimalkin, these people … they're MY people! The tribe I was taken from by the Saxons!"

"Ah." She nodded sagely.

"It's taken me over a score of years to find out who I am."

"Cabbage hearts! Are you really that old?"

He intended to rail at her, even strike her, but in her eyes was a gentle humour that he had never seen there before. Was she actually trying to cheer him up? He relaxed a little and steadied himself. Then he looked at her sheepishly. "To be fair I should thank you," he said, "for that rumpus you caused earlier."

"Really, Brit? Why's that?"

"You stopped me from making a dreadful mistake. I was … I was about to … I was falling in love with … my sister." The confession stung his throat.

"That's bad, is it?" she asked.

"Grimalkin, in the name of Frigg…!"

"Sorry, Brit. Different standards, you know."

He tried to relinquish Grimalkin's support, but he seemed to be trembling all over. The pressure of anger and sorrow and grief was threatening to tear him in pieces.

The pony's large head shook from side to side. "You're having a rotten time, aren't you? Wonder how our Elf-queen's doing?"

Elgiva! The thought of her deepened his shame. "Oh, Frigg! I forgot all about her!"

"Hardly surprising," said Grimalkin. "She'll be all right, though. She's got magic."

Godwin grimaced bitterly. "Oddly, so have I," he said. "My sword was made by Elves."

"All things return full circle, Brit."

He curled his fingers into her mane and tried to explain his heartache. "My father," he gasped, "my father, Gwion … he died a week ago and I … I was too late!"

She snorted sympathetically. "Poor orphan and slave," she said.

"Grimalkin … I can't bear it!" He threw his arms about her neck and surrendered to his tears.

"That's right, old son," she snickered softly, "have a good weep and let it all out. Do you good. Too much on your plate." She stood unmoving, supporting his weight until he regained his composure.

At length, he grew calm and mastered himself. "Where's Trystin?" he wondered bleakly.

"Little whingebag buggered off. Think he was bored," she said. "With all the excitement going on, no wonder he feels left out."

Turning, Godwin leaned on her shoulder, and with a great sigh of spent emotion, expelled all the air from his lungs. He felt like an old rag, hung out to dry. He scrubbed the tears from his eyes. "I thought I tied you up, you old nag?"

"There isn't a rope made that these old teeth can't handle."

"Next time, I'll use a chain." A half-smile touched his lips. "I think I'll go inside and rest."

"Good idea. It's starting to rain."

Godwin looked up at the blackening clouds. "Perhaps I should go and find Elgiva," he said with a worried frown. "She was far too weak to go on her own."

"Have a nap first," advised Grimalkin. "Then everything will be in its proper perspective."

Whatever that is, thought Godwin. He patted her neck, then made to leave.

"I say!" she called, and he glanced back at her. "What is it that was given to you, belongs to you alone, yet is used by your friends more than by you?"

He shrugged.

"Your name!" she said.

"You and your riddles!"

"So," she snickered, "what *IS* your name, Brit?"

He looked at her blankly, then turned away. "Godwin," he replied.

* * *

Chapter Thirty-Four

There was a hammering at the door and someone was calling an unfamiliar name and Godwin turned over on the bed and huddled against the wall, but try as he might to ignore it, the annoying noise persisted. He dragged himself angrily from his rest, stamped towards the door of the hut and quickly heaved it open. An old man stood on the threshold. Rain was filling the hood of his cloak and thunder cracked in the sombre sky behind him. Godwin stared vacantly, fuzzy with sleep.

"Aidan," said the old man, "there are things we need to discuss."

"Oh, for Frigg's sake, leave me alone," yawned Godwin.

"Aidan, this cannot wait!"

"My name is Godwin, old man."

The elder tutted with exasperation. "Godwin. Please … will you come?" he asked. "The elders are waiting to speak to you."

"What if I don't want to speak to *THEM*?" The elder sighed, but said nothing, and Godwin shrugged resignedly. "Oh, very well," he said.

The old man set off across the village and Godwin trudged morosely in his wake. Soon they had reached a large, wooden structure, open on all sides, like a barn that no-one had cared to complete. It sheltered a roaring fire and around the blaze the elders sat, cross-legged and solemn-faced, waiting in silence for them to arrive. A gathering breeze lifted sparks from the fire and they floated like motes of gold-dust above the elders' heads.

The old man took his place with his peers and beckoned Godwin to join them, but Godwin stood outside their circle, his arms folded intractably. Embarrassed by his aloofness, the elders regarded each other and it seemed that none was prepared to speak first.

While Godwin waited with growing impatience, the sound of hoof-beats plodded towards him and Grimalkin sidled up lazily. Moving into the shelter, she took her place beside him, rain steaming off her dun-coloured hide.

“Storm brewing,” she snorted, as another roll of thunder drummed across the sky.

“It looks that way,” muttered Godwin.

“That nag seems to follow you everywhere … brother,” said a soft, sly voice from the circle of elders. “Indeed, you seem to prefer a dumb beast to the company of your own people.”

Aled sat smirking in his direction and provocation flashed in his eyes, but Godwin merely frowned at him, refusing to be baited. Beside the youth sat Ceara, scowling and stiff with contempt.

“Aidan,” said one of the elders, “I am Llewellyn, the oldest here. I welcome you to your long-lost tribe on behalf of all of us.”

“Not all.”

Godwin’s remark sent a spasm of pique across Llewellyn’s face, but he carried on undaunted. “We have heard the news from Angwen. As eldest and strongest surviving child of our late chief Gwion, you will be chief, when Morvyth dies. We acknowledge this as your right.”

The elders waited for Godwin’s response, but he had no words; he was drained of them. Confused and giddy with hunger and sleep, he placed his hand on

Grimalkin's withers and tried to hold himself steady. At least, he would show them no weakness.

"You've all been against me from the start," he said at length, "and I don't see why I should talk to you."

"Circumstances have changed," said Llewellyn. "Morvyth believes that you are truly Aidan, and you bear the Elf-sword."

"That is no proof!" cried Aled. "He could have stolen it!"

"Peace, Aled!" said Llewellyn crossly. "That is unjust."

"Don't speak to me like that!" cried Aled. "I am the son of Gwion and I will say what I choose!"

"Aidan is also Gwion's son, but you treat him with disrespect," said Llewellyn. "No-one here has a greater claim to lead the tribe than he and you must acknowledge that."

"He knows nothing of our ways," sneered Aled. "He is a heathen, raised by barbarians – by the people who robbed us of our land, killed our warriors and raped our women! How is he acceptable? What right has he, after so many years, to claim the title of chief? Angwen knows the ways of our people and she has been prepared for leadership, but he is a stranger who travels with Elves. He knows nothing of how we have suffered…"

"Fit or no, his claim is just."

But I haven't made a claim, thought Godwin. I don't want any part of this.

"Are we not men of honour?" demanded Llewellyn crossly. "We loved and revered his father. Can we now be faithless to his memory? He would not rest easy in his grave, if we spurned his son and heir."

"I will have proof!" cried Aled.

Godwin didn't want to participate, yet he knew that he must before his future was decided for him. Llewellyn was about to speak, but Godwin interposed. "You are my tribe," he told them, "and I acknowledge the right of the elders to choose who will be chief. However," he pointed a finger at Aled, "I do not acknowledge *HIM*. He has no place among the wise and should be with the children of the tribe."

Aled jumped up, his face dark with rage. "I am Chief Gwion's son! I have a right to be here!"

"Insolent whelp!" snorted Grimalkin.

Indeed, thought Godwin, how on earth did I end up with a brother like that?

"Calm yourself!" admonished Llewellyn. "Aidan, you, too, are unjust. It is not meet that brothers should quarrel." The old man smiled placatingly. "It is clear that you share the same father. Gwion also had fire in his eyes. Now, let us sit down and talk peaceably."

With a grimace, Aled reseated himself, and Godwin reluctantly joined the elders sitting round the fire. He forced himself to concentrate, but he desperately wanted to be alone, to untangle the skein of his thoughts. And one thought dominated over the rest: what had become of Elgiva? Her absence gnawed at him like panic. He glanced across the village at the gathering dusk. Even if he searched for her now, he would lose her in the darkness.

"So, Aidan, you are the tanist," said Llewellyn, "and you will lead us when Morvyth dies."

"But is he warrior enough to lead us? We are sorely in need of strength," snarled Ceara, with barely concealed contempt. "Aled requires proof of who he is, but I would like proof of his mettle."

"Well, then, I can't help you," Godwin replied. "I was brought up to serve, not fight. I have no strength, and, furthermore, I don't intend to stay here. I made a vow to protect Elgiva and, until her quest is accomplished…"

"You will spurn your duty to US!" cried Aled.

"Aled, he has made a vow!" exclaimed Llewellyn sharply. "Such things are to be honoured."

"A vow to an Elf?" jeered Ceara. "It smacks of treachery."

"Treachery, indeed," said Aled. "And, speaking of which, how can we be sure his allegiance is not with the Saxons, too? They might have sent him to search out his race and help his masters to destroy it!"

"Aled speaks wisely," Ceara declared. "We cannot trust a man such as he." She jerked her chin in Godwin's direction. "Not only is he a heathen, he consorts with a demon in animal form!"

Godwin almost laughed out loud. In the capering shadows beyond the fire, equine expletives singed the air.

"These accusations are false," stated Godwin wearily. "Not only that, they are bloody ridiculous, but I won't waste my breath in arguing about it. If you need proof of my integrity, then this is all I have and, by Frigg, you can take it or leave it!" He got to his feet, unsheathed Taranuil, and brandished it like a reproof. "I suppose you all know its history?"

"Indeed," said Llewellyn, "its origins are well known to all the elders. It was the birth-gift of an elvish queen."

"It was more than that," said an old man beside him, "it was a token of friendship between our people and theirs."

The elders looked at Godwin thoughtfully. "Yes," he said, "and you know that this sword has a name that awakens its power and only Gwion knew that name. But I, as the sword's rightful owner, have learnt the name..." He hesitated, then cast all caution aside. "I learnt by the grace of good magic, which spoke to me through this very blade. Yes, Aled, jeer at my words. Your ridicule doesn't touch me." He glanced round the circle of firelit faces. "This sword was forged for me alone and it is forbidden to do me harm. If you need proof, I am happy to provide it."

He took half a dozen steps backwards, so nobody would hear him as he whispered to the blade. Then he offered the weapon, hilt first, to the highest -ranking elder. "Llewellyn?"

The old man regarded him quizzically and looked at the others for guidance, but they were all equally baffled. Godwin's unflinching gaze, however, drew him to his feet. He approached and grasped the hilt of the sword. Godwin bared his left arm.

"Cut me. As hard as you like."

Llewellyn's eyebrows lifted in horror. "I cannot!" he protested. "Aidan, there is no need for this!"

I know, thought Godwin, but isn't it fun? He resisted the urge to smile. "Do it!" he snapped impatiently.

The elders stiffened round the fire and became as silent as stones. Godwin frowned at Llewellyn, annoyed by his hesitation. Then Llewellyn moistened his lips.

"I cannot do it," he said.

"Then let me do it!" cried Aled. He ran up and snatched the sword from Llewellyn, a smirk of glee on his face. "I will try this heathen's mettle, and I am stronger than you!" He looked at Godwin smugly. "Shouldn't you brace yourself, brother?"

"Get on with it," rasped Godwin. "I haven't got all day."

Aled's grin faltered briefly, then a cruel frown scored his brow. He lay the cutting edge of the blade on his brother's naked flesh and, with all the strength and speed he could find, he sliced the sword along Godwin's arm.

Godwin felt the drag of the blade and its dull scrape set his teeth on edge.

The elders gasped in sick horror and a flash of lightning ripped through the sky and lit up the night, like the anger of clouds.

Aled's arms went limp with reaction and Llewellyn looked at Godwin with eyes that begged for forgiveness. But there was nothing to forgive. Godwin held out his arm to·them all. There was no cut, no injury of any kind.

Godwin repossessed the sword and stepped to the edge of the shelter. Slicing quickly to the right, he struck at one of the sturdy stanchions that held up the wooden roof. It offered no resistance and the sword cut through it, like a knife through freshly-churned butter. The elders recoiled fearfully, as, with a mournful creaking noise, the roof collapsed on one side, lacking the broken spar's support.

"So there!" snickered Grimalkin.

The elders looked at each other in silence, while rain fell outside the shelter in ever-increasing torrents. Darkness was falling prematurely and the air was devoid of warmth. A flash of lightning overhead roused them from their stupor and they clustered together to share their thoughts.

Godwin turned towards the hills, but whatever he hoped to see there was denied him. Darkness covered everything and rain tumbled down from the sky, as though the clouds were ruptured. But then the elders' voices rose in conflict and the part of his mind that was still vaguely interested drew his attention towards it.

"Call me what you will!" cried an old man, his raw-boned features sharp in the firelight. "But you know that what I say makes sense. How else will we survive?"

Llewellyn's voice was taut with outrage. "Gwydion, what you suggest is unthinkable!"

"Nevertheless," persisted Gwydion, "if we acknowledge Vieldrin, he will free us from the enchantment. We will have more food and more freedom."

"Freedom?" hissed Ceara. "Or greater slavery?"

"We have opposed him," Gwydion said, "and look where it has brought us. We have no defence against magic. If we declare our allegiance to him, perhaps he will treat us more kindly."

"Or take even more than he already has," Ceara countered bitterly.

Aled looked around the circle, determination sharpening his gaze. "You say we have no defence against magic, but it seems to me we do!" He thrust out his arm and pointed at Godwin. "He has a magic sword!"

Godwin winced at the hope in their eyes. "Be reasonable," he said. "I'd have to get close enough to use it and how would I manage that? I am known to Vieldrin."

Aled's grin was reckless and savage. "But I am not!" he cried. "Nor do I fear to make the attempt!"

"I'm pleased to hear it," retorted Godwin. "Unfortunately for you, this is *MY* sword, not yours."

The splenetic youth then got to his feet and prepared for his next attack, but something shifted his gaze.

Godwin turned round to see Angwen and Trystin walking towards the shelter. Both of them were soaked to the skin, but neither appeared to notice.

Trystin looked tired and miserable, lost in the company of so many Wilthkin. It seemed he had been loath to relinquish his rags, as if they were all that remained of his home, but he had put on a pair of sandals, which, being too large for his feet, merely added to his air of awkwardness.

Angwen stepped into the shelter and she had a distraught look in her eyes. "Morvyth is dead," she said quietly.

She directed her gaze at the elders, but she seemed to be looking straight through them. They froze with shock and sadness. Then she turned her face towards Godwin, but both of them were too embarrassed to hold each other's eyes for long. Nobody knew what to say.

Suddenly, Aled strode up to his sister. "Here is our new leader!"

Angwen shook her head. "No, it was Morvyth's wish, her dying wish, that Aidan be our chief!"

The elders looked at her thoughtfully, then at each other, and, finally, at Godwin. He avoided their incisive eyes. On top of everything else, would he now be forced to disregard a dying woman's last, desperate wish?

"Still I do not trust him," said Ceara. "Morvyth's choice is suspect. Her illness deluded her."

Angwen confronted Ceara and her hands were clenched into fists. "You presume to dismiss her dying words as the ravings of infirmity? You bitter, old harridan, show some respect!" The elders visibly winced. "I sat with her all the while and her mind remained clear to the end." A violent cackle of lightning filled the shelter with blue-white light, as though the elemental forces shared Angwen's indignation. "Aidan is Gwion's eldest child and he has the blessing of his aunt ... the blessing of our Chief!"

Godwin watched his sister, touched by the way she defended him and impressed by her determination. He couldn't bear the thought of having to tell her it was all for nothing.

"How can he lead us?" protested Aled. "He is a stranger, a slave ... a heathen!"

"And he stands in your way!" declared Angwen. Aled gaped in surprise. "It is you who aspires to leadership, Aled, and what a leader you would make with your peevish and impulsive ways. Because you have no power within you look for power without!"

"No!" cried Aled, hurt and resentful. "I aspire for you, sister ... for you!" He grasped her arm imploringly, but she pulled herself from his grip.

"Aidan is a warrior," she said, her blue eyes fierce with authority, "but his courage comes from unselfish service. It is not your courage, Aled. Yours is reckless and arrogant. It lacks the foresight of maturity. Morvyth believes that our race will fight back and that the time is soon, and, when it comes, only men like Aidan can lead us against the Saxon hordes."

Godwin's jaw fell open in horror. Battling against the Saxon hordes? As well might an ant try to hold back the ocean! Angwen's fighting spirit was admirable, but she ought to be shown the hard facts of reality.

"When Aidan's friend has disposed of Vieldrin," Angwen continued confidently, "we must begin our search for our people, for they are strong and many in number. Aidan will lead us west to their strongholds and we will flourish as before. Then we will prepare for the war that will rid us of these Saxons forever."

Everyone but Godwin gazed at Angwen mutely, mesmerised by her passionate stance. Then thunder rolled brokenly over the sky and it jolted them out of their silence and everyone seemed to start talking at once. All Godwin felt was irritation; it seemed so remote from what really concerned him. He wanted to know where Elgiva was, what was happening to her. He wanted to escape from the uncomfortable feeling Angwen's presence gave him, the demands that the elders had made of him. Unable to endure another moment of their ceaseless bickering, he turned and left the shelter. Lurching into motion, Grimalkin lumbered after him.

The rain was now falling heavily, transforming the earth to a sticky slime that foiled all desire for haste. He had barely measured out three yards, when someone intercepted him.

Suddenly, Aled blocked his way. "Where are you off to, Saxon-lover?"

Rage erupted in Godwin's breast. Lashing out with the back of his hand, he sprawled the youth in the mud and, before Aled could get to his feet, the lethal tip of Taranuil was resting against his throat.

For several long moments thay stared at each other. Aled clutched the smart on his face and his eyes were round with fear.

"Carve his tripes out," suggested Grimalkin.

Godwin couldn't help smiling at this. Aled mistook his amusement for a sneer of cruelty and his lower lip began to tremble.

"I have only to say one word," threatened Godwin, "and I'd have the power to cut you into a hundred pieces, and with no more effort on my part than it takes to cut up a rotten apple."

Angwen staggered towards them, the mud sucking at her feet. She stopped and watched in horrified silence, clasping her hands at her breast.

"However," continued Godwin, "because you're my brother, I'll spare you. It's your youth that makes you so insolent. But, Aled, mark me well. That won't excuse you forever. You'll have to learn some tact and humility, if you wish to live as long as these elders."

"You … you do not frighten me," vaunted Aled, "you … imposter!"

Godwin shrugged. "Perhaps I am. Perhaps I am a Saxon-lover, a heathen and a slave, but my sword is no imposter!" He jabbed the blade at Aled's throat to underscore his words. "And at least I don't pretend to be anything other then what I am. Now, get up, you arrogant, little worm, and think before you speak. The next insult you hurl at me will be your last, I promise you."

Aled gasped with frustrated anger, but he was powerless to protest. Dragging himself from the mud's wet clench, he shambled back to the fire.

Godwin sheathed Taranuil and turned to the elders with a weary sigh. "If you continue to live in the past, then there's no hope for you," he said. "The present isn't up to much but, for now, it's all you've got. You have to play along with Vieldrin, while those entrusted with the task do what they can to cause his downfall. You've done your part by sheltering us. As for the question of choosing a leader, I refuse to accept the title and grant that dubious honour to Angwen, if she will stoop to take it. I can't stay and listen to your petty squabbles. I belong to a wider world."

He stopped and looked at them all. They were hanging on his every word, like naughty children resigned to chastisement, and for the first time in his life he felt fully the master of a situation and his confidence took him by surprise.

"You can't remain as you are," he went on, "insular and suspicious. There are changes happening in this land and they won't pass you by forever. My knowledge of the Saxon ways might have helped you fight them, but that self-same knowledge tells me that such a fight would be useless. The Saxons are here to stay and they are unstoppable. But there are other ways of defeating an enemy apart from slaying him in battle." He hoped they understood, but their faces were blank and unforthcoming.

With that he turned and walked away, squelching through the mud, and made for Angwen's hut. Trystin and Grimalkin followed, like his personal retinue. The elders stared after him, speechless and bemused, but Angwen hurried to join him. She caught him by the sleeve. With a frown of vexation, he turned to face her and rivulets of rainwater ran into his eyes, forcing him to squint, so that his sister appeared as little more than a benighted blur. But he was relieved not to see her eyes; they were bound to be raw with entreaties.

"Aidan, do not leave us!" she begged. "Not after so many years apart! God has sent you to us."

"Perhaps he has," said Godwin dourly, "but you misread his purpose, sister."

"Aidan ... brother...!"

Her desperation wrenched his heart and he cursed himself for his asperity. He seized her by the shoulders, determined to make her understand, but a flare of lightning showed him her face, livid with pain and loss, and he was bereft of explanations. He grasped her hand and made for the hut.

"Let's get out of the rain," he said.

Together they stumbled into her dwelling and Angwen moved to rekindle the fire. Before Godwin could close the door, Grimalkin squeezed her way over the threshold and stood against a far wall, pretending to be invisible. Angwen looked at Godwin askance, puzzled by his lack of reaction, and decided to ignore the intrusion. Closing the door, she walked to his side and they warmed themselves before the fire, while steam plumed from their clothes.

An uncomfortable silence stretched between them and they feared to catch each other's eyes. Then Angwen ventured to speak.

"Aidan … I…"

"Look, Angwen, I'm leaving as soon as Elgiva returns," Godwin said quickly. He forced himself to meet her gaze and he fancied he saw her blush. "I think it's best," he added, folding his arms defensively.

"Forgive me, brother." She looked away.

"No, Angwen." He relaxed his stance and put his arm around her. "It's you who must forgive."

Tears welled in her lucid eyes. "How were we to know?" she asked sadly.

Godwin sighed. "I've wronged you, sister."

She searched his face, unsure of his tone.

"Yes," he continued, "before I knew we were brother and sister, I was false in my dealings with you. My heart and my duty lie elsewhere. I'm already married. I have a Saxon wife."

"A Saxon wife?" gasped Angwen.

"Angwen, you are still very young and, when this evil is removed, your people can travel and trade again and you'll find someone to help you lead them."

She nodded, but the gesture lacked conviction.

"I've too many duties elsewhere," he told her. "Not only a wife, but children, too. And leadership ill becomes me, Angwen. This is your destiny, not mine."

She looked at him, still uncertain, and chewed her lower lip. He hugged her to him and stroked her hair.

"You told me once that your village was dying and you'd lost too many elders," he said, "but that's no reason for despair. It means you can start afresh. Some of the old ways may have been lost, but they aren't always the best ways. You need to find new ones and I know you have the strength to do it … and I ask you to take this burden from me, in the name of the blood we both share."

She studied his face, then she smiled and hugged him. "I gladly accept then, brother, because it is your wish … but I shall always think of you as leader of this tribe, no matter where you are. I will lead the tribe on your behalf and your humility will be my guide."

He kissed her brow and it struck him how like Elgiva she was. Both seemed too young to be weighted down by frightening responsibilities, yet both had unquenchable inner strength. And neither of them knew it. And both of them needed his love and support. How cruel that he must choose between them. Crueller still that he had to abandon his long-lost family yet again.

It seemed to him that deserting people had become a way of life.

For a while they stood, wrapped in each other's arms, as if they knew that this embrace was going to be their last.

At length, she lifted her eyes to his. "Will you return to us?"

"Who knows what the future holds?"

He held her face between his hands and for a time he looked at her and tried to impress her features onto his mind, so that he would never forget them. Then he lowered his head and kissed her soft mouth and, as he released her, she smiled at him, but the anguish of parting shone in her eyes.

"God be with you, brother," she said, in a small but courageous voice.

"And with you, sister," said Godwin.

She turned and stepped towards the door, then she looked back, smiling broadly. "You are wrong, Aidan," she said.

He raised his eyebrows questioningly.

"Leadership becomes you well." And with that, she was gone.

With a sigh, Godwin turned back to the fire. He felt that his past and his present were either one and the same thing, or at least two parts of the same confused tangle, and trying to cope with all the loose threads would pursue him to the grave.

Suddenly Trystin entered the hut and he carried a basket draped with a cloth. He set the basket on the floor and waited for someone to notice him.

"So, Brit," snorted Grimalkin, "you never pretend to be what you're not. Then why did you let her think you were free?"

"What are you, my bloody conscience?" he rasped.

"Well … if the position's vacant…"

Godwin sighed with exasperation, then he noticed that Trystin was offering him bread. The Elfling gave him a tentative smile, as though he were afraid to speak, and Godwin felt a pang of guilt.

"Come nearer the fire, Trystin," he said. "Your clothes are soaking wet." He put his arm round Trystin's shoulders. "I've been ignoring you, haven't I? I hope you can forgive me."

Trystin pretended that it didn't matter.

"I told you he was bored," said Grimalkin. "Cabbage hearts! Who isn't? But nobody gives a mare's cuss."

Godwin refused to be baited. "Well, you'd know all about that," he said. He turned to the Elfling and smiled. "The storm's here for the night, lad, and, unfortunately for us, we're far too kind to leave a poor creature out to fend for itself." He cocked an eyebrow at the pony. "So we're holed up in here until it stops with some rather dubious company."

"I was thinking the same myself," said Grimalkin.

★ ★ ★

Chapter Thirty-Five

Elgiva felt sure she was near the top, but blinded by rain, it was hard to tell. A loud concussion in the sky made her heart leap into her mouth and she flattened herself against the rocks, panting with shock and exhaustion. For a time she had to rest again, while the rain cascaded down the hill and the blood pounded in her ears.

Too many rests. She would never make it. While she waited for her strength to return, she relived the ordeal of her ascent.

Vieldrin's enchantment had been the first obstacle and getting through it without help had cost her more energy than she could spare, but she triumphed over the spell and very soon she found herself gazing up at the nearest hill. Since then she felt she had climbed for hours, through daylight and into dusk. The hill was taller and steeper than it had appeared from the ground and in places covered by loose, sharp shale that shifted underfoot.

She had started out towards the hills buoyed up by optimism, convinced that her recovery from illness was complete, but it soon became apparent that she didn't have the stamina to undertake the task that she had chosen for herself, and once the enchantment had taken its toll, her fatigue was all the greater. She was barely half way towards her goal, when a feverish trembling overtook her. Forced to rest, she had fallen asleep, and woke up later, gripped by panic.

Then the rain had started and at first her fever welcomed it, but soon the sky grew darker and the rain became a stinging torrent that loosened the shale still further. Her clothes were weighted with rain, her linen shift slimy with mud, and the jagged rocks tore at her cloak. Runnels of rainwater slicked her path and she stumbled on the greasy stones and the sparse and slippery grass.

Still she toiled upwards, gasping for breath, as though she were climbing a waterfall. She couldn't get enough air in her lungs and was often compelled to rest and, each time she stopped, the darkness span round her and she fell into a kind of swoon. Then she would waken suddenly, convinced that a great deal of time had passed; time she couldn't spare.

The air became colder, the higher she climbed, until her bones were aching with it. Eventually, her need for warmth made her summon magic to her aid, but her attempts were useless. Her power was like a candle, snuffed out by a tempest. Then her tears were mixed with the rain and she huddled over the anguish of her battered knees and bleeding fingers and thoughts of Godwin sprang into her mind, filling her heart with loss and longing.

She should never have come alone. Without his help and encouragement, she would never make the summit.

She longed to give in to exhaustion, to become a part of the darkness, sink into it forever and abandon the purpose of her quest, but she forced herself to continue. Godwin would have expected no less.

And so she had struggled ever upwards with blind determination, while the rocks snagged her clothes and scraped the skin from her hands: she had the image of Godwin to carry her through her weakness.

But now she was resting once again and, this time, she feared that her strength had all gone. Yet she knew that she was right. It had to be. It had to be. Because, if not...

She closed her hand around Siriol and it answered her need with a glow of heat.

She strained to see through the helm-cloud that covered the top of the hill, but it hid the summit like a cloak, concealing whatever promises her fevered mind had imagined. So all she could do was clamber on. There was no turning back. She ignored the pain of her bruises and cuts, the pain in her lungs and the flashes of lightning. She was almost there; she had to keep moving.

A hint of light at the top of the hill flooded her mind with relief and hope. She heaved herself higher and spasms of pain tormented her arms and shoulders, while the guttural boom of thunder roared mockery at her toiling form. Then she stopped and squinted through the darkness.

Some yards ahead was a narrow ledge and on it stood a tall, dark shape. Behind this figure was a cave and it gave off a warm and inviting glow. The figure bent a little towards her and its long robe fluttered in the wind, the trailing sleeves and voluminous hood totally hiding its face and limbs.

"You have come this far, my child," said the figure. "A few feet more, that is all."

She struggled on in desperation, scrabbling for holds on the slippery rocks, and her breath sobbed in her throat. "Please," she begged, "your hand!"

His tone was fraught with regret and sadness. "Alas, I cannot!" he said.

"But, I can't make it ... I can't!" she cried.

"Do not surrender now, my child. A little more effort, then you can rest."

He turned and was gone and she tried to recall him, but her voice was a feeble croak. With one, last, pained exertion she managed to reach the ledge. Crawling slowly on all fours, she entered the cave and collapsed on the floor and let out a groan of relief.

Then, like a stone, she dropped into darkness. It covered her like peace and she lay for some time in welcome oblivion and knew that her ordeal was over. At length, she heard a caring voice and it lifted her into the light.

"Forgive me, child. I can do nothing to remedy your distress."

Elgiva lifted her head slowly and her senses drew into focus. In front of her the heat of a cheery fire bled warmth into her bones. When the tightness in her chest had eased, she sat up and scanned her surroundings.

Except for the fire, the cave was bleak and its only sign of habitation was a trestle bed, but the bare frame showed that it hadn't been used. The rear of the cave tapered away into an unadorned blackness and only an overhang of rock protected the cave from the weather. To her surprise, Elgiva saw a raven sitting on a ledge and, to her right, chewing its cud, was a goat with curling horns.

"Greetings," croaked the raven.

"Greetings," bleated the goat.

Hidden within the folds of his robe, the figure watched her across the fire. "You like my little refuge, Elgiva?"

Still puzzling over the figure's companions, Elgiva nodded absently.

"Ah, these are my friends," the figure said. "Rork the raven brings fire in his beak." He indicated a pile of spills lying on the floor. "Eswen the goat carries wood up the hill. But lately I have not needed fire, except to signal my presence. No need for fire to warm my bones, when I have none to warm." Elgiva frowned at this. "You chose a bad night to visit me, child."

"Is … is it you, my lord… uncle?" The dark hood nodded in answer. "Faine's love! I'm so happy to see you!"

"You do not see me," he replied. "Come nearer the fire and dry yourself."

"Uncle, remove your hood."

"I cannot," he said. "I am not in the flesh. I appear to you in spirit, while my body lies sleeping elsewhere. You know that I am in fetters, chained by a spell I cannot break."

"Oh … uncle Bellic!" Her voice cracked with emotion and hot tears burned her eyes. How she longed to embrace this kindly, old Elf who had taught her, protected her, loved her.

"I used to come here in body, too. In sooth, I had thought to bring *YOU* here and teach you the uses of magic," he said. "Well, things did not turn out as planned." He shook his head and she looked at him, raw-eyed with remorse. "My dear, you have been gravely ill. Alas, poor child, I lacked foresight. Is this what I have brought you to?"

"No, uncle Bellic. Don't blame yourself."

"You have been touched by evil magic. Tell me about it, Elgiva."

"Vieldrin." She paused and drew a deep breath. "But I'm free from his spell now, uncle. That's not what I need to discuss. There isn't time … I need your help … so many things I need to ask..."

"You have the Lorestone?" asked the Elf-lord.

"Yes, I have the Lorestone, uncle."

His hood bobbed slowly in satisfaction. "Then all is not lost," he declared.

"But nothing is gained!" she protested. "With the Stone was a parchment which bore a clue to the whereabouts of its name. Without its name, the Lorestone is useless."

"Faine would not wish it to be used without effort. Where is this parchment, Elgiva?"

Elgiva looked away guiltily. "Vieldrin has it," she said.

"I see." He considered this fact for a moment. "Do you remember the words of this clue?" She nodded. "Then please recite them."

Elgiva did her best to recall the verse that was written on the parchment. For a while she felt like a child again, repeating the morning's lesson. Lord Bellic listened, silent and still, until she had finished speaking, and before he could comment on the words, Elgiva gave voice to a nagging suspicion.

"Uncle Bellic," she ventured, "you believe that I am the one ordained to wield the Stone, but … perhaps you are mistaken."

"Why so?"

"For one thing, I didn't find it. It was found by my friend, Godwin, a Briton, who bears a magic sword."

The Elf-lord straightened himself abruptly, as though her words were blows. "Then I have erred! I misread the Ninth Book. Alas, my conclusions were false!"

"Well, one of them at least," she said, "but, be that as it may, we have to find the Nine Wise Men."

"In this I can be of service," he said. "These Nine Wise Men are menhirs, my child. They stand upon a broad glade, a circle of stones surrounded by oaks. The tallest is the kingstone and the others are his eight sons. A Wilthkin legend would have it that Arawn, King of the Otherworld, punished them for their arrogance by turning them into stone, for they were wise as wizards are wise and thought themselves greater than they were. On the night of the summer solstice, they sing their remorse to the sky, or so it is believed."

Elgiva decided to intervene, before this turned into a lesson on Wilthkin myths and legends. "Yes, but *WHERE* are they?" she asked.

"Once you have left these hills behind, you must head towards the south-west. The grove in which you will find the menhirs lies in a hollow in the land. It is like an enormous bowl, ringed by mounds of earth. It should take you two days on foot."

"Two days!"

"Have patience, child. Vieldrin does not have the Stone and were he to find the sarsen ring, the name is as useless without the Stone, as the Stone is without its name."

Elgiva tried to accept his words, but a sense of foreboding clung to her bones and made shivers of panic run up her spine.

"Now, Elgiva, while you are here, what other matters assail you?"

She thought for a moment, tried to be calm, but she felt ridiculous sitting there, when she should have been racing back to her friends to tell them what she had discovered. "Tell me, then, about Siriol."

His hood moved slowly up and down. "It had but one spell and one spell only. Magic for use when there was need, but only for good, of course. The power it held would endure for as long as you wished it to, and no longer. Thereafter as an amulet it was effectively useless. Whatever appeared to happen subsequent to that was entirely down to you. You could say I lied to you, my child, but I had hoped, by providing a focus, that it would help to awaken your powers, that it would give you confidence, and perhaps it would show you your courage. The most important requirement for using magic is belief. You had to believe in Siriol and believe that something would happen. And hopefully, it did."

"I suppose you were right," she admitted reluctantly. But sometimes it made me too confident and gave me more courage than wisdom allowed.

"Perhaps I took a grave risk, but what else could I do at the time? Then Vieldrin arrived in Elindell and I was unable to leave. I suspect he had made himself known to Thallinore some time before you were banished. To Tarkinell also, perhaps. Indeed, he may have suggested your exile to isolate you and test your powers."

"He wants me as an ally." She hesitated. "And as his queen."

The Elf-lord didn't seem surprised. "He must have heirs, no doubt. I am sure that he regards you as the one most suited to his requirements. Alone. Untrained. Having power without knowledge. The ideal prey. Easy to corrupt."

Elgiva lowered her dark eyes, recalling the Elf-king's seductive embrace, his charm and lavish promises. True, she had resisted him, and resisted, too, the addiction of magic that yearned for satisfaction. But she also knew that it hadn't been easy.

Elgiva's self-doubt didn't escape the attention of her great-uncle. "Do not chide yourself, Elgiva, for being a little in love with him. No matter how good we think we are, some darkness lives inside us all."

She glared at him in outrage, but it was futile to protest. It was, she knew, too near to the truth. And, if Vieldrin weren't the evil monster that she knew he was…

"And if it did not," Bellic went on, "we would go against the balance that resides in all of Nature's works. We would not exist."

Elgiva tried to steer the conversation onto a different track. "Vieldrin must know we have the Stone, but perhaps he thinks I'm dead by now, or that my friends have been captured and forced to reveal where the Lorestone is, so I dare say this gives us some space to breath…"

"I fear he must know," sighed Lord Bellic. "We must not underestimate him, and he is sure to have spies."

"Well … at least he has no more power yet than any other Wardain."

"My dear, that may not be the case. He has been trying to summon up the dark things that dwell beneath the earth. These things are called the Fetchen and they are ancient shades of evil. Indeed, in Elindell…" His voice trailed away.

"But how?" she demanded, appalled.

"Best we do not dwell upon it, for there is much in this world and beyond that even the Eldrakin do not know. Our magic is of the Earth and the Wardain use it for good, but again there must be a balance, so evil exists there, too."

Elgiva smiled to herself. Without evil, good has no meaning, she thought.

"And these Nine Men," said Bellic, "are sources of power. They stand in a place where the magic is focused, as do all circles of stone. In such a place many spells may be woven and powerful magic released."

"Such things are beyond me." Elgiva shuddered. "I don't feel equal … to any of it." She looked up at Bellic, her eyes wide with need. "Uncle, I can't use magic and powerful magic frightens me and I feel … I feel like I'm dying. The power is destroying me. Vieldrin overmastered you, yet you are a powerful Wardain. You have years of practice behind you. You can be in two places at once! What hope do I have of succeeding, when my own power turns against me?"

He winced at the fear in her voice. "Elgiva, your magic is very strong, but you yourself are weak. Your aura is faint and you have not been strengthened in preparation. In childhood, all Wardain must struggle this way, but for them, of course, it is easier. They have instruction and practice. But remember that this power is inherent in the Earth and it is right and natural. It is your ally, not your foe."

It doesn't feel like that, she thought. She shook her head despondently. She felt like a scrap of parchment that someone had screwed up and cast aside. She had counted on her great-uncle being able to unfold her and smooth out the creases.

"We are directly in touch with this natural power. It is ours for as long as we are the medium through which it expresses itself. At the final test, it will not fail you."

"No!" she protested. "I still don't know how to summon this power to my aid."

"You do not need to know," he said. "You merely need to feel. And inasmuch as you use the power, that power is using you, for the energy must find some release."

"But I can't sustain it!"

"Because you are weak. Prolonging the magic will come with practice."

"But there's no time for that!" She groaned with exasperation.

"You fear and that is why you fail."

She got to her knees, angry and hurt. "It's true, I'm afraid," she blurted out, "and, by Faine, I have cause to be! All this has been thrust upon me and it's a burden I can't bear!"

"Nevertheless, it is your inheritance."

"Uncle, I've always feared magic, because I believed I had none … and now it's too late to learn otherwise." She glared at him accusingly.

Bellic was unperturbed. "Niece, you do right to rail against me, but it is too late for recriminations. And all I can do is to give you advice, though you would not be blamed for resenting it." He waited for her to calm herself. She sank back slowly onto the floor and folded her hands in her lap. "Magic is passion," he continued. "Does not your power stir most when you are beset by anger or fear?" Reluctantly, she nodded. "Such feelings concentrate the mind, if not the very being, too. Use them to focus yourself on the magic, to become as one with the energy. Your entire being, Elgiva, body, mind and spirit. They must be one with the power. This power is good and will not destroy you, though it leaves you not entirely scatheless."

"I perceive that you are dissatisfied, but I tell you that you must master this power. Do not let it master you. And if you fear that it may surpass you, then channel it through some other medium, something strong and of the Earth. Direct its force away from you. But one day you will have the strength and will wonder then why you were so afraid." He paused to let his words sink in. "We are like the standing stones. We must let the power flow through us, as they do, pure and unhindered by fear and self-doubt."

She shook her head and sighed. You're asking me to let go, to give myself to this terrible force. As always, you ask too much, she thought.

"Hesitancy will undo you. Vieldrin is devious, clever and quick and has struck his opponent long before he has shown any signs of so doing." The Elf-lord paused, then his voice grew stern. "Elgiva, you must listen well, for I need *YOUR* help also."

She gave him a pained and haunted look, as though the idea appalled her.

"It is true, Elgiva," he went on. "Though you will refuse to accept it, you are stronger than I. You must release me from my fetters."

"No," she said. "It's impossible!"

"You have revered me, this I know, but I am a Wardain, not a god, and I am no longer in my prime."

Elgiva covered her face with her hands.

"Do not falter," he told her. "Vieldrin must be stopped. The war must be ended and peace restored and the balance re-established. And, Elgiva, your cousin is dying."

"Dying?"

His hood bobbed briefly in affirmation. "Your throne awaits, Elgiva. Prove yourself worthy to claim it. Nothing that is valuable in life is ever attained without effort."

"But uncle," she protested weakly, "to fight Vieldrin I must break my oath to Faine First-Father. Thallinore…"

"Yes, child, I know. I am sure that Faine will understand."

She gazed at her great-uncle hollow-eyed. She hadn't found the comfort she craved. Her mind had reached out to him in anguish, but he seemed unequal to her need.

"Tell me, Elgiva, how is Trystin?"

The change of subject left her floundering. "Well … I dare say … he is fine."

"Care for him. He is a good Elf. And Godwin, your friend, is a Briton, you say? They are attuned to the power of the Earth. It is well you travel with one."

"That's exactly what your daughter said." A mischievous twinkle lit up her eyes, as she wondered what his reaction would be, but Bellic merely nodded. "I did a spell for Godwin," she went on. "Now he can speak to animals. To Elves and Wilthkin, too. I used my powers to grant him this gift, but it worked much better than I expected and still it endures, but I don't know why."

"This gift was given in love," he explained, "and it will endure as long as your love."

Elgiva found herself blushing slightly.

Suddenly Bellic was standing. "I must depart. And you, also. There is a quicker way down the hill than that by which you ascended. Eswen will be your guide."

"But, uncle … must I … must I go? There's more … there is so much…"

"Have courage, my dear, and trust in Faine. He has chosen you for a purpose and his choices were always well made. Be of a good heart, Elgiva."

Confused by his sudden need for haste, she struggled to her feet. Red motes dappled her vision and the blood surged in her brain, but his stance denied all knowledge of weakness and she knew that she had to be strong. Sadly she turned and walked from the cave.

"Faine guard you," called Bellic from within, "and hasten the day when I may embrace you."

She took one last look at the hooded figure standing beside the fire, then a furry body brushed past her.

"Good-bye and good luck," croaked the raven.

"Follow me," bleated the goat.

* * *

Chapter Thirty-Six

A calm like sea-brume hugged the fields and the village was wrapped in an early autumn haze. Smoke stagnated in the air above the cooking fires and insects droned beneath the eaves of the quiet, wooden dwellings. Warriors sat by the parapet, drowsily sharpening daggers and swords, and on the horizon a shimmering heat-haze blurred the seam that joined earth and sky.

A path snaked out from the stronghold and meandered past a grove of trees and there, in a tall oak's generous shade, sat the village chief's small children: Eluned and her brother, Aidan. They giggled over their spoils, as they plunged their hands in the deep, wicker basket and drew out the dark, sweet fruit. Specks of sunlight danced on their faces.

In the distance the sky was darkening and black clouds rolled towards the village.

For a time, the children ate the fruit, then Eluned's conscience pricked her. "Mustn't eat them all," she said.

The boy thrust out his lower lip and she frowned in exasperation, adopting an adult role.

"Naughty boy. So greedy," she scolded. "Save some for Mother."

Aidan sighed. "I'm bored, Ellie."

"Play with your toys," she told him.

"Don't want to," he retorted.

"We go home soon. Oh, look at the clouds! Aren't they big and black!"

"Ellie, will it rain?" he asked.

Licking the juice from her fingers, Eluned nodded sagely. Aidan peered up through the oak leaves and saw the swollen cloud-mass, a black grume that seemed to devour the sun. He didn't want to go home. Being indoors was dull. He sighed again, determined to sulk, but his mind was diverted from that idea, when he saw his sister busy about some task.

"What you doing, Ellie?"

"A daisy chain. Isn't it pretty?" Her tongue toyed with her upper lip, as she struggled to bend the tiny stems.

Aidan watched with interest. "What you doing it for?"

"For you," she replied. "A crown for you, 'cause you'll be chief one day."

"I won't have a crown, Ellie."

She pouted. "Well, I think you should." She held up the circlet for his inspection.

Aidan leaned forward to accept the gift, which she placed upon his head. Clumsily, he drew his sword, which was far too large for his childish grasp, then he marched up and down on his chubby legs.

"Mother will be angry," said Eluned. "She said to leave the sword at home."

Aidan pulled a face at her and Eluned burst out laughing, and her infant voice was like the sound of sunlight in the trees. "Silly boy!" she giggled. "Will you forget Ellie, when you're chief?"

"Never!" he declared.

"We'll always be together, won't we?"

It took him some time to sheath the sword, his small brow creased with effort, then he knelt at her side and hugged her fondly. The basket of fruit was behind her and slyly he seized the chance to steal a handful of the berries. He crammed them into his mouth.

A drizzle of rain began to fall and they knew that they should go home. Aidan glanced at the curdled sky and chewed his lower lip. He could feel the raindrops on his face.

"Ellie, will it hurt my crown?"

"How can rain hurt flowers?" She laughed.

She was far more sensible than he was, although he was her senior, and her wisdom often made him feel foolish, but he didn't really mind. He felt secure with her.

The rain was heavier now, the oak no longer sufficient shelter. A hint of lightning scoured the sky and the grass was ruffled by a freshening breeze.

"Aidan! Must go home now!" Eluned exclaimed.

A clamour in the village went unheeded by the children, as they gathered up their wooden toys and giggled at the need for haste.

"Hurry, Aidan! We'll get wet!"

They knew that they had been naughty, staying out for so long, and it filled them with delicious fear, which led to further giggling, but then the noise in the village grew louder and they couldn't help but notice it. There were shouts and the sounds of clanging metal. Aidan clung to his sister, his blue eyes wide with alarm.

"Ellie, what is it?" he pleaded.

Clouds of dark smoke curled beyond the trees and the children stood rooted with fear.

"Ellie, I'm afraid!" wailed Aidan.

People were running towards them; people they knew, pursued by strangers. There seemed to be movement everywhere and fighting and cries and panic. The children huddled against the tree and watched as their neighbours were slaughtered. The breeze carried smoke that stung their eyes and they knew that their village was burning.

Two of the raiders spotted the children cowering under the tree. “Take them!” cried one, then he hurried away, his broadsword dripping blood.

The other was quick to obey. Tall and blond with a curling beard, he walked towards the children. In his hand was a death-dealing broadsword, already stained with gore. The children wailed in terror.

The raider seized hold of Aidan. The basket of fruit was overturned and the daisy chain fell to the grass. He crushed the boy under his brawny arm. Eluned sprang to her brother’s aid and kicked at the raider’s shins, her fear overtaken by anger.

“Leave him alone!” she screamed.

She tugged at the warrior’s arm, trying to make him release his captive. The man roared at her in rage, but she kept on kicking and wouldn’t let go. In the distance a horn sounded urgently. The raider, anxious to get away, lashed out with his sword, while Aidan watched in helpless horror.

“Ellie!” screamed Aidan. “Ellie!”

He struggled in the Saxon’s grip and then hysteria clogged his throat, as he saw his sister dead on the grass, among the trampled blackberries and the abandoned toys. In her soft, young neck was a deep, red gash and her blood became one with the rain and the earth.

The raider ran to join the others, Aidan still struggling under his arm, and the boy’s eyes were blinded by acid tears and his screams became part of a roar of darkness that carried him away …

… Carried him away. And he floated with it willingly, until he found himself stretched like a sacrifice, lying on top of a knoll. A ring of flowers encircled him, enclosed him in a peaceful void, as though he were a precious thing they wanted to protect.

And outside the circle of upright blooms, every pain he had ever felt was crouching in the darkness.

⋆ ⋆ ⋆

Godwin sat up with a start.

His chest was heaving with ragged gasps and his heart seemed to be struggling to beat at the bottom of a very deep well. It was dark and he didn't know where he was, nor even who he was. Thunder cracked above him, increasing his alarm.

He swung his legs off the low bed and sat, hunched forwards, hugging his chest. Sweat cooled on his skin and made him shiver.

Eluned.

Was that her name? And was she lost to him forever? He knew now that she wasn't. We'll always be together, she'd said. Nothing was ever lost, only changed.

He straightened himself and took a deep breath, then he looked around the room; in its centre the embers of the fire glowed red and gave off a meagre light. Trystin lay sleeping on his bed, his outline dimmed by darkness, and in the shadows beyond the fire, Grimalkin snuffled softly.

Suddenly the door scraped open.

A figure swayed on the threshold; a silhouette of lightning. Godwin's heart pounded with shock. He sprang to his feet and searched for his sword. A whinny escaped Grimalkin's lips, as she was startled from her sleep.

Then the door creaked shut and the figure walked in and knelt before the fire. Shivers racked her frame. “Sorry I was so long,” she said.

Godwin sagged with relief. Elgiva pushed back the hood of her cloak and, muttering a few words under her breath, she raised her hands to the fire. It threw out tongues of yellow flame and hurled her shadow against the far wall.

“Bring more wood,” she gasped.

Godwin didn’t hesitate. As he fed the fire, he looked at his friend, shocked by her condition. Her arms and legs were cut and bruised, her clothes were torn and soiled and her eyes had a hollow, vacant look. He yearned to offer some comfort, but he felt himself unequal to it.

A distant growl of thunder proclaimed the passing of the storm.

Godwin placed his hand on her shoulder. “I was worried,” he confessed. She lifted her head and looked at him blankly. “What happened?”

Elgiva shrugged. “It rained.”

“The wise man…?”

“Uncle Bellic,” she said. “In spirit only, of course.” With a wry smile she shifted her gaze and stared into the fire. Steam began to coil from her gown, as though her will had turned to vapour.

For a while they sat without speaking. The silence had an abstracted quality that made Godwin feel he might still be dreaming.

“What’s wrong, Elgiva?” he asked, at length.

She sighed. “I expected too much.”

"I know," he said. I know. He slipped his arm around her and she leaned her body against him. "Tell me about it, my dear."

"He told me where to find the Nine Men. They're standing stones," she explained. "He said Thallinore is dying. He said he's been wrong about the Ninth Book. He said that I was weak. He said I must learn to master my powers, but I still don't really know how."

Godwin knew only too well the smart of shattered hopes. "We'll prevail," he assured her.

She shook her head at him doubtfully. "Vieldrin seeks to control the dark forces that slumber in the Earth."

Godwin didn't want to hear about that. "We've got some food here, Elgiva. You should eat," he advised.

Grimalkin took several steps forwards, pricking up her ears.

"Hello, Grimalkin," said Elgiva. "Have you guarded the Lorestone in my absence?"

Grimalkin looked at Godwin and flashed the whites of her eyes.

"Her behaviour can always be relied upon," Godwin said with a wry smile.

The pony emitted a satisfied snort.

"The storm's passing," Elgiva observed. "We should be on our way."

"Indeed," remarked Grimalkin, "we've dallied too long with these clodhoppers."

"I'm sick of your insulting remarks about my people!" Godwin cried.

"I only insult, Brit, but you renounce."

His jaw dropped open in abashment and he found himself strung between anger and shame. Elgiva relinquished his support and turned to face him with a look of concern.

"Godwin, what does she mean?" she asked.

"Why don't you tell her, Aidan, lad?" suggested Grimalkin smugly.

He didn't know where to begin, so he showed Elgiva the dragon ring. "Morvyth gave me this," he said. "The symbol of my race. It belonged to Chief Gwion…" Abruptly he stopped and his artless eyes were clouded with emotion. "By Frigg! Elgiva, you've no idea … it's unbelievable!"

Elgiva frowned at him anxiously. "My friend, what is it?" she asked, placing her hand upon his arm. She sensed that there was something different about him, but she couldn't put a name to it. "In Faine's name, tell me what's happened?"

He gaped at Elgiva helplessly. In Faine's name it had all happened. Taranuil. Faine's Lynn. The Hill-Shrine. Orphan and Slave.

Oh, Grim. Oh, God.

"These are my people!" he blurted out. "And I … I'm Aidan, Gwion's son … his long-lost son … his heir!"

Elgiva gasped with astonishment and he proceeded to tell her the rest. His talk with Morvyth. The Elfblade. The elders. Eluned. Angwen.

But, when he spoke of Angwen, there were things he hadn't the courage to say and he looked at Grimalkin with a silent plea: as I spared you, spare me likewise.

"Godwin, you refused to be chief?" asked Elgiva, astounded.

"But I don't want that," he said. "I'm not trusted here and there are things … more important things I have to do."

"More important than your inheritance?"

They who persecute evil shall prosper … "No!" he protested. "It's not what I want."

"Am I the cause of this?"

He gazed at her forlornly. How could he answer, when he didn't know? He shrugged noncommittally and folded his arms.

Elgiva didn't feel justified in causing her friend further pain by asking him a second time, so she left the question hanging between them, but she sensed that if she had the answer, it would only add to her burden of guilt. She could but hope that by acquitting herself well and accomplishing her quest, she would somehow pay all her debts to him.

Quickly, she got to her feet, crossed to the door and flung it open. The storm had abated and, in its wake, it left the night washed clean. Cool air flowed into the hut and Elgiva inhaled it gratefully. For a while she stood in silence, then, turning, she noticed Trystin. He sat on his bed with his knees drawn up, as though he didn't wish to be seen. She smiled at him and he ran to her and threw his arms about her waist.

As she hugged his malnourished body, tears began to sting her eyes, and they stung all the more, when she realised that she cried for herself and not for him.

"Well, my friends," she said unsteadily. "Time for us to leave."

"I hope you'll take some food," nagged Grimalkin. "We're always lacking in that respect."

"How can we, when they have so little?" Elgiva asked reproachfully.

"Be reasonable," said Godwin. "How else shall we survive?"

"Very well," agreed Elgiva, "but we must wait for daybreak, so we can ask Angwen for provisions."

"No need," snickered Grimalkin. "I know where they keep the food!"

"Shall we be thieves?" retorted Elgiva.

"There are worse crimes," said Grimalkin.

Like Killing, thought Elgiva.

Like cowardice, thought Trystin.

Like abandonment, thought Godwin.

"Let's waste no more time, then," Elgiva sighed resignedly. "We have many leagues to travel before we reach the Nine Wise Men, and many more to Elindell. And first we must brave Vieldrin's enchantment, which reaches to the foothills. I have already braved this Elf-bane and, alone, I could not face it again, but if we work together, as we have done before, then breaking through it won't be a problem."

* * *

Chapter Thirty-Seven

For the next two days the companions travelled, the hills and the Elf-bane behind them. Elgiva knew a quick route through the former, thanks to Eswen the goat, while the latter had been breached by the agency of magic and the united willpower of the quest. Elgiva set a brisk pace and their rest-stops were marred by a nagging feeling that they had no time to waste.

Godwin wondered guiltily what his people would think of him, when they found that he'd fled like a fugitive without a word of thanks, without even saying farewell. Without even asking to see his father's grave.

The last was something he couldn't do until he felt worthy enough. Or brave enough, perhaps.

Elgiva was too preoccupied to spare a thought for her friends. Her eyes flicked constantly to the south-west, where the Nine Men guarded their secret of power.

Trystin trudged behind them, infected by the mood of the quest, while Grimalkin kept him company, at one point giving him a lecture on carrots.

It was later on the second day, when that which they both wanted and feared at last came into view. As they clambered over a ridge of land, they saw below them a grove of oaks. The plain on which these old trees grew was surrounded by ancient earthworks, so that they seemed to be standing in a dish that was moulded out of the land.

The travellers looked at each other and their eyes were full of unspoken questions. Then, with Elgiva at their head, they scrambled down the man-made bank and hastened towards the oaks. At the edge of the grove Elgiva halted and turned to face her friends.

"We must be careful," she warned them. "I dare say Vieldrin has many spies."

They surveyed their surroundings guardedly, but nothing could be seen or heard, only the innocent presence of birds.

"Lady Elgiva," ventured Trystin, "you don't think he's still here … waiting for us?"

"Don't smell him," snorted Grimalkin.

Elgiva squinted through the trees. "I'm sure Vieldrin's been here. He has the parchment and he is lorewise, so he'll know, or has discovered, what the Nine Men are."

"And if he believes we have the Stone, he knows we must come to this place," said Godwin.

"This dithering is getting me down," said Grimalkin. She lowered her ungainly head and snatched at a tuft of grass.

Indecision hung in the air. Suddenly, Godwin unsheathed his sword. "We're getting nowhere standing here."

He made his way slowly into the oaks. Watching and listening intently, his companions followed his lead. Soon they were within the centre, a glade where daisies grew in abundance, and, towering above the tiny blooms, nine monoliths of sandstone were planted in the earth. But the largest stone had been ripped from its roots. It lay on its side and was splintered and charred, the victim of wanton violence. The four friends grouped themselves around it, like mourners paying their last respects.

Elgiva looked down at the riven stone, as though it were a symbol of her broken hopes, and in the hole where the menhir had stood she could see an oblong box made of marble. It gaped open to the air, blank and empty, its lid discarded on the grass. Whatever it had contained was gone.

For a time that seemed like helplessness, they brooded over the shattered kingstone.

"Think we're too late," said Grimalkin, at length.

Elgiva raked her hair with her fingers and distress pinched the skin between her eyes. "I don't know what to do," she confessed. She looked at Godwin, pleading for guidance.

"Well," he said firmly, "whatever happens, we can't let Vieldrin get the Stone. Not now. Now he can use it."

A sigh escaped Elgiva's lips and she nodded despondently. "We're compelled to follow him and he knows it. We have no choice. He must be stopped and the Lorestone is the only way. If he releases the Fetchen … well, then only Faine's magic can stop him. We must find a way to use it."

Godwin nodded and sheathed his sword. "But how do we sneak into Elindell without letting the Stone fall into his hands?"

Elgiva shrugged. "I don't know, Godwin. I must think. Let's camp here tonight. I can't … I need some kind of plan."

He nodded grimly, then turned on his heel and went to get wood for a fire.

⋆ ⋆ ⋆

Night thickened around the ellipse of stones, as if to mimic the gloom that darkened the mood of the Lorestone's guardians. The stars were obscured by clouds that moved like shadows across the sky and in the centre of the circle, the camp-fire seemed small and futile surrounded by so much darkness.

Grimalkin wandered away from her friends and stood at the edge of the circle, while Trystin curled up beside the fire and sought the solace of sleep. The wet, chilled earth on which he lay caused him less distress than the lifelong burden of melancholy that seemed to be a part of his soul.

Elgiva and Godwin sat, side by side, too restless to sleep, too tired to talk. Both of them jumped at the sight of an owl, which swooped, white and silent, over the circle, like a ghost bereft of Heaven and Earth. It flew to the dusky tree-tops to hoot at the veiled moon.

Elgiva found herself clinging to Godwin, like a terrified child beset by ghouls. Ashamed, she prised herself away and wrenched herself to her feet. Impelled by a need for reassurance, she walked to the nearest standing stone. She stretched out her arms as far as she could and flattened herself against it.

Almost at once, she sprang back in surprise, then she reached out her hand and touched the cold stone to verify what she had felt. The dark rock thrummed gently with power, like a cat that purred with drowsy contentment. She knew that such stones sucked up power from the Earth, but she hadn't expected to feel it so strongly. It seemed to suffuse itself into her limbs and it felt like solace and friendship and warmth. It made her smile with the joy of shared power; of oneness with the Earth.

Its balm spiralled deeper until it found the matrix of her might, the place where magic slumbered and grew, and called to it to awaken, to blend with the rhythm of Stone. As the two forces merged without conflict or clash, Elgiva felt her courage renewed and the hurt in her heart was cauterised.

She felt herself floating, as if in a dream, but she needed to stay alert, so she pulled away from the soothing power and slowly withdrew her hand. Remembering what Bellic had said, she beckoned to her friend, and when he approached she took his hand and placed it on the stone.

"Godwin, do you feel it?" she breathed. "The very power of the Earth itself. The life-force that sustains it. It is vigour and fire and green things growing!"

Godwin's eyes widened fractionally. Where his hand touched the menhir, he felt a tingling, faint but unmistakeable. He braced both hands against the rough surface.

"Bellic said that your race are attuned to it. Sensitive to its rhythm," she said. "It's stronger in some places than others, but the power is everywhere. The stones can draw it from the Earth."

"Magic," said Godwin reverently. "Like the magic I took from you. Like my sword … only weaker."

"This is a healing magic," she said. "A gentle magic. Undirected. The stones draw it up like wicks, but they have no will, so they can't use it. They hold it in trust for others. But the Earth contains other forces, too. There are dark, unwholesome beings, trapped and struggling beneath us. They have no flesh and despise the light, yet they long to walk abroad as we do, so they can destroy what they hate." She placed her finger-tips on the stone. She felt that communing with the Earth had granted her a share in its wisdom. "These beings are the Fetchen." And, somehow, I can feel *THEM*, too.

She quickly withdrew her hand.

"And Vieldrin wants to help them get out," said Godwin.

She nodded. "As Smirill did, but they can only be used so much, before they become uncontrollable. In the end they surpass their master in a way that good magic never can."

"So Vieldrin would be destroyed by the Fetchen."

"True," said Elgiva, "but they would be strengthened by his power and that of the Lorestone, too, I dare say, and they would be unleashed forever."

"But can't the Lorestone destroy these things?"

She shook her head. "Not destroy. Destroy darkness and there is no light." She grinned at him mischievously. "I remember somebody saying once that without evil, good has no meaning." Godwin nodded at this and smiled. "They can be contained and imprisoned, but they can't be destroyed. And it all depends on who wields the Lorestone and what their intentions are."

"How can you know this for certain?" he asked.

"I don't." She shrugged. "It's just a feeling."

From somewhere in the tree-tops came the hooting of the owl and its disembodied voice echoed like the mirth of shadows. A shiver skittered up Godwin's spine. Elgiva's mysticism had unnerved him. It reminded him too poignantly of the differences between them: Elf and Wilthkin, knowledge and ignorance, female and male, power and weakness. But perhaps their differences bound them together, made them need each other so much, like two halves of a whole.

Suddenly she turned to him with a look of doubt in her eyes. "You took a great risk in following me. You sacrificed many things. And I know you're torn in many directions and I … I'm ashamed to be the cause. The end of our quest isn't far ahead and I'm afraid … for myself and for you. You've done far more than anyone could have expected you to do and now I can't promise that I'll be able to defend you from … from whatever awaits. So…" She paused and swallowed hard and turned her face away. "So whatever vows you made to me … if you choose to leave, well … no-one could blame you."

He shook his head dismissively. "Don't worry about me," he told her. "Let's see this out together. To the finish." She smiled up at him gratefully. "Perhaps I did give up a lot, but nobody made me do it and it's nothing compared to what I've gained." And I love you so much, it breaks my heart.

"Very well, my friend," she said. She took his hand and squeezed it gently. "Now I think we'd better get some sleep, but I feel we'd do well to be on guard in such a place as this. I'll take the first watch."

⋆ ⋆ ⋆

When Elgiva woke Godwin later to take his turn on watch, he greeted it with a sense of relief. Strange dreams had beset him while he slept, dreams of barrows where dead men lay, rotting among their treasures, and spirits roamed in an earthbound stupor, envious of the living.

It was still several hours before the dawn and a clammy brume rose about the circle and curled round the feet of the lofty stones. The spring night was sharp and cold and Godwin added more wood to the fire and sat close to it, rubbing his hands. The owl hooted urgently from the trees, but Godwin paid it no heed.

But gradually he became aware that something wasn't right. An inexplicable apprehension rode the chill, night breeze. He noticed the strangely coiling mist that rose from the ground like steam, and watched as it crept towards him. It clung to his clothes with pulpy fingers, stroked wetly at his skin. Scanning the darkness on either side he couldn't see anything to account for the dread that writhed in his guts. Elgiva and Trystin were fast asleep and Grimalkin stood with her head lowered on the edge of the circle of stones. Above them all the moon and stars winked between gaps in the clouds.

And, yes, it was far too quiet.

He almost let out a yell of fear, when a ghostly shape swooped past his eyes, scant inches from his face. It was only the owl, but it had been startled and, as it soared noiselessly over the circle, he heard it hoot 'Beware!'

Just then a twig snapped like a dry bone in the blackness somewhere behind him and he stumbled to his feet in panic. Then he heard stealthy movement, sly rustlings in the grove of oaks, and his body tensed with foreboding. The merest hint of a whisper reached his fear-sharpened hearing. It seemed nothing more than the breeze in the leaves, but he realised that the breeze had dropped and the stillness was suddenly stifling, like the build up of pressure before a storm.

His hand shook as he drew out his sword and the noise it made seemed unnaturally loud in the thick and clammy silence. The rustling in the bushes ceased. Whoever he had been listening to, was also listening to him. Godwin hardly dared to move, as he glanced towards Grimalkin. Her ears were twitching in all directions and the firelight showed him the whites of her eyes.

He saw that the mist had thickened and swelled and it seemed to move of its own volition, needing no wind to propel it. It gleamed with an inner glow. He looked down, but he couldn't see his feet, for they were enveloped in fog. Likewise the stones seemed to rise out of clouds. Then he tried to move, but he couldn't. The turgid vapour that hugged his legs gripped him as though it had muscle and bone. He wanted to call out a warning, a protest, but some coercion stopped his throat. With horror squeezing at his heart, he watched the fog seep over the grass and roll towards Grimalkin. It coalesced around her form, like a cloud of pulverised nacre.

And then the rustlings startled again.

Grimalkin whinnied in terror, but then the compulsion of the mist forced her into silence.

Whispering hissed in the shadows and vague shapes scuttled towards the circle. Godwin fought his helplessness and tried to master himself. He tightened his grip on the hilt of his sword and with every ounce of will he possessed, he struggled to gasp out a single word.

"Taranuil..."

The name broke from him like a yelp of pain and the sword responded at once. A shiver of clean power coursed down the blade, flashed retribution at the mist. It helped Godwin to fight his inertia. Stooping, he slashed at the cloying fog and carved it into gaseous chunks. The fog recoiled like a living thing and he was released from its narcotic power.

He hastened to where his friends lay sleeping, cocooned in a cloud of vapour; it drew aside before him. Urgently, he shook them both and they struggled to open their eyes.

"We're attacked!" he cried. "You must wake up! There are creatures beyond the circle!"

Elgiva got quickly to her feet and her gaze flew straight to Grimalkin. The fog was up to her withers and a throbbing pulsated in its depths.

"This fog is unnatural!" Godwin cried. "Elgiva … you must do something!"

"They're after the Stone!" she hissed.

Grimalkin let out a whinny of fear, as the enveloping mist slid away from her, allowing dark shapes to take her captive.

The companions dashed towards Grimalkin, but, long before they reached her, three Elves sprang into the sarsen ring, moonlight glinting on their swords. Godwin ran to confront them, and his sword seemed to pull him behind it. He plied Taranuil to the purpose for which it had been forged and soon two of the Elves lay dead at his feet, their blood pumping in runnels over the grass. The third Elf drew back, a featureless shape against the background of glowing mist. Godwin prepared to attack him.

But then the surrounding vegetation and even the night itself appeared to rise up in a palpable mass and become a wall of darkness. It enclosed the circle of standing stones and boiled with malevolent power.

Weird cacklings and whisperings filled the night air. Trystin screamed with fear and his distress made Godwin hesitate, allowing the third Elf to make his escape. The dark wall opened to let him out before sealing itself up again.

Through the blackness that writhed around the circle, Godwin saw an Elf with a staff mounted on Grimalkin. She reared and bucked with all her strength, but she couldn't dislodge her attacker. The Elf hit her with his staff and Grimalkin whinnied in pain. Godwin ran to her rescue, but he slipped and fell on the blood-soaked grass and then the wall of darkness thickened and Grimalkin was lost from view.

"Grimalkin!" he cried. "Grimalkin!"

But all he could hear was the pounding of hooves, as Grimalkin galloped away and Godwin almost wept at the thought that everything was lost.

Darkness closed in around the companions. It became a flapping, shapeless mass, that looked like a flock of large, deformed birds caught up in a whirlwind. Godwin felt himself pulled towards them and he knew that their touch would be lethal.

"Elgiva! Where are you?" he shouted. "Help me!"

A sudden burst of blue-white force scorched across the circle. Godwin span round to face Elgiva and hurried to her side. She was standing before the camp-fire, which the poisonous air had almost put out, and Trystin was hunched at her feet, his body racked by whimpering cries.

Elgiva's bolt of magic had briefly banished the whirling shapes and they flew to the edge of the sarsen ring, hissing with displeasure. But then they drew slowly inwards again, like a tide of black, polluted water.

Elgiva grabbed Godwin by the sleeve. "Vieldrin left a trap for us! He left some Elves to steal the Stone, but he also left this … darkness! Godwin, these are the Fetchen! They can recognise other powers. They isolated the Lorestone, so the Elves could take it from us."

"And Grimalkin!" Godwin gasped.

"And their reward will be to kill us, before they return to their lairs!" she exclaimed. "But I don't intend to die just yet!"

She threw a bolt of magic at the hissing, fleshless creatures and they instantly recoiled, but those behind Elgiva seethed nearer than before. She span to hurl her power at them and the wall of darkness grew in size, rose higher round the circle. The air above the sarsen ring began to boil with whirling shapes and their whisperings and moanings became like the roar of the sea.

Elgiva knew it was hopeless. She couldn't hold back their loathsome ranks. Godwin watched as the shapes danced above them; though black, they were almost transparent, like veils suspended in the air, pieces of shadows cast adrift. And they flitted ever nearer. He didn't know how to protect himself, but he stabbed his sword at the cackling wisps and the Fetchen capered away from the blade, left it to ache with frustration.

Unhurriedly, the Fetchen revolved within the circle of stones. Their extremities took on the shape of claws and within the blackness of the horde, skeletal faces gibbered with glee. Their voices became an eerie howling that filled the sky with abomination.

Elgiva strained to shout above them, to recite the incantation that she had used against the Fellkin, but it only served to madden the shapes and their howls became ear-splitting shrieks. The noise brought tears to Godwin's eyes and he felt Trystin clutching at his legs, his body tensed with pain.

Elgiva was shaking with anger. A desperate beam of scarlet force sizzled from her finger-tips towards the murky mass. It splashed against their writhing forms and dripped like wasted blood. The Fetchen roared their hate at her and she blasted them again. And again and again she threw out power, until it began to fail.

Elgiva stopped to catch her breath and her head was swimming with effort. And she knew that fear restrained her; fear of the Light as much as the Dark.

Let go, she pleaded with herself. Let go.

But she couldn't. She didn't want to die. Her flesh was too frail to wield magic. The thought of unreined power appalled her. She was unskilled, untutored, weak.

Faine First-Father … help me!

She unleashed her magic once more at the Fetchen, but it was the product of desperation, ill-timed and ill-directed; a widely diffused discharge of power that rebounded off the Fetchens' might. They hurled it back at Elgiva and she and her friends were knocked flat by the blast and it burned on their skin like acid.

Regaining their feet, they clung to each other, while the Fetchen advanced to consume them.

Dazed by the blast, Godwin held up his sword, the only defence he could think of. Elgiva's eyes were drawn to the blade. It was still awake and eager, angered by its master's plight and ready to strike at the enemy. She didn't know the weapon's name, but she knew it was an Elf-blade, and it had been forged in such a way that magic couldn't warp its metal. And it had magic of its own.

She recalled how she had used Godwin's knife, when they were attacked at the Hill-Shrine, and then she remembered Bellic's advice. Channel it, he had said.

A rush of excitement lit up her face. "Godwin! Give me your sword!"

"What?" Godwin asked, bemused, as she tore the weapon from his hand.

She closed both hands around the hilt. Power hummed quietly down the blade. Forgive me, she thought, for the Forest of Shades. Let us now work together as friends. "Get down!" she commanded. "Both of you!"

Godwin and Trystin obeyed at once. Bewildered but trusting, they knelt at her feet, while the black shapes howled about them.

She held the sword out straight before her and summoned up her powers and, suddenly, a beam of light pulsed from the Elf-blade's tip. Like a ray of sunshine, it cut through the Fetchen, scattering them like old, dry leaves. Their shrieks of anger pierced the night. Elgiva turned slowly, round and round, and sliced through the whirling mass, but when the beam had passed them by, the Fetchen regrouped and shared their strength.

Her forehead creased with effort and sweat ran down her face, but this time she wasn't prepared to give up. I have to focus, she told herself. Body, mind and spirit.

The magic shaft intensified, became a blade of azure. Godwin and Trystin shielded their eyes. Taranuil hummed and jerked at the force that scorched along it, but the Elf-blade wasn't surpassed. Adding its own might to Elgiva's, it began to throb with mounting glee.

Let go, it told her. Let go. Let go.

And Elgiva abandoned all her fears and gave herself to the magic. It filled her limbs like ecstasy and nothing else existed. Her entire being revolved around it and power monopolised all her senses. She felt herself to be a part of all the magic that ever was or ever would be again.

Her power flooded into the night, overjoyed at its release, and Taranuil accepted it, channelled it away from her and threw it at the Fetchen. A searing, white beam of destruction, it lit up the whole of the sarsen ring, like an exploding star.

While Taranuil keened with power, Elgiva span round and round, cutting through the ranks of the foe. She stood at the hub of a wheel of might. The Fetchen gyred around her, like pieces of black and helpless anger, trying to swoop towards their prey, but Elgiva's magic pushed them back.

Then a new sound filled the air, a chiming rife with energy. The monoliths were singing!

Laughter welled up in Elgiva's throat. Now she knew what magic was. Magic was ecstasy, abandonment, freedom. Magic was total awareness. Magic was oneness with everything that was natural, pure and good.

The ringing of the sarsens' song rose to the sky, like the voice of the Earth. Awoken from their somnolence, they called to Elgiva's magic and it hummed through their granite hearts like passion.

In a sudden, simultaneous rush, the Fetchen flew from the circle, swirling in all directions with a noise like beating wings. The speed of their departure left a gust of air in its wake. It snatched at Elgiva's clothes and hair and howled off into the distance. The black shapes melted into the night.

But, as they went, their fading cries sounded more like triumph than defeat.

Elgiva extinguished her power. Darkness swooped back into the glade and the menhirs ceased their granite chimes. In her hand the sword gleamed, sated with power, then it reverted to its former state; a thing of cold, dead metal.

Godwin levered himself to his feet, his vision stippled by flashes of light. A smell of singeing hung in the air and the heat drew moisture from his skin. Helping Trystin to his feet, he put his arm around him.

For some time nobody moved or spoke. In the stillness Elgiva's ragged breathing sounded abnormally loud. Godwin suddenly realised that dawn was breaking beyond the trees. Birds were starting their morning songs, as if nothing had happened in the power-scourged glade.

Elgiva's hands were clenched at her sides and her eyes had a far away look. Taranuil lay at her feet and Godwin stooped to retrieve it, Trystin still clinging to his side. As he hefted the blade, he thought again of the differences between them. They had lived all their lives in separate worlds, spanned by a yawning gulf. Taranuil was the bridge.

"So," said Elgiva, "he's done it." She gritted her teeth against her rage, as her breathing slowly returned to normal.

"He has the Lorestone," sighed Godwin.

She flashed a look of hatred at him and an after-glow of magic glinted in her eyes. "I'm a fool!" she cried, gasping with anger, and he winced at the violence that crackled in her gaze, but he knew that it wasn't meant for him. "I should have kept the Lorestone beside me!"

"If we'd been attacked by Elves alone, we'd have been able to stop them," he said, "but those other things..."

"By Faine!" she cried. Blue flames curled along her arms and dripped to the grass with a sizzling sound. Godwin stepped back in alarm. "I'll smash him! I'll burn him! I'll snap every bone in his worthless body!"

With a cry of frustration, she hurled her magic into the pallid sky. Godwin watched as the bolt soared upwards. It burst high above like a monstrous flower, illuminating the sarsen ring down to its roots.

She sank to her knees and began to sob. Squinting against the pain in his eyes, Godwin placed his hand on her shoulder.

"We'd better follow Grimalkin," he said. "Perhaps she's managed to hold them up. We might be able to catch them."

She looked at him, her cheeks wet with tears. "Godwin … I've failed," she groaned.

"No, my dear, there's still a chance." Gently, he pushed Trystin away, so that he could sheath his sword.

"M-Master Godwin … I was afraid!"

"It's over now," said Godwin.

"Those black things…!"

"They're gone," said Elgiva. She ran her fingers through her hair. "They can't endure the light. Not yet."

Godwin felt a lump in his throat at the sight of her hag-ridden gaze. He helped her to her feet and smiled encouragement at both of his friends, in spite of his own despair. "Come on," he said, "we must follow Grimalkin, while her trail is fresh."

★ ★ ★

Chapter Thirty-Eight

For the rest of the day they travelled as quickly as they could, until weariness forced them to slow their pace. At one point they saw the signs of a struggle; a patch of dried blood and trampled grass. Fearing the worst, they hurried on. At length, they stopped beside a small stream and filled their empty stomachs with water.

"We can't go on like this," complained Godwin. "We must find something to eat."

Elgiva nodded half-heartedly and studied the far horizon. All she could think of was Grimalkin, heading away with the precious Lorestone.

"Couldn't your magic help us, Lady?"

"What?" She stared at Trystin and her eyes had a feverish cast. "No, I can't conjure up food. It would have to come from another place." Her gaze flicked back towards the horizon. "My magic's not strong enough to span any distance."

You could try, thought Godwin dourly. "But you are stronger," he said. "Much stronger."

She looked at him askance. "But without your sword…?"

He sighed.

Elgiva shrugged off the cling of despair. "We must pick what we can along the way. Roots, buds or anything else. Trystin, I leave that task to you. You know what things are good to eat."

"But please, no toadstools, lad," said Godwin, trying to be cheerful.

Trystin managed a wan smile.

⋆ ⋆ ⋆

It was half way through the following day, when they came to a ridge in the land. Rocks gleamed like splinters of bone in the grass. Following the pony's trail, they clambered up the slope and, having gained its level crest, they saw the land before them drop sharply down to a vast, flat plain.

Elgiva emitted a gasp of delight and closed her hand on Godwin's arm, her fingers pinching his flesh. "I'd no idea we were so close! Look … over there! Elindell!"

Godwin shook off her painful grasp and followed her jubilant gaze. The horizon had a hint of darkness, but it meant nothing to him. "It must be two leagues away, perhaps more."

They followed the trail along the ridge. Suddenly, the ground fell away and before them was a narrow rift, like a gash in the hump of land. The tracks of Elves ran along the rift and out across the plain, but the hoof marks ended at the edge. They peered into the fissure. A soft moan rose from the darkness below and they gazed at each other in horror. The plaintive murmur was unmistakeable.

"Grimalkin!" cried Elgiva.

"Lady Elgiva, what shall we do?"

"We'll get her out at once!"

All three of them squinted into the rift, not daring to think what injuries the pony had sustained.

"In Frigg's name, how?" asked Godwin, frowning.

"The quickest way," replied Elgiva. "Levitation." She smiled at Trystin. "I've already had some practice."

He returned her smile weakly and chewed his nails, while Godwin knelt upon the grass and peered into the fissure. He didn't know what levitation was, but he prayed that it would work.

"Grimalkin," he called, "can you hear me? Don't worry. We'll soon have you out of there."

Ragged breathing answered him from the darkness of the rift. He looked at Elgiva with hope in his eyes. She drew a deep breath and lifted her hands. Bruised and scraped from her climb up the hill, they seemed meagre tools for the task ahead, but her gaze was firm and steady.

"From out of this abyss, dark and drear,
"Grimalkin, arise, and have no fear.
"The power of Good suspend you high
"Above the sharp rocks where now you lie.
"Float towards me, friend so fair,
"Like a mote that rides the warm spring air."

The companions watched expectantly, then a dim shape rose from the fissure. Godwin glanced at Elgiva, hardly daring to breath for fear of breaking her concentration, but when he saw the effortless way she exercised her power, a thrill of excitement ran up his spine. He hugged his chest and tried to be patient. Elgiva continued her incantation.

"I order you stop, but do not drop.
"And float towards me, slow and sure.
"Lie at my feet; the spell is effete.
"Gently down and heavy once more."

Grimalkin's unconscious body obeyed Elgiva's commands and drifted slowly over the grass, then it came to a halt at Elgiva's feet.

They knelt beside her anxiously and Elgiva ran her sensitive hands over the pony's body. She wasn't badly injured, merely cut and bruised by the fall.

Elgiva smiled with relief. "Nothing broken," she said. "This creature is made of iron!" Godwin and Trystin grinned at each other. "But she's badly bruised," Elgiva went on, "and she's had a bad knock on the head. Thankfully, all the eating she's done since she's been with us has put lots of padding on her bones and saved her from serious damage." She nodded towards Grimalkin's pack, then sat back on her heels. "They've taken the Lorestone, of course."

"They pushed her down there on purpose!" fumed Godwin.

"They were far enough away from us and near enough to Vieldrin," she said. "Grimalkin was no longer needed." She began to unstrap the pony's pack. "And I dare say she played up too much and they were glad to be rid of her."

"The bastards could have just turned her loose," snarled Godwin.

"Poor Grimalkin," sniffed Trystin, his large eyes full of tears. "Lady Elgiva, will she be all right?" The fate of the Lorestone seemed small to him compared to the pain stretched out on the grass.

Elgiva hugged him comfortingly. "Yes, she'll be fine. Don't worry. But she won't be able to travel for a while and we haven't time to wait for her." She swept the tangled hair from her eyes and scanned the darkening sky. "The day grows old. We must go," she said, getting to her feet.

"But we can't just leave her here, all alone!" Trystin's gaze flitted back and forth and finally settled on Godwin.

Godwin smiled reassuringly. "I'll stay with her," he volunteered.

Elgiva turned to face him, questions thronging her gaze. "Godwin, I can't leave *YOU* behind!"

"We'll catch up with you," he assured her. "Anyway, you don't need me. Go to your uncle. He'll know what to do." Attempting to convince her, he added, "Take my sword, if you wish."

"Take your sword? I can't! It's yours!"

His generosity touched her, but it filled Godwin with secret shame. He feared the Forest of Elindell. It was a place of magic and peril, a place where he surely would founder and fail and be a hindrance to his friend.

To the finish. He had promised her that, but the final test had come and it had found him wanting. He found it hard to look at her, undeserving as he was of the love that shone in her eyes.

Suddenly, Trystin jumped to his feet and pointed across the plain and his eyes were wide with wonder. "Lady Elgiva, what is it?" he cried.

His companions followed the line of his gaze. Issuing from Elindell was a cloud of dust and, as it drew nearer, the sound it made resembled thunder. As the nebulous shape approached them, they saw within it a herd of horses. Their coats were white but their manes and tails were black as ebony. They galloped nearer, their necks thrust forward, dirt and grass flying from their hooves.

"The Royal Herd of Elindell!" Elgiva cried with delight.

"They're beautiful!" squealed Trystin.

Godwin was entranced, amazed. He saw the great animals skid to a halt at the bottom of the ridge. They stood there, snorting powerfully, their large hooves raking the earth. Godwin knew little of horses, but he realised that here before him was the finest herd he would ever see.

The horses raised their noble heads to the figures atop the ridge. They thrashed the air with their raven-black tails, which fell to the ground in silken splendour, and their black eyes glittered haughtily, for they knew themselves to be without equal.

Then one of the horses pranced lightly forwards. "I have come for the one who once cleaned my stable, whom now I honour as my Queen."

"Greetings, Alison Fiorin." Elgiva's response was formal, but her voice was full of suppressed excitement. "Greetings to you and the Royal Herd."

"The King is dead," Alison declared. "We have awaited you. Lord Bellic told us you would come."

Elgiva nodded. "Alsion, these are my friends. This is Godwin, who found the thing we sought, and Trystin, who knew where it was hidden. And this poor beast is Grimalkin, who kept it safe as long as she could until she was taken by wicked Elves."

Alison nodded slightly. "You must return at once," she said. "Elindell has a new King."

"Vieldrin, of course," said Elgiva coldly.

Alison snorted contemptuously at the mention of his name. "I am leader of the Royal Herd. I alone have the right to carry you."

Elgiva didn't hesitate. She slithered down the grassy slope and ran towards her friend. Her joy at seeing Alison could no longer be contained and she threw her arms around the horse's neck. Alison glared stonily at the sky, anxious to maintain her dignity.

"Dusk falls soon," she snickered. "Vieldrin has creatures about him at night. And he has the Lorestone. We cannot tarry … my long awaited friend." The Elf-horse nuzzled Elgiva's cheek, then quickly drew back her head.

Elgiva leapt onto the animal's back. "You stay, then, Godwin?" she asked. He nodded. "Trystin, what about you?"

The Elfling chewed his finger and pondered indecisively. His eyes flicked back and forth between Godwin and Elgiva, as though he were unable to decide which of them he loved the most.

"What should I do?" he fretted.

"You'd be safer here," said Elgiva.

"I'm not afraid!" declared Trystin. "And, when you kill Vieldrin, I want to be there to see it!" He straightened himself and tried to look brave, but his thin legs trembled beneath his tunic.

"Girasol will carry you," Alison announced. "He is gentle and surefooted. The best of mounts for a young Elf."

A handsome, young stallion trotted forwards and intercepted Trystin, as he scampered down the slope.

Alison swung her head round. "And what of your human friend, Elgiva?" Elgiva whispered in her ear and the great horse turned and stared at him. "So, Godwin," she said, "is it your intention to follow as soon as that pony revives?"

Godwin nodded stiffly. Alison was only a horse, but he felt humbled by her tone.

"Then I shall leave you my eldest son. Tanarus Aquila will carry you, when you are ready to travel. That pony will not be up to the task."

Giving him her eldest son might have been a compliment, but Godwin would have to decline. "No, really," he said, "there is no need."

"Fear not," said the mare condescendingly. "A recent injury to his leg makes him less swift than the rest of us."

He folded his arms defensively, annoyed that the horse had realised the truth behind his objection.

Trystin swung onto Girasol's back and the herd prepared to leave. Elgiva looked back at Godwin, but neither of them could say good-bye. They might never see each other again, but saying good-bye wouldn't help; it would only make the fear more real.

With a twinge of loss, Godwin watched as the herd thundered off towards the forest and, all too soon, their milky hides were sucked out of sight, like a cloud of vapour.

* * *

Godwin had made a small fire and was sitting beside it, watching the evening fall upon the land. In his lap he cradled Grimalkin's head and he stroked her forehead absently. The few provisions he had found in her pack had done little to fill his emptiness, but the loss of Elgiva bothered him far more than the gnawing of his stomach.

He looked down at the pony. He was glad that she had been unable to speak to the Royal Horses, for her form and manner would have been greeted with nothing but disdain - as he would suffer the scorn of Elves, were he to go to Elindell. Better that both of them stay where they were.

Above him the wispy, spindrift clouds were like brush-strokes across the lambent sky. The sun was falling towards its decline and soon every leaf and blade of grass took on a gleam of crimson. He watched as the daylight melted away and the sun dropped into its abyss of fire.

And, for a while, he fell asleep, but then Grimalkin stirred and woke him. The sky was the colour of charcoal and filled with glittering stars.

Grimalkin staggered to her feet and Godwin made shift to avoid her hooves. She shook her head and then her body and finally her matted tail. She cast off sleep like a chrysalis and emerged with a vigorous snort.

"Cabbage hearts! I'm reborn!" she exclaimed. "Dreamt of warm hay and spring greens."

"I'm glad you're up," said Godwin. "My legs had gone to sleep." He rubbed his thighs to alleviate the stab of returning life. "Your head weighs a lot, for something so empty." He clambered to his feet.

"You make a fine pillow, if nothing else," she snorted. "So where has everyone gone?" Godwin explained the situation. "So, you stayed behind to look after me, eh?" She thrust her long muzzle into his face and tried to lick his cheek. Godwin recoiled in disgust. "I gave them trouble, you know," she went on. "Kicked one in the gizzard. The other thought he was dead." She bared her yellow teeth in triumph.

"Quite brave of you, I suppose," said Godwin, "but they made you suffer for it. They pushed you down that chasm."

"Celery stalks! I've been in worse plights. Suffering's my lot."

"Well, at least you're feeling better."

"I'm in agony!" she protested. "But who am I to complain?" She gave him a large-eyed, martyred look and shook her scruffy mane.

It was then that Godwin's attention was drawn to something in the distance; two parallel lines of lights were moving slowly towards the ridge. He squinted to try to make sense of them. Just then, Alison's son appeared, striding up the bank, his body dim-grey in the darkness. The animals weighed each other up, while Godwin pointed across the plain.

"What's that?" he wondered, slightly alarmed.

"Don't ask me," said Grimalkin.

"It comes from Urith-Endil," Tanarus stated matter-of-factly.

"Should I put out the fire?" asked Godwin.

"We have already been observed," Tanarus replied.

And so they waited.

The strings of light-beads threaded their way closer to the ridge, and, as they drew nearer, Godwin could see that they formed a torchlight procession. Between the two rows was a golden litter carried by eight male Elves and they were all dressed in gold and white.

The procession halted fifty yards from the bottom of the ridge and from its midst four riders came, three bearing golden lances. When they reached the bank, they stopped and looked up and one of them hailed the three companions.

"Who are you and what is your purpose?"

Grimalkin snorted loudly. "None of your business, nosy!"

The Elf who had hailed them scowled at this. "I am Tercel," he said sternly. "Captain of the Guard. My Lady, Queen Gilda, will know your business, if you have any sense."

Grimalkin hissed in Godwin's ear. "Think the old slicer is due for an airing. Better safe than sorry."

Godwin unsheathed his sword.

⋆ ⋆ ⋆

Within a cave in the depths of the forest, sat Bellic, Elgiva and Trystin, while between them a small fire kept the darkness at bay. Merrill, the Captain of the Guard, stood in the maw of the cave, a gloved hand poised on the hilt of his sword, ready to fend off intruders.

"Well, Trystin," the Elf-lord was saying, "it makes my heart glad to see you alive, though I wish we had met at a happier time. But I see that you have left behind more than your former slavery." He reached out and touched the Elfling's cheek.

Trystin flushed with embarrassment, as he recalled the disfiguring scar, then he turned to Elgiva with a grin and his large eyes glowed with affection. Bellic nodded knowingly.

Elgiva was anxious to avoid all talk about her success with magic. "I'm glad to see you alive, too, uncle. Vieldrin hasn't harmed you."

"I have Merrill to thank for that," he said. "He has been my jailer for many months and pretended to be my tormentor, too, to spare me the malice of others."

Elgiva stared at the iron bands on her great-uncle's wrists and ankles and the chains that restricted his movements. "Forgive me, uncle Bellic," she sighed. "I can't break the spell that binds you."

The creases around the Elf-lord's eyes tightened momentarily. "It is better you do not, for now," he said, trying to lighten her mood. "If I am seen without my shackles, it would arouse suspicion."

His remark was unsatisfactory, but Elgiva refrained from comment. Silence settled like dust in the cave. Elgiva tugged at a hank of her hair, while Trystin studied the wielders of magic with barely suppressed anxiety. Then Elgiva lifted her gaze.

"I'll never confront Vieldrin on any terms but his own," she said, "and that's something I can't risk. He can use the Lorestone whenever he likes and he has the Fetchen to boost his power, and compared to that … I'm nothing."

"My dear," said Bellic reproachfully, "you must not give in. There must be a way. I sent out my spirit to speak with Gilda and she is on her way here. Behind her marches an army. Perhaps some diversion can be contrived."

Elgiva frowned at him. "What good will that do?" she demanded.

He winced at the harshness in her tone. For the first time in all their years together, he felt that she held the reins. He stroked his grey beard thoughtfully. "When Vieldrin uses the Lorestone, I think he will use it against you only."

"You think, but you don't *KNOW*."

He disregarded this. "Against his other enemies he will use his personal power and that of his creatures and guards. You must stay here and hide, Elgiva, until Queen Gilda arrives. Possibly the three of us can defeat him in magical combat."

"If we can take him unawares." She gave him a withering look.

"If Gilda's army attacks," he said, "it may distract him long enough for us to use our powers."

Elgiva shook her head doubtfully. "But why should he use the Stone against me? He could destroy me without it. In fact, he could kill us all at once. Postponing the moment makes no sense."

Despite his concern for Elvendom, a tiny voice in Bellic's mind tempted him with memories of quiet study and solitude. He drew a deep breath to dispel his fatigue.

"No-one knows the Lorestone's might, or what it is capable of, my dear, and you have forgotten something. Vieldrin's caprice and arrogance. You defied him, Elgiva. You made him look foolish... and then you escaped. He must make you pay for that, and you must be seen to pay. He will want to gloat on your defeat and his triumph will then be all the sweeter. His hatred for you consumes him and he will want a public display to show the rest of us who is master. We must be thankful that our opponent is bereft of the guidance of reason. It gives us more time to make our plans."

Elgiva was about to respond, but Merrill interrupted. "Forgive me, my Lord. It is time we should go."

"A few minutes more," pleaded Bellic.

"The Fetchen will be out soon," said Merrill. "My Lord, the curfew has passéd."

"Curfew, uncle?" asked Elgiva.

Bellic nodded sadly. "We must keep to our homes after sunset. Those who don't may fall prey to the Fetchen. At night they terrorise the forest, but they must return to their lairs before dawn, until their master finds a way to free them forever by wielding the Stone." Bellic's hands fretted in their chains. "I am unable to defend myself. These chains are a block to my powers and I must fear the Fetchen no less than the lowliest of the nar-Wardain."

"If I can't remove your chains," said Elgiva, "perhaps Queen Gilda can."

"She is a powerful Wardain, my dear, but do not worry on my account."

"It's difficult not to," said Elgiva. "We need your powers, uncle." Bellic seemed disconcerted and Elgiva realised that he had hoped for more personal a concern. "We need all the help we can get," she went on. "I know what evil the Fetchen possess. I dare say their touch could freeze the soul. They attacked us at the circle of stones."

"How did you purchase your escape?"

His question called up thoughts of Godwin and twinges of self-reproach. It had caused her pain to leave him behind. "I told you of my friend, who bears a magic sword? I used that sword to channel my power. I unleashed great force without harming myself."

"You did not bring it with you?"

Elgiva glared at him. "It belongs to Godwin! It was a gift ... his birth-right, uncle Bellic. And I couldn't take it from him, even though he offered me the use of it... I refused."

"Refused?" His eyebrows lifted in surprise.

"He wished to stay with our injured pony," Elgiva said defensively. "How could I take his sole means of protection?"

"I admire your concern for your friend, Elgiva, but the future of Elvendom is more pressing. You should have compelled him to come with you."

"Compelled!" she blazed. "I am not Vieldrin!"

Bellic nodded and then he smiled. "Indeed you are not," he said softly.

"Please, my Lord!" hissed Merrill.

Bellic hauled himself erect and sighed at the stiffness of his joints. "I must go," he stated. "I fear you must put out the fire, lest its light draws prying eyes."

Suddenly, Trystin jumped to his feet. "Why can't we steal the Stone?" he exclaimed.

"It is always at Vieldrin's side and he is surrounded by guards," said Bellic. "Could you steal it without his knowledge?"

"Turn me into a mouse!" cried Trystin. "I'll get into his Hall…"

"And how will you carry the Lorestone, Trystin?" Bellic smiled indulgently.

"Then … I'll make him use it on *ME*!"

"He would not," said the Elf-lord. "You would throw your life away needlessly."

"But we must do *SOMETHING*!"

"For now we must be patient, Trystin. Impetuous acts will only undo us. When Gilda arrives, we will think of a way to foil Vieldrin's plans."

Trystin sat down sulkily. He wished that he were older, then people might listen to what he said.

"Good night, my dear," said Bellic, kissing Elgiva on the brow. "Good night, Trystin. Try to rest. You both are weary and travel-worn. Stay in this cave and you will be safe. I sent the Royal Herd to look for you because they come and go as they please, so their movements do not arouse suspicion. Nobody knows you are here." He turned towards the Captain. "Merrill, I am ready."

Elgiva threw dirt onto the fire and the cave was plunged into darkness and she and Trystin sat in silence, wrestling with their thoughts.

Exhausted by anxiety, Elgiva began to drowse, but Trystin's unease kept him wide awake and he chewed his nails until his teeth ached, but it gave him no relief. He had to do something to help Elgiva, to prove his value to their quest, and if he threw his life away, then at least his last act would be one of courage.

"I don't care … I'm going!" he cried abruptly, springing to his feet.

His sudden departure startled Elgiva and he had gone before she could stop him.

She bolted after the Elfling, fearing to shout incase she was heard by the Fetchen or the guards. She hurled a thin ribbon of harmless fire in his general direction, hoping to bring him to his senses. She knew that she could easily kill him to prevent whatever reckless act he intended to perform, but she loved the Elfling far too much. And so she resolved to make no further attempts to hinder his progress by magic. She feared what her anger might unleash and she couldn't afford to alert whatever patrolled the benighted forest.

She was forced to rely on her native speed, but Trystin was younger and faster and fuelled by determination. He flitted through the underwood and she couldn't catch him up and soon he was swallowed up by the trees and the all-embracing darkness.

★ ★ ★

Chapter Thirty-Nine

Godwin explained the situation as briefly as he could and waited nervously, sword in hand, while Captain Tercel returned to the litter and spoke to its unknown occupant.

At length, the Captain hailed him sternly. "The Queen requests you to descend. She would have speech with you, Wilthkin." His tone made it clear that this was an order, not an invitation.

Godwin clambered down the bank, Grimalkin and the Elf-horse following close behind. He made for the golden litter, escorted by the lance-bearing guards. When he had approached within a few yards the Captain cried, 'Hold!' and he stopped in his tracks. Then the golden drapes were swished aside.

An apparition of loveliness moved gracefully from the litter and set her golden sandals upon the torchlight sward.

Queen Gilda appeared to be middle-aged, old enough to be his mother, but, stunned by the vision before him, Godwin neither knew nor cared. The black hair falling to her waist was streaked with strands of silver, but they seemed an intentional aid to her beauty, not a feature of ageing. Her body was plump but elegant and her face had a comfortable aspect, traced with fine lines that spoke of laughter, while her dark eyes glittered like gems. A circlet of gold stars crowned her head and each star had a pearl at its centre. In the long, white robe that skimmed the grass, she possessed all the trappings of queenship. And she radiated power.

She scrutinised Godwin gently and her eyes seemed to see right through him and she smiled with such warmth that he felt his heart melt. His mouth fell open dumbly.

Godwin was enchanted.

"Invaginate your sword, young man," Queen Gilda commanded softly, her eyebrows arched with mischievous humour.

He lifted the sword and gaped at it stupidly, as though he had lost his wits. The Elf-queen's face lit up with pleasure.

"Come closer," she said urgently.

Woodenly, Godwin stepped towards her. The nearer he was, the greater became Queen Gilda's emanations. She seemed to shimmer with benevolent power. Magic had touched him so many times that now he could easily sense its presence and he knew that before him stood a being whose powers were fully matured; they took his breath away. But with this knowledge came a sudden, unwelcome realisation: Elgiva totally lacked this aura.

"Your sword, if you please," said Queen Gilda.

Godwin extended the weapon and she took it from him with a smile. To his surprise it began to hum, as though overjoyed by her touch.

"Many moons have travelled the sky since last I held you, Taranuil," said the Elf-queen happily. She flashed her glittering eyes at Godwin and he almost dissolved into the grass. "Do I enchant you, Aidan?" she asked him matter-of-factly.

Godwin stood, his mouth hanging open, a yearning for the Elf-queen throbbing in his veins. "You … you're so … so beautiful," was all he managed to say.

She grinned and her mouth appeared to be a repository for pearls. "It would seem that I do. Please forgive me."

The Queen reached out her left hand and touched him on the cheek. For a moment, his brain reeled with desire, then the night congealed about him and suddenly drew into focus.

"Aidan, dear, I am glad to see that you have treasured my gift," she said. "Has it shown you your courage?"

Godwin's mouth fell open again, this time in disbelief. "*YOUR* gift?"

"Use the proper form of address," muttered the Captain beside the litter.

"Quell your indignation, Tercel," chided Queen Gilda gently. "He is unfamiliar with our ways. We will dispense with formalities."

The Captain bowed stiffly. "Yes, Your Majesty."

"How fares your father, Aidan?"

Godwin fought for self-control. It seemed that his life had become a series of startling revelations. "My father is dead, my Lady."

"Ah, me!" Her expression darkened with sorrow. "He was a good Wilthkin. And what of your mother?"

"She, too."

"I am sorry for that."

"My Lady, this is all a bit too much for me to take in. Did you say *YOU* gave me this sword?"

"It was my birth-gift to you," she replied. "The magic it contains is mine."

"Then I must thank you."

"There is no need." She smiled at him affectionately. Her warm, melodic voice took the edge off his confusion and he started to feel at ease.

"You travel with little Elgiva," she said. "She has gone to see Bellic, I was told, and we also are planning to meet him. It is my intention to treat for peace in the hope that this will buy us some time – though how we shall use the time so gained is a matter quite beyond me. I have heard of this Lorestone, of course, but lacking lorewisdom as I do, I know little about such things." She smiled at this confession. "I must hope that Lord Bellic contrives some means of foiling Vieldrin's plans. My army follows close behind. I intend to make camp here and wait for them." She turned towards the Captain. "Tercel, my dear, we will rest here."

"Yes, Your Majesty." The Captain marched off down the procession, barking orders at the Elves.

Queen Gilda glanced at Taranuil. "Sleep now," she said, and, smiling broadly, she handed the sword back to its master. Godwin accepted it with a smile and slid it back into its scabbard.

"Will you eat with us, Aidan?" asked the Queen. "You have a lean and hungry look. A little food would be welcome, I think." She offered him her pale-skinned hand and they strolled towards a heap of wood that the servants had stacked upon the grass. With a glance she set it alight. "When I made you the gift of Taranuil, I also made a promise, my dear," the Queen reminded him. "I offered you my protection, should you ever lose your family. Are you perhaps a little too old to be in need of adoption? Well, being a widow, I suppose that I could give you my hand in marriage."

He scratched the stubble on his chin and gaped at the Elf-queen blankly. Her suggestion seemed to be serious, though her eyes were sparkling with gentle humour. But, if she were in earnest, he felt that he would find it very hard to refuse.

"Fear not, my dear," she said, squeezing his arm, "I am a whimsical creature. Were I to suggest such a union, my counsellors would fall down in a fit. They are a dull assembly and horribly strict about Elven laws." She chuckled merrily. "Well, then, you cannot be my husband, so I will have you as a son, in memory of your dear, kind father. He was so good to my own child. And now I may deal kindly with his. Hold out your right hand, Aidan."

When he complied, she grasped his hand and pressed their palms together. There was a brief sensation of heat and, when she withdrew, he saw that she had left a mark upon his skin. There was a brand in the shape of a star and within it a rune that meant nothing to him. Then he realised that it was identical to the marks on Taranuil.

"That is my mark," explained Queen Gilda. "No matter where you travel, this brand guarantees safe passage through all the Elven lands. Likewise, no Elf who sees this mark will refuse you food or shelter. From now on you are 'Elfryth' – Elf-friend."

Godwin found himself lost for words. All his thoughts revolved around the magic of the Elf-queen's touch. A servant scurried forwards and offered him fruit on a golden tray. He helped himself without looking.

"Henceforth you may call yourself my son and my counsellors must accept it. They will throw up their hands in horror, of course, and fret about the unthinkable – a Wilthkin inheriting Urith-Endil!"

Godwin almost choked on the fruit. Looking up he saw Captain Tercel standing some yards away. His face was grim and humourless and dark with disapproval and, Godwin suspected, a touch of envy.

The Queen's mellifluous laughter rang in Godwin's ears. "Aidan, do not worry. I have two sons and a daughter. They and their issue will rule after me."

Godwin looked at her demurely. From his experience he well knew that the future was nothing if not uncertain and there were no guarantees. He forced a smile to conceal his disquiet.

"I am honoured to be your adopted son," he said, bowing slightly in her direction.

"And I am glad you accept the title. Such eyes as yours are wasted on Wilthkin. They speak of potentials and passions that only an Elf could comprehend."

"Oh … really?" Her candour made him blush.

Queen Gilda laughed. "My son, you enchant me!"

Godwin searched the grass at his feet, looking for some composure, then he remembered his obligations. "Lady, I think I should leave now," he said. Queen Gilda's eyebrows lifted in query. "I intended to follow Elgiva, as soon as our pony was able to travel." He looked out over the landscape. The dawn was breaking in the east.

Gilda nodded with sad acceptance. "Indeed. Your friend is dear to you and you wish to be at her side. Forgive me for detaining you. I am loath to let you go, my dear, but perhaps if you rode on ahead of us, you could forewarn Lord Bellic of our arrival. That lovely Elf-horse will get you there swiftly. Is he bound to you?"

"No," he said hastily. "He's just … a guide."

"But you must be swift." She lowered her voice. "That pony, she is ewe-necked, poor dear, and has too little heart-room. A perilous mount, to be sure. You do not intend to ride her, my son?"

Godwin blinked at Queen Gilda. He didn't intend to ride either of them, but he understood the need for haste and how could he give in to cowardice, when he was the son of an Elven Queen?

As if to mirror his thoughts, she said, "You must ride a beast that accords with your rank."

Godwin saw that he had no choice. Bowing slightly to the Queen, he went grudgingly to meet his fate.

"Hold, my son!" she commanded.

For a second, Godwin ignored her, already forgetting his new-found status. The ensuing silence reminded him and he turned to face the Queen.

"No son of mine, by birth or adoption, shall walk the land like a beggar," she said. "Those filthy rags must be transformed."

Filthy rags? He looked down at himself and saw, as if for the first time, the dried blood that stiffened his trousers. It puzzled him for a moment, until he remembered the sarsen ring and how he had slipped on the gore-caked grass. His clothes were stained and ragged. They were filthy and so was he.

She made a brief gesture in the air and he was engulfed by a golden light. It spiralled about him giddily, then gradually receded. To his astonishment, Godwin found that he was now attired in Queen Gilda's colours. His clothes were essentially still the same, but now they were new and impeccably white and on his tunic, above his heart, a gold star had been embroidered. Runes of gold glittered on his belt and Joskin's cloak now reached to the ground, white and silken and edged with gold braid. His mop of hair had been neatly trimmed, too, and he was clean and shaven. He felt as fresh as the dawn.

He gaped at the transformation. "By Frigg!"

Queen Gilda laughed and her beautiful hands were clasped at her breast with delight. "What a fine Elf you would make, my son!"

Godwin smiled and bowed his thanks and then he turned towards Tanarus. The muscled bulk of the mighty horse reared up in snorting splendour and disdain gleamed in his eyes. He cringed as Godwin touched his mane, but he knew this Wilthkin was Elfryth and could not be refused.

Godwin tried to mount the great horse, while the Queen's attendants muffled their laughter, then a sharp glance from their mistress persuaded them to go to his aid. They heaved the reluctant warrior onto the animal's back. The ground reeled far below him, but between the hard earth and Godwin's fear was the bulk of the haughty stallion, a creature of power and frightening speed.

"Tanarus," asked Godwin gingerly, "can I hang onto your mane?"

"If you must," said Tanarus, stamping his foot.

"Go with all haste," Queen Gilda urged. "We will follow anon. Good-bye, my son."

"Good-bye … er … Mother," said Godwin.

The Queen's eyes sparkled with laughter at this, then she turned to confer with the scowling Captain.

With a horrible jolt, Tanarus set off and Godwin clung desperately to his mane. Every muscle was painfully tensed to stop him from sliding off the smooth back, while the world flew dizzily past him. This was a new experience for Godwin and one that he wouldn't care to repeat. He risked a glance behind him. Grimalkin was tearing after them and he feared that she would overtax herself, but he was grateful for her presence.

"Are you all right, Grimalkin?" he shouted.

"Are you mad?" she whinnied wheezily. "I'm an old woman, I am. Unfit for mad dashes like this."

"Why persist, old crone?" neighed Tanarus, who wasn't even breathing hard. "Your heart will burst for certain."

"Well, I'm tenacious. Grant me that. My race, bred for stamina. We pulled chariots at the gallop. Not like you young whippersnappers. One quick canter and you're finished. Legs like straws, you have."

"Ha!" the Elf-horse snorted. "You are on your knees already!"

"Cabbage hearts! I am, am I?"

With a pang of dread, Godwin sensed the brewing of some mischief. He tensed himself apprehensively and only a moment later Grimalkin lurched forwards and closed the gap. Thrusting out her sinewy neck, she clamped her teeth on the great horse's rump. Tanarus reared up with an ear-splitting shriek, his dignity abandoned, while Godwin held on as best as he could. With an unbelievable turn of speed, Grimalkin charged ahead of them.

"Come on, strawshanks!" she taunted. "I'll race you!"

Tanarus accepted the challenge and thundered after Grimalkin with all the speed he could muster. Godwin hugged the straining neck, as the Elf-horse pursued his tormentor, who goaded him on with derisive remarks.

As they galloped madly towards the forest, Godwin watched his past life flashing before his eyes.

* * *

Trystin knew he must be swift. He ran on through the leafy bowers, avoiding the pathways and glades, where dwellings lay still drugged with sleep. Here was the chance for him to prove himself by redeeming Faine's gift from the clutches of evil. Now was the time to show his friends that he was an asset to them, not merely an item of baggage that they had brought from Misterell; a silly Elfling, ruled by his fears.

At last he arrived at the great Hall. Crouching low in the underwood, he took stock of his surroundings. A handful of guards stood outside the main doors, talking in lowered voices. Torches were set in the ground before them.

Misterell had taught him stealth and he knew how to move without making a sound. He noticed a door at the side of the Hall and crept towards it, like a shadow. A lone guard patrolled the flank of the building and Trystin sat and watched him, chewing his finger nails nervously and wondering how to divert the sentry so he could slip in through the door.

Then it seemed that fate was on his side, when the guards at the main doors started to quarrel and their voices rose in contention. Scowling, the sentry left his post and marched across to join them. Trystin gladly seized his chance and within moments he was at the side door. He lifted the latch. It was unbolted and his heart leapt with joy at his good fortune.

Silently, he slipped inside and found himself in semi-darkness with only the light of a solitary torch that smoked above the hearth. Closing the door behind him, he tiptoed over the wooden floor.

Beside the hearth lay a massive hound. It lifted its head and snarled. The dying embers of the fire cast a reddish light on the animal's back and its large eyes glowed like rubies.

"Hush, friend dog," whispered Trystin, a finger against his lips.

"You're after the King," growled the hound. Trystin's heartbeat quickened its pace, but the hound laid its head between its paws and let out a weary sigh. "You're welcome to him," it said. "Over there. He's sleeping behind those drapes."

Trystin padded the length of the Hall towards the curtained chamber, then, after a moment's hesitation, he summoned up his courage and twitched the hangings aside. Vieldrin lay on a raised bed, a woollen blanket pulled up to his chest. On the bench beside him a chunk of candle glimmered in a sconce. In his arms he cradled the Lorestone, as though it were a baby.

Trystin's heart was in his throat, as he looked at the slumbering king, and his mouth was parched with terror. Yet he wished he had brought a weapon. How easy it would be for him to kill Vieldrin where he lay.

Then he heard a cry from outside and he flinched as though he had been hit. Blades clanged together outside the Hall.

Vieldrin stirred and frowned in his sleep. Horrified, Trystin stepped away and hid himself in an alcove. He heard the Elf-king curse with rage, then the sound of his feet upon the floor. The swish of the drapes made him snatch in his breath.

"What's going on?" demanded the King. "Who dares to wake me with this noise?"

Vieldrin marched across the Hall and the hound stood up and began to bark at the sight of its angry master.

"Silence, you worm-riddled cur!" yelled the King. Picking up a flagon of wine, he flung it at the dog. With a yelp of fear it scuttled away, its tail between its legs.

The King hurled force at the Hall's main doors and they threw themselves open so violently that all of their hinges buckled. Trystin watched with a pounding heart, as Vieldrin strode out into the night.

"I'll have you all throttled with wire!" roared the King. "I'll feed your guts to the hounds! I'll teach you to quarrel, when you're on watch! Get back to your posts this instant!"

Confused and angry as he was, Vieldrin had left the Stone behind. Carefully, Trystin sneaked back through the drapes. The Lorestone lay on the blanket. He darted forwards and snatched it up, a glint of triumph in his eyes. Then, quitting the chamber, he made for the door, grinning at his success. Checking to see that his way was clear, he crept towards the undergrowth.

But there he was caught.

A hand was clamped across his mouth and he was dragged to the grass and he felt that shock and terror would surely burst his heart. But then he recognised his captor and he felt dizzy with relief. Slowly she released him.

"Oh … Lady Elgiva!"

"In Faine's name, what have you done?" she hissed.

"I have it … I have it … Look!" He held out the Stone and she sucked in her breath. Trystin beamed with pride. "Lady Elgiva, take it!"

"What's that noise there?" demanded Vieldrin. He marched from the entrance of the Hall, his fists upon his hips. "Ware, you dogs, we have prowlers!"

"Run!" urged Elgiva. "Back to the cave!"

They fled into the forest.

But they didn't make it back to the cave. They had barely left the great Hall behind, when a wall of darkness blocked their path: a darkness with features and claws.

"By Faine! The Fetchen!" cried Elgiva. "I can't fight them again …I Can't! We mustn't let them touch us, Trystin." She pushed the Elfling behind her.

Shrieking with glee, the Fetchen formed a ring around the Elves, and slowly they were herded back towards the Royal Hall. Then, suddenly, a gap appeared in the writhing wall of shapes and the King strode forward into the ring, a clutch of guards at his back.

"Elgiva, my dear, what a pleasant surprise."

* * *

Grimalkin had reached the edge of the forest some minutes before Tanarus. She collapsed in the grass, her nostrils flaring and her coat all lathered with sweat.

Presently, Tanarus appeared. He came to such a sudden halt, that Godwin slid the length of his neck and into the nearest bush.

"Beat you!" snorted Grimalkin. "I beat you!" Her brown eyes rolled with exertion.

"Half kill yourself and call it victory?" Tanarus neighed contemptuously. "And I was forced to slacken my pace. My leg is not yet healed."

Grimalkin wheezed disdain at him. Godwin pulled himself from the bush and knelt at the pony's side. In his heart he was proud of what she had done. Who would have thought that the elderly nag had such a turn of speed?

"I was weighed down by that human, or I would have beaten you, lame or not," snapped the Elf-horse angrily. "He flops up and down like a sack of turnips."

Grimalkin heaved herself to her feet. "Excuses," she snickered jeeringly. "You're a whingebag and a pain in the arse."

The stallion flashed the whites of his eyes. "Never before has anyone dared to speak to me like that!" he raged.

"Then it's high time they did," said Godwin, spinning round to face him. "By Frigg, you needed a lesson badly! Grimalkin has bested you, like it or not."

Tanarus emitted a snort of outrage. "Insolent, two-pronged bag of turnips!" His large eyes glittered dangerously.

"Get lost!" said Godwin. "You don't frighten me." And, to his surprise, he was speaking the truth.

With a scornful whinny, the horse limped away, assuring them that his mother would learn how he had been insulted.

"When beauty is clothed in vanity, it's an ugly thing," said Godwin.

Grimalkin considered this piece of philosophy, then she shook her large head sagely. "Aye, Brit, that's true," she snickered. "You can't tell a carrot by its leaves."

Godwin grinned and patted her neck. "Queen Gilda said you had too little heart-room. I suppose she meant that your body is too small to hold such a great heart."

"No, Brit, that's not what it means."

"What does it mean, then, Grimalkin?"

"Never mind." She nuzzled his cheek. "I prefer your definition."

The sudden appearance of an armour-clad Elf took them both by surprise. Godwin quickly drew his sword, but the Elf held up his empty hands to show that he meant no harm. His gaze had a distracted look that sent shivers up Godwin's spine.

"Are you Godwin?" he asked. "Elgiva's friend?"

"What if I am?" returned Godwin dourly.

"I'm Merrill, Captain of the Guard. Lord Bellic spoke of you." Godwin narrowed his eyes and said nothing. "I await Queen Gilda's arrival," said Merrill. "Did you see any sign of her on your way here?"

Godwin nodded slowly and Merrill looked him up and down, puzzled to see a Wilthkin dressed in the colours of Urith-Endil, but far too polite to remark upon it.

"Don't doubt me, Godwin," Merrill said. "I'm Elgiva's friend, too, and that's the truth."

"Easily said," remarked Godwin, "but not so easily proven."

The Captain spread his hands apart in a gesture of helplessness, then he let them fall to his sides. A cloud of despair seemed to settle upon him. "Everything goes amiss," he sighed. "Lord Bellic is under close arrest and warriors are marching against Queen Gilda. She can't kill them all, nor would she, for she knows they serve Vieldrin out of fear. I have no power to stop them. I'm helpless, and that's the truth. And..." He paused and looked at Godwin with a mixture of sadness and sympathy. "And, worst of all, my friend, little Elgiva and Trystin are taken."

"Taken?" repeated Godwin, aghast.

"Just before daybreak," said Merrill. "The Elfling tried some hare-brained scheme to get the Lorestone, and failed."

Grimalkin snorted wetly. "That sounds like the little whingebag," she said.

Godwin cursed under his breath. "Are they all right?" he demanded.

"As far as I know," replied Merrill, "but Elgiva seemed to have given up. I offered to take care of their confinement, but Vieldrin said I should go to blazes. He put them under some sort of spell – though by the look of those two wretched creatures, he didn't need magic to subdue them. Then the guards took them off somewhere and others went to get Lord Bellic. I came straight here to wait for Queen Gilda. Didn't know what else to do."

Godwin leant against Grimalkin and let out a sight of despair.

"Please," urged Merrill, stepping forward, "come with me to a place of safety – if there's one to be found. The forest's alive with Vieldrin's guards. And we're all to assemble at sunset. I'll try to hide you till then. Vieldrin says there's to be some sport. Faine knows what he's got in mind." He tugged at Godwin's sleeve. "Come."

"I must help Elgiva!" cried Godwin, snatching back his arm.

"Indeed," said Merrill, "but how? Vieldrin has the Lorestone and the means to use it. There's nothing we can do. I don't even know where they've taken Elgiva. And she'll be well guarded, count on that."

"But you're the Captain of the Guard! Can't you do something … anything?"

"No-one's going to listen to me with Vieldrin breathing down their necks. The truth is, only Queen

Gilda has any chance of beating Vieldrin, but even she can't fight the Lorestone. See sense, man. You must hide."

The Captain turned and hurried away and Godwin gloomily followed him. He felt that the world was about to end.

* * *

Chapter Forty

Dusk was falling over the forest and thick clouds curdled the blood-shot sky. In a clearing specially made for the purpose, the Elves of Elindell were assembled. A handful of armed Elves patrolled the scene, for most of Vieldrin's warriors were guarding the forest's perimeter.

Godwin, Grimalkin and Captain Merrill stood at the rear of the crowd and, despite his fear of what was to come, Godwin had to marvel at the sight of so many Elves. The forest was huge, but still he wondered how so many beings could live within it so unobtrusively.

He looked out over the sea of heads and in front of the crowd he saw two platforms. They stood about twenty feet apart and were raised several feet off the grass. With a knot of dread in his stomach, Godwin surmised their grim purpose.

"There's Bellic," hissed Merrill suddenly.

Godwin started, then turned to the left and followed Merrill's gaze. Flanked by two armed warriors, the Elf-lord shuffled into the glade and his age-lined face was slack with defeat. Iron bands circled his ankles and wrists and were bound together by chains. Behind him trudged a younger Elf in parti-coloured clothes and under his arm he carried a lyre.

"Caspell, the minstrel," Merrill said softly.

Godwin nodded. He knew that he had heard the name before, but he couldn't remember when or where and for some unknown reason it carried with it a pang of nostalgia and loss.

Caspell stood between the platforms and turned to face the crowd. In a quavering voice, he began to sing a refrain in honour of Vieldrin. The strings of the lyre twanged like sorrow.

Muted murmurings ran through the crowd, but not all of them were dismayed. Tarkinell scanned the gathering, a grin on his sharp-featured face. He spotted Merrill at the rear and elbowed his way towards him. Godwin edged into the shadows, as the hawk-faced Elf drew near, but Tarkinell wouldn't have seen him, for his eyes saw only power.

"Well, well," said Tarkinell unctuously, "a great day for Elvendom, would you not say?"

The Captain smiled evasively.

"Power, Merrill, and martial might. A warrior's dream to be sure. You must be proud to be part of all this."

"I obey orders," Merrill said.

"Ah, yes, we must all obey orders, for the sake of the common weal." Tarkinell's eyes glinted greedily. "In doing so we benefit from the rule of law and order."

"Law and order, Chief Counsellor?"

"Indeed. You may think that the King is a little severe with us, but, Merrill, we have grown lazy and lax. Vieldrin must be seen to be strong, for he means to unite Elvendom. We must give him our support."

"But what becomes of freedom?" asked Merrill.

"Tish!" retorted Tarkinell. "A nebulous thing, to be sure. No-one ever attains it, but loses everything else. Freedom to do what?"

At that moment, Caspell's song came to a mournful end and a blare of horns resounded across the clearing. Anxious to be near the King, Tarkinell turned and pushed his way carelessly through the crowd.

All eyes swivelled to the right, as Vieldrin ascended the nearest platform. He wore the Crown of Elindell and his scarlet robe was studded with gems. In the crook of his left arm he cradled the Lorestone. With his elegant frame and handsome face, he looked every inch a monarch. For a while he stood, his eyebrows arched, and contemplated the crowd.

"Well?" he snarled. "No cries of joy to welcome your lord and master?"

The Elves responded half-heartedly. Vieldrin looked upon them all with a cold and steely glare and Godwin found himself clenching his fists, as the dark eyes swept across him.

Vieldrin turned and signalled to his guards beyond the trees. As one, the crowd stared to the left and watched as Elgiva and Trystin were dragged into the glade. The Elfling was made to stand at the front, while two guards pushed Elgiva onto the wooden platform. She stood there blank-faced in her tattered shift, her hands hanging limp at her sides.

She had suffered some ill-treatment and Godwin winced at the sight of her. Raw-eyed and bruised, she looked like a wraith. Despair and fatigue had eroded the pertness of her features and she seemed to have aged prematurely. He wrapped his arms about his chest to still his pounding heart and his mind was labouring frantically.

If only he could get to her, offer her his sword.

Then Vieldrin's voice boomed across the crowd. "People of Elindell," he said, "Elgiva and I are here to provide a little entertainment. You remember Elgiva, do you not? She has aspired to be your queen, but I am about to demonstrate that she is unworthy to rule. Her paltry powers would be useless, if you needed her protection. A ruler must be strong and bold, and lorewise, too, I think. Three virtues that I own in equal measure and I shall provide you with ample proof." His cruel eyes scanned the crowd and he offered them a perfect smile, clearly enjoying himself. "I challenge the upstart Elgiva to a contest of magic. To the death."

Anxious murmurs ran through the crowd and Bellic's weary, desperate voice rose above them all.

"The contest is unfair!" he cried. "You possess the Lorestone!"

Vieldrin frowned. "Be still, old fool. Your senile mumblings grate on my ear. What I have, I have by virtue of my courage and cleverness. Two more attributes I possess that mark me out as fit to rule."

"Then, if you are such a perfect ruler, have you no compassion? Mercy is also a kingly virtue."

Vieldrin glared at Bellic, his eyebrows arched disdainfully. "Showing mercy is not always prudent, especially towards one's enemies. Mercy is for fools and weaklings. Should I show her mercy, then, and have her turn upon me later, like an ungrateful cur? I offered her joint rule, but she made her position clear. There is no other option."

"Then take away her powers!" cried Bellic. "It can be done … You have the Stone!"

Shocked by these words, Elgiva broke the confines of her stupor. She turned towards her great-uncle, her face a mask of outrage beneath her dirty, tangled hair. "How dare you!" she cried angrily. "My powers are my inheritance, to do with as I please. It took me long enough to find them. I don't intend to give them up now! By Faine, I won't surrender and I'll accept no mercy from a cold-blooded killer like him!" She raised her chin defiantly. "I will put my faith in the First-Father and I will endure what I must!" Her tortured gaze fanned out over the crowd and she sensed the presence of friends. A half-smile touched her bloodless lips. "I believe it's better to die once, than die a little every day."

Godwin felt his throat constrict, as he heard her speak these words. He hugged his chest and prayed that her courage would see her through the ordeal ahead.

Vieldrin laughed derisively, though something in his eyes suggested that Elgiva's stance unnerved him. "You see, old man, how no-one listens? You can teach us nothing. A new era dawns and cowards like you can have no place in it. Watch and despair, old fool. Your turn will quickly come." He span to face his warriors. "Night falls. Light your torches. The audience must be able to see everything that happens here. We do not want them disappointed. But stand well back. My friends are a little wary of light." He grinned with cruel pleasure, as the guards carried out his commands.

"Firstly," he went on, arching his brows, "let us have a little prelude to the entertainment."

A restless hush fell on the crowd, as the Elf-king raised an elegant hand and began to chant an incantation.

"I call to those so cruelly banished,
"Come, sweet allies, sage and sear,
"Arise from the clinging darkness here.
"From your deep lairs arise and dance;
"Amuse us with your dalliance.
"The foul sun has been vanquished!"

There was a long drawn out moment of suspense, then, like black fumes seeping from a fissure in the ground, the subterranean Fetchen left their lairs and floated upwards. Rising around the platform, they circled their master with undisguised glee, full of wild joy at being released from the cold, dark caverns of the Earth.

Everyone cringed in horror at the sight of the evil shades, but Vieldrin laughed, as they swooped round his head.

"Soon I shall free you entirely," he promised. "Yes, I shall harness the Lorestone's might and make you immune to the sun. Then its rays will no longer trouble you. Then you shall work my will! But for now, pretty malkins, a dance and a song would be a most welcome diversion. I trust that you came prepared? The audience needs warming up before the contest begins!"

The formless spirits chuckled at this and swarmed between the platforms, where they gathered in a circle. They began to spin like wind-tossed leaves and their voices hissed like serpents.

"Let the sun lie dead and the black mould spread.
"Let the horse be lame that pulls the plough.
"Let the ripe fruit rot; bare be the bough.
"Let the farmer rail and the tall corn fail.
"Let the fungus creep and the children weep.
"Let slime of snail and mildew's scent
"Smother all the innocent."

As their dancing grew more frenzied, so, too, did their eldritch chanting. The Elves recoiled in revulsion, but the horrid fascination of the whirling Fetchen held them where they stood. Vieldrin grinned hugely and clapped his hands, urging his creatures on. Their wild cacophony stunned the trees, profaned the peaceful twilight and sent nocturnal animals scurrying for their dens.

The evil song droned on, eating into the air like gangrene.

"See the gelid dead below;
"To clinging clay the bodies go.
"Cankered buds and mildewed leaves,
"Crippled roots and stunted trees.
"Wither every stinking flower,
"By putrescence be devoured.
"Beauty falls, as we arise
"To poison the water and stain the skies."

Godwin heard weeping in the crowd and saw tiny Elf-children cling to their parents and his heart was suffused with outrage. Cursing at his helplessness, he rested a hand on Grimalkin's neck, knotted his fingers in her mane, and felt her body trembling.

A guard with a torch stood a few feet away, so that Godwin was bathed in a pool of light, but no-one remarked upon his presence; all eyes were enthralled by the dance of the Fetchen.

Godwin's gaze found its way to Elgiva, lost and alone on the platform, and he couldn't imagine what thoughts racked her mind, what hopes she might still be nursing. She seemed subdued and broken, though a flush of anger tinged her pale cheeks, darkening her bruises. If only she could strike Vieldrin before he used the Lorestone, strike him with a lethal blast!

Elgiva's head turned fractionally and she caught Godwin's eye, but all they could do was stare at each other. She saw his fear and desperation and it grieved her beyond endurance, more so because she could give him no comfort. She had failed him. She was weak. Vieldrin had the Lorestone and she would die and so would her friends.

But accepting failure wasn't easy. Surely this couldn't be the reward for all that they had suffered? Had Faine intended evil to win, when he left the Stone for posterity? There must be a chance. There must be.

She wrenched her attention away from her friend. He had seen surrender in her eyes and the hurt in his gaze was unbearable.

Then she looked at Trystin, who was spellbound by the capering Fetchen. His body shook with abhorrence and the hopeless terror in his eyes was like kindling to her anger.

Her friends would die. They would die without hope, the image of her surrender pursuing them to oblivion. For their sakes, if not for hers, she must fight on. Fate had chosen Vieldrin to be the wielder of the Stone, because he had stronger magic, greater will and greater cunning, but love was still worth fighting for, no matter how futile the attempt. Love, innocence and friendship were surely stronger than hatred and cruelty and greed.

And what of the prophecies? Were they all wrong? How had she come to this sorry state? Was it just a mistake?

She studied Vieldrin closely, as he gazed dewy-eyed at his minions, the Lorestone cradled in his hands. His head was tilted to one side and he seemed unaware of her existence. It was as if the purpose of their meeting was forgotten. His beautiful, black eyes widened with pleasure, as he admired the Fetchen, and Elgiva couldn't be certain, but he looked a little older. There were shadows of depravity upon his handsome face. Was evil leaching his youth away? Or was it the torchlight playing tricks on her eyes? Whatever the cause, she drew strength from the sight.

She didn't know that Vieldrin was also watching her, craftily from the tail of his eye, nor did she know that his mind was in conflict. Flushed with anger and loathing, she was beautiful and he desired her. Her defiance had sparked both his hate and his yearning. Never again would he have such a foe on whom to unleash his might. A pity he couldn't ravish her, before he took her life.

He squeezed the Lorestone tighter. Once Faine's power had been unleashed, he would be supreme in Elvendom. But then what challenges would be left?

He frowned. No matter. At least he would finally rid himself of these disturbing emotions. Her death would purge him of such perversities.

Elgiva averted her eyes from the King and followed the dance of the Fetchen. As they spewed forth their hatred of all the things she knew to be good and natural, anguish and wrath welled up in her heart and she screwed up her eyes to hold back her tears. Magic began to shape itself around the hub of her anger and it lifted itself bold and clean, like a new-forged blade preparing to strike.

Faine, I will not believe it, she thought. I will not believe that we are defeated.

The pressure of magic that bulged in her brain demanded to be released and, regardless of the consequences, she had to let it out.

The assembly was suddenly jerked to attention as a blast of blue light burst from Elgiva and spiralled about the clearing, like a whirlwind of magical force. The Fetchen shrieked and capered madly, caught in a gale of power. Howls of confusion tore from their throats, as the light scythed into them.

Scowling ferally, Vieldrin threw up a shield of force to protect himself. Regret simmered beneath his rage; the moment for battle had finally come and his sport would soon be over.

Abruptly, Elgiva's power went out. She was breathing hard, but her eyes gleamed defiance as she turned to face Vieldrin. "Enough," she said. "I won't endure this any longer."

"You will endure what you must," mocked Vieldrin. "You wish me to retaliate?" He held up the Lorestone for all to see and torchlight sparkled on its perfect surface. "Shall I use this now, think you? Or shall I toy with you awhile? The crowd are expecting some entertainment."

"Crown, come down!" commanded Elgiva.

Immediately the Crown of Elindell tumbled from Vieldrin's head, clattered across the platform and rolled into the grass. All eyes watched it wheel and glitter until it came to a halt, midway between the two platforms. Someone hidden in the crowd ventured a nervous giggle.

Vieldrin scowled at the fallen circlet, then his face grew dark with vengeance. He thrust out his arm. The tree immediately behind Elgiva began to topple towards her. It made a great cracking and splintering sound as its roots snapped free from the earth. There were gasps and cries from the crowd.

Quickly, Elgiva raised her hand, her palm towards the tottering giant. "Stop! Don't drop! Ill it boots to leave your roots. Don't lean at all. Stand straight and tall."

As though considering what she had said, the tree paused and swayed, creaking with stress. Then, with agonising slowness, it gradually righted itself and the crowd expelled the air from their lungs in one long sigh of relief.

Elgiva turned to face Vieldrin; her brows were arched and her dark eyes glittered. "Are you trying to amuse yourself, or me?" she asked him with the air of one who knows that they have nothing to lose.

Vieldrin snarled and tore a gem from the sleeve of his scarlet robe, then he hurled it at Elgiva. As it flew through the air it became a large boulder.

"Go home, errant stone!" commanded Elgiva, her hands held up before her, as though to fend it off.

The boulder halted impossibly, hung in the air, then it cast itself back at Vieldrin. He didn't have time to deflect it with magic, so was forced to duck to avoid it. The boulder impacted behind him and splintered the planks at the edge of the platform before it rolled away.

Springing erect, Vieldrin hurled a thread of fire at his enemy. It burst against her shield of force, scattering sparks in all directions. The crowd cried in terror and covered their faces but, shackled by their fear of the King, they didn't dare leave the arena of combat.

Elgiva lowered her magical shield and unleashed a ball of lightning that screamed towards her opponent. With an arc of flame he deflected it and sent it spinning into the sky. It detonated above the forest and illuminated the tree-tops like an exploding comet.

And so they continued, fire against fire, until the air was blistered and their bodies drooped with exhaustion. The atmosphere buzzed and crackled with power and the crowd were crouching on the grass, whimpering with fright.

Finally, Vieldrin threw up a wall of force between himself and Elgiva. It writhed with cold, red flames, and, try as she might, Elgiva couldn't breach it with her darts of power. Then she felt herself weakening and her magic began to falter.

Godwin could bear it no longer.

I made a vow to protect her, he thought. I can't let her die like this! Not alone!

He fought his way through the crowd of Elves and ran to save his friend. As he neared the front, Trystin looked at him and the Elfling's thoughts seemed to mirror his own. Trystin broke away from the guards and together they made for the platform.

"No!" cried Elgiva, extending her hand, and from somewhere deep inside herself she wrenched a bolt of power. It gently stopped them in their tracks and held them where they stood. "You will not sacrifice yourselves!"

"Elgiva … in the name of Faine!" Godwin fell to his knees and wept.

"Godwin … I have faith," she said softly.

Vieldrin's laughter reached their ears. "Distract her, my dark friends!"

The Fetchen converged upon Elgiva, hissing and churning madly, uniting their power against her. She threw weak bolts at their fleshless shapes, but her strength was ebbing quickly. Her well of magic had now run dry and her body could stand no more. She felt a cold paralysis creeping along her limbs. Her magic guttered and went out.

Vieldrin nodded with satisfaction. With a cruel smirk, he surveyed the crowd and their terror filled him with pleasure. "Now the Stone shall work my will!"

Bellic buried his face in his hands, unable to bear Elgiva's defeat, while Godwin pulled Trystin to his side and turned the Elfling's face away to spare him the sight of the horror to come. The Fetchen bobbed around her, their skeletal faces taut with relish, but Elgiva stood calm and resolute, sweat running down her cheeks like tears, and squared her shoulders bravely. There was nothing else she could do.

She needed to look at Godwin; for the last time she had to smile at him in honour of their friendship, in memory of all he had done for her. His artless eyes smiled back at her and she felt a pang in her heart. Perhaps they can get away, she thought. Faine, please let my friends be saved!

Vieldrin was glowing with triumph. He held up the Lorestone with both hands and showed it to the crowd. "Behold, this is the Lorestone and its name is Peronel!"

A gleam lit up inside the Stone and all eyes were drawn towards it.

Vieldrin bent his whole being towards the use of magic and the veins stood out on his forehead. His dark eyes smouldered. His body trembled. And then he began to chant.

"Destroy Elgiva; shrivel her.
"In fire and torment swivel her.
"Wither her; deliver her
"From life and body. Break her.
"Let breath and soul forsake her,
"And all her friends, and any who
"Opposed my will, or thought to do.
"Grant me power greater then
"That combined of Elf and Man,
"Of tree and plant and beast and light,
"Of stone and water, earth and night.
"Sole master make me of this land;
"Put awesome power in my hand,
"And make me with one single spell,
"Heir to Faine's magic, Peronel!"

It seemed that Time then lurched to a halt, that the globe of the Earth had ceased to spin, and a sound like distant thunder rumbled over the clearing. The ground shook. The trees quivered. Every leaf vibrated.

"Behold!" laughed Vieldrin. "The Lorestone's might! It comes! Its wrath is upon you all!"

His laughter rose insanely, as the opal began to glow in his hands.

It became a pulsing sphere of scarlet, like a bead of blood in the wound of the night.

Vieldrin's grin stretched wider.

Then the Stone was a globe of amber; a tiny and perfect sun; a ball as blue as a summer sky; an orb of deepest indigo; a jewel of lavender.

One by one, the colours changed, and then the Stone was a vivid green. It filled the glade with a rich, warm light and the smell of green, growing things and it throbbed like the anger of Nature.

Drunk with power, Vieldrin locked his gaze upon Elgiva. He wanted to savour every moment.

But why ... why was she smiling...?

And then the colours appeared together and a rainbow shot from the heart of the Lorestone and arced across the glade.

Lightning exploded in the air and screamed across the cloud-locked sky and a deafening boom of thunder cracked above the forest, knocking its inhabitants off their feet with one huge detonation.

The might of the Lorestone flooded the glade, hurling the darkness aside. All eyes were sightless before it, all ears were deaf, all mouths were mute, and raw, untrammelled magic rode the night, like the spirit of vengeance.

And as he lay sprawled on the grass, numb to the core of his being, Godwin was aware of nothing; nothing but Taranuil, as it keened in its sheath in fellowship with the Lorestone's awakened power.

Its wordless song was like the laughter of metal.

⋆ ⋆ ⋆

Chapter Forty-One

"Be at peace, Elgiva. All is well."

Elgiva opened her eyes slowly and searched for the source of the voice. "Where am I? Who are you? *WHERE* are you?"

"You are out of the body. You know who I am, and where we are is of no importance."

Elgiva stood wrapped in a pearly mist and she couldn't see beyond it – and she felt that there might be nothing to see. A figure slowly approached her, a young, male Elf in a long, white robe, his black hair falling down to his waist. His large eyes glittered like stars.

"Did you like my trick … the rainbow thing? I thought it would give you hope." The Elfling laughed mischievously.

"First-Father?" wondered Elgiva. He nodded with delight. "But you're so young!" she exclaimed.

"Not really, my child," the Elfling said. "I appear to you as I did in life, when I was at my happiest. It is the custom in Spirit. You see me before I discovered magic, before all my burdens came to me. But perhaps you need me older and wiser." In an instant he changed and his hair turned grey and he was middle-aged.

"Why am I here?" she asked. "Am I dead?"

"You are very much alive, but I brought you here so that we could talk."

"What's happened to my friends?"

"Fear not. They are all quite safe."

"And … Vieldrin?"

"He is … somewhat changed."

"What do you mean?"

"You will see, my child." A smile spread across his face. "The Lorestone contained good magic only and could only be used for good. Would I leave such terrible power to chance? Once awakened, it searched for evil and, having found it, acted upon it and righted what was wrong."

Elgiva frowned in puzzlement. "I don't understand this at all," she said. "This means that Vieldrin couldn't win?"

"It is evil that could not win," said Faine. "Had Vieldrin used the Lorestone to benefit Elvendom, he would have prospered by it. He would have been Elwardain and his name would long be remembered with love in the annals of our people. He would have been my heir … and he would be standing here, not you."

"So I wasn't the chosen one?"

"You were because you chose yourself. You were true to yourself, my child. You resented the burden placed upon you, but even so you accepted it and you never abandoned it. In your heart you knew what was right."

"So the prophecies were wrong," she said.

"The prophecies were not wrong, as you shall understand."

"But they told me I was ordained!" she protested.

"No-one was ordained, my child, only the time of evil. I knew how and when my gift would be found, so that balance could be restored, but everything else was left to the choice and the free will of those involved."

"But … they brought me up as a servant … a slave!"

"And had they not done so, you, my child, would not be who you are. And you have proved yourself worthy, because of your integrity, your struggles and your faith –

and most of all your love. When you faced what you thought was certain death, you made sure that your friends could not intervene. You put their well being before your own and your last thoughts were of them. And even to the very end, you still had faith in good magic … in me. It was always a question of faith." A broad smile lit up his kind, wise face. "And, tell me, had you been the one to unleash the might of the Lorestone, would you have killed Vieldrin?"

"No," she admitted reluctantly.

"Another reason why you prevailed. You would have found another way. Your heart is good, little Elf." He reached out and touched her on the brow. "They who persecute evil shall prosper and come to their inheritance and you, who are most worthy, inherit my power, child. For a twelvemonth only I give you this gift, so the balance is preserved."

Elgiva felt warmth flood into her soul and it filled her with strength and vigour.

"You are supreme in Elvendom and I know you will use this power wisely and act for the welfare of all. There are things you need to do. Go now, Elwardain. It is done."

Elgiva looked at him pleadingly. "Will I see you again, First-Father?"

"You see me now because of the Lorestone. It was a link with my spirit. When it was awakened, it called to me, but the Lorestone is no more. Yes, you will see me again one day, but not for a very long time. And then we will have time to talk. All the time in the world." The grin returned once more to his face and he was again an Elfling, his large eyes twinkling with laughter. "Believe it and it shall be so – and that, my child, is the first rule of magic!"

And the mist rose up and took her away.

* * *

At the moment when the power of the Lorestone was unleashed upon Elindell, Queen Gilda and fifteen-score warriors were engaged in battle with Vieldrin's troops near the border of the forest. The battle had barely started, when the darkness growled with thunder, the earth vibrated under their feet and a flash of lightning seared the sky. Then the blast broke over them and the horses threw their riders and, blinded by a wall of light, the warriors panicked and fell to the ground.

The blast then scaled upwards into a high-pitched whine that mounted towards some dire explosion. The trees whipped back and forth. Queen Gilda's litter was overturned and blown along the grass and everything seemed twisted and tossed in a whirlwind of magical force.

A sudden, silent concussion and it was all over.

Then it was dark and the sky brimmed with stars. Showers of leaves, twigs and dirt that had gathered above the forest, began to fall back to the earth, bringing with them a palpable calm. The warriors looked at each other and then they gathered their wits together. Many hurried to help Queen Gilda and right the golden litter, while others calmed the horses and retrieved the scattered war-gear.

Overtaken by curiosity, their hostilities forgotten, both sides marched into the great forest, Queen Gilda at their head.

They thought that they would find it blasted and burnt, but everything was as it always had been. They stumbled on through the underwood and all around them the trees were singing; the oaks were booming soft and low, while the willows and beech trees tinkled like waterfalls. When they reached the centre of the forest, surprise stopped them in their tracks.

A great crowd of Elves lay strewn on the grass. Some stirred feebly and uttered low moans, while a few had managed to lift their heads and were gazing round in bafflement. A heap of blackened, steaming planks could be seen at one end of the clearing and a golden circlet lay on the grass and glittered in the fitful light of the many abandoned torches.

Queen Gilda and her followers let their gaze stray over the scene to a second platform, still intact, and the figure standing upon it drew their eyes irresistibly.

Just then, Godwin lifted his head, the cool, night air restoring his senses. Something warm was lying beside him and, forcing his gaze into focus, he saw that it was Trystin. Both of them were uninjured, but, to his amazement, Godwin saw that Trystin's bruises had gone and he himself felt whole and well. In fact, he had never felt better.

Then his heart lurched into his throat: what had become of Elgiva! He got to his knees and stared at the platform, fearing what he would see.

There stood Elgiva, robed in white, and her eyes were like embers that smouldered with power. Her pale complexion was flawless and her body gave off a pearly glow, as though she were a creature of moonlight. Her hair fell shimmering down to her waist and, when she moved, it crackled with force.

And Elgiva knew that she was different now. Her old self was no more, but it was right and necessary. Power surged in her veins, but it no longer hurt. It would never hurt again.

And she knew that she and Faine were One; yet there was Faine, and there was no Faine. Faine was a part of the Oneness; Faine was apart from the Oneness. Faine was everywhere and nowhere. She wished she could stay with this feeling forever.

Godwin stumbled to his feet. What had become of his frail, young friend with her bruises and her tattered shift? Now she was a being of fire, Elwardain of Elvendom, and should he approach her as a friend or as a humble subject, a mere creeping thing in her shadow?

He grasped the hilt of Taranuil and begged it to give him the strength to fight the awesome enchantment that flooded his senses. Then he staggered towards the fallen crown and plucked it from the grass. Elgiva's eyes followed him calmly, as he carried the circlet towards her.

Then she frowned slightly and he stopped in his tracks, compelled by her gaze as effectively as if she had uttered a verbal command. Her eyes were terrible wells of power and he felt that his legs would melt beneath him, but her soft mouth curved into a smile and the warmth of it filled him with joy.

"Don't be afraid, my friend," she said, "but I don't think you should touch me yet. I think I might burn you, if you did.The power has not quite been … absorbed."

"What happened, Elgiva?"

"Look," she said, and she pointed towards the other platform.

There before it on the grass Godwin could see the Lorestone, no longer opalescent, but black and neatly cracked in half. A thin wisp of smoke issued from the core.

"Its power is now mine," she said.

A sudden movement caught Godwin's eye. Beside the Stone, its fore-paws raised, a tiny creature sat, twitching its nose. "By Frigg, a mouse!" he said. The creature squeaked and ran away.

Elgiva laughed. "That must be Vieldrin." Godwin stared at her. "The First-Father doesn't approve of killing, when there's another way. Vieldrin will find it very hard to rule Elvendom now! And he'll soon know how his victims felt, when he's living in fear of hawks and owls."

She smiled at him again, a smile of knowledge and consummation, and he knew that she was still his friend, still Elgiva, and she smiled for him alone; and as he watched, her fire faded and the power retreated inwards. Soon she stood before him complete and in control, the magic as much a part of her as her flesh and blood and bones.

She dropped to her knees and sat back on her legs, folding her hands in her lap. As she bowed her head towards him, he placed the crown upon it, marvelling at her beautiful hair. "Faine returned your sacrifice." He reached out and stroked the gleaming tresses.

She nodded, took both his hands in hers, and he took pleasure in the knowledge that he alone was the object of her attention. He glanced to his left and the affrighted faces of many Elves stared back at him, not daring to intervene.

"You are wearing Queen Gilda's colours," she said.

"I'm her adopted son," he replied.

This bald explanation seemed to suffice. The questions could wait for another time, but for now they just wanted to look at each other and share the success of their quest.

Then Bellic stepped forward and bowed to his great-niece and his grey, lined face now glowed with joy. Godwin felt curses spring to his lips at this sudden interruption. After all that he and Elgiva had been through, he felt that they deserved more time to enjoy their triumph and their friendship.

Elgiva glared coldly at her great-uncle, as though she, too, were annoyed by his presence. Reluctantly, she released Godwin's hands and he almost voiced a protest. He felt that he had been severed from the meaning of his existence.

Rising to her feet, Elgiva waved her hand casually in Bellic's direction and the fetters fell from his limbs. Then, as though activated by a single mind, the other Elves cast off their stupor and hurried to pay homage to their Queen. Trystin, however, ignored all formalities. He bounded onto the platform and threw his arms round Elgiva's waist, hugging her fiercely.

"Lady Elgiva, you saved us!" he cried, his large eyes sparkling with happy tears. "We're free of him. We're free!"

Gently, Elgiva pushed him away. "I did nothing," she insisted. "Faine left the Lorestone to combat evil and that's exactly what it did."

"No, no!" protested Trystin. "You're good, Lady Elgiva, and the Lorestone knew it. You saved us all by being yourself."

Elgiva smiled and accepted the compliment, but Godwin saw sadness in her dark eyes and wondered at it. There seemed to be something on her mind and he felt a sudden sense of loss that he didn't understand.

Elgiva turned to the crowd of Elves. "Vieldrin has been dealt with and the Fetchen are back where they belong. It seems to me we should have a celebration. Messengers will be sent out to invite our friends to join us and two weeks hence we will all meet together."

Just then, a figure jumped up and scuttled towards the trees. Elgiva stopped him with a glance and held him in a web of power. He struggled for a moment, but was compelled to turn and look at her. Grinning faces in the crowd watched expectantly.

"Ah, Tarkinell," said Elgiva, a chilling softness in her tone, "conspirator and evil-doer. Your ambitions appear to have come to nothing. I have a mind to banish you, as I was banished."

As she spoke her voice seemed to deepen and mature and it carried great authority. Tarkinell's jaw fell in horror and he stood trembling from head to foot, his hands clasped together, as if to plead for mercy.

"There are bare, bleak mountains far to the north," continued the Elwardain. "It is a place of cold winds and cruel rocks with nothing to eat but coarse grass and bitter roots. Perhaps I shall send you there and confine you by magic, until you have wasted away." Her eyebrows arched mischievously. "I will think about it. Take him away."

The Counsellor collapsed like a broken doll and two grinning warriors heaved him upright and dragged him from the scene.

"Now," said Elgiva, "I call upon Bellic, wise in lore, to offer up thanks to Faine. Sister, would you stand at my side, while we listen to his words?"

All heads turned towards Queen Gilda, who still stood at the edge of the clearing. She gathered her wits about her. "I regret that I was detained in coming to your aid," she said, "but glad that my help was not required. Elgiva, my dear, I shall now be honoured to stand with you – and my dear son, Aidan." Her face broke into a broad smile, revealing her pearly teeth. "My dears, this is truly a night to remember, and thank Lord Faine for our part in it, however humble that might have been."

As she stepped sedately towards the platform, Grimalkin suddenly regained her senses and startled the crowd with a piercing whinny. "Cabbage hearts! What happened?"

"You're safe, you old nag," laughed Godwin. "Everyone's safe and Vieldrin is gone."

"We're about to offer thanks to Lord Faine," said Elgiva, smiling.

"Well, my poor, old body's quite had enough," complained Grimalkin, shaking her head. "But I'll give thanks to old Faine, too. I'll sacrifice some carrots, if there's any to be had. Not the correct observance, but he won't mind. After all, I'm just a dumb beast. See you later, then." She butted the nearest Elf in the back. "Where do you keep the carrots, eh?"

★ ★ ★

Chapter Forty-Two

The day of celebration neared. The Royal Hall was festooned with garlands, new gowns received their final stitches, ovens sweated in the steam-filled kitchens and the boughs of trees were heavy with lanterns.

In his hut some distance from the Hall, Godwin grimaced at his new attire. The tailors had made him a gold-braided tunic, slim-legged trousers and a billowing cloak and they were kingly garments indeed, but they were elvish, and he wasn't. He felt that he should represent his race, but instead the Elves had absorbed him, as if to make him respectable.

Yet, had he been dressed in green and gold – the colours of the Elwardain – he suspected that he might have been happier.

As he left the hut, he saw Grimalkin surrounded by giggling Elves. They capered away as he approached. It seemed that the craze for decoration was going a bit too far. The pony's mane and tail were plaited with ribbons and on her head was a green, felt hat, with two holes cut out for her ears and roses round the brim. Godwin thought he might never stop laughing.

Grimalkin snorted indignantly and tossed her ungainly head and the hat slid over her eyes. "Now we both look ridiculous, Brit." Godwin gave her a pained look and pushed the hat back into position. "We don't belong here," she added.

This observation unnerved him, but he decided to ignore it. "Have you met the other guests yet?"

"Who could see anything stuck out here?"

Inwardly, Godwin agreed with her. It had hurt him to be given quarters so far from the Royal Hall, but, of course, he was a Wilthkin and would never be truly accepted here, no matter how many Elven queens adopted him as their son. At least the pony had kept him company.

"Well," continued Grimalkin, "I did hear dogs yapping. Yap, yap, bloody yap, while I was trying to sleep. What use are dogs, eh? Stupid things. Howling and scrapping and pissing up trees."

"They're wolves, not dogs," snapped Godwin.

"Same stable, different horse."

Godwin strolled up and down for a while, his scabbard slapping against his thigh. He wanted to ask her a question, but was concerned not to seem too needy. "Have you seen Elgiva?" he ventured.

Grimalkin peered from under her hat. "She's too busy to bother with us. Lots to do, I'll warrant. Don't fret. It only *SEEMS* like she's forgotten us."

Godwin tore a leaf from a shrub and studied it intently.

"Why don't you go and see her? Don't tell me you're afraid to." He looked at her indignantly. "Well," continued Grimalkin, "she's a high and mighty ruler now. Daunting, isn't it? But she's still your friend, for all that."

He nodded abjectly at this.

"You're like a cabbage," she snorted.

"What?"

"You're all heart and no head. Always thought you couldn't be as dense as you make out. Now I'm not so sure."

"Don't you ever stop?"

"Brit, if I had a son," she said, gazing into his eyes, "I wouldn't want him to turn out anything like you." She snickered at his indignation. "A son! And why not? There's life in me yet. But I'm fussy, you know. Oswald put me with all sorts of nags, but I kicked their teeth in, the worm-riddled bastards. Only the best for Grimalkin. He realised that in the end."

"What in Frigg's name are you talking about?"

"I know what love is, Godwin."

Godwin was totally taken aback. Never before had she used his name and he knew that for once she was being serious. Gently, he placed his hand on her neck. "You do?" he asked her tentatively.

"Course I do," she snorted. "It's when folk start acting like idiots for no apparent reason."

"By Frigg!" He pulled his hand away angrily.

"But why now, Brit?" she persisted. "You've always been in love with her." Godwin raised his eyebrows at this, but refrained from making a comment. "A terrible thing, rejection."

He turned away and folded his arms. "Now that I'm going to lose her … I know how much she means to me, and my life … well, without her it will be empty."

"Life goes on," she stated. "And you know there'd be no future in it, even if she was just any old Elf. And there's your wife back home."

"Yes. I know. I miss her."

"You going to see Elgiva, then?"

"Well…"

"You'll see her tomorrow, of course, if you can contain yourself. Course, you won't get much chance to talk to her then. Well, while you're dithering, I'll be off.

A gang of Elves is heading this way. Don't want anymore decorating. See you later, Brit."

Godwin stood awhile, deep in thought, then he reached a decision and set off for the Royal Hall.

He soon came to the conclusion that a conspiracy to delay him seemed to be afoot. A group of excited Elflings (they wanted to hear all about his adventures), Trystin (horribly anxious to show off his new clothes), and a wagon with one wheel adrift (the driver begged for his help), had used up most of the afternoon by the time that Godwin reached the great Hall. Once there, the servants were far too busy to stop and answer his questions, and had it not been for a brace of hounds that were sniffing round the kitchens he would have searched the place in vain for a sight of his Elven friend.

They told him that the Elwardain had gone into the forest to find some peace and quiet and Godwin determined to track her down or die in the attempt.

* * *

The Elwardain of Elvendom sat beneath an ancient yew tree deep in the heart of the forest, before her the graves of her ancestors. She didn't stir at the sounds of movement that reached her from the underwood: there was no longer room for fear in her heart.

The foliage parted and Godwin appeared, relieved to have found her at last. Then he saw the headstones and he felt like an intruder.

"Godwin," she said quietly, "come and sit beside me. It's really peaceful here."

Her voice was deeper than he remembered. He sat and leaned against the tree. He was gladdened by the nearness of his friend and the day's frustrations were forgotten.

"You're paying your respects?" he asked.

She pointed at the nearest headstones; two had fresh flowers at their base. "Those two are my parents, King Ner and Queen Erlina." Beside these stones was a smaller one. "That's me. Do you remember? I died when I was a baby. They called me Princess Elfreyan. The grave is empty, of course."

For a moment, Godwin went back in time to Kendra's lonely, little house. "Yes, I remember," he said. He felt acutely uncomfortable and waited for her to speak again.

"Not a name I'd have chosen myself." She looked at him and smiled.

Godwin felt himself relax. "It's so long since I've seen you," he ventured.

Elgiva looked away. When she spoke, there was tension in her voice. "Less than a week, my friend," she said. "I'm sorry it's seemed so long to you. I've been extremely busy. Godwin, you must understand, I'm not merely a Wardain, but an Elwardain as well. I'm ruler of Elvendom, its guide and its protector."

Godwin nodded uselessly, as if he understood, or even cared, but all that really concerned him was Elgiva's translucent beauty.

"This is the oldest tree in the forest," she said inconsequentially.

Godwin wasn't listening. Deep in his heart he nurtured a hope: that she could remove all the obstacles with just one wave of her hand, that she could somehow make everything right and he wouldn't have to leave her.

Suddenly he realised that she was watching him and in her eyes he saw his thoughts, captured and foolishly naked.

"W-what?" He blushed and cursed his weakness.

"This tree is perhaps a thousand years old. It grew here long before we were born and it will still be here, when we are dead. Some things never change. I used to sit here as a child, when life was too grim to bear. It taught me how to endure." She touched the flaky bark with her fingers, as though the tree were a sacred relic. "He sleeps," she said with a smile. "The last time I sat beneath these boughs, I was clad in servant's rags."

"It's a fine, old tree indeed," said Godwin, but to him it was still just a tree.

With a sharp pang of sadness he realised that Elgiva was no longer childlike and frail and in need of his protection, but independent and powerful. Though he needed her now, as a man needs a woman, she had no need of him. She had come to her inheritance.

They sat awhile in silence. The sun had started to sink in the west, staining the clouds with crimson.

Elgiva toyed with a strand of her hair. "I still find it all so hard to believe," she said, at length. "Do you?"

He looked at her. She seemed more relaxed and there was something in her tone that made him think of the old Elgiva. "Yes," he said eagerly. "When we first met – do you remember, Elgiva? – we sheltered under a tree, just like we're sitting now. I was the slave of a warlord, a nothing. Now look at me, a Gododdin chief, the son of an Elf-queen, and Elfryth."

"I, too, began as nothing," she said. "Now I rule the Eldrakin. Their welfare is in my keeping. I'm waited upon by servants. Elders ask my advice. So many decisions and duties. It's strange … ironic, even. By gaining my freedom, I seem to have lost it."

Her wistful tone wrenched Godwin's heart. "A pity we can't go back," he sighed. "Return to our first meeting. To the days when life was simple."

"Was it?" She ran her fingers through her hair. "Godwin, we can never go back. What's happened to us has been for the best. It was all part of Destiny's plan. You always believed in destiny, didn't you, and now I think you were right. Destiny is mapped out for us, but we have the means to alter it by being true, or not, to ourselves. Destiny is like a great wheel and we stand at the hub and it's up to us which way we turn, which spoke of the wheel we travel along. It's the choices we make that cause events to happen as they do. Each spoke is a different lesson, but the destination's the same."

"And what is the destination?" he asked.

"We find out who we are." She paused. "The yew hasn't changed, but everything else has, and, for that change, the Eldrakin owe you a debt of gratitude that can never be repaid. Had you not found the Lorestone…"

"But not without Trystin's help."

"If you hadn't found a way to cure me of Vieldrin's spell…"

"Faine cured you, not me," he protested, suffused with panic at the thought that their conversation was heading away from what he had intended.

"Well. As you wish." She shrugged and stared at the evening sky.

Godwin waited as long as he could before subjecting Elgiva to the severity of his need. "If your people are so indebted to me, then why am I kept at arm's length? It doesn't matter how grateful they are, they still don't trust me, do they?"

Elgiva lowered her eyes. The sky darkened and the clouds were edged with gold and in the branches above them an owl hooted at the coming night.

"Faine spoke to me through the Lorestone," she said. "Well … he put things into my mind. He has a kind voice but his words are cruel." She paused for a moment and Godwin sighed with impatience, convinced that his question would go unanswered. "The Wilthkin are spreading over this land. They encroach upon our domains and they will continue to do so. Conflict is unavoidable, but Faine opposes war, so the Eldrakin will retreat. We must draw deeper into ourselves, like Misterell, but more so. Do you understand? I alone have the power to do this. Elvendom must be removed to another place entirely. To another … dimension."

"Another what?"

"You couldn't understand," she said, "nor do you need to, Godwin. This power I have is given to me for a short time only and I have things to do. I see what I could never see before and I know that the magic of the Eldrakin will fade at some future time, but perhaps I can forestall it by taking my people away."

"But surely," he protested desperately, "that's a long way off."

"Perhaps, but what is time? A circle. An illusion."

Godwin hugged his chest. "I feel that this is the end of everything."

She gave him a sympathetic look, saddened by his dismay. "No, this is the beginning, Godwin, as each new day is another beginning. The old day is dead, but its lessons will never be forgotten. For the Eldrakin another era begins and I am to build a new shrine to Lord Faine to reaffirm our faith. When that has been done, then each of us must face the dawn of another age and my friends must all go back to their homes. That is where their destinies lie."

"Must I?"

She lowered her gaze and nodded slowly. "I've kept you away from your people too long."

"But if I choose to stay here…"

"You would be unhappy," she stated. "You're a Wilthkin. You don't belong here."

"But how can I leave," he protested, "knowing I may never see you again?"

"You will forget."

"Forget *YOU*?"

"We have talked enough," she declared brusquely, "and I have many things to do."

"Talked? We haven't talked at all. There are things I need to say to you!"

She looked at him and sighed, then anger glimmered in her eyes. "Godwin, can't you accept the fact that we can't always have what we want!"

She rose abruptly to her feet and Godwin's heart was in his throat at the thought that he was going to lose her. He jumped up and clasped her cool, white hands.

"But … but, Elgiva, …I love you!" he cried. "I don't know … if I can live without you!"

"How did you live before we met?" Her tone cut through him like a knife.

"I didn't," he stated flatly. "I didn't even know what it meant."

Angrily, she thrust him away, as though he had offended her, and for a moment she glared at him. Her face was grey in the twilight and he realised that she was trembling. "Would you stay and have me watch you grow old and die, while I still live? Would you deny me the right to remember you always as I see you now?"

Godwin's mouth fell open. He hadn't expected this.

"Listen, Godwin," she went on, more kindly, "we have responsibilities, people who depend upon us. We were companions on life's road, but now we must take different paths. Our separate worlds are waiting for us." She smiled at him, though her heart ached, and took his hands in her own. "The dragon ring gives you access to the Britons. Your family gives you access to the Saxons. And, though you are a Wilthkin, you are Elfryth. You have safe passage through Elvendom. Godwin, you can go where you please, do what you please. You can be what you want to be. This is real freedom, my friend, and you have more than earned it." She steadied herself and took a deep breath. "For my part, I must marry a Wardain to secure my line and protect the magic that must be passed to my heirs. I must lead the Eldrakin out of this world to begin another life. You see, Godwin, I am condemned to the loneliness of absolute power."

"By Frigg, it's too cruel!" he cried.

"Do you think I will find it easy to send you away from me?" she pleaded. "That's why I kept you at a distance. I had hoped that you would see the futility of your regard for me, that it would make our parting less hard, that I..." She swallowed thickly and tears sprang to her eyes. "You aren't in love with me, Godwin. You're in love with a dream. You're under a kind of enchantment still, but it's one you created yourself."

With a shuddering sigh, she released his hands. The weight of her words left Godwin speechless. Shortly she continued, her voice now more controlled. "You have a good heart and a good brain, Godwin, and now you also have the chance to put them both to good use. At last you can be your own master. Don't be false to yourself. The future is yours to make of it whatever you want it to be. How many of us can say that?"

Godwin knew that she was right. It had been a selfish hope that they could stay together. He had helped her gain this victory, but that didn't mean she belonged to him, like some prized possession. She belonged to the Eldrakin. She was their gift, not his.

Elgiva stepped forwards and hugged him and Godwin was too taken aback to return her warm embrace. Before he could do so, she had released him.

"In the end, all things are One, and you and I are One," she said. "The physical world is an illusion." Her voice was as mellow as the dusk and her smile filled his heart with peace. "Can you and I ever really be parted? We will always be together. Always."

Quickly she turned and walked away.

Godwin sat down slowly and stared blankly at the sky, trying to make sense of it all.

And perhaps he understood.

While he and Elgiva breathed the same air, trod the same earth, saw the same moon and stars, they could never be apart. But what of this other dimension? He felt his pulse race with a sudden panic and then he remembered what she had said, 'In the end, all things are One', and a feeling of peace washed over him.

Yes, he and Elgiva could never be one in the way that he had hoped and he was being unreasonable if he thought that his problems could all be solved by the intervention of magic. This is the real world, Godwin, he thought. You've been a dreamer too long.

So what was he going to do?

He looked at the mark on the palm of his hand. He could go back with Queen Gilda, but he knew that he wouldn't be wanted there and what would become of his family?

The dragon ring glinted on his finger. Could he see himself as chief of his tribe, riding to Othere's to free his kin and bringing them to live with his people? How would Rowena accept the fact that her people were now the enemy? And what would become of the Britons, when the Saxons tired of peace?

No. He had to return to Rowena, to the wife with whom he had shared so much, the wife he had loved and forsaken. Running away was all part of the dream. And it left too many loose ends in his life. He must go back to Othere's. But he wouldn't be, couldn't be a slave. He would rather die. Yet his place was with the Wilthkin and somehow his marriage seemed to be a symbol of the future. Perhaps one day opposing sides would see that their strength lay in being One.

By Frigg, there were too many choices! And perhaps, like Elgiva, in gaining freedom, he had actually lost it. So, better to see it all as a dream, an adventure, a lesson learned. Better for him to start afresh with everything behind him, with all his experiences on his back, neatly bound like baggage.

At least he now knew who he was and his life had a solid foundation and there was one freedom he had gained: the freedom to be himself.

* * *

Chapter Forty-Three

The night was impaled on a hundred torches and, outside the forest's perimeter, beyond the trees that dripped with streamers, tables stood ranked upon the grass, laden with food and wine. Music wafted through the air, laced with the perfume of flowers, and the Elves and their guests danced in celebration.

On a flat-topped hummock sat the Elwardain, her great-uncle Bellic beside her. Garlands of flowers were strewn at their feet. Elgiva was dressed in green and gold and the Crown of Elindell was on her head, her black, shining hair spilling beneath it. In the folds of her sumptuous robe sat a very old wild-cat, washing its paws.

Bellic smiled at the revelry, but Elgiva was watching the dome of the sky and seemed to be lost in her thoughts.

Among the crowd stood Godwin, resolved to be cheerful in spite of his heartache. At least he was in the company of friends and it was good to see them again.

"Bless me!" Joskin was saying. "Never thought to see Elgiva dressed in all that finery. Looks a bit drowned in it all, eh, Shredwing?"

From Joskin's shoulder, Shredwing agreed.

"She looks wonderful!" said Kendra. "By the stars! Every inch a queen!"

At that moment, Greyflanks and Blacktail appeared and renewed their acquaintance with Godwin and, lost in the face of their conversation, Joskin strode off to the nearest table to sample a tray of cakes.

Lord Bellic turned to his great-niece. "A pity Gilda had to return, but she will visit again before winter." He scanned the merry scene below. "It is good, is it not, to see all your friends so happily brought together?"

The Elwardain shot him a withering glance that smouldered with hidden fire. "I dare say."

Bellic was somewhat aggrieved by her manner and not a little wary. She was no longer a timid child who hung upon his every word and now she surpassed him completely. "Does it not make you happy?" he asked.

She toyed with a strand of her hair. "How can it, when I know that I must lose my dearest friend forever?"

He nodded with sudden understanding. "I fear it must be so."

"Why can't I love him for a short time, Uncle?"

Her petulant tone reminded him of the time when he had influence and his confidence briefly resurfaced. "Do you love him so much you would break his heart?"

"Did you break the heart of Kendra's mother?"

The Elf-lord lowered his gaze. "Mine was the heart that was broken. The Wilthkin are a short-lived race and she I loved has been dead these thirty years."

They sat awhile in silence.

"Without his help I would have failed," Elgiva said, at length.

"What happened was ordained," said Bellic. "All of us played our part."

She frowned at him, but said nothing, and he patted her hand consolingly and decided to change the subject. "You have yet to decide about Tarkinell – where he will be sent."

"Tarkinell?" she asked, annoyed. "Tarkinell's going nowhere. I don't propose to banish him. By Elven law he should have a fair trial, the outcome of which will determine the punishment. He is a clever Elf, but he was corrupted by power. It could happen to anyone."

Her gaze flicked over him like a whip and Bellic felt himself flinch. "You are most merciful," he said.

"I dare say I can afford to be."

"My dear…"

"And I was well taught, was I not?" An unexpected tenderness softened her expression and she reached out and squeezed her great-uncle's hand. "Now, there are things I need to do before this night is over." She signalled to the minstrels and the music ceased abruptly. Then she got to her feet.

"My friends and fellow Eldrakin!" she cried, raising her right hand. The crowd turned towards her expectantly and gradually fell silent. For a while nothing stirred under the moon's cold gaze and even that pallid sphere seemed to be listening. "Now for a spell long awaited!" she declared, and her dark eyes shone with power. She paused for a moment, drew a deep breath, then her clear voice rang out across the stillness.

"From every spinney, tract and height,
"Evanish, stalkers of the night.
"From wood and forest, tor and dell,
"Arise and harken to my spell.
"Expire, demented Fellkin foul;
"Dissolve and die, no longer prowl.
"You things of magic, flesh and bone,
"The Earth no longer is your home.
"You must attend my potent spell
"No matter whereabouts you dwell.
"I charge thee, perish, be no more.
"I bring what you have waited for:

"For your fell bodies death is best,
"But for your souls eternal rest."

A flash of lightning ripped through the sky, startling those assembled, and from the distance a dreadful wail floated through the air. Faint though it was, it blanched their hearts, for it was the sound of a Fellkin dying and they shuddered to think that one of those creatures had come so near to their forest.

Then the Elves began to cheer. Elgiva watched them with a maternal, yet oddly dispassionate gaze.

"Congratulations, Elwardain," said Bellic. "That was indeed well done, but the last line you spoke I had not forseen. You have a kind heart, my dear."

"My next duty," Elgiva announced, "is to choose a new ruler for Misterell, as it would appear that its present monarch is permanently indisposed." The crowd chuckled appreciatively. "There is only one possible candidate, as far as I can see. I intend to establish a precedent by offering the crown of that kingdom to one who is not of Royal blood, but his love for Misterell and for Faine gives him every right to claim kingship. Trystin of Misterell, stand forth!"

Upon hearing his name, the Elfling recoiled and, seeing all eyes turn towards him, he hurried to Godwin and clutched at his sleeve. Elgiva saw him and grinned.

"Will you accept the crown?" she asked gently.

Trystin chewed his finger and looked up at his friend. "Oh, Master Godwin, what shall I do?"

"It's your decision, lad," said Godwin. "What is in your heart?"

Trystin's brow creased thoughtfully. "In my heart ... it says that Misterell is poor and sick ... and it needs help to be beautiful again ... but I..."

"You know how Misterell used to be, what it ought to be," said Godwin, putting his arm round the young Elf's shoulders. "And no-one loves Misterell more than you. You know how to put things right. Misterell deserves such a king."

Trystin fought his indecision, grappled with his shyness, then he stepped forwards, his head held high. "I accept, Elwardain, with all my heart!"

The assembly voiced their approval and Elgiva grinned with delight.

"This pleases me greatly," she said. "You are very young to be a king, but I will send all the help I can and, when you are ready to rule unaided, I'm sure you will be an admirable king and Misterell will once again be the jewel of Elvendom. Don't regret your lack of magic, Trystin. Misterell has more than enough of its own to be going on with." She gave him a mischievous smile. "Some of it may rub off on you."

More cheering greeted her words.

"I have other rewards to bestow," she went on. "Kendra, you will move to Elindell and you are assured of a safe haven here until the end of your days. You I call Elfryth and no-one may offer you insult or injury in this land. Furthermore, as a keeper of knowledge, I entrust you with the archives. The preservation of our lore will be solely in your charge. Greyflanks, you and your family may dwell in my fields and woodland. You will always be under my protection and you may hunt wherever you please. Never again will you need to wander in search of food or shelter. Now, Joskin, what would you ask of me?"

The giant looked up with astonishment. "Bless me!" he declared, blushing slightly. "Could do with some thread and some tools, I suppose, and a bigger perch for Shredwing."

"And that is all you require?"

"I have all I want," replied Joskin.

"What you have asked for is nothing, and yet it shall be done. However, there is more that I can do, though it is much less than you deserve." She pointed at the crippled bird still perched on the giant's shoulder. "Fly to me, skyfarer!" she commanded.

The falcon flapped his damaged wings, took off from Joskin's shoulder, and in an instant his wings became whole; strong, full-feathered and sleek. In ecstasy he soared above the crowd's astonished faces, swooping and climbing joyfully, then he returned to the towering Saxon.

Shredwing's squawks of gratitude were drowned by a tumult of cheers and Joskin gazed at Elgiva, too overcome to speak.

It was then that Godwin realised the import of all their struggles. Everything seemed to centre on this single act of good magic. Shredwing, too, had gained his inheritance: the precious gift of flight, and Godwin was proud to have played his part.

"To Captain Merrill is granted the title of Justice General to the Crown," continued the Elwardain, "for he is a fair-minded, honest Elf. Merrill, I trust you to be the final arbiter in any dispute, if you will accept the position."

In the crowd Captain Merrill made a low bow. "I will be honoured, Elwardain."

"Now, Grimalkin, what would you ask of me?"

Grimalkin stood at the rear of the crowd, sniffing a plate of honey-cakes. She pricked up her ears and looked at Elgiva. "Cabbage hearts!" she snorted. "Haven't had time to think about that, but you can make this hat disappear and get someone to fetch me some more of these buns. I'll have oats for breakfast, too. Apart from that, I'll let you know."

Elgiva smiled, then turned to face Godwin. "My friend," she said, "you far surpass any gifts I could give you."

Godwin squirmed self-consciously, as all eyes turned towards him.

"You have many choices ahead," said Elgiva, "but I think you may want to begin afresh, so I will provide you with gold and gems to purchase your freedom from Othere, and the freedom of your family, if that is what he demands. Build a settlement of your own. You have the courage to do so. But, wherever you decide to live, you and your descendants will be under the Elf-ward of Elindell. You made a vow to protect me once. Now it's my turn I think. I trust that Faine will help me keep my vow as well as you kept yours. Take your pick of my armoury, Godwin, my horses, too, and anything else you may require for your journey. I wish you to ride home in splendour, so the Saxons will see, as I do, a most fearless and constant warrior – Godwin Gildason."

Godwin raised his eyebrows, then smiled. "Thank you, Elwardain," he said politely. He rather liked his new appellation.

"And," said Elgiva, "a certain gift I gave you in the past is yours to keep forever, though it's not in accordance with Elven law, but to take back a gift that was given in love would violate the teachings of Faine."

Godwin stared at Elgiva, puzzled by her humorous smile. What did she mean by 'a certain gift'?

"Also," she went on, "you'll be pleased to know that I have removed the enchantment over Angwen's village. Her people have started rebuilding their lives. Messengers have been sent to assure them of our help and protection. And I will be sending cattle and corn and whatever else I can." She smiled and her dark eyes sparkled with warmth. Then she turned to the crowd. "I dare say you've heard enough talk for one night. Minstrels, your merriest tunes! Enough of the past and the future. The now is all that matters. Let's enjoy it to the full!"

⋆ ⋆ ⋆

Shortly before sunrise, Elgiva and her people and guests made their way to a clearing in the forest. Elgiva stood in the centre, about her a tumble of stones of various sizes and colours that servants had gathered the previous day. Everyone formed a circle around her and stood in respectful silence.

Elgiva slowly lifted her arms and a mist rose up from the ground at her feet and, as it rose, it carried the stones and piled them on top of each other. Where the stones met, they welded together. When the mist evaporated, the new shrine was complete. Three solid walls now stood beneath a roof of polished rock and along the walls were granite benches, plain and unadorned. Elgiva stepped onto the threshold, a smile of accomplishment on her face.

As the rising sun skimmed the tree-tops and touched the clean stone of the shrine, a gasp of approval broke from the crowd. The sunlight made every facet as vivid as a chunk of glass and all the ores trapped in the stones glinted with many colours. It was an inspiring sight, as the simple, granite building became a thing of beauty.

"I dedicate this shrine to Faine, First-Father of Elvendom," said Elgiva, turning to face the crowd. "Like him, it is strong and beautiful. It is humble, yet proud with hidden splendour. It is plain and ornate. It is a thing of both light and shade, created out of the tangible bones of the Earth by the Earth's intangible magic. Let it stand as a reminder of the power of good magic and the balance that sustains the universe. Its separate parts combine into a single, harmonious unity. Thus, it stands as a symbol of Elvendom. It is a place to be apart and a place to be a part of everything. May it and the Eldrakin endure forever."

The Elves applauded Elgiva's words with great enthusiasm. Godwin, however, was only half-listening. There was something he felt he had to do.

Ignoring the scrutiny of hundreds of eyes, he walked towards the shrine and entered. Halting on the smooth, stone floor, he turned to face Elgiva. "There is no altar," he remarked. She shook her head and looked at him quizzically. "It needs something. A focal point."

Slowly, he unsheathed his sword and walked to the rear of the shrine. "Tomorrow, Faine," he said quietly, "I won't be a part of your world anymore, but tomorrow is another day. This Elf-blade has taught me many things. My heart and mind have been opened. In thanks for that, I offer it to you. Let it stay here as a reminder that, when Good is threatened by evil, we need to fight on its behalf."

He selected a central point on the stone floor, then he lifted the sword in both hands and whispered its name so that no-one should hear. Then he plunged the weapon into the floor. It pierced the thick stone easily and buried two-thirds of its length in the granite.

"Farewell, old friend," said Godwin, his tone subdued but not downhearted. "Now I'll face the future alone and stand or fall by my own resources. Remain here in my stead where … where my heart is. But remember, though we are parted, we will always be together." He paused and in the silent glade even the birds were listening. "And by my express command, you will stay here always and never be removed … save by my hand alone."

He finished the last sentence hurriedly, not knowing what motives had prompted it. Perhaps he needed to leave behind a permanent reminder of his existence, something that would live on long after he lay forgotten in some lonely grave. Or perhaps he hoped that leaving the sword would ensure that he would one day return.

Elgiva stepped forwards and put both hands around the hilt of the sword. She pulled, but the weapon refused to move. She smiled and looked up at her friend. "To wield such a sword requires courage," she said, "but far greater courage to give it up."

They gazed at each other, then, linking arms, they walked out into the sunlight.

★ ★ ★

Chapter Forty-Four

Godwin caught sight of the village and a broad smile stretched his lips. Smoke curled cheerily from the huts and people were busy in the fields. He slewed himself round on the back of his horse. Elgiva and her retinue were making their way towards him and, while he waited for them to catch up, he wandered back in his memory to his sad departure from Elindell.

Leaving Trystin had been the worst moment; Godwin had almost come to regard the Elfling as a son. Trystin had clung to Godwin's tunic, his large eyes brimming with tears, and Godwin had done his best to sound stern, as he pushed the Elfling away from him and held him by the shoulders.

"Is this any way for a king to behave?"

"Kings don't cry," said Grimalkin. "They make cruel laws to make others weep."

"Not me!" sniffed Trystin defiantly. He started to chew his finger-nails, but then thought better of it. "I'll be a good king, and brave," he went on, "just like Master Godwin, and I'll never hate Wilthkin or be scared of magic or anything!"

"Care for Misterell, Trystin," said Godwin. "A place of such beauty must be preserved."

"Yes, I will," promised Trystin. "I'll care for it, Master Godwin, and, if I falter, I'll think of you and follow your example. That way, I'll never go wrong."

"Be yourself, lad, and be it well. That's all that's ever required of us." His pretence at fortitude crumbled then and, clasping Trystin to his breast, he hugged him so hard he almost feared that the Elfling's bones would snap.

"Do you wish to visit Angwen?"

Elgiva was now beside him, her green gown draped across Alison's back and her black hair braided with golden ribbons. Her question caught him off guard.

"What? … er … No … No, let's move on," he said. "Can we skirt around the village? Surely there's some ford or bridge downstream where we can cross?"

"If not, I'll make you one," said she, smiling.

He sighed. "I'm pleased with what I see. The cooking fires are burning and children are playing on the grass." He stopped, remembering other children, children past and present. "They have no need of me. I must forget the past, and all this was a part of it. It's better to go forward now."

"If you are sure," she said.

He shrugged. "Yes. Let's move on."

"Move on?" snickered a voice from the rear. "Move on, he says, and here's me thinking I might be in for a rest. My poor, old bones have had enough. Ages since anyone fed me, you know. As for these stones, my poor, old hooves are split and buckled and scuffed so bad, I'll wager I'm crippled for life – what little there's left in my poor, abused body."

Godwin sighed with exasperation at the sight of Grimalkin plodding towards them, but Elgiva grinned mischievously. "I'm sorry, Godwin," she said, "but it was her wish to return with you. I couldn't really stop her."

Godwin nodded resignedly. At least some things would never change.

He turned his horse's head southwards.

* * *

"From here you must travel due east," said Elgiva.

Beside her, Godwin nodded. They were standing on a hillock, one Elgiva remembered well as the place where everything had started for her, and now the adventure was over. The darkening landscape spread out below and on the other side of the hillock her retinue were waiting to turn back for home.

"You have plenty of food for your journey. It shouldn't take long to get home."

Again, he nodded absently. Sighing, Elgiva urged Alison down the grassy slope. Godwin followed with a heavy heart. The horses were left at the foot of the hillock and Godwin stacked wood for a fire.

"Do you like the horse?" asked Elgiva, forcing herself to sound casual. "You didn't really say … but I chose him because he's gentle and not of the Royal Herd. He should give the Saxons no reason to comment."

Godwin stepped back from the firewood and looked at the placid, cream-coloured horse. "Saxons don't need a reason," he said. "By Frigg! what'll they think of me? Bags of gold and dressed like a lord?" He smiled at the Elwardain, aware of the need to appear light-hearted.

"What can they think, but that you surpass them?" Abruptly, she snapped her fingers, as though discharging some pent up emotion, and the firewood blossomed into flame. Folding her arms, she looked at her friend and her gaze held a hint of reproach. "You didn't select a sword," she said. "You left your scabbard behind."

He lowered his eyes self-consciously.

"A warrior can't go abroad unarmed." She cocked an eyebrow at him, then she walked to Alison's saddlebag and drew out an object wrapped in gold cloth. Returning to the camp-fire, she handed the bundle to Godwin. "My parting gift to you," she said.

Inside the cloth was his Elven scabbard, but it had another occupant: an Elf-blade with silver cross-guards. On the hilt were tiny circles and, inside each circle, an Elven rune.

"That is my mark," explained the Elwardain.

Godwin looked up in surprise and delight. "You made this for me?" he asked. Elgiva nodded demurely. "Is it … is it magic?"

"That rather depends on how you use it," Elgiva replied with a mischievous smile.

He fitted the scabbard to his belt and, when he looked up again, their gazes locked together. As if sharing the same compulsion, each made a movement towards the other, as though they meant to embrace.

But then the spell was broken, as something heavy slid down the bank.

Elgiva cleared her throat. "Why, here's Grimalkin, laden with treasure!"

Godwin drew a shuddering breath, torn between anger and relief.

"And what a weight it is, to be sure, by all that's green and edible!" Grimalkin snorted loudly.

Godwin turned towards her and folded his arms across his chest in an attitude of stern amusement. "So, you old nag," he said, "looks like I'm stuck with you forever."

"Gall and wormwood, Brit!" she snickered. "I'm not immortal, you know!"

Laughing, Elgiva sat by the fire and Godwin sat beside her and for a while they watched the flames dance, as dusk fell all around them. It was time to say farewell, but neither wanted to bring to an end their last precious moments together.

"You need a story to tell the Saxons," Elgiva said, at length. "They'll want to know what happened to you and why you have all this gold."

"Don't worry," he said. "I've plenty of time to think of a tale on the way home. I won't mention Elves, of course." He smiled, but Elgiva still looked concerned. "And I'm not going back as Godwin the churl, but as Aidan, son of Gwion, a chief of the Gododdin. My status will dictate my treatment."

"It will?" she asked uncertainly.

"No matter what you think of Othere, he's still an honourable man."

"I dare say you are right."

"But I will tell Rowena the truth. My children, too, when they're older. I want them to know who they are." He paused and looked at Elgiva with his honest, artless eyes. "Knowing you has taught me many things about myself … and everything."

"And in you I met my greatest tutor."

From Elgiva's waiting retinue somewhere behind the hillock there rose a burst of laughter that seemed to profane their intimacy, and they both fell silent again. From the darkness of a distant wood a fox screamed for its mate and its cry was an ache of loneliness.

Now, Elgiva thought grimly, I begin a new chapter, but I am still an exile. But this time I'm exiled by power, not weakness. This time being an exile doesn't mean I can run away, and where in all this great, wide world will I find a friend such as you?

On an impulse, she leaned towards him, threw her arms around his neck and hugged him tenderly. It was time for them to say good-bye, but her lips refused to frame the word. She pulled away from him suddenly, her features tormented by longing.

"Oh, Godwin," she cried, and the tears flowed freely down her cheeks, "we should have been ... we ought to be ... together!"

He gently gripped her upper arms and his eyes were moist with affection. "We are," he insisted firmly. "We always were. We always will be."

They looked at each other in silent anguish, and then they embraced each other, clung together desperately. For a moment that was a lifetime, the gulf between them was closed with a kiss, and in some other dimension where they were and yet were not, their souls touched briefly in an act of love.

Then Elgiva broke away, rose quickly to her feet. "Well, Godwin Gildason, this is where we must part," she said softly. "May Faine always guard you, my friend." No, she thought, I won't say good-bye. My heart is too full for such finality.

She turned and stepped lightly towards her horse. Seizing the golden bridle, she led her to the crest of the hillock and Godwin watched her go, as though she embodied his happiness, which was leaving him forever. A cold and empty feeling flooded through his heart.

Suddenly, the Elwardain stopped, looked back towards her friend. Firelight caught the dampness of her eyes, but a slight smile chased the sadness from her face. It was a smile of defiance, full of mischief and affection; a conspiratorial smile. Her voice carried clearly, when she spoke.

"I love you, Wilthkin."

Then she was gone, Alison beside her, and the drapes of darkness closed behind them, leaving Godwin all alone.

Alone and bereft in a world devoid of magic.

⋆ ⋆ ⋆

Godwin stirred beneath the blankets. It had rained during the night and his coverings were wet. He cast them aside and crawled to his feet. The sun lay on the horizon, like a polished ball of gold, and the dawn was filled with the singing of birds.

After a cursory breakfast, he gathered up his blankets and tied them to Grimalkin's back. "We've some way to go," he said, patting her neck. "I don't want to lose any time. I've been away from home too long."

Home. No, they weren't going home. Othere's settlement wasn't home. Home was an unknown quantity, somewhere in the future. And the thought of it filled him with a sudden excitement.

He had lost Elgiva and his right to lead his tribe, but he could accept that now. He was going back to the Saxons, but he could accept that, too. No matter what life held in store for him, he knew he would accept it all. The road from the past had been long and hard, the road to the future was uncertain, but he faced it all now with his mind uncluttered. At least, he knew who he was. And, more importantly, what he was. And he knew where his duty lay: he was going back to his family.

"Have you gone into a trance, Brit? Thought we were in a hurry?"

Chapter Forty-Four

Godwin caught sight of the village and a broad smile stretched his lips. Smoke curled cheerily from the huts and people were busy in the fields. He slewed himself round on the back of his horse. Elgiva and her retinue were making their way towards him and, while he waited for them to catch up, he wandered back in his memory to his sad departure from Elindell.

Leaving Trystin had been the worst moment; Godwin had almost come to regard the Elfling as a son. Trystin had clung to Godwin's tunic, his large eyes brimming with tears, and Godwin had done his best to sound stern, as he pushed the Elfling away from him and held him by the shoulders.

"Is this any way for a king to behave?"

"Kings don't cry," said Grimalkin. "They make cruel laws to make others weep."

"Not me!" sniffed Trystin defiantly. He started to chew his finger-nails, but then thought better of it. "I'll be a good king, and brave," he went on, "just like Master Godwin, and I'll never hate Wilthkin or be scared of magic or anything!"

"Care for Misterell, Trystin," said Godwin. "A place of such beauty must be preserved."

"Yes, I will," promised Trystin. "I'll care for it, Master Godwin, and, if I falter, I'll think of you and follow your example. That way, I'll never go wrong."

"Be yourself, lad, and be it well. That's all that's ever required of us." His pretence at fortitude crumbled then and, clasping Trystin to his breast, he hugged him so hard he almost feared that the Elfling's bones would snap.

"Do you wish to visit Angwen?"

Elgiva was now beside him, her green gown draped across Alison's back and her black hair braided with golden ribbons. Her question caught him off guard.

"What? … er … No … No, let's move on," he said. "Can we skirt around the village? Surely there's some ford or bridge downstream where we can cross?"

"If not, I'll make you one," said she, smiling.

He sighed. "I'm pleased with what I see. The cooking fires are burning and children are playing on the grass." He stopped, remembering other children, children past and present. "They have no need of me. I must forget the past, and all this was a part of it. It's better to go forward now."

"If you are sure," she said.

He shrugged. "Yes. Let's move on."

"Move on?" snickered a voice from the rear. "Move on, he says, and here's me thinking I might be in for a rest. My poor, old bones have had enough. Ages since anyone fed me, you know. As for these stones, my poor, old hooves are split and buckled and scuffed so bad, I'll wager I'm crippled for life – what little there's left in my poor, abused body."

Godwin sighed with exasperation at the sight of Grimalkin plodding towards them, but Elgiva grinned mischievously. "I'm sorry, Godwin," she said, "but it was her wish to return with you. I couldn't really stop her."

Godwin nodded resignedly. At least some things would never change.

He turned his horse's head southwards.

* * *

"From here you must travel due east," said Elgiva.

Beside her, Godwin nodded. They were standing on a hillock, one Elgiva remembered well as the place where everything had started for her, and now the adventure was over. The darkening landscape spread out below and on the other side of the hillock her retinue were waiting to turn back for home.

"You have plenty of food for your journey. It shouldn't take long to get home."

Again, he nodded absently. Sighing, Elgiva urged Alison down the grassy slope. Godwin followed with a heavy heart. The horses were left at the foot of the hillock and Godwin stacked wood for a fire.

"Do you like the horse?" asked Elgiva, forcing herself to sound casual. "You didn't really say … but I chose him because he's gentle and not of the Royal Herd. He should give the Saxons no reason to comment."

Godwin stepped back from the firewood and looked at the placid, cream-coloured horse. "Saxons don't need a reason," he said. "By Frigg! what'll they think of me? Bags of gold and dressed like a lord?" He smiled at the Elwardain, aware of the need to appear light-hearted.

"What can they think, but that you surpass them?" Abruptly, she snapped her fingers, as though discharging some pent up emotion, and the firewood blossomed into flame. Folding her arms, she looked at her friend and her gaze held a hint of reproach. "You didn't select a sword," she said. "You left your scabbard behind."

He lowered his eyes self-consciously.

"A warrior can't go abroad unarmed." She cocked an eyebrow at him, then she walked to Alison's saddlebag and drew out an object wrapped in gold cloth. Returning to the camp-fire, she handed the bundle to Godwin. "My parting gift to you," she said.

Inside the cloth was his Elven scabbard, but it had another occupant: an Elf-blade with silver cross-guards. On the hilt were tiny circles and, inside each circle, an Elven rune.

"That is my mark," explained the Elwardain.

Godwin looked up in surprise and delight. "You made this for me?" he asked. Elgiva nodded demurely. "Is it … is it magic?"

"That rather depends on how you use it," Elgiva replied with a mischievous smile.

He fitted the scabbard to his belt and, when he looked up again, their gazes locked together. As if sharing the same compulsion, each made a movement towards the other, as though they meant to embrace.

But then the spell was broken, as something heavy slid down the bank.

Elgiva cleared her throat. "Why, here's Grimalkin, laden with treasure!"

Godwin drew a shuddering breath, torn between anger and relief.

"And what a weight it is, to be sure, by all that's green and edible!" Grimalkin snorted loudly.

Godwin turned towards her and folded his arms across his chest in an attitude of stern amusement. "So, you old nag," he said, "looks like I'm stuck with you forever."

"Gall and wormwood, Brit!" she snickered. "I'm not immortal, you know!"

Laughing, Elgiva sat by the fire and Godwin sat beside her and for a while they watched the flames dance, as dusk fell all around them. It was time to say farewell, but neither wanted to bring to an end their last precious moments together.

"You need a story to tell the Saxons," Elgiva said, at length. "They'll want to know what happened to you and why you have all this gold."

"Don't worry," he said. "I've plenty of time to think of a tale on the way home. I won't mention Elves, of course." He smiled, but Elgiva still looked concerned. "And I'm not going back as Godwin the churl, but as Aidan, son of Gwion, a chief of the Gododdin. My status will dictate my treatment."

"It will?" she asked uncertainly.

"No matter what you think of Othere, he's still an honourable man."

"I dare say you are right."

"But I will tell Rowena the truth. My children, too, when they're older. I want them to know who they are." He paused and looked at Elgiva with his honest, artless eyes. "Knowing you has taught me many things about myself … and everything."

"And in you I met my greatest tutor."

From Elgiva's waiting retinue somewhere behind the hillock there rose a burst of laughter that seemed to profane their intimacy, and they both fell silent again. From the darkness of a distant wood a fox screamed for its mate and its cry was an ache of loneliness.

Now, Elgiva thought grimly, I begin a new chapter, but I am still an exile. But this time I'm exiled by power, not weakness. This time being an exile doesn't mean I can run away, and where in all this great, wide world will I find a friend such as you?

On an impulse, she leaned towards him, threw her arms around his neck and hugged him tenderly. It was time for them to say good-bye, but her lips refused to frame the word. She pulled away from him suddenly, her features tormented by longing.

"Oh, Godwin," she cried, and the tears flowed freely down her cheeks, "we should have been ... we ought to be ... together!"

He gently gripped her upper arms and his eyes were moist with affection. "We are," he insisted firmly. "We always were. We always will be."

They looked at each other in silent anguish, and then they embraced each other, clung together desperately. For a moment that was a lifetime, the gulf between them was closed with a kiss, and in some other dimension where they were and yet were not, their souls touched briefly in an act of love.

Then Elgiva broke away, rose quickly to her feet. "Well, Godwin Gildason, this is where we must part," she said softly. "May Faine always guard you, my friend." No, she thought, I won't say good-bye. My heart is too full for such finality.

She turned and stepped lightly towards her horse. Seizing the golden bridle, she led her to the crest of the hillock and Godwin watched her go, as though she embodied his happiness, which was leaving him forever. A cold and empty feeling flooded through his heart.

Suddenly, the Elwardain stopped, looked back towards her friend. Firelight caught the dampness of her eyes, but a slight smile chased the sadness from her face. It was a smile of defiance, full of mischief and affection; a conspiratorial smile. Her voice carried clearly, when she spoke.

"I love you, Wilthkin."

Then she was gone, Alison beside her, and the drapes of darkness closed behind them, leaving Godwin all alone.

Alone and bereft in a world devoid of magic.

* * *

Godwin stirred beneath the blankets. It had rained during the night and his coverings were wet. He cast them aside and crawled to his feet. The sun lay on the horizon, like a polished ball of gold, and the dawn was filled with the singing of birds.

After a cursory breakfast, he gathered up his blankets and tied them to Grimalkin's back. "We've some way to go," he said, patting her neck. "I don't want to lose any time. I've been away from home too long."

Home. No, they weren't going home. Othere's settlement wasn't home. Home was an unknown quantity, somewhere in the future. And the thought of it filled him with a sudden excitement.

He had lost Elgiva and his right to lead his tribe, but he could accept that now. He was going back to the Saxons, but he could accept that, too. No matter what life held in store for him, he knew he would accept it all. The road from the past had been long and hard, the road to the future was uncertain, but he faced it all now with his mind uncluttered. At least, he knew who he was. And, more importantly, what he was. And he knew where his duty lay: he was going back to his family.

"Have you gone into a trance, Brit? Thought we were in a hurry?"

Godwin stared at the pony. "I was just thinking," he said.

"Wondering if it was worth it, eh?"

Godwin walked towards his horse, ignoring this remark.

"Well," persisted Grimalkin, "you got lots of gold for your trouble. What could be better than that?"

"Myself," he stated simply.

"Don't go all philosophical. Too early in the morning," she snickered.

He stood with his hand on his horse's withers and thought of Taranuil, the bridge between his world and that of his Elven friends. That bridge would always be there.

And we will always be together.

He turned towards Grimalkin. Impatience glittered in her blood-shot eyes and a grin spread over his face. They had all been changed by what they'd been through, but, like Grimalkin, like the old yew, like love and faith and hope, some things never changed. They could always be relied upon.

He patted the horse and prepared to mount. "Stand still, Farran, there's a good lad."

As he clambered onto the horse's back, he realised that horses weren't frightening at all, when you knew how to talk to them.

Talk to them? By Frigg!

That was Elgiva's 'certain gift'! He'd forgotten all about it. It seemed as natural now as breathing. He would have to learn how to hide it. The Wilthkin wouldn't understand.

He turned to Grimalkin. "Let's go," he said.

He set off in the direction of home. His heart was lighter than he had expected and summer was blossoming all around him with hope and hidden potential. And the hope was possible, the future was possible, because he had mastered the past.

By Frigg, it had all been a great adventure!

Or perhaps the adventure was just beginning.

THE END